I0720276

By Mike Rousseau

VANGUARDIANS
Scarlet and Sunder
Children of Noctis

VANGUARDIANS: BOOK ONE

MIKE ROUSSEAU

Cover Illustration by Félix Ortiz
Cover Design by STK Kreations

ISBN 978-1-7388419-1-2 (trade paperback)
ISBN 978-1-7388419-0-5 (ebook)

www.mikerousseau.com

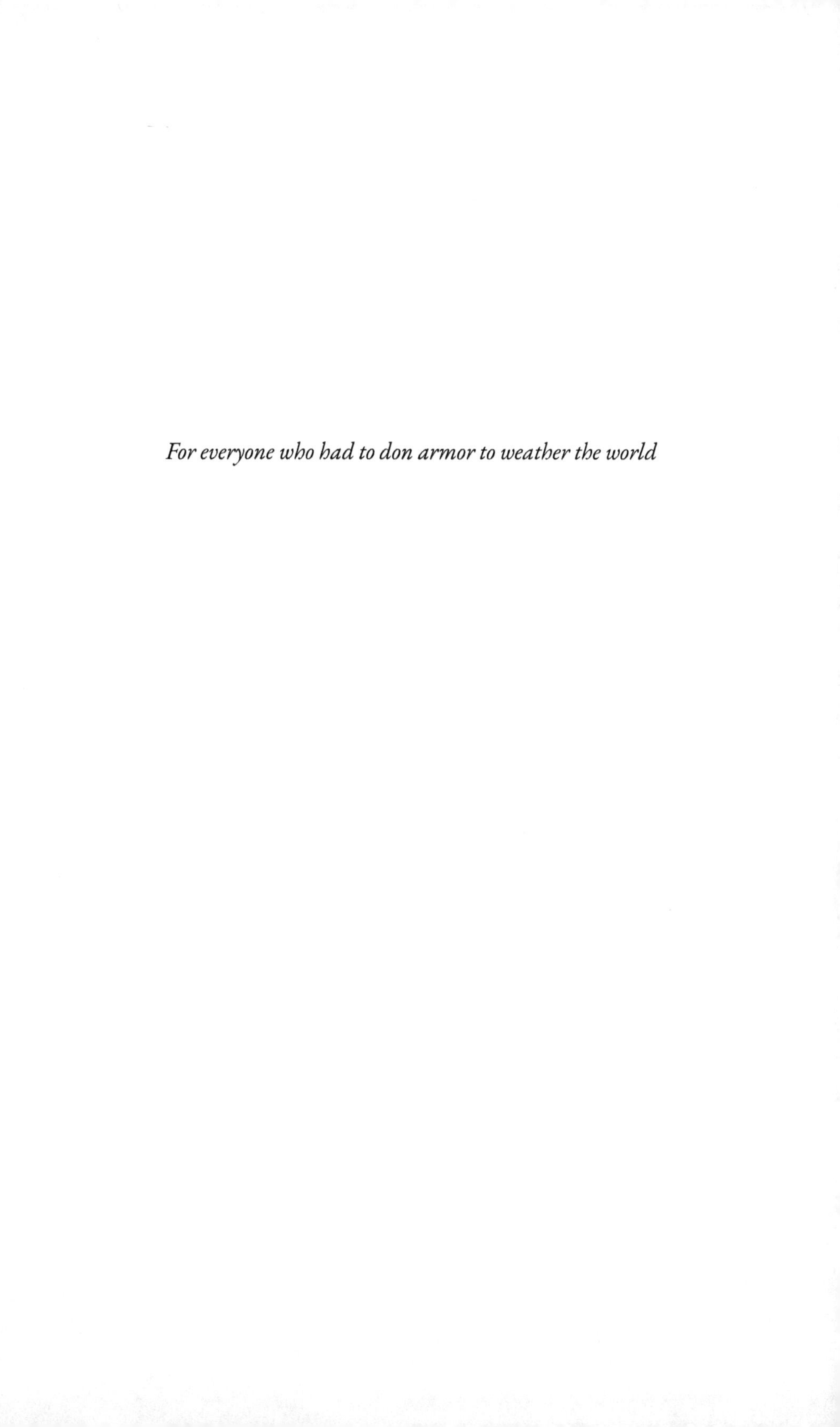

For everyone who had to don armor to weather the world

Part One

The Pilot's Apprentice

Chapter 1
Last Call

It wasn't the first time Maia Sunderland had been shot with a crossbow, but it was the first time she had been shot twice in one night.

Maia regarded the tail end of the quarrel peeking out of her stomach and thanked her luck that at the very least, she didn't have to dig a flintlock bullet out of her mid-section. Bullets always made a bigger mess. She tore the quarrel out with a sharp grunt and a sputter of crimson, then broke it in half with a clench of her fist. The pieces of the bloody bolt tumbled from her trembling fingers and down into the tavern's privy, where they landed with a dull plop.

With the wound clear, the bleeding stopped. In a few minutes, the tingling tear in her stomach would close. Within an hour, it wouldn't even hurt. By the following night, there wouldn't even be a visible scar. That was best. No matter how many of her attackers managed to sneak weapons past the tavern's doorman, she couldn't let them see her pain.

She didn't even hate them for trying to kill her. Anybody who would attempt to murder a Pilot was either monumentally stupid or consumed with vengeance. She held pity for the former and understanding for the latter.

The vengeful ones probably had good reason to want her blood. Maybe Maia had shown up too late to save a loved one. Perhaps she accidentally crushed a distant relative of theirs with her three-hundred-foot-tall walking war machine. Or maybe it was their favorite goat. Many farmers in the Freelands had a favorite goat.

Or it could be that, like many people across the known world, they blamed her for the death of the other four Pilots.

She couldn't rightfully hate them for seeking vengeance. That's why she never called upon her armor and weapons when it came time to defend herself. That's why she only hit them once, just hard enough to ensure she wouldn't see the same face twice.

Maia breathed deep and released the rising heat in her chest through one long exhale. She slid on her easy smile, straightened her torn shirt, and stepped out of the privy. She strutted down the hall and entered the common room of the tavern to raucous applause, taking her place at the end of the bar on the one vacant stool that was hers, and hers alone.

The barkeep approached Maia from the other side of the bar with the cautious steps of a harried fox. She shouted to be heard over the drunken clamor. "Are you okay?"

"It's just a scratch," Maia shouted back.

The barkeep crossed her slender arms. Even wearing worry, Elizabeth Barlowe inspired thoughts as warm as her tawny skin and brown eyes. Maia had no idea how Elizabeth came by whatever she was using to keep her back-length braid of midnight hair so shiny, or where in a run-down crossroads town like Bracken she bought the fine blouses and bodices and velvet chokers she favored. Rather than think about it too much, Maia focused on how lucky she was to be able to enjoy stealing glances at her employer in between nightly bouts of violence.

In another lifetime, Maia would have been more than content settling down with Elizabeth, helping her run her tavern by day and burning through bedsheets with her by night. But it wasn't another lifetime, and Maia needed more liquor if she was going to forget that sobering fact.

"Another bottle," Maia called. The rowdy drunks lining the tavern's benches cheered their hero on.

"The same?" Elizabeth said.

"Always."

Elizabeth's head bobbed beneath the counter. She fished out a thick-bottomed bottle and plopped it down in front of Maia, not bothering to uncork it for her. "Are you taking this one for the road?"

"I may be full of holes, but I'm still your hired muscle." Maia popped the cork and drank deep of the sweet darkness waiting beneath the colored glass. It was almost an insult to call it wine. It tasted more like fruit juice that had taken a wrong turn in a fetid swamp before finding its way into a bottle. Still, it was the strongest wine in the Freelands. Therefore, it had value.

It didn't hurt that it slightly resembled the vintage Maia's mother and father used to bottle. It probably didn't help, either.

"If you stay, you might break your record. You only just set it." Elizabeth rested against the back bar and brushed a rogue strand of hair from her forehead. "Shot twice in under an hour. This might be the worst birthday ever."

Not even close. Maia took another swig and belched loud enough to draw more applause. "Happy twenty-three to me."

Twenty-three. It was four more years than she had expected. Four more than she deserved. And it felt more like turning eighty. She smiled through the thought to keep Elizabeth from reading her.

Elizabeth crossed her arms again. "I'm glad you're having such a good time, getting shot and bloodying up my privy. I'm firing Jacob in the morning."

"It's not his fault. He's new to the doorman game. Lots of ins and outs to navigate. He'll figure it out."

"How daft do you have to be to let two crossbows past in one night? They're huge! If he can't spot a crossbow under a coat, what about something smaller? How many knives do you think are hiding in boots and beneath cloaks right now?"

"Give it another hour, and maybe we'll find out."

"Maybe you don't mind being shot or stabbed, but I have other patrons and myself to worry about."

She had a point. If someone with a grudge and a weapon came at Maia and missed, they might hurt someone who, unlike her, didn't deserve it. Without a witty retort to offer, Maia turned away from Elizabeth's frown and kept drinking. It was a solution that worked for most situations.

The uncomfortable pause lingered for some time until Elizabeth cracked it. "News came today. There was a Feral attack, down in Sanford."

If it had been a Behemoth attack, Maia's Hunter Sense would have detected the creature across any distance. Ferals were trickier; she could only sense them from a distance if they gathered in larger groups, and that was assuming she was sober enough to be receptive to the signs. A few Ferals wouldn't even cause an itch at the back of her skull if she wasn't within a mile of them.

"How many Ferals?" Maia said.

"Three," Elizabeth said.

"How did Sanford fare?"

"Three wounded. Ten dead. The Iron Wardens were slow to act, I'm told."

"Of course they were. You can't trust a Noctean to look after anyone but themselves."

"I hate having Imperials skulking around the Freelands as much as you, but the people need protection," Elizabeth said.

Maia swallowed hard. "Yeah. I guess I'm not enough."

"No, it's not that. I just..." Elizabeth straightened. "Forget it. I'm sorry I brought it up."

She turned on her heels, sending her long black braid flicking at her shoulder. She moved down the bar to serve a group of haggard-looking elves while Maia let her idle gaze bore a hole in her favorite spot on the wall.

Maia let the alcohol do its work. If it failed at the task, she could always get more. In exchange for a few chores and tossing out any guests whose tempers ran a bit too hot, Maia could eat and drink as much as she pleased at Barlowe's Tavern.

"Heroes don't have to pay," Elizabeth told Maia on the night she returned to Bracken a year prior. It was a nice thought, but in the end, everyone paid. Even heroes. In Maia's case, she paid with her own blood.

It didn't take long for word of her return to Bracken to spread. Her challengers started arriving soon after. Some had good reasons for wanting her dead. Others came for the sport, the thrill of challenging the Red Pilot of Fire, the woman who couldn't be killed.

With every cut and broken bone she suffered, Maia watched Elizabeth's heart break just a little more. More than once, Elizabeth pleaded with Maia to leave town, to jump into her war machine and march far away. A few times, Elizabeth even offered to leave the tavern behind and travel the world with her.

Maia never took it to heart. The proposal was nothing but a friendly game they played. Elizabeth would try to guide Maia out of the darkness, back to something resembling an actual life, and Maia would smile and remind herself that she didn't deserve such kindness.

As she headed back Maia's way, Elizabeth adjusted her bodice and straightened her posture. "Sanford isn't really what I wanted to talk about. I need to tell you something. This isn't the best time, but I've been thinking."

"What about?"

Elizabeth moved in closer, lowering her voice. "I've put it off long enough. I've made up my mind. Tomorrow, I'm leaving for Whitehorn. I'm joining Brave Dawn. It's time I did my part."

"You don't even know how to hold a sword." Maia flashed a grin without thinking, a reflex born of habit and necessity. Seeing Elizabeth's frown, she instantly regretted it.

"I can learn. I can help. And...you could come with me. If you like. Even if you don't come to Whitehorn, you could leave Bracken. Maybe you can find something else to do with your life besides getting stuck with sharp things night after night because you're too drunk on free wine to fight back."

Not this again. "We have a good life here. People drink more when they're waiting for a show. It's profitable for both of us. It would be a shame to give all this up just to die for the Resistance."

"I'll give up my full coffers if it means I never have to read a tearful eulogy at your funeral. You deserve better than this."

"Don't worry about me. I'm fine," Maia lied. The rip in her stomach burned as it knitted. She shifted on her stool to hide a pained grimace.

"You're not." Elizabeth reached out, touching Maia's cheek. A bold gesture, one Maia had longed for. But one of Elizabeth's fingers brushed too close to the old scar tissue slicing a jagged line from Maia's forehead, down over her left eye, and across her jaw. That slight touch made Maia flinch as if Elizabeth had raked her with her nails.

A sad smile traced Elizabeth's lips. "Go home, Maia. Take the rest of the night off. Maybe you don't care if you live or die, but some of us do."

"Nobody calls me 'Maia' anymore. I'm Sunder. The Red Pilot of Fire."

Elizabeth shook her head. "At any rate, it's time. Come tomorrow, I'm leaving Bracken for good."

"Sure you are." Maia chuckled, sliding off her stool and grabbing her bottle.

"I mean it this time. It's time we got up and lived our lives. This is goodbye, Maia."

For once, Maia believed it. There was something in the way Elizabeth stood, something firm and defiant that wasn't there the other times they danced this dance.

Maia saluted with her bottle. As she worked her way through the small sea of bodies blocking the tavern door, she concentrated on maintaining her smile so nobody could see the cracks start to work their way through her mask of practiced calm.

The cool night air washed over Maia's face, fluttering through her unruly, scarlet-dyed hair. Lamplight carved through the black, illuminating the unpaved road that wound its way through the center of Bracken, past rows of inns and shops and a single rotating ballista installation meant for warding off Behemoths.

Even those who loved Bracken considered it less a community and more a stop on the way to something better. Most locals lived far outside town in workhouses attached to the many wineries and farms that spread across the countryside, coming into town only for trade and amusement.

Tonight, Bracken sparked with activity, its lifeblood flowing between the town's watering holes long after the lamplighters had gone to bed. Revelry carried by the night breeze blended with the sound of a lute being abused by an unskilled performer. A coterie of beer-fueled drunks wearing simple worker's coats stepped down from a rickety horse-drawn wagon. As they walked arm in arm, they sang one of the many songs written about the exploits of the Pilots, one of the few Maia could stand. She raised her bottle to them, and they returned the gesture.

Further ahead, a Tressille elf sat cross-legged before a group of onlookers, his sweat-laden brow knitted in concentration. He murmured into the thumb-sized seed resting in his shaking hands, coaxing a small strand of magic from beyond the Veil to heed his words. Maia lingered and watched. After three minutes of nothing, a green sprout rose from the seed and blossomed into a little blue flower. The crowd cheered and threw small coins to the elf, who looked ready to faint from the spellcasting effort.

Maia thought about showing the crowd what real magic looked like but decided against it, and left the street mage to his hard-won praise.

Halfway across the rough stone bridge leading over the river and out of town, she stopped to take in the energetic sprawl of Bracken extending behind her. A part of her wanted to take credit for the town's energy, but a single fast-healing drunk could only do so much.

More likely, it was the tension of impending war that drove towns like Bracken all across the Freelands to carry on like each night was their last. Word had come from the border city of Whitehorn that the Noctean Empire had issued the Freelands an ultimatum: Whitehorn was to deliver the head of the cadre of freedom fighters known as Brave Dawn and cease all incursions and opposition against the Empire; if they failed to do so, the Freelands would suffer the wrath of the Emperor's divine might. No threats of trade sanction from the other continental nations would stop them this time, the decree said.

And Elizabeth was about to march to Whitehorn, to join Brave Dawn in their hopeless fight to liberate oppressed Imperial citizens from the Emperor's clutches. Even nestled in a mountain pass, surrounded by thousands of tons of stone with tall walls at each end of the pass, Whitehorn stood as much a chance of surviving a full Noctean siege as a pebble had of breaking a waterfall's flow.

Heavy metal feet shook the stone beneath her feet, breaking Maia's reverie. Two suits of thick armor, coated in white enamel, approached from the far side of the bridge. They towered over her, twelve feet tall and half as wide. Domed helmets connected securely to box-like torsos, hiding the heads of the riders. Stubby metal claws swayed as the armored suits trudged her way. As they drew closer, lamplight danced across the golden lion of Noctis emblazoned on their chests.

Iron Wardens. They were made of steel, not iron, but people took to the name regardless. Anybody could get the plans to build their own from a local scribe for the price of paper and ink, but the act of constructing a Warden proved far more difficult. The complex machinery required to move that much metal carried high costs and required skill beyond the grasp of most local smiths.

How generous of the Noctean Empire, then, to offer Iron Wardens and the soldiers to operate them to any community in the Freelands and the other surrounding nations willing to pay a small fee in exchange. What the Empire lost in steel, they earned in public trust; how could anybody hate a nation willing to deliver peace and protection to those who needed it?

Some people of the Freelands were eager to forget the past. Maia wasn't. She wondered if she ever could.

The Wardens stopped a few strides away from her. A tinny echo tinged one of the rider's voices as it drifted from the hollow steel shell. "Well, look what we have here. Trying out for town drunk, Pilot?"

"Competition's been lacking. I don't think I'll have a problem securing the title," Maia replied, not missing a beat.

The second Warden saluted, his suit's steel claw clinking against his helmet. "Evening, Sunder. Just out for nightly patrol. You heading home?"

"That's the plan, yes," Maia said.

"Why are you getting friendly with her?" The first Warden slapped the other on the arm. "And why tell her our business? She's not in charge of us. She's just a thug who beats up drunks so she can relive her glory days. Isn't that right, Pilot?"

With a carefully chosen middle finger, Maia scratched her eye. "The next time you have a few drinks in you, let me know, and we'll find out. In the meantime, I would love to stay and have a quarrel, but I've been shot with two of them tonight already, so I'll be going. But before I do, settle something for me: are you Imperial shit stains utterly useless at your jobs? Or just cowards? I think the people of Sanford are dying to know."

The surlier Warden took a stomping step toward her, cracking stone beneath his armor's metal foot. "Bold words, Pilot. If you did what you're meant to, we wouldn't have need to be in this piss hole country doing *your* duty. I have half a mind to knock you on your drunken ass."

"And I have half a mind to let you try. The difference between us is that I have another half a mind. I'm off to bed. Don't go rusting on me now, boys."

She pushed past the hulking constructs and continued down the bridge. Five steps later, she heard the groaning sound of the Wardens turning.

"Fuck you, Sunder!" the second Warden cried, his voice laced with the kind of hurt that only comes from being let down by a personal hero. "What makes you think you're better than us?"

A ball of fire was already crackling in her hand as Maia turned. "For starters? How about this?"

For most people gifted with magical talent, spellcasting was an arduous task. The words needed to coax even one strand of magical energy from beyond the Veil were different for each person. It took years to learn where shortcuts could be made, what words could be omitted, while still weaving strands into a proper spell. Even then, the most skilled mages still needed time to cast anything worthwhile, even with the aid of material components.

Maia didn't need words, or time, or anything else. Fire belonged to her.

She dropped the ball of flames onto the stone, willing it to spread into a high and mighty sheet between her and the Wardens. She left the crackling flames behind, dismissing them with a clench of her fist as she reached the other side of the bridge, far from the Warden's colorful shouting.

The dirt road slithered off into the darkness. Maia followed it, letting the shadows swallow her whole. Gradually, her vision adjusted from lamplight to moonlight.

A small dot of fire in the distance grew larger as she trudged on. Maia veered toward it as the road divided. Every night for the last year, her path home brought her here. Some nights, she considered taking the long way around or using another one of her Pilot abilities to magically transport herself home. It was one of those nights, but she reminded herself that avoiding the fire wouldn't be fair. She stayed on course until she reached it.

A raging conflagration of smokeless orange flame roared and licked at the night sky from the depths of a wide crater. Maia could picture where the small winery used to be at the center of the blaze. The blasted remains of the structure had long since turned to ash, but the fire continued to burn without fuel to feed it. In the two years it had raged, the inferno never spread past the edges of the mile-wide crater to the untended vineyard surrounding it, seemingly content with sustaining itself on the memory of what once stood there.

"Hello, Father." Maia took a swig from her bottle. She wondered if things would have been different, had she been there when it happened. No matter how many times she forced the inferno away, the flames returned the second she stopped pushing them down.

There was no way to prove whether it was Noctean mages who had conjured the never-ending blaze, but among her many enemies, Emperor Caelus Noctis

III was the only one with the means. If she was right, that made two parents Maia had lost to the Empire, and there wasn't a gods-damned thing she could do about it without declaring war on an entire nation.

Maia's shoulders went rigid enough to split timber. She took another pull from the bottle, then let it dangle from her fingertips. Her eyes watered from the light of the flames. With her mind in the fire, she almost didn't feel the tingling creeping its way through her chest.

Shit.

A pinch became a tight squeeze, sending radiating waves of pain through her chest and forcing Maia to her knees. She curled into a shaking ball and remained there, teeth clenched until the episode subsided. Maia gasped for breath, sucking in the cool night air with a powerful hunger.

"Well, that was fucking awful." She coughed as she pushed to her feet, drained what wine remained in her bottle, and tossed it into the trees. If no healer in the Freelands could find the source of whatever illness was causing her to suffer agonizing chest pains or discern why they were coming more frequently, at least she had liquor to ease her agony.

With a wave to the dancing flames, she cut into the dense forest. Eventually, she broke through the tree line. Across a quiet field, her massive war machine, clad in gold-trimmed crimson plate armor laid over limbs of gray metal, rested exactly where she had left her.

Scarlet, last of the mighty Vanguardians, stood three hundred feet tall when she wasn't lounging against the sheer cliff face where Maia often left her. Scarlet was made to resemble a knight in full harness, from her thick chest plate down to a set of faulds spreading over her hips. Her head was a single piece of round, shaped metal modeled after a full helm, with a curved visor of strange black glass harder than iron covering the space where her eyes should have been. The flickering flames of several campfires lit the underside of her bent legs. Her one remaining arm rested against the ground at her side, palm up, waiting for Maia to return.

As it often did, Maia's gaze drifted to the ruined remains of Scarlet's left arm, dangling just beneath her flared pauldron. During the first three years of the seven Maia had been her Pilot, Scarlet always recovered from any damage she sustained in battle. Maia couldn't understand why Scarlet had stopped mending herself, why the dents in her chest and the scrapes and tears marring her beautiful crimson frame remained. Something had changed.

"Pilot!" A gaunt figure emerged from beneath the flaps of the largest of the red-tinged tents that dotted the grass beneath Scarlet.

"Brother Tobias." Maia hid her exhaustion with the biggest smile she had left in her.

The priest straightened his red robes and the sharp point of his black beard and pressed his hands together. He looked up with wide, expectant eyes until she returned the gesture. "Oh, Red Pilot of Fire. I fear I have terrible news."

"So do I, but you can go first."

"I'm afraid young Benjamin tried to ascend the goddess tonight and lost his footing. We thought it best to conduct his last rites before you returned. His body has already been committed to the flame."

Maia balled her fist to keep her hand steady. "Tobias, I want you to repeat to me what I told you the last time this happened."

"You said that none of us should attempt to climb Scarlet, the Red Knight Vanguardian, the sole surviving Vanguardian, deliverer of—"

"Great. Now, tell me what I said about throwing bodies into the fire where my childhood home used to be."

"I believe you said that it was against your wishes."

Maia sighed, pressing her fingers to the bridge of her nose. "So, tell me, then, why another of your flock is dead, and why his ashes are swirling around in *my* fire?"

"As I've explained, many in the Order of Scarlet believe that our goddess will grant a boon to whoever is brave enough to ascend and touch Her face and feel Her divine splendor. For some, this is worth the pain of death. I try to dissuade them when I can, but I'm only one man. As for the fire...well, the sacred flame never falters. It is a convenient place for the Order of Scarlet to conduct its rituals."

"Scarlet is a walking pile of metal fused with magic. Not a goddess. If she could talk, I think she would tell you to stop killing yourselves on her behalf. And if she could talk, I would know. I'm her Pilot."

"If she doesn't speak to you, then how do you know Scarlet is a woman?" Tobias said.

The fog from many bottles of wine finally caught up to Maia. "You know what? I'm not answering any more questions tonight. The last person tying me to Bracken is planning to leave town in the morning. If she does, I'm probably going to leave, too."

"I understand." Tobias moved with quick steps to keep up with Maia as she marched toward Scarlet's palm. "I will let the Order know. Where are we headed, Pilot?"

"*We* aren't headed anywhere. *I'm* going to get up early and try to sort this shit out. If I can't, then I'm taking Scarlet somewhere far, far away from here. You're not invited to follow."

"But we need Her! Without Scarlet, we... You would take our goddess from us?"

"I would save your lives." Maia leapt into Scarlet's palm, reaching out to the intangible force that connected them, and willed the knight to lift her hand. Metal ground against metal as the hand started its slow ascent. "Find a new goddess, Tobias. This one has too much blood on her hands already."

Scarlet's hand crossed her chest, depositing Maia neatly on her left shoulder. From there, Maia moved with ginger steps to Scarlet's head, to where a series of overlapping plates formed a hatch at the base of her skull. Maia willed them to open and entered the titanic construct.

Scarlet's cabin had nothing in the way of decor. A pair of old burlap rucksacks holding Maia's meager belongings were crammed into the far corner of the dull, rectangular chamber. A crumpled bedroll was splayed out in the opposite corner, far from the etched circle at the cabin's center and the soft beam of white light that shone down onto it from the ceiling.

Maia looked out through the inside of Scarlet's visor, which covered the far wall and doubled as a viewport. She hated sleeping in Scarlet's cabin. The stale air reminded her more of a mausoleum than the battle station of a marvelous feat of magical engineering. But since the hatch plates would only open for Scarlet's Pilot, the cabin was the one place in the entire world where Maia could truly let down her guard.

She collapsed onto the bedroll. Her shoulders protested as they dug into the hard metal floor underneath the thin fabric. As she stared at the flat, unadorned ceiling, Maia thought of ways to convince Elizabeth to stay in Bracken.

She could always tell Elizabeth about the illness ravaging her. Maybe that would compel her to stay. But that would mean becoming an even greater burden to the only person left in the world who still cared for her. Maia wondered if it would be better to simply leave at first light and walk until whatever was ruining her heart finally ended her. Whatever she intended to do, it would have to be done in the morning—after she sobered up. And after Elizabeth had time to come to her senses.

As she felt herself slide away into the darkness, Maia prayed that she had drank enough wine to sleep too deeply for her nightmares to find her.

Chapter 2
A Bitter Reunion

The sunlight flowing into Scarlet's cabin stung Maia's eyes as she awoke. She never understood why the black glass viewport blocked anyone from seeing inside Scarlet's cabin while allowing the morning sun to intrude on a perfectly good hangover. Like everything else involving Scarlet, magic was probably responsible. Scarlet's creator would know, but she wasn't exactly reachable for questioning.

Maia stretched and rolled to her feet. The sudden motion caused her stomach to make a sound somewhere between a gurgle and a growl. She stumbled to the hatch plates and willed them to open just in time to vomit over the edge and onto the cliff wall behind Scarlet.

"Sorry!" she called to Scarlet and anyone unfortunate enough to be standing below. Maia wiped her mouth with the back of her hand, changed into a less-perforated shirt, and stepped out onto Scarlet's shoulder.

Rather than call Scarlet's hand to ferry her to the ground, Maia stepped off Scarlet's right shoulder, dropping a short distance before the sloping angle of Scarlet's bicep met her worn leather boots. Maia skated and skipped down the length of the long metal limb, her arms wavering as she struggled to keep her balance.

As she reached Scarlet's wrist, her feet crossed, sending her into a rolling tumble. She came to rest in a heap on the trampled grass.

"Majestic," she mumbled, brushing grass and dirt from her black breeches and her shirt, which was a red so deep it could be mistaken for black's distant cousin. By the time she got to her feet, Tobias had emerged from his tent and called to her, so she started jogging in the opposite direction.

Over the past year, Elizabeth had brought up the topic of joining Brave Dawn several times. No matter how determined she sounded, she always found one reason or another to stay in Bracken. Maia began to suspect that she was one of those reasons. She couldn't help but notice the overlong glances Elizabeth stole while Maia was pretending not to do the same. Maia saw the gears turning behind those beautiful brown eyes, as if Elizabeth was puzzling a way to crack her impenetrable shell.

Elizabeth had a big heart, the biggest Maia had ever known, but she wasn't a warrior. Even if Elizabeth believed that leaving town would spare Maia from having to put herself in harm's way every night, Maia couldn't let her leave Bracken to join the Resistance. A quick talk and an apology for whatever she had done to prompt Elizabeth's sudden decision would make everything right again.

Despite the late nights she kept, Elizabeth always rose at dawn's light to prepare for the coming night's patrons. Though the sun was already high in the sky, Maia hoped that if she hurried, she could catch up with her and keep her from making a huge mistake.

Maia's heart thumped too hard in her chest. She didn't have time for a slow, hour-long walk to Bracken, so she elected to abuse another of her Pilot abilities. She stood straight, focusing on a memory of Bracken in her mind's eye. She punched across her body to one side, then the other, willing one of the many spells woven into her body to awaken. Red ethereal wisps of magical energy twisted around her in a tight flurry as she thrust a fist upwards and looked to the sky.

The Teleport spell's energy flowed upward into a beam of crimson light, and Maia floated within it. A moment later, the light subsided, and she found herself standing in Bracken, next to the lone ballista at the center of town. When she arrived at Barlowe's Tavern and saw the barred doors, her smile and swagger sloughed away like cold rain off a duck's back. Maia's eyes traced each line of the red letters painted onto the simple wooden sign hanging on the door. No matter how hard she looked, they refused to change from "Permanently Closed" into "Just Kidding, I Would Never Leave You."

"I thought about leaving a letter." Elizabeth's voice, light as summer rain, startled Maia. "I worried someone might take it before you arrived."

Maia didn't turn around right away. She needed time to cover her panic with a fresh smile. When she did turn, she found Elizabeth dressed for travel, wearing a riding cape and sitting astride a white mare.

"Nice cape," Maia said.

"I like capes. Traveling is a fine excuse to wear one."

"You're actually leaving." Maia approached the horse and pet its head to keep her hands busy.

"I've made up my mind." The words came too rigid. Too straight. Elizabeth must have practiced them until any roughness, any wavering, had been filed away.

"When the Nocteans finally get the stones to attempt another invasion, Whitehorn will fall. Brave Dawn won't be able to stop them."

"They can. They will...with your help. The Freelands need their Pilot."

"Come on. This song is old. You know how it ends. If I go anywhere near the border, the Empire will take it as an act of war. They'll feel threatened and use that as an excuse to attack Whitehorn directly. It's not my place to interfere. Pilots kill Behemoths and Ferals. We don't liberate helpless Imperial citizens."

"If you're not going to help," Elizabeth cut back, anger creeping into the edges of her voice, "then at least leave Bracken. Find somewhere far away from here where you can be at peace. You deserve that much."

Elizabeth turned her mare and stared down at Maia, her eyes pleading. "Why do you let them hurt you? You let them come with their knives, and their spears, and their bows, and you let them take pieces of you. Why? Why don't you fight back or run away? Why do you stay *here,* of all places?"

"I'm the Pilot of a giant walking death machine. There's nowhere to hide. If people want to find me, they'll find me." Maia dared to laugh. "If I can't stop people from coming with their knives and spears and whatever else, at least here, I'm well-watered for the trouble."

Nodding slowly, Elizabeth raised a black-gloved hand to wipe the corner of her eye. "If you want to stay here and drink yourself to death, if that's what you really want, then I can't stop you. I can't think of a person in this world who could. But I'm not about to stay here and watch."

"I'm sorry. Really."

Elizabeth shook her head. "Just come with me. Please? You don't have to fight if you don't want to. You don't have to be alone anymore."

Maia's chest fluttered. She wanted to say yes, a thousand times yes. But when she opened her mouth, her voice stuck, held fast by old promises.

My heart belongs to you, Leona, and no other. The words were easy to say back then. Maia wondered if she would have said them at all if she knew how hard they would be to live by.

Elizabeth looked away, taking Maia's silence as her answer. "Goodbye, Sunder." She wheeled the mare about and took off at a canter. She didn't look back.

Maia's smile held for the time it took her to splinter the bar on the tavern door with a thrust of her palm. She entered the sun-starved expanse and pushed the doors closed behind her.

Fumbling behind the bar, she found the crate of Brackenberry wine Elizabeth kept just for her. One by one, Maia lined up the dark bottles on the counter. Twelve soldiers stood at perfect attention, ready to march on her.

Maia rounded the bar and settled onto her stool. She upended the first bottle, gulping like a suckling babe until it was empty. It tumbled to the ground and shattered, like everything else she touched.

Passing out far from the safety of Scarlet's cabin left Maia vulnerable, but in that empty tavern, she found a significant lack of fucks to give. She uncorked another bottle, and another, until darkness came for her once more.

The new headache that greeted Maia when she woke made the one from that morning seem like a blissful picnic on a warm summer's day. She pushed herself upright, giving her eyes a few moments to adjust to the waking world. Only four bottles of the twelve remained on the bar.

"May have overdid it." Maia slipped off her stool for the last time and left the tavern.

She rarely walked the streets at this hour. The town should have been brighter in the light of day, more colorful than it was at night. Without the crowds and revelry, though, Bracken looked gray and cold. Plain. Had it always been that way?

"So long, Bracken." The words didn't hurt like she thought they would, but the hollow space they left in her chest was worse somehow.

The mid-afternoon sun bore down on Maia's shoulders, making the walk back to Scarlet seem longer than usual. When she finally emerged from the tree line into the clearing, she prepared for Brother Tobias to descend upon her.

But Brother Tobias wasn't there. Neither was the rest of the Order of Scarlet. Large patches of flattened grass and abandoned fire pits were all that remained of the hundreds of lost souls that made up Tobias' flock.

Maia didn't have time to wonder where they had gotten off to. She was too busy staring at the stone cliff face at the end of the clearing where Scarlet's massive body should have been resting.

Panic swept through Maia's chest, lighting her lungs with wildfire. Somehow, Tobias had made off with Scarlet. But that wasn't possible. A Pilot and their Vanguardian were bonded; nobody else could command or guide a bonded Vanguardian, not even another Pilot. Since Vanguardians didn't just go for jaunty strolls on their own, Maia couldn't find another way to explain the sudden disappearance of her walking war machine.

A sudden pulsing throb in the back of Maia's head startled her. She was about to blame it on her hellish hangover when the familiarity of the pulse sent her heart pounding harder in her chest.

It had been over a year since she last felt it. This wasn't the dull, pumping ache that she experienced when a pack of Ferals crossed over into her world from whatever hellscape their masters called home. This sensation pulled harder, too distinct for her prey to be anything but a Behemoth.

A pack of Ferals could wipe out a town's population in hours if left unchecked; a single Behemoth could destroy the town itself in a fraction of that time. And there was no way Maia could defeat a Behemoth without her Vanguardian.

She reached out to the invisible thread that tied her to Scarlet. The connection was strong. Distant. Scarlet was far away, moving with uneven strides toward the source of the pulsing in Maia's head.

Her hands were halfway through the motions for her Teleport spell when she halted the rising flow of magic. If she Teleported, it would be an hour before she could call upon the spell again.

She decided to make her way by foot, so that once she caught up to Tobias, beat the living shit out of him until he explained how he had made off with Scarlet, and handled the Behemoth, she could quickly transport Scarlet somewhere nobody would ever find her.

Maia burned hard for almost three hours, arms and legs pumping with hot adrenaline as she ran. A flurry of worried thoughts flew through her mind faster than the grass passing beneath her, but she let them slip away. There was no room for distractions while Scarlet was under someone else's control. All that mattered was reaching her before Tobias did something stupid with her.

The brisk evening wind failed to soothe her as she sped across a grassy plain. In the distance, the setting sun painted Scarlet's silhouette onto the canvas of the horizon. Spotting several forms crouched in the grass ahead, Maia skidded to an abrupt stop, kicking torn sod into the air. One of the crouched figures rose from his prayer, brushing dirt and grass off his crimson robes.

"Brother Tobias," Maia sighed and cracked her knuckles. "I have many questions."

"Oh, Pilot!" Tobias cried, his eyes gleaming with manic fire. "Come, bear witness to a miracle! Scarlet has awakened! She moves on Her own to strike back against the invading menace!"

"Oh, shut up." She stepped past him, more interested in the other group gathered near Scarlet. The light of the setting sun cast soft gold onto their white armor.

"Nocteans," Tobias said.

Only one man in Noctis would be bold enough to march into the Freelands, break several treaties, and secure a weapon of mass destruction that was impossible to steal.

Except somehow, he *had* stolen it.

"I'm going to go say hello to our neighbors. You should stand back." Maia balled her hands into tight fists. The red-robed fanatics fell back, giving her a wide berth.

Maia couldn't just walk into a retinue of Noctean soldiers looking the way she did. She needed them to know she was serious. She thrust her arms over her head, crossing them as she channeled a Pilot ability that no mage could ever match. Magical energy coursed through her, sparking every inch of her body. Red light swirled over her, joined by thin strands of flame that converged to cover her like a blazing coat.

She brought her crossed arms down to her chest. The swirling fire that enveloped her burst outward and quickly dissipated. Maia stood in the explosion's wake, covered in a suit of gleaming red armor trimmed with gold, like Scarlet's, with a visor of the same black glass covering her eyes. Two long, thin falchions rested across her back, their curved edges hot and glowing.

Maia flexed her gauntlets and began an easy stride toward the Noctean host, confident that the dazzling flames cast by her transformation had let them know exactly who they were dealing with.

Panicked shouts and a row of spears greeted Maia as she approached the Nocteans. A smile spread across her lips beneath the cool, smooth metal of her helmet. To anyone else on the continent, a retinue of Noctean soldiers was a wave of white death ready to roll over them. To Maia, they were a minor inconvenience, at best.

When the spears parted to make way for the group's mounted leader and his officers, Maia's smile faded. His close-cropped hair was the color of salt, complementing his bulky suit of white-enameled armor. It didn't match the raven hair worn by the man Maia had once fought beside, but the silver wolf emblem of House Valerius on his chest and the perfect, deliberate maze of scars etched across his worn sandy face and down his neck left no doubt in Maia's mind as to who she was looking at.

As she suspected and feared, it was General Arcturus Valerius himself leading the Noctean insurgents.

Arcturus had once told Maia that the pattern of razor-thin scars covered most of his body, proof of the mandatory magical modifications he had undergone in his youth. The enchanted metal fused to his bones contained all manner of body magics, granting him strength and endurance that almost matched hers.

Almost.

He brought his horse to a halt a respectful distance away and rested his right arm, a rune-inscribed Blacksteel prosthetic that glowed with multiple enchantments, on the pommel of the similarly enchanted longsword sheathed at his hip.

"Hello, Maia," he said in a warm, fatherly tone.

Maia fought the urge to rip her falchions from her back and take his head from his shoulders. "If it isn't Old Lightning Rod himself," she returned. Her helmet distorted her voice, giving it the edge of vibrating steel.

"That's General Valerius to you, traitor!" a member of Arcturus' entourage shouted from the saddle of his own steed. Maia's gaze snapped to him; the man shrunk back as if she had slapped him.

She didn't rule out doing that very thing if he opened his mouth again.

Arcturus raised his Blacksteel hand in peace. His angular face cooled to a neutral expression. "Tell me, Maia. How have you fared since we last spoke?"

"Nobody calls me that anymore."

"Nevertheless, it's good to see you."

"Can't say I feel the same. You're a long way from home." Maia made a show of looking over his retinue. "Based on the lack of arrow wounds, I'm guessing you didn't come through Whitehorn." She tapped a metal finger against her helmet. "I bet you got passage through Brimholme. The right coin to the wrong people. That's a hell of a detour, going all the way around the mountains."

Arcturus chuckled. "You remain sharp as ever, Maia."

"You have no idea. Now, let's get to the part where you tell me *why* you've snuck into the Freelands, how you managed to make off with Scarlet, and which testicle is your least favorite."

"Maia, I—"

"Because that's the one I'm going to leave you with."

Arcturus opened his mouth to respond, but dull vibrations in the earth and the throbbing of her Hunter Sense pulled Maia's attention past Scarlet to the blurry shape of the approaching Behemoth. An intense drive to fight the monster competed with her desire to see Arcturus' blood soaking the soil at her feet.

With a swift motion that belied his age and the weight of his armor, Arcturus swept down from his mount. He strode past Maia, motioning for her to follow him. "Be at ease. I'm not here to make war with you. I've come not only to reclaim Noctean property, but to bring you a gift. Something you've longed for, in fact."

"First, Scarlet doesn't belong to Noctis—she's mine. Second, what I long for is the Emperor's head on a pike. I don't think you have that stashed in your saddlebag, so."

The old general bristled. His iron gaze narrowed. "Know that I still hold you in high regard for everything you've done in the service of our divine Emperor. And for everything you've suffered, you have my sympathies. That being said, I won't tolerate blasphemy. Especially from a Noctean citizen."

"Is all that rusted metal fused to your skull clogging your mind? I was born in the Freelands."

"We thought so as well. We questioned some old associates who worked with your mother when she was affiliated with Brave Dawn, before she..." He frowned and cleared his throat. "They revealed that she gave birth to you while fleeing Noctis in the back of a wagon. As it happens, you came into this world *before* crossing the border into Whitehorn. That makes you a Noctean. And though I can't read your expression through your helm, I assume you know what this entails."

"What belongs to the Empire's citizens belongs to the Emperor." Maia's stomach turned. "Even if you're not lying, it won't be enough to convince the other continental nations that your little social call isn't a breach of the treaties. But I doubt they'll take action considering you've found out how to steal control of a Vanguardian from a Pilot. Looks like you have the advantage. Still, there's just one problem."

Arcturus smiled. "You'll kill us all before you let me leave with Scarlet."

She pointed at him, cocking her hand like a gun. "Sharp as ever, Arcturus."

"Before we draw swords and spoil this lovely sunset, allow me to present the gift I've brought you."

Maia followed his sweeping hand to the horizon, where a titanic mass shook the earth with each approaching step.

"A Behemoth? You shouldn't have."

"No, Maia. I bring you the gift of freedom," Arcturus said. "I'm told you spend every night drinking yourself into a stupor, content to let our Iron Wardens handle most of the Ferals that cross over into our world. It's obvious that you no longer wish to bear the burden of being a Pilot. You want to leave that life, that past, behind. And yet, you cannot. You're sworn to protect the world from otherworldly invaders. But what if you didn't have to? What if someone else could carry on in your stead, someone willing to endure the hardships that you've faced for so many years?"

Maia's breath caught in her chest. "Son of a bitch. You finally did it. You made a new Pilot."

The memory of her tormentor forced its way into Maia's mind. On the night of their meeting, looking up at her from the steel table she was bound to, she wondered if her captor was some kind of demon. When she began her dark work, Maia was sure of it.

Before she subjected Maia and the other four youths she had captured to nerve-fraying agony, she went to great lengths to describe what she was doing to them, and why. Maia tried to recall the numerous potions and treatments and spells that this monster who called herself Heretic used to re-forge her into a living weapon, but Maia's screams had drowned out what would have no doubt been a fascinating lecture under better circumstances.

What she did retain from the experience was that creating a Pilot wasn't a simple thing. Even a circle of elder mages would likely fumble the task.

But as she watched Scarlet's right hand curl into a tight fist, Maia couldn't deny that somehow, Noctis had finally perfected the process.

"This wasn't how I wanted the two of you to meet," Arcturus said, motioning with his head toward Scarlet. "She was to depart with an armed escort once her training was complete. Apparently, she couldn't wait to see her duty done. She has her mother's tenacity."

Maia looked sidelong at Arcturus. "Who's up there, controlling Scarlet?"

His chest swelled with pride. "My daughter, Serenia. Though, ever since she awoke, she prefers 'Ren.'"

The name sent Maia falling back through her memories to a stained image she hoped she could one day scrub from her mind. The day she first met Arcturus. The day the first Behemoth crossed over. The monster razed the Imperial capital of Noctis without challenge until Maia arrived with Scarlet and put it down. By the time the work was done, the death toll reached well into the thousands.

When she descended from Scarlet to meet with representatives of the city she had just saved from destruction, the first thing Maia saw was the look on Arcturus' face, fresh from the news that his wife and daughter hadn't survived the attack. He looked like a man struggling to comprehend the hole in his breast after his heart had been carved out with a rusted spoon.

In the seven years since that day, Maia's numerous failures had covered her hands with enough blood to drown the world, but none weighed as heavily as her first debt. When Arcturus approached her and pleaded with her to work with the Noctean Empire to prevent future tragedies, guilt overcame her better judgment.

"When the first Behemoth came," Arcturus said, bringing Maia back to the present, "we considered that it might be a weapon set upon us by one of the other nations. Certain nobles were reported dead or missing, for their protection. Serenia survived the Behemoth's attack, though it left her in a coma. Aurelia, my wife, did not.

"Long before you broke ties with the Empire, we took measures to ensure our continued survival. The continental nations closest to us all possessed a native Pilot and a Vanguardian. We did not. We sought to right that imbalance." Arcturus paused as Scarlet's left leg creaked to life, starting an awkward stride toward the approaching Behemoth. "It took time and much sacrifice, but we were finally successful. Not only did the Emperor bring my daughter back to me, he presented us with the means to fight the Behemoths. To win."

"How old is she?"

"We celebrated her sixteenth birthday just last month."

Sixteen. That was the age Maia had been when her powers and duties were thrust upon her, altering her life's course forever.

At sixteen, Maia hadn't been ready. The disaster in the Noctean capital was proof of that. Seeing the awkward way that Scarlet moved, listing to the right with each straight-legged step, it was clear that Serenia was even less prepared than Maia had been. She was a dull knife, more likely to skip and cut her wielder than whatever she was pressed against.

Arcturus placed his Blacksteel hand on Maia's pauldron. "I understand why you left us. You should know, I've never held a grudge. We...I made mistakes."

"You're making a big one right now. You've worked with me. You've seen what it means to be a Pilot. You know what it costs. How could you let any girl, let alone your own *daughter,* suffer that life?"

"Because there is need." He let the words hang between them until their weight settled. "The world needs a defender. Serenia accepts her charge willingly, for the glory of her Emperor and her people. Let go, Maia. Serenia can become our savior in your stead. You can finally rest."

"Bullshit." Maia shrugged his hand away. "You're not saving anybody. You're securing the most dangerous weapon in the known world for a power-hungry madman who thinks he's a god. And with Scarlet at his command, he might as well be."

"Whether you believe that our cause is just or not is irrelevant. Answer me truly, Maia. Do you want to continue being a Pilot? *Can* you continue? I know about the pains. Have they gotten worse?"

Maia's fingers hooked Arcturus' breastplate. She pulled, bringing them face-to-face. Arcturus raised a hand, warding off any reprisal from his soldiers.

"How do you know about that?" Maia growled.

"I don't like having to spy on you, but it's my duty, to the Empire and to the world, to know everything I can about the last remaining Pilot of, as you so succinctly put it, 'the most dangerous weapon in the known world.' Let us help you. We have powerful mages at our disposal. There's every chance they can—"

Any lingering sympathy for Arcturus flew from her heart, replaced with the heat of the never-ending inferno burning in a crater where her childhood home once stood. She shoved him away "Oh, I know all about your powerful mages. Using fire was a nice touch. Was that your way of getting back at me, for...for everything?"

Arcturus turned his gaze to the ground. "I had nothing to do with your father's murder."

Maia's fist tightened, straining the metal of her gauntlets. "At least you're calling it what it is. In case you've lost track, that's two parents I've lost to your glorious Empire. Now, you've come to take the last thing I have left to my name. Even if I believe you, and you didn't have anything to do with my father's death, somebody in Noctis gave the order. You had to have known about it. If you didn't move to stop it, that doesn't make you any less responsible."

Maia's fixed her cold gaze on Scarlet plodding her way toward the approaching

Behemoth. "You came to get your daughter back. Let me fetch her for you. Then, I'm taking Scarlet far away, where you'll never be able to get your hands on her again. And I dare you to try and stop me."

"You can't run from this, Maia. You're not well. We both know it. Who will protect the world when you're gone? Would you leave the world without protection out of spite?"

Maia dropped into a crouch. With a mighty push, she leaped into the air, leaving Arcturus behind with questions she couldn't answer.

Chapter 3
The New Girl

Ren's legs burned with each step, muscles screaming for rest as she drove Scarlet toward her quarry. Her instructors had assured her that once she entered Scarlet's cabin and gained control of the mighty Vanguardian, her training would take over, and she would know exactly what to do.

What they didn't tell her was how difficult it would be to move Scarlet, that the mere act of forcing the metal titan to walk would send hot, stinging pain radiating up her spine. Ren grimaced and wiped sweat from her brow. Scarlet mimicked the motion, grinding the back of her crimson hand against her own forehead.

Ren sighed. Being in total control of Scarlet would take some getting used to. When she first entered the etched circle in the Pilot's cabin, and the soft beam of white light pressed down upon her, Ren panicked. Once she realized that the beam's pressure was meant to slow her so she could match Scarlet's weighty movements, her fear subsided.

The unknown architect of the Vanguardians had to be an artisan of legendary skill to craft such wondrous machines. She longed to meet him. Unfortunately, only the original five Pilots knew for certain where the Vanguardians came from. Four of them were presumed dead, and the one surviving Pilot wasn't exactly forthcoming with details about their origins.

But that didn't mean Scarlet would be the last of the Vanguardians. Soon, Noctean engineers would have a functional Vanguardian to study and replicate, as soon as Ren delivered swift and decisive ruin to the Behemoth plodding her way.

Her mind flooded with visions of thousands of Noctean citizens applauding her. Even the Emperor himself, God among mere mortals, would look up at her with admiration once she returned victorious with Scarlet under her control.

She was so fixated on her pending victory that she barely heard Scarlet's hatch plates open behind her. She snapped out of her daydream as the plates slammed shut in a staccato of dull thuds and froze at the sound of clinking metal footsteps approaching.

She tried and failed to still the hammering beat of her heart. Every noble in Noctis had seen paintings of Sunder. The works often depicted her in the same bulky enameled armor Noctean knights wore. In person, Sunder's crimson Pilot's armor was like nothing from any nation she had studied. It resembled Scarlet in miniature, though sleeker, with thinner plates of gold-trimmed red and gray layered perfectly over a suit of dark chain mesh so fine it appeared woven. The twin falchions on her back held fast to her armor without the aid of a sheath, their edges glowing faintly like simmering coals.

The woman who avenged the death of Ren's mother canted her head, her expression hidden beneath her black glass visor. Ren realized, with a fresh jolt of panic, that she was being measured. She took comfort in the weight of the fine rapier on her left hip and the revolver holstered at the small of her back and stood a little taller under Sunder's scrutinizing gaze.

When she spoke, Sunder's voice carried the cold tinge of tempered steel. "You must be the new girl."

"And you must be Maia Sunderland, the Red Pilot of Fire." Ren set her gaze forward and took another step toward the Behemoth. "I am Serenia Lucretia Valerius, Pilot First Class of the Noctean Imperial Army. My friends call me Ren."

"Serenia it is, then. Get out of my Vanguardian."

"I'm afraid I can't do that. First and foremost, Emperor Caelus Noctis III has tasked me with retrieving Scarlet, and I'm bound to fulfill my sworn duty. Second, it was quite a climb to get up here, and I don't intend to let that effort go to waste. Third, as you can plainly see, I'm rather occupied at present."

Ren motioned with her chin toward the viewport. The hulking Behemoth stomping their way was a head shorter than Scarlet, but Scarlet was three hundred feet tall, so the giant still stood tall enough to crush a house underfoot with ease. It reminded Ren of a lion twisted to walk upright, with wild eyes shining against a mane of bronze fur. The key distinction between this lion-thing and a real lion, aside from its extreme size, was that its muscled body was covered from the neck down in short, sharp quills, much like a porcupine.

The weight of the coming battle sent Ren's heart slamming harder against her sternum, and she lifted her right leg, placing it down straight and sliding it back across the floor of the cabin to simulate a step. One foot in front of the other. That was all she had to do to keep moving forward. To win.

"I don't know how you're able to control Scarlet, but you have no idea what you're doing." Sunder sighed. A flush of warmth flooded Ren's cheeks. Sunder stared at her for a long moment. "Just walk normally. The beam will hold you."

The lion charged, shaking the earth with each titanic stride. Ren planted her foot and took a step. To her surprise, her foot glided in place over the smooth metal floor of the cabin, and she remained within the control beam's soft glow. She took another step. Scarlet moved just as smooth, all lurching gone from her stride.

A rush of confidence spurred Ren into a run. Her opponent grew larger until the beast filled up the viewport. Ren planted her foot, raised her left arm, and launched a quick jab as the Behemoth came into range.

It would have been a potent strike, save for the fact that Scarlet didn't have a left arm. Scarlet's hips turned as she waved the remnants of her upper arm at the Behemoth. The lion creature tackled Scarlet, driving her back and shaking the cabin. Ren's teeth rattled in her skull as she fought to keep standing.

"Okay. Playtime's over, Princess," Sunder said. "Close your eyes to break your connection to Scarlet. I'll take it from here."

"Your assistance is not needed!" Ren shouted. She thrust out with her right hand, and Scarlet launched a cross, narrowly missing the lion's head as it swayed.

Ren kept punching, sending Scarlet's arm pumping through empty air as the nimble monster dodged her barrage. Grunting with effort and frustration, Ren launched a sharp uppercut aimed squarely at the lion's chin. As Scarlet's red knuckles rose into view, the Behemoth stepped back out of range. The beast leaped forward after the blow had passed, slamming its fist into Scarlet's head and turning it.

The control beam's hold wrenched Ren to the side, contorting her body to mimic Scarlet's twisted posture. The sudden jerk sent a flash of pain through her side. So long as Ren remained in the control beam, Ren and Scarlet would mirror each other's movements, for better or worse.

Ren gritted her teeth as she turned and lashed out, kicking in a wide arc. The world outside Scarlet spun as the Vanguardian turned into the motion.

"Too slow," Sunder said.

The lion slipped under Scarlet's leg and vanished. Something smashed into Scarlet from behind, sending Scarlet toppling forward. The ground rushed up to meet her. Ren closed her eyes and covered her face with her hands. She fell from the circle of light, slamming into the black glass of Scarlet's visor.

Sparkles shot through her vision. Ren tried to shake them away, tried to make sense of what had happened. Seeing Scarlet's viewport filled with dirt, cold realization settled over her. The battle was over. Scarlet had fallen. She waited for the Behemoth to finish her off, destroying the last Vanguardian along with her dreams of becoming her people's savior. Then, the beast would be free to march on Noctis, killing everything in its path until her failure was complete.

And there was nothing she could do to stop it.

Ren rolled onto her back and stood, groaning as her vision wavered. Suddenly, the cabin pitched, and she stumbled as Scarlet righted herself.

The soft white light of Scarlet's control beam covered Sunder's shoulders. She meant to take over, to claim victory where Ren couldn't. That was worse than losing her life to a Behemoth.

Ren wanted to scream against the sting of tears forming in the corners of her eyes. She struggled to remain standing as Scarlet whirled to face her opponent, metal creaking as she turned.

Sunder's metallic tone cut like a razor. "For your first and last time piloting a Vanguardian, that was...well, terrible. Since you came all this way, I'll give you a free lesson. Pay attention. First, every Behemoth needs a name, so you can mock them later over drinks. I'm calling this one...Lionheart."

"That's a silly name," Ren said. Ahead, Lionheart was roaring, its muscled arms wide in premature celebration, showing off an underbelly bristling with a coat of spines.

"It doesn't address the quills, but we're short on time. Think you can do better?"

"No." Ren's brain swirled from her fall. She had a hard enough time staying on her feet. She doubted she could even think of a worse name, let alone a better one.

"Lionheart it is, then. Second, don't engage the enemy directly unless you have the advantage. To get the advantage, throw your opponent off their balance." Sunder cleared her throat. It sounded halfway between a cough and two knives raking against each other.

"Hey! Behemoth!" Sunder's voice projected from Scarlet, booming over the battlefield. "Settle a bet. Did your dad fuck a hedgehog or a bucket of nails to father something as ugly as you? I'm thinking both?"

The beast roared at Scarlet, paws thrashing at the air as it charged.

Sunder cocked her head toward Ren. "Most Behemoths can't speak, but they definitely know when they're being insulted. Now he's all riled up. Isn't this fun? Third, always be prepared to adapt."

"And how, exactly, does one adapt to a creature as agile as this one when piloting a massive hunk of walking metal?" Ren seethed through gritted teeth.

Scarlet's right arm drifted up at Sunder's command, parrying a wild haymaker from the thrashing lion. "Fighting isn't about speed. It's about timing and distance. Anticipation. This thing's no faster than you. It just knows you're always going to go for the head."

"Where else can I strike?" Ren shot back. "Perhaps you're forgetting that its whole body is covered in spines?"

"Perhaps you're forgetting that Scarlet is made of metal."

Sunder threw an uppercut, stepping into the blow and diverting it into Lionheart's chest as he tried to duck. The crunch of spines shattering under her knuckles sounded like a copse of trees falling in unison. Lionheart doubled over onto Scarlet's fist, wheezing in a high-pitched whine. Sunder pushed him off with her shoulder and thrust Scarlet's arm out to the side.

The screech of metal bit at Ren's ears. A beaten, notched blade slid from Scarlet's forearm and locked into place. The edges of the blade glowed red hot, like Sunder's swords, causing the air around the blade to waver. Sunder brought her right arm across her body and swung. Scarlet slashed, drawing a gout of sparks from Lionheart's shoulder as its blood kissed the open air. Again and again, she cut the beast, each wound severing spines and lighting up the air between them.

Ren ignored Lionheart's pained, flailing cries. She couldn't take her eyes off the warrior goddess standing before her, guiding Scarlet's fury with such potency and confidence. Slowly, Ren's dumbstruck awe gave way to grief. She had come all this way, fueled by praise from her father and her instructors, to prove her worth; it had only taken a few blows from her first Behemoth to undo three years of intense training and leave her defeated.

What made me think I could be you?

Lionheart fell to its knees, head lolling and body smoldering from its many wounds. The sharp screech of Scarlet's arm blade retracting back into her forearm made Ren jump. Was Sunder going to spare the beast? Ren tried to stand tall, but the wavering in her head left her leaning against the cabin wall.

Sunder swept her leg up and held it nearly vertical, completely unencumbered by the weight of her armor. "One last thing, Princess: if you're going to do anything in this world? Do it with style."

Sunder's leg burst into flame, sending waves of heat rippling through the cabin. Ren shielded her eyes as Scarlet's lifted leg ignited in turn, filling the viewport with blinding light.

"Blazing Axe!" Sunder yelled. Her leg fell, dropping Scarlet's flame-covered heel onto the Behemoth's head. Lionheart slammed chin-first into the earth and went still as crackling flames spread across its body.

Sunder turned Scarlet's back to the Behemoth as it exploded in a violent torrent of fire. When the dust and debris finally settled, nothing remained of Lionheart but a scorched crater at Scarlet's feet.

"You look like shit," Sunder said. "Word of advice, Princess. Give up while you can. Being a Pilot isn't as easy as I make it look."

Ren wanted to lash out, to tell Sunder she was wrong, that she would get stronger. That she would never give up. That she was enough. Instead, she fell to the floor. The agony of controlling Scarlet and the fog in her head stole any indignant retort she could prepare.

She looked up at Sunder, standing so fierce, so infallible. Sunder's steel-lined words barely reached her as she slipped into unconsciousness.

"Lesson over."

Maia's helmet broke apart with a thought. The pieces slid out of sight, stacking behind her head. She looked down at Serenia Valerius, half-curled on the cabin floor. Her once-pristine crown of raven braids had started to unravel and her porcelain skin, shining with sweat, had reddened from exertion. Even as she rested, her chest rising and falling beneath her black, high-collared officer's jacket, Serenia's brow furrowed as if she was aware of being unconscious, and it pissed her off.

That was understandable. If Maia had lost four years of her life to a coma like Serenia had, she would hate sleeping, too.

Somehow, Noctis had found a way to revive the girl and give her the ability to command Scarlet, but clearly, whatever they did to her wasn't enough. Every step Scarlet took taxed her. Whatever Noctis had made Serenia into, she wasn't a Pilot.

Still, there was something there, driving her on, that had compelled Maia to humor her desire to fight the Behemoth. Maia could see it in each determined stride, each failed attack. A defiant spark, warm and familiar, flared behind Serenia's blue eyes as she struggled; despite all she had lost, Serenia seemed determined to press on, to not let the weight of her past drag her down.

Arcturus told Maia so many times that what happened in Noctis wasn't her fault. He had a right to hate her, just as she had a right to despise the Empire for what it tore from her. Instead, he asked her to work with him.

Maia's father had been livid when she told him she had enlisted. How could she join forces with the Empire that took her mother's life? Looking down at Serenia, a living reminder of Maia's many failures, she remembered the answer she had given him.

I owe them. I owe her.

Maia pinched the bridge of her nose. Scarlet was the only thing she could offer as reparations for all Serenia had lost. Even if she gave up Scarlet, it wouldn't bring Serenia's mother back or buy back the time that was stolen from her. She would only be arming the Empire with the means to expand as far as the Emperor desired.

She couldn't just hand a weapon like Scarlet over to Serenia, but what else could she do? Running wasn't an option. Serenia had found Scarlet once already. That spark in her eyes told Maia that she would keep coming, again and again, until Maia was too weakened by the illness wreaking havoc through her body to do anything about it.

None of the other options that came to mind were any better. She couldn't scuttle Scarlet. That would leave the world defenseless against the Behemoths. The ballistae and cannons that had sprung up over the past seven years were a step in the right direction, but they couldn't stop a Behemoth on their own. They could only delay the inevitable.

She didn't even entertain the notion of stopping Serenia by force. Maia had taken enough from her already. And if she did cross that line, what would stop Noctis from doing what they had done to Serenia to another girl? How many would-be Pilots would Maia need to stop before it was over?

The different paths ahead of Maia fell away like petals from a dead flower. One way or another, at some point, Serenia would inherit Scarlet. She would follow Maia down the same bloody path she had walked for seven years.

But before that day came, Maia had time. Not a lot of it, but enough to change things, to give the girl what Maia never had.

Guidance.

Serenia was a dull blade, but she could be sharpened. With care and effort, Maia could potentially undo the mental conditioning that made Serenia blindly loyal to Noctis. She could ensure that if Serenia took on her mantle, she would do it properly.

And more importantly, she could show her young successor firsthand the life she was stepping into. She could make Serenia see all the misery and death that came with being the Pilot of a Vanguardian. Maybe she would begin to understand what Maia had learned long ago, that the Pilots were a mistake. Maybe she would quit. That would be the greatest victory she could hope for.

But Maia didn't have room in her heart for hope. She needed to be realistic. If Maia took Serenia on as her apprentice, she could only see two outcomes. Either Maia would be responsible for sacrificing another girl to a war that was never theirs to fight, or she would doom the entire world by arming her enemies with the ultimate weapon.

She needed time to think, but a sharp, sudden jab in Maia's chest sent her to her knees, reminding her that time wasn't on her side.

You can't keep this up forever. Time to make up your bloody mind.

A dull rumble caught Maia's attention. Something in one of Serenia's belt pouches was pulsing. Maia opened it and pulled out a smooth rectangular black stone that fit neatly in her palm. A litany of carved runes glowed across its face.

It was a Farspeaker, one of Noctis' favorite magical inventions. Each was attuned to its twin, allowing their owners to speak across any distance. It was one of the reasons the Empire had been able to grow so vast. Communication was power. Being able to relay information to all corners of the Empire without the delay of messengers allowed the Emperor and his advisers to manage a vast nation as efficiently as one would run a small village.

Serenia stirred, causing the silver chain running from her jacket's epaulet to the wolf crest pinned to her left breast to jingle. A dull moan escaped her parched lips. She would wake soon. Maia gripped the shaking Farspeaker tighter. Arcturus was trying to contact his daughter. Maia wagered he wouldn't agree to the plan forming in her mind, so she didn't bother asking for his permission.

Entering the circle of light, Maia took control of Scarlet once more. She performed the motions of her Teleport spell, sending a swirling maelstrom of energy churning around Scarlet.

Maia focused her thoughts on the most remote place in the Freelands she could think of as she thrust her fist to the sky, summoning a radiant beam of red light that would take her, Scarlet, and Serenia far from the smoking battlefield.

The sound of crashing waves brought by the evening tide roused Ren. Panic sent her rolling across cool sand and scrambling to her feet. She turned about, reaching for her weapons before she realized where she was. She was on a sandy beach, alone, save for one other soul.

"Evening, Princess." Sunder sat by a small fire, unarmored, hugging her knees as the dancing flames cast a severe shadow over her rosy beige complexion. Far behind her, Scarlet rested in the same pose.

"I told you, my name is Ren."

"That was quite the nap. How are we feeling?"

"Where are we?" Ren moved with ginger steps toward the fire.

"Answering a question with a question is rude." Sunder eased back, bracing herself on her arms. "We're still in the Freelands. West coast. A Pilot's Teleport spell can transport them to their Vanguardians, or to a Behemoth, or a large enough group of Ferals, but we can also travel to places we've been to in the past if we hold an image of that place in our minds."

"I'm well aware of that," Ren lied. The specifics of Pilot Teleportation were a mystery in the Empire. She made a mental note. At least she could bring some useful knowledge back home with her when she returned in defeat.

"This was the first place I thought of. Never been here at night. Or sober."

Ren tensed. "Am I your prisoner?"

"Not at all. You're free to go. The border is about a three-week ride that way." Sunder made a vague sweeping motion with her hand. "Another week to the capital from there, give or take."

Ren smoothed the pouches of her belt, letting her fingers slip over one cleverly concealed pouch. Getting back to the capital wouldn't be a problem. "Why have you brought me here, then? What is it you want from me?"

"I think we should talk."

Ren moved closer, easing down onto the sand on the opposite side of the fire, and regarded Sunder through the crackling flames. She didn't match the paintings Ren had seen, the ones where she wasn't wearing her famous armor. Her hair was a messy, shoulder-length tumble of dyed red that could challenge any comb and likely win. Instead of the stoic look of a hero, she wore a smug smile that provided her with an air of easy confidence, further bolstered by the lean, cord-like muscles that her armor kept hidden.

Then there was the scar. Noctean artists always portrayed Sunder's facial scar as a thin line running over her left eye. One could mistake it as a slip of an artist's brush had it not been featured so consistently in every rendition of her.

But the real scar was not a small thing. It was a rugged, ugly mess, starting on her forehead, ripping into her left brow and eyelid before carving an errant path down her cheek to her jaw. This wasn't the clean, heroic cut that Sunder was said to have earned in defense of Noctis. It looked hateful. Pilots were said to be able to recover from any wound. If that was true, why hadn't this scar ever healed?

Sunder looked up to the night sky, smiling to herself. "So. You want to be a Pilot?"

Ren averted her gaze, both to hide a rush of emotion and to keep from staring at Sunder's marred face. "It is the Emperor's wish that I become Scarlet's Pilot."

"Maybe you didn't hear me. I asked if *you* wanted to be a Pilot."

"Absolutely. I want it more than anything else in this world."

"And if I don't give you Scarlet, I bet you'll keep trying to steal her. Unless, of course, I stop you." Sunder's hand rose, cutting off her response. "Not that I would hurt you. Pilots fight Behemoths and Ferals. We don't hurt people. It's one of the rules we Pilots came up with as a group."

"What rules?"

Sunder shifted to a crouch, locking her piercing brown eyes with Ren's. "That's it, right there. You don't know anything about being a Pilot. You only know whatever horse shit the Empire spoon-fed you about 'bringing glory to Noctis and her people.' You don't know what it's like to be a Pilot. What it means. What it costs."

"I'm prepared to do my duty." Ren sat a little taller and inclined her chin.

Sunder's mocking grin stole a piece of her thunder. "Yeah? What part of 'prepared' involves losing to a Behemoth in under two minutes?" Her grin faded, replaced with a softer smile. Sunder stood and wiped sand from her black breeches. "You can still give up, you know. I never had a choice, but you do. If you take on this fight, it'll own you. Behemoths and Ferals can strike at any time. There's no rest for a Pilot. No happy ending. But you don't have to fight this fight if you don't want to."

"I want this fight." The certainty in Ren's voice surprised her, even as her heart pounded at the memory of her recent defeat. She rose to face her rival, the woman she had trained to surpass. "This is the path I wish to walk."

A sly smirk settled on Sunder's lips. "Okay, Princess. Here's what I propose. You want to be a Pilot, and I won't be around forever, so *someone* will end up taking over for me, eventually. I want you to travel with me. I want to show you what it means to be a Pilot, and I'm going to make sure that *if* I let you walk this path, you'll do right by the people. All the people. Not just Nocteans."

"A-are you serious? You're asking me to become your apprentice?"

Sunder nodded. "I'm going to take you somewhere. There's something you need to see before you commit to the life of a Pilot. Along the way, I'm going to work you hard. Prove to me that you have what it takes, and I'll consider handing Scarlet over to you."

Despite her best effort to appear impassive, Ren's face lit up, but before she could respond, Sunder raised her hand again.

"There are conditions. First, you follow my lead. You do what I say when I say it, how I say. No arguments. Second, I expect you to impress me. I'm not about to hand a walking engine of death to a temperamental child. I'll scuttle Scarlet before I let that happen. And don't even think of thanking me yet. Once we reach the end of this road, and you see what I have to show you, there's a good chance that you won't want to be a Pilot anymore."

Ren nodded slowly, considering the offer. It was possible that Sunder had no intention of giving her Scarlet, that this was all some sort of ploy.

If it came down to it, if there was no other way to secure Scarlet, Ren had very explicit instructions on how to best proceed. The massive revolver resting in the holster at the small of Ren's back, the first and only of its kind, had been a gift for her sixteenth birthday. Ren recalled the lack of joy in her father's eyes as he explained that, if needed, the weapon's thumb-sized cartridges could pierce a Pilot's armor at close range.

To her relief, a much better path had just appeared before her.

"I have a condition of my own," Ren said. She pressed on, ignoring Sunder's raised eyebrow. "If I am to be your student, if you would teach me, then I demand that you remain sober during our time together."

Sunder's glare narrowed to thin knives. The night breeze tousled her wavy hair.

"I can smell the wine on your breath, even from here," Ren continued. "If you demand my best, then I expect the same in return."

With a groan, Sunder slumped her shoulders. "I need alcohol to..." She pushed her hands through her crimson hair. "Fine. No ale."

"No ale, wine, *or* liquor."

"Blue Hells, *fine.* Now, before the Empire tears the Freelands apart looking for you, I want you to contact your father. That Farspeaker of yours is connected to his, I wager."

Ren produced her Farspeaker. She focused her intent on the strands of magic woven into the runes, causing the carvings to glow with faint light. The stone pulsed rhythmically in her hand.

After four pulses, it stopped, and her father's voice drifted from the stone. "Ren? Where has Sunder taken you? Are you hurt?"

She waited for Sunder to nod before daring to answer. "I am well, Father. Sunder has not mistreated me. She merely wanted to speak to me in private."

"I need to be sure that you're unharmed."

Ren took a deep breath, gathering her courage. "Aurelia." They had agreed long ago to use her mother's name as their private code, proof that she was not being coerced. "Sunder has asked me to travel with her. I am to become her apprentice."

"You have a duty to the Emperor to bring Scarlet home. A good soldier always follows orders."

"I haven't forgotten, Father. Everything I've done, everything I intend to do, is a step toward seeing the Emperor's will done. This will bring me closer to achieving my goal. I will return once my duty is complete."

A moment of silence. "How long are you expected to remain by Maia's side?"

"As long as it takes," Sunder cut in. "I'm not taking her hostage. She's free to leave any time she wants. No harm will come to her while she's in my care. In return, you and your soldiers are going to get the fuck out of the Freelands and stay out until we're done what we need to do."

The stone rumbled with her father's growl. "Maia, you've made it more than clear that you hold me responsible for what happened to your father. As I've said, I bear no ill will toward you. However, if any harm comes to Serenia, I will have no choice but to—"

Sunder slipped the Farspeaker from Ren's hand and squeezed it. The stone cracked in her hand. She pressed the two broken pieces back into Ren's palm. "Men and their threats. That just leaves one more thing before we shake." She stood and extended her hand. "No contacting your father. Not until we're finished."

Ren looked down at the broken Farspeaker in her hand, then back at Sunder.

"Yeah, I know," Sunder said. "But you seem like the resourceful type. If you try to call home without my permission, or if I decide you're not worth my time, we're done. I'll drop you on Daddy's doorstep myself. Do we have a deal?"

Ever since Ren woke from her endless nightmare, all she wanted was to become a Pilot and serve her people, to prevent others from suffering her mother's fate. All she needed to do was reach out and take Sunder's hand, and she would be one step closer to achieving that dream.

And yet, she hesitated. She knew the stories. She heard the rumors. Sunder was said to be responsible for the deaths of the other four Pilots. If that was true and she turned on Ren or decided to alter the terms of their arrangement...

Her father's words came to her as they always did in times of need. *A good soldier always follows orders.* She was a good soldier. Her orders were to become Scarlet's Pilot. That's what she would do, regardless of the danger.

Ren placed the two halves of the Farspeaker back in her belt pouch, straightened the cuffs of her black leather gloves, and smoothed her jacket before taking Sunder's hand.

"I humbly accept your offer, Sunder."

With a look somewhere between curiosity and amusement, Sunder regarded her. She released Ren's hand and turned away, making her way back toward Scarlet.

"Everybody calls me Sunder." She looked back over her shoulder. The corner of her mouth teased into a grin. "Call me Maia."

Chapter 4
Breaking Fast

"I fail to see how this is relevant to my Pilot training."

Seven days. It took Serenia seven days to start complaining about her training regimen. That surprised Maia. It was six days longer than she expected.

Ignoring her apprentice, she leaned back against Scarlet's prone foot and poked at the bacon and potatoes sizzling in a skillet on the coals of their campfire. She closed her eyes and basked in the smell of bubbling bacon grease blending with the sunbaked grass of the forest glade to keep from thinking about how badly she needed a cup of wine.

"Maia? Did you hear me?" Serenia said.

"Yeah. Remember the deal," Maia called back. "You do as I say, when I say. Don't like it? Quit."

Serenia stood from her squat so fast that Maia expected her to take off into the sky. She wiped the sweat from her face with the hem of her undershirt. "Is this the best use of our time together? When will we get to actual combat training?"

"Piloting a Vanguardian is about more than hitting hard. Don't think I didn't see how much you were sweating when you fought Lionheart. You need endurance and muscle control. No point in teaching you how to win a fight if you can't get to the fight."

"None of the other Pilots were subjected to endless squatting."

"It's not endless squatting. You're doing push-ups next. And what do you know about the other Pilots, anyway?"

Serenia lifted her chin. "I'll have you know, I was trained by the finest instructors and scholars in Noctis. Their curriculum was based on firsthand accounts gleaned from the works of Dalzin Bonecruncher, the White Pilot of Earth."

On hearing his name, Maia's mind drifted somewhere she didn't want it to go. She watched the neck of Pearl, the White Unicorn Vanguardian, cave in as a gleaming black claw gripped it, squeezed, and twisted. She watched Pearl's head tumble to the cold ground, severed from his body. Dark, spear-like feet descended, piercing the unicorn's white metal skull like it was an empty eggshell. The black claw came for Maia next, hammering over and over until—

Maia stretched, using the motion to hide her shuddering exhale. "Dalzin's songs and books were written to entertain. He was an artist and a performer, not a scholar, and he left out a lot of important details. Why aren't you squatting? I didn't say you could stop."

"A good soldier always follows orders," Serenia grumbled.

That was Arcturus' favorite saying. Maia grew tired of hearing it less than a month after she started working with him. As his daughter, Serenia must have heard it every day of her life, and for that, Maia felt a sliver of pity for the girl. "Maybe we do need a change of pace. Let's work on your banter."

Serenia frowned. "Must we?"

"It's a useful skill. The best opponent is an unbalanced one, Princess."

"For the thousandth time, my name is Ren, or Serenia, or Pilot Valerius if you would prefer to address me more formally. My name is not, nor has it ever been, 'Princess.' How many times must I repeat myself?"

"See how flustered you are? That's what we want. Now, pretend I'm a Behemoth. Say the first thing that comes to mind. Go."

"On behalf of the Noctean Empire," Serenia began, gesticulating like she was acting in a stage play. "Uh...lick your own...ass?"

"What's the second thing that comes to mind? Because that was shit."

"Perhaps I simply can't match your range and expertise when it comes to being crass."

"You'll get there. Have a seat. Breakfast should be ready soon. *Princess.*"

Serenia stomped to the fire and sat cross-legged next to her weapon belt and her neatly folded officer's jacket. She pulled her gun from its holster and began polishing it with a white cloth and a small vial of oil she produced from one of her belt pouches.

The weapon wasn't like any flintlock pistol Maia had ever seen. Its solid hexagon barrel of violet-tinged steel was a hand-and-a-half long, and its bulky frame, thick as her forearm, housed a revolving cylinder. The bullets it held were as thick around as her thumb. Maia thought about how it would feel to be shot with a gun like that and suppressed a shudder.

"That's a nice weapon." Maia motioned with her chin toward the gun. "How does it work?

Serenia stopped polishing. She slid the weapon back into its holster and pulled her weapon belt closer to her side. "It's called a revolver. It's a recent Noctean invention, one that will revolutionize warfare once perfected. Further details are restricted to those with sufficient rank."

Maia nodded and turned her attention back to cooking. She wasn't used to spending this much uninterrupted time with the same person. As the silence lingered between them, she grew aware of her apprentice's attempts to look at her without looking at her. "You're staring. What's on your mind?"

Serenia pivoted to face her. "I was hoping you could fill in some gaps in my teachings."

"What could I possibly teach the girl who knows everything there is to know?" Maia waited for a retort, but all Serenia offered was a dour look. "Fine. What do you want to know?"

"To start, why does the blood of Ferals and Behemoths burn when exposed to air?"

"Don't know. Might be to cauterize their wounds. Might be a defense, meant to blind and disorient."

"Is it related to why Ferals burn up when defeated? And why Behemoths explode?"

"Most likely. Could be intentional, a way to cause extra damage even after they've lost."

"Intentional?" Serenia sat up straighter. "You believe that the Behemoths and Ferals were designed? Bred?"

"I don't think. I know."

"Interesting. And what about Scarlet? She was most definitely designed. How does she function? That is, how does something composed of that much metal move so effortlessly? What force drives her?"

"How in the Blue Hells should I know? Vanguardians are magical. Don't think about it too much. If you spend all your time trying to figure out why things are the way they are, you'll drive yourself mad. Any more questions?"

"I have one more," Serenia said. "It pertains to the Pilots, and...and what happened to them."

Maia always dreaded this moment. She was used to hearing the question sputter from the lips of rowdy drunks emboldened by liquid courage. It was always exhausting. The way Serenia was avoiding eye contact, like she was afraid of the answer, was worse.

"Ask," Maia said.

"What happened to the other Pilots?"

"They died."

"That's what people say, though nobody has been able to... How did they die?"

"They were killed." Maia looked up from the skillet, aware that her mask of smiling calm had slipped, revealing a hint of the coldness waiting beneath it. "That's not the question you really want to ask me, though."

Serenia shut her eyes tight, as if bracing herself. "Did you kill them? The other Pilots? Like the rumors say?"

Maia dared to laugh. "Would you have come along with me if you believed that?"

Serenia didn't answer. She didn't have to. From what little Maia knew of her, one thing was painfully clear: the girl was nothing if not determined. She approached every task Maia gave her with single-minded intensity. She would probably throw herself onto a blade and pull herself down its length if it got her one step closer to her goals.

You and Leona would have gotten along so, so well.

Before she could think up a better deflection for Serenia's question, the presence tingling in the back of Maia's mind for the better part of an hour shifted. The intruder was close. The timing couldn't have been more perfect.

Maia took the skillet off the coals and started portioning bacon and potatoes onto a pair of carved wooden plates. "How hungry are you?" Maia said.

"I don't know." Serenia looked shaken. Maia's answer to her question probably hadn't instilled the confidence the girl was looking for.

"Well, you'll have time to think about it while you greet our guest over there."

Maia gestured with her spatula at a rustling bush at the glade's edge.

The creature that emerged walked like a man, albeit a hunchbacked, skinless man with thick purple muscles that twitched as it moved. Long arms dangled past its knees, ending in wicked clawed fingers. The round mask of solid bone covering its face hinged at the jaw, revealing rows of black fangs. A single eye, yellow and gleaming, peered through a small hole carved into the right side of the bone mask.

"Is that a Feral?" Serenia whispered.

Maia recrossed her legs. "Surprised you didn't feel it coming. Every true Pilot has the Hunter Sense. One of our 'gifts.' It guides us toward Behemoths and Ferals. A lone Feral is hard to notice unless you're within a mile or so. You should be able to feel this one, since it's so close."

Serenia rubbed the back of her head and frowned. "I don't feel anything."

"Well, there it is. You wanted combat training, right?"

"Yes. Practical experience is always best." To her credit, Serenia did a good job of hiding the waver in her voice. She reached for her weapon belt.

"Leave your toys here," Maia said.

Serenia fixed Maia with a questioning look. "But it's a Feral."

Maia jabbed at a chunk of potato on her plate with her fork. "You think you're a real Pilot? Prove it. Show me what you can do, Princess."

Leaving her belt behind, Serenia strode across the glade. There was only a slight shaking in the girl's knees as she dug in with her back foot and turned it outward, falling into a perfect Noctean boxer's stance.

The Feral, standing a full two heads taller than Serenia, accepted her challenge. Its maw opened, birthing a screeching gurgle that sounded somewhere between a screaming baby and a drowning animal. Claw-tipped fingers eagerly scissored the grass as the monster lumbered toward her.

Serenia pushed off with her back foot and rushed inside the Feral's impressive reach before it could raise an arm. Her fist rose, landing a precise uppercut straight into its jaw, just beneath the edge of its mask. The Feral staggered back a half-step, then reared and slashed.

A sliver of alarm jabbed Maia's chest. If Serenia had a Pilot's strength, her blow would have cracked the Feral's jaw. She didn't have her Hunter Sense, either. What else was the girl missing?

Maia had once seen a Feral punch clean through a man's head. If the Feral connected...

Serenia slipped under the swing, grabbing the Feral's arm and shoulder to pull it off-balance. With the beast framed in front of her, Serenia's leg rose, driving hard into the monster's muscled stomach. As it doubled over, Serenia grunted and pivoted, using the momentum to throw her larger attacker over her shoulder.

The beast pushed itself to its feet, looking no worse for wear. "Okay, Princess," Maia shouted. "That's enough. Stand back and let me finish it off before you hurt yourself."

"I'm not through yet." Serenia grunted, stepping back to avoid another wild swing. She advanced as the Feral recovered and drove another sharp kick into its chest. The monster continued its advance, slashing and swinging. Each time, Serenia avoided the attack, countering like a stinging wasp and slipping out of reach before the Feral could kill her.

A bait-and-counter approach would have worked if Serenia had been fighting a person. Against a monster like a Feral, who was built for combat, she would need to be bold. From the way she let the Feral set the tempo, it became clear to Maia that Serenia wasn't confident enough to take control of the fight. She wasn't acting; she was reacting.

Gradually, her movements slowed, while the Feral showed no signs of tiring. "Attack the joints! The joints!" Maia shouted through a mouthful of potatoes.

Serenia looked back, face twisted in confusion as she tried to decode Maia's garbled instructions. The Feral seized the opening and pounced, pinning Serenia to the ground with its bulk.

"Right. Fuck this." Maia put her plate down. Her hand tightened around the handle of the empty skillet. In one fluid motion, she stood and hurled it. The cast iron slammed into the Feral's face with a dull crunch. The beast recoiled; its eye went wide as it felt around the large crack in its bone mask.

Maia thrust her palm forward into the empty air. She couldn't risk harming Serenia by summoning her flames, so she reached for another innate Pilot ability, one she rarely used. Her fingertips tingled as the spell took shape.

The Feral raised its arms above its head, screeched, and swung down at Serenia like a blacksmith hammering an anvil. Fists collided with a curved screen of faint red light framed with bright, brilliant edges. A pulse of magic from the shield repelled the Feral, throwing it back.

Though Pilots all shared common magics, Heretic had granted each of them a unique ability. The other Pilots had been given fantastic powers; Maia always felt that she got the short end of the stick with hers. Outside of saving upstart apprentices, the ability to instantly conjure a floating barrier held little value for Maia, who had magical armor and the power to recover from most injuries.

The Feral raged against her shield, each strike answered by a pulse of red that threw it back further. Maia reached Serenia and hauled her back to the campfire, keeping one hand outstretched to maintain the magical ward.

"The Implacable Defense," Serenia panted, chasing after her breath as she spoke.

"Barrier. The spell is called Barrier."

"I thought it would be bigger."

"How big is yours?"

Serenia shot her a bitter look.

"That's what I thought." Now that the situation was under her control, Maia's panic subsided. "Today's lesson: never go into a fight unarmed, and never attack head-on if you can avoid it. Attack indirectly. Sneak up on your enemy. You're a hunter. An ambush predator. Use every advantage you have."

"But you told me to go in unarmed!" Serenia all but screamed at her.

Maia canted her head. "And if I told you to jump off a cliff, would you flap your arms on the way down? Use your head, Princess. Never willingly give up your advantages. Life isn't fair, so why should we fight as if it is?"

Concentrating, Maia reached out to Scarlet. Guiding her Vanguardian without the direct connection of the control beam was taxing. Complex actions were out of the question; all she could issue were simple orders, such as "lift your hand," or, in this case, "take a step forward."

The ground rumbled as the dark shadow of Scarlet's colossal metal foot passed over them, settled over the Feral, and descended, crushing it flat. When Scarlet's foot lifted, all that remained was a smoldering black stain where the Feral had burned away in death.

After the tremor of Scarlet's stomp subsided, Maia passed Serenia her plate.

They ate in silence. Serenia's eyes stayed on her breakfast until she was finished.

"You did well," Maia offered, shattering the quiet with a hammer. She caught Serenia's glower. "You move well, and you've clearly been—"

"You are a terrible teacher."

The words cut Maia in a way she didn't think was still possible. She forced her jaw to unclench. "You're right. This is my first time taking on a student."

"That much is clear. You only offer criticism after I've failed. You take delight in telling me how little I know, yet you're reluctant to actually show me anything of worth." She scoffed. "I would have fared far better under the tutelage of one of the other Pilots, I think. Windstrider, perhaps."

Windstrider, the Green Pilot of Wind, better known to her people as Amisrala Illandres. To Maia, she was Ami. Serenia was right; Ami would have made an excellent instructor. Like all Reddalian elves, Ami was discouraged from sharing her people's teachings with outsiders. Despite that, Ami loved nothing more than discussing the many artistic and scientific advancements of the Reddalians in great detail to anyone who would listen.

And she did it in a way that any fool could understand. If Maia had any interest in engineering and science, she would have learned so much. Maia didn't doubt that Ami could have told Serenia exactly how Vanguardians worked, down to the specific spells woven into their metal frames that made them move.

"Windstrider would have been a great teacher," Maia said. She swallowed hard. "But she's dead. That leaves you with the second-best teacher life has to offer."

"You?"

"No. Failure." Maia put her plate aside and rose, her care-free smile restored. "That's how I learned. How we all learned. Even Windstrider. See, every step you take in a Vanguardian is a lesson. Whenever you accidentally crush a tree, or an animal, or...or a person. That's a chance to learn, and a chance to improve."

Unable to meet Serenia's gaze, Maia paused to gather herself, pushing another painful memory away. "Failure is a part of being a Pilot. You should make friends with it. It'll always be with you, no matter what. Every battle has a cost. There's no such thing as a perfect victory. Even when you win, you lose. That's the best lesson life can ever teach you."

"Such wisdom, coming from someone who fights with a skillet," Serenia muttered. She stood, donned her black officer's jacket, and strapped on her weapon belt. She looked ready to march away into the forest and never return.

That was for the best. Serenia could command Scarlet, but whatever she was, she wasn't a Pilot. She wouldn't last. It was better for her to quit.

Maia was about to say as much when she remembered what she owed her young apprentice. She found herself standing in front of Serenia.

"A skillet is a weapon," Maia said. "*Everything* is a weapon. Even the ground can be a weapon if you know how to use it. Though my personal favorite is turning an opponent into a weapon. Here. Knuckle up."

Serenia hesitated, then narrowed her eyes and raised her fists, settling into her boxer's stance.

"Try to hit my hand." Maia said. She extended her palm. Serenia's jab came quick and clean. Maia moved her hand back out of range and slapped Serenia's knuckles as her fist retracted. "That's what you do. You dodge and counter. The opponent asks a question, and you answer."

"And what's wrong with that?"

"Nothing." Maia looked down at the rapier hanging from Serenia's belt. "You favor a longer, thinner blade, like most Noctean officers. You're a duelist; you rely on dexterity and finesse to win. When you face an opponent with a heavier blade, you can't parry. You have to dodge and counter. That makes you predictable. Try to hit my hand again."

This time, Maia thrust her palm into Serenia's fist as it extended, pushing her back onto her heels.

"Hey!" Serenia said, rubbing her knuckles.

"Don't wait for the question. Interrupt your opponent with your own. Fighting is a conversation. Try breaking the rhythm." Maia settled into her stance. "Attack your opponent while they're attacking you in a way that keeps you safe. See how I added your strength to mine and used it against you? Try it. Get your palms up."

Maia pushed forward with her open hand. Serenia met it in the middle with a stinging slap. Next, Maia threw a cross, and her apprentice met her again in the middle. Gradually, they fell into a rhythm, slapping with one hand, then the other. Serenia started sneaking in extra strikes out of tempo, disrupting Maia's rhythm and forcing her to adapt. Within minutes, they were circling each other, hands weaving in a flurry of slaps, pushes, and redirections.

When Serenia laughed, Maia couldn't help but smile. She couldn't remember the last time she smiled for any reason other than pure reflex. Joyful warmth radiated through her chest, reaching a part of her she had thought cold and buried, and squeezed.

No. It wasn't joy.

The phantom fingers curled inside Maia's chest, their gentle grip tightening into a clenching fist. Maia collapsed and writhed on the ground, unable to see through the pricks of light and pain scattering her vision.

When she was able to breathe again, she found Serenia kneeling at her side.

"Maia! I'm so sorry! Whatever I've done, I'm sorry. Are you well?"

"Never been better," Maia rasped, coughing as she pushed to her feet. The world spun. Slowly, the throbbing beneath her sternum began to fade. "You didn't do anything wrong. Really."

"What's the matter? What was that?"

"It has nothing to do with you. Leave it alone." Heat flared in her heart, but it simmered when Serenia recoiled. *What did you expect?* she thought. *You let her travel with you. She was bound to see this sooner or later.*

Maia put her hand on Serenia's shoulder, relaxing again into her easy way. "Hey. I'm sorry. I'm fine. Really. I'm going to go forage, so we have something for dinner. Break down camp and see if you can find my skillet. We'll leave when I get back. You're piloting Scarlet this afternoon."

She expected Serenia to jump at the chance to control Scarlet again. It was all the girl seemed to want. Her scrutinizing gaze narrowed. "Are you sure you're well? All Noctean officers receive basic battlefield medical training. I can examine you if you like. Perhaps you just need some water or—"

"Break down camp and find my skillet," Maia said. "That's an order, soldier."

With a dramatic sigh and a weak salute, Serenia started gathering soiled cookware. "A good soldier always follows orders."

Maia waved her off and wandered into the brush. When she was alone, she leaned on a tree for support, grounding herself in the sounds of small forest birds fluttering away at her approach. She took deep breaths until the last of her pains subsided.

Twice in one week. The attacks were coming more often now. Maybe this was how fate decided it would punish her for her many sins.

Did you kill them? The other Pilots? Like the rumors say?

Serenia's words dug into Maia and held on, their sharp nails refusing to let go.

She could only deflect and avoid the question for so long. One day, she would have to summon the nerve to answer it.

Chapter 5
Galford

As a youth, Ren was taught that the Freelands were nothing but a collection of scattered, lawless settlements, where people living in squalor killed and robbed each other to feed their malnourished families. When she stole away and crossed the border into the Freelands by way of Brimholme, she stayed clear of main roads and settlements to avoid unnecessary attention, which gave her little opportunity to confirm what she had been taught.

As the Free City of Galford emerged on the horizon, Ren wondered how a city so vast could exist outside of the Empire and how her instructors had neglected to mention its existence. She surveyed the sprawl of uneven, tightly packed rooftops, where slanted Fennish roofs tiled in green and brown, shingled clay slats favored by Tressille elves, and even some Noctean-inspired flat-topped tenements formed a chaotic and jagged saw against the afternoon sky. Galford's stone walls were much lower than the tall, unshakable barriers of Noctis, and the pure white spire of the bell tower lording over the northern half of the city couldn't approach the grandeur of the Imperial Palace, but Ren couldn't deny being drawn to the city's raw, messy beauty.

Though, if she was being honest, aesthetics were only a small part of what pulled her toward Galford. She was most excited about the prospect of finding something to eat within the city walls.

It had been a day or more since Ren had last enjoyed a proper meal. Two mouths went through supplies faster than one, leaving Maia's provisions exhausted after two months of traveling and training together. Neither Ren nor Maia had much luck scaring up game over the past week. Aside from some foraged berries, neither of them had much of a breakfast that morning.

All Ren had to do was make it to Galford, where whatever passed for good food in this lawless land waited for her. She picked up her pace, pushing harder despite the strain Scarlet was putting on her.

Since Maia had allowed her to regularly pilot Scarlet, Ren had grown accustomed to commanding her Vanguardian, to the point where she often forgot that she was in control of a metal titan that could kill with a step. The weighty heft of her strides didn't hinder her any longer, though she still hadn't been able to adapt to the pain.

It started as a dull ache at the base of her spine, a radiating heat that turned to daggers the longer she remained in Scarlet's control beam. She thought to ask Maia if she shared the same pain, if piloting a Vanguardian was meant to hurt, but feared the answer. Her mind was already overflowing with worries that something had gone wrong during her Pilot ascendance. Compared to Maia, she wasn't as strong or as durable, and she couldn't Regenerate or summon armor or sense Ferals and Behemoths the way her mentor could. If she learned that the pain she felt wasn't normal, that she was somehow broken or wrong...

No. Her abilities would awaken with time. They had to. And if they didn't, she would push through the pain and make her father and her Emperor proud regardless. Ren would let Maia continue to think that the tremors and sweating she suffered were a result of poor physical conditioning. At the end of the day, she had the cool, welcoming metal of Scarlet's cabin floor beneath her bedroll to soothe her aching back. That was all she needed.

"Slow down, Princess." Maia rose from her crouch and pointed through the viewport to a patch of cleared land outside of the city. "Veer around the crater and head that way. Slowly. We don't want to crush any farmers. Or goats. People around here are particular about their goats."

Ren turned Scarlet, each deliberate step weighted by the Vanguardian's size. She took a wide berth around the vast farmlands surrounding the city and a massive crater half-filled with water, the remnant of one of Scarlet's past victories. She veered toward a flattened path of uneven packed earth, one of many "Pilot roads" all over the continent created by the Vanguardians over the years. The path ended just before a wide, fast-moving river that sliced through the city like a cool, blue scar, dividing Galford into two halves. Scarlet entered the river. The light rumbling of the waters parting around Scarlet's leg sent a shiver through Ren. She lingered on the second step, delighting in the fact that even nature had to bend to her Vanguardian's might.

Soon, that might would be rightfully hers. All she had to do was continue to prove herself worthy of it.

Once clear of the river, Ren set Scarlet to rest in a kneeling position near a gate set into the stone and mortar wall surrounding Galford. As Ren stepped out of the control beam, Maia thrust something crumpled into her hands.

"Put this on," Maia said. Ren unfolded the garment. It was a shirt of such deep red that it bordered on black, just like Maia's. "Your accent isn't bad, but that Noctean officer's uniform is going to draw attention, and I can't leave you alone here with Scarlet. You need to blend in."

Despite her heart leaping in her chest, she retained her composure. *We'll look like sisters,* she thought. The idea wasn't unpleasant. Ren slipped the dark red shirt on and adjusted her weapon belt around it. The garment hung a little looser than she liked, but she found she liked the idea of growing into it.

"I want that back," Maia said over her shoulder as she opened the cabin hatch plates with a wave of her hand.

Ren smiled to hide her disappointment and slipped on her black gloves. Maia quirked the corner of her mouth. "I said you need you to blend in. Bring your weapons, but leave the gloves. You look like a tiny pirate."

Ren tossed them onto her folded uniform and jacket. "Of course. We wouldn't want that."

"While we're getting supplies, we'll find you something else to wear. Got any coin?"

"I only have this." Ren produced a small disk of pressed platinum from one of her belt pouches. It was the only coin she would ever need in the Empire. An officer's challenge coin entitled them to any goods and services they required in service of the Emperor, no questions asked.

"Fancy. Mine was only bronze," Maia said. "Challenge coins don't spend in the Freelands. Looks like we'll need to make an honest living. Come on."

When Maia exited the cabin, Ren lingered, enjoying the moment she had alone with Scarlet. Maia often complained about having to sleep in Scarlet, though she warned Ren that resting anywhere else would leave her too vulnerable. Though

Maia often likened it to a coffin, Ren felt at home among the perfect edges and metal seams of Scarlet's cabin.

Home. Ren placed the challenge coin back in her pouch and reached into another, feeling the broken halves of the Farspeaker she had forced back together. She doubted it would work again, and Maia forbade her from trying to use it, but it calmed her knowing that somewhere, her father was holding the stone's twin, waiting for her safe return.

With her confidence swelling, Ren left the cabin and made her way across Scarlet's shoulder and onto her raised palm. She nearly stumbled as she looked to the ground below. Raucous cheers from the massive crowd gathered by the gates swept over her like a furious storm. Maia waved at the citizens below as a large ensemble launched into an upbeat tune. Channeling her father's stoicism, Ren resisted the urge to join Maia in waving to the crowd.

You haven't earned their love yet. Give it time.

When Scarlet's hand reached the ground, Ren followed Maia through the open gate. Wide rows of armored soldiers formed walls with their rectangular shields, pressing the frenzied masses back against either side of the wide avenue. A short, gray-bearded man in a stately brown vest and jacket waited with a small escort.

As they approached, Ren marked the man as a Granrum dwarf, hailing from the nation of Brimholme to the east. The points of his ears and brown skin, however, showed elven ancestry. Reddalian, specifically. He had a warmth to his smile that clashed with the cacophony raging around them.

The dwarf's hands swept wide. Maia bent and offered him a warm embrace.

"Sunder! It's been too long, far, far too long!" he boomed, his voice lacking the accent typical of the Granrum.

"You're looking well, Forguth." Maia released him and rose.

"And who might this be?" the dwarf said, looking back and forth between Maia and Ren.

"This is...Sara," Maia said. "My niece. We're just taking in the sights. She's never been to a big city before."

"Niece? I didn't know you had extended family. Or siblings, for that matter."

For a second, the corners of Maia's mouth dipped toward a frown. She recovered and lifted her face into an even wider smile. "Well, she's definitely my niece!"

Forguth matched her grin and turned to Ren, taking one of her hands from her side and holding it in both of his. "Sara. I'm Forguth Drenchwood, the mayor of Galford. It's an absolute pleasure to meet one of our Pilot's kin. Speaking of loved ones, where is your Leona? When we saw you approaching, we expected she would be traveling with you."

This time, Maia's smile failed completely, pulling into a grimace that twisted the line of her scar.

"Oh. I'm sorry, Sunder," Forguth said. "Whatever happened, that's your business. Forgive me."

It was common knowledge that Maia had been briefly involved with Edgar Ragnarson, the Black Pilot of Water. The records of Maia's exploits never mentioned anyone named Leona. How had she kept a relationship secret from Noctis' extensive spy network?

"Galford is looking lively," Maia said, deftly changing the subject. "All thanks to your leadership, no doubt."

"Oh. Yes. The people are cared for, and that's what matters to me." Forguth motioned to one of the soldiers, and his escort encircled them as they strolled down the street. "You know, Sunder, I should probably be turning you away from my gates."

"I apologized to that farmer a thousand times. Is he still on about that goat?"

Forguth stopped, moving in closer to be heard over the cheering crowd. "I'm talking about the Nocteans. The ones we employ to protect us with their Iron Wardens. Word's come that they've been ordered to stand down and abandon their duties in the Freelands until the Noctean officer you kidnapped is returned. The young *female* officer. With black hair." He fixed his gaze on Ren.

Maia's laugh was loud and forced. "Come on, Forguth. The Empire just wants to stir up trouble. If I kidnapped a Noctean officer, would I bring her into a city full of people who would tear her apart if they had the slightest idea who she was?" Maia aimed her smile at Ren, raising her brows to make her point known. "Besides, Wardens are slow to act and near-useless in a real fight. All they protect you from is your coin."

Forguth waved his hands. "It all sounds like bollocks to me, anyway. An excuse for the Empire to defame our beloved Red Pilot of Fire. Between you and me,

Sunder, I've never been comfortable having the Wardens here, but the people demand protection, and a mayor's duty is to ensure his people survive to appreciate his efforts, yes? Maybe they'll think differently about the Wardens once they hear that our would-be saviors are spreading scandalous rumors."

Maia motioned to the street ahead, and they continued. Forguth and Maia chatted like old friends the whole way. Ren couldn't make out what they were saying, and even if she could, the notion that her disappearance had caused trouble in the Empire and for the people of the Freelands weighed heavy on her heart. Silently, she prayed to the Emperor to grant her, as well as the people of the Freelands, the strength to endure this trying time until her goal was achieved.

The roar of the crowd served as a pleasant distraction. The people of the Freelands loved their Pilot and weren't afraid to show it with cries of affection and gratitude. Only a few voices seemed fueled by anger, though they were swept away in the commotion and quickly lost.

One face in the crowd gave Ren pause. The man stood unmoving like a stone jutting from fervent waters. A dirty mop of hair fell over his vacant face. The patch he wore over one eye deflected her focus to the cold stare of the other. Every time she looked up, he was there, having moved to keep pace with them.

Maia turned back and cocked her head Ren's way. "Sara will help out. It'll be good experience for her."

"Oh, of course." Forguth clapped his hands together. "And thank you again, Sunder. I'll see to the arrangements immediately." The crowd ahead thinned out. The initial excitement of the Pilot's arrival and the impromptu parade had run its course. While Forguth stayed to address those who remained, Maia and Ren to carried on.

"What exactly am I to be assisting you with?" Ren asked as Maia led her down an empty side street. "I had trouble hearing over the fanfare."

"We need coin, so I asked Forguth to set up a charity banquet this evening."

"We're to be taking charity, now? From common rabble?"

"Not exactly." Maia turned down an alley and motioned for Ren to follow. "We'll be working the banquet. The proceeds will go to those in need after the workers take a fair wage. No work goes unpaid in the Freelands. It's the law."

"I have several questions." Ren stopped, crossing her arms. "First, it was my understanding that the Freelands were...well, free. You have laws here?"

Matching her posture, Maia leaned against the alley wall. "Everybody has laws. Even animals follow the laws of nature. We have elected officials, local lords, trade kings, that kind of thing. The difference is we aren't the property of an overreaching Emperor."

"Our Emperor guides the people under his care toward a common purpose and sees to our communal well-being. It's much more efficient that way." Ren cleared her throat. "What role will you serve at this banquet?"

"Entertainment and cooking."

"Cooking? You?"

As they walked, Maia looked off into the distance. "I like it. Sometimes it feels like all I can do for people is kill the things that are trying to kill them. It's nice, being able to help in another way. Doing something normal, for once."

"Normalcy is overrated. We're Pilots. Ours is a higher calling. What role will *Sara* be expected to play at this banquet?"

"Am I right in assuming you've never worked a day in your life?"

Ren shook her head. Her father's help took care of all her needs ever since she was a child, and as an officer, she never had to bother herself with menial tasks.

Maia clapped her hands together. "Then you'll be preparing and serving. It'll be good for you to get your hands dirty for once."

A wave of vague disgust rolled through Ren. Such base duties didn't befit a Pilot. She choked down her displeasure. "Understood. One more question, if I may. Where, precisely, are we headed right now?"

Maia tilted her head. "To a tavern, of course. It'll take Forguth a few hours to make the arrangements and spread the word, so we have some time to burn."

"Need I remind you that not only am I *sixteen,* you also agreed to remain sober during our travels?"

"Right. I forgot both of those things. Not used to hanging out with children. Guess we'll find something else to pass the time."

They weaved back to the main street, following its curving path over a long, arching stone bridge and into a bustling market. They strolled through the crowd, passing by vendor stalls selling everything from clothing to tonics for male impotency. Wafting clouds of cooking smoke from grilled meats and vegetables, heavily sauced and served on skewers, made Ren's stomach rumble.

Ren was about to ask Maia if *she* had any coin to spare for a bite when the ground began to shake rhythmically. Since she lacked the ability to sense the presence of Ferals and Behemoths, she looked to Maia for guidance.

Maia crossed her arms and planted her feet as the crowd parted to make way for two dozen Iron Wardens marching in unison through the middle of the market, their steel feet pounding a steady beat.

Like a whisper in the night, Ren faded back and slipped into the crowd. She doubted any of the Wardens would recognize her, but she didn't want to run the risk of being discovered and sent home prematurely. The lead Warden, clad in a white and gold lion-emblazoned half-cape that marked him as captain, ground to a halt a few feet from Maia. She looked up at the white dome peering down at her.

The captain's sigh resonated inside his hollow armor. "Stand aside, citizen. We don't wish to trample you."

"Do you know who I am?" Maia called, loud enough so the crowd could hear her.

"Yes, Pilot. We're very impressed by your grand display of civil disobedience. Now, kindly move aside. We have our orders."

"Last I heard, your orders are to stand down," Maia said with a sneer. "I think you owe these people an explanation. You were paid to protect them. Why have you been ordered to abandon your duty?"

The captain's Warden turned to the crowd, then back to Maia. "I'm under no obligation to explain myself to you or anyone else, Pilot," he growled.

Maia had invited the captain to vilify her as a kidnapper in front of a crowded marketplace, and he had refused. Either he was afraid of the repercussions of a public accusation, or he had been instructed to keep Ren's absence relatively quiet. The Emperor likely wouldn't want to risk the embarrassment of losing Noctis' only Pilot to another nation.

That meant that by falling in with Maia, Ren may have angered him. Her heart beat faster, and she said another quiet prayer to her savior, begging for his divine forgiveness and promising him that she remained true to his will.

"Well, this doesn't look much like standing down," Maia said. "This looks like a bunch of metal-clad babies spreading fear by waddling through a public market, just so they can feel big and strong."

"I'm warning you, Pilot," the captain said. "Stand aside. I won't ask again. As you can plainly see, you're outnumbered."

"Yeah? What else is new." Maia kept her arms crossed and waited. A moment later, the captain's Warden turned, joints whirring.

"The path ahead is blocked by a dangerous killer of men," he called to his retinue. "I'm not about to sacrifice Noctean lives to sate her bloodlust. About face!"

The Wardens pivoted as one and marched back the way they came. The cadence of hurled stones bouncing off their backs blended with the crowd's jeering. Once the quaking of the Warden's steps subsided and the people went back to their business, a short man in a simple tunic and breeches approached Maia.

"Many thanks, Pilot," he said. "Just like Nocteans to cut and run. They couldn't face us in the War of Bones without their walkin' dead, and they can't face us now. Cowards, the lot of them! I hope that blasted dragon takes them on their way back home!"

Ren bit her tongue to keep from berating him. From what her instructors had told her, the people of the Freelands refused to let go of the memory of the War of Bones and chose to extend their prejudices against the necromancers who started the war to all Nocteans. That conflict ended over seventy years ago, and the Emperor paid all reparations asked of him on behalf of those responsible for launching the failed campaign without his knowledge. Some of the demands the other continental nations placed on the Empire were unfair, yet he agreed to all sanctions, including the banning of necromancy throughout the Empire. What more did these ingrates want?

"What blasted dragon?" Maia said.

"Oh! 'Bout six or more months back, we started seein' this big dragon flyin' by, oh, once a week or so? Usually around sunset or durin' the evenin'. You just missed her a few days back. Think it might be a green. Hard to see it clear."

"Greens are territorial," Maia said. "They roost in Brimholme or the Southlands, and they don't stray far. Unless this one's migrated for some reason. But then, it would be hunting."

"Hasn't caused us any bother yet, but maybe it's got a taste for Wardens, eh?

We'll see soon enough." The man bowed to Maia and headed back to his stall to tend to his grill.

"What is it?" Ren asked, noting Maia's furrowed brow.

"I don't like this. A green dragon roaming the Freelands is one thing. I'm more worried about the Wardens withdrawing. It looks like your Emperor wants you back home sooner than we planned. But he knows the other nations would sweep in to help if he tried to invade again, and Scarlet is too big of a threat to him. This is just posturing. If things escalate, though, if people learn why the Wardens are standing down, and they figure out who you are, somebody could get hurt. Maybe it's time to take you home, Princess."

"I'm sure this is all just a misunderstanding. Perhaps if I could contact my father, he could speak to the Emperor, and—"

"Your Farspeaker is broken, and I'm not about to ask a Warden to borrow his. Besides, we had a deal. No contacting Arcturus."

Ren raised her hands, warding off her mentor's ire. "I admit, the situation isn't ideal. I'm not suggesting that we put innocent lives in danger, but until we see no other alternative, please, allow me to remain serving as your apprentice. As you said yourself, you're in need of a successor."

Maia stood in thought for some time. Finally, she nodded. "Okay. For now."

"Excellent!" Ren fell in step beside Maia. "Now, about that dragon. Do Pilots ever engage in monster hunting?"

"I have, on occasion, but our job is to fight Ferals and Behemoths. We're not really dragon slayers."

"If there is indeed a green dragon roaming the Freelands, we may have to be. I shudder to think how a city, even one as vast as Galford, would fare against a fully grown wyrm without the aid of the Iron Wardens."

Maia covered her mouth to hide her laughter. "Really? Iron Wardens, fighting a dragon."

"What is so amusing?" Ren said. "Some Wardens are equipped with ranged weaponry. It's tactically feasible."

"Have you ever actually seen a Warden in action? It takes two or three of them to take down one Feral. Your engineers made too many alterations to the original Fennish design after they stole it."

After hearing a litany of insults directed at her people without challenge, Ren couldn't contain her frustration any longer. "The Iron Wardens are a Noctean invention, one of our greatest feats of mechanical engineering. I doubt the brightest minds of the Freelands could even come close to such a wonder."

"That's what the Empire wants you to think, that you're responsible for everything good under the sun." Maia's face twisted into a smug, superior smirk. "Engineers from the Fen Islands built the first Iron Warden. Noctis stole their work and modified it to cover the theft. Now, they're too heavy on top, and the riders can't see for shit. Too many blind spots. Too easy to topple. They couldn't figure out how to make their own Vanguardian, so they stole the next best thing and turned it into a walking joke."

"That's not true. You're lying." Ren crossed her arms and puffed out her chest. "Take it back. Now."

"First lesson of the day, Princess: not everything you hear is true. Maybe it's time you started thinking for yourself."

As Maia walked away, Ren's mind drifted back to the time her father had taken her and her mother on a visit to the Fen Islands. She was six, perhaps seven at the time. The first Behemoth wouldn't arrive in Noctis to steal her mother's life for another two years.

Her father had leveraged Noctis' strong trade relationship with the islands to gain entry to the cloistered kingdom for a rare vacation. She remembered dancing through an endless field of rich purple flowers; their shade instantly became her favorite color. And though the massive volcano that thrust from an island at the center of a far-off atoll filled her young heart with awe and wonder, Ren had been most delighted by the sight of the strange rolling contraptions the Fennish people used to harvest their fields.

When she saw a similar machine the following year in Noctis, she always assumed that the Fennish people had borrowed the idea from Noctean engineers. But what if Maia was telling the truth? Like most Freelanders, she seemed to hold an unreasonable grudge toward Noctis, yet Ren's mentor was a woman of honor, not prone to telling lies. Had the design for the Wardens come from Fen? If it had, then what other lies had Ren been told?

Chapter 6
Foreign Relations

"You're doing that all wrong," Maia said.

Ren wondered if that sentence would become permanently etched into her psyche given how often Maia repeated it. She averted her eyes to keep from glaring at her mentor.

Wearing an apron and a loose white hat that covered her crimson hair, Maia somehow seemed more at home in a kitchen than she did crushing Behemoths. She moved like a smooth breeze through the crowded kitchen, calling out orders to the two dozen cooks under her charge. They called back each instruction, following her lead with the practiced confidence of elite soldiers.

Ren was an elite soldier, but kitchen work vexed her. Attempting to peel potatoes, which should have been a simple task, had resulted in a cut finger. The chickens she tried to clean and prepare ended up in a state of butchery that might have been considered a war crime in some parts of the world. And when her mentor sent her to scrub pots just before the night's service began, she couldn't get the caked-on, heat-crusted leavings off more than half of them.

Pilots were meant for greater things than peeling potatoes and scrubbing pots. She should have been able to master such menial tasks in short order.

"I can't do this." Ren stepped back from the wash basin.

"Sure you can," Maia said as she passed by. "It just takes time. You won't become a *seasoned* cook overnight. Don't worry. I have lots of *sage* advice to *pepper* into your training."

The kitchen broke into laughter. Maia paraded down the line, hands held high in mock triumph.

They only love her because she's a Pilot, Ren thought. Without her powers, her armor, and Scarlet, Maia was just common rabble like all the rest.

Ren removed her dirty apron and wiped her hands on it, straightened her hair, and smoothed down her shirt. She pushed her resentment down into a hard, black ball in the pit of her stomach. There was still work to be done.

All she had to do for the rest of the evening was bring food to the guests and smile. Any fool could do that.

Outside the kitchen, Ren fell in line with the other servers waiting near a long banquet table while a pair of young boys scrambled to light the wrought-iron braziers dotting the hall. When the sun waned in the sky, the doors to the hall opened. The murmur of pre-dinner conversation overtook the clinking of coins leaving hands as patrons filtered in. Within ten minutes, there wasn't an empty seat left at any of the long tables stretching down the hall's length.

The doors to the hall shut. Ren glanced around for Maia. Her mentor was nowhere to be seen.

A girl to Ren's right leaned in. "First time?" she whispered. She must have taken Ren's wandering gaze as a sign of anxiety.

Ren regarded the girl out of the corner of her eye, afraid to turn her head or break rank. She had sandy blond hair and pale skin with too many freckles, and her clothes were so drab that they hurt to look at.

"Just relax," the girl said, offering Ren a reassuring, if crooked, smile. "Try to have fun."

A common wastrel from the Freelands had no business offering a Pilot advice. Ren forced a polite smile. Practice, for the night ahead.

The guests clamored for food and wine, but none of the servers moved. They had been told to wait, so Ren followed orders, trying her best to ignore the knot twisting tighter in her stomach with each passing moment.

A loud bang silenced the hall. The doors flew open, and Maia strolled in, clad in her crimson armor. She looked about the room, rolled her neck, and broke into a run.

A third of the way down the hall, Maia launched into a series of back-to-back tumbles that carried her the rest of the way across the room in a red blur. With one last push, she spun through the air in an upside-down pirouette, arms stretched wide as tongues of flame lashed out from her palms.

She landed in a crouch with her head lowered. When she rose, one of the serving girls stepped forward and tied a white apron around her waist. The silent room exploded into a frenzy of claps and cheers for the Pilot of the Freelands and her antics.

Maia's steel-tinged voice filled the hall. "People of Galford! Thank you for coming to dine with us tonight. I'm sure most of you have heard by now that Noctis has ordered its Iron Wardens to stand down." She paused, allowing a litany of boos and jeers to run its course. "That's fine. We're the Free People, and we don't need the Imperials or their toy soldiers!"

While many of the patrons cheered, Ren noticed quite a few frowns and some half-hearted applause coming from sections of the crowd. Not everyone was so quick to condemn the peace and prosperity Noctis promised to bring to the world, it seemed.

In time, the rest would come to realize that the Emperor was offering an open hand, not the closed fist they had been told to expect.

"That's why we're here tonight," Maia continued. "Most of the coin you've generously parted with will go toward providing food and shelter to those in need. The Freelands takes care of its own. Always has. Always will. Enjoy your night, Galford!"

With a salute to Forguth, Maia passed by the small head table and took her place with the other cooks behind the long banquet table. When she was in position, the servers around Ren burst to life, grabbing serving carts, loading dishes, and striding toward their assigned rows.

She recited the instructions she had been given. Ask the guest: chicken or beef? Deliver the chicken, deliver the beef. How could it be any simpler?

"Half chicken, half beef," one patron demanded.

"Extra potatoes," shouted another.

"No salt on the green beans."

"Was the beef butchered locally in Galford?"

"Just white meat—no dark."

The patrons asked their stupid questions and barked demands at her as if she were a mere commoner, not an elite soldier worthy of praise and respect. Ren struggled to remember who had requested what as she pushed her rickety wooden cart to the serving table.

"Just beef or chicken," the closest cook said, not bothering to look up at her as he prepared another identical-looking plate. "Every plate, the same. Fair."

"But I have several requests for—"

"I've got it." The serving girl with the sandy blond hair placed a hand on Ren's shoulder, and it was then that Ren became aware she was trembling. "They'll trample you if you let them. You need to be firm."

"Why do they have to behave like this?" Ren whispered. "Why is 'chicken or beef' such a complicated concept for these ingrates?"

The girl looked at Ren as if she had grown a second head. "They're just hungry and excited. Who wouldn't want to meet the Red Pilot of Fire?"

Ren scoffed. "She's nothing special."

That was, of course, a lie. Maia Sunderland was everything Ren hoped to become one day. Skillful. Brave. Confident.

But Ren wouldn't only become her. She would surpass Maia. She would grow stronger. The world would celebrate her the way they celebrated Maia. One day, they would see her worth.

"Are you okay? You can take a minute if you need," the girl said. "I'll handle the first table in your row. Go to the next one and carry on from there. And remember: it's just a one-night job. Nothing is at stake here. Just steak." The girl chuckled at her own joke, gave Ren's shoulder a squeeze, and left her at the serving table.

Ren imagined herself in Scarlet's cabin, channeling the feeling of commanding a walking weapon of immense power as she approached the second table in her row. "Chicken or beef?" she almost shouted at the back of the closest guest, whose worn brown robes may have once been part of a burlap sack.

"I only eat vegetables," the patron said, each syllable deliberate and measured as he forced hard t's through his thick accent. His cracked, pallid skin and tight gray ponytail made him look older than her father by at least twenty years.

"I apologize, but I'm afraid that's not an option. Chicken or beef?"

The old man cleared his throat. "I do not partake in the harm or consumption of any living creature. I only eat vegetables."

"I'm afraid the chickens and cows we're serving tonight are beyond saving at this point. Can't you pick around the meat?" Ren offered. The old man stared back, saying nothing. "Very well, then." She wheeled her cart back to the serving table, pushing her way through the other servers. "May I have a plate with only vegetables, please?"

The cook didn't look up at her. "Chicken or beef."

"I have a request for a plate of vegetables from a guest. Is such a simple thing beyond your skills?"

That did it. The cook looked up, fixing a scrutinizing glare on her. "What's your problem, girl?"

"Girl?" Ren huffed. "The only problem I have is that I have a room full of common rabble to feed with this *detritus* you've prepared, and I have an old vagabond demanding a plate with only vegetables, but you seem to be too much of a fool to fulfill his inane request!"

The room fell quiet faster than light leaving a snuffed candle. Ren hadn't meant to yell. Every eye in the room fell on her. As the first shouts and thrown cups reached her, Maia was there, her metal hand firm on Ren's shoulder as she guided her from the hall and back into the kitchen.

Maia dismissed her helmet and propped a hand under her chin, tucking the other into her armpit. "What does 'detritus' mean?"

"Waste. Debris. Refuse."

"Ah. You learn something new every day." She leaned against the wall near a rack of knives. "So. What happened in there was not good."

"I apologize for my outburst. I was out of line. But this common rabble is trying my patience, and I—"

"Blue Hells, stop calling them that!" Maia pushed off the wall. She was only a few inches taller than Ren, but in her armor, she held the stature of a giant. "There's nothing common about any of these people. Just because they're not highborn nobles with sticks up their asses doesn't make their lives worth less than yours. You don't know them. That elder in your row with the gray hair, for instance? The one who, I'm guessing, asked for only vegetables? That's Gaston Turner."

Ren rolled her eyes. "Am I supposed to know who that is?"

"The famous artificer? He invented the flash pan lid used on modern flintlocks before he became a pacifist. And a cream for treating burn scars, but I figure you would be more interested in gun stuff. He apprenticed in Inemelle, the capital of Reddalia, for most of his life. The Reddalians don't often share their knowledge with outsiders. You should be honored to be serving him, and everyone else in that room. Every person in the world has a story. Every life has value."

"He invented the flash pan lid? Preposterous. The flintlock and all of its components are a Noctean invention."

It was Maia's turn to roll her eyes. "Keep thinking you're the center of the world if it makes you happy. Next, you're going to tell me that your Emperor shat out the sun himself and lights it every day at dawn with one of his flaming farts."

Warmth flushed Ren's cheeks. She angled her chin up toward her mentor, fighting to remain calm in the face of such blasphemy. "How was I to know who he was?"

"You shouldn't need to know someone's history to treat them with respect."

"Can you guarantee that none of those people out there are killers and thieves?" Ren said. "What, then? I should extend everyone I meet the same fealty I would give the Emperor himself, even if that person may secretly be a criminal? I should welcome them all with open arms despite the fact that any one of them would knife me in the back if it provided a way to escape the poverty they've dug themselves into?"

"You're not getting it." Maia rubbed her face with her hands. "How would you feel if I called you a necromancer? You know, since all Nocteans are necromancers."

The simmering anger frothing in Ren's chest tipped over into boiling. "That would be most unfair," she hissed through gritted teeth. "As you're no doubt aware, necromancy has been outlawed across the Empire following the War of Bones. Since you were raised in the Freelands, what you may *not* know is that insinuating that *any* Noctean citizen would dare sully themselves by delving into the forbidden arts is pure bigotry and tantamount...to..."

Maia had trapped her, and there was no way to talk herself out of the cage. In that moment, Ren wanted nothing more than to punch Maia right in her smug, superior mouth.

"Now she gets it," Maia said. "Oh, and that crap about outlawing necromancy? Don't fool yourself, Princess. How else can you explain why your Emperor is still walking around well over two hundred years after he claims he was born?"

"Not through necromancy, I assure you. Emperor Caelus Noctis III is our immortal savior, and through his gifts and grace, we—"

"*Gifts* and *grace?*" With no more than a glower, Maia drove her back against the wall. "I wonder if your instructors ever told you what the Empire does to noble children born without any magical talent. How they cut them open and graft enchanted metal to their bones as a 'gift.'"

Ren was familiar with the procedure. Her father underwent magical modification as a youth. The Emperor was quite open in his desire for every Noctean noble child to wield the gift of magic, as opposed to regular citizens, who were strictly regulated in their practice. If a noble child didn't display magical aptitude, if they couldn't pull a strand of magic from beyond the Veil and bend it to their will in some way, the Emperor elevated them so they would stand equal with their peers. Some who lacked faith in the Emperor perished during the ceremony, but that was their own fault.

Wasn't it?

Maia leaned forward. "You should know all about it. They did it to Arcturus and to my..." She pushed her breath out as if she were venting steam. "Don't talk to me about the Emperor and his 'gifts and grace' ever again. It's time you stopped being a good little soldier and learned to question the *detritus* the Empire has been feeding you."

Maia took a moment to find her breath. "Stay here. I'll be back for you once the feast is done. Then, I'm taking you back home. We're through."

"What? Over something as trivial as this? Surely you can't... No. *No!*"

Without another word, Maia stormed from the kitchen, her metal boots thudding in a heavy rhythm over Ren's protests. The door closed behind her, leaving Ren alone in the dimly lit kitchen. She wiped the corners of her eyes, unable to control the heaving of her chest and shoulders and the curdling in her twisting stomach.

She grabbed her belt from where it hung near the back door of the kitchen and pushed out into the alley. She didn't give any thoughts time to form, letting the panic running through her veins fuel her as she bolted down the alley, eager to put as much distance between herself and the Red Pilot of Fire as she could.

Chapter 7
Making New Friends

Ren ran until her lungs burned with each wheezing breath. When her legs turned to jelly, she slowed to a resigned, meandering walk through Galford's many identical-looking alleys until the thunder in her heart finally died.

The first sliver of morning light slipped blade-like over the steeple of the massive bell tower standing watch over Galford. She had been out all night. Somehow, she made it all the way to the docks on the north shore.

Was Maia out looking for her? Would she be mad at Ren for running off? Did it matter? Either way, Ren was no longer her apprentice.

The realization crashed into her like a horse-drawn wagon. She stopped in the middle of the street as the weight of her failure bore down on her. A very real horse-drawn wagon ripped past, almost running her down and pulling her out of her torpor. The driver cursed at her, and she yelled back a series of vulgar retorts, the most potent of which contained the phrase "fecal scraping."

I can't even curse properly.

Ren ventured down the creaking docks and leaned against a stack of barrels, too crestfallen to take another step. Further down the dock, workers hurried to unload cargo from a river barge as wide as Scarlet's foot. Most of the workers were young, only a few years older than her by the looks of them, though there were a few gray beards among them.

Perhaps some of those older dock hands had heard tales of the War of Bones from their parents, who may have very well fought their own parents during the conflict. The Noctean necromancers who swept through the Freelands, claiming to be taking back lands rightfully belonging to the Emperor, bolstered their ranks with dead from both sides. How many of the Free People had gone mad at the sight of their own fallen kin marching on them with hungry eyes and gnashing jaws?

It took the intervention of the rest of the continental nations to force the rogue necromancers to cede their campaign, which they claimed to have waged on the Emperor's behalf. The Emperor was held accountable for his subjects' actions, and the accords that followed banned all necromantic practices, even the most benign ones, and weakened the Empire's position considerably.

That Maia would even suggest an Imperial officer, let alone the Emperor himself, would ever stoop so low as to practice the dark arts that had brought shame to her homeland made Ren burn in ways she didn't think possible. And within that anger, she found the deepest depths of her failure.

Ren carried great pride for her homeland. She wanted nothing more than to make her father and her Emperor proud. To be lumped in with villains had wounded her. Especially when she realized it was no different than the way she had behaved from the moment she first set foot in Galford.

Just as there were still rogue necromancers caught and tried for practicing the forbidden arts, there were likely citizens of Galford who strayed toward the wrong side of the law...but that didn't mean all of them did. And those who did likely had good reason, at least in their minds. Ren herself had broken several laws by sneaking into the Freelands to steal Scarlet! Those who didn't know her story, who didn't know that she acted in the name of the greater good, might judge her as she had judged the people of Galford, including Gaston, the artificer she had called a vagabond.

Along with an apparent affinity for guns, she and Gaston had much in common. Both were a long way from home, and both deserved respect and compassion. To Gaston, she had offered neither.

Ren pushed away from the stack of barrels, rubbing her tired eyes. She needed to make things right, regardless of whether it restored her place at Maia's side. It was the honorable thing to do. Before she could be honorable, though, Ren needed to get her bearings and find her way back to the banquet hall.

The bell tower. That was as good a landmark as any. Perhaps from there, she could find directions. There was still time to—

"Hey!"

As Ren spun on the man who had approached her, her left hand shot to the handle of the revolver holstered at the small of her back.

The man scratched his flat nose and showed all three of his teeth in a wide smile. He reeked of cheap wine and pipe smoke. Ren relaxed her grip, letting her fingers slide off the revolver's smooth wood handle.

"Apologies, good sir. I do not have any coin to spare," Ren said, forcing a weak smile.

The man stepped back, eyes wide, and wagged a finger at her. "See now, that's the problem with the world nowadays, innit? Gettin' so a man can't talk to folks without them thinkin' he's just askin' for a handout. It's…it's reductive! That's what that is!"

He was right. Ren didn't know his story and had assumed the worst. Again.

She smiled even wider. "I apologize. I meant no offense. What can I do for you?"

"Well—and this is embarassin'—I actually *was* wonderin' if you had any coin to spare. Can't very well sit out here all day without whet for my whistle, eh?"

As her smile melted, Ren turned and walked until she could no longer hear the man shouting after her about his whistle. At the edge of a vacant jetty, she sat and let her feet dangle over the edge. A cool breeze swept past, and she hugged herself against the morning chill. Ren quickly lost herself in the black flowing morass of the mighty river that cut Galford in two, not unlike the crack that ran through her Farspeaker.

She reached into her belt pouch and withdrew the etched stone. The two halves fit together perfectly. The break was clean; she couldn't even see the crack unless she squinted. Ren sighed. If only every broken thing could be so easily mended.

When the Farspeaker vibrated in her hand, she almost dropped it into the water. Dim light rose from a few of the intricate runes carved into it. It still worked! Some of the strands of woven magic forming the enchantment must have survived.

The urge to answer the hail gnawed at her. Maia ordered her not to contact her father, and a good soldier always followed orders. No matter how she longed to hear her father's voice, to find comfort in something familiar, she couldn't betray her word.

Then again, she was no longer Maia's apprentice, which meant she didn't have to adhere to her former mentor's terms. And even if Maia experienced a change of heart, Ren's promise was quite specific. She couldn't attempt to contact her father.

Answering his summons wasn't the same as contacting him. Not really. And Maia might even be glad that she had answered once Ren bade her father to petition the Emperor to reconsider any action that might harm the people of the Freelands.

The latent energy remaining in the stone beckoned, and she allowed it to course through her palm. The etched runes wavered and crackled.

"Serenia? Are you there?" Her father's voice lifted from the stone, dull and distant, as if he were speaking underwater.

"It's me, Father. By the Emperor's light, it's so good to hear your voice. Where are you?"

"I can barely hear you, my dear."

"Father, where are you?"

"We have safely crossed the border. When the connection between our stones died, I feared the worst. Has Maia hurt you? Where are you? Are you well?"

"'Aurelia.' I'm fine, Father. We're in a city called Galford. I haven't been ill-treated." Ren exhaled and steadied herself. "Though, I fear I may have failed my mission."

"Nothing is over until we return to dust and darkness. Why don't you return home?" Though he was whispering, his tone was warm, reminding her of the hearth where she used to curl up on his lap as a child while he regaled her with stories of conquest and bravery. "We can devise another plan to obtain Scarlet. The Freelands are not safe right now."

"I was hoping to ask you about that. Why has the Emperor ordered the Iron Wardens to stand down? I'm not being held against my will, so there's no need to punish the Free People for my decision."

A pause. She could picture him furrowing his brow. When he spoke, the warmth in his voice faded, replaced by steel and duty. "I am a blade of the Empire, and a servant of the Emperor's will. If he wishes the Iron Wardens to stand down until you return, including the ones stationed in the Empire, it is my duty to see it done. It's not my place to question his will. The Emperor also wishes you to know that he has ordered a halt to the construction of Lion's Roar."

She clenched the Farspeaker tighter. Lion's Roar was Noctis' best defense against Behemoths. It had been under various stages of construction for years. The Wardens could handle any Ferals that attacked the capital, but if a Behemoth came, and Lion's Roar wasn't completed in time...

"Father, this is madness. I'm not a hostage, but you've made one out of the entire continent. The Emperor holds my people's lives at my throat like a knife unless I'm able to accomplish the impossible! Please, speak to him. I beg you. I can convince Maia to make me her apprentice once more. She may yet give me Scarlet if she deems me worthy."

"And if she decides you're not?"

She had no answer for that, so her father provided her with one. "Your mission comes first, Serenia. You know what to do. One shot. Aim for the head. She deserves a quick end in light of her service to the Empire. To be perfectly blunt, you'll be doing her a favor."

Ren hefted her revolver from its holster, not bothering to see who might be looking. Her eyes traced over the purple-hued metal finish and the simple wolf's head glyph etched into the long, hexagonal barrel. Less of a handgun and more of a hand cannon, her wolf's bite was keener than even the long flintlock rifles some Noctean sharpshooters employed, capable of killing a Feral at range in a single shot.

But the large hand-made cartridges it employed weren't just for hunting Ferals. They were crafted specifically to pierce the unique magical metal of a Pilot's armor. They had yet to be tested on a living Pilot, but based on the way they tore apart everything else, Ren had no doubt that at close range, Maia's armor couldn't stop her wolf's bite.

That was assuming, of course, that Ren found the nerve to pull the trigger. And that Maia didn't kill her first.

"You have one week to return to Noctis, with or without Scarlet. If you haven't arrived by that time, I will come to retrieve you," her father said. "You know what must be done. Contact me when you're ready to return home."

"I understand. Father? I love you."

"I love you too." She pictured a warm smile, despite his stone-like tone.

The Farspeaker's runes went dim. Ren put it back in her pouch, careful not to damage it further. She cradled her revolver in her hands, tracing the wolf glyph again with her finger, seeking distraction in the cool metal carving.

The boards of the jetty creaked, their rhythm discordant with the pulse of the river below. Someone was approaching.

"As I said before, I don't have any coin," she said.

"Beggin' your pardon, miss. I'm not after your coin." The voice didn't belong to the beggar. The words flowed fast, blending into the smooth, lulling accent common in the southern Freelands.

Ren was on her feet in the span of a breath, her revolver in her left hand and her rapier drawn and ready in the right. She rested the barrel of her revolver on her right arm for support. The owner of the voice held up his hands. His features were indistinct with the light of the morning sun at his back.

He moved closer, stopping a few paces away. Ren could see him clearly then. Human. Almost six feet tall. Age, somewhere between sixteen and eighteen years old, riding the razor's edge between a boy and a man. Black leathers fitted with a hood, the kind a ranger would wear. Or a thief.

No sleeves. Fingerless black gloves. Two daggers sheathed at his hip, eighteen inches long each. Bronze skin. Black hair, artfully mussed. Piercing eyes.

He teased the corner of his lips into a grin. Ren trained her revolver on his chest. "Come no closer."

He ran a hand through his hair, pushing a few errant strands back from his forehead. "Sorry. Didn't mean to startle you. Sometimes I forget how quiet I am. Name's Kasper. You can call me Kas."

"I don't care what your name is. A thief is a thief." She cocked the revolver's hammer.

"What? Oh." He smoothed his vest, then raised his hands again when Ren cleared her throat, reminding him that she still had a gun pointed at his heart. "I'm no thief. I'm a Feral Hunter. See these?" He shook his hip, jostling his sheathed daggers. "These are for Ferals. One for each heart. Surest way to take them down."

"Wonderful. As you can plainly see, there are no Ferals here. That being the case, what do you want, Kas?"

The revolver started to waver in Ren's hand. She had never fired at a person before. If he made a move, she wasn't sure she would be able to squeeze the trigger, and the longer they talked, the less sure she felt.

"Was just walkin' by. Saw you lookin' sullen. Thought I would make sure you were okay."

"Do I look sullen now?"

"Nah. You look downright fierce. Though, I'm gonna put my hands down now, if it's all the same to you."

"It's not. And you must think me a fool. Your excuse is thinner than Fennish parchment. Tell me the truth. Unless you would prefer to tell your tales to a gravedigger instead."

Kas laughed; he stopped when the tip of Ren's rapier pressed against his throat. "Okay. Steady, now. Look, you don't know me, but I promise, I'm a friend. I wasn't lyin' when I said I was a Feral Hunter. Damn good one, too. But the truth is... I'm also a spy."

The point of Ren's rapier pushed into Kas' throat, and he backpedaled. Ren advanced, seeking to drive him into a nearby stack of crates, but then her rapier twisted out of her hand, and her revolver turned in her grasp, and when she regained her footing, she was bare-handed.

Kas held her rapier by the blade and her revolver by the barrel. Ren barely felt either weapon leave her hands. She knew she should be angry or panicked now that she was defenseless, but the way Kas had disarmed her so cleanly...

Blue Hells, he's good. She scowled, not just at him, but at the incessant fluttering in her chest.

"I know it doesn't sound like it, but I swear," Kas said again, "I'm a friend." He used his thumb to reset the revolver's hammer and offered both weapons back to her.

Ren snatched them from his grasp.

The Noctean spy network had skilled operatives working all over the Freelands to uncover any potential threats to the Empire. Even her father was forced to rely on their intricate web of shadow-skulking rogues from time to time. The fact that he hadn't warned her that she was being followed stung, though. Did he still think of her as a child in need of his constant protection?

"Friend or not, I have my own shadow. I don't need another. I wish to be alone."

"Hey," Kas said, drawing her eyes back to his. "I get it. You won't see me again. I'm sorry for startlin' you. If you don't mind keepin' the fact that I revealed myself a secret, that would really help me out."

"I make no promises," Ren said. She looked down at her revolver. She had drawn arms on the first person in the Freelands who seemed to care whether she lived or died, someone who had likely disobeyed orders by revealing himself, all out of concern for her.

Can't I do anything right?

"Fair play, I suppose," Kas said. "Sorry, again. Keep that chin up, okay? Whatever's got you down, you'll get through it. Take care of yourself."

When she looked up, he was gone.

With a shiver, Ren sheathed her weapons. Her heart wouldn't stop thumping. When drilling disarms with her instructions, Ren had never felt anything so smooth, so effortless. Any time one of them took her weapon in training, she paid for it in pain and vowed to return the favor when it was her turn to try.

Kas could have hurt her. He had a right to—she had advanced on him with intent to wound. He was simply defending himself. And instead of escalating, he had been gentle with her. That was more compassion than anyone had shown her in quite some time.

Stop it. Grow up. How dare she allow her nerves to be broken by warm eyes and a handsome smile? Such childishness was unbecoming of a Pilot. A quick, brisk walk to realign herself to her purpose would put things in order.

At the end of the jetty, near a stack of crates and tackle, the old beggar waited. As Ren stepped past him, he screamed, shrill as a banshee.

"What is *wrong* with you!" Ren cried, spinning to face him.

"Oh, nothin'. They told me they'd get me a hot meal and a bath if I could get you to look this way."

Two strong arms wrapped around Ren from behind. She struggled, thrusting her head backward into where her attacker's nose should be. Something hard came down atop her skull. She felt her body grow light as a dusty sack came down over her head, and then she was floating in the dark alone.

Ren woke with the taste of copper in her mouth. The walls of what looked to be a warehouse moved of their own accord. When her vision finally settled, she fixed her gaze on the one-eyed man hunched on a wooden stool in front of her.

"I remember you." Ren's voice was little more than a croak. Had she been knocked unconscious? She didn't remember how she had come to be lashed by her hands with rough hemp rope to a vertical beam in a run-down warehouse. All she remembered was waves, and the rocking of a small boat...but the time before and after that seemed to be missing.

Whatever the case, the blow to her head hadn't rattled her brain enough to dislodge the memory of the one-eyed man following her through the crowd with his piercing stare.

"There isn't much for us to say to each other." He stood and stalked around her. She could see now that one of his coat sleeves was pinned up to the elbow. In his remaining hand, he held a short dagger. Ren straightened when he stepped behind the pillar, out of sight. "Truth is, you don't matter."

"Then release me at once," Ren said.

A dozen men and women padded in through the narrow side entrance of the warehouse. Each brandished a heavy crossbow, the kind that needed to be cranked before loading.

"You don't matter," the man repeated, "but the Pilot does." He came back into view, waving his dagger.

Maia. Everything has to be about her, doesn't it? "You should know that I've received extensive training in interrogation tactics. Your attempts to intimidate me will prove unsuccessful."

"No reason for you to feel intimidated. This isn't about you. You're going to sit there as quiet or as loud as you like. And when the Pilot comes to rescue you, you're going to watch us gut her like a sow."

"I'm afraid you'll be sorely disappointed," Ren said with a chuckle. "Sunder and I aren't on the best of terms at present. I doubt she would deign me worthy of her spittle let alone come to my rescue. Best to just let me go, and we'll forget this ever happened."

"She'll come." The cold certainty in his voice matched the relentless furor in his eye.

"What's this all about? Why do you want to hurt her? What has she done to the world but save it time and time again?"

The man stepped closer. His breath blew hot against her cheek. "You think she's a hero? The Behemoths, the Ferals... I don't know if you're old enough to remember, kid, but they weren't always here. They only started showing up when the Pilots did. Isn't that funny?"

"You think those monsters and the Pilots are connected?" She dared to laugh at him. "Whoever created the Pilots and the Vanguardians did so to *fight* Behemoths and Ferals!"

"Nah. Nah, see, to me, that seems just a little too convenient. That's what the people in power want you to think. I'm thinking it's the other way around. What if the monsters came to hunt the Pilots? What if the Pilots are the cause of all this mess? Maybe the invaders are going through us to get to them?" He reached up and removed his eye patch, revealing a hollow mess of scarred flesh. "Lost this and my arm because that Pilot of yours didn't show up when she was supposed to. And I'm one of the lucky ones. My family, my little girl..." His voice cracked. "You've never lost anything to the invaders, have you?"

Just four years of my life and my mother, you ungrateful waste of flesh. She wanted to scream at him, but he was a coward and a kidnapper. He didn't deserve to know her pain.

Ren gritted her teeth and balled her hands into fists, tensing against her bonds. With more time, she could escape and use her captor's underestimation of her skills to her advantage. All she had to do was keep the man talking long enough for a plan to form.

"That's what I thought." He swept his arm across the room, toward the dozen angry men and women gathered there. "Everyone here's lost something, and that bitch is to blame. She has to pay. But she's hard to kill. She's been stabbed. Shot. Burned. I hear people even tried drowning her, once. Bitch just walks away, fresh and unbloodied. It's not natural. She gets to walk away without a scratch while we're torn apart by the demons she set loose on us. She gets to walk away and be the big hero."

He leaned in closer to Ren, spitting as he spoke, "Fuck. That."

Ren winced at the hot spittle splashing her cheek. "So what, precisely, is your plan, if Maia is so hard to kill? What is your genius strategy to take her down?"

"She's tough, but she *can* die. Look at the other Pilots she murdered if you need proof. She has weaknesses, like any living thing." He stepped back, wagging his blade at her. "For some reason, you matter to her. She'll come for you. And when she does, she'll surrender, or you're going to pay in her place. Then she'll finally know what real loss feels like."

"You think she'll simply surrender if you ask? Have you *met* her?"

One of the knots started to slip. Ren wrapped her legs around the beam. As she was about to pull at her bindings, screams and shouts from outside pierced the air.

"That would be her." Ren smiled at her captor. "Now, if you wish to get out of this situation unharmed, I suggest you... Oh."

Ren struggled to finish her thought as a hulking mass of twitching purple muscle ducked through the side entrance. Three more followed close behind. They resembled the Feral she had fought and lost to, save for the curved blades of sharp, yellowed bone hanging from their right arms where claws should have been.

She thought about bargaining with her captors, begging them to release her and return her weapons so that she could help them make a stand. As the one-eyed man shouted orders to his followers and crossbows thrummed, Ren realized they were too occupied to pay her any heed.

She pulled, straining so hard against her bonds she feared she might snap before her bindings did. Her hands went numb from the rope's bite as the first of her captors fell, his body split halfway down the middle by the lead Feral's cruel bone blade.

There, as the fear of her impending demise gripped her chest, she found the rest of the thought she had left unfinished. It wasn't elegant, it wasn't proper, but it did sum up her current predicament in a way that would have made Maia proud.

"We're positively fucked."

Chapter 8
Awakening

Maia's uppercut broke the messenger's jaw, relieving him of at least one of his good chewing teeth. She was already running through the streets of Galford before he hit the ground.

Though she was in a hurry, she spared a moment to congratulate herself for her restraint. She didn't hit the messenger right away; she waited until he repeated his message, confirming that Serenia was being held in a warehouse by the southern docks and that the man's friends would kill her if Maia didn't come alone and unarmored.

And she only hit him once, just enough to ruin his self-satisfied smile. That was something to be proud of. She would celebrate later when Serenia was safe.

The people of Galford threw themselves clear of Maia's charge as she swept her arms into a cross above her head and brought them down to her chest, summoning her armor in a flash of fire and purpose. She didn't stop to see if the flames had caused any damage. She had more important things to focus on, like berating herself for being so careless.

Long after the banquet ended, Maia lingered to entertain her guests until the sun rose. She completely forgot about the young apprentice she had left waiting for her in the kitchen.

Of course Serenia would run off. Of course she would get into trouble. It wasn't her fault. The current situation Maia found herself in owed less to Serenia being young, highborn, and impulsive. It had more to do with how stupid Maia had been in thinking that taking on an apprentice in the first place was a sound idea.

This is what happens when you let people get near you.

With crimson panic humming in her veins, Maia pushed into a mighty leap.

She landed on a nearby rooftop and took off, each blazing step leaving cracked roof tiles in her wake. Her momentum carried her forward as she cleared the gaps between buildings with short hops.

The town's white bell tower loomed ahead, rivaling Scarlet's full standing height. Maia gathered her feet and launched toward the tower, drew one of her hot-edged falchions from her back, and buried it in the stone.

She flipped onto the embedded blade, using it as a makeshift perch. Her eyes flicked over the city below, mapping out the quickest path across the river. With a route committed to memory, she planted her foot against the tower. She was about to push off when a sudden pressure bore down on her mind.

Six distended black disks of rippling liquid appeared over Galford, each flat as canvas. Their bottoms sagged and stretched under the weight of whatever was struggling to rip through. One by one, the shadowy membranes tore, dumping their contents in streams of bubbling black smoke.

The Ferals tumbled from the torn sky, some dashing against rooftops, others landing in the river. Most landed safely, kicking up large clouds of dust as they touched down and filled the air with their horrendous shrieking.

Six breaches. That meant that up to six dozen Ferals—more than Maia had ever encountered in one place—had been set loose upon Galford.

The black disks shrank into pin pricks and vanished. Her Hunter Sense drew her in too many directions at once; Maia didn't know where to begin. Her heart pounded like a war drum, matching the dull throb in the base of her skull. This was the best part, right before the hunt, when her blood was fire and she could hardly keep from shaking in anticipation. She hated her creator for sewing this bloodlust into her. She hated herself more for liking it.

Down below, the people of Galford flowed through the streets in a churning mass of chaos. The hulking beasts of solid muscle and bone swept their long arms through screaming crowds, sending broken bodies sailing through the air like rag dolls. The cries of the dead and dying floated up to Maia, competing with the drumming beat of her heart for her attention.

Every fiber of her body howled the same keening note. It took everything Maia had to ignore the voices in her head whispering bloody murder and pull her gaze from the carnage below, shifting her focus to a warehouse on the other side of the river.

She needs you. You owe her.

Maia leaped straight into the air from her blade perch. Her flight brought her level with the massive wrought-iron bell that hung at the top of the tower, and she kicked it. Metal rang against metal, sending a dull toll over the city, the beginning of a funeral dirge.

Hopefully, it would alert any guards who were still sleeping in their barracks. Maia told herself that that was all she could do for the people of Galford as she fell past her falchion, tore it from the wall, and kicked off the bell tower, leaving the screams behind her.

The one-eyed man looked up at Ren from the ground. A thin line of blood trickled from the corner of a mouth forever frozen in a defiant scream. As the last of her captors screamed and fell silent, Ren tensed and twisted her wrists again, but her bonds wouldn't give.

The Feral who killed the one-eyed man approached, its dangling knife-hand tracing a bloody trail across the warehouse floor. Her belt, along with her weapons and the contents of her concealed pouch, sat atop a crate that seemed miles away.

Ren fought to keep from trembling, but her body seized into one solid mess of panic as the beast drew near. When the Feral stepped within range, Ren screamed and pulled hard on her bindings. Her training took over. She contracted her abdominal muscles and lifted her numb legs, aimed at the inside of the Feral's knee, and thrust out. Her kick turned the monster's hip outward, causing it to stumble and drive its bone knife into the ground. The blade broke with a dull crack under the Feral's weight. Before it could stand, Ren landed another double-footed stomp to the side of its masked head.

One down. Three to go. Breathe. You can do this!

The fallen Feral stirred as soon as its back touched the ground. A second Feral stepped over its body, knife raised. Its head cocked to the side, gurgling nonsense as it considered her.

In a flash, it hacked at her neck. Ren screamed and kicked it in the chest, pushing it back. The knife swiped just short of her throat. Her arms flexed. Her muscles tightened. Her legs lifted high over her head and dropped heel-first, crashing down on the Feral's skull. It wasn't enough to fell it, but the monster staggered backward and tripped over its rising ally. They both collapsed into a thrashing, snarling mass.

She flexed again but couldn't lift her legs. Fear had stolen what energy she had left. With her weapons, she stood a chance. Four against one, bound by the wrists…

This is it. This is where it ends. I'm going to die here.

Ren cried out, first for her father, then for Maia, but she knew in her thundering heart that neither of them would come for her. The four Ferals would set upon her with wicked blades and sharp claws. And if she somehow managed the impossible and fought them off, there were eight more approaching the warehouse, with dozens more roaming the city beyond.

Ren froze. She could feel how many were in the city. The dull pulsing in her head matched her hammering heartbeat. Her mind lit up with sparks, each one pulling her along an unseen path toward an individual Feral.

The sensation stole what little breath she had. *I can feel them. Why? Why now?*

Pain answered her. Ren's body contracted, her muscles spasming against her will. She stretched against her seams, straining against an invisible force so intense she thought it might tear her apart.

When it did, all she could do was scream.

Muscles ripped. Bones cracked. A rush of heat and pressure and utter agony seared her to the core. Ren leaned into the burning wave, letting her pained scream rise into a furious war cry. She lost her vision to flashes of red, then white, then black as she finally succumbed to the pain.

She was gone only a moment. Her eyes flicked open. Her chest heaved as she sucked air through her sore throat. Her destroyed body mended itself in the span of a breath, leaving behind a cool, hard strength that made her feel like she was made of tempered steel.

With one jerk of her hands, Ren snapped her bindings. The cracked, jagged remnant of the first Feral's bony knife thrust at her stomach as her feet touched the ground. Ren stepped around the attack, leaped up, and snapped her foot into the Feral's chest. Bone crunched under her boot. The monster flew into its partner, sending them both careening into a stack of crates.

Her muscles thrummed with new power, enough to put a Feral on its back with an ungrounded strike. She didn't know how it had happened. She didn't know why it had taken so long. It didn't matter. All Ren cared about was that the moment she had yearned for had finally come.

"I'm a Pilot."

Ren suppressed a shudder. Now that she had awakened into her true self, she couldn't lose.

She rushed toward her belt, hopping back as a bony knife sliced through the air. One of the Ferals moved to block her path to her weapons. The Feral thrust, and she twisted too late.

The edge glided over her left shoulder. Her hand went to the wound, clamping down as she fell back.

Perhaps she could still lose after all.

Ren backed away as the monster waded in. Her eyes locked on the bone razor, slick with her own blood. The other three Ferals closed on her, forming a semicircle that grew tighter with each step. Fresh pain arced from her shoulder like lightning, dividing her focus as Ren's mind worked to find a way to get to her weapons.

A loud crack and a flash of light split the air. The furthest Feral squealed and clawed frantically at the flames licking at its back. The other three monsters turned their masked heads, tracking a shape darting between short stacks of crates. Two more quick explosions sent another Feral reeling backward, arms flailing, as hungry flames covered its chest.

"Maia!" Ren cried. She wasn't about to waste the moment her mentor had bought her. Ren dashed toward the Feral who had cut her and leaped, planting her hands on its shoulders and vaulting over its head. As she touched down, she threw herself into a roll, avoiding the beast's lazy turning swing. The maneuver brought her to her belt, and she ripped her rapier and revolver free.

Before she could take aim and fire, the darting shape collided with the Feral in front of her. The monster stood straight, as if called to attention by a distant voice, before collapsing onto its face. The Feral's killer rode its body to the ground, ripping his stiletto daggers free from the monster's twin hearts and sending fountains of sparking lifeblood erupting into the air.

He shielded his face and stepped off the body as rolling flames burned it to ash in seconds. When his eyes met Ren's, he flashed her a sly grin.

"Kas? What in the Blue Hells…"

"Sorry. I know I said you wouldn't see me again," he called back as he dropped to his knees and slid under the next Feral's swing. "I didn't say I would stop keepin' an eye on you, though. I've got a job to do." He plunged a dagger into the Feral's knee, angling his face away from the spray of sparking blood. "Don't worry. I'll get you out of here."

"I can handle this myself, thank you!"

Three more Ferals pushed their way through the narrow side door. At the same moment, the Feral with the broken knife, the one whose ribs she had cracked, grunted and wailed as it threw itself at her. She wished she had something clever to say that would unbalance her foe, but she lacked Maia's rapier wit.

Fortunately, she did have a rapier. A fine one, at that.

She thrust it into the Feral's bicep as it passed and fell back into a receiving posture before it registered the damage. It howled and swung its broken knife hand at her in a wild arc. She slipped under the blow and countered. Two new wounds blossomed on the Feral's right flank. The creature didn't seem to care. As it swept both arms down in a hammer blow, Ren twisted and stepped, landing a strike to the Feral's neck as she retreated.

A second Feral moved to flank her. In all the excitement, Ren had completely forgotten about her revolver. Even with three years of strength training, Ren still had difficulty hefting and firing such a large weapon with any semblance of accuracy even if she held it in both hands. Trusting in her newfound strength, she raised the revolver one-handed and squeezed the trigger.

Her wolf leaped, barely moving in her grip as its thundering bark tore the air. The advancing Feral's right hand disappeared, replaced with a flower of sparks and mangled flesh.

Four shells left, she reminded herself.

Ren squeezed again. The shot took the Feral in the mask, piercing the thick bone. The Feral's body was already awash with flames before it crumpled to the ground.

Three.

Ren let her attention drift to where Kas was attempting to hold his ground. Two more Ferals had made their way inside the warehouse. Kas spun and dodged their swings, flicking his wrist and tossing what looked like blackened walnut shells at their chests. The shells cracked and burst on impact, showering them with fire.

His eyes locked with hers for the briefest of moments. Perhaps it was the way the corner of his mouth pulled at a playful smirk or the intensity of his gaze that made her cheeks flush. The cause of the new pain in her left forearm, however, was far easier to discern. The Feral she had briefly ignored had dug long gashes into her skin with its claws while she was distracted.

Ren yelped and brought her revolver to bear, but the Feral lowered its shoulder and slammed into her, bungling her shot and driving her onto her back.

Two.

The Feral pinned Ren's sword arm flat against the ground. As its knife hand reared back, she lifted her revolver and placed it against its mask. Before she could squeeze the trigger and end its life, the Feral pushed its face past the end of the barrel.

She had to give the Feral credit for being a quick learner. Fortunately, she was quicker.

She turned the revolver sideways, loosened her grip, and fired. The revolver's recoil sent the mass of forged metal crashing into the side of the Feral's face.

One.

The monster howled and rolled to the side, clutching the shattered remains of its mask in its hands. Ren pushed to her feet, leaving her rapier on the ground. As chunks of bone crumbled through its grip, the Feral looked up at Ren, showing her what the mask had been protecting. Its left eye, once hidden behind its mask, was a distended yellow oval with a cat-like iris that took up a commanding portion the Feral's face.

With its most vulnerable point exposed, the Feral broke into a screeching wail. A point-blank shot to the face ended its misery, painting the floor with a sunset of burning ichor.

Zero.

With her path temporarily clear, Ren retrieved her belt. She rested the revolver in the crook of her elbow and broke it open. Nimble fingers removed spent casings from the cylinder's five chambers and replaced them with fresh death from one of her larger belt pouches. Ren slammed the weapon closed and gave the cylinder a quick spin to align it, turning her attention back to Kas now that she had a moment to breathe.

She looked up just in time to watch him sidestep a Feral's wild slash. Its partner caught him flat-footed with a tackle, wrapping Kas up in a bear hug and driving him into the wall. Wood planks cracked under their combined weight, and Kas and the Feral fell through the wall and out of sight.

"Kas!" Ren cried. She slipped past the growing throng of Ferals and braced against the edges of the hole. It was then that Ren realized the whole warehouse was on raised stilts over the river, and that beyond the wall was a sheer drop into the flowing waters below.

The world fell away. She didn't know how long she remained there, staring in shock at the floating chunks of wood being swept away by the current before she realized she should try to save Kas.

As she was about to dive in after him, the sound of cracking timber forced her to turn. A Feral rolled onto its back, shaking off the debris of the support beam it had been thrown through. Maia stalked in, clad in her crimson armor and brandishing her falchions, whose edges burned brighter than ever.

The Feral rose, curled its clawed fingers into a fist, and smashed Maia in the stomach. She didn't even flinch. In response, she slammed her helmeted head into the Feral's mask, driving it back. Her blades leaped to life in her hands. Glowing edges passed through the muscle and bone of the Feral's neck like parchment. She pushed the burning body away as it fell and sent both blades spinning end over end through the air and into another Feral's chest. Maia walked past the burning Feral, ripping her blades free of its twin hearts and placing them on her back in one fluid motion.

The warehouse was suspiciously empty, save for the bodies of her kidnappers, but Ren noted several piles of ash that had not been there before.

"Princess," Maia growled. She grabbed Ren by the shoulders. "Are you hurt?"

She looked down to her bloodied arm. The gashes had already pulled closed, and her shoulder no longer ached. In the chaos of battle, she hadn't noticed.

"I...believe I'm fine." Ren took a moment to steady herself. "But there was a boy. He fell into the river with a Feral, and he..."

Maia glanced at the waters and shook her head. "Sorry to say, but he's probably done for. Come on, Princess. We need to get back to Scarlet. You'll be safe there."

Ren pushed back her tears. She would have time to cry for Kas later. She walked to where she had dropped her rapier and scooped it up. "Not yet. There are several dozen more Ferals we must deal with. We must do our duty."

"No, *I* must do our duty. You..." Maia canted her head. "Hold on. You can feel them?"

Ren nodded.

Maia stared at her through the black glass of her visor for a long moment. "So, you've—"

"Yes. I have."

"Huh. Well, it doesn't change anything. It's my duty to keep you safe."

"No, it's your duty to train me. This is as good an opportunity for a practical lesson as we're likely to get. The good people of this city need our assistance. Shall we get to it?"

Maia put a hand to her visor. She sighed, her helmet warping the sound into something resembling a hiss. Finally, she gestured to the door. "After you, Princess."

Ren gritted her teeth, forcing her thoughts onto the task at hand and away from the boy in the water as she ran from the warehouse. The sound of clinking metal boots followed close behind.

Chapter 9

Payment Due

A flash of Maia's blades took another Feral's arm clean off its body. She marched through the spark shower bursting from its shoulder and worked her falchions through a dizzying series of slices, each angry blade advancing to cover the retreat of its twin.

Behemoth and Feral attacks had slowed over the last year, giving Maia fewer chances to properly ply her craft. She forgot how good it felt. She hated how much she missed it. All of it, from the indescribable feeling of piloting Scarlet to the unique smell of Feral blood burning as it kissed the air, brought her back to a version of herself she thought lost.

The Feral fell to its knees, sparking and bleeding all over. She thrust her swords into its chest, striking the twin hearts beneath its sternum. As it burned away in death, the memory of the fight was already fading, blurring into a day-long haze of violence. She hadn't given any one of her foes much thought. Her experienced hands knew how to move her blades where they needed to be.

A breeze caught the Feral's ashes and whipped them past her. It had taken all afternoon to hunt the remaining Ferals across Galford; with her latest kill, she could sense no more.

That didn't mean they were all dead. There were close to two score unaccounted for. They had likely roamed beyond the city limits, spreading too thin for her to locate as a pack. That meant days of traveling the countryside to track down the stragglers.

Maia grinned beneath her helmet. Shivers raced up her spine. This life was better than wine. Better than sex. Better by far than the all-consuming numbness she felt most days. Hunting Ferals and Behemoths defined her, made her who she was. How could she have ever thought about quitting?

The last drops of bloodlust drained from Maia's head and hands, and with clear eyes, she took in a ruined town square strewn with broken and torn bodies and so much ash. The mournful wails of the survivors pierced the safety of her helmet. Reality slammed into her chest like an iron fist. Within the destruction painting the square, Maia saw the end result of every battle she had ever waged. She remembered why she longed to leave this life behind.

Maia slid her blades into place on her back and dismissed her armor in a flash of light and fire. Serenia approached and stood at her side. The girl had done well. Though Maia was reluctant to take her along, Serenia pulled her weight, taking down a half dozen Ferals over the course of the day. And it wasn't solely that giant revolver that had made her a threat. Something had changed inside her.

Whatever it was, it made her strong, and fast, and confident. And dangerous.

Maia would deal with that later. A churning crowd formed a wide perimeter around them. The most important part of the day's lesson was still to come.

"People of Galford!" Maia shouted, "I am truly sorry for your losses. Rest assured, the Ferals within the city have all been dealt with. You have nothing to fear. In the coming days, my apprentice and I will—"

"This is *your* fault!" A woman screamed. She cradled the body of a boy roughly Serenia's age in her arms. "You fled! I saw you! You looked down at us, and you ran! Now you come back after the demons have had their fill so we can praise you as a hero? My boy is dead because of *you!*"

There it was. The rage. The blame. Maia couldn't think of anything she could say that would give back what had been taken, so she said nothing. Even if she hadn't chosen Serenia's life over theirs, lives would have been lost. The people of Galford were entitled to their anger.

They had a right to hate her. So, she let them. Serenia needed to see what being a Pilot really looked like.

A man with a shaved head shouldered through the crowd. "I bet she's in league with the demons! Barely any come around here for years, then they show as soon as she comes to town. I say we put a stop to this, once and for all!" His eyes held the look of a desperate man about to make a huge mistake. Grief had that effect on people.

He broke into a screaming charge. She saw the knife before it found his hand.

She stepped in front of Serenia, spread her arms wide, and waited.

Come on, then, she thought. *Come get your piece of me.*

The man stopped suddenly and grunted. He dropped to his knees, eyes wide, too stunned to cry out. As the knife clinked against the stone, Maia followed the thin line of steel leading from the crook of his elbow, under her own arm, and back to Serenia's hand.

"Attack your opponent while they're attacking you, in a way that keeps you safe," Serenia said in an icy monotone. She withdrew her rapier's tip from the man's arm. That was his cue to bawl.

Before she could berate her brash apprentice, something flashed in the corner of Maia's eye. She would have easily avoided it, but a heaviness in her chest she mistook for fatigue became a wrenching twist. The sharp, sudden pain froze her in place. Based on the way the missile shattered against her scarred temple, it must have been a bottle. The blood dripping into her eye was a small worry. The pressure of phantasmal fingers squeezing her heart had her full attention.

The world flashed as the grip expanded and contracted, crushing Maia's insides. She struggled through the shapes and colors blasting her vision. She didn't remember falling, but the cold stone against her cheek told her she had. Her heart tensed and constricted so tight she thought she might snap. A gout of blood spewed from her lips, staining the ground where she lay.

When the attack finally subsided, Maia struggled to see through hot tears. She had kept her illness a secret for so long, but there it was, on display for the world to see. Word would spread. The lingering faith the people had in their lone protector would fade; based on the sea of horrified stares aimed her way, she had already lost the people of Galford forever.

And if she hadn't, then Serenia drawing her revolver and sweeping it across the crowd would certainly do the trick.

"How *dare* you!" Serenia boomed. "This is your *Pilot!* She fights for you! Bleeds for you! And this is how you repay her? By taking up arms against her?"

"My son is dead because of her!" yelled a grieving man.

"And my wife!" another said.

"I lost my business!"

"I lost an eye!"

The people shouted, tallying up their losses and placing them at Maia's feet. She coughed up another mouthful of blood and propped herself up on her elbow.

With a thrust of her gun, Serenia forced the crowd back. "And how many of you are alive today because of her? How many of you would be dead if you didn't have Scarlet and Sunder fighting to protect you?"

The man with the knife stood with difficulty, cradling his injured elbow. "We're supposed to thank her? While our kin lay dead in the streets? Maybe we show the Pilot what it's like to lose, eh? Might be we bleed you out in front of her. Let that be a lesson."

Serenia's aim flicked to him. "Speaking of lessons: perhaps you haven't learned yours." She squeezed the trigger. A flagstone next to the man's feet exploded in a shower of dust and stone. Before it cleared, he was already running.

"If anyone else is in need of instruction, I can happily oblige." She waggled her revolver. "Perhaps you'll overtake us, but I have four more bullets in this cannon of mine. Who wishes to roll the dice?"

"Hey. Enough." Maia reached up and touched Serenia on the leg, forcing a smile as the last of her spasms subsided. "Leave it be. Let's get out of here. Okay?"

Forguth emerged from the parted crowd, picking his way forward with care, hands raised in a show of peace. "We don't want any more trouble than has already befallen us. We thank you for your service, Sunder. Go in peace. Galford wishes you safe travels."

And good riddance. Maia didn't miss the coldness in his tone.

"Here." Maia stood, catching herself before she fell again, and ripped the money pouch from her belt. She tossed it to Forguth. The mayor caught it, hefting the bag of clinking coins.

"Your wages from last night?" he said. "This won't bring the dead back, I'm afraid."

"Nothing ever will. That's for supplies." Maia accepted Serenia's shoulder, draping her arm over it for support. "Bread. Bacon. Root vegetables. No eggs. They break too easily."

Maia looked down at Serenia and her torn red shirt. "And some clothes for the girl. What's your color?"

"Oh...purple?" Serenia replied.

"And some purple dye. I know it's hard to come by. Make it happen. Have everything delivered to Scarlet, and we'll be out of your hair by morning. Let's go, Princess."

As the crowd started to disperse, Serenia craned her neck. "Hello there! Sir! Mister Turner!" she called. The artificer stopped at the sound of his name and turned.

"Mister Turner? Do you have a moment?" Serenia said. "I'm glad to see you unharmed. Should I call you 'mister?' I've never spoken to a master artificer before. I'm afraid I'm not sure how to best address you."

"Then ask me, instead of waiting for me to educate you," he said.

"Of course. How should I address you?"

"You may call me Gaston. And what shall I call you?"

She looked up at Maia, who nodded. "You can call me Ren," Serenia said.

"It is good to meet you, Ren."

"Gaston, I wish to apologize for last night, for disrespecting you and the people of Galford. I'm sorry. My behavior was inexcusable. Nobody deserves to be spoken to with such disregard."

Gaston nodded. "I accept that you are sorry. However, I accept neither you nor your apology."

Serenia stiffened. "I'm afraid I don't understand," she said.

"I do not doubt that you feel sorry for what you said. I also do not argue that just now, with that man, you were acting in self-defense. That being said, it is not my duty to absolve you of guilt." Gaston closed his eyes. "If you travel with Sunder, if you aid her in her duty, then you are our protector, as she is. Your words and actions carry great weight. Don't be sorry. Be better."

"Oh." Serenia bowed her head. "I understand. Thank you. I will be better. I promise."

Gaston inclined his head to Serenia, then to Maia. The two women left the bloody square, weathering a storm of angry glares from those who remained.

"Are you well?" Serenia asked when they were alone in an alley. "That episode was worse than the one at the campsite. Is it your heart?"

"Let's start a list of things we're not going to talk about," Maia replied. "Starting with that."

"Mmm."

"I know you think that I only focus on your failures, but you shouldn't have threatened that crowd. Also, you stabbed somebody. A person."

Serenia swallowed. "I know. It wasn't becoming of a Pilot. I feel terrible about it. Gaston was right. I must do better."

Better than me, at least. "We fight Ferals and Behemoths. We don't hurt people. We don't get involved in their affairs."

"You got involved at the marketplace. You stood up to the Iron Wardens."

"Yeah." Maia coughed, clearing blood from her throat. "Maybe I'm not the best example to follow. Thank you, though. For stabbing that guy."

"You were going to let him hurt you. Why?"

"I was protecting you. I've been cut before. It's nothing." Maia didn't want to admit to her apprentice that she wanted him to hurt her. That she deserved to be punished for everything she had done. For everything she might do.

"Were all the Pilots treated this way? Did people try to stab them as well?"

"For as much as the people loved us for protecting them, some hated us for not being able to save everyone. We were all attacked from time to time, except for Dalzin. Everybody liked Dalzin."

"I believe I'm beginning to understand how thankless this calling can be. Why you wanted to quit."

"We have to protect them, even if they hate us. That's not why I wish I could leave this life behind, though."

"Is it because of Leona?"

Maia pushed away from Serenia and turned to face her. *My heart belongs to you, Leona, and no other.* "Where did you hear that name?"

"Yesterday. When we first arrived in Galford. Forguth mentioned her, and you said... I thought, maybe..."

Maia placed her hands on Serenia's shoulders, looking the girl square in the eyes and putting on her widest smile. "You don't know me very well, so I can't be mad at you for asking about her. But if you ever bring her up again, the next words you speak will be from your doorstep in Noctis. Is that clear?"

Serenia's eyes widened. She quickly found her composure. "Very well. I'll add her to the list of things we're never to discuss, right next to whatever illness is afflicting your heart."

"Above. Put her above my heart." They continued walking. "I need to ask. Back there, in the warehouse. What happened?"

Serenia looked down at herself as if she was seeing her body for the first time. Maybe she was. Her muscles had grown visibly, and Maia could have sworn she had gained an inch or more in height. "I was about to die. I knew I was. Then there was this pain, bright and blinding, and then... I'm not sure words can convey. I felt like I was torn apart and remade anew. Does that make sense?"

"That's what it feels like to become a Pilot." Before it could take hold in her mind, Maia pushed away the memory of her own sundering. "If you're like the rest of us, from now on, you'll be able to feel Ferals and Behemoths with your Hunter Sense. You'll recover from injuries that you shouldn't be able to walk away from with Regeneration. And you'll be faster. Stronger. That means you need to be more careful. The bloodlust... If you're not careful, it'll own you."

"Bloodlust?"

"Yeah. When you sense Ferals and Behemoths. That force that drives you to rip them apart. You felt it, right?"

"Oh, of course. Yes." Serenia's mouth pulled into a tight line.

"You don't have all your powers. Not yet. Teleportation, armor, those come with—"

"Why now, though? Why did my powers remain dormant all this time?"

"Not sure. It wasn't like that for me. At any rate, making a Pilot is complicated. Maybe your mages got something wrong."

"Doubtful. I have the utmost confidence in my...my..."

As they rounded the corner, Serenia's words slipped from her lips and pooled at her feet, mixing with the blood slicking the street. Six Iron Wardens were strewn across the ground, their white armored frames caked in blood and ash. What was left of the captain's body dangled from the top of his Warden. Crimson ichor dripped from a horrid gash in his neck, staining the Warden's cape and its golden lion emblem.

The Wardens were on orders to stand down. This street wasn't anywhere near their barracks. They had sought this fight deliberately, even though they were ordered not to. The black ash staining their bodies told Maia that they disposed of at least a few Ferals before they were overwhelmed.

Serenia moved to the fallen metal husks, her steps rigid and forced. She crumbled to her knees before the captain's Warden and rubbed her hand over the grime and blood covering the white lacquer of his breastplate, accomplishing little more than dirtying her own hands.

Maia kept her distance. "I'm sorry, Princess."

"I've told you countless times. That's not my name. But...thank you." She let her hand rest on the bloodied armor. "They stayed and fought. They disobeyed their orders."

"Not all good soldiers follow orders," Maia said. "They made a choice. So did the boy who helped you. So did the fellow who tried to stab me. So did you. The only difference is that as a Pilot, your decisions weigh more." Maia drew a little closer. "You've seen a lot of horrible things today. I understand if you want to quit. If you don't want to be a Pilot anymore."

"I had thought that you already made that decision for me." Traces of venom laced Serenia's words. She let her hand fall from the Warden's armor. "Thank you for coming to my aid, but I don't understand why you did. All you had to do was leave me to my kidnappers and the Ferals, and I would no longer be a burden to you."

Maia grimaced. *Is that who you think I am?* "I couldn't leave you. The truth is, I... Your father would bring the Empire down on the Freelands if you... He would make the War of Bones look like a child's birthday party if anything happened to you, is all."

"Hmm," Serenia said. "I see."

Maia smoothed her hair back and took a deep breath. "Look. The thing is, I don't know how to do this. Any of this. I wish you had a teacher like Amisrala, but you're stuck with me. I'm a fighter. When I have a problem, I attack it. But I'm supposed to be your teacher. I should be a better example for you to follow."

"You were right to scold me, after the banquet. I understand, now, what I must become." Serenia looked back over her shoulder and sniffled. "Do you wish for me to continue as your apprentice?"

Maia sighed. *You're making a mistake,* she thought. *If you let her in, if you let her see what you really are, it won't end well.* "If we met six months ago, no. But between that Behemoth we fought and the Ferals we faced today, it looks like this war is far from over. Whether I like it or not, I need to keep training you. The world needs a protector after I'm gone." Maia cleared her throat. "It's up to you if you want to continue. There's no shame in quitting. Not after what you've seen."

"The Wardens stayed and fought."

"So they did."

"We're not all as bad as you think," Serenia said. "Nocteans, I mean."

"You might be right about that."

"Then we've both learned something. The Wardens stayed. They fought against all odds. So, I'll stay and fight as well."

Maia offered a pitying smile. "You're hopeless."

"No. I should say I have quite a bit of hope. And like the people of Galford, I know what it is to lose someone to these monsters. I can't leave this fight. Not yet."

The urge to tell Serenia the truth about the day her mother died, to ruin everything that had started to form between them, tugged at her harder than a Behemoth. Serenia scrunched up her brow. "What is it?"

"It's just my heart." Maia forced a smile.

Serenia looked back to the Wardens. "They may not receive a proper burial. Not by these people."

Maia gestured with her chin. Together, they carried the bodies of the fallen Noctean riders into the center of the street, arranging them in a row on top of some wooden debris Serenia gathered. Once they were in place, Maia summoned fire with a thought, sending a screeching plume of orange flame from her palm to ignite the makeshift pyre.

"May the Emperor's light guide you across the Veil to your eternal rest." Serenia bowed her head and clasped her hands together. "In His name."

Maia gave her a few minutes to grieve in silence. "Come on," she said. "We're not safe out here. We need to get back to Scarlet before dark." She slipped an arm over Serenia's shoulder, even though she had recovered enough to walk the rest of the way on her own. Serenia slid an arm around Maia's waist, pulling her in tight as they stepped past the dancing flames.

There was so much she wanted to say to the girl, more than the full extent of Maia's failure on the day Serenia's mother died. The space between them just wouldn't hold it. The day had been too long already. Too bloody. As they trudged along in silence together, Maia gave Serenia's shoulder a squeeze, hoping the simple gesture would carry at least a sliver of what she had left unsaid.

Part Two

Old Wounds

Chapter 10

Ashen Lady

The cloaked shape slipped through the shadowy woods, unhindered by the clouds obscuring the moon's light. She didn't need sight to hunt. She moved through the gnarled, leafless forest, quiet as a shadow despite the deadwood beneath her feet. She didn't need to fear what lurked in the dark around her. The night was hers, and whatever crept beneath its cover knew better than to cross her path.

She shifted her vision, trading night sight for another of her gifts. The souls she sought appeared as white splotches of bright light in the distance. Even without her ability to sense the living, she would have found her quarry eventually. Between the roaring bonfire throwing dancing flames high into the night sky and the echoing cries of drunken revelry, the bandits had all but mailed her an invitation to their camp.

It didn't seem fair. She had to skulk in the dark, hidden from the world, while these Imperial turncoats were free to do as they pleased. In this case, "do as they pleased" consisted of robbing Noctean convoys bound for the border and carousing like blithering fools.

It wasn't some altruistic need to make the Empire a safer place that drove her to hunt this particular group. It had more to do with the fact that she was hungry, and nobody would waste effort investigating the deaths of some Imperial traitors in a remote forest.

As she approached the camp, the bandits' voices reached her through the night, breaking what would have been deathly stillness. "You believe that horse shit?" The furthest bandit, a burly man in scratched leathers, doubled over in laughter. "Hey, I've got a castle in the Fen Islands to sell. Real cheap. You can move in tomorrow."

The cloaked shadow paused outside the clearing and waited.

"I swear on the Emperor's golden sack!" a second man added. "They say she haunts the capital. Creeps up in the dark of night and feasts on her victim's blood."

"That's vampires. You're thinking of vampires." This voice, hard like gravel, belonged to a woman. The leader, no doubt.

"Hey, lots of things drink blood! Giant spiders. Leeches. Zombies." The burly bandit shifted on the log he was sitting on.

"Zombies eat brains," the other bandit said.

"Isn't that a myth? Whatever. You know what I mean. Just because she feasts on blood doesn't mean she's a vampire."

"What is she, then?" the leader said with a sigh. "A ghost? A witch?"

"Something else entirely, I'm afraid." The shadow stepped into the clearing, delighting in the frenzy of activity as the six thieves grabbed their weapons and formed a defensive perimeter.

"Who goes there? Show yourself!" the burly one shouted.

"Just a hungry traveler. Seeking a warm fire, shelter and... Ah, to the Blue Hells with this. I'm too hungry for this shit. Run, or fight. I don't care. Let's get to the killing."

She threw back her hood, revealing lifeless gray skin and a mane of bone-white hair running down to her hips. Her veins pulsed blue, though their dim glow paled next to the brilliance of the raging bonfire.

The necromantic fluid that maintained her was failing. Thankfully, a six-course meal had just been served.

"It's her!" The burly bandit's spear tip shook as he spoke. "The Night Bitch!"

"Night Bitch! I haven't heard that one before. Not my favorite nickname, I have to say. There once was a girl who called me 'Ashen Lady.' I liked that quite a bit." She paced around the fire. Spear and sword tips followed her path. "I couldn't spare her, though. I had just made her an orphan, and I thought it would be a kindness to...I...wait." She scrunched her face. "Sorry. I'm rambling. I sometimes lose myself when my blood goes stale. I'm back now. Where were we?"

The burly one's war cry gave her ample warning, but she didn't bother avoiding his charge. She allowed the spear's tip to plunge into her abdomen. It wouldn't kill her. At this point, aside from blood death, she wondered if anything could.

Her taloned fingers tightened around the spear shaft, and she pulled on it, drawing herself close enough to smell his fear. "It's rude not to introduce yourself to a lady before penetrating her. Mind you, I don't really have a name to offer in return. I had one once, but that name, that life, was taken from me. I'm not the woman I used to be. For the time being, since we're so close and all... why don't you call me Ash?"

The trembling bandit clung to the spear's shaft as if it would save him. As if anything could. "By the Emperor's golden sack... What in the Blue Hells are you?"

"Ask him," Ash said. "He made me."

Her fingers thrust through his sternum like it was made of soft clay. Ash's hand closed into a fist, clenching the bandit's heart as a dull orange glow emanated from beneath his skin. He opened his mouth to scream, but his life, his breath, was hers.

Rippling waves of power crawled up her arm as she fed on his essence. The bandit leader offered up a rallying cry and charged, her gravelly voice cracking. Her sword never found its mark. Ash's free hand shot out, clamping around her neck. Talons pierced tender flesh. The woman's face lit up with unholy orange light as Ash drank her fill.

When there was nothing left to drain, she released her victims, watching their empty husks crumble to the dirt and scatter in a burst of gray ashes and discarded leathers. A quick swat of her hand broke the shaft of the spear still protruding from her stomach. With a jerk, she pulled the other half out through her back. The edges of the wound pulled shut. Within seconds, it was fully knitted.

The remaining four bandits turned to flee. Ash hurled what was left of the spear at the closest one, piercing the bandit in the thigh and sending him scream-ing to the ground. Before she could move in to feed, an unseen force gripped her torso and held her in place. She prepared to draw on her magic to defend herself when she recognized a familiar presence approaching.

"Release me," Ash hissed. "I need to eat."

The force binding her fell away, and she shifted her vision back to day sight as she turned on the intruder. He floated just off the ground, carried through the air by the same gravity magic that he had used to hold her in place.

The light of the bonfire danced across his dark blue skin and glistening red eyes. His hair, a brighter white than hers, wafted in the air behind him, though there was no wind that night. Two long blue horns protruded from his crown and curved back over his head, giving him the appearance of a demon. His posture remained perfectly straight as he approached, hands folded neatly into the sleeves of his billowing black robes.

Ash's pitch-black eyes met the Kith's blood-red gaze. She decided long ago that one day, she would kill him, and she would enjoy it.

"Professor," she said. "Come to share a meal?"

"This is a fruitless endeavor." He spoke in the same droning monotone as always, each clockwork syllable even and blunt, as if the whole of the world bored him with its simplicity. "You must return for your transfusion."

"It's too early. I can hold on a little while longer."

"It is precisely the correct time. You know this. Do not act like an infant." He withdrew one of his long, slender hands from the sleeves of his robes and flicked his fingers in the direction of the wounded thief. The man's terrified scream grew sharp as he lifted into the air. With a twist of Professor's wrist, the man's body tore in two.

"I was going to eat that," Ash said.

"Your blood has expired. It will no longer sustain energy siphoned from an external source." Professor gestured down to her arms. Beneath her gray flesh, the brilliant blue glow, strengthened by the lives she had taken, had already started to fade.

She waved her hand, urging him to get on with it. Professor reached into his robes. One hand produced a thick vial filled with a black concoction while the other traced loose spirals in the air. "My supply of reagents is running low. Coming to fetch you is a waste of precious resources."

He murmured the words of his spell for close to five minutes before the vial shattered and the black fluid slithered sideways through the air, spreading until it formed a flat disk.

They moved as one, pushing against the rippling surface of the disk until it snapped. They stepped through the fissure and emerged on the other side shrouded in black smoke. As it cleared, familiar cavern walls came into view.

Home, sweet home. How Ash tired of these tunnels. Being surrounded by this much dirt and rock was tantamount to being buried alive. The catacombs that ran under the Imperial Palace of Noctis stretched for miles, forming a winding labyrinth that Ash had yet to fully explore in her nights of endless wandering.

If Professor upheld his end of the bargain, she would be free of her torment in a few months. Compared to the years she had spent skulking beneath Noctis, that wasn't so long to wait.

They emerged from the ragged, twisting tunnels into angular halls of worked stone. Ash followed Professor through an open steel doorway and into a circular chamber. She struggled to find even a single sheet of parchment out of place in Professor's private laboratory. He kept all of his apparatus in immaculate shape, from the racks of vials and flasks to the glowing, metal banded crystal that projected a view of Noctis into the empty air.

Only the flat, black door at the far end of the laboratory seemed like it didn't belong. It blended into the wall seamlessly, like an unnerving obelisk abandoned partway through excavation. Ash had yet to find a way to open it. The door had no handle, or keyhole, or any kind of locking mechanism. Brute force hadn't been successful, either.

Whatever was behind that door, it was important and secret. She didn't like Professor having secrets. The balance of power in their relationship was already a tenuous thing. Wherever that door led, it could be hiding something that might be used to shift the balance against her.

Ash approached the steel chair bolted to the floor at the center of the room, and the strange machine next to it, fitted with pumps that reminded her of a blacksmith's bellows.

"The machine has finished processing the final transfusion," Professor said.

Final, Ash thought. *Not next. Final.*

Professor had often impressed on her the pains he had gone through to produce her replacement blood, which was far more effective than the short-lived slurry the Emperor had gifted her with when he raised her from the grave. The process of creating her blood required many rare ingredients, most of which were no longer obtainable. Without them, she could only borrow against fate for so long before payment was due.

She ground her teeth as she settled into the cold steel chair. She had hoped to siphon enough life essence to maintain her current transfusion for a few more days, but Professor's calculations, as much as she loathed to admit it, were never wrong. She needed a transfusion, and she needed it immediately.

The extra time would have been welcome, but Ash didn't dwell on it. Replacing her blood had always been a temporary measure while they worked toward a more permanent solution. That solution would arrive soon. According to Professor's faultless calculations, her final transfusion wouldn't last much longer beyond its arrival.

Professor fixed her feet in the chair's stirrups and clamped thick metal restraints onto her right arm. He pierced one of her dim glowing veins with a cold needle, and the machine surged to life, pumping and thudding. Luminous blue ichor crept as slow as frozen molasses from a glass container atop the contraption, through a clear length of tubing, and into the needle in her arm.

"Has Arcturus reported?" Ash said, hoping to take her mind off the pain she knew was coming. Professor levitated over to one of the room's many tables, returning with a sealed letter. He broke the thin wax and handed the transcription to her.

The Noctean Spymaster had such neat handwriting. Ash could only imagine what the original note Arcturus scrawled had looked like before transcription. She pictured malformed letters slipping from fingers trembling with restrained anger. Desperate pleas for help in seeing Serenia returned to Noctis, regardless of whether she had Scarlet in her possession, crossed out and re-written in a formal, more appeasing tone. Perhaps a long-winded tirade promising revenge if any harm came to *his* daughter if she was lucky.

Of course he would put emphasis on "his." Ash loved reminding him that Serenia was *their* daughter, just to see his perfect demeanor crack.

The corners of Ash's mouth raised in a smile as she read. "Sunder's condition is getting worse, and Serenia's powers have awakened." She tipped her head back and let the paper rest in her lap. "You were right about the missing catalyst. I was beginning to think the conversion had failed."

"I do not make mistakes," Professor said. "The process by which Heretic created the Pilots is now evident. I will inform my people that your request to send valuable assets to a city of little importance, weakening our position so close to the activation of the Aperture, was not a total squandering of our resources."

Ash ignored him. This was cause for celebration. She had originally planned to reveal herself to Serenia after her final transfusion. Sunder was too unpredictable an opponent to face alone, even with Ash's many gifts. Ash needed Serenia. Together, as mother and daughter, they would storm the Freelands, gain control of Scarlet, and avenge themselves against Sunder.

Then Serenia had to run off, out of some misplaced sense of filial duty, to play hero. It was Ash's idea to have Professor contact his Kith brethren and have them send a Behemoth to her world as a distraction, giving Sunder something to focus on while Serenia moved into position.

She hadn't counted on Serenia actually succeeding in stealing Scarlet, or choosing to fight the Behemoth herself, and nobody could have predicted that Sunder would be moved by the display to the point of taking Serenia as her apprentice.

Sending Ferals to Galford to had been an even riskier play. Noctis wouldn't be able to replace Serenia if she fell to the Kith's foot soldiers, and Ash would lose Arcturus' support if their daughter perished. Her plans hinged on Serenia's survival. Now that Serenia had awakened to her true potential, Ash was one step closer to getting back everything Sunder had taken from her.

The searing pain of artificial blood creeping into her body cut her internal celebration short. Lancing shocks radiated through her as the thick ichor coursed through her veins, devouring old blood and leaving behind raw, pulsing strength.

"Relay a message," Ash said when the aching subsided. Professor used his gravity magic to float a quill from one of his worktables and into her hand. She scrawled her instructions on the other side of the parchment. "I want Arcturus to hold position and wait. There's no use in him marching back into the Freelands and complicating things. Serenia will return, sooner or later. Until then, she's a knife poised to strike Sunder between her shoulder blades. When Sunder is weak enough and the time comes to spring our trap, I want to pull that knife out slowly after I give it a jaunty twist."

"We cannot afford to lose the girl," Professor said.

"We won't. Trust me, for once." Ash blew on the paper to dry the ink and held it between two fingers. "Speaking of your precious resources, we'll need to squander them further. Your instructions are at the bottom, along with a list of other things I require."

Professor guided the letter from Ash's hand and into his own. He snarled as he read, revealing the tips of his sharp white canines. "The chemical you have requested is a trite thing. Precision deployment of additional Behemoths from our world via umbral portals, however, will tax us even further. Every remaining Behemoth has been allocated and has its place in—"

"The Exodus. Yes, yes, I know." Ash sighed. "There won't *be* a fucking Exodus if you don't provide me with what I need. If you want to save your people, this is what we need to make that dream a reality. If we don't keep giving Sunder things to fight, she might not see the need to train an apprentice. Without Serenia at her side, we'll lose our best play if my trap fails. And you need time to put the finishing touches on Lion's Roar, as I recall. Go on. Tell me I'm wrong."

Professor shook his head as he folded the paper into a thin square. "You are playing a dangerous game. Sunder is not the only one whose condition is degrading. Attacking now would be prudent."

"Then by all means, go after her yourself." Ash put her hand over her mouth, feigning surprise. "Oh. That's right! She would sense you coming before you got close enough to strike. You're not of this world." She smirked at her blue companion. "You need me to kill Sunder and keep the Emperor in check. I need the Kith, so I might survive past the Exodus. I may not care if the Kith die out, but I very much want to live. If you don't trust me, then trust that."

He shot her a diamond-cutting glare and floated from the room, not bothering to release her from the transfusion chair.

Rude.

Ash wrenched herself free of the steel restraints, standing so fast that the surge of new vigor coursing through her veins caused her to stagger. With no more use for the chair, she raised her leg and dropped her heel onto it. Bolts cracked as the throne fell to pieces. She left the mess for Professor to deal with and left the laboratory, her mind swimming with visions of gleeful vengeance.

She made her way through the worked tunnels and back into the catacombs. Her wandering, as it often did, brought her through twists and turns to a particular sepulcher and a particular stone coffin.

Ash slid the engraved top halfway off the coffin. When she reached inside, her fingers stuck to the sleek surface of the ice block resting within. There were several of these frozen tombs scattered through the catacombs. Complex enchantments kept the ice in the coffins from ever melting, preserving the important figures contained within until Noctean necromancy advanced to the point where they could be restored properly.

Ash had been a test of those advances, the first true Lich raised in Noctis' history. She was too important to be allowed to stay in her grave, too potent a weapon to remain in the sheath. Unlike most undead, who were rendered little more than mindless, flesh-craving monsters after reanimation, Ash retained her faculties, bringing back greater power and understanding from her soul's return journey through the Veil's sweet caress.

The corpse entombed in this block of ice, another of Sunder's many victims, wouldn't receive the same cursed blessing. If needed, the corpse could be re-animated by calling its soul back from beyond the Veil and tethering it to its former body, but it would be nothing more than a shambling corpse. For now, it remained preserved, a card to be played if the situation demanded it and discarded when it had served its purpose.

Ash smiled to herself. Despite all she had lost, all she had been forced to endure, fate was about to turn her way and grant her everything she ever wanted.

For that, she was grateful. After all, how often did one have the chance to kill their own murderer?

Chapter 11
Getting to Know You

Maia awoke from her short nap to the sound of thumps and creaking wood. Raindrops pinged against her armor from a leak in the long awning covering the farmhouse deck.

The bar holding the barn doors shut stressed as the Ferals trapped inside, still weakened and sluggish from sleep, struggled to escape their makeshift prison. Using a slaughtered cow treated with a potent herbal mixture as bait, the owner of the farm had lured five of the wandering monsters inside.

The Ferals devoured the entire cow in minutes, and the herbs sent them into a deep slumber. Their gathering triggered Maia's Hunter Sense, bringing her and Serenia to the farm just in time to save the old farmer from a sixth Feral that he hadn't noticed.

The kill had gone to Serenia, who had rushed the Feral, thrusting the tip of her rapier through the eye hole of its mask and striking each of its hearts before it had a chance to recover.

When they first met, Serenia hadn't been able to take on a single Feral on her own. After a week of hunting Ferals across the countryside, she was facing them head-on with the confidence of a seasoned killer. Maia wanted to be proud, but the reckless way the girl flung herself into combat worried her.

That was why Maia had decided to wait under the slanted awning of the farmhouse for the Ferals to break free. She could have taken all five of them in the dark of the barn by herself. A more tactical approach would set a better example for her brash apprentice. Maia thought about having Scarlet crush the barn, but her suggestion sent the farmer into a yelling tirade that turned his face a shade of red so deep that it matched Scarlet's armor. The next best option was to wait for the Ferals to awaken and take them at the entrance, once at a time, as they emerged.

Maia yawned and sat up. Serenia snapped awake at the sudden movement, uncrossing her arms and pushing away from the door frame she was leaning against. She rubbed sleep from her eyes and straightened her new purple shirt and black vest.

"Has the time come?" the girl said.

"Just about. Let's get into position. They're going to come through that door very, very soon." Maia grunted as she stood.

"Excellent. What say we make this hunt a tad more interesting?" Serenia didn't wait for Maia to respond. "I have devised a new game. It's called 'Tell Me Something I Don't Know.' The rules are simple. For every Feral I slay, you owe me an interesting fact about yourself, and the same goes for you and any Ferals you put down. Only killing blows count. I'm already up one today, so do try to keep up."

"First, I haven't agreed to play anything," Maia said. "Second, hunting Ferals isn't a game. It's serious work. Third... You're counting that kill? That was hours ago. How is that fair?"

Serenia grinned and drew her revolver. "I seem to recall it was you who said that life isn't fair. Why should we fight as if it is?"

Serenia charged out into the rain, pounding through puddles as she ran. Cursing under her breath, Maia pulled her blades from her back and stalked toward the barn. Though Serenia had grown into an even sharper pain in Maia's ass, having a partner fighting at her side wasn't the worst thing in the world. It reminded Maia of the old days, fighting a new Behemoth every week, then retiring to drink at some tavern or another to laugh at the ridiculous names she and the other Pilots had given the monsters they fought.

Maia winced. Those days were long gone, and so were the people she had shared them with, so she smothered the memories as the barn door started to splinter. Unlike Maia's lost friends, Serenia didn't have Pilot armor to protect her. Maia needed to focus.

"You'll miss all the fun!" Serenia shouted as she ran.

"Look out!" Maia called back.

Serenia reached the barn doors just as they heaved off their hinges. She skidded to a stop and threw herself clear with a sidelong roll, muddying her new clothes.

The doors slapped down hard against the wet earth. The first of the Ferals stumbled over the fallen door, its momentum carrying it onto the mud.

Maia seized the moment, sprinting over to it and driving both blades into its chest. The beast toppled, smoking as drops of rain hissed against its flame-engulfed body.

One to one, she thought.

"Don't think you've won yet!" Serenia shouted. She wiped mud off her revolver with her palm and rose from her crouch. "I believe you still owe me something I don't know."

"My favorite color is blue!" Maia yelled as she spun to the next Feral's rear, taking its hamstrings with a pair of clean slices and dropping it to the ground.

"That's now how this works! I get to ask you a question!" Serenia hefted her weapon and squeezed the trigger. The thundering blast caught the closest Feral in the mask, leaving little left above the neck.

One to two. "Ask away then, Princess." The Feral at Maia's feet grabbed her leg and yanked her onto her back. That earned the monster a metal-clad boot to the face that cracked its mask and left it dazed. Maia reversed her grip on one of her swords and jammed it twice into the prone Feral's back.

Two to two.

"First question," Serenia said. "How did you get your scar?"

That wasn't a pleasant tale. The memory of that day caught Maia as she rose, sticking her in place. One of the two remaining Ferals swept its clawed hands upwards, catching her in the chin. The world spun. Her right shoulder crunched as she splashed down onto the muddy ground.

Maia dismissed her mud-covered helmet so she could see. The Feral charged. She vaulted over it, pushing down and driving it into the mud. "I got it when I was almost fifteen, about a year before I became a Pilot. Injuries from before we became Pilots don't heal. As for the how, it was a training accident. Which reminds me: we really should start sparring with live blades soon."

It was Serenia's turn to freeze. Whatever answer she had been expecting, that definitely wasn't it. The Feral closest to Serenia seized the opportunity and kicked her in the chest, blasting her onto her back. She groaned and clutched her ribs as she stood.

Maia circled her own Feral as it struggled to stand.

Arms spread and back on its feet, the Feral threw itself at Maia. She leaped and twisted, landing on the monster's shoulders. "Second question?"

Serenia's Feral swiped at her, forcing her to abandon her aim and stay on the defensive. "I'll admit, I'm curious. If your favorite color is blue, why did you become the Red Pilot of Fire?" she panted.

Maia drove one of her curved swords into the top of her Feral's head, leaning back and splitting its skull open. She rolled backward off the dead Feral's hunched back as it fell and burned. *Three to two.* "We didn't get to choose our colors. Red was chosen for me. So, I started dyeing my hair and clothes red. Made the Red Pilot of Fire my identity. Blue would have been nice, but it would have been better to not be a Pilot at all."

Serenia scoffed. "I don't understand how you can feel that way. Becoming a Pilot is the greatest gift I could ever receive."

"You say that now."

Serenia's Feral swung wide, leaving it off-balance. She raised her revolver to fire. Maia suddenly remembered she was in the middle of a competition and hurled her swords at the Feral. The blades struck home, sinking into the Feral's tough, muscled chest half a breath after the bark of Serenia's revolver took its face clean off.

Three to three. A tie.

The rain stopped. Maia rolled her hurt shoulder and stooped down to pick up her falchions, not bothering to wipe off the mushy ash clinging to their blades. She motioned for Serenia to follow, and together, they lifted the fallen doors and leaned them awkwardly against the side of the barn.

"You would have been happier being the Blue Pilot of Lightning, then?" Serenia asked. "Come to think of it, that's what I should have asked about. The Blue Bolt. I don't know anything about him."

That's not my story to tell. Maia waved to the farmer, who was peering at them from the safety of his farmhouse. "Blue liked to live a private life."

"Unlike Dalzin, the White Pilot of Earth." They made their way around the farmhouse, back toward Scarlet, who was kneeling near a wide corral filled with cattle. "I've seen quite a few of his paintings. My favorite is his rendition of

Amisrala, the Green Pilot of Wind. How I would have loved to have seen her Vanguardian! I've often wondered how something that large could fly, being made of metal and all. Though, if I could only meet one Pilot, discounting you, of course, I would have to choose Edgar, the Black Pilot of Water. My father told me a story of the time he—"

The sharp crack of Maia's fist thrusting through the side of the farmhouse made Serenia jump. Maia wrenched her hand free and stared at it, willing her fingers to stop trembling and forcing Edgar's name to leave her mind. She motioned with her chin. "Hey. Go get some water. That tree is on fire."

"What? No, it isn't."

"Yes, it is." Maia's hand shot out. A small ball of fire whistled from her palm and burst against the tree's trunk, spreading orange flames across wet wood.

"Emperor's Grace!" Serenia took off toward the barn, shouting something about a bucket. When she was gone, Maia willed the flames away and leaned against the side of the house.

She placed a hand on her belly and breathed slow and deep, eyes fixed on a far-off point. Once her heart slowed, she could dislodge the terrible images that had taken root in her mind with barbed fingers.

A black, rigid claw descended on Scarlet, hammering her chest over and over. The shriek of rent metal ripped into Maia's ears. Then came the screaming, blending with hers into a horrific harmony.

Maia suddenly became aware of just how heavy her armor had become, how heavy *she* had become. She stepped clear of the farmhouse and dismissed her suit in a flash of light and fire. The smell of the smoldering tree anchored her in the present until the unbidden memories floated back into the dark of her mind where she kept unpleasant things.

"If you can dispel flames as easily as you can summon them, why did you send me running?" Serenia shouted. She set a full washbasin down on the wet grass and knelt by it, splashing collected rainwater over her face and hair to wash the mud off. "Perhaps you would like to explain what that little outburst was about?"

Maia donned her mask of smiles, though she couldn't get her grin to reach her eyes. "Remember that list of things we're not going to talk about? Add Edgar Ragnarson to it."

"Shall I place him above Leona and your heart?"

Maia ignored her sharp tone. "Below Leona. And definitely below my heart. That was always the problem, wasn't it?"

"Am I to attempt to answer that? Are you making that one of your three questions?"

"Right, I forgot. Your little game." Maia walked around the corner of the farmhouse so that Serenia couldn't see her rubbing her temples.

The girl's voice found her. "We have no other pressing engagements. Go on. Ask me a question."

Heat flared in Maia's chest. If her apprentice wanted to push, she would push back. "Fine. Just how scared were you the first time you faced a Behemoth?"

The sound of splashing water stopped. "Are you referring to Lionheart? Or the unnamed Behemoth that crushed my home, killing my mother and stealing four years of my life? Technically, the latter was my first experience, but I would have to say I wasn't especially afraid of it, as I had little idea what was happening at the time."

Maia's smile shattered. Her heart beat faster. Serenia's words confirmed what Maia had suspected since their first meeting. Arcturus hadn't told his daughter the truth of that day. All this time, training to become Maia's successor, learning how to control Scarlet, and nobody had told Serenia that it was Scarlet that had crushed her home and took her mother's life. Scarlet, not a Behemoth, that left Serenia trapped in darkness for four years.

Maia scratched the back of her neck and swallowed hard. "It was my fault, you know. What happened, it... If I had been better at my job, maybe your mother..."

"I don't hold you responsible. Besides, you succeeded in avenging us both by defeating the Behemoth who took her from me." Maia could hear Serenia's smile in her voice from around the corner. "I owe you for that."

No. I owe you. More than I can ever repay. "Yeah, I... What was she like? Aurelia, I mean. Your mother."

"I'll take that as your second question." Serenia paused. "I remember her cutting wit, most of all. I also remember thinking that she used too much profanity. Quite unbecoming of a noblewoman. She was a fierce warrior, terrifyingly strong both physically and magically. I know she loved me, it's just... After I was born, she had to abandon her military career to care for me. I think, deep down, she resented me for having to give up that life. I once overheard her and my father arguing about sending me to live with relatives in the southern reaches of the Empire so that she could serve again."

"Well, Princess, if she could see you now from beyond the Veil, I think she would be proud of you."

Serenia peaked around the corner. Her face beamed. "Perhaps my ears are still filled with mud. Could you repeat that? It almost sounded like a compliment."

Careful. She's growing on you. "You heard me. I don't like repeating myself."

"You adore repeating yourself."

They walked back to Scarlet's waiting palm. The rain had washed most of the dirt from her, and the sun peeking out from the parting rain clouds made her wet crimson metal shine like new, despite the many gashes dug into her body.

Maia's gaze drifted, as it always did, to where Scarlet's left arm should be. Early in her career, Maia fought a Behemoth she named Venomole on account of it being an odd cross between a mole and a venomous centipede. After its caustic spray had melted through a large part of Scarlet's right forearm, it took Scarlet some time to repair herself.

Vanguardians could recover from almost any damage, just like their Pilots. But for the last four years, Scarlet seemed to have given up. Her missing left arm had never repaired itself.

Even if Scarlet had quit, Maia couldn't. Not yet. Not while she had a wild blade of an apprentice to deal with, one who deserved an explanation for why her life had taken such a drastic turn.

Maia stopped in front of Scarlet's palm. "About the first Behemoth attack in Noctis. There's something else you need to—wait. Do you feel that?"

Serenia nodded and closed her eyes. "Yes. It's like...a heavy wave, crashing over and over. Pulling me...northeast of here." She pointed in the same direction the matching pulse in Maia's head was pulling. "It's akin to what I feel from a gathering of Ferals. But heavier. Is this what a Behemoth feels like?"

Maia sighed. "Yeah. That's a Behemoth. It's near Whitehorn, along the Noctean border. And you're not fighting it."

"W-what?" Serenia's eyes snapped open. "Why?"

"Back there at the barn, you were reckless. Careless. You're like the trigger on that revolver of yours. A little bit of pressure, and you unleash hell in whatever direction you're facing. You have power, now. You need to be more careful with it. You need to be better. Remember?"

"I believe Gaston meant for me to be kinder and more considerate toward the people I'm protecting, not Ferals and Behemoths. Am I to start showing compassion to monsters? What have I done wrong? I struck first and sought the initiative, just as you taught me."

"You can be ruthless and still be careful." Maia rubbed her face. "You were more concerned with winning your little game than anything else. So no, I don't trust you to fight a Behemoth just yet."

"How am I to grow as a Pilot, then? I need to fight this Behemoth. How else can I redeem myself for my previous failure?"

"That's another reason you're not fighting it. Right now, you care more about saving your bruised ego than saving lives. Look. I know what it's like. The rush of power. That feeling, like you can take on the entire world and win. But we're not immortal. We can bleed, and we can die. Until you understand that, until you can prove to me that you can fight with a clear head, you're not setting foot in Scarlet's control beam."

Serenia exhaled sharply. "Perhaps I've been a tad rash. I promise to conduct myself with the utmost care while piloting Scarlet."

"I can't trust you to stay calm when you're clearly in pain. The conditioning hasn't helped. Every time you take control of Scarlet, your face scrunches up. It's more than discomfort. You look like you're about to shit a boulder."

The girl wilted under her stare. "It hurts. Is it supposed to?"

"No. It's not. And that tells me that whatever Noctis did to make you a Pilot, they fucked it up. I have no way of telling what else might be wrong with you. What I do know is that if you're keeping things like this from me, then I definitely can't trust you."

"What, then?" Serenia's hands flopped against her sides. "What must I do to convince you that I'm worthy?"

"Lift Scarlet's palm," Maia said. "It takes patience and a calm mind to issue the simplest of commands when you're outside the control beam. Lift us up to her shoulder. Do that, and I'll let you fight."

"Bull fucking horse shit. Fuck!" The girl didn't swear often, but when she did, she made it count. "This isn't a lesson. You're merely trying to find excuses to keep me from... Wait. Where did the Behemoth go?"

"I don't know." The throbbing in Maia's head was gone. She had only known her Hunter Sense to quiet once the Behemoth or Feral it detected had been destroyed.

But Scarlet was the only force on the continent powerful enough to fell a Behemoth. And Scarlet was kneeling next to a small farm, waiting for her two Pilots to quit bickering.

"Do you think it was the dragon, the one that man in Galford spoke of?" Serenia asked.

"I doubt it. There's no reason for a dragon to seek out a Behemoth. Does the Empire have a secret weapon up by the border that you haven't told me about?"

"It couldn't have been any Noctean secret weapon."

"But Noctis *does* have a secret weapon?" Maia countered.

"I don't know! Perhaps we can contact my father and ask him if the Empire has any new defensive measures we may not be aware of."

"Even if your Farspeaker wasn't in pieces, that piece of garbage is the last person I want to hear from today."

That got Serenia's hackles to rise. "What quarrel do you have with my father that you would deign to speak of him so rudely? He always spoke of you with the utmost respect. What happened between the two of you?"

"Let's add that one to the list, too, shall we?"

"No," Serenia said. "I killed three Ferals today. So did you. We each have one question remaining. I'm asking mine. Why do you hate my father so?"

Maia reached out to Scarlet and ordered the Vanguardian to raise the middle finger of her resting palm. She leaned against it. "Fine. Let me tell you a story about a girl. A wine maker's daughter. She was a wisp of a thing, nothing special, really, until her sixteenth birthday. A demon took her in the night, turned her into a living weapon, and sent her to fight a war that wasn't hers. Kind of like her mother, who died in a battle nobody asked her to fight. You can imagine how upset the girl's father was when the girl went to work for the Empire who killed her mother."

"The first Behemoth," Serenia said. "You enlisted shortly after you defeated it. I know all of this."

"Then you know that I was assigned to your father's command. Back then, Behemoths attacked weekly. The Pilots hadn't organized yet. We didn't know or trust each other. We stuck to defending our homelands. Edgar protected Kaldrsteinn in the north. Dalzin had Brimholme in the southeast. Amisrala covered the Shining Sands and the Southlands beyond. Blue Bolt and I took different parts of the Freelands. I handled Noctis alone. Behemoths and Ferals rarely touched the Fen Islands, so any targets there were first come, first serve. And Sinadaria...well, it never happened, but if a Behemoth landed up there, I doubt the Sinadarian elves would even need our help.

"Arcturus and I worked together for almost a year. When more than one Behemoth appeared, he took charge. Sent me to where I was needed most. Sometimes, he had me lure the bastards to places where our fighting would cause less damage. When it came to strategy, he was never wrong, your dad. We saved a lot of lives together."

"Then why do you hate him so?" Serenia said.

"Hush. I'm getting to that. When there were no Behemoths or Ferals to hunt, I was still a Noctean officer. Arcturus sent me on other assignments. Mostly, I went to places the Empire couldn't reach to get things the Emperor didn't have. It didn't matter what Arcturus asked. I did it. 'A good soldier always follows orders,' remember?"

Maia moved closer to Serenia. "Then came the day he gave me an order I couldn't follow, something he *never* should have asked me to do."

"What was the order?" Serenia asked.

"He wanted me to 'suppress an uprising,' which is Noctean for 'murder a village full of innocent people.' And when I wouldn't do it, he had a captain by the name of Salvian carry out the order instead."

"I don't believe you," Serenia said. "My father is a just and righteous blade in the service of the Emperor. He would never give such an order."

"He did. And I'm also fairly sure that he's the one who had my father killed, or at very least, he knew about it and didn't stop it. All that's left of my father and my family homestead is a pile of ashes and a fire that never stops burning. Only Noctean mages could do that, and your father has plenty of reasons to want revenge. Believe me, or don't. I don't care. But you asked."

Serenia's face contorted like she had just swallowed a whole lemon. "My father has no reason to hate you. He doesn't blame you for what happened to my mother. To me. And neither do I. He's not the man you claim him to be."

"Then ask him about the village of Aquila next time you see him," Maia said.

"Don't be ridiculous. There's no village in the Empire called Aquila."

"No, there isn't. Ask him why that is."

Serenia crunched her fists so tight her arms quaked. Maia wondered if the girl would throw a punch. Instead, she spoke in a low, frosty tone. "As your apprentice, it is my duty to follow your instructions and remain open to your wisdom and guidance. I must apologize. I forget, at times, that our relationship is that of a master and her student. I apologize for overstepping that boundary in my attempts to get to know you better. I would also like to apologize for any trouble I've caused you by acting recklessly. I will endeavor to show you the respect and obedience you demand from me."

She moved so close that her breath touched Maia's cheek. "However, if you speak ill of my father in my presence again, your words will not go unanswered. Put anything you have to say against him at the top of *my* list."

Maia stepped back and regarded her apprentice, unsure whether she should be angry or impressed by her threat. In the end, she was a bit of both.

She motioned to Scarlet's palm. Now that all the Ferals in the lands surrounding Galford were accounted for, they could continue their journey.

Brimholme, their final destination, was still a long way off. She considered Teleporting Scarlet there to save them both time and pain, as the longer she spent traveling with her young apprentice, the harder it would be to part ways.

At the southeast edge of Brimholme, near the coastline, at the bottom of a deep crater, Serenia would see what Maia longed to show her. She would quit her quest and return to Noctis. At the very least, Maia could rest knowing she had saved another girl from sharing her fate.

But what if Serenia didn't quit? She hadn't seen enough of a Pilot's life yet. What waited in the crater might not be enough to break her resolve. It was too early for Brimholme. If Maia showed her hand and Serenia decided to stay the course like a good little Noctean soldier, there would be no other cards left to play.

Brimholme could wait. There were more pressing matters to attend to. Serenia was growing sharper by the day; now, Maia would have to set her focus on prying her from the Emperor's grip and tempering her wild edge.

That, and figuring out how a dragon, even a great wyrm, could stand toe-to-toe with a Behemoth and win. And if the dragon wasn't responsible for the Behemoth's destruction, who—or what—had destroyed it?

Scarlet's palm shuddered as it rose. Serenia slipped on the wet metal, and Maia caught her by the arm before she fell over the edge.

"I guess you've calmed down, then," Maia said.

Serenia shook her head. "You're not doing this?"

"No. Must be you. Scarlet can't move on her own."

"Oh. Perhaps I willed it without thinking about it?"

"Maybe. Either way, good job."

They shared a smile, a fleeting thing that broke apart as soon as they reached Scarlet's cabin and shuffled inside in silence. Maia stepped into the control beam and started walking. With each stride, she could feel the rift widening between them, and wondered if letting it continue to grow would make everything easier for both of them.

Chapter 12

Where There Is Need

Whatever foul creature had crawled between the two pieces of bread in her hands and died, Ren pitied it almost as much as she pitied herself for having to eat it. Maia had insisted that this remote roadside inn served the best sandwiches in the Freelands. Aside from a terse "good night" and "good morning," it was the most Maia had said to her since their argument the day before, so Ren feigned enthusiasm and accepted the lunch offer for the peace offering she hoped it was.

It wouldn't have mattered if the foul-smelling sandwich *was* the best in the Freelands. Ren wasn't hungry. She had spent most of the morning cleaning blood from the inside of Scarlet's viewport while Maia drove their Vanguardian forward in sullen silence. Neither of them said anything about Maia's latest episode or the blood she vomited before she collapsed in a shivering wreck. Worries over whether this would be the day her mentor died had all but destroyed Ren's appetite.

Ren ate the sandwich anyway. The innkeeper was an admirer of Maia's and hadn't charged them for their lunch. Not only would it have been rude to refuse, but they were once again out of supplies. A free meal, however terrible, wasn't something she could turn down. She needed to keep her strength up. Her father had vowed to come and retrieve her, and the date he gave her to return of her own volition had come and gone.

Was he already on his way? How long would it take for him to re-enter the Freelands and find her? And what would he do to Maia if she stood against him?

She took a steadying breath. Regardless of her father's wishes, it wasn't time to return to Noctis. Not yet. Gaining ownership of Scarlet was her duty, but she still had to discover the nature of her mentor's illness. There was much to be done before she could allow her father to take her from her place at Maia's side.

And, truth be told, Ren was enjoying her time as Maia's apprentice. She was growing steadily under Maia's tutelage, such as it was. More than that, Maia was the only person in the world who Ren could share her struggles with, the only one who could understand the great destiny they were entrusted with. She was a kindred weapon forged of the same mettle as her. Being by her side felt right.

If Maia felt anything like the swelling warmth blossoming in Ren's chest, she didn't show it. She ate in silence. Though there was only a short length of wooden table between them, Maia looked like her thoughts had taken her a thousand leagues away. Her long expression pulled at the edges of her eyes and changed the run of her scar, making her look far older than she was.

She has her own worries, Ren thought. *She doesn't care for you.*

Ren looked down at the brilliant purple of her new shirt and realized that that simply wasn't true. Maia could have used the money spent on purple dye for food. Instead, Maia gave her something uniquely her own. That wasn't a sign of indifference. And if she no longer cared for Ren following their disagreement, she would have deposited her back in Noctis or abandoned her in the Freelands to fend for herself.

Ren tried to think of a joke, or a story, or anything else she could use to clear the fetid air lingering between them. There had to be a way for them to move forward. Once they were on speaking terms again, they could find it—together.

"I'm sorry," Maia said, startling Ren. She hadn't expected Maia to make the first move. Two simple words slit through the barrier, leaving a space just big enough for Ren to crawl through.

"You are?" she said.

"I am." Maia pushed her plate away. "I'm supposed to be your teacher. I'm supposed to guide you. But, sometimes, I get stuck in the past. I feel that, in a way, I've failed you."

Ren was expecting an argument, not an apology, so she didn't have a response ready. "Oh," was all she could say.

"Yeah." Maia looked away and scratched the back of her neck. "I know I said these were the best sandwiches in the Freelands, but I may have been drunk when I came here. I don't remember them being this bad. So, I'm sorry."

It wasn't becoming of a Noctean officer to shout until she lost consciousness, so Ren elected to scream internally. She pushed her own plate away. "I forgive you."

"They taste like...detritus?" One corner of Maia's mouth lifted in a smirk. "Is that the word? Detritus?"

"Yes. That's the one."

Maia pushed to her feet. "Come on. Let's get out of here. I'll figure something out for dinner. I'm still not used to feeding two bellies."

Feeling more than ever like a burden, Ren left Maia to say her goodbyes to the innkeeper. Outside, near the dusty road running past the inn, she found a well-lathered horse hitched to a post. Maia and Ren were the only two patrons, so she wondered where the horse's owner was.

Ren approached the chestnut mare and scratched its neck as it drank from a trough of water set near the base of the post. "Where's your friend, huh?" she cooed.

"Probably pissing in the back," Maia said as she approached. She froze mid-step. "Or, they're over there, touching my fucking Vanguardian."

Ren jogged to keep up with Maia. She could barely make out the sliver of black standing next to Scarlet's red foot. As they drew closer, the figure turned.

Black leathers. Two daggers on his belt. A quirked smile that sent a flush through Ren's cheeks.

"Wait," Ren called ahead to Maia. "I know him!"

Maia slowed to a walk. Ren knew she should warn Maia that there might be more of her father's agents, or perhaps her father himself, concealed nearby, but the sight of Kas alive and well stole her good sense.

"What are you doing here?" Ren said.

"Turns out I'm a better swimmer than I thought. Took me a bit to find you." Kas shielded his eyes from the afternoon sun with his hand and winked at her. Ren fought to keep her heart still in her chest.

"I'm just relieved you're safe," Ren said. "Maia, this is the boy I was telling you about. The man, I mean. The person? At any rate, he tried to help me back in the warehouse."

"Tried?" Kas put a hand to his chest, feigning shock.

"Yes, well... Maia, this is—"

"Kasper." Maia's carefree smile returned.

"You two know each other?"

"Hey, Sun." Kas casually saluted with two fingers. "Been a while."

"It has been a while, hasn't it?" Maia strolled closer. "I mean...look at you. You're not a kid anymore. You're a man now. All grown up. How old are you? Eighteen?"

"Almost, give or take a few—"

Maia's fist slammed into Kas' gut with enough force to send him flying backward. He landed hard, rolled twice, and came to rest on his back, wheezing.

"Close enough," Maia said.

"What in the Blue Hells is wrong with you!" Ren cried. She ran to Kas and knelt next to him, checking him over for injuries.

"Good to see you too, Sun," Kasper said between coughs.

"I hope you know you had that coming." Maia stepped onto Scarlet's waiting palm. "Come on, Princess. Leave that *detritus* on the ground where it belongs. And Kasper? Don't follow us. Next time I see you, I won't hold back."

"That was holding back?" Ren pulled Kas to his feet and stomped after Maia. "Would you mind telling me precisely what is going on?"

"Long story," Kas groaned. "Sun and I—"

Maia spun on her heel and jabbed the air with her finger. "Say one more word, and whatever follows will have to creep around my knuckles."

"Very well," Ren said. "How about—"

"Because I'm going to ram my fist down your throat," Maia finished.

"Stop, please! If you don't want Kas to tell me, that's fine. *You* tell me what's going on!"

Maia narrowed her eyes. "Kasper is Leona's brother. *Adopted* brother. She took him in when he was a pup. All you need to know is that he's a piece of shit, and I'll never forgive him for what he did. Put him on the list of things we're not going to speak about again, beneath everything else, where he belongs."

That would be hard to do. A living piece of Maia's history, the most reliable tie Ren had to her mentor's past, was sitting right in front of her. Kas might be able to provide insight into Maia's affliction. How could she not ask the million questions fluttering through her head?

Kas raised his hand. "Can I say somethin'?"

Maia stared hard at him. After a moment, she nodded.

"Promise not to hit me again?"

"No. Just say what you came to say," Maia said.

"I know you're still sore about what happened, and believe me, the last thing I want to do is open old wounds. But I'm here on business." Kas pushed onto one shaking knee. "Truth is, I'm a spy. I've been trackin' you both since before you came to Galford."

When Maia turned her glare on Ren, the intensity of it made her take a step back instinctively. "Did you know he was a Noctean spy?"

"I'm not with Noctis." Kas held both hands out as he stood. As if they would do anything to stop Maia if she decided to charge at him. "I work for Brave Dawn."

Ren's father hadn't sent him. Relief mixed with confusion. She looked hard at him. "What business does Brave Dawn have with Maia?"

"I was asked to keep an eye on her, to stick close, just in case." He reached into a belt pouch and produced a Farspeaker. "A few days ago, I was told to make contact. They thought that, what with us knowin' each other and all, she might listen to what I have to say."

Maia threw her hands up. "Roderick sent you? I told that bastard a thousand times, I can't get involved! If I side with Brave Dawn, I'm declaring war on the Empire. The other nations would be forced to intervene. Blood, everywhere." She looked back and forth between Ren and Kas. "Why doesn't anybody seem to understand that? And why in the Blue Hells did anyone think I would listen to *you?*"

"I know, Sun. I told Roderick it was a bad idea. But orders are orders. You know how it is, what with your Noctean military trainin' and all."

Whether he meant it as a jab or not, Maia must have taken it as one. Ren barely managed to block her path before she reached Kas. "What does Brave Dawn want Maia to do?" Ren asked. "We won't take part in any insurrection."

"More of that good old Noctean learning," Maia said. "That's not what Brave Dawn does. They help Noctean citizens who want to get out from under the Emperor's thumb. People who are sick of losing loved ones to a tyrannical dictator. Especially nobles. Do you know how many noble children die every year to forced magical modification? Not everyone's like your father. Not everyone survives the process."

"Noctean magical modifications are perfectly safe. That's what the Emperor says," Ren shot back.

"Whatever you say. Everything they told you back home has been right so far, hasn't it? You really need to start thinking for yourself."

Ren bristled and turned to Kas, eager to change the subject. "So, what exactly does Roderick want?"

"Things are gettin' complicated at the border," Kas said. "Noctis is amassin' troops. If they move on Whitehorn, a lot of people'll die. On both sides."

"Figures. Right after she leaves to go do her part and help the downtrodden," Maia mumbled. "Roderick wants me to fight, then. Even though he knows I can't."

"Roderick wants Scarlet to stand guard. Give the Nocteans somethin' to think about before they come knockin' on our door. Just a stern presence. Nothin' more. So, here I am, deliverin' the message. Then I'm bound for Whitehorn to let them know you aren't interested."

Maia stepped up onto Scarlet's waiting palm. "Okay. Let's go." When neither Ren nor Kas moved, she stooped down and slapped her thighs with her hands. "Come on, children, unless you plan on walking all the way to Whitehorn. After I drop Kasper off and have some choice words with Roderick, I need to check on a friend. Maybe get her to leave town before things go to shit."

"There's also the matter of the Behemoth that vanished near Whitehorn," Ren added.

Maia pointed at Ren. "Thanks for reminding me. We'll ask about that, too. But we're not staying. We're not getting involved."

"Wait," Ren said. "Before we leave, I want you to promise me that you won't hand me over to my father's men if they are indeed waiting at the border."

"If it stops a war, I might have to. I can promise you I won't make a decision until I see the situation for myself. Good enough?"

Reluctantly, Ren followed Kas onto Scarlet's palm. It hurt that Maia would even consider sending her home, but deep down, she knew Maia would do what was best for her people.

She didn't agree with it, but at least she could understand it.

"What about my horse?" Kas said.

"I'm not taking a horse in the cabin," Maia replied. "I'm sure someone will give her a good home."

"I like that horse."

When they reached Scarlet's shoulder, Kas moved with cat-like grace, slipping inside the open hatch plates at the back of Scarlet's head. Ren steadied herself and joined him and Maia in the cabin.

"So," Ren said, sliding closer to where Kas was leaning against the back wall. "You're Leona's ward?"

"I am."

"I have so many questions. Perhaps, if you have some time later?"

"Remember the list," Maia said as she busied herself with securing her rucksacks. "We're not talking about her. End of discussion."

Ren rolled her eyes at her mentor's back and turned her focus back to Kas. "If you're not a Noctean spy, how did you know who I was when you approached me on the docks?"

"I was supposed to watch Sun and report. Nothin' more. Then we got word that Sun kidnapped a Noctean officer. Roderick wanted me to investigate and report back. I figured it had to be you since you were travelin' with her. Though, I was expectin' some grizzled old veteran, not..." He smiled and looked away.

"A young female Pilot?"

Kas chuckled. "No, definitely not. So, what's your name?"

Out of habit, Ren saluted. "Serenia Valerius. Though, I prefer Ren. I definitely do *not* enjoy being called Princess."

"Ren," Kas said, trying it on for size. "I like the way that sounds."

Hearing him say her name sent a jolt through her belly, like panic, but warmer and far more pleasant. She knew she should focus on her duty and reel herself in, but all she could think about was hearing what other words would sound like on his lips. "So, why did you approach me?"

"When I saw you on the docks, lookin' the way you did... I thought you could use a friend, is all."

"It's been a long time since I've had one. Thank you for your kindness, even if it almost cost you your life."

"Can I get some quiet in here?" Maia growled. "I'm trying to picture a good spot to Teleport to so I don't wipe out half of Whitehorn when we arrive."

Ren saluted again, and she and Kas shared a chuckle. "How is your stomach?" Ren whispered.

"Still aches. Sun has a mean right hand. But if you ate at that inn, you probably feel worse than I do," Kas replied.

Ren giggled and covered her mouth with her gloved hand. She never giggled. What was happening to her?

Maia swept her arms through the motions of her Teleport spell. "Hold onto something. Or don't. I really don't care." A swirling nimbus of red lights whirled across Scarlet's viewport. When Maia shot her fist to the sky, Scarlet lifted in a beam of red light, and for a moment, Ren felt weightless.

She touched back down as the red light faded. A few miles away, nestled in a mountain pass and barely visible in the light of the late afternoon sun sat a grand city awash with flickering lights.

No. Not lights. Flames.

"Is that Whitehorn?" Ren asked.

Maia didn't answer with words. She threw Scarlet forward in a mad dash, forcing Ren into a crouch to keep from being thrown to the floor as the cabin pitched with each thunderous step.

Whitehorn, and the flames covering almost a third of the city, grew larger in the viewport as Scarlet approached. As Maia pumped her legs and arms, she prayed to whatever goddess was listening that Elizabeth wasn't in one of the many stone and wood townhouses wreathed in hungry orange flames.

As Scarlet approached Whitehorn's Freelands-facing outer wall, Maia dropped into a crouch, sending the Vanguardian into a long skid that rocked the cabin. Torn sod and dirt spewed into the air ahead of Scarlet as she slid clean through the hewn stone wall like it was made of paper. Maia shut her eyes, severing her connection to Scarlet, and moved to the cabin's hatch. Outside, she crossed her arms over her head and brought them down as she leaped from Scarlet's shoulder, summoning her armor in a brilliant flare and sliding down her arm. Before the light faded, she was rushing down the street leading deeper into the city.

Up ahead, a group of burly men with wet rags tied over their mouths were filling buckets with water from a large barrel fixed to a cart. They hauled the buckets toward a two-story inn covered in flames. A line of several identical carts extended back toward a massive wooden water tower set up on long stilts at the center of town.

"Make way!" Maia shouted. The men fell over themselves, scrambling to clear a path for the crimson knight charging their way. Lowering her shoulder, Maia smashed through the wooden wall of the inn. Amid the roaring flames, she spread her arms wide. The fire responded to her will, resonating with the flame that burned eternally within her. She told the roaring blaze to die, and it obeyed, perishing with an audible hiss.

Maia exited the smoking inn. She pointed to the firefighters. "You two! Get in there and look for survivors. You! What in the Blue Hells caused this? Was it a dragon?"

One of the firefighters, not the one Maia had addressed, pulled down his rag. "Dragon? That was yesterday! Green bastard saved us from a Behemoth and took off. This was the bloody Nocteans and their fuckin' wizards!"

Maia gritted her teeth and took in the full breadth of the destruction. Fireballs hurled over the high stone wall were likely responsible for the creeping fire slowly picking up speed as it worked its way through the valley where Whitehorn stood.

With time, Maia could quell the fires, but not before they took most of the city with them.

"Elizabeth, I never should have let you come here." Maia focused her intent on Scarlet. "Hey, Princess!" she shouted, hoping that Scarlet's ability to project her voice beyond the cabin worked in reverse. "If you can hear me, take control of Scarlet. Don't argue; just do it. I have a plan."

Scarlet rose from her crouch with a dull groan. She stood tall, raised her arm, and saluted.

"Okay. See that water tower at the center of town? That thing that looks like a giant barrel? Pick it up and hold it over the city. Be careful with it. Go, now!"

With tentative steps, Scarlet waded through the city. She slid her hand underneath the tower and lifted. The barrel-like structure shifted and groaned as its struts broke off.

"Good!" Maia shouted as she ran. "When I tell you, toss it straight up." She dug her foot into the ground, skidding to a stop beneath Scarlet's hand. "Hold. Not yet." Maia summoned fire, collecting it in her legs and compressing it until the flames demanded release. "Hold... Hold... *Now!*"

Scarlet lobbed the water tower into the air. Maia released the gathered fire in one controlled burst. The explosion ripped from her feet as she leaped, hurling her into the sky like a flaming bullet. In the span of a breath, she reached the wooden tower and smashed clean through it.

The tower blew to pieces, cascading water and splintered wood over half of Whitehorn. Maia looked down as she reached the top of her leap high above Scarlet's head. A sea of hissing smoke erupted from below, clouding her view of the ground. There were still fires that needed her attention, but the blaze had been weakened enough to be controlled with well water. Maia turned her body as she fell, using short bursts of flame to right herself and slow her descent. The smoke rushed up to meet her.

As she entered the thick black cloud, the phantom grip returned. Her heart seized. Maia lurched, unable to control her fall. She met a roof head-first, smashing clear through it, the second floor, and the ground floor until she slammed into the hard rock ground of the house's cellar.

Maia lay on her back, wheezing through blood-stained teeth. Before she could stand, the townhouse she had flown through decided it had suffered enough. Beams groaned and cracked. Debris and timber rushed down to meet Maia, entombing her in darkness.

When the phantom fingers released their hold on her heart and the shock of impact wore off, all that was left was a lancing pain of her right shoulder, no doubt dislocated, and the immense pressure of the world bearing down on her. Something shifted in the dark. Debris pushed harder against her chest, stealing what little breath she had just found, sending her mind back to that terrible day, unable to stand, with a black claw hammering over and over and over.

Fire sprang to life like webbing between her shaking armored fingers. Maia snaked her left hand upwards. With one grand blast, she could be free. But fire wasn't a thing to be treated lightly. Any time she used her gift, she was taking a risk. No doubt, the people of Whitehorn saw her fall. Knowing she was their best chance for survival if the Nocteans attacked again, they may have already gathered to find a way down to her.

She focused as much as she could with the weight on her chest and let a small blast rip from her left hand. Two more followed. Hopefully, whoever had crowded around the destruction would know to stand clear.

The next blast erupted from her entire body, hurling the dark weight up and away. When the rain of dirt and chips of wood and rock settled, she clawed her way out of her makeshift grave.

"Maia! Are you hurt?" Serenia shouted as she scrambled over the wreckage, Kasper following close behind. Maia had to turn her head to see them around the crack in the right side of her visor.

"Me? I'm bloody fantastic." Maia swallowed, choking down blood. Her right pauldron had split, leaving a gap in her armor and mail that left her dislocated shoulder exposed. She grabbed her right forearm and wrenched it toward the ground. Her shoulder crunched as it popped back into place, and she ground her teeth to keep from crying out. Pain was only temporary. Her shoulder, and her armor, would repair themselves like they always did. She stumbled off the pile of debris. There was still work to be done.

It took until sunset to finish quelling the remaining fires. Maia suppressed as much of the inferno as she could, one building at a time, leaving Kasper and Serenia to help search for survivors in the wreckage. When they had done what they could, they took a moment to rest.

"Hey," Maia called to a passing firefighter, "where's Roderick?"

The woman pulled her rag down, revealing a frown. "Sorry to say, ma'am, but he fell when the Nocteans attacked."

The Emperor got his wish. The leader of Brave Dawn was dead. "Then who's leading?"

The woman pointed to a thin man in a peasant's tunic addressing a small group. Even without his red robes and bangles, he stood with a bearing of unshakable faith, his pointed beard still as stone.

"Brother Tobias?" Maia shouted.

He turned at the sound of her voice. "Just Tobias, now." The energy and vibrancy of his fanatical devotion had left him. What remained held a graven seriousness. "That was quite a tumble. Are you well?"

"I'm fine." Maia had many questions, including how a mad priest like Tobias had made his way to Whitehorn and had come to oversee the city, and by extension, Brave Dawn, but there were other, more pressing matters on her mind. "Tell me what happened here."

"A Brave Dawn caravan was attacked while escorting Noctean refugees bound for our borders," Tobias said. "Noctean forces recovered the refugees, killed half of the escort, and took the rest back to stand trial."

"To Castle Blackwood?" It was the closest outpost Maia could think of, an old fortress built against the Sinadaria Mountains to the east.

Tobias nodded. "A few of our people escaped. A detachment chased them all the way to our walls, whereupon they bombarded us with fire. Roderick and the rest of Brave Dawn's leadership were in council at the time. Theirs was one of the first buildings hit. In one stroke, they cut off our head. And then, you arrived."

"You're lucky I did."

"I agree. This is why Roderick wanted you here." Tobias smoothed his face with his hands, rubbing more soot into weathered wrinkles Maia had never noticed before. "With your help, we're going to get our people back."

"If I cross the border in Scarlet without a Behemoth attacking an Imperial city as an excuse for intruding, the Freelands will suffer."

"Look around, Sunder. We're already suffering."

Maia did look around, taking in the whole of the chaos. Firefighters were digging through smoldering, charred husks of what used to be people's homes. Other townsfolk helped the injured haul their burnt and broken bodies to a tavern-turned-hospice, all the while choking on ash and smoke. Some lay in the mud, unmoving, never to rise again.

Noctis had broken the accords and attacked the Freelands. The Emperor would use Serenia's "abduction" as justification for the attack. Or, he might frame it as retaliation for Brave Dawn "kidnapping" his people. Perhaps both.

The story didn't matter. The Emperor would fight to make it stick, using his Farspeakers and his spies to spread his version of the truth to the corners of the continent and rally forces to his cause before any of the other nations could move to stop him.

Whitehorn was built after the War of Bones to defend the Freelands border, but it couldn't hold against the entire Noctean army. People would die, all because Brave Dawn couldn't mind its own business. All because Maia had made Serenia hers.

Guilt gnawed at her, but she couldn't let it alter her path. "We'll stay the night. The Imperials won't attack while we're here," Maia said. "After that, we're back on the road. Pilots fight Behemoths. Not Nocteans. You should focus on fleeing town or preparing for a siege. I'm sorry, but if your people were taken, they're as good as dead already."

Tobias inclined his head. "Quite possibly, yes. They knew the fight they were signing on for. That doesn't mean we're about to give up on them. Brave Dawn, and the people of Whitehorn, owe you a great debt, Sunder. If there's any way we can repay you, let me know."

"I feel bad for asking, given all that's happened, but I'm looking for someone. Her name is Elizabeth Barlowe. She's about my height? Brunette? Fennish? Has this look like you've disappointed her? Though, that might be reserved for me." Maia shook her head vigorously, clearing her thoughts. "I need to know she's okay. Have you seen her?"

"I'll ask about her. It will be some time before everyone is accounted for. If she's here, we'll find her. I promise you that." Tobias turned to the gathered crowd, voice booming as he called out instructions. Citizens broke off into groups to see to their assignments.

Serenia tapped Maia on her injured shoulder, drawing a wince. "Apologies. May I have a word?" She guided her away from the crowd, leaving Kasper behind. "There may be more we can do to aid these people. I believe I can negotiate the safe return of the Brave Dawn fighters taken in the attack."

Maia scoffed. "You want to help Brave Dawn? What would Daddy say?"

"I wish to avoid a war, to stop blood from spilling on both sides. I'm sure this is all a misunderstanding. The Empire would never attack a border settlement, even if provoked. The traitors—" Serenia took a deep breath. "The Noctean citizens involved in this ordeal will have to remain in the Empire, where they belong, but I believe I can help coordinate the return of the Brave Dawn captives."

"And I believe, sometimes, that I can shit rainbows. That doesn't make it true. We're not getting involved."

"Please, let me try. I'm an officer of the Noctean Empire. And my father may be coordinating this campaign. I can speak to him. I can—"

"We had a deal. You do what I say when I say it, or I drop you back in Noctis. I doubt the Emperor will stop his advance even if I do return you to him, but I'm willing to try." Maia crossed her arms and looked down her nose at her upstart apprentice. "Go on. Keep pushing me. I dare you."

Mimicking her posture, Serenia marched right up to her, unfazed by the threat. "Was it not you who told me I should start thinking for myself? That is precisely what I'm doing. I intend to speak to the commander at Castle Blackwood, which may very well be my father, to get to the bottom of this and, Emperor willing, save as many lives as I can. You may feel that a Pilot's sole duty is to fight Behemoths and Ferals, but I disagree. That's not the kind of Pilot I wish to be. I would rather be a Pilot who goes where there is need and helps in any way she can."

"And are you willing to kill your own countrymen?" Maia said. Serenia averted her eyes. "Because when your negotiations fail, and they will fail, you might have to. Can you do that? Can you put a bullet, or the tip of that fancy rapier of yours, into the heart of another Noctean? What about your own father, if it means saving all those people you suddenly care so much about?"

When Serenia offered no answer, Maia nodded slowly at her silence. "That's what I thought."

Tobias waved her over. "Pilot!" he shouted.

"Did you find her?"

Tobias crossed his hands over his belt. "Sunder, I'm not sure how to tell you this..."

"Just out with it. Please."

"I spoke to one of the survivors of the escort. She says a newcomer, a Fennish-looking woman named Elizabeth, was a part of her cohort. We're not yet sure if she fell in the attack or was taken back to Castle Blackwood, but she never made it back to—"

Tobias fell to the dirt as Maia pushed past him. She thanked her cracked visor for hiding her panic. Numbness spread to her legs as she darted by burned-out homes and ran for the bolstered gates separating the Freelands from the Noctean Empire. Maia prepared to clear the city wall with one fiery leap. Her feet tangled. She fell to her belly and crawled the last few feet.

Firm hands grabbed her shoulders. Someone turned her over and hauled her into a seated position against the border wall. Maia dismissed her helmet, gasping for air as the plates slid away. No matter how much breath she took in, her heart wouldn't stop racing.

"Take it easy, now." Kasper placed a hand on her uninjured shoulder, holding her in place.

"Let. Me. Go," Maia panted between gulps of air.

Serenia knelt at her other side. "Maia, is it your..." She pointed to her own chest.

"No. It's not that." Maia covered her face with her hands. "Let me go. I need to go. It's my fault she's out there. I need to get her back. I need to..."

You need to what? she thought. *Attack a Noctean outpost? Declare war on the Empire, on the off chance a tavern owner with no combat experience managed to survive an encounter with seasoned Noctean soldiers?*

The hammering in Maia's chest told her that that was exactly what she needed and exactly what she intended to do.

She slapped Kasper's hand away and got her legs under her, leaning on the wall for support. "Princess. Go to Tobias. Help him however you can. He's in charge of you until I return."

"Sun, slow down," Kasper said.

"Elizabeth might still be alive!" Maia slammed her fist into the wall. "They already took my mother, and my father, and my..." She struck the wall again, splintering the rock. "They can't have her. I won't let them have her!"

"We need to think rationally," Serenia said. "We can resolve this without bloodshed. Let me help! I know I can do this, Maia."

"Not risking you, too."

"Maia, I—"

"Go. To. Tobias. A good soldier always follows orders, yeah? I'm giving you an order, Princess. Follow it."

Serenia let out a long breath that peaked at the beginning of a frustrated growl. She offered a weak salute and marched back toward the center of town with her shoulders tight. It had been years since Maia had met anyone so reckless. So hotheaded. And so, so brave.

She had no place in what was to come. What Maia intended to do wasn't a brave thing.

Kasper stepped into Maia's line of sight and lifted his chin. "I'm comin' with you. Before you say no, remember who taught me how to track. You want to get to Castle Blackwood fast, under cover of night? I can get you there."

Of all the people Maia would ever rely on as she planned a suicidal foray into dangerous territory, Kasper wasn't even on the list. But he was right. Leona was the finest hunter Maia had ever known, and she taught Kasper everything she knew.

If Maia meant to get to Elizabeth and the other prisoners before any further harm came to them, she needed Kasper's help.

Despite that fact, she couldn't stand to look at him. "This doesn't make things right with us. What you did..."

"I know, Sun. I know. Come on. We're wastin' time."

Kasper followed her back to town, where a group of Brave Dawn fighters was gearing up. Maia found Tobias and Serenia helping a quartermaster pass blades and spears from large barrels into eager hands.

"Too many," Maia said.

"Too many what?" Tobias said.

"We need to move fast and quiet. We can't do that with this many fighters. Pick a dozen of your best. Have them dress in black. Give each of them two falchions. More, if they can carry them. Have them meet me at the gates within the hour."

Tobias fixed her with a quizzical look. "You've changed your mind? You're coming with us?"

"No. You're coming with me."

Chapter 13
Blades In

Night draped over Maia's group like a cool blanket. She led her party through the rolling hills outside Whitehorn and across the short stretch of neutral territory that separated the Freelands and the Empire. The fighters moved in two long lines, forgoing the aid of torches. Kasper stalked just ahead of the host. The moon's silver gleam shone just bright enough for Maia to make out his silhouette and follow his footfalls.

When they came to an open plain, they veered wide and fell to their bellies to crawl past the site of the caravan massacre. The danger of being spotted by a patrol was great; the risk of recognizing a familiar face among the fallen and sinking into despair was greater. There would be time to count the dead once the living were safe.

A few hours before midnight, Castle Blackwood came into view. The castle was rammed up against the titanic Sinadaria Mountains, whose individual rocky spires bled together into one monumental mass of sloping stone that thrust into the sky and up beyond the clouds. Maia wondered if Noctis had consulted the Sinadarian elves who lived atop those mountains, so high above the world, when they built a castle next to the base of the elves' kingdom. She also wondered if the Sinadarians would even care; they rarely noticed the rest of the world on the ground far below.

If they did care, perhaps they would agree with Maia that Castle Blackwood was a terrible name for the fortress. It was neither black nor made of wood. The castle's dated, simplistic design consisted of four strong outer walls of ageless, fitted stone and mortar, with towers rising where the walls joined. The outer walls also contained the barracks, which were large enough to host an entire battalion. A simple drawbridge past a small barbican granted passage across a slow-moving moat, fed by an underground river running beneath the mountain range.

A tall, square keep lay at the far end of the castle grounds. The prisoners and refugees, if they still lived, would be in the dungeon below. They had to be. Maia wasn't sure what she would do if they weren't.

Kasper signaled back to her. The group huddled close to keep their whispers masked by the night breeze. The fighters wore dark leathers, at Maia's request, with black cloth wraps covering their heads, leaving only their eyes exposed.

"Down there, part of the river branches off, goes beneath the castle," Kasper said.

"That's their water supply. If the way through is barred, I can take care of it," Maia whispered. "We'll need to weave past the patrols."

"That won't be a problem," one of the masked fighters said. "We know their patrol patterns."

Maia recognized the voice and bit back her sigh. "Tobias. Is that you?"

The masked man waved.

"I said I wanted a dozen fighters, not eleven fighters and a priest. Do you even know how to use those swords?" Maia said.

The fabric of his mask lifted. He was smiling beneath it. "Far better than I wish I did. It's a long story."

"Dying to hear that tale. Wait. Do you feel that?"

Rhythmic vibrations in the earth grew stronger until the sound of giant metal feet stamping down on moist sod came so close that Maia and her group barely had time to clear the way and avoid Scarlet trampling them flat.

If Serenia noticed, it didn't stop her. She continued her forward march, driving the giant war machine straight toward Castle Blackwood.

"What's she doin'? Kasper hissed.

"Thinking for herself. And she's going to get us all killed," Maia said as she quickly weighed her options. "We'll use the distraction as cover."

"I'll go around back, scale the wall, and keep an eye on Ren. She might need help," Kasper said. He didn't wait for her response before shuffling off into the dark.

As the night swallowed him. Maia held back some of her most creative curses. "If he gets caught, we're all dead. We need to get to the river. Stay low. Go, now!"

They scurried toward the castle. All the while, Maia kept her focus firmly on the guard towers and ramparts. Large ballistae, along with several archers roused by the commotion, trained their sights on the Vanguardian stomping their way. Neither would hinder Scarlet, but if just one set of eyes veered from the spectacle, down toward the moat…

Magical fire swelled within Maia, ready to be launched at a moment's notice. She hoped it wouldn't come to that. Before Maia left, Serenia made her promise not to take any Noctean lives. Maia assured her that she had no need to worry, that they were going "blades in." The thin, curved falchions that the fighters of the Freelands favored were only sharpened on the front edge. Turning the blades inward and striking with the back edge lessened the chance of a fatal blow.

I doubt we'll get the same courtesy from them if we're spotted.

Maia slipped into the river with the rest of her party close behind. The water's cold embrace gripped her, causing her breath to quicken once her feet no longer touched the river's bottom. Her fire rose within her, defeating its chill. She paddled on and let the current drift her toward a metal grating at the base of the castle wall.

One by one, the Brave Dawn fighters crossed the river. As they reached the other side, they linked arms in a human chain to keep from being swept downstream. Maia grabbed one of the vertical iron bars for support and focused her fire into her free hand.

When mages used their gifts, they pulled small strands of infinity from beyond the Veil and spoke to them, coaxing them to change their form and function to form spells. A strand could be sealed inside of an object, forming an enchantment, or woven together with other strands to create more complex spells and enchantments.

Though Heretic had stitched many strands of infinity into Maia's body when she twisted her into a living weapon, she hadn't given Maia a strand of fire. She imbued Maia with a whole sliver, a slice of pure primordial fire capable of channeling more flames in the blink of an eye than an arch mage could ever conjure.

The first time Maia tried to command the flaming sliver inside her, she almost burned down an entire copse of Brackenberry trees. It took time, and practice, to rein in her hellish flames and learn how to focus them.

Maia breathed out slowly. A thin, fast-moving orange flame extended from her fingertips. She looked away as it hissed into the first of the iron bars to avoid blinding herself.

Molten metal dripped from the bright cut, little droplets hissing as they kissed the water. It was slow work, but there was no faster way to get her group inside and free the prisoners before Serenia or Kasper got them all killed.

Ren dropped Scarlet into a kneeling position a short distance from the castle walls. She couldn't command Scarlet from outside the control beam like Maia could, so using Scarlet's hand as an elevator wasn't an option. Instead, she angled Scarlet's arm toward the ground and took a long, careful stroll down the length of it. She dropped off the end of the hand, touching down on the worn dirt road leading to Castle Blackwood.

She lit a borrowed torch and placed her tinder kit back in the pocket of her officer's jacket. It had been so long since she last wore her old uniform, but apparently, it had been long enough for her to think of it as her old uniform. The tight, high collar of her jacket stifled her, so she unbuttoned it, letting the cool night breeze quench her nerves.

With deliberate steps, she made her way to the iron gate of the castle's barbican, aware that at least two score archers had their bows trained on her. White-armored guards yelled from beyond the safety of the gate, demanding that Ren identify herself while doing their best not to gawk at the crimson giant kneeling behind her. With nimble fingers, Ren fished her challenge coin from her belt pouch and held it high. The platinum finish glimmered in the light of the barbican's sconces.

She wasn't disobeying Maia's orders. Not really. Maia told her to stay and heed Tobias. And she had stayed...up until he left to join Maia's party. Without Tobias around to direct her, what was there left to do but fall back on Maia's previous directive and think for herself?

"I am Serenia Lucretia Valerius, Pilot First Class of the Noctean Imperial Army," Ren shouted. "I require an audience with the commander of this outpost.”

The guards stared at her, unmoving. “Open the bloody gate!” Ren yelled, channeling a touch of her mentor's charm. The men scrambled, and the gate soon rose with a protesting groan. She had never used her authority to command much of anything. It didn't hold a candle to the raw power she felt when piloting Scarlet or the rush of fighting Ferals, but being in charge felt nice.

The draw bridge touched down just as she reached it. Ren tossed her torch to one of the gate guards, who dropped his spear to catch it. With a jerk of her head, she bade him to follow her, never breaking stride.

Show them who's in command. Don't give them a chance to deny you.

Maia had likened Ren to the trigger of her revolver, prone to firing with a little bit of pressure. Hopefully, once Ren solved this mess, Maia would see that a trigger didn't need to be squeezed to be effective. The threat of one weapon could keep many in their sheaths. If she played her part right, she could end this madness without any further bloodshed.

It was a risk, bringing Scarlet onto Noctean soil, but lives were at stake. Timid people rarely made history.

Across the courtyard, the doors to the castle keep creaked open, giving way to a modest waiting area with two stone staircases snaking up to join a high balcony. Beneath the balcony, a corridor led to the rest of the keep's main floor. Castle guards and attendants lined up at the edges of the room beneath bright banners bearing the golden lion of Noctis.

“Bring me the commander of this base at once,” Ren barked to nobody in particular. A uniformed attendant broke off from the gathered ranks with a hasty salute and sprinted up the stairs, leaving through a doorway leading off the balcony. She expected to be seen immediately, given the way the rest of the outpost had fallen over itself at her behest, but she waited close to ten minutes before anyone appeared on the balcony.

Instead of her father's stern face peering down at her, she looked up to see a whip of a man, tall and slender, with a hooked nose and shrewd eyes that reminded her of a crow. His slicked black hair had receded into a widow's peak in its eagerness to escape his pale face and deep, resentful frown. His officer's jacket, a near match to hers, only differed in the emblem pinned to his breast, a pair of crossed feathers. On his hip rested a thin rapier much like hers but with a complex, ornate guard. Like many officers of his age and rank, he was likely an orthodox fencer, trained in one of the old styles.

The commander crossed his hands behind his back and waited at the balcony's edge. His raised brow told Ren that he would not speak first. His elevated position, like his delayed arrival, was meant to remind her that though she technically held superior military rank, only the Emperor himself outranked a citizen of the Empire in their own house.

You walked here in a walking war machine, Ren reminded herself. *Stand your ground.*

They sized each other up for several moments until, finally, the commander's lips parted with a sigh. "Serenia Valerius. What brings you to Castle Blackwood?"

"*Pilot* Valerius. You have me at a disadvantage. May I know the name of Castle Blackwood's commander?"

"My name is Salvian. I don't know if you remember me, but we met once when you were younger, before..." He made circles with a gloved finger, leaving her to fill in the rest.

Ren smiled, hoping that he hadn't seen her eyes widen as he spoke his name. Maia told her that a man named Salvian had carried out the destruction of Aquila. "I'm afraid that the years I lost to slumber have dulled my memory. Do not take offense."

"I don't." Salvian peered down his nose at her. "You look disappointed. Were you expecting to see your father?"

"Does he not command the invasion forces?"

"Invasion? Preposterous. We're merely protecting the Emperor's lands from unwashed heathens. Dull work for a man of your father's rank and station."

Despite having seen the result of that "dull work" firsthand in Whitehorn, Ren held her tongue. Any retort she offered might start a grand melee, and she was grossly outnumbered.

"Last I heard, your father had returned to Noctis," Salvian continued. "At any rate, I'm glad to see you returned to us safe and sound. Word reached us that you had been kidnapped." He left the unspoken question of her sudden appearance dangling in the air.

"I escaped. My duty is complete. I've secured Scarlet for Noctis." Ren had never lied to an officer before. If he found out—*when* he found out—there would be consequences.

Worry about that later, she thought. *There are people who need your help. They need a hero.*

"Your father will be overjoyed." Salvian cleared his throat. "Not that I don't appreciate the visit, even at this late hour, but if you're in search of lodging for the night, my aide can make you most comfortable. If there's nothing else..."

"There is. I would prefer to speak in private, officer to officer. Are you prepared to receive me?"

A look of annoyance flashed across his face. He offered the curtest of nods. Salvian stroked his stubble and whispered something to his aide, who scurried away like a rat. "This way."

Salvian led her up a long, winding stone stairwell to the fifth floor of the keep, where he held his office. The commander offered Ren a seat in one of the two plush chairs sitting near a bookshelf that spanned an entire wall of the long chamber. He stopped at a window near an ornate wooden desk at the back of the room and shuttered it on his way to a small bar set up in the corner. As he busied himself there, Ren eyed the large revolver holstered at the small of his back. It looked identical to hers, save for its black finish.

Her wolf was a custom piece, one of a kind. Reproductions had apparently started making their way to other high-ranking officers. Her father had neglected to mention that. What else had he kept secret from her? The village of Aquila pushed its way into the forefront of her thoughts. She held it there. All in due time.

Salvian returned with two goblets. He handed one to Ren and sat opposite her.

Why do adults keep forgetting that, by Imperial law, I'm too young to drink? The wine, if that's what it was, tasted sweet, but it burned the back of Ren's throat. She swallowed with a gulp, swirling the remaining liquid in her goblet as she had seen adults do. All the while, Salvian stared at her as if trying to solve a puzzle.

"You were blond." He leaned forward and set his glass down on the short end table next to his chair. "I distinctly remember you being blond."

Ren patted her crown of black braids. "I was, yes. I'm told it's one of the unfortunate side effects of the Pilot conversion procedures I underwent. I do miss my old fashion, but it's a small price to pay for the many benefits I enjoy as a Pilot. Tell me, Commander Salvian. You said we were acquainted. When, precisely, did we first meet?"

"A few days before the first Behemoth attacked Noctis. I'm not surprised you don't remember, given all you've been through. Terrible thing, what happened to you."

Without thinking, she rubbed the back of her shoulder, where a piece of tumbling ceiling had smashed the wind out of her despite her mother's broken body shielding her. That shoulder always itched when she remembered that night. "Thank you for your sympathy. Losing four years of my life, as well as my mother, has been difficult. Emperor rest her soul."

"I'm referring to the fact that your father saw fit to turn you into...whatever it is you are now. Not entirely human anymore, are you?"

Ignoring the cut, Ren forced an agreeable smile. It wasn't the first jab she had suffered from an ignorant noble on the subject of her Pilot ascension. "No less so than any noblewoman born without magic who then finds herself blessed by the Emperor's grace. I'm grateful to our lord and savior for affording me another chance to serve the Empire. Whatever I am now, I am what the Emperor wishes me to be."

That shut his mouth. No officer would ever dare to speak ill of the Emperor or criticize his actions. By slighting her, Salvian had inadvertently questioned the Emperor's will, and that misstep would unbalance him. It was time to strike.

Ren took another sip of wine, stifled a choking cough, and placed her cup down. "That's well enough for pleasantries, I think. On to business. I'm here to inquire after the Brave Dawn fighters and Noctean refugees you're holding in your dungeon."

Salvian snorted. "I have no refugees here, only traitors bound for the gallows. They were in league with Brave Dawn, selling information regarding the disposition of our defenses. Their deaths will save countless Imperial lives."

"That's not the story I've heard. I would like to speak to your prisoners, to learn what I can and make up my own mind on the matter. I have it on authority, from a very trusted source, that those Nocteans you recovered were seeking emancipation from the Empire. Surely, the Emperor can forgive them for their momentary madness, as well as the Brave Dawn fighters who, though misguided, were only trying to help their neighbors."

"Interesting that you should speak of authority when you have none. Does the Pilot purview now include investigating traitors to the Empire? Or perhaps, coming to their defense?" Salvian stood and paced toward his desk. He crossed his arms behind his back, knuckles hovering just over his revolver's polished handle.

"As Pilot First Class of the Noctean Imperial Army, acting in the name of Emperor Caelus Noctis III, you cannot refuse me." Ren produced her platinum challenge coin, waving it slowly to hide the shaking in her hand.

He faced her. A grin so slight she almost missed it curled Salvian's lip. She balanced the coin on her thumb and flicked it to him. Before his revolver rose above his hip, before the coin touched the carpet, Ren already had her own gun drawn and trained on his forehead, hammer cocked.

"I should have offered you a bath before receiving you," Salvian said. "You reek of smoke. I wonder where you picked up such an odor?"

"You reek of blood and deceit. No amount of bathing will remove that wretched stench."

"Precisely how long have you been a traitor to the Empire?" Salvian spat on the carpeted floor of his own office as if that would somehow offend her.

"I'm no traitor. I serve the Emperor in all things." The barrel of Ren's revolver wavered. The wrongness of aiming it at a person still made her stomach churn.

"Beautiful words, but they don't match your actions. You have her over-inflated sense of self-importance, you know that? That blasted Pilot. Sunder." He raised his gun and took aim. "She was too afraid to act, to do what needed to be done. You're just like her. You won't fire. Drop your weapon and surrender."

"I must admit, I'm growing quite tired of people telling me what to do."

Ren squeezed the trigger. Her wolf thundered. The corner of Salvian's desk exploded in a shower of wood chips and splinters, sending him shrieking and flailing.

"Stupid child!" Salvian screeched.

"*I'm* the child? Which one of us screams like a little girl?" Ren swallowed hard and gripped her nerve tight before it left her. "Two things will happen. You will escort me down to your dungeon, whereupon every living soul I find there who wishes to leave with me will do so. Before that, you're going to tell me precisely what happened in Aquila. What did my father order Maia to do? What did he order *you* to do?"

"Why not ask him yourself? He's right behind you."

"Once again, I wonder aloud, which one of us is the child? Did you really think that would work?"

"Actually, I was hoping it wouldn't." Salvian's face was too relaxed. Reacting on instinct, Ren whipped her revolver's barrel toward the door behind her. An iron grip clenched her wrist. She followed the length of the Blacksteel arm all the way up to her father's frowning face.

"Serenia. Let it go."

She obeyed, ever the dutiful soldier. Her purple-hued revolver thudded to the carpet. When her father released her wrist, she rubbed it to bring the feeling back.

"When I heard you were seen with Maia in Whitehorn..." Her father paused, taking in a deep breath. "When I heard that you may have turned against the Emperor, I had to see for myself if it was true. I'm so disappointed in you."

The pained timbre of his voice pulled at her heartstrings, but Ren pushed her chin higher. "Speak true, father. Are those prisoners down in the dungeon refugees or traitors?"

Her father's face sagged. "Both," he said after a long pause.

"But were they traitors who became refugees? Or refugees who were branded traitors?"

The iron returned to her father's demeanor. "Those who spurn the Emperor are not worthy of his protection. All Nocteans are gifted with a purpose. Whether their strength is granted by the Emperor or intrinsic, it belongs to him. To attempt to leave the Empire, to take that strength away from the Emperor, is unforgivable."

"I'm afraid our disappointment is mutual, father. This is not what the Empire you raised me to follow stands for. This isn't our way!"

Salvian stepped toward her, revolver still raised. "Arcturus, this is pointless. Don't waste wind explaining yourself to her. She's a traitor to the crown!"

"Do *not* point that gun at my daughter." Her father's tone stopped Salvian like a wall of stone. The commander fell back, dipping his barrel to the floor.

"He's good at following orders." Ren crossed her arms, emboldened by righteous anger. "What orders did he follow in Aquila? Maia said you demanded that she wipe the town off the map, and when she wouldn't, you had Salvian do it. I wish to hear the truth from you."

"Aquila isn't... Serenia, there are some things that—"

"What were the orders?" Ren all but screamed. Her father wouldn't meet her gaze. His silence told her everything. "Maia was right. You ordered the deaths of innocents. Did you have her father killed, as well?"

A fury she seldom saw, normally reserved for the battlefield, flashed across his face. "I am the Emperor's sword. I live only to execute his will. The purge of Aquila will always be a bloody stone around my neck. I will bear that weight for all my days, proudly, for the Emperor wishes it so. But I swear to you, on my life, that I did not have any hand in what happened to Maia's father."

"How am I to believe you?" Ren let her hands drop helplessly to her sides. "You told me all my life that the Emperor's wish was to unite the world under his protection. Why would a benevolent god treat his subjects with such hatred and disdain? You've been lying to me my entire life. Was any of what you told me real? What about the War of Bones? Was it truly started by rogue necromancers? Or was that a convenient excuse to cover the Emperor's unlawful advance into the Freelands?"

"Serenia, cease this heresy." Her father took a heavy step toward her, and she retreated. Her heel brushed against her dropped revolver. "Your duty is fulfilled. You have Scarlet. You can return to Noctis a hero. Don't tarnish your victory. Do you still have your Snapstone?"

Her hand unconsciously went to the small steel box she held in a secret belt pouch. "Give it to me," he commanded, extending his Blacksteel hand. "You will remain here with Salvian while I put an end to this night's folly. Then, we're going home."

"What are you talking about?"

"Serenia." Her father's frown deepened. "Don't think me a fool. If you're here, Maia must be nearby. What was your role in all of this? To act as a diversion? Give me your Snapstone."

Maia. She was likely already well on her way to the dungeon. Or perhaps, she had already escaped with the prisoners. It was more likely that she had been discovered and needed Ren's help. Her father blocked her escape; with the aid of the enchanted rune-inscribed steel grafted to his bones and the potent magics each strip contained, she would never get past him. Salvian barred her way to the window, beyond which waited a long drop to the ground that would likely kill her. Without a miracle, she had no chance to escape.

A dull boom from far beneath her feet grew into a rumbling tremor, drawing her father's attention downward. It wasn't exactly the miracle she had hoped for, but whatever caused the commotion, Ren wasn't about to let it go to waste. Not while Maia needed her.

She pivoted, hooked her foot under her revolver, and kicked it into the air ahead of her. Two steps brought her to it. She snatched it as she veered and ducked to avoid Salvian's aim. A boom and a flash leaped from the barrel of his revolver. The shot missed her, hitting the bookshelf instead. Bits of wood and paper hit Ren like a sideways hailstorm, but she kept running, lining her gun up with the shuttered window.

She fired. What remained of the shutters blew outward. Her father shouted. Ren spared a glance back. He had wrenched the revolver from Salvian's grip and pushed him to the floor. His eyes met hers.

In front of the open window, Ren froze, suddenly aware of what she was doing. If she took the plunge out into the cold dark of night, she might survive the five-story fall to the ground below thanks to her newfound Pilot gifts. But she would be turning her back on her father, the only family she had left, the only one who hadn't forgotten her while she was trapped in the eternal darkness of her coma.

And Ren would be defying him so she could rush to the aid of a woman who didn't much care for her, a woman who wouldn't shed a tear if Ren died. A woman who had broken her own iron law, risking war with the Empire, just to save one person.

A woman who, unlike her father, had never lied to her.

Ren slid her revolver back into its holster. A rush of air, displaced by her father's magically enhanced speed, tickled her face. He switched speed for strength and hurled Salvian's desk out of the way with one hand. Before the wood slammed into the far wall of the office, Ren had already leaped, arms stretched wide as she embraced the open night air.

Chapter 14

Still More to Lose

"Would you mind repeating that?" Ash said.

Professor looked up from his workbench, where he was presumably hard at work preparing the concoction Ash had requested over a week ago. He wore a blank gaze that told Ash he was in no mood to repeat himself. She stared at him until he did.

"General Valerius has reported that your daughter has resurfaced at Castle Blackwood. Sunder is expected to be nearby. General Valerius will recover the girl and deal with the Pilot himself."

"That's what I thought you said. I wanted to be sure." Ash leaned against the cold stone of the laboratory wall. "I told him to stand down. If we bring Serenia back now, we lose our best chance to trap Sunder. Lion's Roar isn't ready yet, I take it?"

"Correct."

"Then call him back! He's going to ruin everything I've planned!"

"This is not a plan. This is a farce, one I no longer find amusing. Sunder must die, and the girl must be returned. She is too valuable of an asset to be allowed to roam free. If you are too afraid to face the Pilot yourself, then leave the task to General Valerius. There is more at stake than your petty revenge."

Ash ran her hands through her white hair. If something happened to Serenia, then the ultimate revenge she had dreamed of for so long, as well as any hopes of living beyond the Exodus, would crumble like a dead leaf in a stiff breeze. Professor was right about that. But his faith in Arcturus was misplaced. With all the enchantments melded to his bones, and his equally blessed runic Blacksteel arm and longsword, he stood a fair chance of beating Sunder in her current state.

So long as any latent feelings for Sunder stayed his hand. And Arcturus was nothing if not sentimental.

"Open an umbral portal," Ash said. Professor blinked. She had caught him off guard. "My apologies. Did I stutter?"

"As I have stated, the reagents necessary for umbral portal conjuration are in increasingly short supply. More to the point: what has led to you changing your stance?"

"Opportunity." Arcturus would no doubt fail in his task. Ash was sure of it. However, she had the element of surprise on her side. Her daughter's impulsiveness may have tied an even tighter noose around Maia's neck than the one Ash was so close to knotting. "If this is the direction the night is headed, I intend to take advantage of it. I'll return shortly. I need to make a stop at the armory before you send me on my merry way."

Ash closed her eyes and smiled, affording herself one lingering moment to bask in the excitement surging through her veins.

Her only regret was that if the weapon she was on her way to pick up worked as intended, Sunder would never know who ended her pathetic life.

⚔

With the gate breached, Maia led her Brave Dawn fighters through a narrow cistern. The thud of the drawbridge touching down above spurred the crew to quicken their pace. They crested the top of the well and gathered in a dark corner near the castle courtyard, where more Noctean soldiers than Maia could count stood at attention.

All eyes were on Serenia as she marched, straight as the stick up her ass, toward the keep's main entrance. Any thoughts Maia had of escaping Castle Blackwood without a fight crumbled to dust, though she had to begrudgingly admit that a high-ranking Noctean officer visiting a remote outpost was quite a good distraction. She needed to find Elizabeth and the other prisoners, fast.

"On me. Remember: blades in," Maia whispered to Tobias and the rest of her fighters. They moved as one, blending into a single liquid shadow flowing silently in her wake.

A shuttered window at the base of the keep gave them access to a well-stocked pantry near the kitchen. The late hour and the commotion caused by Serenia's arrival left only two guards to deal with on the way to the spiral stairway leading down to the dungeon. Tobias' hand flashed a signal Maia wasn't familiar with; two of her fighters broke rank and rushed the guards, choking them out with the blunted back edges of their blades and guiding them to the floor without a sound.

I definitely want to know more about your life before priesthood, when this is all over, Maia thought. She led her crew down the torch-lit stairway. At the bottom, they fanned out to form two neat lines on either side of the thick steel door that blocked their way to the dungeon proper.

Maia peeked through the door's grated slat. Rows of prison cells lined a stone corridor wide enough for five people to walk abreast. Halfway down the hall, a passage cutting to the left led to more cells. At the hallway's end, the path split to the left and right.

She didn't see any guards. Maia slowly slid the bolt and gave the door a nudge. It didn't move.

"Barred from the inside," Maia whispered. "What an odd prison."

"A trap?" Tobias said.

"A trap. They must be expecting a rescue. You might have a spy in Brave Dawn." Maia ran her hands over the iron door. "It'll take too long to cut through this much metal. Get back up the stairs. When you hear my signal, rush in. Take the left passage. I'll cover you and go on ahead."

"What's the signal?"

Wearing her widest grin, Maia pressed her back to the door and crossed her arms over her head. Tobias cursed and ushered his fighters up the spiral stairs.

When they were around the corner, Maia dropped her arms to her chest. The burst of fire that came with her summoned armor and weapons tore the door from its frame and sent it tumbling. When the sound of metal crashing against stone settled, she turned, drawing her blades and charging to the first intersection. Her fighters poured in behind her, tapping her on the shoulder as they angled down the left passage.

Six taps in, the first cell door swung open at the end of the corridor. Something bright and round arced through the air. Maia slashed at it reflexively, realizing too late what it was.

The flask exploded, bathing her in burning oil. Fire couldn't harm her, but one of Tobias' fighters screamed as splashes of sticky flame slipped past her and clung to his clothes.

Maia willed the fire away as dozens of Noctean soldiers, clad in white cuirasses and dark gambesons, poured from every cell in the hallway. More than half of them had flintlock rifles held at the ready. She hauled the burnt Brave Dawn fighter to his feet and shoved him into the arms of another, ordering both fighters down the side passage. The first bullet caught her in the back, plinking off her armor like a drop of rain. The storm of bullets that followed filled the air, cutting down two of Tobias' fighters before they made it around the corner.

Their blood splattered across Maia's cracked visor. She turned from the bodies of the fallen, as furious with the Noctean riflemen as she was with herself for forgetting to use her Barrier to protect them. Spent flintlocks fell to the ground. Swords were drawn. Unsure of whether she could safely disable her opponents while armed, Maia sheathed her own blades and charged down the hall, a fierce growl surging in her throat.

She slammed into the Noctean wave, dropping her shoulder and pushing through until she was swimming in a sea of bodies. They lashed out with their swords, thrusting and cutting. She put her balance on the balls of her feet, weathering their meager strikes and countering with metal-clad punches, each blow sending another of her attackers slumping to the ground.

One of the soldiers gripped his sword by the middle, maneuvering its tip like a short spear. He dug it into the crack in her right pauldron. Maia bit back a yelp and backhanded the sword, snapping it and leaving the end embedded in her shoulder. A kick to the stomach flung its owner into the crowd, bowling over three of his companions.

More soldiers surged around the corners at the end of the hallway, two for every attacker she felled. The wounded slumped against the bars of the cells or laid at her feet, groaning and nursing their wounds if they were still conscious enough to do so. The flow of fresh fighters continued.

Good. Let them come. Focus on me. That'll give Tobias and the rest time to—

Around the crack in her visor, through the steel raining down on her, Maia saw a figure in a tattered brown cloak round the corner. The hooded newcomer moved like they were taking a casual stroll through a market, though the Black-steel rifle they carried, half as thick as their torso, was unlike anything Maia had ever seen in any vendor's stall. From the butt of the thick stock to the tip of its notched hexagonal barrel, the weapon dwarfed its owner's height by several inches. A long scope was affixed to the top, similar to the kind Fennish hunters used with their bow guns.

"Hold her!" the hooded figure yelled in a woman's voice that seemed to blend with a darker echo of itself, a sound so discordant it sent a shiver up Maia's spine.

The soldiers threw themselves at her, wrapping her up in their arms. She punched down at them, but they piled on faster than she could dislodge them. The soldiers further down the hall flattened against the walls and floor, leaving a clear path between Maia and the cloaked figure. The rifle's barrel dipped toward the ground. The figure grabbed a long handle on the gun's side and ripped it back. Gray-skinned fingers reached beneath the cloak's folds, producing a finger-length piece of pointed metal. The gunner slid it into a breach running down the rifle and jerked the handle, sending it sliding back into place with a metallic shriek.

With just one hand, the gunner raised the monster of a weapon. She tilted her head to put her eye in line with the gun's scope. The barest hint of a gray-lipped smile peeking from beneath the cloak's hood sent Maia's heart leaping in her chest.

Maia struggled against the weight of the soldiers holding her legs in place. Her instincts screamed danger. Heat built in her chest, threatening to burst outward. She kept her flames at bay, unable to stomach the thought of turning her fire on a person, even an enemy.

She wrenched a leg free, thrashing her body to shake the rest of herself loose, but a flash from the end of the hall stopped her mid-stride.

The bullet struck Maia before the air-shattering bark of the rifle did. Her head jerked back and to the right. A splash of red took her sight. Screaming, she grabbed her head, shutting her eyes tight against the slicing agony tearing through her face and the horrible ringing in her ears.

The soldiers fell away, giving her a wide berth. Maia tried to force her eyes open. Only the left obeyed. She took her shaking hands away from her face and looked down at them. Shattered bits of red metal and black glass, mixed with her blood, fell through her open fingers and onto the dungeon floor. What remained of her helmet tumbled away, clanging to the ground in broken chunks behind her.

Maia's breath quickened. Her fingers moved to the right side of her face. As they traced over the ruin left by the bullet, she understood why she couldn't open her other eye.

It wasn't there anymore.

A torrent of nausea blasted through Maia. Her head lolled, too heavy for her neck. When the dizziness left her, she was on her knees, a bolt of fresh pain arcing through her head like cruel lightning.

Before she could fully register what had happened, how Noctis had found a weapon that could kill her, a longsword crashed down on her bent back. Maia pushed to her feet and regarded the soldier who had struck her. Her breath came in short, quick gasps as his gaze flickered from her ruined face to the cracked blade in his hands.

Her one remaining eye drilled into him. Flames she had struggled to contain raged at her edges. The soldier dropped his sword and held his hands up in surrender.

As was her way, Maia only hit him once. Bone crunched beneath her knuckles as she slammed her fist into his chest. The soldier looked down at her hand, then up at her, face twisted in confusion as if he was trying to comprehend why she had caved his chest in with her fist. The light left his eyes as his heart beat its last. He slumped onto Maia's arm, then slid off her fist and onto the cold ground.

Pain and rage and shame mixed with the fire running through her veins and fueled the war cry that ripped from her throat. Flames danced over her armor as she screamed herself hoarse. Swords hit the floor. Noctean soldiers fell over themselves trying to flee from her. At the end of the hall, the cloaked assassin was wrenching the handle of her gun, reloading for another shot.

Maia had never been hurt like this. She wasn't sure if her Regeneration would restore her missing eye. Even if it did, the memory of that Blacksteel rifle and the way it had almost torn her head apart with a glancing shot would stick with her for the rest of her life. With a weapon like that in Noctis' hands, a weapon that anyone could use to pierce her armor from a distance, she would never be safe again.

The flames swirled from her sliver and gathered in Maia's palm. She knew she should try and regain control. This wasn't the way. This wasn't *her* way. Even though the Empire continued to find new ways to take what little she had left, Maia knew that even in the most corrupt reaches of the Empire, there were good people fighting for change.

Hopefully, none of them were in that corridor with her.

Maia thrust her palm toward the assassin and let her fury fly. A roaring sphere of twisting flames tore through the air, narrowly missed the assassin, and exploded behind her. A screeching wall of fire sped back toward Maia, chased by crumbling stone and the screams of the dying. The inferno washed over her, covering her like a warm cloak.

When the fires finally died, Maia was alone in the dark, surrounded by the putrid stink of burnt flesh. She braced against a charred stone wall and heaved, tossing up what was left of the terrible sandwiches she and Serenia had suffered through at lunch.

Princess. Maia had forgotten about her. She had to be somewhere in the keep. Even if her negotiations had succeeded, she would share the blame for what Maia had done. The Empire wouldn't let an attack on one of its outposts go unchallenged.

Nothing could stop the war now. Serenia would be thrust into it, just as Maia had been thrust into the war against the Behemoths and their masters.

The difference was that Serenia had a choice. She didn't have to bloody her hands the way Maia had. She could be saved. There was still time.

Footsteps drew Maia's attention back to the spiral stairs. Tobias was there, guiding the freed prisoners through the destroyed doorway. The surviving freedom fighters held out the spare blades Maia had ordered them to bring, passing them into the prisoner's hands. Through the soot and dust, Maia couldn't make out Elizabeth among the throng of bodies pushing through the doorway. Hopefully, she was somewhere in the middle of the crowd, where the fighting might not reach her.

She tried not to think of the alternative, that Elizabeth was rotting somewhere in the dark of the countryside. An unbearable flash of stinging pain in her head brought her back from that horrid thought. Maia stumbled through black smoke on unsteady legs, coughing and hacking the whole way.

Tobias waited for her at the stairs. "Sunder! We're headed back to the well, as planned. We'll hold there while...oh. Oh, no. Sunder. What did they do to you?"

His hands were empty. He had given both of his weapons away. Maia reached for the length of sword still jammed in her right shoulder, missing it twice before managing to grip it. The broken blade came free with a tug, and she placed it in Tobias' gloved hand.

"Help the others escape," Maia said. "I have to find my apprentice. Don't wait. Leave without us." Her hand went to where her eye once was, hovering there as daggers radiated from the wound.

Tobias opened his mouth to speak, but the smoke made him cough, stealing his words. He made for the stairs, stopping to glance one last time at Maia before he disappeared around the corner. When he was well out of sight, Maia allowed the raging flames still roiling inside her to seep out from her back and shoulders, forming a flaming cloak. The flowing blaze licked at the floor and walls, spreading with every trudging step up the staircase.

I'm coming, Princess. Please, don't be dead.

Ash emerged from a cloud of black dust and slammed into the wall of Professor's laboratory. She flopped to the ground in a broken heap.

Sunder's fireball had caught her by surprise. Her ambush would have gone much smoother if, instead of reloading to take another shot, she had taken the time to prepare her defenses against Sunder's magic.

As an orange glow pulsed through her body and her shattered bones and dislocated joints mended themselves, Ash berated herself for her mistake. Shame on her for letting Professor's chiding stoke her lust for revenge. Now, Sunder knew that Noctis possessed rifles that could shatter her armor. She might work out that Serenia's revolver could do the same. That would complicate things.

This was precisely the sort of thing that happened when one deviated from a carefully laid plan.

As Ash rolled over to find Professor hovering over her with a look of casual disgust on his face, she couldn't help but smile. With one impulsive, bungled shot, she may have ruined their plans, but the sheer thrill of seeing Sunder in pain and knowing she had been the cause of that exquisite anguish brought her no small amount of joy.

"Here's an interesting fact," Ash said. "When you use a Snapstone, you maintain whatever speed you were moving at when you emerge." She spat a glob of glowing blue blood onto the floor.

"This is not new information." Professor looked her up and down. "You have suffered extensive injuries."

"It's nothing I can't walk away from. Send in a few guards. Once I feed, I'll be good as new."

"Were you successful?"

Ash considered her reply. She sank inside herself for a moment, reliving the memory of Sunder's head whipping back, her helmet breaking, and the beautiful music of her cries. "She flinched."

"Then, you failed."

"Not entirely. She's in an unspeakable amount of pain right now. I can promise you that."

"Hmm." One corner of Professor's mouth lifted, ever-so-slightly, in a rare grin. "Good."

Ash matched his smile. Even if Arcturus failed, even if her plans were ruined, it was still one of the best nights of her unlife.

Chapter 15
Blades Out

Cold wind slapped Ren in the face as she threw herself from the window and into the dark night. Instinct forced her body into a twist to get her feet beneath her, but something slammed into her from the side, stealing her wind. Arms wrapped around her, pulling her into a lazy arc back toward the keep.

"Hold on!" someone shouted into her ear.

Ren crashed into the wall, her impact softened by whoever had grabbed her. They dangled there, suspended by a long rope leading up to the parapet of the keep. She fought the urge to struggle once she looked down at the ground below and realized just how far a five-story drop was.

"You're heavier than you look," her savior grunted.

"Kas? What are you doing here?" She clutched him in a tight hug.

"Thought I would try savin' you again."

"I have to go to Maia. She needs me."

"Rope won't go all the way to the ground." Kas shifted her to his back, where she wrapped her arms around his neck. He began his ascent, dragging her further from where she was needed.

As they passed the window, Kas jerked to the side. A Blacksteel grip extended from the opening and clamped around Kas' leg.

"Ren! Grab the rope!" As soon as she wrapped her fingers around the rough woven rope, Kas drew one of his stilettos and sawed at where he had tied the rope about his waist.

When the rope gave way, Kas fell a short distance and dangled by the leg from her father's hand.

"Get to the top! I have another hook and rope set up on the other side that'll get you down to the—"

Her father hauled Kas through the window and into Salvian's office before he could finish. Whatever happened next was brief, punctuated by the keen of metal on metal, a pained cry, and silence.

Panic kept her fingers wound tightly around the rope. Even with her Pilot abilities, she had no delusions about facing her father head-on and succeeding.

For all she had become, she wasn't enough. Not enough to save Kas. Not enough to help Maia. Not enough to save the prisoners in the dungeon below. Maia was right. How could she have ever thought she could change anything?

Ren bit back tears and braced her legs against the sheer wall of the keep. Each pull of the rope, each step toward the top, brought her further from a life she could never return to, further from the boy who had fallen twice trying to save her.

Maia caught a fleeing soldier by the neck and lifted him off his feet. Maybe it was the sight of her ruined face that twisted his in horror. It could have very well been the encroaching blaze trailing behind her that terrified him. Regardless, he answered her question with a stammer, letting Maia know that Serenia wasn't on the ground floor of the keep. She had gone up to the fifth floor to meet with the base's commander.

Maia thanked the soldier for his help and hurled him against the wall, not bothering to check if he survived the impact. Hungry flames spread from her back and shoulders, crossing the floor and climbing the walls. She didn't linger to watch the banners burn. The climb up to the waiting area's balcony took longer than Maia thought. With each step, she fought the urge to turn around, leave the keep, and follow the shouts to the courtyard, where the fighting was.

Brave Dawn had their duty. Maia had hers. She had already broken promises that night. No matter what, she couldn't break another. She needed to make sure Serenia was safe.

Maia entered another spiral stairwell and trudged upwards. Rolling waves of pain blasted through the right side of her skull. Maia braced one hand against the curving wall for support as she climbed, the other hand clutching her falchion.

A few remaining soldiers tried to rush past her, but Maia's trail of flames left nowhere to run. She cut them down, reversing her grip and slamming her blade through the last soldier's chest and pinning them to the stone wall.

When she ripped her sword free, the body tumbled. Maia looked down at the face of a girl not much older than Serenia, her face frozen in pleading confusion.

For a moment, the weight of the night caught up with Maia, pressing down on her until she could barely draw breath. What kind of woman would her latest victim have grown into had Maia not ended her story so abruptly? And what of the other lives she had taken when she broke her oath to never use her powers against a person? So many souls sent across the Veil in an instant. Could one of them have made a difference? Could one of them have been the key to a new Noctis?

The stabbing pain of her destroyed eye returned her to the flaming stairwell. The rush of heat from her cloak of flames flared out, covering the stairwell's walls. The damage was done. Even if she wanted to, she couldn't take any of it back.

Eventually, there would be a reckoning. Until Serenia was safe, guilt and consequences would have to wait.

Maia stopped at each exit of the stairwell to call out for Serenia. Her flames continued to spread as she climbed, slithering to wood and tapestries and consuming everything they touched. When she reached the fifth floor and called, someone else answered. She forced down her cloak of flames and stumbled through an open doorway. In what she presumed was the commander's office, she found Kasper slumped against the wall near an open window and a hefty, overturned wooden desk. Bits of wood and paper littered the carpet. Kasper grimaced and clutched his side with bloody fingers.

"Sun," he said, though his voice was weak. "You need to find Ren. Her father's here. She's headed for the roof." Kasper's face sank as he regarded her. "Blue Hells, Sun. Your face."

"Arcturus is here?"

Kasper winced as he nodded. "He went after her with the commander of the castle, some ass named Salvian."

"You're sure you heard, right? His name was Salvian? Are you sure of what you heard?"

"Yeah. I was outside the window, waitin' for an openin'. Ren was askin' him and her father about a place called Aquila."

Adrenaline pumped through her searing blood, and she squinted against the haze muddying her vision. "Can you walk?"

"Yeah."

She hauled him to his feet. The wound in his side looked deep, but the slow trickle of blood told her it wasn't fatal.

"Hold still." Maia reached beneath Kasper's leathers and released the slightest wisp of her fire magic. Kasper yelped and shut his eyes tight, breathing against the sting as Maia sealed his wound.

She wanted to yell at him. Compared to her injury, his was nothing. With the bit of control she had left, Maia forced most of her hatred of him aside. "Turn around."

Kasper did as he was told. The wound in her right shoulder still ached, so Maia grabbed Kasper by the leathers with her left hand, lifted him, and hurled him out the window.

"Thanks for everything," she called after him.

His scream trailed off into the night, followed by a splash. She meant to throw him onto the rampart atop the outer wall, but the moat worked, too. He couldn't very well go down the way they came, after all. The stairs were on fire.

She returned to the stairwell, allowing her cloak of flames to consume the rest of the room. Eventually, the curling path straightened out, leading to a barred iron door.

With no time to cut through the door, Maia gathered her flames into a churning ball, looked up to the stone ceiling, and let it fly.

Ren hauled herself over the lip of the keep's crenellated parapet and landed in a crouch. Flaming sconces lit the corners of the flat square roof, though their light didn't reach far, leaving most of the expanse shrouded in darkness. It was through that blanket of shadow that Ren's father and Salvian emerged, rising from a stairway cut into the far side of the roof.

Faint sounds of combat drifted up from the courtyard below, and long tendrils of black smoke curled up over the edges of the parapet. Smoke meant fire. Fire meant Maia.

"Serenia, cease this foolishness," her father said.

She tried to think of a petulant response, but the middle of the roof heaved upward in a mighty explosion, tossing Ren, her father, and Salvian onto their backs as a wide pillar of fire rose from below and raged against the night sky. Ren covered her head and curled into a ball as bits of hot stone rained down on her. Not ten feet away from her, Salvian stirred. Her father was already on his feet and headed her way, bleeding from a gash along his jaw.

He turned his head and leaped back, narrowly avoiding a snaking trail of fire racing across the rooftop. Ren followed the line of flames back to the churning column of fire. A hunched silhouette lurched from the inferno.

"Arcturus!" Maia screamed. The maelstrom died, leaving only the burning barrier that divided the roof, separating Ren and Salvian from her father and Maia. Stumbling, Maia drove her sword into the ground to keep her balance. Her other hand fumbled for the second blade at her back.

The wall of fire illuminated Maia's haggard form. Gritty soot blackened her armor, leaving only splotches of crimson peeking through in places, and she wasn't wearing her helmet. Sweat matted her hair to her head. She grimaced as she walked, baring bloodstained teeth.

When Maia turned to look at her, Ren's heart seized in her chest at the sight of the hole where her right eye should have been, and she couldn't help but scream.

Maia locked her focus on Arcturus as he drew his longsword from his hip. Runes etched into the blade's Blacksteel surface sprung to life. The sets of runes along his arm glowed bright blue in response, ready to lend whatever stored power he required.

Her chest heaved with each ragged breath. Splinters of pain punched through her head. She let her gaze drift over the wall of fire, finding Salvian's icy glare and matching it.

One stroke and he would fall. The people of Aquila would be avenged. But first, she had to deal with Arcturus.

"Maia, don't!" Serenia cried. She stepped toward the wall of fire that separated them but fell back, shielding her face from the intense heat. "Don't hurt my father! Please! You promised! Blades in! That's what you said!"

"Think you can keep that crow-faced shit stain occupied?" Maia shouted back.

"Maia! You *promised* me!"

"Keep Salvian busy!" Maia let the tips of her swords drift to the ground as she walked. The glowing ember edges hissed as they kissed cold stone. "Remember what I taught you. You'll be fine."

Arcturus tightened his grip on his blade and fell into a low guard. "Maia, stand down."

"I have a better idea, Lightning Rod. Why don't you hold still while I shove that sword up your ass?"

He stood his ground. "I don't want to hurt you."

"You already have." Maia pointed a sword at Arcturus. "You can beg my father for his forgiveness once I send you to meet him."

"Look at yourself!" Arcturus roared. "You can barely stand. You're half-blind. You can't defeat me!"

"I don't need to defeat you. I just need to keep you here until the keep collapses under your feet."

"Then you'll die as well!"

Maia shrugged. "Guess I'll introduce you to my father myself, then."

Summoning strength from her dwindling reserves, she hurled forward in a mad dash, bringing both blades down hard. They fell short. The world was a very different place with only one eye.

Arcturus cut in a wide arc, forcing her back. "How many times must I tell you, I had nothing to do with your father's death! I don't wish you any harm. I don't blame you for what happened to us!" He spared a sidelong glance across the wall of flames to his daughter. His point lowered, and he pushed a lazy thrust. Maia crossed her swords and drove Arcturus' blade down, sliding along its length until their faces were inches away.

"Even if that's true," she growled, "you still have to die."

"Why? Why must you—"

Maia answered him by smashing her forehead into his nose. Pain flashed through the side of her head. She lashed out with one of her falchions, narrowly missing Arcturus as he staggered away. "You betrayed me and everything we fought for. That should be enough to want you dead. But there's so much more. Tell me. Do you know my parents' names?"

Arcturus pulled his hand from his bloody nose. "Bianca and Alain Sunderland."

"Those were the names of the simple winemakers they became when they fled Noctis and came to the Freelands." Maia worked her swords through a flurry of wild slashes, forcing him to fall back and focus on parrying her assault. "In Noctis, their names were Galeria and Lucius Liberalis."

There was no way Arcturus wasn't acquainted with those names. House Liberalis had been one of Noctis' great noble families before their ancestral home went up in flames, claiming the lives of a lord and lady who had lost their only daughter a year prior. Lady Galeria Avita Liberalis had, sadly, been with child at the time. Arcturus froze, a look of realization spreading across his face. Maia pressed on, slipping past his guard. The burning edges of her falchions cut glowing gashes in Arcturus' pristine white armor. He winced and fell back, touching the cooling cuts.

She circled him like a prowling beast. "They faked their deaths and fled the Empire. All my mother wanted was to make sure I would be free of the Emperor's clutches, to keep what happened to my sister from happening to me. If I knew then what I know now, I wouldn't have worked with you. My father only told me the truth after you ordered Aquila razed to the ground. He told me why my mother *really* had to leave me behind, time after time, to fight for people who didn't deserve her. She was trying to keep other children from being butchered like my sister!"

The ground beneath them shook violently. The wall of fire rose to match her rage, crackling higher as tongues of flame whipped up around the edges of the roof.

Arcturus grimaced. "I had no idea, Maia. Your mother wore a mask when she fought against us. Her choice of weapons gave us pause, yet there was no way we could have known who... I'm sorry. Truly."

"No, you're not. But you will be." Maia shut her eye, unable to keep from trembling. "You told me once that when they fused that enchanted metal to your bones, you recovered so quickly that the Emperor ordered a second round of enhancements. Some children don't survive their first. Barely any make it through two. But you were special, so they kept going. Eight times, they cut you open and played god with your insides.

"You were special. My sister, Aemilia, was even more special. They must have been inspired by your success. Do you know how many times they cut into her?"

"Maia, I—"

"Fifteen times! She died on her sixteenth surgery! My sister died because you showed the Emperor just how far he could push special people. What happened to my family is on your head. Once I knew the truth, I vowed that one day I would burn you until your ashes remembered nothing but the memory of their names."

The tips of her heated blades parted the stone as she drove them into the ground. "I could have killed you in the Freelands. I wanted to. But that's not the Pilot's way. We don't kill people. We don't seek revenge. You were going to be my exception. For what you've done to me, I should kill you ten times over." The flames binding the roof faltered. "But I can't. Not for that. Not for any of it."

Arcturus relaxed his stance, standing up a little straighter. He fell back and shielded his face as a furious explosion erupted from Maia, bathing her in thick rolling flames and sundering the moment of silence with a piercing screech.

"But I'll be fucking *damned* if I'm going to let you take her." Maia pointed her flame-covered hand at the dividing fire and beyond to Serenia. "I can't change what happened to her, what you *let* happen, but I can keep her from becoming an Imperial tool, like you. I can still save her."

Maia tore her blades from the ground, letting her flames caress and wash over them until they shone like the sun, and threw herself at Arcturus. Each feverish strike rang off his longsword, filling the air with the notes of their own discordant song and painting the night sky with gouts of flaming rage.

Ren stood transfixed by the sight of Maia's sharp yet feral movements. Through the flurry of exchanged blows, neither fighter seemed to be gaining ground. They floated around their half of the roof like dancers, each strike a step in a complex, savage, beautiful waltz.

The raging fire splashing off Maia never touched Ren's father. The flames seemed to curl toward his Blacksteel arm, disappearing into a series of runes that glowed a different color than the others. He shifted enchantments, increasing his speed to keep up with Maia's furious barrage.

All Ren wanted was for them to stop hurting each other. And yet, for all her wanting, her knees buckled at the notion of standing between the two titans.

The sound of a blade leaving its scabbard cut over the din of ringing steel. Ren had forgotten about Salvian, so little and insignificant as he was compared to the two living legends battling through years of resentment on the other side of the wall of fire. She pulled her own rapier from her hip, stepping back to maintain distance as the castle's commander approached.

"Regardless of how this little drama plays out, I'm afraid you're still returning to Noctis," Salvian said. "You would be wise to lay down your weapons."

"I should say the same to you."

"Ah. The audacity of youth. Suit yourself. I challenge you to a duel to first blood, without the use of secondary weapons, as befits our rank and station. As an officer, you cannot refuse me."

He was right. She couldn't refuse. By the Emperor's law, Noctean nobles and high-ranking members of the military had the right to seek satisfaction for any slight, perceived or otherwise, through crossed blades. The practice sounded so romantic and elegant when Ren's instructors regaled her with stories of famous duels fought throughout Noctean history and the disputes they settled. Given everything she had learned about her homeland since then, she wondered if the tradition wasn't just another method of control, a way for the strong to keep others in their places through threat of violence.

"Very well." She pressed the hilt of her rapier to her forehead in salute and fell back into a receiving stance, leaving most of her weight on her rear leg. Her empty left hand hovered near her brow, ready to defend her vital areas if Salvian's blade slipped through her guard.

Salvian returned the salute and took an even-weighted posture with his sword held parallel to the ground. His off-hand pressed against his rear hip, forming a perfect loop like the handle on a teacup.

His stance confirmed what Ren had suspected from the design of his rapier. Salvian practiced an old school of fencing that had fallen out of fashion years before Serenia was old enough to lift a blade. He wouldn't be able to deploy his off-hand in that position and would be relying entirely on the deftness of his rapier's tip to win.

To win with that style, one had to be bold in their approach. She would use that against him and take control of the line.

Ren let her tip trail slightly to the left, opening a door for him on her right. Taking the bait, Salvian lunged, his measure longer than she anticipated. His tip danced around hers with a deft flick as she moved to intercept. Her gloved free hand diverted the sharp tip as she retreated, resetting for the next exchange.

They darted in and out in a steady tempo, seeking chances to commit to a thrust as their blades weaved and vied for control. Ren had her youth and Pilot agility, but Salvian had decades of experience. Whenever Ren found an opportunity to strike, she hesitated, unsure if the opening was an opportunity or a trap laid by her more cunning foe.

Thinking he might be similarly intimidated by her youth and physical superiority, Ren presented a ruse of her own and allowed Salvian to settle his blade atop hers. He closed the line with a deft push and drove his tip toward her shoulder. Ren's left hand moved in perfect time, diverting the thrust as she retreated and prepared her own counterstrike.

She only touched the edge of his blade for a moment. Salvian must have anticipated the maneuver. He flicked over her hand and into her face, drawing it down and cutting a sharp line from the side of her nose down to her jaw.

Ren cried out and fell back, patting the wound. The cut had gone deep, but the pain was already dimming as her Pilot gifts saw to the injury.

"Oh, now I've gone and done it," Salvian said. "Well, no matter. I'm told that you abominations recover quickly. Your father will be relieved. No real harm done."

Across the fire, Maia's guard was wilting under the weight of Ren's father's fierce overhand swings. Ren turned back to Salvian. "We bleed just the same as you. Is our pain worth less than yours because we don't keep our scars as proof?"

"It doesn't matter. I've drawn first blood. You've lost."

"I don't care about first blood," Ren growled. "Last blood is all that matters, you...piece of detritus!"

Salvian huffed. "Detritus?"

"Detritus."

"You impertinent little... You *dare* defy the rules of engagement?"

The rules. Of course. Ren almost smacked herself for forgetting the most important lesson her mentor had imparted on her.

Life isn't fair, so why should we fight as if it is?

Ren dropped her rapier's tip and bounced back and forth on the balls of her feet. "Come now. Is that all the fight you have? If a couple of weak strokes is what you call a thrilling exchange, it's no wonder you've yet to find a wife."

Salvian's face turned pink as he scowled at her. He rushed in, a bestial growl rumbling from his throat. Ren's tip remained low, beneath his guard, where it posed no threat. She fell back as he advanced, slipping away from his angry thrusts. If she couldn't out-fence him, she wouldn't fence him at all.

There were other ways to win. Maia had shown her that.

She squared her posture, leaving her chest unprotected. "Do you need a moment? A hot cloth, perhaps?"

His thrust came right up her center line, as she had anticipated. Bringing her feet together, Ren spun to the side, rolling along the rapier's length and sending the tip rushing past her. Her left hand snapped to her revolver's handle at the small of her back. She couldn't draw it in such close quarters, so she left it in its holster, angled it, and squeezed the trigger.

Everything is a weapon. Even the ground can be a weapon if you know how to use it.

Her wolf roared, tearing through the bottom of Ren's holster and striking the ground at Salvian's feet, tossing a spray of dust and stone into his face. He reeled and stumbled, shaking his head and clawing at his eyes with his free hand. Ren completed her turn, lifted her blade, and thrust.

Her rapier entered his right shoulder as he turned to face her, slipping clean through him with such ease, it sent her stomach rolling. Salvian's arm went limp. His sword fell from his grasp.

"Blue Hells!" the commander screeched. "You dishonorable little brat! You don't fight fair!"

Ren tilted her head and dared to smile. "No. I suppose I don't."

She debated pushing the blade in deeper, forcing Salvian to his knees, but the old commander gripped the blade of her rapier and drew himself down its length until he was close enough for her to count his nose hairs. His foot slipped behind hers. His free hand pushed her shoulder, twisting her torso and breaking her balance. She fell on her side, losing her grip on her rapier. Salvian stood over her, his left hand moving toward the handle of his own revolver.

As always, Ren was faster. She had her purple-hued gun trained on his forehead before his weapon left its holster.

She knew she should fire. Every bit of her screamed for it. She had no choice. If she didn't take his life, he would take hers.

And yet, her finger wouldn't move, even as the barrel of Salvian's revolver slowly drifted toward her face and his thumb cocked the hammer back.

Ren shut her eyes. Salvian grunted. Her hand clenched. Her wolf leaped in her hand, its howl drowning out the world, taking what remained of her honor with it.

Maia staggered back, her injured right shoulder stinging after parrying one of Arcturus' mighty two-handed blows. Even in his old age, he fought like an entire garrison of soldiers, fueled by the runic steel fused to his bones. Runic items, like his longsword and prosthetic arm, granted their wielders great power, but they paled in comparison to the magical might of enchanted material implanted inside a living body.

Having two swords normally meant Maia could attack while defending, just as she had taught Serenia to do. Against Arcturus, she had to devote both swords to defense. A protracted assault would stress his runics, causing them to falter and even break if he pushed them too hard, but Arcturus had an internal arsenal like no other. Maia fought to keep up with him as he seamlessly switched between his enchantments with a thought, calling on the woven magic stored in his grafted steel to add force to his strikes or lighten his step to avoid Maia's counters.

As the battle dragged on and the pain of Maia's gunshot wound sapped her strength, she reached the grim realization that she wouldn't last long enough for Arcturus to overwork his runics. Her armor grew heavier with each clumsy dodge. She considered dismissing it to create a quick distraction that she could use to end the fight quickly. If she failed to finish him in that instant, though, the next blow from Arcturus would end her. Of that, she was certain.

On the other side of the wall of flames, Serenia and Salvian were locked in combat. Their thin blades flicked impossibly fast through the air, almost imperceptible. Serenia was holding her own, but she was fighting fair. Salvian's superior skill would eventually prove the deciding factor.

The moment of distraction cost Maia dearly. When she set her focus back on Arcturus, the general wasn't there. She realized too late that he had slipped to her right, into her blind spot. His metal grip clamped down around her throat, and she gurgled as he lifted her off her feet.

"This ends *now!*" Arcturus shouted. "For the last time, I had no hand in your father's murder. Had I known about of any attempt on his life, I would have stopped it." Something in his voice gave Maia pause. He held every advantage. He didn't need to keep lying to her.

What if he was telling the truth? Who, then, had the Emperor tasked to burn her father to death in his own home, if not his most loyal and capable servant? Was the Empire involved at all? Who else had the resources to conjure a flame that would never die?

Arcturus' grip tightened. "Whether you believe me matters not. I will not allow you to take my daughter away from me. Forgive me for what I must do, Maia."

She expected the sharp pain of a blade slipping between her ribs; what Arcturus did instead made Maia wish he had used his sword. The flames sweeping over her body ripped back inside her. A thin line of agony traced its way from her chest, up her throat, and into Arcturus' Blacksteel arm. The false limb thrummed with energy as Arcturus siphoned the very fire bound to Maia's soul.

Panic took the reins. Her leg shot up, catching Arcturus in the chin. The gray-haired general reeled. She kicked him over and over, thumping her armored boot against his steel-lined skull. After six kicks, he relented.

Reaching down to where her sliver resided deep inside her, Maia found her flame still burning, hot and angry, but smaller than it was. Empty space hung at her edges, something vacant and wrong where there had once been more of her.

As always, Noctis found new ways to take what little she had left. Whatever complex enchantments had been set into those strange runes on Arcturus' arm, they held the power to draw her sliver from her body.

Her breath came in heaving gasps. Settling back into her fighting posture, Maia stepped back and let her right sword drop low to parry Arcturus' sidelong swing, unable to commit both weapons to her defense. The longsword passed unimpeded, snapping Maia's worn and chipped blade in two and smashing into her flank.

Her crimson armor held, though it couldn't absorb the force of the blow entirely. From the sharp pain spidering through her side, Maia knew at least one of her ribs was broken. Arcturus spun to cleave at her head from the opposite side. With only one blade, she couldn't parry the blow, so she threw her shoulder into the arc of his swing, blasting into his forearms and stealing most of the strength from the swing. As Arcturus stepped back to create distance, Maia pushed off the ground as hard as she could, planted both legs on Arcturus' breastplate, and kicked.

The old general flew back, giving Maia time to crawl back to her feet. She checked on her weapons, one broken two-thirds to the hilt, the other close to cracking. She didn't dare get into a close-range exchange with him again. Fighting at a distance wasn't an option, either. No doubt, he would swallow up whatever fire she threw at him with those special runes of his.

A gunshot rippled through the air, drawing Maia's attention beyond the wall of fire. Serenia emerged from a cloud of dust and debris and drove her rapier into Salvian's shoulder. Instead of finishing him off, she hesitated. Salvian took her to the ground and drew his own revolver. Before it got halfway out of its holster,

Serenia had her own gun in hand.

Horror ripped into Maia's chest, reverberating through her pounding heart. She had seen what Serenia's revolver could do. If Salvian's gun was anything like it, one shot from it would utterly destroy her.

What sent Maia's heart racing faster was the alternative. If Serenia fired first, she wouldn't become a weapon of the Empire like Arcturus. She would become a murderer. Like Maia.

That, she couldn't allow.

She lifted her arms and swung her blades downward as if she was about to throw her falchions, prompting Arcturus to guard. At the last moment, Maia pivoted. Her crimson-handled swords spun through the wall of fire, whistling as they cut through the night.

The broken blade caught Salvian in the neck, sinking to the hilt. The other flew past his hand, severing it and flinging his revolver away. Gurgling, he staggered back as Serenia fired. Her bullet tore through the empty air where Salvian had been standing and trailed off until the starry sky swallowed it.

Salvian crumpled. Serenia stood and looked across the flames to Maia, her face bearing a look of panic and disgust.

Maia's victory was short-lived. She had saved Serenia, but only for the moment. Arcturus raised his sword in a high guard near his cheek, tip poised and ready to thrust.

Perhaps her armor would hold against the blow. It didn't matter. He would continue hammering on her until his enhanced strength broke through or until the body beneath her armor was too beaten to stand.

Then, he would take Serenia back to Noctis, along with Scarlet, and the world would suffer for her failure.

Without a weapon, Maia couldn't defend against Arcturus' next attack. She took a deep breath and resigned herself to the only remaining play she had left. If her armor couldn't protect her, then she would turn it into the weapon she needed. Maia crossed her arms over her head and brought them to her chest, dismissing her crimson plates in a flash of light. The sudden loss of her armor's support caused Maia to slump. Arcturus watched her with keen eyes, waiting for her next trick, but Maia stood where she was, arms outstretched.

"Go on, then. End it," Maia said, allowing defeat to creep into her voice. Arcturus hesitated, glancing at Serenia out of the corner of his eye. "If you don't," Maia added, "I'll never stop coming. I'll take her. I'll take her from you."

That did it. Arcturus howled and charged, driving his longsword into Maia's abdomen. She felt the tip slip through her back, felt her blood spray into the cold night. When she looked up from the length of Blacksteel protruding from her stomach to the man that held it, Arcturus was frowning.

"I can't lose her. To you, or anyone. I'm sorry, Maia."

"I'm sorry too," Maia said, spitting blood onto Arcturus' white breastplate. "For this."

With her trembling arms crossed over her head, she brought them sharply down as soon as she felt the surge of power gathering in her chest. Her armor returned in a blazing nova, giving Arcturus no time to absorb the sudden explosion. The blast folded him, sending him hurtling across the roof like an arrow until he slammed into the far edge of the parapet with a sickening crunch.

Maia collapsed to her knees, clutching her gouged stomach. The wall of fire fell with her. Arcturus' sword lay shattered beneath her, though she could feel a length of it still lodged in her abdomen, cleanly sheared off by her armor's summoning. Despite the comforting weight of her armor, Maia became lighter, and then she was floating toward the ground. Something halted her descent and eased her down gently.

She opened her eye. Tears that weren't her own splashed against her soot-stained cheek.

"What did you do?" the girl whispered, half of her face flickering in the firelight.

Through her spinning head, anguish and exhaustion jumbled Maia's thoughts into an addled mess. "I killed a lot of people. I killed the king in his castle." She blinked. "And I think I broke your dad."

Serenia looked to where her father had fallen. "He's gone, Maia."

"I'm sorry. I didn't want to kill him. I couldn't let him take you."

"No, he's *gone.*" Serenia rummaged in one of her many belt pouches and produced a small metal box. She opened it and fished out a square-cut purple rock that looked like a packed cake of powder. "This is a Snapstone. When you break it, it transports you to wherever its twin rests." She gripped the rock tighter and held it against her forehead. "My father has his own. He must have used it to escape. That means he's alive, at least. Back in Noctis. Someone will help him."

"You had a magic...thing, all this time? Why didn't you fly away from me? Like a little bird?"

Serenia laughed through her tears. "Clearly, I'm not ready to leave you yet, you colossal fool."

Maia opened her mouth to return fire. All that came out was a groan. Serenia shook her. "Hey, hey," she said, "stay with me. We'll get you some help."

"I'll stay with you. I will," Maia croaked. "Nowhere else to go. Keep's on fire. Can't think enough to make it not burn. No way down." She reached up with trembling fingers, pushing Serenia's grip tighter around the Snapstone. "Go."

Pulling her hand free from Maia's grasp, Serenia returned the Snapstone to its pouch. With a grunt of effort, she hefted Maia to her feet and forced her to take her shoulder for support. The world tipped and bobbed with each labored step. "You're heavier than you look."

"Put me down. I hurt so many people. I hurt you. I have to answer for it."

"Right now, you need to survive, so I can be extremely upset with you later."

As they neared the edge of the roof where the flames were thinnest, the keep quaked beneath them. Maia hoped that before the whole castle collapsed, Serenia would have the good sense to abandon her, like she should have done long ago.

The quaking grew louder, closer, more rhythmic. The last thing Maia saw before slipping into darkness was a giant red form stepping through the outer wall of the courtyard, reaching out for them with an open hand.

Chapter 16
Child of Gray

Ash walked alone through the streets of Noctis. She rarely risked leaving the catacombs beneath the Imperial Palace without good reason. That night, she had one.

Rows of tightly packed tenements of identical height and shape spread down either side of the lamp-lit street. Most of Noctis looked like this, a perfectly planned city uniform in its mediocrity, which made finding one's way through the many same-looking white stone avenues something of a chore for most people. Ash wasn't people anymore. The life force she was seeking pulsed wildly, drawing her like a beacon to a particularly bland two-story box of a building.

Ash approached the front door and lowered her hood. At the sight of her, the two armored guards stationed there exchanged glances. One leveled his spear toward her. "You're in violation of curfew. Return to your home," the guard said.

Ash turned to the other guard, a woman who looked to be around the age Ash was when she died. "He doesn't know who I am. Do you?"

She nodded.

"Good. Let him know when he wakes up." Ash slipped inside the reach of the guard's spear and slapped him hard enough to snap his head to the side. He fell back against the door frame and slid to the ground, unconscious. "Might I enter now?"

The remaining guard opened the door and let Ash pass. She followed the pulsing life force up a creaking wooden stairway to the second floor.

After the destruction of the old Valerius estate during the first Behemoth attack, Arcturus chose to live in the most basic housing he could find, using his remaining fortune to fund advances in magical research that might see Serenia restored. The main room of Arcturus' quarters doubled as both a living area and a kitchen, with simple unstained wooden furnishings and no hearth. Arcturus was laid out across the kitchen table, naked to the waist and groaning in agony. Three robed healers, hands glowing with arcane energy as they drew strands from beyond the Veil to weave into spells, stood over Arcturus. Three more slumped on chairs off to the side, sweating and spent.

Ash drifted into the lamplight. "How does he fare?"

One of the seated healers, an older man with thinning hair, rose and approached her. "Mistress, the general has suffered extensive injuries. We've mended his broken ribs, but his spine will take time to restore. It's delicate work."

"I don't have time for delicacy." The healers working on Arcturus backed away. Ash wiped the sweat from his puckered brow, then caressed his cheek. "Home so soon. Did you miss me that much?"

He recoiled as if she had struck him. "Don't lay your hands on me, demon. Leave the healers to do their work."

"Ah, orders. My favorite! But I prefer to give than to receive. Tell me what happened."

Arcturus straightened where he lay, lifting his chin higher. "I'm through with your scheming. I won't be a party to your plans any longer, and neither will Serenia."

Ash sighed. "Why does everything have to be a debacle with you?" She gripped Arcturus' forehead. His eyes rolled back into his head, showing bone white as he fought against her efforts. The runics grafted to his bones stopped her from reaching deep enough to render him a slave to her will, but she could still take what she needed from his memories.

Plunging into his mind, she weaved through the cracks before he had time to resist. Ash grabbed hold of a moment that looked interesting and followed the thread tied to it. She saw Serenia walking through the courtyard of Castle Blackwood from Arcturus' vantage point along the parapet. Then, their confrontation in Salvian's office. She felt the pounding in Arcturus' chest as the base commander raised his weapon and aimed it at their daughter.

She continued down the thread to a rooftop alive with blazing fire. Ash took her time, reveling in every second of Arcturus' bout with Sunder. Arcturus' metal hand clamped around Sunder's throat, drawing the fire inside her into a set of runes designed to drain and contain magic for later use.

Foolish, Ash thought, projecting her words into Arcturus' mind. *We'll deal with that problem shortly. But first...*

Deeper, she found the figment of Arcturus driving his sword through Sunder's stomach. She reeled. She expected Arcturus to feel some satisfaction as he dealt the fatal blow to his enemy. Instead, the whole memory was stained with thick, bitter regret.

Then came the explosion. Ash released Arcturus before he struck the edge of the parapet. No use experiencing that pain if she didn't have to. She could piece together what happened next.

"You almost had her," Ash said. "I wonder how you would have fared if I hadn't softened her up for you."

Arcturus thrashed and cried out. "You violate me, witch!"

"Not yet, but I'm about to." Ash beckoned the six healers closer. "Come, brothers. Join hands." The healers formed a circle around Ash and Arcturus. "Good. Now, close your eyes, and pray."

"Pray?" one of the healers said. "Our power does not come from prayer, mistress."

"Oh, I know. I just thought you might like to let your maker know that you're on your way to meet them."

Ash grabbed the closest healer by the throat with one hand and Arcturus' living arm with the other. The healers screamed in chorus as an orange glow ripped through them, traveling from body to body. She focused the stolen life force into Arcturus' spine, pulling together and mending fragments of bone and sinew until he was whole again.

She released the healer and blew on his cheek. The desiccated, hollow remains of the man, along with his five brethren, crumbled to dust at her feet.

"I hope you appreciate the gift. You're so hard to shop for."

Arcturus rolled onto his feet. He grabbed the edge of the table with his Black-steel hand and hurled it aside, splintering it against the wall. "If you ever befoul me with your dark magics again, you bloody abomination, I will end you. Do you understand me?"

"Demon. Witch. 'Bloody abomination.' Settle on a pet name, would you?"

Ash waved him away. "Necromancy from 'healers' is fine, but when I do it, I'm a monster. Get dressed. We have one more thing left to attend to tonight."

"What? Murdering orphans? Defiling a church? Perhaps a blood sacrifice?"

"Those are all wonderful ideas, but save them for the new moon. I thought we might stop you from exploding and taking thousands of lives."

Arcturus followed her gaze down to the blazing runes on his arm. Ash picked up one of the healer's dusty cloaks from the floor, shook it off, and pushed it into Arcturus' chest. He slipped it on, unable to take his eyes off the searing brands on his arm as she hurried him from the room.

She led Arcturus back down the same-looking streets the way she came, back to the sheer-faced mountain at the center of Noctis and the white stone palace perched atop it. They ignored the gatehouse and the long, winding road extending up and around to the palace's garden high above and instead ventured into a thick copse of dark trees at the back of the mountain.

When they arrived at a familiar boulder, Ash reached down inside herself and found the magic she needed. She flicked her wrist. The boulder lifted without a sound. She guided Arcturus beneath it and into the catacombs.

They jogged through the twisting tunnels, passing shelves dug into the walls that held the bones of long-deceased Nocteans. She felt Professor's presence long before he drifted from his laboratory at the end of the tunnel. Ash turned left, pushing through a thick metal door to one of the many expansive steel-lined bays strewn throughout the catacombs. The echo of her boots clicking on the railed catwalk disappeared into the thick blackness below.

Professor floated to her side as they crossed onto a wide platform, set against the wall halfway between the floor and ceiling. "I have news from the Spymaster."

"Shh. Busy." Ash motioned for Arcturus to join her. "You've done a very silly thing, absorbing some of Sunder's power. It's not properly bonded to your body, and your arm isn't a suitable container. We need to release what you took."

With beckoning gestures, Ash drew out the flames sealed in those troublesome runes. Blazing lines drifted in arcs, gathering into a compressed orb that pulsed and glowed like a tiny sun.

She aimed the sphere at the darkness at the end of the bay and gave the orb a nudge. A roaring conflagration tore from the sphere, bringing light to darkness.

Flames swirled and screeched for several moments, then died as quickly as they came, leaving behind the tangy smell of hot metal.

"She had that much power within her?" Arcturus said.

"That, and more," Ash said. "Strands of magic, drawn from beyond the Veil and put to purpose, are like drops of water. Complex woven spells, like the ones sealed in your enchanted arm and the ones that grant Pilots their other gifts, are closer to puddles.

"Each Pilot is bonded with a sliver of pure, primordial magic, attuned to a specific element. A slice of infinity from beyond the Veil. It acts as a conduit, allowing a Pilot to channel magic at will without the need for incantations. If strands are droplets and spells are puddles, then a sliver is a channel to the ocean, connected to all the water in the world. You carved a piece of that channel. You're lucky I was able to draw it out of you and release it before you made a mess everywhere. Though…"

"What?"

"It's not the worst thing. A Pilot's intrinsic magics are strengthened by the presence of a sliver. A diminished sliver will still act as a conduit, but a smaller one. It will weaken her other gifts. This might provide the advantage we need."

"Does Serenia have a sliver of fire inside her, as well?"

"Yes. And no. You don't have to worry about her. She's—" Ash became aware of Professor's piercing gaze.

The Kith slipped his hands into the sleeves of his robes. His blue nostrils flared. "I have news from the Spymaster," he repeated.

"Oh, yes." Ash leaned back on the railing. "Now that the night's entertainment has concluded, please. Regale us with the Spymaster's news."

"Scarlet was seen leaving Castle Blackwood for Whitehorn with your daughter and the Pilot. Sunder survived." An opened letter floated from his sleeve and into Ash's hand.

Ash's head bobbed from side to side as she considered the news. On one hand, Sunder's survival meant everything they were working toward was in jeopardy. On the other hand, Ash had another opportunity to draw out her punishment.

"News of the Brave Dawn attack on Castle Blackwood will circulate through the Empire and to the surrounding nations," Professor continued. "The Spymaster has seen to it."

Not that it would accomplish anything. It was all posturing. A way to guilt
Serenia into returning. There was no time to organize a sufficient force and make
good on their idle threat to invade the Freelands. The Aperture would open far
sooner, and once the Exodus began, petty squabbles over land would no longer
matter.

Ash's blood would run out just beyond that day, according to Professor's
faultless calculations. She had done well by taking control of the Emperor's mind
and bidding him to provide Professor with all the labor and materials he needed.
The Kith would save Ash. Assuming, of course, that Professor remained true to
his word.

"The situation has become too complex. We must recall the vessel," Professor
said.

Gritting her teeth, Ash hid her tension behind a forced smile. "We have time.
I'm not ready to pull them apart just yet. Serenia is in the best position to finish
Sunder off if our trap fails." Ash crossed her arms. "We need the rest of the
Behemoths I requested."

"The last one we deployed was defeated in minutes. A great waste of resources."

"I'm sorry. I must have somehow given the impression that I was asking. This
trail requires more breadcrumbs. Bring them. She'll follow. Don't worry."

"We will squander no more resources. Sunder is weakened. Go to Whitehorn,
kill the Pilot, and retrieve the vessel."

Attempting to attack Sunder directly had almost ruined everything. She
wouldn't repeat that mistake. "No. You'll do as I say. And if you don't, I'll release
the Emperor from my thrall. You can explain to him yourself what those five
towers you've been building around Noctis are for."

"If you persist in this foolishness," Professor said, "I will end our agreement.
You are aware of what that entails."

She was. A lost soul could only be brought back and stitched back into its
body once. When a soul passed back through the Veil for the second time, the
soul didn't return to the sweet hereafter for a peaceful, eternal rest. It was drawn
back with the speed of a cannonball. As it crossed the Veil, the soul would be rent
apart. Destroyed. And that would absolutely happen to Ash once her replacement

blood lost its potency, causing her unliving body to decay until she died for good.

But if a soul was removed from its body and placed in another, a person could cheat death an infinite number of times if they had the means to repeat the process.

The Kith had the means. So long as Ash kept up her end of their bargain, removing Sunder as a threat and ensuring Noctis cooperated with the construction of the Aperture, she would soon have the means as well.

She wasn't about to let Professor ruin that for her. "Go ahead, then. End our alliance. Watch as I finish the war between the Pilots and the Kith with a flick of my wrist. You stand to lose much more than I do."

"I do not find your bluff amusing."

"You don't find much of anything amusing." Ash placed her hands on his shoulders, pulling him closer to the ground and looking him deep in his blood-red eyes. "You don't have anything to worry about. Get me those Behemoths. I'll recall Serenia when the time is right, and then you can be the true savior of the Kith like you always wanted, and I can have my life back. We all win, so long as you get me what I want."

Before Professor could respond, a mighty roar rippled through the walls and vibrated the platform beneath them. From a door at the other end of the bay, a wide-eyed guard ran across the catwalk, clutching a Farspeaker in his trembling fingers.

Ash grinned, happy for the distraction. She released Professor. "How fares my other child?"

The guard, a fresh-faced young man, wiped his sweat-laden brow. "Uh, mistress, you see, it—"

"He," she corrected, squeezing his pauldron.

"Yes. He. Uh, as you can hear, he's...unhappy today."

"You don't say." She patted him on the shoulder, and he jumped, startled by the sudden movement.

They crossed through several connected bays, all identical to the one where she had released Arcturus' stolen fire. The electric lights that lined the walls cut out just beyond the walkway in the final bay. There, high above in the black expanse, a red strip of bright light sliced the dark.

The red light bobbed as a towering shape rushed toward the platform, filling the air with the thunder of heavy steps and grinding metal. The shape stopped at the end of the thick chains binding him, just shy of the light's touch. His titanic, pained roar reverberated through Ash's chest.

"Your mistake remains ornery," Professor said. "I maintain that we should destroy it."

"*Our* mistake, Professor. If he's ornery, it's as much your fault as it is mine. But don't fret. He just needs his mother's touch." Ash approached the edge of the platform and reached for the giant in the dark. As he knelt, his head slipped into the light.

Though she meant for him to take the form of a mighty knight in shining silver, Ash's second child, Slate, was an imperfect thing, all awkward angles and jutting edges of drab gray metal. He resembled a misshapen cross between a lizard and a man, with wide gnashing jaws, long, clawed limbs, and a segmented tail that trailed behind him in the darkness. His visor, a long, jagged strip of hardened glass, was red when it should have been black.

In many ways, Slate was a disappointment. That didn't mean he was useless. Every gambler needed a hidden card up their sleeve. Slate, flawed as he was, would be hers.

She reached out to him, working with what semblance of a mind he still had, and compelled him to be calm. The intense resentment flowing from the hulking form ceased.

"The Kith are fleshcrafters," Professor said. "Working with living metal is blasphemy. It is not where our strengths lie. You are lucky that this *thing* functions at all."

"I do feel lucky. Now, go see about the Behemoths I requested, won't you?"

Professor gave Slate one last hateful look, shuddered, and drifted from the room. Arcturus paced the catwalk, staring daggers at Ash as if there wasn't a three-hundred-foot-tall mass of metal and barely contained rage looming over them.

"Out with it, then," Ash said.

His Blacksteel arm swept across the bay. "Why do you need Scarlet when you have this...thing? Professor is right, much as I'm loathe to admit it. End this nonsense. Use this abomination, remove Scarlet as a threat, and bring my daughter back to me!"

The thought had crossed her mind. At that moment, Sunder was vulnerable. A quick, decisive attack on Whitehorn and the deed would be done.

Though Slate was more than a match for Scarlet, his wild nature made him difficult to control. Once she set him loose on Whitehorn, there would be no way to stop him from razing the entire city. That put Serenia at great risk.

The only way Ash could guarantee Slate's compliance was to bond with him. She wasn't in a rush to make that pact until she had no other options available to her. From what Professor told her, it wouldn't be a pleasant process.

"Arcturus, you forget. I'm doing this for you," Ash said. "For us. We deserve our revenge. Sunder will die, I promise you that. But before she does, I want her destroyed."

"I don't want revenge. I want my daughter! The longer Serenia stays by Maia's side, the more danger she faces. She could have died at Castle Blackwood! If you don't care for her, then remember what purpose she serves! Without her, you'll never live again!"

Ash flexed her taloned fingers at her sides. "You need to follow orders, little soldier. I may not be able to control your mind with all those runics lining your skull, but that doesn't mean I can't hurt you. I can work her memories. I can make sure she never remembers a single thing about you. Better yet, I can make her hate you. I can twist her memories until you're nothing more than a monster to her. If you thought losing Serenia was painful the first time, perhaps losing her a second time will—"

She caught Arcturus' hand, stopping the knife an inch from her chest. Which of the guards had he taken it from? "I'm actually not sure if a knife to the heart would even hurt me," Ash said, leaning in closer. "I don't know if I ever told you, but when Scarlet broke me, I didn't die right away. There was a moment, a few seconds, perhaps, where I was aware of every shattered part of my ruined body. I've returned from the grave stronger than I was. Pain is nothing but an inconvenience to me, now. Do you think you can end me with a simple knife? I almost want you to try. But what if you succeeded? Who would stop the Kith if they decided to break our contract? Do you believe Serenia is up to the task of defending the world by herself?"

Ash let go of his hand, inching forward so the tip of the knife pressed against her breast. "Kill me if you think you can. Doom Serenia. What use do the Kith have for her when I'm gone?"

The knife shook in Arcturus' hand. He wouldn't meet her gaze. After a long moment, he cried out and threw the blade past Ash's head and over the railing.

"Good," Ash said. "Back to business, then. Keep your Farspeaker close. Serenia will likely try to contact you to see if you're well. Don't answer. Give her some time to worry for your health. She'll be more pliable when you finally make contact."

"And what shall we discuss when she calls, my daughter and I?" Arcturus asked. "How I've lied to her? How I've betrayed her?"

"You're going to remind Serenia that her mission is to put a fucking bullet in Sunder's head and bring Scarlet back to us."

Arcturus' eyes met hers. "She won't do it. She can't. She's not... It can't be her that does it."

"Give her a reason. Perhaps the truth of her mother's demise will motivate her. After the massacre at Castle Blackwood, Serenia has seen who Sunder really is. She will believe you. If it results in her pulling the trigger, wonderful! Our problems are solved. If not, we'll lead Sunder into our trap as planned. Either way, the work will be done. Go home for now. You've done well. Rest, and think of how wonderful it will be to have our daughter back when this is all over."

When Arcturus and his slumped, defeated shoulders had left her, Ash turned her attention to Slate. She laid her cold hand on him again. As soon as she connected with her child, he sent Ash an image of his clawed fist slamming down onto the platform, pulping her and leaving nothing but a smear behind.

Without me, you have no purpose, she thought. *You'll stay where you are, buried in the dark, forgotten in this metal tomb.* Ash showed him what that would look like. She expected him to throw another tantrum. To her surprise, the gray giant lowered his head and retreated, each pounding step taking him further back into the darkness.

It had been a good day for gambling. Ash had pressed her luck multiple times and won every exchange. If she had failed to cow Professor, or Arcturus, or Slate, any one of them could have shattered what remained of her plans. She allowed herself a moment to bask in victory. Soon, Ash would have the means to regain the life she lost.

Unfortunately, Serenia wouldn't survive the process. Two consciousnesses, two souls, simply couldn't inhabit the same vessel. Once Professor transferred Ash's essence into her daughter's body, the parts of Serenia that mattered most would cease to be. But so long as Arcturus still believed that she and Serenia would be sharing her body, he would do whatever she asked of him.

The pang in her chest, the first real emotion she had felt since her reanimation that wasn't rage or grim satisfaction, didn't surprise her. It did, however, bother her. Arcturus was a good man, despite the evil he had been forced to commit in the Emperor's name. And Serenia was, for lack of a better word, innocent. Neither of them deserved the fate she had in store for them.

Then again, Ash didn't deserve her fate, either. Nobody should have to die twice. If she couldn't return to the afterlife, then at least she could cling to her second life, miserable as it was.

I'm a victim, Ash told herself as she left the bay, letting bubbling rage seep through every part of her until the pang of guilt was replaced with the anticipation of the sweet, bloody revenge that awaited her.

Chapter 17
Mending

Broken waves slapped against Maia's bare knees. She worked her toes deeper into the sandbar until her feet were rooted in the earth while the chill of the ocean waters numbed her skin and worked its way into her bones.

Her lover would return soon. And when he did, she would take him to her favorite spot: a pristine, secluded pool on a plateau high in the Sinadaria Mountains, but not so high that the Sinadarian elves would notice them. With a bit of her fire magic, she would transform the pool into a pleasant hot spring.

Maia's flames surged within her, attempting to protect her from the ocean's bite. She held them at bay. The chill of the ocean was the only thing Maia liked about Kaldrsteinn, whose elevation left most of the nation locked in frigid winter even in the spring months. It was one of the few places in the world she could still feel cold, like a normal person. She often had to go to great lengths to remember what that was like. If she stayed long enough among the waves, maybe they would wash away her sins and leave her better, purer than she was.

As if anything could wash the blood away.

A lithe form breached the ocean's surface and stood upon the water as if it was solid ground. He rode the waves back to her, arms crossed over his scarred chest, a long blond braid draped over one shoulder. He smiled at Maia, a wicked grin full of promises, and her heart jumped in her chest. When he reached her, he took her up in his arms, turning her about as he stepped from the water and onto the shore.

Just as Maia couldn't be burned, Edgar Ragnarson, the Black Pilot of Water, would never drown or freeze. He put her down and brushed her hair from her eyes. Maia grabbed the back of his neck, pulling his mouth down onto hers. When her fire met his frost, she could almost hear a hiss rising from somewhere deep within them.

When they separated, Edgar laughed and led her away from the beach. That wasn't right. He hadn't laughed. Maia had said something playful about his dive taking too long, and he had snarled at her. Called her "woman." Ruined the whole day. They spent the rest of the afternoon sitting in the hot spring in silence, spending far too much energy ignoring each other.

But today, Edgar laughed. Even if she didn't miss him, she wished she could hear him laugh again.

Someone barred the path ahead. She wore brown leathers lined with fur, worn and scratched from use, and clutched a leaf-tipped spear made for hunting boar. Her jet-black hair lay in the elaborate braids of her father's people, the elves who lived high atop the cloud-piercing Sinadaria Mountains. She had her human mother's blue eyes, eyes that shone with a danger that made Maia's knees weak.

This wasn't right, either. This wasn't how they met.

Maia floated away from Edgar, away from his quick temper and childish moods. She drifted toward the huntress, slowly at first, then faster, hurtling like a cannonball. That part was just like she remembered. Once she started falling for her, Maia couldn't stop.

A hand gripped Maia's wrist and spun her around. Edgar loomed over her, his hands changing shape until they were thick and huge, like the pincers of a deep-sea crab. He brought a claw down on her, knocking her to the ground. He battered her chest, over and over, screaming of betrayal and calling her every name he could think of.

A primal scream tore from Maia's throat. She threw Edgar off and mounted him. She thrust her hands out, and fire poured from them, covering Edgar like a blanket.

As he burned, his body contorted and shifted. He became something else, something that screamed from each of its fang-lined mouths. The creature flailed its many long, barbed lashes, cutting deep into her skin. Flames screeched from Maia's palms until her own cries drowned them out, and all that remained was a black silhouette edged in orange and yellow and red.

"Maia." The voice was too musical, too gentle to belong to her nightmares.

When her blurry vision cleared, Maia was staring into Elizabeth Barlowe's deep brown eyes, heavy and rimmed with worry.

"She's awake! Go! Get Ren!" Elizabeth said to a boy standing guard by the door. His footsteps echoed down the hall as he rushed down the stairs.

Wood stairs. Wood walls. A straw pillow wrapped in a linen sheath. This wasn't Scarlet's cabin. Maia thrashed, pushing herself away from Elizabeth and flattening against the wall.

"No!" Maia cried. "I can't be out here! I can't…" She shut her eye so tight it ached. She remembered now. Her right eye wouldn't open, not just because it was covered with a thick bandage, but because she didn't have a right eye anymore.

She bit back her tears. She wasn't about to break in front of Elizabeth.

Elizabeth broke for both of them, laughing as she cried. "It's okay, Maia. You're safe, in Whitehorn. You're back."

"Oh." Maia got a better look at Elizabeth. A white cloth sling pulled her left arm against the laced bodice and simple white blouse she wore. She had a finely stitched gash over her left eyebrow. "Are you okay?"

"I got a little banged up during our escape. We wouldn't have made it out without you. Do you remember? You came to rescue me."

"I came to rescue you." Maia choked on her own breath at the memory of the red flash ripping through the side of her face as that horrible night returned to her. "How long?"

"Seven days. You've been asleep since Ren brought you back. Well, mostly. You woke up twice. Do you remember?"

Maia shook her head.

"You were shaking. You spit up blood. Ren said it's happened before."

Maia nodded. "Since before I returned to Bracken. More, over the last year."

Elizabeth's lips pinched into a thin, disapproving line. "You should have told me. Do you know what's causing it?"

"No. Whatever it is, there's no cure."

"Oh, Maia." She reached out to touch Maia's scarred cheek. Maia didn't move to stop her, steeling herself so she wouldn't flinch. The warmth from Elizabeth's fingers drifted through her, making her dizzy.

Elizabeth's features softened. "I'm so, so sorry," she said. "This is my fault."

With only one eye, Maia's aim wasn't what it had been. She carefully reached out and touched the underside of Elizabeth's chin, gently nudging her face so that their eyes met. "Noctis did this to me. And to you. You're not to blame."

"No. You were right. I shouldn't have run off to play soldier. What was I thinking?"

"You were thinking that people needed help, so you helped. That makes you the bravest woman I know. If you still want to use a sword, I'll show you how after this is all over."

"I thought I was your apprentice?" The sound of Serenia's voice sent a jolt through Maia's heart. The bags under her eyes were as dark as her raven hair, which she had tied up in a messy bun in lieu of the perfect crown of braids she usually wore.

"Princess." Maia settled back against the wall. "Are you okay?"

"I am, thanks to you," Serenia moved to Maia's bedside and handed her a carved wooden mug from the end table. Maia tipped it to her lips.

Water. She was hoping for wine. She drank deep anyway, surprised at how thirsty she had become.

Elizabeth stood and offered her stool to Serenia. Maia wanted to reach for her and tangle their fingers together, anything to keep them from ever separating again. There would be time, later, to say all the things she had been too much of a coward to say.

On her way out, Elizabeth stopped by the door. "Thank you. For coming for me. Whether you think so or not, you're a hero, Maia. You're *my* hero. And you always will be."

When Elizabeth left, Maia's face hardened to match Serenia's dour expression. The girl had seen the real Maia, the furious, rage-fueled engine of death designed to bring ruin to everything she touched. There was no point in hiding behind fake smiles any longer. Not with her. "How did we get back to Whitehorn?"

"The keep was crumbling beneath us," Serenia said. "I considered leaping for the moat. I wasn't confident we would make it. Kas left a backup grapnel on the roof, but I panicked and forgot about it in the moment. He's fine, by the way. He says you threw him?"

"I did. Yeah."

"He came to help me, you know. You should be kinder to him."

"Mmm." Maia couldn't deny that she felt a small bit of relief knowing that Kasper had survived.

"At any rate," Serenia continued, "the keep collapsed. We fell. Scarlet saved us. She smashed through the outer wall and caught us halfway to the ground. Then, she led the refugees and Brave Dawn fighters back to Whitehorn. Since then, she's been standing guard, just beyond the gates, while you've been sleeping. You'll have to tell me how you managed to control Scarlet while unconscious. I wasn't aware you could do that."

Neither was I, Maia thought. *Because it's not possible.* Had Serenia formed a connection to Scarlet deep enough to allow her to guide the Vanguardian from outside the control beam? Had Maia guided Scarlet in her sleep?

Or had Scarlet moved on her own?

Maia cleared her throat and changed the subject, not wanting to worry Serenia with the possibility that Scarlet might be breaking free of her Pilot's control. "How many made it back?"

Serenia exhaled slowly. "More than half of the refugees and Brave Dawn fighters. Many of the survivors were injured. Some may never fight again."

"Is Noctis planning a counterattack?"

"I don't know. I haven't made contact with the Empire. As per your wishes." Serenia shifted in her seat, pulling one knee up to her chest and hugging it.

"They'll come. This is the excuse the Emperor's been waiting for. What about the dragon? Did you find out anything?"

"Nothing we didn't already know. It was a green dragon. It defeated the Behemoth too quickly for anybody to get a close look at it and left immediately after, according to Tobias. I'm told he was the one who saved Elizabeth during the escape. I already thanked him on your behalf." A frown settled on her tired face as she looked Maia up and down. "How are you feeling?"

Maia went still and let her pain tell her its tale. Her broken ribs had mostly mended. Her gut still ached from being ran through with a longsword. The wound had closed but hadn't fully healed, same as the stab wound in her shoulder. Maia reached up and touched the bandage wrapped around her eye. She bowed her head, lifted the wrapping, and felt around beneath it. Maia winced. The bone of her eye socket and the skin around it had been restored, but the recess was hollow. Empty.

"Arcturus did something to me," Maia said. "I felt him taking my fire. Something's wrong. I'm not healing like I should."

"I'm sorry for that. And for all you've suffered. Truly. I pray your powers return in earnest with time." Serenia inched the stool closer and released her knee. "There probably isn't an opportune time for this, but we do need to talk."

Maia straightened against the wall. "Yeah. Okay."

"You broke your promise."

Maia thought for a moment. "You'll have to be more specific."

"You hurt my father." Serenia's hands tightened around the edge of the stool. "I don't know how badly he's injured, or even if he still draws breath. You promised you wouldn't hurt any Nocteans, and you did anyway."

"I wish there had been another way, but there wasn't. Not one I could see. He wasn't about to let us go, and I wasn't going to leave you." Maia reached up and untied her bandage. Serenia looked away. "Look at me. I want you to look at me. See this?" She pointed to her lost eye. "They can hurt me, Princess. They have a weapon that anybody with a working trigger finger can use to kill me." She let the back of her head thud against the wall. "I was hurt and scared. I lost myself. I'm sorry for the Nocteans I killed, for the Brave Dawn fighters and refugees who died, and for hurting your father. But I don't seem to recall you asking him not to hurt me."

Serenia peered sidelong at her. "I didn't think he would harm you. I didn't think anybody could. I don't think he meant to kill you. His blade missed your vitals."

"How very fucking kind of him."

"Well, it wouldn't have happened if you had trusted me to negotiate."

Maia crossed her legs and leaned forward. "You walked into a trap. If I hadn't been there, you and Scarlet would be back in Noctis right now, and a lot more people would be dead."

"For all we know, you were discovered before I arrived!"

"Or maybe, we would have made it in and out safely if you hadn't waltzed in with Scarlet and woke up the whole castle." Maia forced her shoulder muscles to loosen. "Did you hear what I said to your father when we were fighting?"

Serenia nodded.

"And Salvian. Did you ask him about Aquila?"

"I did."

"Look. I don't care if you believe any of it. My sister's death. My father's murder. Arcturus ordering Salvian to wipe out a whole village. Or the fact that Nocteans still practice necromancy in secret. All I care about is making sure you don't go down the same road I did. This?" Maia pointed to her missing eye. "I don't think it's coming back. And you know what? It's a small price to pay. I killed those Nocteans to save innocent lives, including Elizabeth's. I killed Salvian to save you, in more ways than you know. I tried to kill your father to keep him from taking you and turning you into what I used to be, what he still is. What I did will haunt me, and I'm sorry it went the way it did. But if it means saving Elizabeth and saving you, I would do it again in a heartbeat."

Serenia shot to her feet so fast, she knocked her stool over. "You slaughtered my countrymen, killed Salvian, and hurt my father, all for revenge. For yourself. Don't pretend that any of it was for my sake. I didn't ask you for *any* of those things!"

"Then take that gun of yours and do what you need to do." Maia pointed to the weapon with her chin. "Get justice for all the harm I've done. I'm guessing that pistol was made to break my armor, same as that rifle they used on me."

Serenia paused. "It was."

"I wonder when you were going to tell me."

"I never intended to use it on you!"

"I don't know how I'm supposed to believe that. For all I know, you never meant to negotiate the release of the prisoners. Could be, you just went to Castle Blackwood to tell your father what we were up to. I don't have a way of knowing for sure."

"No, you don't!" Serenia said. "And it doesn't matter what I say, does it? You don't trust me. You've *never* trusted me! I don't even know why you took me on as your apprentice! You've never believed in me for one second!"

"Give me a reason to trust you! Tell me that if we keep going, if I keep training you, that you won't bring Scarlet back to Noctis. Tell me, *promise* me, that you'll use her only for what she was intended. To protect the people. Can you promise me that?"

"If I refuse, what happens then? Am I no longer your apprentice?"

"That's exactly what happens. What's it going to be, Princess?"

Serenia kicked the fallen stool into the wall so hard it broke apart. She leaned against the door frame, looking up at the ceiling for a long time before she spoke. "My father lied to me. Perhaps the Emperor has been lying to all of us, and the Empire I love is nothing but a clever deception hiding something dark and sinister. Perhaps everything you've told me is true. Perhaps only some of it is. Either way, I'm a traitor to the Empire for helping Brave Dawn. I can't go back. Not now. Maybe not ever. Not even to see if my father still lives.

"If I'm ever able to return home, I have questions that demand answers. And I intend to get them. Until that day comes, I remain open to the possibility that I may be ill-informed about a great many things. I will make up my own mind, and pick the best course of action to follow, once I have my answers." Serenia pursed her lips and nodded to herself. "That's the best I can offer you. Take it or leave it."

Finally. Progress. "I'll take it."

"I'm sorry I didn't tell you about my revolver. Believe me when I say I was unaware that there were more weapons like it put into service."

"I have to believe that. You're a pain in my ass, Princess, but you've always been honest with me. I'll give you that."

The way Serenia looked away, it was as if the comment stung her. "I'm sorry you lost your eye."

"I'm sorry I broke my promise, and I'm sorry about your father. I hope he survived. Really."

Serenia nodded and made to leave. "Wait," Maia said. There was still one wound that needed tending, an old, festering gash that Maia had put off treating for too long. "There's something else. Something you need to know."

With her stool in pieces in the corner, Serenia sat on the edge of Maia's bed instead. "Have I done something else to displease you?"

"No. No, Princess. It's nothing like that." Maia sighed. "I want to talk about what your father said. About how he didn't blame me for what happened to you and your mother."

"He doesn't. And neither do I. You killed the Behemoth that killed my mother."

"It wasn't the Behemoth." Maia's nails bit into her palms. She let out a shuddering breath. "It was Scarlet. No. It was me." She met Serenia's gaze. "I'm responsible for your mother's death and for what happened to you."

Serenia looked down at her hands. "Is that why you offered to train me?"

"Partly. Yes."

"Hmm." Serenia got up and moved to the door. "I don't want you to feel you need to bear the burden of what happened to my mother. You didn't send that Behemoth to Noctis."

"No, but I—"

"Maia. Please." When she turned, there were tears rimming her eyes. "Shut up and listen to me, for once in your bloody life. I can't be your apprentice if you're only training me out of a sense of obligation. If I am to become Scarlet's Pilot, then it must be because I'm worthy. The world deserves a competent Pilot, and if I'm unable to prove myself capable, I need to know you won't endanger the world out of a sense of lingering guilt for something that wasn't your doing."

Maia wanted to correct her, to make her understand that she *was* responsible, that it was Scarlet who crushed her home, not the Behemoth. If she did that, Serenia would leave. That would accomplish her goal, to dissuade Serenia, to make her understand what Maia already knew, that the Pilots were a mistake. That all they brought was pain, and death, and despair. Training Serenia to take over as Scarlet's Pilot was simply preparing for the worst in case Maia's plan failed.

But that was just another lie. If she really wanted Serenia gone, she wouldn't have rescued her in Galford or climbed to the top of Castle Blackwood to fight for her. There was something there, something more than her guilt and a nostalgic yearning for the days when Maia didn't have to fight monsters alone.

Blue Hells. She really did care for her stuck-up apprentice.

They had both suffered enough for one lifetime. That rotting wound that Maia thought needed tending was nothing but an ugly scar. There was no point in opening it again.

"Okay," Maia said.

"Good. I'll let you get some rest. Tobias has advised the people of Whitehorn to evacuate. He fears Imperial reprisal, and only those who wish to stay and fight are bound to. There are festivities this evening. I'm told that the best way to honor the dead and send off the living in the Freelands is to get 'shit-faced,' as one of the townsfolk so eloquently put it. The main event, I'm told, is taking place at the Goat's Beard."

"The largest tavern in Whitehorn survived. There is a goddess after all, and she loves me."

"Do I need to remind you that you promised to remain sober? Regardless, if you're feeling well enough, you should attend. Kas and I are going together."

Maia arched the eyebrow above her missing eye. "Together?"

"Yes. Together." Serenia beamed, brighter than she had the first time Maia let her pilot Scarlet.

That wasn't a good sign. It made Maia's head ache in new ways. "I'll think about it. Close the door on your way out. I'll yell for someone if I need anything."

Before she left, Serenia reached down to the small of her back, unclasping the damaged holster for her revolver and placing it at the end of Maia's bed.

"I'm leaving this with you," she said. "I want you to feel safe while you recover. Until you feel you can trust me."

Maia said nothing as Serenia left, closing the door behind her. When her apprentice's footsteps faded into distant taps and she was sure she was alone, she reached up and felt around her empty eye socket.

A flash of red. Blood on her hands. Soot coating her body and clogging her throat. Screams. Fire. Unbearable pain. The pressure caught up to Maia, slamming her chest like Arcturus' metal fist.

Her heaving gasps came hard and fast. She lashed out, knocking the terrible purple-hued revolver off the bed so she didn't have to look at it anymore. Maia got her pillow to her face just in time to muffle her wailing cries as she finally allowed herself to break, alone, where nobody could see.

Chapter 18
Dedication

After leaving Maia to her rest, Ren returned to the caravan gathered near what was left of Whitehorn's Freelands-facing gates, where she had been working before the errand boy came to fetch her. Her instructors had told her that Whitehorn was a small village of little importance, nestled between a chain of impassable mountains, where the upstart group known as Brave Dawn skulked and schemed in between cowardly attacks on the Empire. Having spent the last week providing aid to the city, she could see it now for what it really was. Whitehorn wasn't a village of rogues. It was a fine city, woefully unprepared to withstand a full Imperial siege, but a fine city nonetheless, home to a tight-knit community of good, honest people.

Ren knelt and wrapped her arms around one of the many large sacks of grain waiting to be loaded. With all the wreckage cleared and scoured for salvage, and the dead gathered and buried, the only work she could find was preparing for the evacuation. Her muscles protested despite the strength her Pilot awakening had granted her, but she didn't mind the work. It was a Pilot's duty to help those in need, and manual labor, for once, was a welcome distraction.

Without something mundane to focus on, she would have spent the past week worrying about Maia, or her father, who had yet to attempt to contact her through her reassembled Farspeaker.

A man bumped into her, apologized, and veered around. Ren realized she had stopped halfway to the wagon, interrupting the loading line. Her grip loosened on the sack she was hauling. She let it topple from her arms, not caring if it split. Maia was awake. The thoughts Ren had been trying to out-pace all week caught up to her.

She remembered that moment when Maia turned her head, revealing her ruined face. She saw her father laying in a twisted mess against the parapet and the way his face sank when she ran to Maia's aid instead of his, right before he crushed his Snapstone and vanished. The two scenes repeated over and over in her mind, taking root and digging in until there was nothing else.

A pair of hands settled on her shoulders and scattered her worries. A firm, familiar grip started working through the taut kinks in her muscles.

"By the Emperor, that feels amazing." Ren closed her eyes and melted. She turned, looking up at Kas and crinkling her nose in confusion. "You're not Tobias."

Kas smirked, and she melted a little more. She pressed her head into his chest and wrapped her arms around him. He enveloped her, resting his cheek atop her head.

With Maia injured and her father potentially lost to her, nothing felt right anymore. Nothing, except the way Kas held her. The warm smell of his leathers, of dirt roads and fresh grass, mixed with the faint scent of oil and smoke from his week helping in the smithy. The blend filled her head with a haze of sparkling clouds.

When she started to drift away, Ren broke their embrace. "Maia is awake."

"I heard," Kas said. "Figured I'd find you with her."

"We spoke briefly. There's still much to be done. How are you feeling?"

"Movin' a little better." He twisted at the waist. Ren had already apologized for her father stabbing Kas. Thankfully, Kas didn't seem to be one to hold a grudge and admitted he tried to stab her father first, so they were even in his mind.

Kas surveyed the wagons. "I'm sure they can get by for a bit without you. It's not like Noctis'll invade tonight. Why not go wash up? Party's startin' soon."

"Yes. The party. That's something."

"So are you." He took her hand in his. Warm sparks fluttered through her fingers. Ren thought that they would have faded by now, but the sensation was as strong as it had been a week after he first took her hand in his.

It had been so long since anyone had shown her affection. Ren couldn't remember the last time her father held her, and her training back in the Noctis had left little time for suitors. Not that there were any. She didn't realize how starved for touch she had been until that first night back in Whitehorn, where Kas had found Ren by Maia's bedside and tied up her fingers in his own, pulling her up from the pit of grief threatening to swallow her whole.

As they walked, she focused on the warmth of Kas' palm pressed against hers. A moment's relaxation allowed another thought to sneak up on her, one she had avoided confronting. "I would have killed him."

Kas stopped and turned to her, waiting, the line of his brow asking a wordless question.

"Salvian," Ren said. "If Maia hadn't intervened, I would have shot him. I would have destroyed him. And you would be holding hands with a killer."

"But you didn't. And I'm not. Sun saved you."

"Should she have?"

"What are you talkin' about? Of course she should have."

Ren hugged herself. "Perhaps she wouldn't have had to if I had listened to her."

"Maybe. Maybe not. All I know is you're no murderer. Even if you meant to kill Salvian, you were defendin' yourself. And I'm glad you did. I would have done the same in your boots."

"Then you would have blood on your hands, as well."

"Ren." He placed a hand on her shoulder. "I already do."

"Ferals hardly qualify. They're animals. Monsters."

"Not just Ferals. Things haven't always been easy for me, livin' on my own. Sometimes, you have to do things you're not always proud of."

She could see them, now, the same hard facial lines her mother had, born from a practiced scowl. Lines a boy on the edge of manhood shouldn't have.

"Do you regret it?" she asked.

"All the time. And I know Sun does, too. You sure *you're* okay, holdin' a killer's hand?"

"I'm sure you did what you did out of necessity. It must have been difficult." Ren took Kas' hand and turned it over. She traced her fingers over his hardened callouses. "I've only known you a short time, yet I believe you to be a good man."

"I don't think about it that way. I'm not good or bad. I'm a person doing his best. I hope that's enough."

Ren pondered his words. She never denied the fact that her father had taken lives in service of the Empire and her people. Was that any different than what

Brave Dawn was doing? Or what Maia felt she had to do to protect the world?

Good people lived in the Empire. There were also some, like Salvian, who could wipe out entire settlements without losing sleep over it. Likewise, for every scoundrel like her one-eyed kidnapper in Galford, there were heroes like Tobias and Elizabeth and Kas living in the Freelands, people who would risk their own lives to protect others if the need arose.

Then there was Maia. She had saved countless lives during her Pilot career, but in addition to all the Nocteans she had killed at Castle Blackwood, including Salvian, there was still the matter of what happened to the other four Pilots.

If the rumors were true, and they all died by Maia's hand, there must have been a reason why. There had to be. There was goodness in Maia, a sense of purpose and honor beneath all the blood and dirt staining her.

Good and evil. Black and white. Those were the hard lines Ren had been raised to follow growing up in the Noctean Empire, lines that blurred the longer she spent away from home. She snaked an arm around Kas' waist and pulled him in closer, content to have found some solace within the murky gray.

✕

Plucked notes from a well-tuned lute drifted through the night air, blending with drums and the rumble of stomping feet. Ren followed the sound to the Goat's Head Tavern, where the party was already in full swing.

Kas held the door open for her. She responded with a mock curtsy before wading into the bustling tavern. On a raised stage along the far wall, a four-piece band was in the middle of a jaunty tune that brought beer sloshing from the mugs of two Tressille elves who danced, arms linked, across one of the long tables.

One of the elves stopped, nearly toppling as his partner carried on. He knocked the carved wooden mug in his hand against the other elf's head and pointed, directing his partner's gaze to Ren.

The backs of her legs tightened as the two elves marched grim-faced down the length of the table. When they reached her, they lifted their mugs into the air and roared. The crowd around them responded, adding their own voices and mugs to the cheer.

Many of the Brave Dawn's fighters who had approached her over the past week attributed more than a little of the success of Maia's rescue efforts to the distraction Ren created when she marched up to Castle Blackwood in Scarlet. Whether she had made the situation worse or not, the people of Whitehorn viewed her as a hero.

I've earned this, Ren thought. She waved to the crowd. Her heart rose a little bit higher.

"Everyone," one of the elves shouted, "three cheers for the Turncoat Pilot!"

Ren's hand lowered. She forced her smile to remain as her heart broke. By the time the third "hip hip" had been answered, her legs had softened to jelly.

Turncoat. Deserter. Traitor. That's what she feared she had become, and hearing it from the lips of others made it real.

Kas grabbed her hand and led her toward the stairs to the upper floor, where a wide balcony reached around the perimeter of the tavern's common area. "Are you okay?" he asked.

"I am fine," Ren lied.

"They shouldn't be callin' you that. I'm sorry."

They wove through the standing crowd, across creaking wood, to several smaller tables above the stage. When they sat down, Kas dropped Ren's hand so fast she wondered if she had somehow burned him.

Following his gaze to the next table, Ren understood why. Maia sat with her chin in her palm, boring a hole into Kas' skull with all the concentrated ire her one eye could muster. Ren couldn't help but notice the six empty tankards lined up in front of Maia, protecting her like a castle wall. Her lips tightened. It was her turn to glare.

"I've been meaning to ask," Ren called over the clamor of the tavern, "does becoming a Pilot increase your alcohol tolerance? I suspect you're an expert on the subject, as well as the practice of breaking promises."

Maia's mouth curled into an amused grin. She didn't offer a retort. Ren was about to press the issue when a burly man with a curled mustache approached the table, hefting two full tankards of ale.

"Pardon me, Sunder. Evenin'. Wanted to thank you for what you did for us. Mighty brave, and all. And thanks, for everythin' else, really. Big thanks to you."

He thrust the second tankard her way, spilling foamy ale on the rough wooden table.

Maia sat up straight. "No thanks needed. It's a Pilot's duty." She cast a quick glance Ren's way. "I appreciate the offer, but I have to stay sharp in case the Nocteans come back. Would you do the honors?"

The man slapped the tankard against his wide chest in salute, then raised it to his lips, emptying it and slamming it down next to the others on the table. After he stumbled away, Ren found Maia staring at her.

"That's been happening since I got here," Maia said, sweeping her hand over the empty mugs. "I'm sorry. What was your question, again?"

"Let it go, Sun," Kas said. "She's been through a lot."

In the span of a heartbeat, Maia blasted to her feet and cleared the distance between her and Kas.

"You." Maia crossed her arms over her chest, tilting her head back to study him while Ren tensed for whatever violence was coming. "You said you were going to help her, but all you ended up doing was getting yourself stabbed."

She slapped his shoulder. "You bought me enough time to get to her on the roof, though. It doesn't change a bloody thing between us. Still, I appreciate the effort. Thanks, Kasper."

Maia left them at the table and stalked down the stairs to be swallowed by the crowd below. Kas wore a dumbfounded look that somehow made him look even more adorable.

"Kas, I—"

"Hold on. Let me enjoy this for a moment. Sun's never thanked me before." He closed his eyes and smiled. "Okay. I'm good."

They sat at Maia's table, which had a better view of the lower level. Below, Maia worked her way toward the door. Every few steps, she was stopped by some reveler or another. She exchanged a few words with each one, then excused herself, jerking her thumb toward the door.

Maia was trying to leave a room full of people who wanted nothing more than to celebrate her. She had sacrificed for these people. She bloodied her hands for them. She deserved this party, even more than Ren did.

Ren rubbed her face with her hands. She turned to Kas, who canted his head.

"You didn't hear a word I just said, did you?"

"I'm sorry. I'm a little more tired than I thought."

"Right." He leaned closer. "Look, I know you're worried. I've known Sun for years. She's a one-woman army. She can take care of herself. What about you? What's next for you?"

"I aim to continue my training. There's an end to this road we're on. Something Maia wants to show me. I owe it to her and to myself to see this through."

"And what if you don't like what she has to show you?"

Ren shrugged. "I suppose we'll see, won't we? What about you? What are your plans?"

"I've been talkin' to Tobias." Kas slid his chair closer to her and slipped an arm over her shoulder. "He says that if Noctis invades... *When* Noctis invades, havin' contact with Sun is critical. He wants me to go with you when you leave."

Lightning jolted her chest, leaving a warm tingling behind. "With me?"

"Yeah. With you. The road'll be rough, and I figure you could use a friend."

"A friend? Nothing more?"

A hand on Kas' shoulder drew his attention up and away from her as he opened his mouth to speak. Elizabeth smiled down at him. She had brushed out her dark hair and tied it in a simple ponytail that fell near her hips. Even with her arm in a sling and a bandage on her brow, she commanded stares.

Ren hoped that when she grew up, she was half as beautiful.

"Good evening, friends," Elizabeth sang. She eyed the seven empty tankards on the table.

"Gifts for Maia. From the people of Whitehorn," Ren said.

"Is she still here?"

"She's down there. I believe she's headed for the door." Ren pointed to the crowd. "If you hurry, you might be able to catch her."

"Thanks." She looked Kas up and down, winked at Ren, and made for the stairs.

Ren wanted nothing more than to talk to Kas about traveling together, but she couldn't keep her eyes off Elizabeth as she shouldered her way through the crowd.

Elizabeth reached Maia as she neared the door, touching her elbow to catch her attention. When Maia turned, her mask cracked in a way Ren had never seen before. Her face lit up like the morning sun on the first day of spring.

They talked. Elizabeth said something that must have been funny because Maia laughed, covering her mouth with one hand. Her fingers lingered there, half-concealing her parted lips.

Elizabeth took Maia's hand in hers and tried to lead her back to the floor with a gentle tug. Maia shook her head and gestured for the door. A few more tugs and she relented, allowing herself to be pulled back into the crowd.

The song ended, and as the band returned their instruments to their cases and the crowd broke into raucous applause, Maia became a rock and would move no further.

Their fingers slipped free. Maia said something, pushed her hair behind her ear, and turned toward the door.

Ren marched to the balcony railing and vaulted over, landing on the stage in a crouch. She slid onto a still-warm stool and pulled a lute from its leather-bound case. Though Ren's Pilot training in Noctis had taken up almost all her daylight hours, she was still expected to pursue the same classic education as any other noble daughter of the Empire.

That included, among other things, musical instruction. The lute happened to be among the three instruments within her focus.

It was considered rude to use another musician's instrument without permission, but Ren had no time to spare. Maia had bled for her and for Whitehorn. She continued to suffer as an unknown affliction ravaged her body.

If a song was all that was missing for Maia to have one night for herself, one night with the woman she was clearly smitten with, then she would have it.

Ren's fingers curled around the lute's wooden neck. The first few notes she plucked formed the beginning of a distinct melody. Her music tutor had taught her the ballad in private, remarking that while it was an important piece of history, and relevant to her Pilot studies, Ren was cautioned against ever playing it in public for two reasons.

First, it wasn't permitted in Noctean courts and thus had no value beyond curiosity. Second, it was an incredibly difficult song, technically demanding and unforgiving. Even attempting to play it in front of an audience was considered arrogant.

It also happened to be exactly what Ren needed to turn the night around.

The din of the tavern settled beneath her. Across the room, Maia turned. She must have recognized the tune. Ren's fingers continued their intricate dance across the lute's strings. When she opened her mouth to sing, she worried the pounding of her chest would force her voice to emerge as a croak.

But when she sang, dozens of other voices from the crowd joined hers. "Strider on the Winds" was a favorite of the Free People in their taverns, though most lutenists favored a much simpler variation that almost any player could perform. It was time to show the people of Whitehorn the song's true form. She picked up her pace, heart swelling and pouring out through her fingers and lips like the rising wind the ballad was meant to evoke.

The song's prelude told the story of Amisrala Illandres, the Green Pilot of Wind, and the day she and Emerald, the Green Eagle Vanguardian, single-handedly defeated three Behemoths. It was customary to pause after the prelude, to give the listener time to settle while giving the lutenist time to rest their fingers.

Whatever was gripping Maia's heart and stealing her life had struck twice that week. There was no time for pauses. Life moved ever forward, often violently. Ren would keep pace however she could.

She swept into the first verse, introducing the first of Amisrala's foes, a massive worm Behemoth. For every mistake Ren made in her fingering, she repeated it in the next measure, masking it as an artistic choice. Not that anyone noticed. By the time she reached the chorus, with its pounding rhythm and simple repeated refrains, the whole tavern was dancing and shouting. Elizabeth had coaxed Maia back onto the floor, and they lightly moved to the rhythm, mindful of their injuries.

At the end of the chorus, Ren saw a flicker of movement out of the corner of her eye. Kas had taken the stool next to her. With sticks in hand, he followed her lead on a large drum as she sped into the second verse, the most demanding part of the song.

With one foe defeated, Amisrala had to face the two remaining Behemoths simultaneously. In the truest rendition of the ballad, this required the lutenist to play two blending melodies at once. The crowd roared and stomped. The tavern rumbled. A bald man in a torn tunic climbed onto the stage, threw his hands into the air, and leaped back into the shifting mass. Many hands held him aloft and carried him over the crowd. He disappeared somewhere near the bar to the sound of breaking wood and more cheers.

The muscles in her wrists ached and pleaded for rest. At least two of her fingertips were bleeding. Ren had pushed too far. If she faltered, the crowd wouldn't think any less of her. She had done more than anyone expected already, but it wasn't enough. The daughter of General Arcturus Valerius didn't surrender. Not while there was greatness within her grasp.

She drove into the chorus once more and let the crowd carry the lyrics. Halfway through, she turned to Kas and bobbed her head slowly. He nodded, matching her tempo as she gradually let up speed. The crowd adjusted to the subtle shift. The pounding of feet became a low rumble through the tavern floorboards.

The chorus ended, and Ren let the song drop to the floor. Whispers rode the wave of quiet rolling through the room. Ren tensed against a shiver and flowed into the final verse alone, her voice expanding to take up the space the people of Whitehorn left open for her.

Amisrala and Emerald were on the verge of ruin. One Behemoth remained standing. Ren drew out each note, giving herself time to recover. A rush of relief fluttered through her aching hands.

Red-faced couples, sweaty from carousing, leaned on each other for support. Ren's heart flared in her chest when she spotted Elizabeth resting her head on Maia's shoulder. The pair swayed to the gentle rhythm. Maia stood rigid, as if she had been struck by lightning. Eventually, her posture softened, and she folded her arms around Elizabeth.

When her strength returned, Ren began her ascent. Kas struck a marching beat to match. The march became a canter, then a full gallop. Ren stood and balanced the lute on her knee, shouting the words of the final verse at the top of her lungs. The tavern answered her call to war. Clapping in time, they followed her all the way to Amisrala's triumphant victory over the final Behemoth, roaring all the way.

She picked up speed, strumming and plucking so fast she worried she would break a string. The crowd's fervor lifted her higher. Ren crashed into the chorus one last time, easing off at the very end and leaving Kas' steady beat and the crowd's chanting to bring them the rest of the way. When it was over, she spread her arms and let their applause roll over her like an avalanche, burying her completely.

"Thank you ever so much, Whitehorn!" Ren shouted. "I must offer my apologies to the owner of this lute. Please see me if you would care for some lessons." When the crowd's laughter faded, she found herself wanting more. More laughter. More cheers. For herself and for Maia. "I believe I can muster another song if you'll indulge me. What do you say, Whitehorn?"

She reveled in their enthusiastic stomping reply and settled back down on her stool. Though it wasn't as impressive a composition as "Strider on the Winds," when it came to Pilot ballads, Ren always preferred "The Chosen Five," chiefly because it gave each Pilot their due and ended with Sunder, the mightiest of them all.

That would give Maia more time to spend with Elizabeth and a chance to bring the crowd's focus to their attending hero. She couldn't think of a more perfect selection.

Ren picked through the first few notes of the melody. This song was more commonly played than "Strider on the Winds," so she knew the crowd, including Maia, wouldn't be strangers to the tune.

As she wove through the first verse, Ren looked up, eager to gauge Maia's reaction. Maia wasn't there. A path had been carved through the crowd all the way to the door, strewn with fallen, cursing drinkers.

Oh no. Her heart.

Ren left the lute on the stool and flung herself from the stage. She cleared most of the crowd in a single leap, landing near the fallen patrons near the door, and chased Maia out into the night.

Chapter 19
More Broken Promises

The world collapsed around Maia, tumbling toward her in waves of indistinct shape and sound. She bolted through the night, half-running, half-falling. Cutting around corners. Breath coming in haggard gasps. Which way to Scarlet? She needed to get back. The cabin was safe.

Serenia's second song had roused something terrible inside her. Though it was a song about all the Pilots, it was written specifically as a love letter to Maia. A gift from Edgar, given to Dalzin to perform.

Serenia couldn't know it would hurt her. Neither did Maia. She didn't know it would make her so small. Her skin boiled. She needed to leave it behind. Shed it all. The armor, the blood, the memories. It all had to go.

She saw the black claw, hammering her chest, over and over and over and over. She pulled thinning air into her lungs. Not enough to keep her. Maia fell against a wall.

She slid down, down, down. The dirt caught her. Then, she was sitting, heaving.

"Deep breaths." Elizabeth propped Maia up against her chest. She wiped Maia's brow and smoothed her hair with careful fingers.

"It's not the...not my heart. I can't. Scarlet. It's not safe. I need her. I can't."

Elizabeth turned over one of Maia's hands and traced circles in her palm with her fingers. "How does Scarlet work?"

"What?"

"How does she work? What makes her move? Is she alive?"

Maia reached into a haze of half-formed thoughts and found something resembling an answer. "Gears. Magic. They make her joints move. She has a core, in her chest. I think that's 'her.' The rest is a shell."

"A core? Like a soul? What does it look like?"

"A cage of light. She has a sliver of fire, like me, mixed with…something bright. You can't look right at it." Maia swallowed. "Ami showed me once. How to make Scarlet open up and show me."

"Who's Ami? Tell me about her."

"Amisrala. The Green Pilot of Wind. You've heard of her," Maia said. "I was so jealous of her. I can make shields with my Barrier magic. She had the gift of Perception. She could see the way things worked and what people would do before they did it."

Elizabeth gave her hand a squeeze. "How did you meet?"

"The Pilots weren't working together yet. We stuck to our own lands. We were wary. She had been watching me fight and found a way to talk to me through my Vanguardian. She needed me to know that if somehow, Scarlet's core was exposed, and it took a clean hit, it could explode. Scarlet could destroy an entire city. When she reached out to me, to warn me, what I really wanted was a friend, someone like me who could understand. I asked her to have lunch with me, on a cliff in Brimholme, near…"

Maia looked up at Elizabeth. "I'm the first Pilot she removed her armor in front of. She showed me how to dye my hair red. We went for picnics on tall cliffs and… Why are you asking about all of this?"

"How do you feel?"

Maia's breath had returned. Her chest didn't ache as much. The song was gone. She couldn't recall how it went. "I don't know. I just…feel."

"Will you come with me? We can go someplace quiet. Or, I can take you back to Scarlet. I'll stay with you. You don't have to be alone."

Scarlet loomed over the gate at the edge of town. If Maia went back there, Serenia would find her, and she would have to explain herself. Or lie. She wasn't ready to do either.

"I'll go with you," Maia said.

Elizabeth led Maia to a long house divided into smaller units that resembled Noctean apartments. The door to Elizabeth's home creaked as it opened. The main room was about the size of Scarlet's cabin. A simple wooden bed without a headboard or posts was tucked into the back of the room. A small stove sat in the far corner. Her shelves held simple sundries, and a plain knee-height table took up the middle of the room.

Cramped. Confined. Perfect. Maia breathed easier.

"Home, sweet home," Elizabeth untied the front of her leather bodice. "Help me with this?"

Maia loosened the weaving leather cords, removed the bodice, and helped Elizabeth re-tie her sling.

"Much better," Elizabeth said, turning at the hips and adjusting her blouse.

"Maybe you shouldn't wear that until you're healed."

"It makes me feel like my old self. Less like a fool who ran off to play soldier. Care for some tea?"

"Got anything stronger?"

Elizabeth cocked an eyebrow. "Is that a good idea right now?"

Maia wrung her hands together. "It helps with the chest pains I've been having. I doubt you have enough liquor to get a Pilot drunk, anyway. I promise to behave."

Elizabeth went to one of her shelves and returned with a long, tapered bottle of Brackenberry wine. "I brought this with me. I wanted something to remind me of what I left behind, what matters most to me."

"The tavern?"

Elizabeth looked away. Her lips set in a soft smile.

There were no words. The flush of warmth in Maia's cheeks was too distracting. Elizabeth popped the cork and poured some of the sickly black wine into two cups and handed one to Maia.

Maia sat down on the bed, resisting the incredible urge to gulp the whole cup down. She deserved a drink, even if she promised not to have one. Serenia would have to understand. She also didn't need to know about it.

A small sip. Just a taste. The Brackenberry wine was as terrible as Maia remembered. "I'm sorry for driving you away. I know I can be...difficult."

Elizabeth leaned against the shelf, cradling her cup. "It's true that you do piss me off sometimes. I want to knock sense into you on a daily basis. But that's not why I left. I thought this would be best—for the Freelands and for me. And for you. Especially you. I thought you needed a push, so you could find yourself again." She tilted her cup and grimaced at it. "And here I am, helping you slide back into bad habits. I'm sorry. I shouldn't be—"

"Elizabeth, I'm dying."

Maia downed the rest of the wine in her cup. She reached for the open bottle and chugged until only a little remained.

Elizabeth put her cup on the table, sat next to Maia on the bed, and waited.

"It's my heart," Maia said. "It started about four years ago. After the other Pilots... After that. I felt this sharp pain in my chest. Like fingers squeezing and tearing my insides. It was a year until it happened again. And a year after that. After my father was murdered and I left Bracken, it started happening more often. Since I've been back in Bracken over the last year, it's been every month. Now, it's more than once a week."

"You said before, at the inn, that you don't know what's causing it?" Elizabeth said.

Maia shrugged her uninjured shoulder. "I've been all over the Freelands. Healers don't know what's wrong with me. Serenia knows something is wrong. And others have seen it. I can't hide it anymore. Whatever's happening to me, I think I deserve it."

"I know it feels that way. You must know, deep down, that that isn't true. Right?"

"I deserve it," Maia said. The Pilots. Serenia's mother. Salvian. So many Nocteans. Countless people she had crushed by accident or failed to save. Maia had to pay for them all, eventually.

She lifted a leg onto the bed and turned to Elizabeth. "I wanted to work on my family's vineyard and stain my hands and feet purple making bad wine. I wanted to wear dresses, grow my hair long, and settle down with a nice girl. I never wanted to pick up a sword. Heretic, the one who did this to us, never asked what we wanted. She put vengeance in my blood. Remade me into a weapon to fight her war. And that's what I'm for. That's all I'm for. I want to quit and leave it all behind, but I can't. Either I kill every Behemoth they send until they have none left, or they kill me. There's no other way this ends."

Maia touched her bandage and lightly pushed a finger into the depression beneath it. "What scares me more is that she might end up the same way, or worse.”

"Ren?”

"Yeah. I've lived longer than any Pilot. Maybe what's happening to me happens to all of us eventually. She's just a kid. She can't protect the whole world alone. That's why there were five of us, I think. Soon, when I'm gone, she'll be alone, like me. She'll make terrible mistakes like I did, and the world will take from her like it took from me. I don't want this life for her.”

Elizabeth nodded, taking in her words. "May I say something? You've lost more than one person should ever have to. I'm so, so sorry for all of it. You were hurt saving me, and I can't ever repay you for your sacrifice. But you're not alone, Maia. Not in this fight and not in any other. There are people who want to fight for you. Because you're Maia Sunderland, the bravest, kindest person I've ever met.

"I know you, and I see you. The real you. The tender, beautiful girl you armor with that smug smile of yours. And I know Ren. I've only had a week with her, but Maia... I see so much of you in her. She doesn't have to be alone, either. If we can't fix this, whatever it is, I'll be there for her. I'll look after her. She'll be okay. I'll bloody well make sure of that.”

"I don't know what to say,” Maia said.

"I didn't know you were hurting this much. I thought we would have more time. I should have said something sooner. You don't have to love me, Maia. And you don't have to let me love you. But if you don't want to be alone, you don't have to be. It doesn't have to be anything more than that.”

That was the problem. With Elizabeth, it would always be more. The only way to be with a woman like her was to fall headfirst with a smile on your lips. Maia teetered on the precipice, breathing through the tightness in her chest. "You should know, I was married once. Her name was Leona.”

"Tell me about her?”

"She was half Sinadarian, if you can believe that. A hunter and a hedge mage. Brilliant. Cunning. I left Edgar for her. We were together for only a year when she asked me to marry her. It seemed sudden, and we were young, but I wanted to make her happy. Leona wanted a Tressille bonding rite for our ceremony. I never asked why. We drew and shared our blood. We made vows. I told her that my heart belonged to her and no other. I said the words.” Maia crossed her legs.

"I said the words. I *promised.* Just because we're not together anymore, it doesn't mean I can..."

"What?" Elizabeth asked. She shifted to match Maia's posture, her soft eyes settling on her like she was the only thing in the world that mattered.

"I gave my heart to her. I can't take it back and give it to someone else. Even though I want to."

A strange smile crossed Elizabeth's face. "I'm not asking for your heart, Maia. I'm not asking for anything. I only want you to know that I'm here if you need me."

After the death of the Pilots and her father, Maia had difficulty finding a reason to carry on. Her heart had been poisoned. Salted. Nothing new would ever grow there. To pay for her crimes, she had to treat joy like a stranger. If she let somebody in, if she let them dig into the deepest part of her, it would hurt even more when the world inevitably ripped them away, as it always did.

Sitting there on Elizabeth's too-firm bed, Maia didn't care. She leaned into the heat flushing her cheeks and spreading to her stomach, and she allowed herself, for the first time in so many years, to reach for what she wanted. "I don't want to be alone. I want to be with you."

Maia found Elizabeth's hand and brushed it with the tips of her fingers. "Is this okay?" Elizabeth asked. "I can't tell you how much I've wanted this. But I don't want you to think you have to do anything just because I want to."

"I've never done anything I didn't want to do," Maia said.

Maia leaned in slowly. As their lips met, a rush of fire filled Maia's chest and flowed to her head, leaving her dizzy and floating. She reached for Elizabeth, careful not to jostle her injured arm. Pulling her close, Maia drank deep.

My heart belongs to you, Leona, and no other. Along with the wine, that was two promises broken in one night.

She let the shards of her vows scatter. In that moment, there was only Elizabeth.

Maia traced her fingers down her back, gently, deliberately. Elizabeth folded into her. They took their time, exploring each other with tender care as the hours of the night faded around them. For the first time in so many years, Maia surrendered herself to what her heart wanted, instead of dwelling on what she had lost.

Chapter 20
The Road Ahead

After an hour spent running through the streets and alleys of Whitehorn like a frightened chicken free of its coop, Ren found someone who could help her. An elderly couple had seen Maia leaving with Elizabeth, looking weakened but otherwise fine. No blood. No convulsions.

After letting Kas know it was safe to call off their search, Ren headed back to the inn. She thought to stay with Scarlet in case Maia came back in the middle of the night, but decided against it. If Maia intended to keep her as her apprentice, they would be spending many more days together in Scarlet's cabin. Another night apart would do them both some good.

Just before sunrise, Ren was lying awake in her bed at the inn, wondering how she could convince Maia to let Kas travel with them, when a low rattling startled her. She sprung from her bed and moved to where she had hung her belt. Her Farspeaker buzzed against the wooden wall.

Ren's ripped the stone from the pouch, willed the runes carved into its surface to light, and rushed back to bed. She threw the covers over her head and whispered against the fuzzy noise pouring from the device.

"Father?" Ren cleared her throat to keep her voice from cracking. "Are you there?"

"Serenia, it's so good to hear your voice. I—"

"Aurelia."

"Aurelia. I'm glad you're well." His voice was lower than usual, like the fire that lit it had gone out and only cold embers remained.

"Never mind me. Are you hurt? I worried you might be dead."

"Very nearly. Our healers have...mended me."

"Oh, thank the Emperor. I've been trying to raise you all week." Her relief faded, replaced with something molten and raw. "Father, this may not be the right time. There never seems to be a right time. While I can't tell you how happy I am to hear you're well, I have questions, and given everything that has transpired, I would have answers."

"I suppose that's only fair." A sigh and a pause. "Go on, then."

"Is the Empire preparing to invade the Freelands?"

"Yes," her father replied without hesitation. "A Pilot of the Freelands attacked a Noctean outpost. That aggression cannot go unanswered."

"I thought she was a Noctean Pilot, and Scarlet was rightfully ours?"

"Maia has made her allegiances clear. She sides with Brave Dawn, and Brave Dawn has ignored our demands."

"They did not present you with the head of their leader, no. Yet you took it all the same."

"The leader of Brave Dawn is dead?"

Ren cursed inwardly. That wasn't her news to share.

"Nevertheless, our retaliation must be swift," her father said.

"They only attacked Castle Blackwood to liberate their comrades. It wasn't a baseless assault. I'm starting to think that Maia has the right of it. How much of what she said that night atop the keep was true?"

"I did not know who her parents really were." Her father exhaled. Through the damaged Farspeaker, it came through as a hiss. "There were experiments conducted on their daughter, Aemilia. That much is true. She was a marvel. The secrets of her ability to adapt to her modifications, when uncovered, would have saved countless Noctean lives and granted the Empire immeasurable strength. I only learned the extent of those studies after her unfortunate death."

"Had you known how far they would go, what the cost would be for that knowledge, I wonder, would you have stopped them?"

"How can you say that?" her father said. "Maia has poisoned your mind and turned you against me and your homeland. You think me an uncaring beast. You don't know what I've sacrificed to keep you safe. To make you strong again. To bring you back. You wound me with your words."

"Have the healers mend you, then." She regretted the jab as soon as she launched it, but she didn't dare lose her momentum. "You brought me up to believe that the Empire was just. We distributed Farspeakers and used them to organize individual states into an efficient nation where all are cared and provided for. We created the Iron Wardens to further protect our people against Ferals. We have no vagabonds. No orphans. Everyone has a place and a purpose in the Empire. Yet for all that light we bring, we cast a shadow so deep that I feel foolish for never seeing it."

"Every light casts a shadow. You think the Freelands are so different?" her father said. "Don't be naive. Freedom spreads its own darkness. Trade kings tax their tenants until they're forced to resort to thievery. Rapists and murderers roam the countryside. There is no unified force to deter them, just local militia with shoddy pikes and patchwork armor. The people watch and do nothing as their brethren are eaten alive by their own. Do you love them more than your own people? Are they so much better?"

"No. Yet neither do I believe that Nocteans are superior to anyone else. I have come to know that every one of us, regardless of where we hail from, is a broken, messy creature. What breaks my heart is that you kept me from seeing the shadows creeping across our own backyard. What else have you kept from me?"

Her father started to speak, but he stopped himself. There was a long silence, a deafening voice where he had carved away something heavy.

"Father? What else have you kept from me?"

"No matter what, you're still my daughter. It's my duty to protect you."

"Tell me!" Ren hissed in a tight whisper. "Tell me now or lose me forever."

Another sigh. "Know that everything I've told you tonight has been the truth. What I'm about to tell you is also the truth, though it may pain you to hear it."

"Blue Hells, just say it!"

"Maia killed your mother."

Her head drifted, light and airy, as if she had taken a sharp hook to the jaw. "What?"

"You know of the first Behemoth, the one that attacked Noctis. Maia defeated it and avenged us all. But it wasn't the Behemoth that crushed our home and stole your mother from us. It was Scarlet."

Her father's words sent a flood of recollection rolling through her. Liquid fear lifted her memories like a rising tide. The black beneath the covers gripped her tighter.

Ren had been asleep when the Behemoth came. The rumbling of the dueling titans woke her. She rushed to the main hall, looking on from the top of the staircase in confusion.

Her mother found her and wrapped Ren in her arms, something she hadn't done in some time. A massive foot sheared through the ceiling of their home. The main hall lay divided by that armor-clad foot. The rest of the ceiling collapsed in an expanding wave. Aurelia Valerius fell on top of her daughter, shielding her from the debris.

And just before her world snapped to darkness, a darkness that would steal four years of her life, Ren saw the blood-red metal of her ruiner. How had she forgotten? How long had that image lurked in the back of her mind, waiting to be coaxed forth?

When her father called her name, she found herself back under the covers, shivering and covered in sweat.

"Yes, father. I'm still here."

"I'm sorry. I should never have kept this from you. The Emperor thought it best. You were to become a Pilot and inherit Scarlet. He feared your anger would drive you to confront Maia directly. We...I didn't want her to take you from me. But in a way, it seems she already has."

Maia had tried to tell her the truth earlier that day, and Ren hadn't given her room to explain herself. Still, that didn't account for months of opportunities Maia had squandered, where she could have told the truth.

"She couldn't have done it on purpose," Ren said. "It must have been an accident. She must have slipped. She must have."

"Serenia... I've known Maia far longer than you. And in that time, from the day I watched her battle that Behemoth attacking our great city to the final task I assigned her before she left us, I have never known her to slip. She fights as if she was born to command a Vanguardian." Her father swallowed hard. "No, my daughter. Either she destroyed our home out of malice, or she simply didn't care where she stepped. And I am unsure which is worse."

As Ren's chest heaved, her hand went to the small of her back, to her revolver. Her fingers curled around nothing.

Maia was dying. She should have been spending her waning days with Elizabeth. Instead, she chose to train an unwanted, unworthy successor. Maia had come to rescue her—twice—and lost an eye for her efforts. And yet, for a fleeting moment, Ren wanted nothing more than to put her revolver to Maia's head, look her in the eyes, and squeeze the fucking trigger.

"She didn't mean it," Ren whispered. "She couldn't have."

"I don't wish her harm for what she did. It wasn't vengeance that drove my blade that night atop the castle keep. It was a fear of losing you that bade me to do the unthinkable. It took time for me to find forgiveness for Maia. Someday, perhaps you will, as well. Though I fear it doesn't change what you must do."

"What do you mean?"

"The Emperor is willing to forgive your transgressions and welcome you back into his graces. However, his benevolence does not come without cost. You are to return with Scarlet, as per your original orders. The Emperor has also decreed that you are to bring him Sunder's body, as well."

"No. You can't ask that of me."

"I'm not. Your Emperor is. Time is running short. Behemoth attacks are on the rise. The world needs protection. It needs Vanguardians. You must bring Scarlet to us and eliminate any other claim to her if we're to answer this threat."

So, this was the General Valerius that Ren had heard so many tales of. When he spoke of her as an old friend and colleague, she was Maia. When he was ordering her death and acting as the Emperor's blade, she wasn't Maia anymore. She was Sunder. A claim to Scarlet. An objective waiting to be met.

"Father, I can't. If I bring Scarlet home and we're successful in creating others like her, what's to stop the Emperor from using them to expand the Empire by force once the Behemoths and their masters are dealt with?"

"I assure you, that is not the Emperor's will. Didn't we provide Iron Wardens to the other nations? Haven't we done all we can to care for our neighbors, despite their continued hatred and judgment? We don't desire war. We seek peace for the Empire. For everyone. You can't bring peace to the world by yourself, and Maia won't be around forever. The kindest thing you can do for the world, for her, is to end her suffering, so we can all move forward as one."

His words sent a chill surging through her veins. "I have to go. I'm glad you're well. I—"

"Serenia." Iron and fire returned, stoking the bellows of his voice. "If you wish to return home, you will fulfill your oath. A good soldier follows orders. I have given you yours. Don't trade your life for the woman who murdered your mother because she didn't care enough to—"

"I will speak with you another time. Please advise the Emperor that it's in his best interests to return the Wardens to active service and complete the construction of Lion's Roar. In addition, please inform him that a war with the Freelands will not go unanswered."

Ren didn't say goodbye. She didn't say "I love you." She pulled the Farspeaker apart and marched to where her belt hung. The two halves of the Farspeaker went into different pouches, so far away that there was no way they would ever make contact accidentally.

She had just told her father, the man who had given everything he had to bring her back from the darkness of her eternal slumber, that she would go to war with him.

Her heavy feet rooted to the floor, and Ren became aware of where she now stood.

Maia lingered in the open doorway far longer than she intended to, burning the bleak copper of the rising sun into her mind. As soon as she stepped out into the morning, the night would be over. What remained of her life would never compare to what she was about to walk away from.

Even though she knew Elizabeth was near, Maia still flinched when she felt warm fingers caress her shoulder.

"You have to go," Elizabeth said. Half question, half statement.

"I have to go." Maia turned from the sunrise and looked at Elizabeth. She didn't need to burn her face into her memory. She couldn't shake the glow of her tawny skin, smooth cheeks, and hopeful brown eyes from her mind if she wanted to. And she didn't want to.

"About last night," Elizabeth began. She held up her hand to stop Maia from interrupting. "I know that you promised your heart to somebody else. What we did...it wasn't a promise. You don't owe me anything. I have no regrets. I'm glad that it happened, and I hope you are, too."

Maia didn't have words to express just how much that one night of respite had meant to her. Or how much she wanted to stay and make that night last forever, if only she wasn't tasked with her cursed duty. "What'll you do now?"

"Well. I've decided to leave Brave Dawn." Elizabeth looked down at the sling wrapping her arm. "I don't think I'm cut out for this kind of fight. I sold my horse when I arrived in Whitehorn, so I'm going to hitch a ride with one of the caravans heading back west. One will be passing near the Hinterlands."

The Hinterlands lay just south of the Kaldrsteinn border, in the mountains of the northern Freelands. "You're headed to your parents' place in Steadbrook?"

Elizabeth exhaled through her teeth. "Whether they'll welcome me back or not, I'll feel better knowing they're close by if the Nocteans come. Not that I can do much to protect them. My time in Whitehorn has made it painfully clear that I'm not much of a fighter."

Maia propped Elizabeth's chin up with her finger. "Maybe not with a sword. But in every other sense of the word, you are."

Elizabeth guided Maia's hand to her cheek. It was warm, there. So very warm. "Thank you, Maia."

"What'll you do in Steadbrook?"

"I figure I'll get a cabin near the village with a comfy little hearth, and I'll chop wood and make soup and enjoy the snowfall."

"That sounds really nice."

"Hey." Elizabeth's fingers found Maia's. "The world needs heroes, but it doesn't always have to be you who answers the call, you know. It's cold up in Steadbrook. After you're finished training Ren and you find a cure for whatever is hurting you, you could come find me. If you wanted to. You could help keep me warm."

"I'd like that."

"Yeah?"

"Yeah." She fought the urge to ask Elizabeth to come away with her. The further she was from Maia, the safer she would be. "When this is over, I'll come find you. I promise."

"You don't have to promise. Just come, if you like."

"I promise." Maia leaned in and stole one last overlong kiss. "Goodbye, Elizabeth."

A new pang sliced into Maia's chest as she made her way back to Scarlet. Her latest vow had lasted seconds. A new low, even for her. Maia's feet dragged through the broken pieces of it, each step cutting deeper.

There was no cure. No "after." No happy ending. Just her duty, followed by a lonely, painful death.

After a quick stop at the inn to gather her things, Maia returned to Scarlet. She found Serenia waiting with a crowd gathered to see their "heroes" off. Serenia had washed and re-braided her hair into a tight crown. She wore a scowl that made Maia's shoulders tighten.

"Good morning. Did you have a relaxing evening?" Serenia said. "I had no way of knowing if you were dead in a rut alongside a road somewhere, so I chose to believe that you had a pleasant time, if only to keep from dying of worry."

"I'm fine, mother. I was with Elizabeth."

"Yes, I heard. How wonderful it would have been if you told me yourself."

"Last I checked, I didn't need your permission to catch up with a friend over drinks."

Serenia's eyes narrowed. "Drinks."

Shit. "Drink. I only had one."

"Cup?"

"Bottle."

"Another broken promise." Serenia buried her face in her palm. "I can't believe you've done this."

"If you can afford to cut me a bit of slack, I'll take it. It's been a bit of a rough week, in case you haven't been keeping up." Maia's fingers circled the space where her right eye used to be as she walked past Serenia, turning the gesture into a wave to the gathered crowd.

"You're right. I apologize. I should be more sensitive and understanding."

Maia whirled on Serenia. "Oh, sweet merciful crap. Why are you apologizing? I'm the one who messed up."

"Then pray, tell me, what do you want from me? Empathy? Or nagging?"

"You're in the Freelands. Act like it. If you want to be mad, then be mad. Goddess above knows you have every right to be. Just make up your mind, for once."

"Pilot!" Tobias emerged from the crowd, wearing the wide smile he favored when he was still the leader of a band of religious fanatics. Maia thought to smile back, but her face sank when she saw Kasper walking beside him, hauling a rucksack, a bedroll, and a hunter's bow and quiver. Like he was going somewhere.

"What's all this?" Maia said.

"Kas is coming with us," Serenia said, appearing at her side.

"Blue Hells he is."

"May I have a word?" Tobias stepped between Maia and Kasper and ushered her off to the side, near a pile of rubble that had once been a part of the city walls before Scarlet blasted through them.

"Look, I'm sorry I made things worse for you," Maia said, cutting Tobias off before he could speak. "It's my fault you have to leave Whitehorn. I was born here, and even though I have no real memories of it, I hate to see the city in a state like this. But I'm not a member of Brave Dawn. So, I definitely don't need a representative of Brave Dawn keeping me company." She jabbed her chin at Kasper. "Especially that one."

"I'm aware that there's some history between the two of you."

"History?" Maia stepped into Tobias' space. He staggered back. "You have no idea. If you did, you wouldn't be asking me to take him in."

"Whatever happened between you, he couldn't have been more than a child at the time," Tobias said.

"Doesn't matter how old he was. He knew what he was doing. Believe me, I wish I could forgive him. I just can't. Don't ask me to."

"I wasn't about to." Tobias crossed his hands behind his back and paced. "Brave Dawn is finished. There's no way for us to stand against a formal invasion force. We have no reinforcements coming. All we can do is disperse, warn the people, and hope the trade kings organize a defensive front in time. Many will die. I'm not asking you to forgive young Kasper. I want you to save him."

"You're insane. You can take the leader out of the cult..."

"I never once believed Scarlet was a goddess, you know." Tobias' features stiffened. "Not in the traditional sense. Yet, she did change my life and the lives of my followers. I wasn't always a spiritual leader."

"You definitely weren't a baker, either. I'm told you're handy with a sword."

A grimace, probably attached to a bloody memory, pulled at Tobias' wrinkles. "I was in Noctis during your first battle. I'm ashamed to say that I was not there on pleasant business." He kicked at a piece of stone buried in the dirt at his feet. "Then, the Behemoth came, and you with it, and everything changed."

He cleared his throat. "I looked out the window of the house I had stolen into, and all I could see was Scarlet's shadow, spread across the entire block. I looked at the knife in my hand and the monster you were fighting, and I realized that the real enemy was far bigger than I had ever imagined." Tobias pointed to the sky. "It was out there, somewhere. Coming for us all. I've never felt so powerless in my life."

"You had a change of heart."

"I did. I wandered for a time, lost and without purpose."

"Been there."

"I found others who had also become lost in a changing world, people in need of a home and something to believe in," Tobias said. "In a way, the shepherd was found by his flock."

"And then I left you, so you wandered to Whitehorn to die for a lost cause," Maia said.

"We came here to continue your mission. To save others, as you and Scarlet saved us, and honor those we've lost. That day in Noctis, I was mistaken. The real enemy is up there, beyond our reach, yet that doesn't mean there's nothing we can do down here, in the dirt, to make the world better. I didn't ask to lead Brave Dawn, and I never asked to become the head of a false religion. I simply went where I was needed and did what was expected of me, as you have. As I'm asking you to do now, by saving the life of a boy who shouldn't have had to grow up as fast as he did."

Had he prepared that impassioned speech in advance? Or did he craft it on the spot? Maia could see why his flock, and now Brave Dawn, had chosen him to lead.

She looked back to Scarlet, to Serenia and Kasper, who grinned and waved. He wore that same grin the day Leona introduced him as her younger brother, Kasper Carver. She even gave him her family name.

Maia never asked why she chose Kasper, of all people, to be her ward. She always figured that Leona was driven by sympathy. One orphan looking after another. Maybe there was something more to him. Maybe not.

Either way, he meant something to Leona, so Maia tolerated him. And by the way Serenia was all but swooning over him, it was starting to look like she would have to tolerate him a little while longer.

Maia pursed her lips. "You saved Elizabeth."

"It's entirely possible that I did. To be perfectly honest, once I have blade in hand, what follows is usually a blur."

She nodded, knowing that feeling all too well. "Then I owe you. Kasper can come. But if he steps out of line even once, I'll feed him to a Feral myself."

With his arms spread wide, Tobias smiled. "I would expect no less. Thank you, Maia. Before you go, I have something else to offer you. A small token of my gratitude."

He handed her a folded piece of fine cloth. She unfurled it and studied the markings. "A map?"

"Being the leader of a resistance movement affords me access to a great deal of information. There are rumors of a dead forest in the Freelands, beneath the southern peaks of the Sinadaria Mountains closest to the Brimholme border. In the center of that dead forest, I'm told, there's a glade, rich and green and alive. In that glade grows a plant that can't be found anywhere else. Ancient Tressille writings called it Heartflower. It's said to be a panacea for almost any ailment."

"Blue Hells," Maia said. "Does everybody in the fucking Freelands know about my problems now?" She willed her calm to return and swallowed hard. "Heartflower is a myth. It doesn't exist. And even if it does... Did you tell Serenia about this?"

"No. This is my gift to you. It's yours to do with as you like."

Maia nodded in thanks and returned to Scarlet, wearing the best look of contentment she could still muster.

"Kas is coming with us," Serenia said as she marched up to her.

"Is that so?"

"It is. And I won't be silenced by your threats of dismissal any longer." Serenia stood up a little straighter. "Kas can be of great benefit to my training. He's an accomplished hunter and tracker. Those skills would be valuable to any Pilot."

"Okay," Maia said. "He can come with us."

"Wait. R-really? You mean it?" By the tension in her posture, Serenia had clearly been expecting more of a fight.

"Yes, really. But he's sleeping outside. The cabin is cramped enough already. And he'll be doing all the cooking and cleaning, too. Those are my terms. Now, get in the palm before I change my mind."

Serenia and Kasper boarded Scarlet's hand. Maia lingered, gazing upward at Scarlet's black glass visor. Was there a consciousness hidden deep beneath all that red metal, a will that might eventually break free of her? The damage Arcturus had done to Maia's sliver had weakened her other Pilot abilities. She had to hope that if her control over Scarlet faltered and her Vanguardian was able to choose her own path, she would continue to act as a protector, as she had at Castle Blackwood.

"Thanks, Scarlet. I owe you everything," Maia whispered.

Maybe it was a trick of the morning light, maybe it was just her imagination, but Maia could have sworn she saw Scarlet's head incline in the slightest of nods.

The three of them rose on Scarlet's hand, waving to the people of Whitehorn as they ascended. Inside Scarlet's cabin, Maia slid the map into her bag and dumped it next to the rest of her things. She tried not to think of where it led. There was no use getting anyone's hopes up just yet. Not even her own.

And yet, she felt a surge of anticipation in her chest as she patted the bag. Maybe this wasn't goodbye for her and Elizabeth after all.

"So, where are we headed?" Kasper said, his voice as bright as the birds chirping outside the cabin.

"We were on a course before we Teleported to Whitehorn," Serenia said. "It will take some time for us to get back to where we were."

"It will," Maia said. "But we'll get there. We're going to stick to the Pilot roads.

South, along the Sinadaria Mountains. There's a place I want to visit on the way to Brimholme."

"Brimholme," Serenia said. "What awaits us in Brimholme?"

"The end of the road." Maia clenched her hand to keep it from shaking. "You have until we get there to show me you can be the kind of Pilot the world deserves."

Kasper laid his hands on Serenia's shoulders. She covered them with her own. When they saw Maia was staring at them, they separated, taking to opposite ends of the cabin.

Letting Kasper come along was a mistake. Young love never lasted, and Maia didn't relish the thought of having to guide Serenia through her first broken heart. The air in the cabin thickened. As the oldest and most responsible, Maia had to make the first move, or none of them would survive the journey.

"Kasper, get ready to guide me out," Maia said. "You know the land. Make sure I don't step on anything important."

He wore a confused look that vanished when Maia arched her eyebrow at him. With a quick salute, he took his place in a crouch near Scarlet's viewport. He was smiling.

"Oh, and Princess?" Maia went back to the bag where she had hidden the map, reached in, and pulled out Serenia's revolver, still in its torn holster. Her hand trembled as she handed it over. "Keep that handy. Only for emergencies, yeah?"

Serenia didn't nod, didn't respond at all as Maia took her place in Scarlet's control beam. When Maia brought Scarlet to her feet and made her way over what remained of Whitehorn's outer wall, she could see from the corner of her eye that Serenia hadn't moved an inch. She was staring at the revolver in her hands, transfixed on it, probably overcome with the weight of Maia's gesture.

After some time, she fastened the revolver's holster to her belt and took her place at Maia's side, completely silent as they left Whitehorn behind.

Part Three

Haunted

Chapter 21

Deadwood

"So, Princess," Maia said as Scarlet's cabin shook like the lid on a boiling kettle. "What can you tell me about our current situation?"

On the other side of the viewport, a Behemoth resembling a heavy-set anteater with pink fur buckled Scarlet's knee with a brutal snap from one of the four orange tentacles it had in place of forelegs.

Serenia bent her legs and thrust her arms out for balance. "It appears that rather than letting me face this Behemoth and gain much-needed experience, you would rather demonstrate the myriad ways one can lose a fight."

Maia ignored her apprentice's sarcasm, which she was secretly proud of, and hunkered down. The Behemoth dipped in and out of her blind spot. This was the second Behemoth they had encountered in the months since they left Whitehorn, and it was giving her more trouble than what she was used to.

Though she had learned to compensate for the loss of her eye, the aches from her many half-healed injuries didn't help. And try as she might, she couldn't connect her sliver to Scarlet's to project flames from her Vanguardian's arms and legs to even the odds.

Maia could have used any number of excuses to explain why she was struggling. Excuses wouldn't keep them from dying a horrible death, so she kept them to herself.

The Behemoth, which Maia had named Slapdash, slipped around Scarlet with an agility she hadn't expected from such a large creature. When one of its slick orange tentacles cracked against Scarlet, another was already arcing in. All the while, it flanked Scarlet with darting leaps she could barely follow.

Scarlet shuddered and listed to the side as another volley struck home. Maia drove her left leg into the floor of the cabin. Scarlet crouched lower with her one arm poised to protect her head. Her metal body was strong, but she wasn't invulnerable. She couldn't withstand this assault forever.

Maia hoped her apprentice couldn't see the sweat beading her brow. "And what am I *not* doing?" she said.

"Winning?" Serenia caught Maia's jagged glare and sighed. "You're not employing Scarlet's arm blade or launching any kind of offense. You're allowing the Behemoth to set the tempo."

"Good. Now, the big question: why?"

"You're waiting for an opportunity so you can interrupt it. Slapdash has the reach advantage, and its attack cadence hasn't yet afforded you the opening you seek. As I see it, the only way to win this fight is for Scarlet to close the distance, yet I don't see how that's possible."

Neither did Maia. Outside, Slapdash reared up and launched another flurry. Maia's teeth rattled in her skull with each impact. Her helmet would have filtered the vibrations, but it hadn't returned to her when she summoned her cracked armor and damaged blades before the fight.

It was bad enough that her Regeneration failed to fully mend her wounds; now, her armor and weapons were refusing to repair themselves. Just like Scarlet's lost arm. Whatever Arcturus had done to her sliver had far-reaching effects. Dwelling on it wouldn't change anything; it was done, and nothing could undo it. There was always a way to win. Maia just needed to find it.

She looked at the floor of the cabin and listened to the rhythm of the slapping tentacles. Four strikes, a pause while Slapdash relocated, then four more. Every time she thought she had worked out a pattern, Slapdash smashed a different tentacle into Scarlet, covering the advance of the one she had anticipated.

Each tentacle covered the next, and that one covered the one to follow, the same way she employed her twin falchions. One strike from each tentacle in succession. That meant that even if she couldn't predict the first three...

One. Two. Three. Maia thrust Scarlet's hand down and to the right on four. Crimson metal clamped around thick, rubbery flesh. "Hold on!" she said.

Maia braced her injured right shoulder with her left hand, twisted her hips, and pulled. Slapdash stumbled into range, running snout-first into Scarlet's thrusting forehead. As the monster reeled, Scarlet slipped in and launched a kick from the right. Two tentacles wound around Scarlet's leg, stopping it halfway to its target.

"That was a good fight," Maia said.

"Was?" Serenia said.

"Was."

Maia dropped her leg, using Scarlet's weight to pull Slapdash to the ground. Scarlet's arm blade screeched free from its hiding place in her forearm, chipped edges gleaming orange. Maia brought it down. The remains of two severed tentacles writhed at Scarlet's feet. With a screech, Slapdash threw itself into a sidelong roll away from her, but by the time it managed to stand, Scarlet's right leg was already on its way. Maia landed three hard kicks to its unprotected flank. As Slapdash groaned and crumpled, Scarlet's knee rose to meet it, catching it in the jaw and snapping its head back.

"Back to the lesson," Maia said. "It's a good idea to start thinking about a finishing move. Something decisive, brutal, and too risky to use on a fresh opponent. Something with a brilliant name that people will remember and be inspired by." She looked down at Slapdash, who kept stumbling as it tried to stand. "I could have finished our friend here with a thrust to the heart. But why waste a perfectly good chance to mold young minds?"

The lesson was only part of the reason why Maia hadn't finished the fight already. The bout had awakened her bloodlust, sending it pumping like lit lamp oil through Maia's veins, blurring her vision and bringing her back to the dungeons of Castle Blackwood and that horrid red flash.

It wasn't enough for the Behemoth to die. It had to take her pain, as much as she could throw at it, before it broke.

"Scarlet Kick!" Maia shouted, pushing into a dashing leap. Scarlet left the ground, careening through the air toward Slapdash with her right leg leading. With Scarlet's full weight behind the kick, Slapdash was blasted to the earth. Its broken body exploded, leaving behind a smoldering crater in the middle of an otherwise pristine stretch of verdant countryside.

"That was just a leaping side kick," Serenia said.

"When Scarlet does it, it's a 'Scarlet Kick.' It's harder than it looks."

"I wouldn't know. You won't let me try." Serenia uncrossed her arms and pointed out the viewport. "Look, up there!"

Canting Scarlet's head upward, Maia followed Serenia's finger to the sky. Powerful wings propelled a distinct silhouette through a sea of blue.

"Blue Hells," Maia breathed. It was the dragon. The morning sun blurred the wyrm's details into a solid splash of deep green burned into the sky, but there was no mistaking it for what it was.

The dragon dipped its head, looking down at them as it flew past. "That's the second time it's shown itself to us," Serenia said. The dragon had been about to engage the last Behemoth they encountered since leaving Whitehorn before Scarlet arrived to face it, sending the dragon fleeing to the skies as they approached.

"I still want to know why it's hunting Behemoths," Maia said.

"Behemoths disturb the natural order. Perhaps it's asserting its dominance. Regardless, staring at it won't do us any good. We should get back. Kas is waiting for us."

The mystery of the dragon would have to wait. When Maia's Teleport spell replenished, she cast it, bringing them back to the small campsite where they had left Kasper. Though Maia forbade him from sleeping in the cabin, he seemed more than happy camping in his tent, and he always had breakfast prepared for Maia and Serenia by the time they returned from morning training.

They descended in Scarlet's palm and approached the smothered remains of a cooking fire. Two bowls waited for them on a small boulder near Kasper's tent.

Maia dismissed her damaged armor and looked past the camp to the gnarled, leafless forest melding into the base of the Sinadaria Mountains. The woods spread like gray death, as if a painter had set out to draw a gorgeous forest vista and only had charcoal to work with. But from Scarlet's cabin, Maia had spied the small splash of green at the center of the canvas, barely visible in the shadow cast by the looming mountains.

More than once in their travels, she steered Scarlet away from the mountains, claiming she was taking a detour or guiding them toward an interesting landmark. Now that they had reached the spot marked on Tobias' map, Maia knew why she had delayed coming to this forest. Hope was foreign to her. There was no telling what kind of hell it would wreak if she let it run amok in her heart.

She grabbed one of the still-steaming bowls and flicked away a small beetle clinging to its lip. Poached eggs and tomato sauce. Maia sniffed the vapors rising from the bowl and cleared her throat to cover the sound of her growling stomach. Serenia held her own bowl in one hand and a piece of parchment in the other.

"What's that?" Maia said.

"It's a note from Kas." Her parted lips rose into a smile that reached all the way to her eyes. "He says he's off to find supplies and hopes our hunt went well, and…oh, he's so sweet."

"Save it until after I'm done eating, so I have something to throw up."

Serenia rolled her eyes and wandered off, taking her meal on the other side of camp. Maia tucked into her food, cursing Kasper for being such a bloody good cook. And a great navigator. And for doing all the chores and taking all her caustic jabs with a smile.

The bastard wasn't giving her new reasons to hate him. Not that she needed any. The ones she had were enough. Still, he was trying to make amends. She could spare him an inch and see how it felt. When morning training was complete, Maia decided that she would compliment Kasper on his cooking. That was as good a first step as any.

When they had finished eating in silence, Maia set her bowl on the boulder and clapped her hands. "Okay. Time to get to work. For the rest of the morning, we'll focus on striking. Today is kicks. Yours are lacking. Scarlet only has one arm, so you'll need to get used to using all of her other tools."

"I believe we've trained together enough for one morning. That Behemoth encounter was quite informative." Serenia turned and headed for the edge of the dead woods.

"Hey. Don't forget: you ran off with Scarlet and marched on Castle Blackwood in the dead of night. You could have killed somebody. Until I know you can use her responsibly, I fight the Behemoths, and you watch."

"Whatever you say. I'm off to see if Kas requires my assistance. I'll be training with him for the rest of the day."

"Again?" Maia called after her. "That's three days in a row. We have work to do!"

Serenia disappeared into the twisted darkness of the tree line.

"Hey! I want you back here at midday! Kicks! Do you hear me?"

A sudden jolt of pain knifed into Maia's breast, followed by a numb wave. It subsided quickly, leaving behind a dull ache. Maia pulled Tobias' map from her pocket.

With the rest of the morning to herself, there was no reason to put off venturing into the gnarled woods any longer. Whether or not Tobias' information bore fruit, or in this case, flowers, nobody else had to know about it until Maia had good news to share.

And even if the Heartflower was a hoax, Maia could spend the hike back concocting an even more grueling training plan, something that would make her apprentice think twice about shirking her responsibilities.

Maybe the day held promise after all.

Every contorted tree in the mangled forest looked the same to Ren. High above in the rotting branches, mottled crows looked down at her from their gnarled perches. Occasionally, one would squawk, which prompted a sharp retort from another in its murder, continuing until each corvid in earshot had its say.

Ren pressed on through the dead woods, trying to keep her path straight and direct so that she could easily retrace her steps. Hopefully, Kas wasn't cross with her for leaving him behind when she and Maia rushed off to fight that Behemoth. Maia had insisted they had no time to waste, even though the Behemoth had appeared far from any settlements, and elected to leave Kas behind without telling him where they were headed. It was just another way for her to treat Kas poorly, despite his efforts to endear himself to her.

And what gave Maia the right to lecture her on responsibility when she was the one responsible for the death of Ren's mother? Or the deaths of so many Noctean soldiers, right after she espoused how important it was for Pilots to not involve themselves in political matters?

Those were mistakes, Ren told herself. She had to believe that. Maia was in pain, and she was doing her best.

Perhaps Kas would know how to cut through the thickening tension dividing them. He had known Maia far longer than she had, and he was smarter than Maia gave him credit for. And stronger. And more handsome. Ren particularly enjoyed the way one corner of his mouth quirked up higher than the other when he smiled, and the way his tanned complexion gleamed in the morning light.

Ren quickened her pace, pushing past brittle bushes whose branches snapped cleanly with only light pressure. She came across a tree as wide as a horse-drawn coach, with brown and black bark peeling off its trunk in chunks. Its thick, deadened roots snaked in and out of the barren, packed soil at her feet. Ren vaulted over a root and called out to Kas.

A flutter of movement from beyond the trunk of the dead tree startled her. A lizard as long as her forearm skittered across the dirt, nails kicking up dust. Before it could escape, an arrow whistled from above, taking it in the tail.

Ren leaped back over the root and drew her revolver. She rested it on the curling deadwood for support as she scanned the treetops for the archer. The lizard, pinned to the earth, thrashed and squirmed until its tail tore off. It flitted away, disappearing beneath some thorny underbrush.

"Thanks," Kas called to her. He shouldered his bow and leaped from his perch in the dead tree, landing next to Ren without a sound. "Couldn't get a clear shot until you spooked it. We make a good team."

"You scared the Blue Hells out of me!" She holstered her revolver and threw her arms around him. "Though I fear that tail won't be enough to feed all three of us tonight."

When she released him, he retrieved his arrow, removed the still-wriggling tail from the tip, and placed it in one of his pouches. "Pyrosaurs aren't for eatin'," he said.

"Is that what that was?"

"Yeah. A young one. His tail'll grow back. In a few years, he'll be bigger than me. I was hopin' there was a nest out here. They like dry places. Some creatures have a bit of magic to them. Pyrosaurs can shoot flames like Sun can. The tail is what I was after. They make great spell components. Add a bit of sulfur, some charcoal, and you can conjure a nice little flame."

"Ah, you're making more of those grenades of yours," Ren said. "Where did you learn to make them?"

"From Leona. She taught me a lot of things." Kas winced. "Ah, shit. Don't tell Sun I mentioned 'you know who.' It'll just make her mad."

"As if I care what she thinks."

"Hey." Kas threaded his fingers with hers, pushing apart the fist she hadn't realized she was making. "You can be mad at her and still worry about her, you know."

"What makes you think I'm worried about her?"

Kas made a show of raising an eyebrow. "Come on."

"She refuses to travel to Noctis and seek a more experienced healer. If her illness progresses, the world will suffer without her."

"More than that, you'll lose somebody you love. Now, don't try and deny it. The way you two spar some days, you'd think you wanted each other dead. But I see it. She means a lot to you. I just wish I knew how to help her. And you."

Ren squeezed his hand tighter. "You're doing wonderfully. Thank you for weathering the storm and fury that is Maia Sunderland. I do appreciate it."

He clucked his tongue and flashed her a quick wink. "I've got enough tails. All that's left is to scare up somethin' for dinner. Keep your eyes peeled. Might be bigger pyrosaurs nestin' deeper in."

The thought of Kas-sized lizards brought Ren's revolver quietly into her hand as he guided her deeper into the bush.

"I've been meanin' to ask," Kas said, motioning with his chin. "Why the wolf? On your gun, I mean."

Ren glanced down at the wolf's head etched into the purple-hued steel of her revolver. "Oh. Yes. High-ranking nobles are permitted to wear their own house crests in lieu of the Emperor's golden lion if they wish. This is for my father."

"Your parents are wolves?"

Ren punched him in the arm. "It's the crest of House Valerius. My father is no wolf. You've met him."

"He hits hard." Kas rubbed his arm. "So do you."

"So did my mother, I'm told." A tightness spread through Ren's chest. "I don't think she ever lost a fight before I was born. She once told me I was the one who finally defeated her. I used to look a lot like her."

"Used to?" Kas paused, turning to her.

"Yes." Ren ran a hand over her crown of black braids. "I used to have blond hair, like hers. Becoming a Pilot darkened it."

"What was becomin' a Pilot like for you? Did it hurt?"

"I was asleep for close to four years before I was selected for ascension. The ritual is a closely guarded secret. There were many failures before the Emperor succeeded and brought me back from the brink. I'm not sure what exactly was done to me, but whatever it was, it didn't hurt, as I wasn't conscious at the time. Though, when I awakened my abilities in that warehouse in Galford, that certainly wasn't pleasant."

"Do you ever wish it hadn't happened to you?"

"Not at all. I've been given a wondrous gift. I still don't have an elemental affinity, or a unique Pilot ability like Maia's Barrier, or the capacity to Teleport, and I can't summon armor or weapons. Still, I'm grateful for all I've been granted. I don't regret being made into a Pilot."

"Sun does. I mean, she regrets being made into a Pilot herself." Kas looked away. "I shouldn't have said that."

"No, please. Tell me. What did she say? I promise she won't know we spoke."

Kas' voice lowered. "She said it was the worst thing that ever happened to her. This monster comes for her in the night, takes her and four other folks her age. Ties them to metal tables. Pumps their blood full of elixirs. Casts spell after spell on them until they black out from the pain of their muscles and bones tearin' and knittin'. Except Sun says she was awake the whole time. Screamed right through the pain. She wouldn't give in to the darkness. That's how she is. Once she's set her mind to somethin'..."

Ren stowed her revolver and pulled Kas to her. "I know she's terrible to you, but I'm glad she trusted you enough, at one point, to tell you her story. She's lucky to have you."

"What about you? Do you feel lucky?"

"To have you?" Ren said.

"Yeah," Kas said. "You do, you know. Have me. No matter what."

The space between them shrank until she could feel the warmth of Kas' breath on her lips. She closed her eyes. His fingers brushed her cheek, sending a tingling bolt coursing through her. At the same time, something twisted in her gut, quickening her heart for all the wrong reasons.

Ren pulled away as their lips touched. "I'm sorry."

"I should have asked first."

She climbed onto a nearby fallen log and hugged her knees. "I just can't get my mind to settle." She motioned to the decayed forest surrounding them. "Besides, this place doesn't feel like a fitting place for my first kiss."

"First?" Kas took a seat next to her.

"My Pilot training was quite intensive. I didn't have time to pursue...entanglements. I doubt my father would have approved, anyway."

Kas stared ahead. "You sure it's just the scenery? It doesn't have anythin' to do with Sun?"

"What do you mean?"

"She doesn't approve. You know. Of us."

"It...may have something to do with that." Ren put her hand on Kas'. "I don't doubt that she's overreacting, but if I knew what happened between the two of you, it may help me understand."

Kas frowned. "If I tell you, Sun can never know."

"Of course."

"I'm serious. You can't tell her. Ever."

"I promise."

He picked at the peeling, dead bark of the log. "Leona's dad was a Sinadarian elf. He lived high on the mountains, above the clouds, with the rest of his kind. The way she tells it, he came down to learn more about the people of the world below. He ended up in a scrape with a brown bear. Leona's mother found him and nursed him back to health. You can guess what happened next."

Ren nodded. "They fell in love, and soon after, she was with child."

"When Leona turned twelve, they tried to go back to Sinadaria. Her dad wanted his girl to see where he came from." Kas paused, rubbing his forehead. "I don't know what you know about the Sinadarians, but they don't much care for us 'ground dwellers.' They put Leona's dad to the sword for fallin' for an outsider. They took pity on Leona and her mother and banished them. Didn't think they were worth killing."

Resisting the urge to ask how this related to Kas and Maia, Ren settled in, waiting for the thread to reveal itself.

"Leona's mother moved on, found a new partner," Kas continued. "Nasty, hateful man, I'm told. Had it in for Leona right from the start. It's not long until things get ugly. Leona's mother does what she needs to do to protect her daughter. Pays for Leona's life with her own. So Leona spends the next few years on her own, fightin' to get by, usin' what her mother taught her to survive.

"My parents were necromancers. They were executed for it. Leona found me when I was eleven or so. Took me in. Passed on everythin' she knew, so I could be a survivor, like her."

"You're Noctean too?" Ren almost choked on the lump rising in her throat. "Did you... Have you ever practiced necromancy yourself?"

"No. Not even once. When I was old enough to know what they were up to, I was disgusted by what my parents had done. They were wrong. So were the people who killed them. Hypocrites, the whole lot of them. The Empire is broken. That's why I joined up with Brave Dawn. I wanted to make things better. For everyone.

"Anyway, Leona took me in. She met Maia, who left the Pilot she was with to be with her. Things were good for a while. One day, Leona asks me about my parent's magic. Wants me to take her to where they kept their books and such. So, I take her." When Kas turned to Ren, his eyes were glossy with tears yet to break. "How could I say no? I had to do it. For her, I had to."

"It's okay," Ren said. "You can stop if you like."

"I was like kin to Leona, so much that she gave me her last name. But she wanted a family of her own. A child of her own. She was obsessed with it. Her and Sun couldn't have one themselves, so she used the books my parents hid." Kas pushed his palms hard into his thighs. "That creature Leona made from her blood and Sun's, it was wrong in every way. Tentacles. Barbs. So many mouths. I still see it, sometimes, in my nightmares. I still remember its cry."

Ren reached for him, but Kas pushed to his feet and busied himself straightening the daggers and quiver at his belt. "Come on. We should get back. Sun'll be lookin' for us soon enough."

She stood in his path. "Kas. I'm sorry I pressed you. I need to know that you're okay. Is there anything I can do?"

His breath left him all at once. His shoulders heaved, and his face finally cracked. Kas enveloped Ren in his arms and cradled her head, sobbing next to her ear.

"It's all my fault, Ren. Sun couldn't let that thing live. She had to kill it. It wasn't right. It wasn't right."

"I don't believe it. Maia could never do something like that. Even if the child was... No. She couldn't."

"She did," Kas said, his voice even as steel. He released her and wiped his eyes with the back of one of his fingerless gloves. "And she blames me for it."

"It's not your fault. You were just a child. You were only doing as Leona asked."

"Tell that to Sun."

"Maybe I will." Ren kicked up dirt as she paced. "Perhaps there's a way to mend things between Maia and Leona. Maybe then she can forgive you, and she won't have cause to stand between us. Do you know where Leona is now? Have you kept in touch?"

"I think I know where to find her," Kas said.

"Excellent. All we need to do is—"

"Ren."

"It's okay. It's all going to be okay. I—"

"Ren!" Kas placed his hands on her shoulders. "You want to help. I get it. More than anyone, I get it. But take it from me: sometimes, the best way you can help is to leave things alone."

"No. I can't accept that. We must try. There's always something that can be done."

"Not this time. I can take you to Leona if you want. But no amount of tryin' can fix this mess."

"Why?" Ren all but cried.

When Kas looked her dead in the eyes, his stare was cold and flat. "Because Leona's dead, Ren. And I think Maia is the one who killed her."

Chapter 22

Hope in Flames

It took Maia about an hour to make it to the green clearing nestled deep in the heart of the dead woods. Whatever sort of creeping death had fallen on the rest of the forest had passed over the glade, allowing lush beds of wildflowers to thrive in the sheets of sunlight piercing through an emerald canopy. A single tree thrust up from the rainbow sea at the glade's center. Maia stepped gingerly over the flowers to make sure she didn't crush the one she was looking for.

When she made it to the center, she realized that she had no idea what a Heartflower even looked like. She picked her away around the tree, examining each bloom with a careful eye. Amid a wash of yellow and orange flowers, a single red bulb caught her eye. Unlike the rest of the flowers, the red bulb remained closed, tight as a fist. Its tapered end and fat bottom reminded her of a heart's shape.

"Could you be what I'm looking for?" Maia whispered. She bent down and sniffed the flower. She almost placed its scent when something sharp bit into her right side.

Reflexively, Maia twisted and threw herself into a roll. Her many injuries screamed at her as she came up from the sudden dive. She pressed her back to the massive tree trunk and slid behind it, sparing a glance down to where a crossbow quarrel had punctured the meat of her hip and dangled from the leather of her now-torn pants.

She peeked around the trunk. A flash of movement brought her back behind cover as another quarrel thrummed into the thick wood.

"Apologies, fair lady. This thing pulls a little to the right. I hoped for a clean kill."

"By shooting me between my ass cheeks?" Maia ripped the quarrel from her hip with a grunt. "Look, I'm just here to pick a flower. Once I have it, I'm on my way. No need for things to get messy."

"Well, that was a common tulip you were admiring," the voice called back. "The red ones are quite striking, I will admit. I wager that's not what you were after, though. And speaking to your request, now that you've entered my woods, I'm afraid 'messy' is all but assured at this point. You're no use to me alive, after all."

"I'm looking for a flower that can heal people. Do you have anything like that out here, or not?"

Boisterous laughter echoed through the glade. "I see word has spread. A whisper in the right ear is all it takes for a message to take flight, drawing wayward souls to places they should never tread, all in the name of salvation. You're much healthier than most. Those who make their way here are often on their last leg. Sometimes, literally."

"I'm not hearing an answer to my question. So that's two," Maia shouted back.

"Two what?"

"Broken bones. Want to go for three?"

"I don't think you're in a position to be making threats."

Maia peaked out again. She saw the shooter, a short, bald man with pale skin wearing a monk's robes and holding a heavy Fennish bow gun with a hunter's scope attached. He fired again. The quarrel struck the trunk a few inches to her left.

"I know a tavern where you'd fight right in. Everyone there is as bad a shot as you are!" Maia shouted.

"I told you, the blasted thing pulls to the right. The previous owner isn't around to service it." The man swore under his breath. "How about this. You come out, and we'll go visit your two friends wandering in my woods. The young man is strong. I can use him. Give him to me, and I'll give you what you're after. I might be able to do something about that eye of yours, as well. What do you say? Do we have a deal? If not, I may have to find a use for the girl as well."

A rush of anger brought Maia out from behind the tree before she knew what she was doing. She didn't dare call on her fire or summon her armor. The blast that came with it would set the surrounding area ablaze, and she doubted her ability to control a fire of that size after what Arcturus had done to her sliver.

No fire. No armor or weapons. The situation called for a subtle approach. But since Maia and subtlety had not been on speaking terms for many years, and the man with the bow gun had just threatened Serenia's life, she opted to cross her arms over her head and charge full speed with an animal's growl rising in her throat.

The bow gun clicked. Maia veered to the side. The quarrel skipped across her ribs, but she didn't slow. When she reached the monk, she cleared the bow gun from his hand with a backhand slap and kicked him square in the chest. He flew back a dozen feet, crashing into a bramble bush at the edge of the glade.

"That was...more than...two bones!" the man wheezed. He stumbled from the bush, face covered in thorns, and broke into an awkward run.

"I don't have time for this." Maia hooked her toe under the bow gun and kicked it up into her hands. A quick pump of the handle on the underside of the weapon loaded a quarrel from its hopper. Though her dominant eye was destroyed, nobody could miss with a Fennish scope.

The quarrel whistled beyond the glade, its flight followed by a yelp and a thud. Maia followed the sound of the man's groans and found him rolling on the ground, clenching his right ass cheek.

"You weren't kidding. It does pull to the right." Maia shattered the bow gun against a tree and stalked toward the man, grabbing him and dangling him off the ground by the scruff of his robes. "That sounded expensive. What's your name?"

"Len."

"Okay, Lenny, let's—"

"It's short for Lenbraham."

"Lenny, I need you to listen to me. Very carefully. You strike me as the type of fellow that probably lives in a shitty hut. Which way is it?"

He gestured vaguely in the direction opposite the way she came, deeper into the dead woods. "Okay," Maia said. "We're going to your hut, and we're going to see what you have for me. If I find what I'm looking for, maybe I turn you over to one of the nicer magistrates. What do you say? Do we have a deal? I'll give you a moment to consider."

Maia dropped Lenny and snapped the quarrel sticking out of his rear, causing him to screech. He clenched his left side all the way back to his hut, nursing what were no doubt broken ribs. A mangled mass of dead branches formed a canopy covering that, though leafless, managed to block almost all the midday sun. An awning extended off the cone-shaped roof of the shitty hut, covering a simple workshop.

Curious, Maia veered toward the covered workshop. Caked blood stained the rough wood of the worktable. Curved metal tools, the kind hunters used to skin and clean game, hung from rusted hooks on a board fixed to the side of the hut, though Maia hadn't spotted any signs of wild game during her hike.

Having seen enough, Maia marched Lenny to the door of the hut and threw him over the threshold. Her breath caught in her throat. A shelf along one wall held potions and tonics sealed in stoppered glass bottles, while another held larger containers filled with viscera suspended in luminous fluid. On a small table next to a simple straw bed, she found a yellowed tome. Maia couldn't read the writing, but the diagrams of human and elven bodies in various stages of dismemberment she found as she leafed through the book told her all she needed to know.

"You're a necromancer," she growled.

"Indeed. This forest has been kind to me. By draining its life essence, I've lived quite a long and happy life."

"I'm not the first person who came here looking for a cure. Tell me what you did with the others."

"They were practice," Lenny replied, earning him a backhand to the face.

"Tell me where their bodies are!"

Lenny showed his bloodied teeth. "Everywhere. They're bound to me, now. While we were walking, I bade a few of my treasured friends to go and keep your companions company."

"If I kill you, whatever you've raised will die." Maia flexed and curled her fingers. It would be such an easy thing. Easier than the Nocteans she had killed. She wouldn't need her weapons or her fire. Just a tight grip on his neck and a sharp jerk, and he would be gone.

"You know your necromantic laws. But know that I don't fear you. You're no killer."

"I've killed before." She clenched the front of his robe, making a fist so tight it hurt. "You would be surprised."

"I would be," Lenny said. His grub-like face softened, and for a moment, he looked less like a mad hedge mage and more like a person capable of reason. "I've met many people in my long life. Killed more than half of them. Some come to my woods in search of the means to save a dying loved one. Others come to harvest the herbs that grow here to sell to the needy and desperate. Some are hard men, the kind whose stories can be penned in the blood they've spilled, with plenty of 'ink' to spare."

"Your point?"

"It's safe to say that, inside and out, figuratively and quite literally, I know people. And having peered into the depths of you, I know you, too. You've killed, but you're no killer. Now that I know that, I no longer fear you. You may bruise me or break me. I will recover with time. Without fear of death, there's no need to lie anymore. There is no Heartflower. Not here, anyway. I concocted that rumor to lead people to my woods so they might aid in my experiments. And even if I did have a Heartflower, it wouldn't help you. I'm afraid what's killing you is beyond its purported restorative powers."

Maia let Lenny slide from her grip and turned from him, eager to hide her frustrated scowl. "I guess you were lying when you said you didn't need to lie anymore. I've been to the best healers in the Freelands. None of them have seen anything like what I have. I'm supposed to believe that you know what it is."

"I would wager that none of those healers were necromancers," Lenny said. "You probably think our arts end at making corpses walk. I speak to dead kings and revel in their knowledge. I manipulate life in all its forms. If you believe nothing else I've told you, trust me when I say that I'm an expert in matters involving death magics. And I know enough of curses to know one when I feel it."

A curse. That wasn't possible. One of the healers would have discovered it. Maia scoffed. "So, it's just a curse, then. That's it?"

"It's just a curse in the way that a Flaming Archwolf is just a puppy with a mild case of heartburn." Lenny closed his eyes and felt the air with spread fingers. "This is an exquisite, ancient thing that's crushing your heart. Beautiful work. Whoever laid this on you, even I would be proud to call them master. It would take me months to even begin breaking something as perfect as this. It grows like a muscle, resisting your...huh."

Lenny screwed up his face. "Your body, it's... Living flesh can't hold that much magic. Just who are you?"

Maia pushed Lenny back through the doorway of the hut. "I thought you said you knew me."

She crossed her arms over her head and brought them down with a grunt. The hut exploded in a wash of fire, casting burning debris into the dead forest around them. Flames spread, fed by dry kindling and crackling with excitement. Maia stepped down from the charred remains of the hut clad in her damaged red armor.

"You're a Pilot?" Lenny screeched.

"Indeed. And since my apprentice doesn't appreciate my teachings, I have all the time in the world for you."

Lenny shrank back from her. "What do you intend to do?"

"I won't kill you. You're right about that. But I'm going to make sure you answer for your crimes. Before that, you're going to tell me every fucking thing you can about this curse, and you'll do what you can to break it. Then, you're going to take a look at my apprentice. I need to know if she's in danger. If she's cursed, too."

She shoved Lenny into a march, leading him away from the growing inferno feeding on the forest behind them.

Ren and Kas walked in silence. She wasn't sure if they were headed deeper into the dead woods or back toward Scarlet. It was hard to focus on anything other than the thought that Maia might be capable of the terrible things Kas suggested.

They had only known each other for a few months, but aside from his initial, necessary deception, Kas had never lied to her. He believed what he told her. But that didn't mean there wasn't more to the story.

Kas said something as they approached a large dirt mound. He disappeared over the top before Ren could ask him to repeat himself. Whatever it was, it couldn't have been that important. Not compared to the heavy thoughts she was contending with.

He reappeared at the top of the mound, waving his arms and shouting to her, then slipped back over the top. Ren trudged up the incline after him. In her distracted haze, she barely reacted in time to sidestep a flaming log hurtling over the top of the hill. When it tumbled to the bottom, it unfurled in a tangled heap, and she realized it wasn't a log. It was a body. And it wasn't her troubled thoughts clouding her vision. It was smoke.

"Ren!" Kas shouted. Two small explosions followed. He flew over the top of the mound and rolled sidelong down the hill. Dirt stuck to the black ichor smearing his face and bare arms, and his bow was missing. She went to help him to his feet, but he pushed her aside, drawing one of his stilettos and letting it fly.

The flaming body at the base of the mound, now on its feet, pawed at the length of steel sticking from its forehead for a moment, then collapsed. Kas marched to it and ripped his dagger free, wincing as he brushed at an errant flame that had stuck to his glove. "Didn't you hear me? They're comin'!"

She heard their cries shortly before they clambered over the top of the hill. Mottled gray flesh sloughed off their mismatched, sewn-on limbs. Their harmonized wails mixed with the crackling flames rising behind them, creating a mournful ballad that sent a shiver down Ren's back.

Zombies. But how? Necromancy was forbidden, especially in the Freelands, where the memory of the War of Bones remained strong. Who would dare raise this many corpses?

Her revolver leaped into her hand. Maia said it was only for emergencies; Ren decided in a heartbeat that a horde of flesh-eating ghouls and a roaring conflagration certainly qualified.

She took aim and squeezed the trigger, rendering the nearest zombie's head into a fine paste. She fired again, taking another zombie's torso off its body. Kas ran to the fallen half-zombie and plunged a stiletto into its forehead, completing the kill.

Ren fired again and again, stopping only to crack open her revolver and replace the spent shells with fresh death from her pouch. Five shots. Reload. Repeat. When her reaching fingers felt more of the leather walls of the pouch than spare shells, Ren began to worry. The walking corpses kept coming. Severed arms and hands inched across the sand toward them. A pair of legs, separated from the rest of their body, stumbled around aimlessly. Kas darted in and out of the fray, daggers flashing, tossing his walnut shell grenades and scattering ghouls with bursts of flame.

Sweat rolled down Ren's face. She blinked through the salty droplets blurring her vision. Eventually, the herd started to thin. Her left hand throbbed from her revolver's fierce, repeated kicks. She thought about drawing her rapier to conserve what little ammo remained when a shambling form in brown robes emerged from around the base of the hill, clutching its left side.

Ren's wolf pivoted into position, and without a second thought, she fired. The shot took the zombie in the chest, throwing it back against the trunk of a tree with a sickening crunch. One breath later, Maia was there, standing where the zombie had been, wearing her damaged armor and a wide-eyed look of sheer terror.

"What the fuck!" Maia yelled. Her shocked gaze lingered on the dead zombie. When she approached Ren, her face was flushed and tight. "You just shot the only... You could have shot me! What did I tell you? Only for emergencies!" She turned to an approaching, flame-covered zombie, planted her foot on its chest, and launched the putrid corpse back. "Come on. We have to go. I set the zombie forest on fire."

Her mentor's outburst left Ren shaken. "What?" was all Ren could muster.

"I set the zombie forest on fire. What part of that don't you understand? Kas! Get your ass over here! We're retreating!"

Maia brought Scarlet's foot thundering down. Smoke and flames carrying the memories of everything that happened in the horrible forest curled around the Vanguardian's foot and drifted into the sky to be forgotten in the heavens.

Stomping out a burning zombie forest was a lot like stomping Brackenberries back at her family's vineyard. Maia could almost feel the purple pulp squishing between her toes every time Scarlet crushed a copse of burning trees.

By the time she was finished, those simpler days filled with berries and laughter were the furthest thing from her mind. She could only think about how at some point, while stomping out what remained of the burning forest, she had stepped on the body of the necromancer Serenia had murdered, a necromancer who had told her that her insides were being crushed by a powerful curse that had no known cure.

Apart from the organized crew that had kidnapped Serenia in Galford to get to her, most of Maia's enemies tended to come at her directly. They used crossbows. Knives. One time, a pig strapped with some very primitive alchemical explosives. Who among her enemies had the skill, the means, and the sheer darkness in their heart needed to lay such a powerful curse on her?

The Emperor, most definitely, but from what little Maia knew of curses, a mage needed to be close to perform them, and it would be obvious what they were attempting. Could Heretic have cursed her when she remade her? Maybe all Pilots had a fuse that would eventually burn out to keep them from turning on their creator once their duty was done.

Maia had no answers. Serenia had put a fist-sized bullet hole in the chest of the one person who might have been able to tell her anything. Necromancers were not only hard to find, they also weren't typically forthcoming about the intricacies of their art. She wouldn't find another so easily, and if she did, she couldn't count on them to be skilled enough to help.

She wanted to scream at Serenia for ending two lives with a single misplaced bullet. Three, if Serenia also shared her curse. Instead, Maia kept stomping the forest long after the crushed wood and blackened dirt stopped smoldering, until her rage had been squelched as well.

If she told Serenia the full extent of the damage she had caused, it might be enough. Serenia might quit her quest to become a Pilot. This was an opportunity. A lesson. Actions had consequences, and not everything could be made right with an apology.

But that meant telling Serenia that she was a murderer, that she was just as filthy and unworthy as Maia. The idea stung her heart in a way her curse never could.

Hurting Serenia wasn't the goal. Maia's duty was to stop her from walking the same path she walked, and if that proved impossible, to divert her down a better one. She could spare her unlikely apprentice this pain, at least. She could save her for a little while longer.

Maia didn't realize she had stopped moving until she felt the tingling of her aching muscles finally getting a brief rest. When she looked up, Serenia was standing in front of her, head bowed, presenting her revolver to Maia like she was making an offering at a temple.

The weapon hurt to look at and stung to touch even though she was still wearing her gauntlets, but Maia managed to nudge the revolver back toward Serenia.

The girl needed to understand the weight of her actions. But not today.

"It's okay," Maia said in a soft voice that nobody had bothered to offer her when she failed. "You didn't hurt me. I was frightened, that's all. I'm sorry for yelling at you."

"I feel like I continue to fail you." Serenia holstered her weapon. "You were right. I haven't been taking my training seriously, and I've been allowing my feelings for Kas to get in the way of our duty. But those are just excuses. The truth is, I've been angry with you for some time, and I haven't felt free to speak my mind."

The crunch of an apple turned Maia and Serenia's heads. "Hey. Just wanted to say I'm still here," Kasper said with a weak wave. "Did you want me to—"

Maia willed Scarlet's hatch plates to open. Kasper hurried outside onto Scarlet's shoulder.

"I know why you're angry with me," Maia said.

"You do?"

"Yeah. I've been keeping something from you for a while now. Something I should have told you a long time ago."

"Oh?" Serenia crossed her hands behind her back.

Maia nodded gravely. "And I promise, I'll tell you about what happened between Kasper and me, why I give him such a hard time. Sometime. I promise."

"Oh. *That's* what you want to talk about."

"Is there something else on your mind?"

Serenia crossed her arms and regarded Maia for a long time. "I suppose not."

"Great." Maia forced a smile. "Now, let Kasper back in so we can get going. You're piloting Scarlet for the rest of the day."

"Really?"

"You were right, too. You'll never learn if I don't give you a chance. You can stop if the pain gets to be too much."

Serenia took her place in the control beam. The hatch plates opened. Kasper tossed the core of his apple over his shoulder as they shut behind him. "Everyone okay?"

"More or less," Serenia said.

"Hey," Maia said. "They were just zombies. Okay? They were monsters. They had to be destroyed. You didn't do anything wrong."

"I know. Thank you."

"Oh, and Kasper?" Maia said, angling her head back over her shoulder. "Breakfast was great. Thank you."

"Well, you're more than welcome, Sun," he said.

Serenia cleared her throat. "So, what's our next destination? I assume you have some additional training planned?"

Maia looked out Scarlet's viewport at the ruin she had caused by daring to hope. "No more training for today. I don't know about you two, but I'm exhausted. We'll take it easy. Tomorrow, after morning training, we'll go someplace special. Keep following the mountains, toward Brimholme. That way." She pointed out the corner of the viewport.

Brimholme. Maia wasn't looking forward to exhuming the truth that waited for them there, but it couldn't stay buried forever. Serenia needed to see the extent of Maia's greatest failure. She had to know the secret Maia had kept to herself for the last four years, had to understand that the Pilots were a mistake. The last thing Maia wanted to do was go digging through the past, but for both of their sakes, it had to be done.

It had to be done.

Chapter 23
A Brief Reprieve

Scarlet's cabin rumbled as Ren worked one of the Vanguardian's feet into a crag in the mountain face. Since Scarlet had only one arm, and the mere act of piloting sent pain swelling up Ren's spine, her ascent up the mountain had taken most of the morning.

"Just admit it," Maia said, thrusting a finger at Kas and whittling away some of Ren's much-needed focus. "Say I'm right."

Kas sat cross-legged in the corner of the cabin, cupping a rune-inscribed walnut shell and a small, conjured flame in his hands. Sweat ran down his brow as he shifted and swayed with Scarlet's jerky movements. "I don't know, Sun."

"Seems simple to me. Living things can't hold enchantments for long. Non-living things can. That's how necromancy works. Once a body isn't living anymore, you can enchant it like those cute little nuts of yours. You're changing what something is, the way it behaves. Enchanting and necromancy are two sides of the same coin."

At least they were talking again. After the dead forest, the three of them spent the rest of the day and the following night in relative silence. Ren wondered if they had nightmares that night like she had. Maia seemed the least bothered by what had happened. That worried Ren. That practiced mask of calm, with its easy smile and hollow eyes, had returned thicker and sturdier than ever. Such a mighty defense would have to be protecting something raw and tender.

Whatever it was, when Ren looked at Maia, she kept asking herself who she was looking at. Maia had killed so many Nocteans. And Salvian. Could she be capable of killing her own child? Or her partner?

Ren had Kas' half of the story. She needed the rest, so she could understand. That was the first step.

Kas peered up at Maia. "I'm not sure you're makin' the point you want to make."

A chip fell from Maia's mask. Her lip quivered. "Come again?"

"Well," Kas said, shifting his focus back to the dwindling flame in his hands. "Say you're right. Can't enchant a livin' thing. You're a livin' thing, and you're plenty magical."

"Something about the way Pilots are made changed us. I can't explain it."

"You've been enchanted. You could say that, right? Well, if enchantment is the same as necromancy, and you've been enchanted, then you're sayin' you and Ren have more in common with those zombies we fought than with regular folk. Is that what you're tryin' to argue?"

Maia showed her teeth. "I have to ask: are you looking to be thrown headfirst off a mountain? And not necessarily this mountain. Maybe I'll drag you down this one, up another, and then toss you off that one. How about that?"

"Maia, please, stop antagonizing him," Ren said. "And Kas, can't you wait to do that until we reach the plateau?"

Kas pushed the flickering flame into the walnut shell and held it shut. It hissed for a moment as it blackened and sealed shut. "You won't drop us. I trust you. We couldn't be safer."

"As much as I appreciate the sentiment, truly, your work is quite distracting."

The cabin shifted as Scarlet worked to find her next foothold. "You're distracted. Good," Maia said. "Fighting is chaotic. You need to be able to keep your focus, whether you're dealing with screaming townsfolk, enemies coming at you from all sides, or your boyfriend making magical fire nuts in the cabin of your walking war machine."

"It's more than a simple distraction that I can simply tune out," Ren said. She found her hold and pushed off, launching Scarlet up the mountain face and grabbing onto an outcropping large enough to support her weight. "It's the fire he's conjuring. I can feel it."

Maia crossed her arms behind her back and squinted. "You shouldn't be able to feel any heat from that far. They're baby flames. I'm surprised Kasper actually hurts anything with them. But you're saying you can feel them."

"Yes, I can. And could you put out the fire in your hands, as well? I'm about to slip."

A breath left Maia's lips, and she revealed the flickering flames licking up from her palm. "You felt this, too."

"Makes sense," Kas said. "She's a Pilot."

"She just might be," Maia said. Her jaw trembled as she stared into the flames. Slowly, they shrank back into her palm. She panted from the effort.

"Are you okay?" Ren said.

"I'm fine. Don't look at me. Look at the mountain. Once you get to the top, we can begin the day's training."

"I thought the climb was the training!" Ren said.

"I never said that. This is just a warm-up. Besides, you're the one who wanted more time with Scarlet."

"Why didn't you just Teleport us to the top? For that matter, why haven't we Teleported to Brimholme, so I might see whatever it is you're dying to show me?"

Maia approached the viewport. "That's the problem with Nocteans. You're always looking to the end of the road. You don't care about the path you have to walk to get there. I suppose that explains why the Emperor thought he could achieve world peace by summoning an army of the living dead and turning them loose on the people he wanted to rule."

"I hardly think that my desire to avoid falling to our deaths and the War of Bones are comparable," Ren said.

"There's a reason for everything. We'll get to Brimholme when it's time for us to get there. We're not Teleporting to the plateau because I want you tired for your training. It'll keep you focused on technique over strength. Besides, controlling Scarlet is an amazing feeling. I don't know why you would want to miss a single moment."

Ren flattened Scarlet against the wall of jutting stone and inched her fingers up toward the next handhold. When she first connected with Scarlet, she could barely get her to respond to her movements. With training, Scarlet's limbs had become her own. Maia was right. Nothing else in the world compared to the sheer power and thrill of piloting a Vanguardian, and Ren couldn't think of a good reason why Maia would ever want to give it up.

Perhaps she didn't intend to. Ren tried not to entertain that possibility. One way or another, she had to secure ownership of Scarlet. If she didn't believe with all her heart that she would accomplish her goal, she was doomed to fail.

There was still the matter of what to do with Scarlet once Ren had her. She knew that, at some point, she needed to return to Noctis, to her father. Beyond that, she didn't have a plan. She recalled what her father had said about the need for more Vanguardians. It was true that she couldn't save the world alone. Was creating an army of war machines the only option?

And what of Maia and her condition? And Kas? What would their futures look like if Ren returned to Noctis and submitted to the Emperor's will?

Her concentration faltered. Scarlet's fingers slipped from the rock. Ren scrambled for purchase as the world tipped backward, finding nothing but empty air in her grasp.

A pair of hands wrapped around her waist. She closed her eyes, breaking her connection with Scarlet, and allowed Maia to throw her clear as they had planned. Maia stepped into the control beam. With three thrusts of her fists, the spinning world outside of the cabin became wreathed in swirling red lights. A second later, Ren fell into Kas, who grabbed her and shielded her with his body as they tumbled against the back wall of the cabin.

"Well, that was bracing. Any further, and Scarlet might not have been able to absorb the impact." Maia brought Scarlet back to her feet and allowed Ren to retake her place in the control beam. Scarlet stood at the edge of a long plateau dotted with patches of grass and exposed rock that blended into thick bunches of pine trees. Behind them, over the edge of the cliff Ren had failed to scale, the Freelands extended further than she could see. In the distance, stretches of tilled farmland looked like little flicks of an artist's brush next to a village so tiny she almost missed it entirely.

Ren had never felt so small in her entire life. When she looked past the trees to the end of the plateau, where the Sinadaria Mountains continued their sharp thrust up through a billowing sheet of clouds, she felt even smaller.

"Is it safe for us to be up this high?" Ren said.

"Don't worry," Maia said. "We're not even close to the summit. Sinadarians don't like to look down. Well, they look down on the people who live on the ground, but you know what I mean."

"Have you ever been up there?"

"Not even I'm that brave. Forget the elves. It's time to get to work. Head to that outcropping. That's where you'll be training today."

Ren approached the large, jagged spire Maia had pointed to, a rocky protrusion half as tall as Scarlet that melded with the wall of the cliff behind it. She couldn't place the type of stone, but it looked dense and sturdy.

"Okay," Maia said. "Your job is to kick that thing."

"That's all?" Ren said.

"Of course that's not all. Scarlet can't punch from the left, so you need a weapon on that side. You need to get comfortable using kicks at a moment's notice." Maia raised her knee and launched three quick turning kicks without touching her foot down. "Your goal is to do that."

Scarlet's weight shifted to her right leg. Ren lifted her left knee and angled it toward the rock in preparation. She let her foot drift back to the earth. "I don't mean to question your methods, but Scarlet can easily smash through the rock. Don't I run the risk of causing an avalanche? I'm worried I may hurt somebody on the ground below."

This time, when Maia smiled, it reached all the way up to her eye. She laid a hand on Ren's shoulder. "You're absolutely right, Princess. You've already passed today's test." She retrieved a rucksack from the corner, headed for the hatch, and motioned for Kas to join her. "This exercise is about control. Hit the rock, but don't destroy it. Soft touches only. Come find us at the far end of the plateau when you're done."

"What'll we do in the meantime?" Kas said.

"There's a delightful little hot spring tucked in past those trees. We could all use a soak." Maia waved to Ren. "When you're finished, we'll be there."

Ren offered a salute and willed Scarlet's hatch to open. Once Maia and Kas stepped onto Scarlet's palm, she lowered them to the ground. She waited until they vanished into the trees before she dropped Scarlet into a fighting stance and set about her task.

Hours later, Ren arrived at camp, having followed a thin trail of smoke snaking into the sky from beyond a small copse of pine trees. Kas greeted her with fried bacon, some bread, and a hug. When he pulled away, his black leathers were darkened by large splotches of Ren's sweat.

"How was it?" Kas said.

"Laborious."

"Sun's waitin' for you at the spring. Follow that path around by those boulders."

"You're not joining us?" Ren asked.

"I'll go later. Wouldn't be proper for us to bathe together just yet."

"Oh! Of course. What with the nudity and... Yes, thank you for the meal. I'll be going now."

Ren scurried away before her face turned completely red. She ate as she walked. The path ended in a circle of small boulders surrounding a calm, stream-fed pool of the bluest water she had ever seen.

And yet, there was a distinct lack of steam rising from the pool. Ren's shoulders slumped. Maia had promised her a hot spring. Still, cold water was better than no water. Once she was out of her sweat-drenched clothes, Ren waded in.

"Death from above!" came a booming voice. Something dropped from the sky like a shooting star and crashed into the pool. Ren fell onto her rear, shielding herself from the massive splash with her arms. When she finished drying her eyes, Maia was standing in the middle of the water, naked as the day she was born, laughing and clutching her injured side.

"What is wrong with you!" Ren cried. "You need to be more careful! You're still injured. And you got your bandages all wet!"

Maia poked at the squishy, wet wrapping covering her eye. "Yeah. You're right. I suppose I'm starting to get used to... I'm sorry. I'll leave you to it."

"No, wait," Ren said, grabbing Maia's wrist as she waded past her. "Stay. Please. I'm sorry." She splashed Maia. "Look. I'm having fun, see? How often do we get to relax halfway between the land and the heavens? I can see why you've been meaning to take us here for some time."

"What?" Maia said.

"When we left Whitehorn. You said there was a place you wanted to visit before we reached Brimholme."

"Oh!" Maia rubbed her shoulder and looked past her. "Yeah. Yeah, this is where I wanted to go. I needed to see if this spring was still here. I was thinking about taking Elizabeth up here. When this is all over."

Ren saw the lie for what it was, a diversion from something more painful, but there was nothing dishonest about the warmth in Maia's voice when she spoke of Elizabeth, so she didn't press further.

"Well, it appears that this spring is no longer hot," Ren said.

Maia squatted in the water. With her fists clenched at her sides, her face softened into a vacant expression like she was staring through the fabric of time itself.

"What are you doing?" Ren asked.

"Trying to. Warm up. The water," Maia grunted. A large bubbles breached the surface of the spring.

"That's disgusting!"

"Just wait." Maia exhaled, long and slow. Waves of thin flame radiated off her body. From the depths of the pool, more bubbles churned in steady streams.

"Oh. Oh!" Ren sat down and let the soothing heat take her.

When a fine mist hung over the water, Maia slumped and leaned back, panting. "See? Hot spring. I thought it would be good for your back."

"Mmm." It was the perfect gift for a sore Pilot. Ren's aches melted away like a bad dream. "How did you find this place?"

"When everyone in the world knows who you are, you start going places people can't. Edgar and I found this spot. It was one of our favorites."

Edgar was on the list of things Maia forbade Ren from talking about, so she had nothing to say in response. The silence expanded between them, filled with all the things Ren wanted to ask and needed to know.

"What are you thinking about?" Maia said. "You're doing that thing with your forehead."

"What thing?" Ren said.

"That thing you do when you're thinking really hard." Maia creased her forehead and puffed out her cheeks. "Like this."

Ren splashed her with the back of her hand. "I do not look like that! If you must know, I was thinking about Kas."

"Of course."

"Not like that. We talked, in the forest, before the zombies and the fire and the yelling."

"I know. You asked him about Leona," Maia said.

Despite the tranquil heat of the spring, the tension returned to Ren's back and shoulders. "How did you know that?"

"I didn't. You just told me."

Ren sprang to her feet. "You're horrible. I'm leaving."

"Wait. Don't go. I just wanted to know if you talked to him first so I have an idea of what you might already know."

"You could have asked me! This just shows how little you respect me. Enjoy your bath."

"Hey, wait. I'm sorry I tricked you. That wasn't fair." Maia patted the surface of the water. "Come on. Sit. Please?

Ren complied, not yet ready to leave the soothing warmth behind just yet.

"I don't know exactly what Kasper told you," Maia said. "I can guess. And if I'm right, then everything he told you is the truth. Or a version of it. He has a right to hate me too, you know. I can't fault him for that."

"I don't think he hates you, Maia. Perhaps if you sat and talked with him for once, instead of tearing into him all the time, you both might find common cause. A way forward."

"I wish I had the luxury of being able to move past what he did. He's a reminder of a life I can't go back to. A life I wish I could forget."

"But you can't."

"No. I can't." Maia cracked her neck. "Tell you what. You wanted honesty. Even though you used up your three questions from our game, I'll let you have another. Forget the rules. Ask me anything."

Ren's mind raced. She could ask about Kas. Or Leona. Or the fate of the Pilots. Or why Maia had lied about the death of Ren's mother. Whatever she chose, it needed to be strategic. Decisive. Too much time had passed, and she hadn't made up her mind. When the heat started to fade, Maia left the pool and shook the water out of her hair.

Finally, Ren made her choice. "Why didn't you take Elizabeth with us?"

Maia turned, clutching her shirt to her chest, wearing confusion.

"We took Kas along," Ren continued, "and you don't even care for him, yet it's obvious you care for Elizabeth a great deal. Why didn't you ask her to come with you?"

"It's because I care about her that I can't take her with me," Maia said. She looked down at herself, at the many scars and bruises which should have already healed. "I don't want her seeing this. The Sunder she doesn't know. The one who's mad all the time. Hurt all the time. Dying. She deserves better than me."

If Maia was set on denying herself the happiness she deserved, there wasn't much left to say. Feeling defeated, Ren left the spring and dried off. While they were dressing, Maia tapped her arm and presented her with a cotton cloth.

"That's a little small for drying off," Ren said.

"Oh. It's not for that. It's that time again, right?"

Her monthly blood. Of course. "Thank you." The tension she had left in the hot spring returned.

When she awoke from her four-year slumber, none of Ren's cousins or childhood friends would see her. On the rare occasions where she found time to be social, she mostly spent her time in parlors with daughters of other noble military families her father favored.

One day, when she was feeling especially comfortable, she let slip that she only had her monthly blood every other month. That had been a mistake. One of the girls remarked on how unusual that was for a noble daughter. Soon, they stopped calling on her. She never told another soul after that.

Then, when she turned sixteen, her father neglected to arrange a debut party for her. Instead, he gifted Ren a fine rapier and a wolf-engraved revolver, weapons fit for an officer, not a young lady. Did he know that something wasn't right with her? Was he trying to hide her? Was he ashamed? If she didn't engage in the usual ceremony of pomp and circumstance that all noble daughters went through, would she ever become a woman?

Ren had dashed those thoughts from her mind and relied on her never-ending training to keep herself occupied. All that mattered was becoming a Pilot. Now that circumstances had left her with room for more than training, the thoughts were creeping in through her seams, tagging along with the many new worries she had to contend with.

Ren handed the cloth back to Maia. "That won't be necessary. Thank you, though."

"Oh." Maia crumpled the cloth in her hand. Her scar shifted with her frown. "I guess they did a better job than I thought."

"What do you mean?"

"You have your monthly blood every two months. Same as me. Same as any female Pilot. Which means you... Blue Hells. I bet they never told you." Maia ran a hand through her damp hair. "Pilots can't have children."

Once she woke from her coma, Ren decided that she would spend her new life becoming the best possible version of herself, no matter the cost.

She hadn't yet settled on whether that best self was also a mother. Apparently, that choice had already been made for her.

"How do you know for sure? How can you know?" Ren said.

"Because our creator told me so." Maia donned her shirt and breeches, laced up her boots, and sat on one of the small boulders surrounding the pool. "I was out chopping wood on the night of my sixteenth birthday when she came."

"You were chopping wood on your birthday?" Ren said.

"I guess you have servants for that sort of thing. In the Freelands, most of us have to do for ourselves. No wood, no fire. So, I was out chopping wood. The next thing I know, I'm tied to a metal table while a devil pumps my blood full of alchemical bullshit that makes my whole body feel like it's one raw nerve. She remade all five of us, piece by piece. When she was done, she put a sliver of fire inside me. A small piece of pure primordial magic from beyond the Veil, attuned to flame. She said it would bolster the other magics. With it, I could bond with my Vanguardian, which would awaken the rest of my gifts."

Ren finished dressing and took a seat next to Maia on the boulder. For the second time in two days, she sat and waited patiently, ready to receive a painful lesson in history.

"I've never told anyone this. Not all of it." Maia swallowed. Her breath quivered. "I remember asking her why. Why she was doing this to us. She told us that her name was Heretic. She was making us into weapons to fight a war against her people, the Kith, and said we—"

"The Kith?"

"They command the Behemoths and Ferals. They're fleshcrafters from another world. Now they want ours."

"One of *them* turned you all into Pilots?"

"Yes," Maia said. "Heretic is a Kith, but her people cast her out. She never said why. She made us to fight for her, to stop them from taking over our world." Maia turned to Ren, eyes heavy and sullen. "All five of us agreed to never tell the world about the Kith. Better that people think the Behemoths and Ferals are mindless, acting on instinct. Otherwise, people might try to seek out whoever was in control. Maybe they might try to make a deal with them. Besides, would you trust a protector who was armed by the same people raining destruction down on you?

"When Heretic was done telling us about our purpose, she explained our new 'gifts.' She wove spells into us that allowed us to detect the Kith's creations, and even the Kith themselves, if they ever made it to our world and we were close enough to sense them. But the combination of spells and alchemics used to remake us robbed us of the ability to have children. She gave us all this power, but she took from us, too. She never asked. It would have been nice to have been asked."

With every breath, Maia's shoulders heaved. The binding will that had been holding her together all these long years was unraveling, falling off in strips until only a sobbing husk remained.

Through the cracks in the weathered shell, Ren could see where Maia had broken, sharp and jagged, forcing herself back together time and time again until the pieces didn't fit together quite right anymore. It didn't stop her from enduring, from doing what was expected of her, long after she broke past the point of repair. Even then, after all her suffering, she continued to do her duty, taking on an apprentice she never wanted.

When Ren looked at Maia, all she could see were the lingering scars of a life lived too fast. Her seven years as a Pilot must have felt like an eternity. The thought didn't do anything to sate the anger boiling in Ren's chest, or the need for answers regarding her mother's death, or the reckoning she knew would follow. That anger could wait. Instead, Ren allowed her heart to break for her teacher who, for all her many faults, was doing the best she could with what she had.

She wrapped her arms around Maia, cradling her head. Maia bawled into Ren's chest as she shattered, gripping her with the fervor of someone holding on for dear life.

For all Ren knew, she might very well have been.

They clung to each other until Maia ran out of tears and her breathing calmed. "Thanks," Maia said as she pulled away. "I think you might be the only living person who could ever understand."

"We're Pilots. We're in this fight together." While Maia rebuilt herself, Ren started to gather her own pieces and found one that wouldn't slide back into place. "Maia?" she said, her voice barely a whisper. "How will I know when I've become a woman?"

Slowly, Maia put her arms around Ren's shoulders and held her gaze. "Listen to me, Princess. If there's one thing the world has no shortage of, it's people with opinions. Some folks say you're a woman when you have your first blood, or when you take a lover, or when you bear a child. Or when you have one of those stupid Noctean coming-out parties. None of that shit matters. Some women don't have monthly blood, or sometimes, they skip a month. Some never take lovers or bear children. Some never have coming-out parties. You're a woman when *you* feel like you're a woman. You'll just know."

Their foreheads touched. "Blue Hells, kid," Maia said. "If you throw away everything else I've taught you, please, *please* remember this one thing. Nobody in this world can ever tell you who and what you are. Only you can decide that. That's your power. Don't ever let anybody else have it. Okay?"

A warm swell pushed its way through Ren's shuddering heart. "I understand." She wanted to say more, so much more, but a sudden throbbing ache in the back of her head set her heart beating faster and harder.

"Behemoth," Ren whispered. "Do you think we can get to it before the dragon does?"

Maia sniffled and coughed. "Definitely." She wiped her eye, pushed off the boulder, and marched toward the path, motioning for Ren to follow. "What are you waiting for, Princess?"

"Go on ahead. I need to tell Kas where you're headed so he doesn't think we've abandoned him."

"No. You're coming with me. You're fighting the Behemoth."

Ren froze. "A-are you serious? You told me I wasn't ready, that I was reckless and looking to sate my own ego, and after what happened in the dead forest and Castle Blackwood... I thought..."

"Hey. A good soldier always follows orders," Maia said. "I'm ordering you to kill that fucking Behemoth. Do you have a problem with that?"

The excitement coursing through her body like bottled lightning propelled Ren into a mad dash. Maia kept pace despite her many wounds, her arms and legs pumping faster than the guiding pulse they shared. Ren called to Kas as she passed by the camp, and he chased after them.

As they bolted toward Scarlet, the thumping in the back of Ren's head told her exactly where her foe waited. And when she got there, she would show Maia and Kas just how far she had come.

Chapter 24

A Second Chance

As the churning nimbus of light outside Scarlet's viewport faded, Ren dropped into a crouch to avoid being hurled across the cabin as Scarlet lurched violently to the side.

Outside, rent stone chunks rained down, throwing up large gouts of water as they plunged into the sea surrounding them. Sheets of amber and pink cast by the fading sun glimmered over the lake's surface when it finally settled.

"Welcome to the Sea of Knives!" Maia said.

"What in the Blue Hells just happened?" Ren said.

"We Teleported into something. One of those rock things," Maia said, pointing to one of the many jagged claws of porous stone curling up from the water at odd angles. They must have been what gave the narrow sea its name.

"Haven't you Teleported here before, Sun?" Kas said from where he lay sprawled on the cabin floor. He groaned and rolled over.

Maia shut her eye and stepped from the control beam so Ren could take her place. "If I'm going by memory, the landscape may have changed. When I'm tracking a Behemoth or a pack of Ferals, the image is rough. Hazy. Mistakes happen. Two solid things can't be in the same place at the same time. One has to give. Looks like the rock lost this one."

Ren blinked. "And what, pray tell, would happen if we Teleported inside something much larger than Scarlet?"

"Worry about that when it happens."

"*When* it happens?"

"*If* it happens. Now, focus," Maia said, pointing across the sea. "It's coming."

The Behemoth's landing sent frothy surf jetting into the air. The sea rolled in soft waves as the Behemoth started its approach, each step matching the incessant pulsing in the back of Ren's mind.

If anyone ever asked her to describe what a winged, purple-skinned frog walking on two legs might look like, Ren would have a fine visual reference to draw from. Layers of white bandages covered the frog Behemoth's thin, gangling limbs and torso. Black, bat-like wings folded over its shoulders like a mantle, a stark contrast to the jaundiced yellow of its bulbous eyes.

Its cream-colored throat puffed up, and the Behemoth croaked loud enough to shake the stone spires thrusting from the sea around it. Muscles expanded beneath elastic skin, bulking up its frame until it bore the carved physique of a traveling strongman.

All the Behemoths Ren had seen in her short time as a Pilot were Scarlet's size or smaller. This frog-bat monster stood an entire head taller than her Vanguardian.

"Should I get out for this?" Kas asked.

"No. This is the safest place in the world right now," Ren said.

"She's right," Maia said. She leaned against the back wall of the cabin with her arms crossed. "A few miles behind us is the town of Fulton. We won't make it there and back in time to drop you off. Princess needs to win before the Behemoth makes landfall."

Ren rolled her neck. The control beam sent hot splinters of pain up her spine. "What is our plan, should I fail?"

"Don't have one. My right arm's still injured. That fight with Slapdash only made it worse. You're on your own, Princess. Better get moving. First, you'll need to—"

"Name it," Ren finished. "'Wartwing' seems appropriate. May I proceed?"

Maia held her hands up. "This is your fight."

Wartwing had its arms thrust out to either side. It opened its mouth. "The time of your death draws near, Pilot!" Wartwing screamed in a high falsetto. Ren expected a deeper tone, something to match the timbre of its stone-shaking bellow. Since she was staring at a titanic walking frog-bat, something that shouldn't exist to begin with, she tempered the rest of her expectations.

"Great, we've got a talker," Maia muttered.

"It changes nothing." Ren reached out to Scarlet, extending her will. She had never pushed her voice beyond the cabin, as Maia often did, and was surprised to hear her words booming over the water. "Surrender, Behemoth, and I promise you a quick and painless death!"

"Surrender?" Wartwing cried. "It is you who should be surrendering, Pilot!" The beast's dark wings unfurled, drinking the caramel sunset. "I am the terror that flies in the night! There is no hope left for you, pathetic little creature. Hide in your child's toy, that broken plaything you traipse around in, if you must. It will only make your defeat and ultimate demise that much sweeter when I—"

"I'm sorry," Ren shouted. "I can't understand a word you're saying. Your voice is utterly ridiculous. Would you mind repeating all that?"

Throw your opponent off their balance.

Wartwing puffed up and released another deafening croak. The sheer force of the expelled wind whipped the water between them into small waves. Ren settled back into her fighting stance with her right arm leading.

Her opponent was bigger than she was, but that meant it would be slower. She lifted her chin a little higher and took an advancing step.

Before her foot touched down, the pink, squishy tip of Wartwing's tongue slapped Scarlet's viewport and held fast. Ren's back bent painfully as Wartwing wrenched Scarlet forward into the water.

She managed to get Scarlet's arm under her. Metal fingers dug into the soft seabed. As she pushed up, something slammed into Scarlet's back and drove her under.

Wet, loose sand filled Scarlet's viewport. Maia and Kas crouched on the glass that had become the new floor of the cabin, shielding their heads from a falling rucksack filled with pots and pans.

Short, quick breaths were all Ren could manage. The thrumming of her racing heart doubled the throbbing in her head, filling her ears with a maddening rhythm that scattered her thoughts and left only the memory of her fight with Lionheart.

She was going to die. Maia was going to die. And Kas. And the people of Fulton and everyone else in the world. All because she couldn't master her bloody Vanguardian, despite all her training.

Her body slackened. All she had to do was close her eyes, and the burning spreading up her back would stop. The burden of being the world's protector would slip from her shoulders. She could rest. She wanted to rest. All Ren had done for the last several years was struggle and toil. All that pushing, all for nothing.

As the lids of her eyes started to close, Scarlet's cabin rocked. Ren's back arched. Wartwing stomped on Scarlet again.

It laughed, the sound somewhere between a croak and a chuckle. "Pathetic! I was told that Pilots were formidable opponents. Such a disappointment!"

Disappointment. To the daughter of Arcturus Valerius, being a disappointment was worse than death. It was unacceptable.

She wouldn't lose. Couldn't lose. Not here. Not ever again.

Ren growled through gritted teeth and tensed until she was as taut as iron. She focused on the direction Wartwing's voice had come from, drew her right leg in, and snapped it out behind her.

Metal connected with flesh and bone. Ren pulled both legs in and brought Scarlet onto her feet while Wartwing pulled on a rock spire to right itself. When its tongue came lashing again, Ren was ready with a duck and a weave that brought her beneath Wartwing's jaw.

A muscled arm arced in low from the left, where Scarlet had no arm to defend with. Ren angled away. Wartwing's hook rode the slope of Scarlet's body and skipped off the remnant of her left arm, missing her head completely. Ren couldn't reach its head, so she drove Scarlet's fist into its flexed trunk and threw her metal bulk into the blow.

Despite its size advantage, Wartwing staggered. Ren pressed the advantage, pounding Wartwing's ribs as it struggled to regain its balance. The fight was reaching its conclusion. One quick flick of her wrist to summon Scarlet's arm blade. One thrust and it would be over.

As Wartwing teetered and fell, it planted both legs on Scarlet's chest and pushed, throwing her away. Scarlet's back smashed into one of the stone talons extending from the sea bottom. Ren rolled around it, taking cover from another tongue lash.

"You need to close the distance!" Maia shouted.

"I am well aware!" Ren called back. Wartwing's tongue whipped the air next to her head when she tried to leave her hiding place. Now that it knew how dangerous Scarlet was up close, it would likely keep its distance, seeking to disable her with its tongue before moving in for the kill.

She wouldn't be able to drag the Behemoth to her as Maia had done with Slapdash. One jerk of its tongue had toppled Scarlet, despite her incredible weight. What else could she do?

On foot, against a foe her size, she would have employed her revolver. But Scarlet didn't have a revolver. All she had was a fist, two feet, and an arm blade that wouldn't help her unless she could get close enough to use it.

Ren's lower back had gone almost completely numb from the pain lancing through her spine. She circled the rock, keeping it between her and her foe while she tried to work out a path to victory.

"Fool! You can't hide forever! My tongue will seek you out!" Wartwing cried. Its tongue snapped into the spire, the whipping blow shaking the rock. Small, broken shards of porous stone tinkled against Scarlet's chest.

The falling stones plucked at a fresh memory. Earlier that day, during her training, Ren had taken great care to avoid causing an avalanche. A shower of falling rocks could be devastating. And out in the middle of the sea, with no chance of harming innocent bystanders, a little devastation was exactly what Ren needed.

Always be prepared to adapt. Thank you for the reminder.

Ren moved Scarlet to the side of the sprouting stone, raised her right knee, and blasted the rock with a low kick, just above the water line. The spire cracked and fell away in chunks. Without touching the ground, just like Maia had made her practice, she chambered Scarlet's leg and fired another turning kick, breaking almost all the way through the spire.

With her third kick, she angled high. Scarlet's shin smashed the top half of the spire as it teetered, sending the mass of rock sailing through the air.

It wasn't a revolver bullet, but Ren's impromptu projectile had the benefit of being too large for Wartwing to dodge. Tons of rock collided with the Behemoth's head and shattered. Wartwing wobbled, eyes half-closed, swinging its hands at the empty air in a daze.

The thumping in her head and the slamming beat of her heart united like a single thundering war drum. With fist and feet, she hammered Wartwing's chest and head over and over, ending her assault with a flying side kick.

As Scarlet's foot crunched into Wartwing's chest and the Behemoth flew backward through the air, Ren knew she had erred. With space to breathe, Wartwing spread its black wings wide and flapped to right itself. It croaked. At such a close range, the reverberation resonated like a blacksmith's anvil ringing inside her skull.

When she had shaken the dizziness away and her vision cleared, she caught the barest glimpse of Wartwing's tongue snapping from its jaws. Ren raised Scarlet's arm to deflect it. The fleshy tongue bent over Scarlet's fist, wrapping around her torso and binding her.

Powerful wings flapped and took Wartwing off into the coming twilight. Ren jerked forward as the tongue went taught and pulled Scarlet into the air after it. With Scarlet's legs dragging through the water, she tilted her body as best she could to avoid the sharp spires speeding her way.

"Princess, let me take over," Maia said. She swayed with the rocking of the cabin.

"The Behemoth isn't defeated yet," Ren said.

"You did a great job. Couldn't be happier. But you need to let me take over and finish this."

Ren ignored her master. Beyond the viewport, the town of Fulton drew closer. Sailors on the docks fled their short-masted fishing boats and ran for their lives. She had no idea how much Scarlet weighed, but she didn't doubt that at this speed, she was heavy enough to sheer through the town's sprawl of wood and stone dwellings like a red-hot knife through warmed butter.

If she did nothing, Wartwing would pull her through Fulton, destroying most of the town. If she deployed Scarlet's arm blade and tried to cut herself free of Wartwing's grip, Scarlet's momentum would still carry her past the docks and cause considerable damage to the town. Neither Ren nor Maia could stop Scarlet in time to prevent the destruction of, at best, half of Fulton.

"Stand down," Maia said. "I'll take over."

"The Behemoth isn't defeated yet," Ren repeated.

"A good soldier always follows orders, right? I order you to stand down! Now!"

"To the Blue Hells with being a good soldier!" Ren roared. "I'm not a soldier. I'm a Pilot!"

Ren couldn't stop Scarlet, so she didn't try to. When Scarlet's feet grazed the seabed closer to the shore, she planted her feet and threw Scarlet into the sky. She reached up, grabbed higher onto Wartwing's tongue, and pulled with all the might her quaking muscles could muster. Scarlet's legs kicked skyward, clamping shut and sandwiching Wartwing's tongue between her feet.

Kas and Maia flew into the cabin ceiling. Tiled roofs sped past the viewport, narrowly missing Scarlet's head as she hung upside-down from the frog-bat's tongue. Despite how ridiculous she knew she looked, Ren had avoided damaging the town.

When she spied a stone deity atop a rather large church, arms spread wide in benediction, Ren realized Fulton could still damage her.

"Oh god!" Kas cried.

"One of them, yes!" Ren twisted her neck and shoulders, sending Scarlet swinging like a pendulum. The stone idol, denied a high-speed embrace, settled for drawing a long gash along the left side of Scarlet's helm with one of its outstretched hands.

"That was too close!" Maia shouted. The slope of a large mountain looming beyond the edge of town grabbed Ren's full attention. Wartwing was headed straight for it. No amount of swinging would circumvent something of that size.

"Mountain," Kas said. "Ren, mountain!"

Just a few more seconds.

"Princess," Maia said.

She could almost count the needles on the thick green pines dotting the hillside.

"Princess!"

"Hold on!" Ren yelled.

Scarlet's arm blade squealed from its hiding place and pierced Wartwing's tongue. The Behemoth howled. Its tongue slackened and flickered back into its mouth, releasing its hold on Scarlet in an instant. Ren landed Scarlet on her shoulder and rolled to her feet, sending Maia and Kas bouncing around the cabin like dice in a gambler's cup.

Fury drove the exhaustion from Ren's legs. She broke into a run up the side of the sloping hill, crushing trees to pulp with each burning stride.

As Wartwing floated above, she kept her eyes locked on it. She pushed harder despite her aching, screaming muscles and the pain in her spine, roaring against the agony and denying its hold on her. The peak approached. With one final burst of speed, Ren kicked off the top of the mountain, throwing Scarlet into the air.

Scarlet twisted to face her opponent. Ren took a moment to appreciate the look of confusion on Wartwing's face as she appeared directly in his path of flight.

If you're going to do anything in this world? Do it with style.

"Final Divider!" Ren shouted. She drove Scarlet's blade into the top of Wartwing's head and bore down with all her weight. They fell onto the back slope of the mountain, churning earth as Scarlet skated with Wartwing's limp body dragging behind her.

As she came to rest at the bottom, Ren ripped Scarlet's blade free, ushering a streaming shower of sparks from what remained of Wartwing's head. She put Scarlet's back to the Behemoth as small fountains of flame erupted across Wartwing's body.

"Lesson over," Ren said.

The roaring explosion shook the earth and rattled her bones. She shut her eyes until the ground settled. "Is anybody hurt?"

"Bruised, but fine," Kas groaned. "Sun, you good?"

Maia rose on wobbling legs and stumbled toward Ren. She ran a hand through her sweat-matted hair. She wore a look of confusion, like she didn't recognize the girl standing in her Vanguardian's control beam.

"Feel like a woman yet?" Maia said.

Ren beamed. "Yes. In fact, I do."

Maia patted her shoulder as she passed by and busied herself cleaning up displaced cookware.

When Ren shut her eyes and stepped away from the control beam, pressure left her shoulders. A wave of relief drifted through her muscles like a cool night wind.

"That was somethin'," Kas said. He rubbed his neck and winced. "I haven't been in a fight like that in a long time. Not that I did anythin', but—"

She pulled him close, cutting him short. "I would very much like to kiss you right now. May I?"

Kas nodded, and she pressed her lips against his. With a soft, surprised whimper, he melted into her. As the sparkling faded and they pulled apart, the cabin air ran cool around Ren's lips.

"Was that okay?" Ren said.

"Definitely. I...yeah. Yeah." Kas wandered away, wearing a dreamy smile that looked the way a hot spring felt. Maia handed him a bag as he passed, and he veered away to find a place to stow it.

"Now, there's just one thing left to do," Maia said.

Ren's stomach dropped to the floor, pulling her heart along with it. Brimholme. That was where Maia meant to take her once her training was completed to Maia's satisfaction. Now that she had proved she could defeat a Behemoth on her own, it was time for their journey together to end.

But she didn't want it to end. The thought of anything but traveling with Kas and Maia, training and bickering, left her feeling hollow. She wasn't ready to say goodbye to that life.

"Oh. Of course. When?" Ren said.

"Right now." Maia entered the control beam. "I think you're ready."

"Yes. I suppose I am."

Maia looked back at her over her shoulder. "Why the long face? You should be proud." When she turned back to the viewport, Ren could have sworn she heard her sniffle. "I know I am."

"I am. Very much so. It's just..." Ren's lips pulled thin. "I thought there would be more time."

"Well, we can leave it up to you, then. One way or another, I'm going. You can join me if you want. You're a little young, but I don't see the harm so long as you take it slow. I'll watch over you."

"Hey, Sun?" Kas crept in from the side. "I think you two are talkin' about different things."

"I'm talking about getting shit-faced. I mean, you probably shouldn't, but you know. You kill a Behemoth, you go out for drinks and accept gratitude from an adoring town saved from the brink of destruction. It's tradition. I know I made a promise, but I already broke it, and your first Behemoth kill is a special occasion and all, so."

"Of course. Drinks and revelry. That's what I meant as well." Ren met Kas' gaze and smiled. "Onward to Fulton, then. The night is young, and so are we."

Maia flashed a toothy grin. "Aren't we just?"

While Maia walked Scarlet back toward town, Ren savored the lingering rush of her battle, doing her best to ignore the way time slipped away with each step Scarlet took.

Chapter 25
Nightcap

The deep blue of the night sky blurred Fulton's rooftops into a single soft silhouette. Maia followed the clamor of voices pouring through the night like wine from a tipped and forgotten bottle. As she neared their source, the voices grew loud enough to overtake the jingle of the full coin purse shifting back and forth in her hand.

In older, better times, whenever she stopped by the Fisherman's Folly for a drink with the other Pilots, Maia liked to make a point of reminding her friends that it was technically a tavern. That always sparked a debate. She felt that the thatched roof, long bar, tables, and worn wooden platform serving as a floor made the Fisherman's Folly a tavern. The most prominent argument against it being a tavern was that taverns had walls, and the Folly didn't.

The Pilots never came to an agreement. Regardless, the Folly was always a welcome change of scenery from the steel coffin Maia slept in every night and the cramped, tangy-smelling backwater holes she usually spent her time in.

She worked her way through the crowd spilling out from under the Folly's cover, returning nods where she could. Her mood sagged a bit when she found Serenia and Kasper locked in what looked to be a passionate kiss. She hid a smile when her traveling companions spotted her approach and pulled apart at neck-breaking speed.

Edgar had kissed Maia that same way when they were still fresh and new and perfect. Thinking of him made the unwanted memories waiting at the edge of her mind less blurry, more distinct. It wasn't anything sixteen cups of wine couldn't sort.

From the looks of it, her companions had begun the night without her. Serenia had a mug of ale in front of her, and Kasper seemed to be on his second. It wouldn't be hard for Maia to catch up.

"Evening, kids. Business is settled." Maia tossed her coin purse onto the candlelit table, satisfied by the heavy noise it made. She grabbed the bottle of red waiting on the table, pulled the cork out with her teeth, and poured generously. "Thanks for ordering for me."

"Where did you get that money?" Serenia said, her tone disapproving.

"I stopped by the magistrate's place for a quick chat. No work goes unpaid in the Freelands." Maia held her hands up and waved away Serenia's scowl. "He offered! You defeated the Behemoth without damaging the town or killing anybody. People tend to be grateful for that sort of thing, and we need to eat. And drink. Blue Hells, do I need to drink."

"And you feel that this behavior, charging for protecting innocent people, is befitting a hero?"

Maia paused mid-sip. "We're not heroes. We're Pilots. There's a world of difference. Relax and enjoy yourself, for once. Tonight is special."

"Damned right it is!" bellowed a muscular woman with deep brown skin and a crooked smirk. She raised her mug as she rounded the table. "Cheers to Sunder, and to Scarlet, for savin' us all!"

Mugs raised across the Folly. Voices united into a single roar. Maia lifted her index finger off her cup and pointed at Serenia. "Actually, your hero is sitting right there."

The woman peered at Serenia. "You're tellin' me this little bean rode that titan of yours and beat that Behemoth?"

"She did indeed."

"Well, piss in my mouth and call it brandy!" The woman's shoulder slap nearly crumpled Serenia. "Fair play to you, little lady. Didn't know the Red Pilot of Fire had an apprentice. Would have tried out myself had I known that was on the table. On behalf of the good folk of Fulton, thanks to you and your crew. Sad I missed the fight."

"How could you have missed it?" Kasper said. He was beaming wider than usual. "That Behemoth lit up the sky like a Fennish fire rocket show, all thanks to my girl."

My girl. Maia drained her cup.

"Felt the rumble," the woman said and took a long pull from her mug. "Was tendin' to my horses. You sure spooked them good."

"My apologies," Serenia said, bowing her head.

"A couple of scared horses is a small price to pay for a show like that," Kasper said.

"Next time one of those bastards sets down on us, I'll be sure to spare a glance. Thanks again, all around. Fulton's in your debt." The woman looked Maia up and down. "Once the young ones are tucked into bed, how about we crack another bottle together? I've always been partial to red."

"Oh!" Maia cleared her throat. "I would, but there's somebody I... I mean, I—"

"Relax. Offer's open if you change your mind. Hope to be seein' you around all the same. Folks."

There's somebody. The answer came as a reflex, a backhand slap against anything approaching her heart. Had she been thinking of Elizabeth or Leona when she said it?

When the woman left, Serenia wore a smile so wide that Maia worried her face might stick that way.

"You seem quite pleased with yourself," Maia said.

'Should I not be?"

"You should." Maia leaned in. "You're still reckless, but you're improving. You took down a Behemoth, and nobody died. That's the second-best day a Pilot can hope for."

"What's the best?"

"One with no Behemoths at all."

"I suppose you're right. Though I will admit, I felt quite a rush at the end of that fight. Is that allowed?"

"You're allowed to feel what you feel. I only wish piloting Scarlet didn't hurt you."

"Yes." Serenia took the smallest sip of ale Maia had ever seen. "Though, we work with what we have."

"You don't just work with it," Kasper said. He threw his arm around Serenia's shoulders and pulled her close. "You make art with it. You were amazin' out there. I could never take down a Behemoth. It's the Feral huntin' life for me." He took back his arm and pulled his daggers from their scabbards. "See, the trick for Ferals, for us regular folk, is to stab them in both their hearts at once. Put 'em down in one blow if you can." He jabbed at the air.

"Put those away. You're in public," Maia said.

Kasper frowned and sheathed his daggers as a serving girl with her hair wound in a high and tight bun approached the table carrying a roast chicken on a tray. She watched Kasper out of the corner of her eye as she placed it down. "Problem here?"

"Oh, no, he's just a fool." Maia winked and handed the woman a handful of coins that she hadn't bothered to count. "Thanks so much."

"So," Serenia said. She put her elbows on the table and leaned over them. "I've slain my first Behemoth. I've come up with my own finishing move. By the way, was the name I chose acceptable? 'Final Divider' just came to me. Has that been used before?"

Maia shook her head. "I've used 'Final Uppercut' and 'Infernal Divider,' but not 'Final Divider.' That one's yours."

"That one's mine." Serenia took a swig of her drink and wiped her mouth with the back of her hand. "Oh, yes, as I was saying." She stared at her mug as if it had just appeared in her hands out of nowhere. "This isn't half bad. Yes, as I was saying. I've slain my first Behemoth, and I've developed a finishing move, albeit a highly situational one."

"Yeah. You did," Maia said.

"So, having achieved all that, I feel it's time I pick my Pilot name."

"I think 'Princess' fits." Maia ripped a leg off the roast chicken. "Do you two want some potatoes? I'm thinking about some fried potato wedges for the table. If I got some fried potato wedges to share, you'd have some, right?"

"I don't know why you insist on calling me 'Princess.' I'm a general's daughter, not royalty. Furthermore, I'm only thirty-eighth in line for the throne."

"Closer than I am," Maia said. "Why even have a line for the throne? Isn't your Emperor supposed to be immortal?"

Serenia exhaled sharply. "Please, focus." She used the tips of two fingers to work a piece of meat from the chicken. She mostly got skin. "You're Sunder. Everybody calls you that. Amisrala Illandres, the Green Pilot of Wind, was known as Windstrider to her people. And, of course, there's the Blue Bolt. I should have a Pilot name, as well. It so happens that I have one in mind."

Maia traced a circle in the air with her chicken leg. "Picking your own nickname is in poor taste. Besides, it's a bit early. You're not a Pilot yet."

"But you told me that nobody can tell me who or what I am," Serenia said a little too loudly. "And I feel like a Pilot."

"Yeah, sure," Maia said around a mouthful of chicken. "You're a Pilot. To a point. You can command Scarlet and you can fight Behemoths. But you're not all the way there yet."

"What, exactly, am I missing?"

"Armor, for starters."

"The ritual that transformed me into a Pilot did not grant me armor." Serenia slapped her forehead and groaned. "One mug of this vile swill, and I'm saying things I shouldn't. That was supposed to be a secret."

After Maia had stripped the last of the meat from her chicken leg, she waved the bone as she chewed. "It's fine. If you had armor, I figure you would have summoned it by now."

"Then, when do I get my armor?"

"Awakening as a Pilot makes you faster. Stronger. Tougher. It also gives you your Hunter Sense and Regeneration. But your sliver is the most important part. It lets you bond with your Vanguardian."

"Your sliver?" Kasper said.

"Shh, women are talking. Once you bond with a Vanguardian, the rest of the magic woven into your body takes shape. You get your armor and weapons. You gain the ability to Teleport, as well as your unique, innate magic. In my case, Barrier, which is about as useless as an asshole right here." Maia tapped her elbow with the chicken bone. "The problem is, I don't think you have a sliver."

"But I was made to be a Pilot, like you." Serenia looked back and forth between Kasper and Maia. "When I awoke, they told me they performed the rituals exactly. If you have a sliver, I must have one as well."

Maia pointed to the thick candle sitting at the center of their table. "You can feel that flame."

"Yes. I can."

"Move it."

"What?"

"A sliver gives you mastery over the thing it's attuned to. So, prove it. Move the flame."

Serenia set her mug down, curled her fingers into claws, and swiped at the air, beckoning the candle's flame to move. It flickered slightly, pushed only by the wind of her motions.

It's the ale," Serenia said. "Besides, I'm sure it all comes down to practice, like any other skill."

Maia put her own drink down. "You learn finesse over time, but if you have a sliver of fire in you, then sensing, controlling, and creating fire should be as natural as breathing. You should be able to shoot flames out your ass on command if you're so inclined."

"Is that...something you can do?" Kasper said.

"Never ask a lady that question." Maia dropped her bone, took a swig of wine, and belched.

The last bit of joy from the day's victory had drained from Serenia's face. "Look," Maia said. "I don't know what was done to you. You shouldn't be able to command Scarlet without a sliver of fire. Maybe the Emperor found a way around that. That means you're probably not protected from heat like I am, so you shouldn't go sticking your hand in a fireplace anytime soon. Still, you still might be able to bond with Scarlet and become a full Pilot someday."

"But you're bonded with Scarlet," Kasper said.

Maia grimaced. "Yes, Kasper. I am. And I don't know if Scarlet can bond with two Pilots at once. It's never really come up." She stared at Serenia until the girl met her gaze. "So, even if I decide to let you have Scarlet, you might not be able to bond with her and become a complete Pilot until I'm gone, or we find a way for me to pass the torch. I still haven't decided if I'm turning Scarlet over to you, though."

Serenia leaned back in her chair and crossed her arms. Her features twisted into something halfway between a scowl and a pout. "I saved this entire town by defeating a Behemoth in spectacular fashion. I've done everything you asked. Yet nothing I do is ever good enough for you, is it?" She slapped the table. "I'm starting to think that you had no intention of giving Scarlet up to begin with!"

"You did promise her, Sun," Kasper said.

"Stay out of this," Maia warned as she refilled her cup. "Yeah, you fight well. But there's more to being a Pilot than fighting. What you do when you're not piloting Scarlet is just as important."

"Stop speaking in vagaries and get to the point. What is it you want from me?" Serenia said.

"I think I'm the one who's owed an answer. I have one question left from that little game we played on the farm."

"Let's have it, then. What's your question?"

"If I hand Scarlet over to you, what do you plan to do with her?"

"The Emperor has ordered me to return Scarlet to Noctis, whereupon he will—"

"No. I asked what *you* plan to do with her. I don't care what the Emperor wants. What do you want?"

Serenia lifted her mug to her lips and drank until it was empty, then folded her hands on the table, lacing her fingers together. "I haven't quite decided. I thought it *responsible* to abstain from a decision until our training was concluded and I had Scarlet in my possession. Though, if you're demanding an answer right this instant, I see merit in carrying out my orders. I am to return Scarlet to Noctis, so our engineers can replicate her design and create additional Vanguardians in her likeness."

It was Maia's turn to slam the table. The difference was that, unlike her apprentice's petulant smack, the sound of Maia's hand striking dense wood silenced the tavern. Her right shoulder blossomed with fresh pain from the sudden movement. "After everything you've seen, you want to help build an army of Vanguardians for the Empire."

"No, I don't. I'm not blind to the truth any longer. Our Emperor isn't the man I thought he was. Yet the Noctean Empire remains the only nation with the knowledge and resources necessary to create new Vanguardians. I'm certain of that. That's why, when I return, I will demand that the Vanguardians we create are distributed evenly across the continent, to ensure no nation has an advantage over another. The world needs protection, Maia. This isn't a fight for just one person."

"What's funny about everything you just said—and believe me, it's all ridiculous—is that you really think the Emperor will listen to you. It hasn't occurred to you that you can be replaced. He made you. He can make another Pilot to take your place."

"Hold up, Sun," Kasper said, his hands raised and pleading. "Let's all take a step back and—"

"You don't know what you're talking about!" Serenia shot back. "The Emperor himself promised that I will be promoted to Pilot Commander of the new Vanguardians and any new Pilots we create. He said this—publicly. Think what you will of him, but he will not go back on his word. He's bound by his own laws to honor it."

"Wonderful! Maybe you'll get a blue Vanguardian, just like your hero, Blue Bolt," Maia said.

"Perhaps I will! Or maybe I'll ask for one in purple! I'll be Pilot Commander! I can do whatever I want!"

"Hells, I feel stupid. I thought that maybe, just maybe, if I trained you the right way, some of my good sense might rub off on you." Maia pushed to her feet. "You haven't changed a bit. You're still nothing but a good little Noctean soldier. I must have been out of my mind to think I could mold you into a proper Pilot. If I knew you were aiming to make an army of Scarlets when we shook hands, I would have scuttled her right there on that beach."

"You would doom us all just to spite me? You talk about responsibility, but what of your responsibility to the world?" Now Serenia was on her feet, leaning on her hands and huffing. "If you don't wish to be a Pilot, fine. You say that I can be replaced? Well, so can you, Maia."

"How many times do you think they tried?" Maia said, her tone frosted and even.

"What?"

"You have to know you're not the first Pilot Noctis tried to make. While I worked under your father, Noctean mages worked to figure out how Heretic did what she did to us. The Emperor couldn't stand not having his own Pilot and Vanguardian when other continental nations had one, so they didn't waste any time trying to replace me after I left." Maia folded her arms and leaned in. "I wonder if they told you what happened to all the failures that came before you. Or where their bodies are buried."

The blow landed. Serenia went so rigid, a gentle breeze would have knocked her over. Maia clenched her jaw and took another swing.

"All that power you have was paid for in blood. Knowing that, I hope you can see why hearing what you plan to do has me so bloody furious. You've seen the damage Scarlet can do with a single step. What's more, Scarlet's already moving around on her own without one of us controlling her. If your engineers get it wrong, and your new fleet goes on a rampage, I have a hard time believing that yelling 'I'm the Pilot Commander' like a spoiled brat will do anything to stop them from crushing you flat."

Serenia met her icy glare. "I didn't know what happened to the potential Pilots who came before me. That's... I can't begin to describe how that weighs on my heart. Nevertheless, if I quit now, I would be rendering their sacrifices meaningless. I can't bring back the dead. All I can do is work to ensure a better future for everyone who still draws breath. There are good people in the Empire, and I have to hope that they'll do the right thing when given the chance. I have to hope. I can't turn into you, so cynical and bitter and selfish. You would rather let the world die than allow it to forget you."

As far as counterattacks went, it wasn't bad. Betrayal always stung, no matter how many times it slipped between Maia's shoulder blades. "I don't want you to end up like me either," Maia said. "I don't want you waking up at night, praying for death just so the pain and the nightmares will finally stop. I don't want you flailing in the dirt, struggling to breathe while your insides twist and rip. I don't want you to have this much blood on your hands. Why can't you see that I'm trying to help you?"

Though more than half the tavern was staring, Maia ignored them. She gripped her wine bottle's slender neck and drained what was left. That gave her time to ponder whether she had gone too far.

"Pilot!" The voice sliced through the night air, a hint of anger quivering beneath a refined nobleman's accent.

Maia let the empty wine bottle tumble to the floor. "Great. Yet another vengeful prick with a crossbow." With her arms spread, Maia spun to face the owner of the voice. "Okay, what's the—"

A wedge-shaped space had opened behind her, framed by tavern patrons scrambling to get out of the way of the three men standing at the edge of the Folly's roof. All three were clean shaved, with wavy, well-kept hair. They wore fine tunics, breeches, and overcoats untouched by the dust of the road. The man in the middle, with his fair skin and ringed fingers, probably only knew of hard work by reading about it in a leather-bound book.

His foppish demeanor didn't make the throbbing coming from the space where Maia's right eye used to be any less intense, as the man was holding an ornate flintlock pistol with the steadiness of a practiced hunter.

"Pilot!" the man repeated. His upper lip rose in a gilded sneer.

"I heard you the first time," She didn't dare try to summon her armor and weapons for fear of startling him. Words were the only weapons she had left. "Listen, I—"

The snap of the flintlock's hammer heralded the flash of powder, and then Maia was on her back, blood pooling from the hole the iron ball tore into her body.

Chapter 26

Big Day Tomorrow

It wasn't the first time Maia Sunderland had been shot with a flintlock, but it was the first time she had been shot without the full benefit of her Regeneration.

She looked down at her left arm, thanking whatever deity had seen fit to spare her the downward glance that caused the bullet to pass clean through the meat of her upper arm.

Her Barrier would have saved her had she thought to use it. It always slipped her mind. What use was a magical shield to an armored hunter who could heal from almost any wound?

Except Maia didn't have her cracked and damaged armor on, and her Regeneration had almost completely abandoned her. Would her Barrier have even come if she called it? Had she lost that, too?

A dull ache rolled up Maia's back as she tried to rise from what was left of the table. She didn't remember falling through it. How long had she been on the ground?

Serenia's hands slipped under Maia's armpits. Once she got her legs under her, Maia pushed her apprentice off and shoved past Kasper, who had placed himself between her and the shooter. The fair-skinned man passed the empty flintlock to the man on his left while the one on his right presented him with an identical pistol, which he accepted with a nod.

Maia stumbled to a halt, putting pressure on her wound and grimacing against fresh bolts of anguish.

The shooter trained his weapon on Maia and canted his head to the man on his left. "I thought you said she would heal. She's still bleeding."

"Apologies, Master Bartholomew." The man to his left drew a small clockwork watch from his overcoat pocket. "Give it a minute, perhaps?"

"My coin only covers violence against the Pilot. I don't fancy having to pay an additional fine for injuring some random whore."

"Oh, you got the right woman. Wrong night, though." Maia winced with each staggering step. "Bartholomew, was it?"

"It was, and I suggest you stay where you are." He let the barrel of the gun drift past Maia's head. "I don't want to have to pay for the young lady, as well. I don't think—"

Maia didn't think either. She simply reacted. Flames erupted from her hands, ripping into two screeching lines that sped across the wooden floor of the Folly and off into the night, locking her in a V-shaped space with the three men.

"You will not touch her!" Maia roared. The patrons of the Folly scrambled to escape, shielding their faces from the heat with their hands.

With trembling fingers, Maia forced the flames to die. The effort left her winded and sweating. The acrid stench of burnt wood lingered. "Leave her out of this. Remember, it's me you're trying to murder."

"I would hardly call putting down a beast like you 'murder'." Bartholomew's voice wavered as he spoke. He coughed and waved at the black smoke curling from the tavern's scorched floor.

"And you think that makes it okay for you to shoot me."

"I think you're making a rather big deal out of nothing," Bartholomew said, though his two friends backed away. "I shot you in the arm. If you're really the last remaining Pilot, you'll heal. If the tales are true, you won't even have a scar. How can that be considered a crime?"

The dizziness and nausea falling on her in waves made Maia's slow nod more of a drooping of her head. "I heal, so it's like it never happened. No crime." She shuffled toward him. "Let me tell you something, Bart. I'll remember that shaped piece of iron boring through my body for the rest of my days. The fine people who came here to relax, they'll remember you walking into their favorite tavern, drawing a gun, and shooting somebody, just because you could. Because you're rich enough to get away with it. There will *always* be a scar."

"A necessary scar. I'm doing the world a favor." Bartholomew advanced to meet her, pistol leading. "Think of it as cutting out a malignant growth. You have a lot of blood on your hands. I only intended to wound you, but perhaps I should put another bullet through your skull and deliver the punishment you so richly deserve."

Her left arm was too heavy, too slow, so Maia snapped up her bloodied right hand, grabbed the barrel of the flintlock, and pulled it into her forehead.

The way Bartholomew yelped, Maia expected him to pull the trigger. A moment passed, and another. Maia let go of the barrel to hide the tremors in her hand.

"What, am I supposed to be intimidated?" Bartholomew hissed.

"No. You're supposed to keep the gun aimed at me, where it belongs." Maia took a deep breath. "Everybody who's still here, go home! Don't stop to talk to any guards on the way. It's okay. Everything is going to be okay."

The floor rumbled as the remaining customers rushed from the Folly like blood streaming from an open wound. Maia didn't have to turn to know that Serenia and Kasper had stayed behind, so she kept her head pressed into the end of the gun's barrel.

Maia sighed. "I'm sick of this, you know. Every time one of you comes looking for revenge, you take a piece of me with you. And I let you do it because I think I owe you a debt. It has to stop. There isn't much of me left to give."

A drop of sweat traced its way down Bartholomew's brow. It took everything she had to keep from burying her fist in his chest, if only to spare the world from the day he decided to shoot someone else for sport...if he hadn't done so already.

"Maia," Serenia said from somewhere behind her. "Don't do anything you'll regret."

"Don't worry. I won't." When she pushed into the barrel, Bartholomew stepped back. "But I could. I know pain better than most. I could ruin you in ways that wouldn't leave a mark, Bart. Nobody would even know unless they looked into your eyes, real close, and saw the way firelight refused to dance in the hollow pits carved out by the memory of what I did to you. And they'll know, just by looking at you, how badly you want to step into the flames and let them swallow you, just to make the pain stop. The flames won't take me. I can't get rid of my past. My pain. You have no idea what haunts me when I close my eye at night. You don't know what I've had to suffer to be your 'hero.' To keep you safe."

Bartholomew's face twisted like he had just swallowed something bitter.

With a gentleness she reserved for lovers, Maia touched the barrel with her bloodied hand and pushed it down. "You don't have to love me. You don't have to welcome me. But you can't treat me this way. No matter how mad you are, no matter what you've lost, it doesn't give you the right to hurt me. I'm doing what I can to keep this world safe. I'm sorry if that's not good enough, but I'm all you have."

Bartholomew swallowed hard. "So what, then? If we walk away, what's to say you won't come for us?"

"Well, clearly, you didn't think this all the way through, then, because if you've heard anything about me, you know that I always trade blows. But I'm about to pass out unless I get a binding around this wound, so here's what we'll do instead. You're going to tell me how I hurt you. Who I took from you, or who I couldn't save. I'll listen to your pain. Then, we're going to part ways. Nobody else has to get hurt tonight."

"Oh." Bartholomew let his pistol dangle at his side. He scratched the back of his neck and avoided her gaze. "You see, the boys and I are traveling, getting in one last hurrah before I'm to be wed in the autumn. You know how it is. Truthfully, before tonight, I had yet to lay eyes on a Behemoth, or your Vanguardian, for that matter. I'm not here seeking vengeance. I merely wanted to settle a standing bet we've had pertaining to how quickly a Pilot can heal from a bullet wound."

"Huh." Maia blinked. "By any chance, does that pistol of yours pull to the right?"

In one smooth motion, Maia snapped the gun from Bartholomew's hand and turned it over in her hand. She squeezed the trigger.

The bullet cut into the ground between Bartholomew's feet, spurring him to leap and dance away, yelping as if the ground was made of hot lava. When he turned to run, Maia let him get roughly ten paces away before she hurled the spent pistol into the back of his head. He collapsed to the dirt, landing on his face with his ass pointing to the moon.

"Right. Good talk."

The serving girl from before approached tentatively with a strip of cloth clutched in her shaking hands. Maia smiled as she took it from her, using her fingers and teeth to bind her bleeding arm. She teetered as she stumbled from the Folly and out into the night. Footsteps rushed toward her from behind. They stopped when she raised her hand.

"Don't," she said. Whatever was left of her mask shattered like glass. She didn't bother to pick up any of the pieces.

"Maia, let Kas tend to your wound. Please. You've lost a lot of blood," Serenia pleaded.

"I said, don't." Maia looked back over her shoulder. "We're through. Tomorrow, we're Teleporting to Brimholme."

"No. Maia, please. I have so much more to learn from you. I'm not ready to… Don't do this. Please."

"I have one more lesson to teach you, Princess. Once it's over, if you still want Scarlet, if you still want to be a Pilot, you can have her. Go get some sleep. Big day tomorrow."

Wherever Maia was when she awoke, she was outside, and it was still nighttime. She was sitting with her legs splayed and her back supported by solid wood.

A sting in her left arm sent Maia thrashing. Beyond the edge of the light cast by a single lantern, a figure cowered, arms held up in peace.

"What the fuck do you want?" Maia yelled.

"Easy, Sun. Easy." Kasper stayed low and kept his hands raised as he moved into the light. He held a healer's needle and a length of catgut. "That wound needs stitchin'. You can't do it on your own."

Maybe it was the wine or the loss of blood, but Maia felt lighter than she had in a long time and found herself nodding. Kasper approached, set the lantern closer, and went back to work.

"Where am I?" Maia said.

"Still in Fulton. Halfway across town from the covered court we were drinkin' at."

"It's a tavern."

"What?"

"Never mind"

"This isn't that bad," he said. "The bullet went clean through. Didn't touch the bone. Looks like your healin's not all the way gone. The bleedin' stopped, but you lost a lot of blood. Drink this."

He passed her a hardened gourd topped with a stopper. Maia sniffed it. "Is this water? Or poison that smells like water?"

He rolled his eyes. "Water doesn't smell."

She hadn't realized how thirsty she was until the gourd was empty. She blew against the rim, coaxing a hollow tone from inside. "Thanks."

"There's also this." Kasper pulled a glass bottle from his bag and passed it to her.

Maia held it closer so she could read the label in the flickering lamplight. "Rum?"

"That servin' girl you overpaid wanted you to have it. Said she felt bad for what happened. And, a pretty girl like you deserves it after all you've been through."

"Her words?"

Kasper nodded.

Maia held the bottle between her thighs and pulled the cork. She drank deep. It wasn't wine, but it brought much-needed warmth. "Does her royal highness know you're here?"

"I told her I would find you, make sure you're okay. She stayed behind at the—" Kasper met her gaze. "At the tavern." Leaning in, he bit the excess thread. "All done." When he was done stowing his supplies, he sat down against the side of the house, far enough away that she had to lean to pass him the bottle of rum. He took a short sip and let out a deep, deliberate sigh.

"Got something to say?" Maia said.

"She knows, Sun."

Maia's spine tightened. "What does she know?"

"About your part in her mother's death." He took a bigger pull and handed the rum to her. "Farspeakers can only talk to the other Farspeaker they're bound to. For some reason, mine's been pickin' up conversations from Ren's whenever I'm near. Sounds distant, like she's talkin' underwater. I know it's not right to listen, but..."

"Her Farspeaker is broken."

"No, it isn't."

Maia chuckled. Her student really had been following her example. She knew how to break a promise. "You said 'conversations.' More than one."

"I shouldn't say any more."

"You shouldn't have said anything at all, and yet, here we are. What else has she been talking about behind my back? And how many times has she done this?"

Kasper pulled his knees in closer to his chest. "Twice, far as I know. Once in Galford, when I was trackin' you, and again back in Whitehorn, the night before we left town. I didn't hear everythin', but the Emperor's set to invade the Freelands, and he won't bring back the Iron Wardens or complete Lion's Roar unless..."

"Unless she kills me."

"Yeah."

The rum had reached her much sooner than it should have. Yet another side effect of her weakened Regeneration, which normally made it difficult for her to get properly drunk. "What's Lion's Roar?"

Kasper shrugged. "Probably some kind of weapon."

Maia let her head fall back and smack against the wall. "Do you think she'll do it?"

"I don't think so. But you should talk to her. Sort it out."

"Fuck you. I didn't ask for your opinion."

"Oh, shove it up your ass, Sun!" Kasper yelled. He had never raised his voice to her before. In the distance, a dog barked at the echo. "I go out of my way to be nice. I put up with your insults. I cook and clean. I find you and stitch you up and try to help you, and you still treat me like a piece of horse shit. You can't stop hatin' me for one second, can you?"

"No, I can't! You fucking know why I can't." Maia's left arm was too weak to support her, and her right arm still ached, so she braced her back against the wall and used her legs to push to her feet. "What I want to know is why you're even bothering. Trying to earn her majesty's favor? Is that why you can't admit that you hate me, too?"

"Of course I hate you." Kasper pursed his lips. "Of course I do. Whether or not you killed her yourself, Leona's death was your fault, and I'll never forgive you for that. But, you were important to her. She wouldn't want us fightin', I think."

For a long time, Maia didn't say anything. She counted her pained heartbeats. After a few dozen, she could only think of one thing to say. "It was an accident."

"I know," Kasper said.

"And Princess, and her mother."

"She knows."

"I guess it doesn't change much."

"You know what will?" Kasper said. "Letting go. You've been through plenty. Let Ren have Scarlet. Let her go and make her own mistakes. Let her learn and grow from them like you did."

"She'll turn out like me," Maia said.

"I know you think that's a terrible thing. Given all that you've suffered, I don't think anybody could have done a better job in your boots."

She had no words to offer in return, just a heavy heart and a wish that things could have been different. "You'd better get back. We have an early start tomorrow."

Kasper shouldered his bag. "Brimholme."

"That's right."

"Is that where you—"

"Yes. It is."

Kasper looked away. "Do you really think that'll help? Showing her that?"

"No." Maia's lips curled in a bittersweet smile. "But it might hurt. And it'll save her. That's more important. Now leave me alone."

Kasper scooped up his lantern and stormed away, leaving Maia alone in the dark where she belonged. Before she could take another sip, phantom fingers crept up her sternum and curled around her heart.

The fingers clenched. Maia lurched, dropped her bottle, and fell to her knees. The unseen force of the curse tightened, squeezing harder than she thought possible. She opened her mouth to scream, to call for Kasper to come back so she wouldn't have to die alone, but only a bloody gurgle escaped her lips.

Spasms racked her body. She pulled her knees into her chest as sharp nails carved a trail through her insides. In between the rapid pulses, she prayed that she could hold on for one more day, long enough to do what was needed, and if she couldn't, that the darkness would be merciful and claim her life quickly.

Chapter 27
End of the Road

Waking up to a woman's screams didn't rank high on Maia's list of preferred ways to start her day. It placed somewhere above waking up to find a knife buried in her chest and far below waking up swaddled in furs with warm, naked skin pressed against hers. As the scream bounced around the inside of her skull and the blinding light of day raked her vision, Maia decided that today, she would have preferred the knife.

With a bandage covering her missing eye and dried blood covering her neck and chest, Maia must have looked an awful lot like a corpse, which is probably why the woman who found her had run screaming from the alley. When Maia tried to move, twinges of pain arced through her chest. The ghostly remnant of the curse's grip felt an awful lot like that blade she had wished for. Every breath sent spikes through her lungs, so she kept her breathing short and shallow.

Maia lay there helpless until one of the town guards returned with the screaming woman. Both looked surprised to find her awake and alive.

They helped her to her feet, and after a short explanation, Maia was brought to the guard house to clean up and take a bit of bread and ale. All the while, she struggled to find a way to move that wouldn't aggravate her injured ribs, the wound in her stomach that hadn't fully healed, or her aching, damaged arms. Unable to find relief, she pushed on. With each step, the spiking pains in her chest became more familiar, joining the many burdens she had to carry.

When Maia staggered back to Scarlet, Serenia and Kasper were waiting for her.

A look of shock crossed her apprentice's face. "Emperor's Grace, Maia. You look... What happened?"

"I slept in. How's my hair?" Maia brought them up to Scarlet's cabin and stepped into the control beam. Each thrust of her injured arms brought her more twinges, but she pushed on and completed the Teleport spell.

Moments later, the swirling red lights from the spell faded. Maia looked out across the barren, rocky slope that lay ahead, identical to the picture of it she kept locked in her deepest memories.

"Behold. Brimholme. And not the nice part." When Maia turned her head, Scarlet panned to follow her. Dirt and rocks led to more dirt and rocks, all the way up the incline ahead of them and back down behind them to a wasteland that stretched for miles. "We're deep in the southern reaches. Ever hear of Thenmar's Crater, Princess?"

"Maia, please, stop for a moment. Let's talk. You don't—"

"It's named for the first Granrum dwarf to make it up here," Maia continued, pushing Scarlet forward with a labored step that made the cabin shudder. "Thenmar came here chasing a falling star and found this big crater. No star, though. So, he said, 'this is my crater' and fucked off. The terrain's too treacherous to make it down to the bottom to dig for whatever fell here, so the Granrum never bothered. That makes it nice and private. Just beyond is the ocean. Shittiest beach you'll ever see."

Maia tried to take another step, but her leg wouldn't budge. She stumbled. Scarlet pitched as Maia righted herself. Despite how hard she strained, Scarlet wouldn't move.

What's wrong, girl? Are you afraid of being back here? Maia closed her eye, breaking their connection for a moment, and cracked her neck. *I don't blame you. But we have a job to do. She needs to see. I need her to see that I'm right. Please. I need your help.*

This time, when she pushed, Scarlet responded. The Vanguardian's metal joints ground with each stride, wailing like a mourner at a funeral. Every time her foot came down, Maia had to work harder to lift it again.

There were only a few dozen steps left, and when they were used up, that would be it. Her time with Serenia would come to an end. Whether she gave up Scarlet, whether Serenia followed through on her orders and tried to take Maia's life, she would be alone again.

One more day. She had begged and pleaded for it as the curse crushed the life from her. If one day was all she had, she intended to make the most of it by sparing an annoying, reckless, wonderful young woman from the same bloody fate Maia had been forced into.

"You might want to put on your jacket, Princess. It's about to get chilly." She rolled her eye at Kasper's bare arms. "You're on your own, Sleeveless."

One more push. When Scarlet's head peered over the top of the crater, Serenia gasped. Maia couldn't really blame her. Thenmar's Crater was beautiful, in a horrible way, with thick waves of ice expanding outward from the pit's center like a stormy ocean frozen in time. The looming Sinadaria Mountains, combined with the crater's depth, kept it shielded from the sun most of the time, giving the melting ice plenty of time to refreeze in the shade. From above, the crater looked like a molten, tooth-filled maw, with fangs facing the wrong way.

"Hold on." Maia crouched and pushed off. Scarlet fell for close to a hundred feet before she hit the side of the crater.

Ground-up chunks of ice and snow sprayed the viewport as Scarlet skated down the incline to the bottom, coming to rest on a flat sheet of perfect winter. Maia guided Scarlet toward the center of the crater with small steps. Sunlight glinted off the moisture-slick tips of the frozen spires littering their path.

When Scarlet came to a stop, the echo of her final footstep bounced off the crater walls. The three passengers rode Scarlet's hand together down to the ice.

"From here, we go on foot," Maia said. "There are tunnels and pockets of air running through the whole glacier. Watch your step. If the ground gives way, that's it."

"What could have caused something like this?" Serenia said. "I feel as though I'm looking at an explosion of ice?"

"You're not far off. The crater wasn't always like this. When we found this place, it was just a hole filled with dirt and jagged obsidian. This is the way we left it."

"We?" Serenia said. "Maia, why are we here?"

"You asked me, once, what happened to the other Pilots. You wanted to know if I killed them, like people say. We've traveled together for some time now. What do you think?"

Serenia started and stopped twice before she finally spoke. "I know you. You could never do something like that."

"That's why we're here. Your final lesson is a history lesson. I told you that after coming here, you might not want to be a Pilot anymore. I wanted you to see what Pilots and Vanguardians are really capable of. I wanted you to know that it was a mistake, giving any person this much power. Most of all, I wanted to show you what happens when you think you know everything about something. Or someone."

The hammering in her breast wouldn't slow, no matter how many breaths she took, so Maia pressed on, racing ahead of her raging heart.

"This isn't just a crater." Maia swallowed and turned to Serenia. "It's a graveyard. This is where I killed my best friends."

Chapter 28
Cold Blood

On the morning of Maia's nineteenth birthday, a voice projected through Scarlet's cabin, crashing into her skull like a bag of hammers. She rolled over and stared at the cabin's polished metal ceiling. With a deep breath, she held back her anger until the liquid shape of the words turned solid.

"Maia. It's time to wake up. We're to meet at Thenmar's Crater in three hours. Maia?"

Hard k's and deep, rolling r's. A Kaldrsteinn accent.

Maia's groan roughened into a snarl. She silently cursed Ami for teaching the other Pilots how to use their Vanguardians to communicate with each other. "Edgar. What did I tell you the last time you hailed me?"

A pause. "You said that I'm not to contact Scarlet directly unless the situation is dire."

"And why is that?"

"Because we aren't together anymore and have not been together for a year and a half."

"Go on."

"Must I?"

"Edgar!" Maia slapped the cabin floor. "Focus. What else did I tell you?"

"That even if the situation *is* dire, and my crotch is on fire, and every other Pilot has died a terrible, gruesome death, I'm not to hail you before midday after you've been out drinking."

"And what nights do I go out drinking?" Maia said.

She could picture him clenching his jaw and forcing the words through his teeth. "All of them. Yet I don't know what corner of the continent you're currently in, or if you're in Fen, for that matter, so there's no way for me to know if it's midday where you are."

"Fair." Maia looked out Scarlet's viewport, shielding her face with her fingers. It was well past midday where she was, but Edgar didn't need to know that. "If you want to meet in three hours, then this isn't a dire situation. So, fuck off, and don't call on me again." She slumped back down onto her thin bedroll.

"I thought we agreed to be civil." Edgar's voice carried a low rumble. Maia's heart thumped faster in remembrance, giving her the rush of purpose she used to need to escape him before the rumble became a roar.

"I'll be civil when you stop trying to worm your way back into my life. Is there actually a meeting in three hours? It hasn't been a fortnight since the last one." Or since Maia had last seen Leona. She wanted to tell somebody what had happened, what she had done to the thing Leona had created by combining their blood with forbidden magics. Edgar was as good a person to confide in as anyone else. He would judge her and tell her what she already knew—that she was horrible and didn't deserve to live.

"This is dire, I assure you. I can't say any more right now," Edgar said. "Three hours. Thenmar's Crater."

Maia waited for the little clicking noise that signaled that the connection between their Vanguardians had been severed. It didn't come. "Edgar, are you still there?"

"Yes."

"Is there something else?"

"Yes." Edgar swallowed. "Happy Birthday, Maia."

Click.

Maia pushed out a long sigh until there was nothing left in her chest but hollow silence. She sat up again and reached for the wine bottle waiting patiently next to her bedroll. Her father had reserved this vintage just for her, same as the previous year. And the year before that. It was her mother's favorite. She had given Maia her first cup of it on her fifteenth birthday, the night she left once again to aid Brave Dawn in its fight against the Noctean Empire.

Six months after that, Maia would take another taste of that bitter wine when word reached them that Bianca Sunderland had been killed trying to bring Noctean refugees to the Brimholme border. Another six months later, Maia would be kidnapped and made into a Pilot on the night of her sixteenth birthday.

The next few hadn't been much better. One birthday without disaster would have been just wonderful.

Over the next hour, Maia nursed what was left of her birthday present and wondered what could have worried Edgar to the point of risking her ire. She scowled at her reflection in the viewport. "I have the biggest Vanguardian. I'm practically the fucking leader. You don't tell me when to show. I'll come when I bloody well please."

Maia ran a hand through her ruddy dyed hair and stepped into Scarlet's control beam. A thrust of her fist across her body to either side and one to the sky lifted Scarlet in a swirling storm of red light. When the Teleport spell was complete, she stood near the center of Thenmar's Crater.

Scarlet wrenched to the side. The crash of metal on metal sent a jolt through Maia's chest. Maia planted her foot to stop Scarlet from falling and summoned her armor and blades reflexively, filling the cabin with a nimbus of light and flame. She stepped back, throwing Scarlet's fists up to defend against whatever had struck her.

Pearl, the White Unicorn Vanguardian, with seams of gold and a shining crystal horn, lay on his side in the dirt at Scarlet's feet. Scratches and gouges covered his formerly pristine frame.

"Dalzin!" Maia cried, reaching out and opening a connection between the two Vanguardians. "Are you hurt? I—"

The sharp keen of scraping metal filled the air. At the center of the crater, amid a field of crushed obsidian spires, Onyx, the Black Crab Vanguardian, skittered to the side as Emerald, the Green Eagle Vanguardian, swooped toward him. The black crab swung his right pincer, an oversized mass of dark metal half as large as the rest of him. Flapping her wings, Emerald halted her descent, causing Onyx's blow to fall short. The green eagle dove in behind the swing, drawing sparks with her razor talons.

Edgar's voice slammed into Scarlet's cabin like a breaking wave. "Maia! Amisrala has turned on us! Help us! We need to—"

"Sunder, please assist me." Ami's voice floated in, even and steady, cutting off Edgar. "Edgar has betrayed the Pilots. He attacked me upon my arrival. I'll need your help to—"

"Maia, what are you waiting for! Help us!" cried Edgar. "Amisrala struck first when she learned I was planning to reveal her treachery to the group. She has aligned herself with Noctis!"

Onyx nipped at Emerald's talons with his smaller, thinner claw, keeping his massive hammer claw hovering at the ready. Emerald broke off and flapped her mighty wings, flying higher and putting distance between them.

"Sunder, I'll need your help if I'm to defeat Edgar and Dalzin simultaneously," Ami said. "Are you there? Please, respond."

Maia reached out again to Pearl. "Dalzin, if you're there, I need you to tell me what happened."

Silence. Maia could feel the link between their Vanguardians, but she couldn't tell if Dalzin was conscious. Or alive.

Maia focused her gaze on the space between the dueling Vanguardians until they became little more than soft, colored shapes dancing in a sea of brown dirt and black glass. Inside one Vanguardian was Maia's best friend. In the other, a former lover she didn't particularly care for, though he was still an ally in their war against the Kith.

Maia projected her voice to the other Vanguardians. "Hey, stop! Let's talk this through!"

Neither stopped their assault. She would have to make them stand down. But when she tried to move, her legs grew heavy. Maia couldn't make Scarlet take another step. A step had to lead somewhere. A step was a choice. Maia hadn't made hers yet.

"Sunder. Maia." Ami's voice started to warble. "Are you hesitating to intervene due to what I said at our last meeting?"

That was it. That was what made Maia's legs turn to unyielding stone. The last time the Pilots met, Ami told them that Noctis had approached her, trying to recruit her to their cause after Maia continuously refused to return to the Empire. Ami also mentioned that she was seriously considering their offer.

A pair of Behemoths had appeared, one in northern Kaldrsteinn and one across the Shining Sands, bringing an end to the meeting before Ami could assure them, could assure Maia, that the idea of working with Noctis was ridiculous. That she would never turn her back on the Pilots by serving Noctis as Maia once had.

Then, Leona had surprised Maia with their new child. In the weeks that followed that horrible day, little things like checking in on her best friend to ask if she had defected to an evil empire had slipped Maia's mind.

Maia looked down at Pearl. The gashes and scrapes marring his body were deeper than she thought. This wasn't a spat. Whether in self-defense or not, Ami was going for the kill.

With a grunt, Maia jerked her leg forward, forcing Scarlet into a jog. She kept her focus on the two dueling shapes and hoped she would know which Vanguardian to attack when she closed the distance.

Edgar feinted with his smaller claw and thrust the larger one forward as Ami evaded. Two geysers of steam spewed from the base of Onyx's massive right claw, propelling the hunk of black metal at Emerald. The chain tethering it to his arm droned as it unwound from its hidden spool.

Of all the unique traits that separated each Pilot from one another, Ami's Perception was the ability Maia coveted most. Among other things, it allowed her to see her opponent's attacks before they happened. But seeing a blow and reacting to a blow were two different things.

Ami sent Emerald twisting beneath the claw, allowing it to pass harmlessly overhead. Once the claw moved beyond her vision, the chain seized. Onyx ripped his arm downward. Black metal smashed into Emerald's left wing from behind and pulled her spiraling down to the ground.

Scarlet shook the earth with each thundering step. By the time Onyx's claw retracted, Scarlet was upon him. Maia smashed Scarlet's foot into Onyx's clacking mandibles and sent him skittering back.

"Leave her alone!" Maia boomed. With a flick of her wrists, Scarlet's blades slid from her forearms, locking into place with a loud clang. She pointed one at Onyx. "Edgar, I'm warning you."

"Edgar." Dalzin's voice was little more than a whisper. "Let's stop, okay? Somebody's gonna get hurt."

"Dalzin, you promised me." Edgar said, his voice cracking. "You said you loved me. You said you would be there for me whenever I needed you!" Onyx squared up to Scarlet. The chain wound back into his arm, bringing his black hammer slamming back into place. "If you don't help me, they're going to kill me!"

"Nobody's getting killed!" Maia pointed Scarlet's other blade at Emerald, just in case she was wrong about her friend. She backed away, keeping both Vanguardians in her line of sight.

"Edgar, I'm sorry," Dalzin said. Pearl rose on shaky legs and broke into a canter. His long neck dropped, leveling his shining horn at Onyx like a jouster's lance. Maia didn't need Ami's Perception to see what was about to happen. In every Behemoth fight they had been in together, whenever he had his choice of targets, Dalzin opened with the same attack every time.

Halfway to Onyx, Pearl's canter became a gallop, and he angled his body and threw himself at Scarlet instead. Maia crossed Scarlet's blades and bore down, catching the unicorn's horn and driving it into the ground. Pearl's neck shuddered as the horn caught in the dirt. His momentum sent him flipping over her head.

Before she could recover, Onyx was upon her, snapping at Scarlet with both hungry claws. Maia twisted into the barrage and drove her knee into Onyx's face. As the crab staggered, she retracted Scarlet's blades, planted both hands on top of Onyx's curved shell, and vaulted clean over him.

Emerald rose, testing her bent wing.

"Don't move!" Maia shouted. "Nobody's going anywhere until we sort this out!"

"I don't believe words will help," Ami answered. "I must withdraw. You should do the same. If we stay and continue fighting, we risk a Vanguardian core rupture."

Maia weighed Ami's words. Before the last meeting of the Pilots, she would have followed Ami into the Blue Hells if Ami asked her to. After learning that Ami had actually entertained the idea of working for the Empire, after seeing the violation of nature Leona had created, Maia's faith in others had severely dwindled.

But it wasn't gone. Not completely.

"Can you fly? You might need to lift us out of here. My Teleport won't be ready for—"

"Behind!" Ami shouted.

Scarlet crouched and twisted too late. Onyx's massive right claw slammed into her leg and clamped down. The chain dangling behind it retracted with a high-pitched whine, and then the world outside Scarlet's cabin was spinning.

Maia's neck snapped back as Scarlet slammed onto her back. Black metal consumed her view of a slate gray sheet of clouds as Onyx scuttled onto Scarlet, pinning her chest and arms to the earth. Though smaller than Scarlet, his lower center of balance and considerable bulk left Maia with few options for escape.

With a great deal of thrashing, Maia managed to work Scarlet's left arm free of the hammer claw's grip. Her arm blade came out partway, adding a hot, glowing tip to the end of Scarlet's fist.

One clean blow, directly into Onyx's visor. That was all it would take to end Edgar's life. That's all it would take to rob the world of one of its greatest protectors.

Edgar took advantage of her hesitation, slamming Onyx's hammer into Scarlet's chest. Pain lanced through Maia's neck as her head was thrown back again. She punched out, but her arm wouldn't move.

Onyx clamped down on Scarlet's left arm, just above the elbow. This time, the grip was firm. Complete. The hammer claw squeezed. Metal groaned, then shrieked. A bolt of panic hit Maia as Onyx twisted and jerked, shearing through Scarlet's bicep.

Maia watched Scarlet's severed arm sail through the air as Onyx tossed it aside. It hovered for a moment before it fell behind the black hulk bearing down on her.

Emerald stirred. "I'm sorry, Sunder," Ami said. "I don't think I'll be able to save us both."

Maia barely heard her. Her connection to Scarlet didn't allow her to feel pain when her Vanguardian was damaged, but the shock of having her arm torn from her body made her queasy and lightheaded. Her head drifted from side to side. She watched Emerald take to the air, her bent wing causing her to veer to one side as she gained height.

Onyx's legs drummed the earth as he pivoted to face Emerald. A hissing spray of steam ripped from his back in a tight line as the back half of his shell lifted, revealing a dozen stacked cannon barrels that quickly telescoped to their full length.

"Oh, Maia," Edgar sighed. "Why couldn't you have just loved me like you were meant to?"

"Edgar! *No!*"

The screeching of the cannons erupting one after another drowned out Maia's scream. Bursts of steam sent twelve black projectiles tearing into the air like Fennish fire rockets. Tendrils of smoke trailed behind them as they crisscrossed in lazy arcs toward Emerald.

"I can't evade," Ami said. "Sunder, I—"

The missiles converged and exploded in a storm of light and fury. What was left of Emerald's mangled body spun from the edge of the rapidly expanding dust cloud, her neck and head hanging from her torso by a thin strip of metal.

Click.

Emerald's burning body disappeared over the lip of the crater, sailing toward the ocean beyond. Maia was holding her breath, and the scream waiting behind it, when a bass note smashed into her, so loud and low that it stole her hearing. A sizable chunk of the crater's lip flew apart, torn asunder by an expanding squall of wind and water. A sheet of water, dirt, and obsidian debris spread through the sky, falling in an arc and crashing down at the far end of the crater.

Maia stared dumbfounded at the droplets pattering against Scarlet's viewport. "You killed her."

"Shut up." Edgar brought Onyx's claw down onto Scarlet's chest. "Don't make me fracture your core, too."

The blow scattered Maia's thoughts. It took some time for the fragments to reform into shapes she could recognize. A picnic lunch on a tall cliff. Warm fingers, sticky with red dye, running through her hair. Cool green eyes and a promise that Maia wouldn't have to fight this bloody war alone.

Her memories of Ami faded, replaced by what she imagined the detonation of Emerald's core must have looked like as it scattered Maia's best friend in every direction.

"What did you do?" Dalzin whimpered.

"What did *we* do," Edgar corrected.

"I didn't! I—" Dalzin drew in a shuddering breath. "You said we were gonna capture them. We were gonna reason with them. That's what you said."

"Maia ruined everything." Onyx's black claw hammered Scarlet's chest again. "This is on her head."

"Stop it. Edgar. Stop!"

As Pearl approached, Onyx lashed out with his longer, thinner pincer, catching the unicorn in the snout. "If you want to leave, leave," Edgar snarled. "I'll do this with or without you. But unless you want to share Amisrala's fate, stay out of my way."

"Dalzin," Maia said, struggling to push her words through the depths of the dark pit Ami's death had cast her into. "Just go. He'll turn on you, too."

The hammer claw rose again and fell, thundering into Scarlet's chest. Her armor groaned, straining against the hit, and the next. Maia bounced with each strike. Her gaze drifted through Scarlet's viewport to Pearl's. She wondered what Dalzin Bonecruncher looked like, standing in the control beam of his Vanguardian. What did his face look like as he watched his partner beat the life out of her?

Maia opened her mouth to tell Dalzin that he wasn't alone, that he didn't need to be afraid of Edgar, but Pearl was already moving. His shimmering horn sunk into Onyx's side, sliding between the seam of his upper and lower shell.

"Bastard!" Edgar cried. Onyx twisted. His considerable weight snapped Pearl's horn off, taking a piece of the unicorn's white metal forehead with it. That terrible hammer claw thrust out and clamped around Pearl's neck.

Pearl thrashed as the claw collapsed his throat. Metal grated and moaned, forming a wordless plea. With a twist, Onyx tore Pearl's head off.

The claw opened, dropping the unicorn's head and its Pilot to the earth. Pearl's headless body crumpled, severed from his Pilot and his control beam.

Edgar didn't curse. He didn't yell. He didn't say goodbye. He simply lifted two of Onyx's spear-like legs and used his Vanguardian's bulk to drive them downward. Black metal flashed through the viewport, piercing Pearl's head—and the Pilot inside—like it was an empty eggshell.

Click.

"Look what you made me do. I cared for him. I really did." Edgar resumed beating Scarlet's chest. Thick red metal plates groaned. Soon, they would cave in, exposing her core. "You weren't meant to arrive until well after we had dealt with

Amisrala. Seeing you now, so broken and pathetic, I needn't have worried about facing you both at once."

Maia managed to force out a single word. The only word that still mattered. "Why?"

"Oh, yes, this is the part where I reveal my sinister plot. You know, like the villains do in those old plays you used to drag me to," Edgar said. "Amisrala wasn't the only one the Emperor approached with a proposition. I could say that I accepted that offer. I could say that one of the terms of our arrangement involved your death. That would make things nice and simple, wouldn't it?"

Onyx stopped hammering Scarlet's chest and shifted lower so his visor was even with Scarlet's. "But just between us? I would never align myself with Noctean curs. No. This is personal. This is the end of a road we've been traveling down ever since you left me for that half-elf bitch. Did you really think I would let you walk away from me? From us? Did you think I would keep suffering the indignity of seeing you with her? She took what was mine. You should know, before I send you across the Veil, that she's not coming for you. She can't save you. I made sure of that."

Leona.

Panic gripped Maia by the chest and pulled her up from the darkness, back into the light and all the pain that was waiting for her there. "What?"

"She thought she was so clever, disguising herself, masking her voice, never removing her armor in our presence. Making us all believe she was a man. But I'm not as stupid as you take me for. I know everything."

"Edgar." His name burned Maia's tongue. "What did you do?"

"What did I do?" When Edgar laughed, Maia could just barely make out his silhouette through Onyx's viewport. "I crushed her bones. I painted the side of a mountain with her blood. And I laughed while I did it. What do you think of that, you little—"

A fiery explosion ripped from Scarlet's body with a ferocity so great, it knocked the wind from Maia's lungs. Onyx hurtled like a shooting star to the edge of the crater. From within a twisting maelstrom of volcanic fury that stretched upward like a spear thrusting into the heavens, Scarlet rose. Rolling waves of heat baked the sand and dirt at her feet until it was glass.

Maia pulled molten air into her lungs and roared until her throat was raw and she could taste blood, until her breath was nothing but acrid smoke. And then Scarlet was running, tearing the glassed earth apart with each step.

The black metal crab rose on shaky legs. A vent of steam sliced through the black cloud of smoke snaking off his smoldering shell. Thin legs dug into the earth. A blare of cannon fire followed a procession of light and smoke.

Maia counted six missiles spinning her way. That left as many as eighteen in reserve. Maia grunted with every breath she pulled into her aching chest. The screeching missiles curved to meet her as she sprinted to the side, sending Scarlet leaping and rolling to avoid them. Obsidian chunks crunched under her shoulder as she touched down. The force of the thundering explosions pushed Scarlet from behind, granting her more speed.

A flick of Maia's taut wrist brought Scarlet's remaining arm blade speeding from its hiding place. The glow of its edges spread until the whole blade burned bright, like an ingot fresh from the forge.

Onyx scuttled backward up the crater wall as she neared. Maia dropped Scarlet into a low skid and spun, licking flames following the arc of her blade as it sheared through one of Onyx's legs like it was nothing but parchment. The crab retreated further up the slope. Maia hacked again, severing two more legs.

The bludgeoning claw rose, and the sight of it stole a beat from Maia's heart. She cried out and swung upward, turning the hammer wide enough to miss Scarlet's head. Maia drove her hips into the blow, turning a full circle and slamming her blazing blade down. Red-hot metal dug into the joint behind Onyx's massive claw. She bore down, pushing harder with each pained cry until her voice died and became a raspy wheeze.

With one last drive, Scarlet's blade passed through and hissed into the earth. Onyx's claw thudded to the ground. Edgar yelled something that started as a word and curled into feral noise as he lashed out with the remaining pincer. Scarlet guided it into her armpit and clamped her arm down over it. Maia pivoted and wrenched, dragging the black crab in a wide arc. Her shoulder muscles tightened, threatening to split, but Maia continued her spin, using the momentum to hurl Onyx toward the pit's center.

Maia swallowed and winced. Her ravaged throat throbbed as she stalked to where her foe had landed. When the crab flipped to his feet, Maia greeted him by way of a sideways slash. The tip of Scarlet's red-hot blade sheared through Onyx's visor, spraying black glass shards onto the ground. Edgar cried out. She could see him through the rapidly cooling edges of the hole she had carved, shielding his head with his arms.

Scarlet's blade slid back into her forearm as she clamped her hand down on Onyx's head, putting her palm flush with the gash in his visor.

A voice in Maia's head told her to stop, to show mercy. But then she remembered the three people Edgar had taken from her in one day, and that voice shut its bloody mouth.

The fire bonded to her soul resonated with the blaze burning within Scarlet's core. It flowed from Scarlet's hand like a river, spewing hot vengeance into Onyx's cabin. As he burned, Edgar's low, defiant shout rose into a keening wail that eventually died and became a pained whimper. Then, nothing.

The curling flames faded. Maia released Onyx's head, letting it list toward the ground. When she bent over and put her hands on her knees, she could hear her heartbeat in her head, pumping with such ferocity that she worried she might pass out. She dared to close her eyes for a second.

Groaning, grinding metal brought her back. Onyx's cannon barrels lined up with her chest. Sheer terror sent Maia into a low crouch. She threw Scarlet's shoulder into Onyx, pitching his aim high. She didn't need to count to know that the sputtering barrels had launched all eighteen remaining missiles into the sky. Edgar no longer had a reason to hold back.

With one last shudder, Onyx collapsed against Scarlet. A spiral of black dots painted the sky, twirling as they rose and scattered across the endless gray. The clouds ate their streaming trails as they started to fall and a gurgling noise halfway between a laugh and a cough filled Scarlet's cabin.

Click.

The black crab's dead weight bore down on Scarlet, but Maia didn't move to push him off. There was no reason to, with Leona gone. No reason to remain in a world that offered nothing but suffering and punishment. The fallen were avenged. The missiles would reach her soon. Once Edgar's final attack sent her across the Veil, she could finally rest.

As Maia resigned herself to her fate, she let her gaze drop from the sky to the lip of the crater. There, she spied a glinting splash of color on the horizon. Her chest seized. Even from so far away, the proud blue silhouette of Cobalt, the Blue Panther Vanguardian, stood bold and true against the cold gray sky.

A rush of blood slammed into Maia. For the first time in her life, she was happy to have been lied to. Leona was alive. Maia still had something to hold onto. A reason to live.

Up in the sky, the missiles formed a tight ring, falling far too fast for her to outrun. Even Emerald had been unable to avoid that many. The sight of Emerald disappearing over the horizon, followed by a titanic blast of wind as her core ruptured and released the full force of its contained sliver, stuck in Maia's mind.

And from that image, a very stupid plan formed. Scarlet pivoted, throwing Onyx onto his back. Pearl's crystal horn was still wedged in Onyx's side. Dalzin often boasted that it was harder than diamond. Maia prayed that he wasn't just blowing his own horn as she tore it out and brought it down hard on the thin line where Onyx's chest plates joined.

After three thrusts, the seam gave. The horn glided through the gap and into Onyx's core.

An exploding ocean of water erupted from Onyx's chest, shaking Maia's skull and stealing a moment of her consciousness. The raging waters rushed from the Black Crab Vanguardian's core as its water sliver broke free of its shackles. Scarlet flew upwards, battered by the swift current.

A deep crunch followed, like a thousand bones breaking at once. Outside the viewport, there was nothing but darkness. The crackling ice that now surrounded Scarlet drank all the light from the world above. For a moment, Maia couldn't hear her own breathing from within the deafening silence of her frozen tomb.

The cabin shook as the missiles collided with the ice. Cracks raced through the glacier outside the viewport. The world crumbled around her. When she opened her eyes, a single ray of light pierced through Scarlet's visor.

Scarlet was laying at the base of a deep, icy ravine.

Maia dug Scarlet's hand into the side of the pit and hauled herself from the mountain of crushed ice covering her torso. Fatigue pulled at her limbs and lungs and heart as she ascended, but Maia kept scrambling until Scarlet was free from the ravine. The rutty glacier birthed by Onyx's ruptured core spread across the bottom of Thenmar's Crater, filling it halfway to the top. Jagged waves of icy fangs curved away from the center. A fresh sheet of snow fell so slowly that the flakes didn't look like they were moving at all.

The sound of crunching ice roused Maia, and she saw Cobalt padding her way across the uneven ice. Apologies and explanations and promises formed in her mind, each fighting through the jumbled mess to reach her lips and become real.

"I'm sorry," Maia tried to say, but the croak that left her raw, ravaged throat couldn't hold its shape.

The panther's maw opened. Flickering tendrils of lightning gathered into a misshapen sphere between his fangs. Maia threw Scarlet to the side as a bolt as thick as her Vanguardian's arm snapped from Cobalt's mouth and struck the ice where she had been standing, painting the air with a shower of slush and snow. Cobalt leaped through it, slamming into Scarlet's side as she rose and throwing her back down.

"You killed him!" Leona's first words to Maia in over a week flitted into Scarlet's cabin like sabers. "Traitor! You killed them all!"

"No, I—" Maia coughed. She forced her words out slow and even. "I. Can. Explain."

Maia pushed into a roll, avoiding Cobalt's second pounce. Gleaming claws scraped long, angry ruts in the ice.

"Were you going to kill me next, just like you killed our daughter?" Cobalt's fangs crackled with lightning. Scarlet darted between the prismatic web lashing into the ground all around her. "We could have been a family, and you ruined it. You ruined everything!"

A bolt crashed down near Scarlet's foot and sent her stumbling. Behind her, the massive ravine she had crawled from waited like an angry, hellish maw. Cobalt continued his advance. Ribbons of lightning poured off the blue panther's sleek, deadly frame.

Leona's heavy breathing filled Scarlet's cabin. "Remember your promise? Your heart belongs to me. You broke mine, so I'm going to crush yours."

Arcs of yellow and blue dug into the glacier. The ice groaned and pitched as it gave way and crumbled beneath them. Maia cut to the side, running along the edge of the ravine. The collapsing ground caught up with her after ten strides. Scarlet fell onto her back and rode a sea of white and blue down into the fissure, touching down in a crouch that twisted Maia's knee to the side. Snow and ice cascaded around Scarlet, burying her to the waist.

Up above, Cobalt hung on the opposite edge of the ravine, having leapt clear of the avalanche. His back paws scraped against sheer ice, scrambling for purchase. He found it right as the lip of the ledge broke off.

Cobalt twisted, trying to land on his feet, but chunks of falling ice rushed past him and knocked him about. He crashed back-first on a jagged piece of ice thrusting from the ravine's floor, bending his body in a way it wasn't made to bend. He slipped off it and landed on his belly. After a short pause, he dug his front paws into the rough ground. Slowly, he pulled himself down the ravine's length toward Scarlet.

"Stop," Maia rasped. "It. Wasn't me. Was. Edgar."

"I'll never forgive you. For any of it."

After dragging himself another half a body length, Cobalt shuddered and went still. A crack, thin as a razor's edge, spread across his visor.

"Run if you want. I'll hunt you to the end of the world. You won't find rest. Or peace." More cracks branched from the first, forming a ragged filigree. "And when I find you, when I stand over your bloody, beaten body, and rip your still-beating heart from your chest …"

The visor exploded outward. From the hole, the Blue Pilot of Lightning emerged, clad in her deep blue armor and her panther-styled helmet, gripping the shaft of her spear so tight that her hands shook.

"Then you'll know just how I feel."

Click.

Leona crouched and leaped from Cobalt's head. Lightning arced from the tip of her spear as she raised it over her head.

A flash of panic struck Maia. Instinct made her lash out against the streaking bolt of hate-fueled blue metal careening her way. She closed her eyes too late to break her connection with the three-hundred-foot-tall war machine following her every movement.

A cut-off scream punctured the cold air of Scarlet's cabin. There was no way to know if Leona died the second Scarlet's titanic hand struck her, or when she crunched into the ravine wall, or when she landed in a broken heap on the ice below. It all happened so fast.

Night had fallen by the time Maia was finally able to look away from Leona's mangled body. By then, the image had burned so deep into her mind that she couldn't see anything else.

Scarlet lowered her to the ravine floor. It took some time to find Leona in the dim moonlight. By then, ice had taken her in its cold embrace and fused her armor to the ground. She stared up at Maia through the shattered wreck of her helm, eyes wide and empty.

"It wasn't me. It was Edgar," Maia whispered. She pulled Leona from the binding frost, dismissed her helmet, and rested her head on her partner's shoulder. The frozen metal of Leona's pauldron bit into her cheek. "It wasn't me. It wasn't me." She shut her eyes and repeated the words over and over, hoping that they might be enough to call Leona back from beyond the Veil and turn the corpse in her arms back into the woman she loved.

Maia barely felt the frigid armor ripping a layer of skin from her face when she finally pulled away. Crystallized tears fused her eye lashes and trailed icy lines down her cheeks. Maia brushed them away and staggered to her feet. She trudged like a zombie, gathering crude chunks of ice and dragging them back to Leona's body, placing them on top of her until she couldn't see any blue poking out from beneath.

Her helmet snapped back into place, shielding her from the world. Mechanical steps brought Maia away from the makeshift cairn and back to Scarlet's cabin. When she managed to climb out of the fissure, Maia called on her hateful fire one more time. Flames leaped into a ball in Scarlet's waiting palm, and she lobbed the orb into the far wall of the ravine. It took three blasts to crumble it, sending waves of ice and snow sweeping in to seal the unmarked grave that held three of her friends.

Maia turned Scarlet away from the tomb, away from Leona, Edgar, Dalzin, and what remained of their Vanguardians. She would have found Ami and Emerald and brought them back to join her the rest in their frozen tomb, but the thought of holding another dead friend in her arms sent Maia into a wracking fit of sobs.

She focused on the memory of her family's vineyard and moved her arms through familiar motions. A burst of light and color followed, and she was gone.

Chapter 29
No Turning Back

When Maia finished her story, she found herself staring at the missing chunk of the crater's lip. A few deep breaths later, her heart slowed enough for her to catch up to it. She cleared her throat and flicked away a thin strand of ice trailing from her eye. "That's what happened here."

She didn't tell them what came after, when she arrived near Bracken, walking in a daze from where Scarlet had collapsed and destroyed most of her father's crop. She didn't bother to dismiss her armor as her father ran to her and took her up in his bear-like grasp. She didn't feel the caress of his hard, calloused hands through the metal of her helmet as he comforted her. He didn't ask her what had happened or where she was hurt. He simply held her as her shoulders bobbed with silent sobs and stinging tears slipped through the seams of her helmet.

That pain wasn't for them. It was hers alone.

"Leona was Blue Bolt," Serenia said. Her teeth were chattering and her voice barely had any breath to it. "She was a Pilot."

"Yeah," Maia replied. "She didn't want anybody knowing. When you have power like ours, people try to make you do things. Leona didn't want to be anyone's weapon."

"And you killed her," Kasper said, his tone as hard as the ice at their feet. "I knew she was dead. Didn't know for sure if it was you who ended her."

"It was. And I killed Edgar. I could have spared him, maybe taken him captive. But I lost control. This anger, this bloodlust, it's... I killed them. And I'm responsible for Ami and Dalzin, too. I killed them all."

When Maia met Serenia's gaze, she tried to read her expression and came away with nothing. "Look at this place. Imagine if this happened near a city. Or within one. This is the kind of destruction that comes with giving any one person the kind of power we have. This is how it always ends. I hope you can see that now."

The wind whistled between the frozen spires surrounding them. Maia listened to its song and waited. Finally, Serenia closed the distance with measured, deliberate steps, the way one would approach a cornered animal.

"Thank you," she said.

"Thank you?"

"Yes. Thank you. For everything. For taking me in as your apprentice, and training me, and bringing me here. Now that I know the truth, I understand what you've really been trying to teach me."

Maia couldn't hold back her long, heavy sigh. Worry slipped from her chest and into her breath to be carried away by the wind. She had done it. Finally, Maia had gotten through. It cost Serenia her innocence. It cost Maia an eye. It would cost the Freelands much more in the months to come.

But it was all worth it. Serenia was saved. The cycle was broken. That's what mattered. Now, they could both rest.

"I don't know what to say," Maia said.

Serenia reached for Maia's hands and took them in hers, the way a sister would. "You don't need to say anything. You've suffered so much, waging this war that you never wished to fight. You lost family and friends. You've held on for so long, all by yourself. I see, now, what it costs to be a Pilot, and where my future might lead if I can't properly control the gifts I've been given.

"Now that I know the dangers of the path that lies ahead, I can avoid them. I promise you, when I'm Pilot Commander of my own team of Vanguardians, I won't go down the same road you walked. I *will* be better. Together, Scarlet and I will finish what you began."

The entirety of Maia's body pulled as taught as a winch line on a loaded catapult. "I don't understand."

"I do. I know, now, why you want to give up. Why you wanted *me* to give up. But I accept this charge and everything that may come with a glad heart. You can rest, Maia. I'll carry the torch for you. If any sacrifices need to be made to bring peace to the world, let me shoulder the burden. I'm prepared."

"No." Maia ripped her hands from Serenia's grip. "No! How can you still want to be a Pilot after everything you've seen? What about Galford? Whitehorn?

Castle Blackwood? That fucking zombie forest? Were you paying attention for any of it? Look at how many lives I've ruined! That's what Pilots do. We ruin, and we kill. Is that what you want to be? A killer?"

When Serenia lifted her chin, her face had hardened. She didn't look like a girl of sixteen years anymore. That bright spark in her eyes remained, but something rigid and fierce had taken root alongside it. "What I want is to be a protector of the people. I want to fight for them."

"You don't want this fight. You only think you do because they burned it into your mind when they butchered you and made you into their weapon. What else do I have to do to make you see that you're making a mistake? Dig up Edgar and Dalzin and Leona so you can see where you're headed? Let's go, then! I'll get in Scarlet, and I'll dig them up. Maybe seeing their fucking corpses will—"

"Maia, stop!" Serenia shut her eyes tight and curled her hands into claws at her sides. "I spent four years in a coma, doing nothing but dreaming terrible dreams. When I finally woke up, I rarely slept through an entire night for a long while. I was fed up with sleep. It stole so much from me. It took time for me to realize that sleep was necessary, no matter how much I loathed it. I wouldn't have asked anyone else to forgo sleep simply because I had my fill of it. You've been through so much as Scarlet's Pilot, but that doesn't mean that being her Pilot is a terrible thing. You've had enough sleep. That's all. It's time to make way for another dreamer."

"After everything you've seen, you haven't learned a bloody thing," Maia said.

"What I've seen is a beautiful, diverse, wonderful world in peril. It's worth fighting for. Nothing you can say will change my mind. This is the path I've chosen, and I intend to follow it."

"Follow it on foot, then. You're not taking Scarlet."

"That isn't fair, Sun," Kasper said. "You promised."

Serenia held out a hand to him. "I don't need you to fight my battles for me."

"Is that what this is now?" Maia said. "A battle?"

"I don't wish it to be." Serenia folded her arms. "Kas has the right of it, though. You promised me. You said that after your final lesson, if I still wished to become Scarlet's Pilot, you would hand her over to me. I've seen this journey through to its end, and I've decided that I still want to bear this burden. I expect you to stay true to your word. You owe me."

The words cut into Maia's spine, forcing her to straighten. "I took you in. Trained you. Tried to guide you down the right path. Gave you the best of the time I have left in this world. After all that, you think I owe you more?"

"Yes. You owe me for lying to me about killing my mother and stealing four years of my life."

Maia fought hard to suppress a powerful shudder. There was no avoiding the confrontation they had both been hurtling toward since Serenia awakened. "It was my first fight. I was focused on winning. I should have been more careful. It was an accident."

"I'm sure it was. It doesn't change what happened or the fact that you allowed me to believe, all this time, that you were our avenger. When you told me that you were responsible for my mother's death, I misunderstood you. You could have corrected me. You had so many opportunities to make the truth known. Our relationship is built on a lie and paved with broken promises. For that, I feel I'm owed."

There were more cards left for Maia to play before she was ready to fold. "When did you learn the truth? The first time you called your father? Or the second?"

Serenia's mouth fell open. "Why do you think I called my father? You broke my Farspeaker."

Maia turned her one-eyed gaze to Kasper, who had frozen like a deer staring down a hunter's bow. As much as she wanted to tear them apart, breaking Serenia's confidence in him by revealing that he had betrayed her trust would only drive her further from Maia. She let that card fall from her hand. "I heard you speaking to him in Whitehorn," she lied. "You fixed your Farspeaker, and you broke your promise. I'm assuming it wasn't the first time."

"I did break my word, I suppose. Yet it doesn't compare, in any way, to what you've done."

"What I've done is keep you safe," Maia said, trudging forward and staring down at her apprentice. "Everything I've done has been to protect you."

"All you've protected me from is the truth! How does that serve me?"

A card flicked from Maia's sleeve and into her hand. It wasn't fair play. Maia couldn't take it back once she touched it down on the table.

She played it anyway. There was no other way to win.

"It protected you from knowing that you're a murderer, just like me."

"What?"

"In the dead woods. That robed man you shot right before I arrived. Before I yelled at you. He wasn't a zombie."

"You're lying." This time, Serenia's shivers weren't from the cold.

"I'm not. Not this time. That man was a necromancer. He was alive. Human. Flesh and blood. Nowhere close to innocent, but he knew something about the curse that's slowly killing me. You misused your power, like all Pilots eventually do. You made a mistake, just like I did. You killed him. You killed me. Hells, maybe you killed yourself, too, if all Pilots carry the same curse. We'll never know now."

"You're lying," Serenia repeated. Her voice trembled. "You would have told me if I did something so... You would have told me."

"I didn't. I kept the truth from you because I knew what it would do to you. I wanted to save you. I still can."

Serenia wrapped her arms around herself and pulled away. Maia let her have her tears. When Kasper went to her, she shook her head and shrugged away from his grasp. Maia wondered if she had gone too far, if she had broken her beyond repair. But when the sobs ended and Serenia spun to face Maia, her eyes gleamed like embers.

"So what if I'm a killer? I can still be better. Better than you. Better than any other Pilot. Give me Scarlet like you promised and I'll show you. I'll show everyone."

"I told you. You're not taking her."

Serenia's nodded slowly, her mouth set in a hard line. "I see now. You never intended to hand Scarlet over to me. You only took me on as your apprentice to assuage your guilty conscience."

Maia walked to one of the ice spires surrounding them and placed her hand on it. With her weakened sliver unable to fully warm her, a cold chill bit her palm. "You're right. If I'm being honest—"

"That would be a first," Serenia cut back.

"If I'm being honest, I guess I never thought you would still want Scarlet after coming here, after knowing the whole story. I made a deal I never thought I would have to keep. Yes, I took you in because I felt guilty. It gave me a chance to make you change your mind. But if you think guilt is all that brought us here, you're wrong."

"What else, then?" Serenia scoffed. "Pity? Or perhaps genuine, tingling joy at the idea of shattering my dreams and leaving me—"

"I care about you!" Maia roared. She ran her cold, numb hand down her face. The wind stopped as if her outburst had frightened it away. "I couldn't save myself from this fate. I couldn't save the others. But I can save you. You just have to let me."

"I care about you, as well," Serenia said. She wiped her runny nose with the back of her gloved hand and sniffled. "But I can't allow you to stand in the way of my duty. I need Scarlet, and I'll do what needs to be done to secure her."

Silence fell, settling like fallen snow. Maia didn't know who moved first, but when she blinked, she and Serenia had both fallen back into their fighting stances, bodies coiled and tensed for violence.

"You don't want to do this, Princess," Maia said, pushing a growl into her voice that she hoped would intimidate.

"Stop calling me that, and stop telling me what I want!" Serenia shouted back.

"If you come any closer, that's it. There'll be no turning back. Do you think you stand a chance against me, even on your best day?"

A smirk spread across Serenia's lips. "Look at you, Maia. You can barely lift your arms. You're dragging your feet like one of those zombies we fought. You're suffering from injured ribs and a half-healed stomach wound. You're missing an eye. And if what you say is true, a curse is slowly crushing the life out of you." She edged forward. "Perhaps I can't beat you on my best day, but today is far from yours."

"Okay. Fuck this." Maia pushed, deep and hard. Flames screeched from her hand. She raked her palm over the ground between them, raising a wall of fiery death that hissed against the ice. "It's over, Princess. We're done here."

Serenia approached the fire. She looked down at her gloved hands, turning them over as if they were brand new to her. She stretched them toward the flames, closed her eyes, and gritted her teeth.

As Serenia's arms shook from strain, Maia felt it. Some force other than Maia's sliver was pushing against the flames. The fiery curtain collapsed in the middle. The gap spread to the edges of the wall until there was nothing between the two Pilots but a steaming divot in the ice. Panting, Serenia stepped through the mist. It clung to her hair and froze instantly, coating her crown of braids in a sheen of frost.

"Fire is mine to control as well, it seems. I have everything you have." Serenia fell back into her fighter's stance. "Do you see, now? Do you see how much I've grown? I've become more than a match for you."

With a heavy heart, Maia added her latest failure to her never-ending list and flexed her fingers into fists.

"I guess we'll find out. Won't we?"

Chapter 30
A Decisive Blow

Ren ground her rear leg into the snow-covered glacial ground until she was sure she had the footing to push off and strike. Across from her, Maia struggled to maintain her posture. The deepness of her stance caused her legs to tremble, and the ward she formed with her arms had already begun to sag.

Seeing her mentor in such a weakened state pulled at Ren's chest. She vowed to end the fight quickly. One decisive blow. That was all she needed to end the fight, fulfill her duty, and prove herself worthy. Her rapier hung at her side. Her revolver rested at the small of her back. Once she drew either weapon, the fight would begin. Then, eventually, as all fights did, it would end. One of them had to lose.

Maia moved first. As a burst of adrenaline hit Ren, covering her vision in stars and dust, she caught herself mid-step. Maia hadn't advanced. She had merely risen from her fighting posture to stand naturally with her arms at her sides. Her smirk told Ren that she had seen the twitch.

Maia opened her mouth, probably to say as much, but instead of firing off a scathing remark, she pushed away and skidded toward the curved ice pillar at her back. Kas' fist passed through empty air, right where her head had been.

Ren hadn't seen him slip away and move to flank. With his surprise foiled, he threw himself at Maia, firing off a quick jab from the left. Maia's head tilted to the side, slipping the blow.

"Is this because you didn't get a go at the hot spring?" Maia said.

"You took her from me!" Kas yelled and threw a hook from the right, putting all his weight behind the blow. Stepping inside the arc of the swing, Maia smashed the crown of her skull into Kas' nose.

He reeled, one hand covering his bloody face, the other extended to defend.

Maia grabbed his outstretched wrist, pivoted her hips, and twisted.

It was a subtle movement, with barely any muscle behind it, but the motion sent Kas flipping into the ice column. The sheer perfection of the technique took Ren's breath away right before the column took Kas'. He crumpled to the ground and laid there, moaning as he cradled his bleeding nose.

"Even on my worst day, I don't need strength to win," Maia said, flashing a coy smile. "I don't want to hurt you, Princess. Give up, okay?"

Ren wanted to. She wanted to go back to her days of laborious training, hunting Ferals, eating bacon and bread, and wondering where they would find money to feed themselves the following day. More than anything, she wished she could live those days forever.

But she promised to bring Scarlet home, and Maia had just hurt Kas again. Ren let go of the reins keeping her breath in check and ripped her rapier from her belt. Her resolve hardened to match the steel in her hand. "Summon your armor and weapons," she growled. "I won't strike an unarmed opponent."

Maia had the audacity to laugh, though it sent her into a short coughing fit. "Really?" She forced her injured arms into a trembling cross above her head. "What did I tell you about playing fair?"

The cross lowered, blocking Maia's sight for a fraction of a second. From a dozen paces away, Ren drew her revolver and fired. The bullet ripped past Maia's head and tore into the ice behind her. A panicked cry burst from her lips, and she tilted away from the shattered ice pelting her back. Ren was already running. Three paces from her target, she raised her rapier's tip, fell into a lunge, and slid.

The tip slipped through Maia's right shoulder and dug into the ice behind it. Ren pushed down nausea as realization dawned on her. She had just impaled her mentor. "I'm not playing fair."

With her right shoulder wound opened and her left freshly injured, Maia wouldn't be able to continue. It wasn't a kindness to end their friendship with a thrust of her sword, but Maia would walk away from the fight. It was the best victory Ren could ask for.

"You missed," Maia said with a sharp gasp.

"No, I didn't. I struck you exactly where I meant to," Ren said.

"Then you're a fool."

Maia gripped the blade with her shaking left hand. Slowly, a dull orange spread across its length as she poured heat into it.

"Stop! Let go!" Ren cried and yanked as hard as she could. At the same time, Maia twisted. The heated blade snapped. Little more than a foot of rapidly cooling steel remained of the fine sword her father had given her.

"Blue fucking Hells!" Ren screamed, throwing the ruined blade down. Before she could bring her revolver to bear, Maia's foot snapped into her jaw, sending her sprawling onto her rear. Her gun fell from her grasp and slid across the ice.

With a grunt, Maia pulled the other half of Ren's broken rapier from her shoulder and cast it aside. Something had changed in her eye, a subtle shift that Ren had never seen before. The playful, cocky glimmer was gone, replaced with a grim stillness. A cold spark lit up Ren's spine. Was this what Ferals saw right before Maia tore them to pieces with her ember-edged blades?

"You'll have to do better than that if you want to really hurt me," Maia said. "I've never backed down from a fight before, and I'm sure as shit not going to—"

Kas kicked the back of Maia's knee from the ground, sending her stumbling. Seizing the opening, Ren charged. She planted her foot and spun, lashing out with her back leg, catching Maia across the jaw and drawing an arc of blood from her mouth. Before Maia could recover, Ren darted into her blind spot and slammed a fist into her kidney.

Maia stuttered to the side with a groan. Ren aimed a left hook at the back of her head. This was it. Her decisive blow.

She let her fist fly. A light pressure closed around her wrist. Her hand twisted until it couldn't go any further, and her arm followed, then the rest of her. The world spun. Her shoulder crunched against the hard ground, followed by her head, filling her vision with stardust.

It was the same technique Maia had used on Kas. Had she left that opening on purpose?

While Ren struggled to stand, Kas found his second wind. He moved like he was lighter than air, darting around the ice and hurling crisp punches and kicks at Maia. Though her movements were jerky and labored, she floated just beyond his reach, drawing his stance wider each time.

Kas lunged to pursue her. Maia slipped around to his back with a deft step.

With a twist of her hips, her dangling right arm snapped up and out like a whip, catching him in the back of the head. He furrowed his brow, then fell onto his face, unconscious.

Maia was panting. Her body listed hard to the right. "Stay down, Princess. If you keep coming, I won't hold back."

"Then don't! Give me everything you have!" Ren strode to Maia, chambered her leg, and kicked. Maia accepted the blow, folding into it and grabbing Ren's ankle. As soon as Ren felt the grip, she wrenched her leg back, drawing Maia to her.

Her fist snapped into the corner of Maia's jaw. When Maia released her and pulled away, Ren snaked her hands behind her neck, clasped them together, and pulled her knee into Maia's stomach, over and over.

"You were right, back at the tavern," Ren growled into Maia's ear as she pummeled her, driving her back toward the icy spire. "You're not a hero. You're a coward, and a traitor, and a murderer! Give up! You're in no condition to be Scarlet's Pilot any longer!" She shoved Maia into the spire, reared back, and threw all her weight behind a cunning right cross.

When her blow struck home, her hand lit up with bright agony. Blood streamed from her knuckles through the split leather of her glove. She cradled it against her stomach and curled around it to protect it. She couldn't stop her hand from quivering, and when she tried to make a fist, she nearly vomited from the pain. The column of ice bore a heavy dent and a splotch of her blood where she had struck it.

Maia shakily stood from her crouch. She must have waited until the last possible moment to dodge.

"Stop! Now!" Maia gripped Ren's shoulder, pushed her against the column, and held her there. "All I wanted was to save you. Why couldn't you just let me? Why are you doing this? Is it for your father? Your bloody Emperor? *Why do you want this so much?*"

Ren gritted her teeth and remembered Maia's words. *You'll have to do better than that if you want to really hurt me.*

She leaned closer, pushing her forehead into Maia's. "Why? Because unlike you, I care about the world and the people in it. I have something worth fighting for. You talk about duty, but you only fight the Kith because you're afraid of how worthless you would be if you didn't. By keeping Scarlet for yourself, you're not trying to save me. You can't let her go because you know, deep down, you aren't anything special. Without Scarlet, without your powers, you are *nothing!*"

Maia's face crunched up. Her glare lost its edge. She fell back as if Ren had emptied her revolver into her chest. "I—"

Ren's fist shut her mouth. She carried forward, driving her shoulder into Maia's chest and sending her onto her back, sliding across the ice until she slid to a stop near a glint of purple peeking out from beneath a light sheet of fresh snow.

If Maia got to the revolver first...

Panic whipped Ren, burning through her fatigue. Quick strides brought her to her lost gun. Her fingers closed around it, sticking to the cold metal at the edges of the wooden grip. She whipped her weapon in a wide arc, bringing it to bear.

Something struck her wrist, throwing her aim wide. Maia's left hand was cocked back, palm open and trembling as if she was struggling to restrain the claw her fingers had formed. Whatever that stance was, Ren had never seen anything like it.

When Maia thrust, every part of Ren's body screamed at once, tightening into one solid horrified mass. When she opened her eyes and looked down, and saw the claw hovering just above her breast, she let out a shuddering breath and knew that for a brief moment, she had tasted death.

"I would have had you," Maia said. She looked right through Ren, at something far off in the distance, with a stare so blank it chilled Ren's blood.

Something warm slapped Ren's face. She reached up and wiped her cheek. Blood covered her gloved fingers. Maia collapsed to the ground and hacked up more blood, convulsing as she fought for her life against her invisible nemesis.

Ren backed away, keeping clear of Maia's thrashing legs. A firm hand closed on her shoulder.

"Kas, I didn't...I mean, I..." Ren couldn't think of anything she could say, anything she could do, that could save Maia. All she could do was watch her writhe through the spasms tearing her body apart from within until, with one last cough of blood followed by a pained gurgle, Maia shut her eyes and fell silent.

"She's gone," Kas said. He bent down and reached for her.

"No!" Ren gripped his forearm. "Don't touch her. She wouldn't want..."

The rest of her words fell away. It was over. She was the only living person who could command Scarlet, now. When she returned to Noctis, it would be as a conquering hero. She had everything she needed to make the world a better place, to save it from the brink of destruction. To make her father proud.

It was everything Ren ever wanted. And none of it mattered now that Maia was gone.

"What now?" Kas said.

Ren answered with the slightest of shrugs. She expected her heart to break at any moment, once the horror of her mentor's death worked its way through the numbness. She looked to where Scarlet was kneeling and had a hard time seeing anything but a bloodstained giant, bought and paid for with the life of her best friend.

"We should cover her up at least," Kas said. "Nobody deserves to—"

"I'm not dead yet," Maia whispered.

Ren screamed. Reflex brought her revolver in line with Maia's head. "Emperor's fucking Grace!"

Maia opened her eye and shifted onto her left elbow. Her whole body pitched with each breath. "You didn't shoot."

Ren shook her head.

"But you have orders."

Ren nodded.

With a frustrated sigh, Maia collapsed onto her back. She gazed up at the sky, her chest rising and falling with deep, labored breaths. "Maybe you should pull the trigger. I have a lot to answer for."

What malice remained in Ren's heart bled away. She let her revolver hang at her side. "Did I really take a life back in the dead woods? A person's life?"

"Yes."

"I see." Later, once the weight of her sin had settled, when there was time to break and hate herself, she would indulge. "What are we to do now?"

"You tell me. You're the one with the gun."

"I don't know what to do. My duty is to retrieve Scarlet, yet the only way I can achieve my goal is... And I can't. I just can't."

"Then you have a problem." With a great, shaking effort, Maia pushed up onto her feet. "You can't have it both ways. You have to choose."

"No. I can't. I won't. There has to be another way."

"You can always wait for me to die." Maia's breath wheezed. Her back hunched. "Or, like always, you can rely on me to make all of your decisions for you."

Maia's left hand snapped up with speed she shouldn't have been capable of in her condition. She grabbed the revolver's barrel and pressed it to her head. "Do it," she growled. "Go on. This is what they made you for."

"Maia, no. Stop this." Ren pulled against Maia's grip. "Please!"

"You think I only took you in because I felt guilty? Maybe that's true. But you only came with me because it was your duty. So do your duty. Punish me. Take what's yours. Be a good little Noctean and end this!"

"Ren?" Kas said. "Don't mean to interrupt, but... Is Scarlet supposed to do that?"

The blood red Vanguardian rose from her crouch with a metallic groan. Her forearm blade came singing out, its edges glowing bright. She sank the scorching blade into the ground. Steam screeched from the long gash she carved into the glacier as she trudged their way.

"It's Sun!" Kas wrapped an arm around her waist, pulling her away from the titan's advance.

"Maia!" Ren cried. "What are you doing? You'll kill us all!"

"It's not me!" Maia's face twisted with effort as she held an unsteady hand out toward Scarlet. "She's moving on her own. She's not listening to me. I can't stop her!"

"Ren, come on!" Kas pulled her again. This time, she let him lead her away.

Maia trundled away until she was clear of Scarlet's path. The Vanguardian continued past them unabated. At the end of her march, she sheathed her burning blade, raised her foot, and slammed it down on the seam she had carved. A deep crunch reverberated through the glacier. Then another. The icy mass beneath Ren quaked, throwing her off her feet. Kas dropped on top of her, covering her head and holding her tight as icy spires toppled around them.

When the glacier's anger ceased, Ren opened her eyes and stood. She gasped at the sight of the two-hundred-foot-wide canyon stretching from Scarlet's foot for nearly a mile. At the end of the frozen scar, Scarlet stood tall, pointing a single finger into the depths of the chasm.

Maia's haggard form slumped against a hulking mass of broken ice on the other side of the chasm. Ren yelled to her. If her voice carried all the way across the gap, Maia didn't react to it. She turned and staggered in Scarlet's general direction, disappearing behind a pile of shattered debris.

"Come on. We have to get back to Scarlet before she does," Kas said, and broke off into a run. When he realized Ren hadn't moved to follow, he slid to a stop. "Ren! She might leave us here! If you still want Scarlet, we have to go now!"

"I'll catch up." Ren made a weak motion with her broken hand. "Please? I only need a moment."

He nodded and sped off. When she couldn't hear his crunching footsteps any longer, Ren approached the lip of the chasm. She placed her revolver in the crook of her arm and jerked the cylinder open. With her arm tensed to hold the weapon steady, she reached in, drawing out her last remaining shell. Her fingers wrapped around it, clenching so hard she thought it might burst in her hand.

The memory of her wolf's bark sending a brown-robed man slamming into a tree played over and over in her mind. She hadn't seen his face, but in her mind, she pictured his mouth twisted, as if to ask her "why?"

Because I'm a failure.

The tears she worked so hard to keep at bay came all at once, the sheer weight of the torrent crumpling her to her knees. She breathed into her sobs, forcing them into raspy whispers so that there was no chance the wind would carry them to anyone else's ears.

Dust fell from the tunnel's ceiling, shaken free by the deep, pained cries reverberating through the dense stone. The electric lights lining the walls flickered, then faded to black. Ash swept through the shadows. She didn't need sight to guide her to Professor's laboratory. She knew the way like the back of her cold, dead hand.

The lights flicked back to life as she crossed the threshold into the circular chamber. Professor's head snapped in her direction. Cold rage poured from his red eyes.

"It is not in your best interests to approach without announcing your presence," he said. "You should be tending to that abomination of yours."

"It's time for Serenia to come home." Ash looked to the ceiling as another roar, shriller than before, rippled through the stone.

"Are you certain? Have you run out of ways to further endanger our most valuable asset?"

Ash rolled her pupil-less eyes. "I've received word from the Spymaster. Last night, Sunder was shot at the Fisherman's Folly in Fulton. Unfortunately, she survived, but she spoke of her journey with Serenia coming to an end. They left town this morning."

Professor floated around to the other side of the table, busying himself with some complex schema that he had painstakingly traced onto thick parchment. "And?"

"Well, my dear blue friend, I should add that Sunder also mentioned that they were headed for Brimholme. That means she's taking Serenia to Thenmar's Crater. Perhaps for a history lesson. What if they go digging through the past? They won't like what they find."

"Hmm." Professor nodded. "That would create complications. I will request four dozen Ferals. That should be sufficient to draw their attention."

"I don't want Ferals. I told you before, we need Behemoths. And I know exactly where to send them."

"We are too close to the Exodus to—"

Ash slammed the wall with her fist. Chunks of rock tumbled over her arm and cracked against the floor. "Don't make me repeat myself. This is what you wanted, right? Sunder, dead? Scarlet in our control? If you want your precious Exodus, then do as I say, contact your people, and tell them I want my bloody Behemoths!"

The Kith's eyes narrowed into red slits. "It will take some time to make the necessary arrangements."

"As soon as possible," Ash said with a dismissive wave. "Is Lion's Roar ready?"

"Yes, though it has not been tested."

"Let's hope you're every bit the genius you think you are, then. I doubt we'll need to use it, but just in case..."

When Professor slid his hands into his sleeves, Ash heard him cracking his knuckles. "Is there anything else?"

"Actually, there is. Help the guards bring our frozen friend from the thirteenth crypt up to the palace," Ash called back over her shoulder as she left the chamber. "It's almost time for her to play her part."

Chapter 31
Dilemma

The sharp crack of a wedge of ice breaking off the lip of the ravine pulled Maia from her reverie. Somewhere along the way back to Sunder, she had stopped walking. The sun, eager to be free from such a terrible place, had fled Thenmar's Crater while Maia was lost in her trance. Only a small sliver of its light remained, peeking out at her from beyond the crater's rim as it retreated. Soon, the moon would take its reluctant vigil over the frozen graveyard, just as it had the night Maia killed the love of her life.

That night, four years ago, taught Maia a valuable lesson: attachments always led to loss, and loss meant pain. There was no other way for that dance to end. And it always had to end, at some point. Why, then, had she repeated the same mistake by letting Elizabeth into her heart? And again with Serenia? Why had she let anyone get close enough to be burned by her?

Maia looked over the edge of the yawning maw and found no answers there. *Guess I'm a fool, too.*

The wind cut into her fresh wounds. A wave of dizziness and a powerful thirst made Maia wonder how she had survived losing so much blood. She scooped up some crushed ice in her left hand and put it on her tongue, working it around her mouth to warm it. Maia suppressed a shiver. Her damaged sliver no longer protected her from the cold with its radiant heat. She had all but forgotten how frigid nights could be, even when she wasn't standing on an unnatural glacier stretching across the base of a forgotten crater in the middle of nowhere.

Without Scarlet, without your powers, you are nothing. The deafening echo of Serenia's words forced its way back into her thoughts. Her young apprentice had taken her greatest fear and sharpened it into a weapon.

And she was right. Who was Maia without Scarlet? Just a poor, scarred wine maker's daughter. Not especially skilled or attractive. Cocky. Crass. Confrontational. Who would dare look at her twice? Who could ever love her?

Without Scarlet and the horrid duty that set her apart from normal folk, Maia doubted she would have shone bright enough for anyone to notice her. Not Edgar, or Leona, or Elizabeth, or even Ren.

Ren. Not Princess. Ren. All this time, Maia hadn't even afforded her the simple dignity of calling her by her own name. Had she ever actually intended to train Ren properly? Or had she merely been looking for someone to tell her she was right, that running away from the life of a Pilot was the right thing to do?

Maia's left hand trembled. In that last moment of their battle, with the curse creeping up her sternum, desperation drove her to throw the last of her strength into her deadliest technique. Had the curse not interrupted her, would she have followed through? Even though Ren was holding a weapon capable of splitting Maia's skull like a ripe melon with the slightest flex of her index finger, would she have fired?

The wide-eyed look Ren wore as Maia's hand streaked toward her matched the absolute terror that spread through Maia's chest when she saw that cursed revolver swinging toward her. "When am I going to stop failing you?" Maia whispered into the chill wind.

Night had fallen over the crater by the time she arrived at Scarlet. Ren and Kasper huddled inside a crude roofless shelter made of stacked hunks of ice. Ren's officer's jacket was draped over their shoulders like a small blanket.

"Are you two okay?" Maia said. Ren stared at the ground beyond her crossed legs. Her jawline was tight as she cradled her bandaged right hand. Hours earlier, that hand had guided a rapier through Maia's shoulder. Indignant fire returned to Maia's lips. "What? You're mad because you lost?"

Ren's glare scythed up to meet hers. "Aren't you?"

"No. I'm mad that we came to blows at all. I'm supposed to be the responsible one. I should never have let this happen."

"You know, Maia, not everything is under your control." Ren's eyes softened and lowered back to the icy ground. "I drew arms against you. I'm as much to blame as you are for what happened."

"Fine, you're both terrible," Kasper sighed. "So, what now?"

"I guess I bring you two back to Noctis," Maia said.

Ren shook her head. "Kas is a member of Brave Dawn. He wouldn't be welcome in the capital. And neither would I, for that matter, if I return in failure."

"Well, you need to pick somewhere else to go, then, because you can't travel with me anymore."

"Why not?" Ren shot to her feet, casting her jacket off her shoulders. "My place is with Scarlet, whether you like it or not."

"You stabbed me!"

"You threw me!"

"You shot at me!"

"I shot *near* you. You broke my hand!"

"You broke your own hand!" Maia winced. "Look. This is for your own good. Go somewhere safe. Rest. Take some time and think about what *you* want. Not what the Emperor or your father told you to want. Figure yourself out. Grow up a bit. Maybe our paths will cross again someday, when things are different, and we can try this again."

"Will you last that long?" Ren said. She took a tentative step, looked Maia up and down, and grimaced. "You need help."

There was no helping Maia, not without a necromancer versed in ancient curses. Whether death came that night or sometime the following day, she couldn't outrun it for much longer. When Maia was gone, Ren would undoubtedly find Scarlet. If she didn't, someone else would, and everything Maia had fought for would be undone.

She could still scuttle Scarlet. Maybe that would be best. Twice now, Scarlet had moved of her own accord and resisted Maia's commands. Was she losing control? What if, after her Pilot died, Scarlet acted out again? She was supposed to be a weapon, a machine, as useless without a Pilot as Maia was without her.

And yet, as she held Ren's revolver to her head and bade her to shoot, Maia could have sworn that the voice in her mind crying "enough" had come from Scarlet. There was a will lurking deep inside her Vanguardian, forged of the same metal as the rest of her. What if Maia's waning control was the only thing keeping Scarlet from launching a bloody rampage that would put any Behemoth attack in history to shame?

Destroying Scarlet might save countless lives. Maybe the world would learn to live without Vanguardians. The people could find other ways to fight Behemoths. Lion's Roar, whatever it was, might be a solution. Who could say what the brilliant engineers of Fen might come up with? The future didn't necessarily have to rest on a Vanguardian's shoulders. Or a Pilot's.

And if she was wrong, the corpses of the dead would pile up to the heavens. Maia had an important decision to make. But first, she needed to get her former apprentice and her wife's ward somewhere warm and safe.

"We'll figure out where I'm taking you later. For now, let's get warm." Maia looked up at Scarlet and frowned. "Why didn't you wait inside Scarlet?" *Or take her and leave?*

"I still can't command her from outside the control beam," Ren said through chattering teeth. "And if she's indeed acting of her own volition, then she's chosen to ignore us. She just stands there, pointing at the ravine." She tilted her head up to Scarlet. "Yes, you made that! We're all very impressed! Wonderful work."

When Maia reached out to Scarlet and willed her to lower her hand, nothing happened. "She's not listening to me either." She pushed harder, bearing down on Scarlet with what force of will she had left. With a dull creaking, Scarlet bent over and looked at Maia. She drew her hand back and thrust it toward the ravine.

"What in the Blue…" Maia followed Scarlet's finger into the ravine, down into the hungry dark. It took a moment for understanding to hit her, but when it did, it smashed into her chest, sending frantic urgency rippling through her. "Oh. Fuck."

"What's wrong?" Ren said.

"Scarlet! I get it now! I understand! Bring us down there, now!"

Scarlet's open hand crashed into the icy ground hard enough to throw all three of them off their feet. Maia scrambled into Scarlet's hand and waited in her palm for Ren and Kasper to join her.

"Go, now!" Maia shouted. Scarlet didn't deposit them on her shoulder. Instead, she took two strides forward. The third took her over the edge of the ravine.

Maia's stomach fluttered as they fell into the black. Ren and Kasper screamed in unison as Scarlet hit the base of the ravine with a shudder and a crash, dipping her hand to soften her passengers' fall.

When Scarlet's hand turned and tipped them onto the broken ground, Maia clambered off into the dark as fast as her weakened body would allow. A quick, painful burst of flame from her palm lit her way, revealing a fork in the path that branched off into a covered, worked tunnel big enough for Scarlet to walk through upright. At the end of the passage, Maia came to a stop near the edge of an even deeper hole.

With a yelp, she forced another quick jet of fire from her aching hand, spreading it in an arc over the pit. Some of the flames clung to the edge of the pit, near the long rope ladders set into the lip with thick metal spikes, while the rest of the fiery burst snaked down to be swallowed by the darkness. Though she couldn't see to its bottom, Maia knew what was down there. Or rather, what had been down there.

"What are we doing here?" Ren shouted. Kasper caught her as she skidded to a stop near the edge of the pit. "What is this?"

Maia whirled on her. "You tell me. Doesn't this hole look a little too perfect to you? Like somebody went digging. Like they knew what they were looking for."

"Why would anyone... Oh, no."

Maia grabbed Ren by the shoulder and pulled her closer. "You know what I think? I think the Emperor heard about what happened here. I think he sent his best to find what was left of Onyx and Pearl. I think they found Cobalt and Leona, too, and took them all back to Noctis. I wondered how the Empire had worked out the secret to making Pilots. I left before they could figure it out from the blood they took from me during those 'routine examinations' they put me through. I bet Leona's body told them everything they needed to know. And I think you knew about it this whole fucking time."

The tip of Kasper's stiletto pressed against her throat. "Sun, let her go. You're bein' paranoid."

"I bet everyone thinks that about me."

"It's okay, Kas." Ren gently pushed the tip of the dagger away. She took Maia's hand and lifted it off her shoulder. Her blue eyes glowed in the light of the dying flames. "Please, believe me. I didn't know that this was... I was told that we were in possession of material from a Pilot's body. Frozen and preserved. Our mages used the knowledge they gleaned from studying it to grant me a Pilot's powers and wake me from my slumber. There was no way I could have known who it came from, Maia. I assumed it was one of the samples they collected from you. How could I have known it was hers?"

"You could have asked!" Maia pushed past Ren and made her way back to Scarlet.

"Maia?" Ren called. "Where are you going? I'm sorry, Maia. Please, wait!"

Moonlight from beyond the ravine bathed Scarlet's hand with a soft sheen. Maia climbed on and waited until Ren and Kasper had joined her before ordering Scarlet to lift them. When they entered the cabin, she stepped into the control beam.

"Maia! Please, talk to me!" Ren shouted.

"I want both of you in front of me, where I can see you," Maia said through gritted teeth. "I'm going to Noctis. I'm getting Leona's body back—and everything else they stole. I'll tear the Imperial Palace down brick by fucking brick if I need to. Now, if you...want to..."

Their gazes locked, drawn together by a harsh, shared pulsing in the back of their minds, pulling them to a distant place.

"Behemoth," they said in unison.

Maia reached out, letting her Hunter Sense form an image in her mind's eye. Rows of carefully placed buildings lined streets of white stone that spread along the banks of the many waterways running through the city. A ring of thick, green acreages extended beyond the large estates bordering the city, right up to the massive, curving wall of perfectly cut stone encompassing it. Thick black towers, almost as tall as Sunder, sprung seemingly at random from the perfect, planned majesty of the city, extending like spears toward the night sky.

At the city's center, beyond a mile-long courtyard, a palace of white marble, pristine and eternal, stood atop a mighty, steep mountain.

"Noctis," Ren said. "The Behemoth is in the capital!"

The pounding in the back of Maia's head shifted. Another pulse slipped out from beneath the first, forming a trotting beat with its twin.

A second Behemoth.

Maia focused on that pulse, slowly bringing the Behemoth's surroundings into view. A dirt road cut through a small town of wooden buildings, all laid in a ragged strip. A single ballista built of worn, cheap wood held a lonely watch at the center of what could barely be considered a town.

It wasn't normally a breathtaking place, but the sight of Bracken, the town that had been a part of Maia's life for as long as she could remember, left her lungs empty.

"The second Behemoth is in Bracken," Maia said. "I can only Teleport once per hour. We can't get to both Behemoths in time."

"Oh." Ren looked down at her feet. "I'm sorry, Maia. Truly."

"Don't be. We're heading for Bracken. Noctis can wait." Maia wasn't sure she could still form a cross above her head to summon her armor, but she was sure she could whip her injured arms in a close enough motion to manage a Teleport. She conjured an image of Bracken in her mind's eye.

"Sun, we need to go to Noctis," Kasper said. He approached from the side, leaning in to cross her sight line. "Sun? Are you listenin'?"

"He's right," Ren said. "I'm sorry, but Noctis' population far exceeds Bracken's. We need to think clearly."

"No, *you* need to think clearly. Call your father. Tell him to get Lion's Roar ready," Maia barked. "I don't know what it is, but it was important enough to use as a bargaining chip, so I wager it's enough to defend the capital."

Ren fished the two halves of her broken Farspeaker out of her belt pouches and pressed them together. She shut her eyes. The runes pulsed. "Father? I—"

The runes went dark.

"No!" Ren shouted. "We need to go to Noctis! Please, Maia. My father is in danger!"

"I don't care! I have to protect my home!"

"So do I! What about the dragon? It patrols the Freelands, yes? It already beat us to a Behemoth once and almost succeeded two more times. Perhaps it will make it in time to protect Bracken?"

"I can't take that chance. Shut up and let me concentrate!"

"While we're arguin', people are dyin'!" Kasper yelled. "Look, Sun, it's your call. You're the one with the magic. You decide where we go."

She thought she *had* made her choice, but the worry twisting her apprentice's face reached Maia's distant heart, coaxing a competing image into her mind's eye.

Wherever she chose to go, people would die. While she stood there, paralyzed by indecision, they likely already were.

Maia threw her right arm across her body with as much force as she could muster. She repeated with her left, yelping against the pain of her torn stitches. Her right shoulder screamed at her as she pumped her fist to the sky. The arm collapsed to her side as the red lights outside of the cabin churned faster and faster.

When they reached a fevered pitch, a single image remained in her thoughts. The canyon's icy walls vanished as a beam of scarlet light lifted Scarlet from Thenmar's Crater.

The bright beam faded as quickly as it came. As Maia surveyed the destruction in the distance, she hoped that no matter what happened next, history wouldn't judge her any more harshly than it already had.

Chapter 32

Homecoming

Rain plinked off Scarlet's head, filling the cabin with hard patter. Maia took a moment to steady herself as she drank in her surroundings. Through the moon's clouded shine, she spotted cannons and ballistae angled up at her from the flat sconce-lit roofs of buildings across the capital city of Noctis. From the black stone towers scattered around the city, mages gathered on long balconies to begin the arduous task of spellcasting.

Maia tried to push Bracken as far from her mind as she could. As much as it pained her to admit it, Ren was right. Theirs was a war of attrition, of loss. Comparing Bracken's population of several hundred to the hundreds of thousands residing in Noctis, sacrificing Bracken was the sensible choice.

That didn't make it any easier for her heart to bear.

Beyond the thick, continuous wall surrounding the capital, Maia counted five spires of plain stone all curling in toward the city like claws. Those weren't there the last time she visited the capital. What they were for, she couldn't begin to guess. She was more interested in the eastern part of the city, where lazy tendrils of smoke drifted from the many smithies and workhouses lining the edges of a large channel.

There, in the light of a smoldering stretch of trampled debris, her foe waited. The Behemoth was some sort of humanoid beetle, with two thick supporting legs allowing it to walk upright. Slick black chitin plates covered its body, all smooth and bulbous. Luminescent wings draped over its shoulders like a shimmering cloak, concealing its two massive forearms. The beetle-thing turned to Scarlet and inclined its head in a slight bow, dipping the long horn curving from the center of its crown.

As she turned Scarlet's body sideways to shuffle toward her prey through the capital's wide streets, Maia's only solace was that by choosing to save Noctis, she might be able to persuade the Emperor to call off the invasion of the Freelands in exchange. She doubted her countrymen would forgive her for her betrayal, for choosing Noctis over Bracken, but at least they would live to hate her.

Cannons flashed in the distance. Bolts from large ballistae, as well as fireballs, lightning bolts, and ice shards launched by the mages in their high towers, joined the barrage. More than half of the attacks were directed toward her rather than the Behemoth, though they did little to stop Scarlet's advance.

Ren recoiled from the viewport as a bolt of lightning peeled over the glass. She still had her Farspeaker gripped in her hand. "Why are they firing on us? We're their only hope!"

That was a good question, but Maia didn't have time to think of a reasonable explanation for why the citizens of Noctis viewed her arrival as more of a threat than the Behemoth already wreaking havoc on their home. Her focus was split between the many fragile lives scurrying to avoid her footfalls and the second throbbing pulse in the back of her head.

No matter what she did, people would die. Here, and in Bracken. All Maia could do that night was lower the death toll.

The Behemoth stayed where it was, watching her approach with keen interest. When she cleared the sea of cramped tenements and reached a vast courtyard stretching toward the mountain where the Imperial Palace perched high above the city, Maia gave herself a moment to catch her runaway breath.

She spared a glance upwards, past the palace, to a jutting mountain just beyond the city. An enormous tower of riveted Blacksteel, with wide struts and a domed top, sprung up from the rocky summit, its height affording it a commanding view of the entire capital. All told, the tower looked like a giant metal pepper shaker. If this was Lion's Roar, it didn't look very threatening.

The thumping in the back of Maia's mind sent bloodlust rising and coursing through her veins, dashing her curiosity and bringing her attention back to the task at hand. With a pained flick of her right hand, she brought Scarlet's blade to bear. It slid halfway from its hiding place and stuck with a sharp, grinding wail that made Ren and Kasper cover their ears.

The Behemoth responded to her challenge. One of its wings retracted and slid back under the safety of its shell, revealing its left arm. Instead of a claw, its wrist ended in a long, serrated sickle-sword that curved outward. The Behemoth thrust its wicked blade into the ground and dragged it, drawing a line between them. Two more warehouses erupted in fiery explosions as the blade passed, casting bits of smoking debris into the night air.

"We must engage the enemy!" Ren shouted from behind.

"Sun. You should let Ren pilot," Kasper said. "You're in no condition to fight. You can barely lift your arms."

Maia worked her jaw back and forth, grinding her teeth. "I can still kick."

The Behemoth strode toward a nearby mage tower. Lightning streamed from the parapet and split across the beetle's chitin, but it didn't slow. It sheared through the top half of the tower with a backhand slash of its blade, sending most of the tower tumbling to the ground below. The earth shook as tons upon tons of stone crashed to the earth, ending countless Noctean lives.

The muscles in Maia's right arm shook as she raised Scarlet's. A stabbing pain ripped into her shoulder. Wet warmth spread down her arm from her stab wound. She clenched her jaw harder and marched on.

She had no love for the people of Noctis, who had taken so much from her, but Maia was a Pilot. These people were still under her protection.

"What will you call this one, then?" Ren said.

Maia struggled to think of a name. The muscles in her neck and shoulder spasmed as she fought to keep her trembling arm raised. The nameless Behemoth waited, straight as a spear, until Scarlet was ten long strides away. Then, it folded back its other wing and presented its right arm to her.

She expected another curved blade, not a thick, vice-like pincer pulled straight from the dark of her nightmares. Pressure clamped Maia's chest, stealing her breath. Whatever thoughts had started to form in her mind shattered and jumbled into a mess of bloody red.

Like lightning, the Behemoth closed the gap and snapped the tip of its bulky pincer into Scarlet's visor. Maia shut her eye and screamed. Her legs became liquid, and then she was on her belly, crawling across the cabin floor toward the darkest corner she could find.

"I can't, I can't," Maia chanted, over and over, between hungry gasps of air. She pushed herself into the corner and huddled there, making herself as small as she could. She drew in tighter as the pincer knocked Scarlet's head back again.

"Maia!" Ren slid on her knees, bringing her to where Maia was cowering. "Is it your heart? Is it the curse?"

With what strength she had left, Maia grabbed the purple fabric of Ren's shirt and wrenched her close enough for their cheeks to press together. "Kill. That. Fucking. Thing," she rasped.

Ren's pressed her forehead into Maia's. "I'll make you proud."

When Maia opened her eye, Ren had discarded her jacket and weapon belt and was standing in the control beam, bathed in soft light.

Scarlet stirred.

><

As soon as Ren felt the weight of the control beam settle and the burning pain began its creeping path up her spine, Ren lifted her right leg and kicked.

Scarlet's metal foot slammed into the Behemoth's chest and sent it skittering back. Its shuffling feet cut through a small block of townhouses. Though Ren couldn't hear the screams of whoever had been inside, she could imagine their cutting pitch.

Fighting this Behemoth was nothing like her flawless victory against Wartwing. Her attack hadn't harmed the Behemoth in any noticeable way, and its stumble had cost innocent lives. Nausea gurgled in Ren's stomach at the thought of the mangled bodies buried in the wreckage below. More would join them beyond the Veil before the night was over.

She spared a look back at Maia. The unflappable Pilot, forged of equal parts iron and wit, the woman she had been proud to call master, was gone. Ren didn't recognize what was left. Maia stared out the rain-slick viewport in a daze, as if she had woken from a nightmare but left an important part of herself in its clutches while struggling to escape.

She wasn't shaking. She wasn't spitting up blood. This wasn't the work of the curse. Maia was terrified of a Behemoth, a Behemoth that didn't even have a name.

"The Behemoth's name is Grimclaw," Ren announced. No objections came from Maia's corner. She looked to the other corner, where Kas was crouching with his arms pressed to the cabin walls for support. He nodded.

Now that it had a name, it was time for her opponent to die.

Grimclaw ran its blade through the grip of its pincer, sharpening the serrated chitin edges. When it slashed, Ren brought Scarlet low, stepping and weaving beneath the arc. Scarlet's shortened arm blade drove up into the beetle's abdomen. Spark spurted from the shallow dig in its armor, sizzling and smoking in the falling rain. Scarlet stepped past, crushing several tenements before she could stop her charge.

Another light wound, paid for in blood. Finally, Ren understood what Maia had been trying so hard to teach her. For Pilots, there was no victory. There were only varying degrees of loss.

Ren tightened her grip on her Farspeaker. If her father tried to contact her, she needed to be ready. She focused on the remembrance of his face and voice to keep from wincing as Scarlet sent sharp knives of pain driving into her back.

I can take it. I can do this.

Scarlet advanced. When she entered its measure, Grimclaw thrust straight at her face. Ren dropped low again, aiming for the fleshy pink of its armpit, where it had no armor. Grimclaw bent its arm at the elbow and dropped it mid-thrust, pushing Scarlet's arm off course. With the tip of its blade now in line with Scarlet, Grimclaw jabbed.

The serrated edge cut like a saw, taking a piece of Scarlet's pauldron from her shoulder and filling the air with crimson sparks. The razor cry of rent metal made Ren's teeth ache. She regained her footing and countered. The two titans slashed and parried as they moved in a wide circle. Bits of Scarlet's armor and shredded black chunks of carapace littered the flattened ruins of the city blocks crushed underfoot in their mad waltz.

As Ren grew tired and the pain reached the base of her skull, Grimclaw started slipping through her guard more and more often. Her foe had two weapons, both longer than her shortened blade. It found the angles she couldn't defend. Any time she brought her leg up to kick, it slammed her knee back down and punished her for the effort. She blinked through dripping sweat and waited for a chance to turn the tide.

It came in the form of a hammer blow, like the one Ren's first Feral had attempted to finish her off with. Ren whirled around the descending claws, making a full turn and ending her stride at Grimclaw's back, pivoting her hips and aiming her blade at the base of the Behemoth's neck.

"Serenia!"

Her father's voice burst from her Farspeaker in a hail of crackling noise, startling Ren and ruining her strike. Scarlet's blade skipped off Grimclaw's armored head. It turned as she recovered. Something black and fast crashed into the viewport, and then Ren was falling. Her neck snapped forward as Scarlet hit the ground on her back, quaking the earth and kicking up a thick cloud of dust. A long, thin crack crept from one corner of the viewport toward the center.

The Behemoth squatted on Scarlet's hips. Ren bent her knees and dug Scarlet's feet into the ground, but she couldn't pitch her opponent off. With its weight bearing down and its serrated blade braced against Scarlet's arm, Grimclaw brought its gripping pincer down onto Scarlet's chest. Over and over, it hammered her, each slow blow drawing a sound halfway between a whimper and a plea from Maia.

"Serenia, are you there? Stand down! If you surrender, the Behemoth will not harm you."

"You don't know that," Ren said. She jerked her arm, trying to slip free of Grimclaw's bind.

"You must trust me! I can only guarantee your safety if you yield!"

The crack in the viewport spread. A chip of glass bounced off Ren's arm. The cabin continued to rock. Maia was crying now, muttering something Ren couldn't make out.

"It's okay," Kas said. "We'll find a way to save Maia, but we can't do that if we're dead."

Every inch of Ren screamed at her to keep struggling, to battle to her last breath. Maia's sobs and Kas' smile softened her body's silent battle cry. "I surrender," she said, casting her voice through Scarlet.

Grimclaw paused mid-swing and looked toward the courtyard. Then it nodded, stood, and fell back a few paces, standing vigil over the fallen Vanguardian. The rain of cannonballs and ballista bolts and magic ceased.

"Father." Ren cleared her throat. "Before the night is over, I would know how you've come to be able to command Behemoths. But before that, I have a more pressing question."

Ren worked the tip of Scarlet's foot into the ground and kicked upwards. A shower of stone and earth buffeted Grimclaw's face, causing it to raise its arms and recoil.

Ren slammed Scarlet's arm against the ground. The jolt loosened the stuck arm blade and sent the rest of its length speeding from Scarlet's forearm. She rocked Scarlet onto her feet and dashed forward.

"What makes you think…"

The nicked and battered blade flashed upward, sinking into Grimclaw's left armpit and bursting out the top of its pauldron-like shell.

"…that a daughter of House Valerius…"

Ren twisted and wrenched.

"…would *ever* surrender?"

Grimclaw's left arm, and the long, serrated blade attached to it, flew free of its shoulder in a cascade of sparking blood. Ren spun on her back heel, whipping into a high roundhouse kick. Scarlet's foot rocketed into the side of Grimclaw's head with a dull crunch, and as it fell, Ren continued her rotation and crouched low, cleaving through darkened armor with her blade and drawing more sparks from the soft flesh beneath it.

As Grimclaw fell, Ren turned her back to it. One of the pulses in the back of her mind faded. She left the dead Behemoth where it lay, her mind already moving onward to her impending confrontation with her father as she marched Scarlet back to the massive courtyard, where several companies of white-armored soldiers had assembled. At the rear, on a wheeled platform lit with sconces, stood her father. Two cloaked figures flanked him.

"That was not conduct befitting an officer," Ren's father said in a low, even tone.

"I fear I've spent too much time with Maia," Ren said. "For better or worse, I'm not the same person I was when I departed from Noctis."

"And yet, you have succeeded all the same. You've brought Scarlet back to Noctis. People of the Empire! Your Pilot is victorious!"

It started as a slow, rolling cheer, building in intensity until a hundred thousand voices across the city lifted it high into the sky. The victory cry slammed into Ren's chest, sending her heart leaping and skipping.

This was the moment she had fought so hard for. The agony wracking her back and neck didn't bother her any longer. She forgot Maia and Kas and the many Noctean lives she had ended during her struggle as she let the people's adulation wash over her. The many years she had spent trying to fill the void left by her mother's passing had come to an end. Now, she would finally be whole again.

The fleeting moment passed. The cheers gradually quieted. Without them, there was nothing to keep Ren aloft. She drifted back down to Scarlet's cabin and found herself standing over the wreckage of a sizable portion of the residential district of Noctis, now a mass grave. The hole in her chest remained, as gaping and raw as it ever was. The sounds of celebration had only filled it for a moment.

I've been a fool.

Ren took another step and nearly blacked out from a sharp, twisting pain splintering her mind. It pulsed again, like the throb of a Behemoth, but sharper. Keener. The newness of it faded, and it became bearable. It wasn't a Feral or a Behemoth. Whatever it belonged to was something different, and based on the way her Hunter Sense reacted, something far worse.

The needling rhythm came from the cloaked figure on her father's left. Ren didn't know how she knew what kind of monster those robes concealed. She just knew.

"You're working with the Kith," Ren said, both into the Farspeaker and through Scarlet. She drove Scarlet onward until she was standing at the edge of the perfect grid of soldiers, looking down on her father from on high. "That's how you were able to issue orders to that Behemoth. You've partnered with its master."

The clamoring soldiers fell as quiet as the dead of night. "We have much to discuss, you and I," her father said. "Come down from Scarlet, my daughter, and attend me."

"No. Not until you explain yourself."

"Attend me. That's an order."

"A good soldier always follows orders. Yet I am no soldier, father. Whether I have a Vanguardian of my own or not, I am a Pilot. I protect and serve the people. The Kith are my enemy, as are any who stand with them against the good people of this land."

The other cloaked figure, the one at her father's right side, whispered something into his ear. He nodded. "If you surrender Scarlet, you have my word that no harm will come to you or Maia. All hostilities against the Freelands will cease. That includes the Behemoth laying waste to Bracken."

A hand grabbed Ren's shoulder. Maia pulled on Ren for support, her hunched back heaving with every breath as she fought to remain standing. "Don't."

"But Maia, your home." Ren swallowed hard. "Your Teleport won't be ready in time."

"Please. Don't give Scarlet to them. Whatever it costs. Don't."

Ren held the Farspeaker closer, so it would catch her words clearly. "Scarlet isn't mine to give. I've yet to earn her. And since you've sought an alliance with the Kith, I can no longer, in good conscience, follow your orders."

"Enough!" Her father's voice carried a razor edge that made her shrink back. "You're still a child. You can't possibly—"

"You're right, father. I'm a child," Ren said. She let her voice rise, emboldened by the warmth of Maia's hand on her shoulder. "I'm *your* child. I'm also a child of Noctis, tasked with delivering salvation to her people. I thought I could fulfill that duty by becoming Scarlet's Pilot, yet now I see that we will never be saved by seeking power from without. We can only move forward by confronting the darkness lurking in our own homeland. I've traveled far beyond the Empire's borders. I've seen how the people of other realms live. And I've seen the lingering wounds we've left in our effort to unite everyone under the Emperor's banner. We are not the saviors we claim to be.

"We don't spread peace and unity. We sow fear and death. We turn on our brothers and sisters if they dare defy our Emperor's wishes. He, who claims to be our protector! Our god! And then we ally ourselves with the Kith, the same invaders who send monsters to grind us down until we're nothing but dust and mortar beneath their heels. Until we grow past our dark history, until we end the madness continuing to grip us and forge a just path forward, Noctis cannot be allowed to possess a weapon like Scarlet. I will not allow it, so long as I draw breath."

Cold silence wrapped around her fading words. She waited for her father to reply, so she could know if somewhere, beneath the white-enameled steel encasing General Arcturus Valerius' chest, her father's heart still beat. "Is Maia still with you? Can she hear me?" he said.

"She is," Ren said. "She can."

"I speak to both of you, now." Her father gestured to the robed Kith, who beckoned at the empty air. A wide, black-lidded sarcophagus rose from behind the platform and floated to him, carried by some unseen force. "Do you know what this is?"

"A coffin."

"It's so much more than that. The Emperor is not without mercy. If you agree to cease this foolishness and turn Scarlet over to the Empire, you will be rewarded with the restored lives of both Aurelia Valerius and Leona Carver."

Ren's blood froze in her veins. Memories of the snarling, decrepit ghouls she faced in the dead woods clawed their way into her thoughts. "You think to appease me by defiling mother's soul? By using forbidden necromancy to bring her back? What makes you think that I would wish for her to return to me as a shambling, mindless corpse?"

"You underestimate the Emperor's power, my child. Surrender Scarlet to us, and you can have your mother back...just the way she was."

"Is it... Is that even possible?"

"It is. Wouldn't you like that? To be a family again? Wouldn't you want that for Maia, as well?"

Maia's grip on Ren's shoulder tightened. "Don't," she said again, though her plea was so quiet that Ren barely heard her. Ren looked back at Kas, who was scowling at the floor. Her heart broke for him. Leona was his family, as well. All she had to do was give in, and everyone in Scarlet's cabin could have their fondest wishes fulfilled.

And the world would burn for it.

"Forgive me, Kas. Please, forgive me." The Farspeaker shook in Ren's trembling hand. "General Valerius. My mother would never abide by what you're proposing. And neither would my father, who must be lost to me as well, because

I'm afraid I don't recognize the man attempting to bribe me with such travesties. I hereby resign as Pilot First Class of the Noctean Imperial Army, forgoing all rights and privileges granted by Imperial decree. Effective immediately."

"Serenia," her father said. "Ren. Consider my words carefully. Once you cross this line, there will be no turning back. You will be branded a traitor, a formal enemy of the Empire. You will be charged with high treason and hunted like a dog, and neither you nor Maia will ever be reunited with those you've lost. Are you certain this is what you want?"

"This is what I want." Ren's voice swelled, gaining power as she spoke. "This is what *I* want. I will not allow the world to fall under Noctis' dark grip! I will protect it from any who would threaten it, starting with this Kith standing by your side!"

Another pause. "I've never been prouder to call you my daughter."

"I... What?"

"You're a terrible soldier, Serenia. But you make a fine Pilot. Now run, child! Leave this place, and never return! Hurry, before—"

Her father flew from the edge of the platform. Ren didn't see what struck him. She only heard the thud of his Farspeaker, still connected to hers, bouncing across wood.

"This farce ends now," a faint voice said. Ren didn't recognize the deep timbre. "Activate Lion's Roar."

"No!" The cry came from a second, distorted voice. A woman's voice. "You'll hit her!"

The rumbling drone of grinding steel and whirring gears drew Ren's attention to a dark tower springing from the top of a mountain just beyond Noctis. The domed top shuddered as a section split and folded in on itself. As it rotated to face her, a long cannon barrel as thick as Scarlet's arm extended from within.

Before dread could set in, before she could turn and look for a way to avoid the Emperor's mightiest weapon without killing thousands in her attempt to flee, something smashed into Scarlet. Ren fought to keep her footing as a great weight wrapped around Scarlet's waist and forced her down on one knee.

Looking down at the beetle monster gripping Scarlet, Ren realized her error. Ren had been too preoccupied to notice that when Grimclaw fell, he hadn't exploded. She simply assumed that the fading pulse in her head meant her foe had been defeated, and she had been too distracted to trace the remaining throb back to its source.

That dying pulse wasn't Grimclaw's. It belonged to the other Behemoth, the one attacking Bracken.

Kas called Ren's name. She thrashed against Grimclaw's grip as blue lightning arced up the length of the metal cannon barrel.

When the humming became a whine and a distended sphere of crackling fury expanded from the tip of the weapon, Ren threw Scarlet's arm in front of her face.

As a child, Ren loved to listen to the boom of thunderclaps erupting from distant storms. She often wondered what it would be like up there in the clouds, close enough to feel the air split right in front of her.

When Scarlet's viewport imploded in a brilliant flash of light, she no longer had to wonder.

Maia shook her head to clear the ringing from her ears. The acrid smell of hot metal filled her nostrils and made her gag. She tried to push to her feet, but for some reason, her legs wouldn't move.

When she tried to roll onto her back, she understood why. It probably had something to do with the three-foot shard of Scarlet's visor piercing through her abdomen, clean through her spine.

Maia looked to the corner of the cabin where Kasper had been standing. That part of the cabin no longer existed. Rain fell through the darkness stretching beyond the smoldering, jagged edge where half of Scarlet's head had been blasted away.

Ren. Where was she? She flailed her arms about, searching the cabin floor. Her hand touched something. Boots, attached to legs, still standing in the control beam's flickering light.

Maia pulled on her leg. "Hey, Princess. Hey. Come on. We have to get out of here before they fire again. Come on, Ren."

"Huh." Ren patted the wedge of black glass sticking out of her chest. She looked down at Maia. Her right eye, along with most of that side of her face, had been burned away. She formed a sad smile with what was left of her lips. "You called me by my name."

Her eye closed as she folded onto the floor.

"No, no no no!" Maia clawed at the floor, trying to drag herself to where Ren had fallen, but her arms wouldn't support her weight. "Hey, we've got to get up now, okay? It's time to go. Get up, Ren!"

She strained as far as her hand would reach. Something warm and tingling brushed against her fingertips. Maia raked it until it slid into her palm.

Ren's Farspeaker. The runes were still lit, pulsing dimly in the dark. She gripped the stone as tightly as she could.

"Arcturus?" Maia choked down a lump in her throat and shut her eye hard against welling tears. "It's Maia. I yield. Scarlet is yours. Come and get her. Bring help. Ren's hurt. She's... Come quickly. Please."

The Farspeaker slipped from her fingers. With the last wisps of her strength, and a final push, Maia found Ren's hand. She moved her thumb across the back of her apprentice's knuckles in slow circles, the way her own mother used to do on nights when she couldn't sleep.

"You're going to be just fine," Maia whispered to her. "We're all going to be just fine. All of us."

Of all the lies Maia had told in her life, it was by far her favorite.

Chapter 33

Death from Above

"Ren's hurt. She's... Come quickly. Please."

Sunder's words drifted through the Farspeaker, causing Ash's entire body to clench in an effort to keep the tremors of her rage at bay. Professor floated from the platform, out of her reach, and gestured to his Behemoth. The black beetle released its hold on Scarlet's waist and retreated, portions of its back shell still red-hot from where Lion's Roar had scraped over it.

All Ash wanted was to grab the Kith's neck with both hands and squeeze until her fingers formed fists, even though it would mean the end of their alliance. That would doom her to a slow, painful unraveling.

There would be time to deal with Professor once Serenia was safe. Ash marched to the end of the platform, where Arcturus was hauling himself up. She grabbed his breastplate and lifted him the rest of the way.

"Our daughter needs us," Ash said with a snarl. "Gather what healers you can find."

She followed Arcturus' vacant gaze as it floated past her to where Scarlet knelt. The right half of the Vanguardian's head had been blown apart, as well as her right arm and shoulder. A portion of her chest had been carved away, as well. Smoke curled up from the burned metal edges where Lion's Roar had torn her apart.

"Arcturus! Go, now!"

He turned to her. "I don't know what to do."

"I just told you what to do!"

"Look at all of this." Arcturus swept a limp hand across the vista, passing over the one-armed Behemoth, what remained of Scarlet, and the crumbled remains of so many futures cut short. "Look at this destruction. If Serenia lives, this madness will continue until the whole world is reduced to ashes. Perhaps letting her die would be a kindness. For her, and for us all."

A part of Ash wanted to comfort him. Arcturus had already lost Serenia once. No father should ever have to lose a daughter twice. And yet, there he was, ready to give her up to the Veil to save her, and the world, from further suffering.

Once, she would have agreed with him. The world had never been kind to her. For everything it gave, it took twice its share in return. The woman Ash had once been had often wondered if oblivion was preferable to continual suffering.

Then, she died. In that endless realm beyond the Veil, she knew peace. Dull, seamless, numbing peace. Though it lacked the thrills and fleeting pleasures of the living world, no pain could touch her as she drifted through the ether, completely and utterly alone. She grew used to the bleakness of infinity after a time.

But then the Emperor stole her soul back from the quiet. The next time she died, her soul wouldn't be returned to the monotonous black. It would be ripped back across the Veil with such force that it would shatter. Instead of an eternity of miserable, calm sameness, Ash would know nothing at all.

With a young, empowered body, she could survive. She could make full use of all the knowledge she brought back from infinity with her. She could change the way of things. If Arcturus wasn't willing to follow her toward a brighter future, she would drag him, kicking and screaming, into the light.

Her hand tightened on his pauldron, bending it inward. "What did you think would happen? Did you really believe that aligning ourselves with the Kith would be painless? That at the end of it all, the people of both our worlds would link hands and dance together under a fucking rainbow?" Ash shoved him away. "This is war. Sacrifices must be made. I've made mine. Why are you losing heart now when we're so close to victory? We can still have our daughter back. Don't tell me you came all this way only to—"

"Better for her to die up there, in the arms of someone who truly cares for her. Better that than survive and become a vessel for a monster like you."

"To the Blue Hells with you, then." Ash pointed at a guard captain who was trying in vain to calm his panicked retinue. "You! Fetch healers and meet me at the foot of that Vanguardian!" She turned to Professor as he floated toward her. "And *you*. Don't think I've forgotten about you. I've always wondered what color your blood is. Help me save Serenia, and perhaps I won't have to find out."

"We have a complication," Professor said.

"That's not what I want to hear."

"The second Behemoth has expired."

"Expired? As in, it died?" Ash shook her head. "Impossible. Lion's Roar is one of a kind, and Scarlet is barely standing. What in the Freelands could have done it?"

Professor wouldn't meet her gaze. His lip curled and showed a hint of his fangs. "I do not know."

Long before Heretic took Maia's choice away from her, she wasn't sure that she ever wanted to have children of her own. There wasn't enough left of her to give to anyone, especially a child.

Being a mother wouldn't fill the gashes carved into her heart. Nothing could. No matter what joy and warmth anybody in her life could offer her, they would take so much more with them when they inevitably left her.

She hadn't meant to care for Elizabeth. Or Ren. But her weak heart, her dying, hopeless heart, had betrayed her. She cursed it, wishing she had the strength to tear it from her chest and stop the anguish it continued to inflict on her. Had she known that she would spend the extra day she wished for watching her apprentice die on the ground next to her, Maia would have prayed for death instead.

The sound of clinking metal came from the missing half of the cabin. A grapnel wiggled between two swept edges of jagged metal flooring. With a groan of effort, a tired, rain-soaked fool clambered over the edge and rolled onto his back.

"Hell of a climb," Kasper gasped. "Oh, shit." He rushed over to Maia.

"Kasper?"

"I'm here, Sun."

"Leave me. Help Ren."

The rain had stopped at some point. Kasper gently shifted Ren's body toward the sliver of moonlight slicing through the parting clouds and into Scarlet's cabin. "Ren? Can you hear me?"

Ren moaned and shifted. "Maia."

"I'm here. Everything is going to be fine. Kasper will help you."

"I need more light," Kasper said.

Maia's found what remained of her sliver and pushed against fresh agony until a small droplet of fire blossomed on her fingertip. It dripped onto the cabin floor, blossoming into a small flame.

She had to look away while Kasper examined Ren's wounds in the dancing firelight. Whether the gunner in charge of Lion's Roar had aimed for a glancing blow or simply missed his mark, the heat cast by the coil of crackling lightning ripping from its barrel and through Scarlet's head was enough to burn Ren worse than Maia originally thought. It wasn't an image she wanted to take beyond the Veil with her when she died.

"Can you save her?" Maia said. "You have to save her."

"She's lost a lot of blood," Kasper said. "I don't think I can take this thing out of her chest without killin' her." He bent down and pressed his ear to her chest next to the protruding glass shard. "I don't know how her heart is still beatin'. It's a miracle she's alive."

"Oh." Maia's head lolled.

"Sun?"

"I think I'm dying." Her chest was so cold. She couldn't feel her arms anymore. She felt herself growing light, so very light, like she would float away if she closed her eyes one more time. "No," she said when Kasper shifted over to her. "Get her out of here. Keep her alive. Do you understand me?"

A cross between a roar and a shriek ripped through the night sky. Maia's eye snapped shut. When she opened it, she was surprised to find that she was still alive.

"Did they miss?" she said.

Kasper's jaw dropped as he searched the clouds above. "That wasn't Lion's Roar."

Another booming screech tore the air, closer this time. Its vibration made the visor shards littering the floor of Scarlet's cabin dance and jingle. "Then what the fuck was that?" Maia said.

She followed Kasper's gaze upward. Grimclaw also turned his horned head to the sky as a dark, winged form crashed onto its shoulders and bore it to the ground.

Wind-blasted dust rolled away from the impact. Claws raked, casting sparks in arcing showers. The dark shape took to the air with long flaps of its wings, still clutching the Behemoth in its claws.

A mighty cry blasted from the beast's long, fanged jaws. The dark form threw its body into a backward loop and hurled the Behemoth away. Grimclaw blasted through Noctis' outer wall and flipped into the darkness beyond, leaving a hundred-foot-wide gap in the wall's smooth stone face.

The shape hovered in the sky, filling the air with the rhythmic flapping of heavy wings. Moonlight painted its green, rain-covered silhouette.

It was the dragon, the same one that had been patrolling the Freelands, the same one that had been competing with them for Behemoth kills. Maia choked on her delirious laughter. The darkness slipped in to take her beyond the Veil, but the panic that accompanied the rising wail of Lion's Roar charging for another shot pulled her back from death's embrace.

The dragon pushed higher into the sky and coasted over the Imperial Palace on spread wings. Lion's Roar swiveled to track it. The dragon closed the distance and swooped down at its barrel, gripping it in its talons and shaking it. A few jerks later, Lion's Roar stopped whining and went silent.

Down below, Noctean soldiers shouted and dispersed as the dragon made its way back and touched down at the edge of the courtyard, stomping toward Scarlet on all fours. Stone cracked beneath its sharp claws with every earth-shaking step.

As the dragon came closer, Maia saw it for what it really was. It was green, like she had assumed, but it wasn't a dragon. It was merely built to look like one. Its entire body was forged of sleek, shining metal plates, from its angular, crested head, down its segmented neck and continuing over its body to the flicking tip of its pointed tail.

The creature reared onto its hind legs and craned its neck so the black visor above its snout, where its eyes should be, was level with Scarlet's head.

A voice projected into Scarlet's cabin, laced with a metallic timbre that sent Maia's weakened heart fluttering. "Sunder. I'll fly us to safety."

"Ami?" Maia shuddered. "Ami, is that you?"

"Remain where you are." The dragon Vanguardian leaped and dug its claws into Scarlet's shoulder and chest. Scarlet's head tipped back, sending all three of her passengers sliding toward the one safe corner left in the cabin. Before Maia could protest, they lurched into the air.

Whipping wind howled through the missing half of Scarlet's cabin. When Maia tilted her head and looked through the jagged hole where Scarlet's visor used to be, she saw the moon shining bright and full above a sea of clouds. A few minutes later, Maia heard dull footsteps over the groan of metal wings flapping above. Something dropped from the hole in the ceiling and clanged against the tilted floor.

The crouched body stood and unfurled. She stood over six feet tall, covered head to toe in interlocking plates of green and gray metal trimmed with gold, worn over a dark gray mesh suit. Her helmet was styled after a dragon's head, with her black, glass-like visor sitting between its serrated jaws.

"Ami? How are you... How?" Maia rasped.

The Green Pilot didn't answer. She reached into a case strapped to the small of her back, between the folded metal hunter's bow that rested on her upper back and the quiver hanging from her hip, and produced a vial filled with glowing red liquid.

She straightened the needle attached to the end of the vial, gave it a few flicks with her finger, and touched the plunger at the end. A short spray of bright red, like lava, spewed from the needle's tip. The Green Pilot seemed to be sizing Ren up. "Interesting."

"Can you help her?" Kasper said.

The Green Pilot knelt next to Maia and turned to Kasper. "Kasper Carver. Leona Carver's ward. I didn't expect to find you here. Who is this?"

"Her name is Ren," Maia gasped. "She's... She's my apprentice. My friend. Please. Help her."

"I can save her, but I must attend to you first. Kasper. I need you to remove the obstruction from Sunder's abdomen."

Kasper blanched. "That doesn't sound like a good idea. Are you sure?"

The Green Pilot tilted her head back and forth, considering. "Nearly always."

Maia was in no condition to resist as Kasper tentatively wrapped his fingers around the edges of the black glass shard piercing her midsection and started pulling. New lances of pain arced through her body. She shut her eye and bit down hard to keep from screaming as the shard came free.

Something struck Maia's chest. The needle-capped vial protruded from her sternum. "I apologize," The Green Pilot said. "This won't be pleasant." She pushed down on the plunger at the end of the vial, forcing the luminous red liquid into Maia's body.

Maia fell away. The world whipped past her, then snapped back and wobbled like jelly. An uncomfortable rising heat spread through her body. When it subsided, all that remained was a light tingling and a sudden urge to run until her legs gave out.

Her legs wouldn't listen to her, so Maia pushed against the floor with both arms, arms that shouldn't have been able to support her, and propped herself against the cabin wall. With the visor shard removed, the gaping wound in Maia's stomach sucked shut like a thick bog swallowing a boot.

A flash of sickness made Maia turn her head and vomit. "What in the Hells did you stick me with?"

"It's better that you don't know." The Pilot fumbled in the case at her back and drew a second vial filled with the same shining red. "You would likely vomit again if I listed the ingredients. It's an invention of mine. An Amplifier. When absorbed into living tissue, it improves and strengthens the flow of magic. In this case, a Pilot's gift of Regeneration. It isn't particularly useful for those without magical aptitude. Through extensive trial and error, I've found that a direct injection has the most pronounced results. Kasper. Please remove the obstruction from Ren's chest."

Kasper shook his head. "She'll bleed out!"

"She won't. Her second heart will sustain her while the Amplifier seals her wounds," the Green Pilot said, as casually as if she were explaining that water was wet.

"Her *what?*" Maia said.

"She has two hearts." The Green Pilot gestured toward Ren's chest. "Were you not aware? Her sliver is also of particular interest. We should discuss that later, once I've stabilized her."

The Green Pilot's gift was Perception. The magic sewn into her allowed her to see things that others couldn't. It was part of what made Amisrala Illandres arguably the deadliest of all the Pilots; being able to spot weaknesses in an enemy's defenses and predict their attacks was far more useful than a puny shield of red light.

If Ami said Ren had two hearts, then she had two hearts. Why she had two hearts was a question that could wait until Ren was safe. "Kasper. Pull it out," Maia said.

Kasper grabbed the spear-like blade, shut his eyes, and jerked it out with a whimper. A gout of blood spurted from the open wound. Ren's eye flicked open. She arched her back and screamed.

The Green Pilot slammed the needle into her chest, injecting the vial's slick redness into her. Ren shuddered, then melted into the floor, her chest rising and falling with gentle snores. The flow of blood stopped, and her wounds pulled themselves shut as Maia's had. Kasper took her up in his arms and cradled her, pressing his head against hers as he rocked her back and forth.

The Green Pilot canted her helmeted head as she regarded Maia. "You took a full dose. You shouldn't be conscious right now. You never fail to surprise me, Sunder." She walked to the end of the cabin floor, leaped up, and grabbed the edge of the roof with her talon-tipped fingers. "Rest here. It will take some time to fly to our destination. I'm not certain what will happen if I Teleport while carrying Scarlet. I don't want you to plummet to your death if the spell only affects Viridian and not anything she's holding. I should test that sometime."

"Viridian?" Maia said. "What happened to Emerald?" Maia's eye went wide. "And how is Viridian flying without you in the cabin? And how are you even alive?"

"You need to rest. We'll speak soon. There's much to discuss." The Green Pilot pulled herself onto the roof and vanished.

"Ami!" Maia yelled as her head filled with a soft, flowing haze she could only describe as her brain turning to melted butter.

A green helmet peeked down from the hole in the roof. "Yes, Sunder?"

"Was it you?" Maia said. "Did you kill the other Behemoth? The one in Bracken?"

"Yes. When the two Behemoths appeared, I was closer to the one attacking Bracken. Not knowing if you would react to either Behemoth in time, I elected to fly to Bracken, destroy the Behemoth, and expend my Teleport to reach Noctis. I named my Behemoth Barkneck. What did you call yours?"

Hearing her old friend talk about hunting Behemoths like it was a normal thing that normal people did filled Maia with a small measure of peace. "Ren named it Grimclaw."

"Appropriate. I didn't have time to deliver a killing blow to Grimclaw. We will have to return at some point to defeat it."

"Whatever you say. And, thanks, by the way. For saving Ren. And for Bracken. It's not much to look at, but for me, it's home."

The Green Pilot cocked her head. "Sunder, the Behemoth had already destroyed the town by the time I arrived. With the appearance of two Behemoths, and the time required to replenish my Teleport spell between uses, I couldn't afford to... I'm sorry, Sunder."

The green helmet slipped out of sight. A new pressure, heavy and consuming, pressed down on Maia, pushing her into the cabin floor.

"I lied," Maia said as sleep rushed to meet her. "Everything is not going to be fine."

Part Four

Borrowed Time

Chapter 34

Going Underground

Maia awoke several times during Viridian's long flight over the Shining Sands. The hazy thickness of deep sleep refused to leave her, and every time she tried to sit up, it swallowed her, again and again.

Only scattered bits of the journey stuck with her. Drifting over a sea of dunes that glowed in the blistering sun and seeing herself reflected in their endless nothingness. Thanking Kasper for tending to Ren. Passing over the lush plains and forests of Reddalia, and the sprawling capital city of Inemelle, with its turquoise brick buildings and grand windmills and waterwheels. A slow descent into a deep chasm with a river raging at its bottom. The encroaching darkness of a massive cave hidden near the base of the ravine, followed by a brief flutter of excitement at the realization that Ami was taking them to the Hollow.

Maia had always wanted to visit Ami's underground hideaway. That large gap in the chasm wall led to a network of caves running through the region. That was where Ami and Emerald lived, away from her people, while she pursued her many interests.

If only they were visiting under better circumstances. If the Green Pilot of Wind was bringing visitors to her secluded home, then the situation was worse than Maia thought.

And in her mind, it was already dire.

Sleep took hold of her one last time as Viridian set Scarlet down on the floor of a massive open cavern. When she awoke again, Maia was in a small cave, covered in thick blankets, with her head propped up on a thin pillow stuffed with down. When she pulled the covers back, she found that her dark red shirt and black leather breeches had been replaced with a loose cream-colored shirt and matching pants that itched her skin and were far too baggy for her liking.

In the flickering light of several candles lining a shelf carved into the opposite wall, Maia didn't find much else in the way of furnishings, save for a wheelchair like the kind Noctean hospices used. This one was forged of steel. She continued taking in her surroundings, nearly jumping out of her skin when she saw Ami standing in the doorway, still clad in her green and gray armor.

"Blue Hells!" Maia yelped. "Stop lurking."

Green metal boots clinked against the cave's stone floor. "It's been seven days since we fled Noctis," Ami said. "We're in the Southlands. In Reddalia. More specifically, the Hollow. You're safe here."

Maia had so many questions for her friend, namely how she survived a Vanguardian core explosion and where she had been for the last four years, but one question pushed its way to the head of the pack. "I'm afraid to ask. Is Ren okay?" Maia hid her face in her hands. "Hells, tell me she's okay. Lie to me."

Ami cocked her head. "Ren died on the way to the Hollow. She never recuperated, even after a second dose of Amplifier. She was too weak to survive her injuries, unlike you. You're going to live a long, healthy life."

A clutch of panic rose and fell, leaving a crushing emptiness in Maia's breast. She thought she should be angry, that she should scream and cry and break expensive things that didn't belong to her, but all she wanted in that moment was to lay where she was and let the darkness take her.

"Wait," Maia said. "When I said, 'lie to me,' did you take that literally?"

"Yes, though I thought it was an odd request."

"Ami. The truth, then?"

"Ren is well. She's fully recovered, thanks to my Amplifier hastening her Pilot Regeneration. She's going to be fine. Unfortunately, you aren't. The damage to your spine is extensive. You'll never walk again. Your wounds have closed, but your Regeneration is failing to keep pace with your many injuries and the magics crushing your insides. By my estimation, you'll die in ten days."

"Fuck." Maia pushed herself up onto her elbows. "I missed you."

"I missed you as well. Happy Birthday. I forgot to say that in Noctis."

Though Ami had just saved her life, and more importantly, Ren's life, it wasn't enough to keep the hurt boiling in Maia's chest from spilling over into her words. "'Happy Birthday?' You'll have to be more specific. Happy nineteenth? As in, the one where you left me to die in Thenmar's Crater? Or how about my twentieth, when you were out there hiding somewhere, letting me think you were dead? Maybe you mean my twenty-first, when Noctis burned my father to death with some sort of fire magic that never dies?"

Maia snapped her fingers. "Oh, I know! My twenty-second, right after I returned from spending a year wandering the Therion Kingdoms, alone, just south of your doorstep, before I went back to Bracken to settle in and drink myself to death without a word from my best friend. But you probably meant my twenty-third, which was the day before I took on an apprentice and almost got her killed because the smartest person I've ever met wasn't around to tell me how stupid an idea it was to take an apprentice in the first place!"

"You're upset," Ami said. "You have every right to be."

"Upset? Oh, we're way beyond that. You owe me some answers."

"If you're referring to the battle at Thenmar's Crater, then I—"

"Of course that's what I mean!"

Ami took a deep breath. Her helmet warped it into a hiss, like quenching metal. "Edgar asked me to meet. He said you were defecting to the Empire."

"Me? You're the one who said you got an offer from them! And you were considering it!"

"The two Behemoths that appeared during our meeting cut my explanation short before I could elaborate further. I intended to convey my plan to tentatively agree to Noctis' offer as a means to investigate their research into producing new Pilots. I intended to revisit the topic at our next meeting. I assumed that you and the other Pilots would agree that out of all of us, I'm the least likely to actually side with Noctis. I should have clarified. Later, when Edgar contacted me with news that you had defected, I thought it best to meet with him to glean what information he had to offer, then draw a conclusion after speaking with you directly. He and Dalzin attacked me immediately. They said that I was just a step on the path to you. I suspect his aim was to single us out and dispose of us one at a time. He likely started with me because I'm the strongest Pilot."

"Strongest Pilot?" Maia half-laughed, half-coughed. "Scarlet is bigger than Emerald."

Ami stared at Maia, her expression hidden under her helmet. When the silence became awkward, Maia continued. "How did you survive, then? Emerald's core ruptured. We saw it."

"With Perception, I was able to predict the flight path of Onyx's missiles. However, Emerald was in no condition to avoid them, so I positioned her to lessen the impact. We still suffered catastrophic damage. That explosion of wind you witnessed when we crashed into the ocean was not a compromised core. I utilized an incredibly potent concussive blast of wind to cushion our fall. It's a technique I had been developing in private, an attack that maximizes the magical output that a Pilot and Vanguardian can generate together by utilizing their slivers in tandem."

The memory of the blast replayed in Maia's mind. She knew firsthand how much damage a single sliver could cause. Combining the destructive might of two slivers wasn't something Maia had ever thought possible.

And yet, Ami had accomplished it. *Maybe she is the strongest Pilot.*

"Utilizing that technique," Ami continued, "I was able to—"

"You left me to die," Maia seethed. "If you had stayed, we could have stopped Edgar. You could have stopped *me*. Nobody had to die."

"Including Leona," Ami said, her voice almost a whisper.

"You knew she was the Blue Bolt?"

"Yes, despite the great lengths she took to hide her identity from us. Though our armor is somewhat resistant to magic, including Pilot gifts like my Perception, once the two of you became romantically involved, there were changes in your behavior. It was not a difficult puzzle to solve."

Maia shook her head. "I lost almost everyone I cared for in the same day. If I had you, these last four years, I..."

When Ami's helmet tipped forward, Maia could hear her breathing heavier. "My gift of Perception allows me to see what others can't. It's up to me to determine how to best react to what it shows me. I don't always make the best choices. I didn't see a way for us both to survive, so I took steps to ensure at least one of us would escape to continue defending our world from the Kith."

"That's it?" With great effort, Maia forced herself into a sitting position. "That's your excuse? That doesn't explain why you've been living under a rock for over four years. Literally, under a fucking rock!" Maia gestured to the cavern walls and fell back onto the bed.

"I didn't spend the entire time isolated in the Hollow. Over the last year, I've resumed regular patrols. I thought I could help you if the Kith resumed their invasion in earnest."

"Why didn't you come to me, then? You must have known where I was. The whole bloody continent seemed to."

"When I returned from Thenmar's Crater, my people thought it best that I distance myself from any surviving Pilots and let the world believe I was dead, to keep from bringing further attention to Reddalia. Though, truthfully, it has more to do with the fact that I was afraid to face you."

"So, you wait until I'm almost dead." The rising venom in Maia's voice terrified her, but she couldn't stop the years of pain from pouring out of her like rancid vomit. "Well, here I am, Ami! I can barely move. I'll be dead in ten days. There isn't enough left of me to fear. I think it's time to take off your bloody armor and look me in the eye! Or are you too much of a bloody coward to face me without it?"

"That's...not why I keep my armor on." When Ami sat in the wheelchair, it creaked under the weight of her curved metal armor. She raised her arms in a cross above her head and slowly lowered them, dispelling her armor in a gust of swirling wind and brilliant green light.

When the wind died, Maia pushed her dirty hair from her eye and took in what had become of Amisrala Illandres. What was left of Maia's dying heart crumbled. "Oh, Ami. No."

Ami offered a weak smile that shifted the many jagged slashes running across her face and shaved head. One of her ears was missing its point and had healed into a rough, rounded edge. She wore a sleeveless, cropped black tunic that left many of the burns and half-healed scars marring her deep umber skin exposed. The wounds stretched tight over her twisting muscles as if her whole body was straining against their grip.

With one push of her powerful arms, Ami wheeled herself closer to Maia. "When Edgar's missiles detonated, both Emerald and I suffered extensive injuries. We combined the force of our wind slivers to cushion our impact as Emerald crashed just offshore. I remained trapped in her cabin for several days, pinned by wreckage. My Pilot gift of Regeneration went to work repairing my body, but the number and severity of my injuries taxed its effectiveness and spread it quite thin. This resulted in my death."

Maia blinked. "You died?"

Ami nodded gravely. "It isn't unheard of. I've read several accounts of similar incidents where individuals have expired and returned to life before their souls become untethered and cross over the Veil. I wasn't gone long. Minutes, at most. When I regained consciousness, I learned that the complex spells and treatments woven into all Pilots persist in death. We retain our Vanguardian bonds and slivers, as well. However, I discovered a flaw in Heretic's design. Our Regeneration ability isn't designed to heal our injuries in the stricter sense. The spell seeks to restore our bodies to the state they were in when we became Pilots, minus changes caused by natural aging. The final catalyst of our Pilot awakening requires us to die for just a few moments. Dying again appears to have reset my Regeneration. It will now only return me to the moment I awakened from my temporary death, which it has incorrectly marked as the point I awakened as a Pilot."

Maia remembered that brief moment of darkness at the end of her torture at Heretic's hands before she came back to life brimming with power. "Oh no." She touched the long scar running down the left side of her face, the one that would never heal. The one she received before becoming a Pilot.

"Precisely. My wounds had already started to mend before I became temporarily deceased, though it appears that due to the fault in our Regeneration's design, which Heretic couldn't have reasonably accounted for, I'll never fully recover. If I exert myself, I aggravate my injuries. My body is constantly trying to repair the damage I incur by simply continuing to exist. I'm no longer capable of walking at all without my armor to support me, either."

"Does it hurt?" Maia said. She immediately regretted asking such a stupid question. How could it not?

"Constantly. I created the Amplifier solution to alleviate my distress. In small doses, it allows me to bolster my Regeneration and continue my work. However, the effects are temporary, and if not carefully controlled and administered, Amplifier can prove harmful. Fatal, even."

Maia reached out to touch Ami's leg but pulled her hand back. "I'm sorry. I didn't know."

"How could you know?" Ami offered a genuine, warm smile that reached all the way up to her shining green eyes. "Ironically, had I remained dead, my Regeneration would have repaired my entire body given enough time, though I wouldn't have been alive to enjoy it. I don't want you to pity me. I'm alive. I'm no less than I was. With the aid of my chair and my armor, I'm able to continue my work. I don't mind spending so much time inside my armor. I feel safe with my helmet on. Secure. The pressure and weight are comforting."

"I'm so sorry, Ami. I'm sorry I yelled at you," Maia said, right as she lost the battle against her tears. "You did what you thought was right. It's my fault for not believing in you. Right after you told us about Noctis trying to recruit you, Leona did something horrible. After that, I didn't have a lot of trust left for anyone. If I had taken your side, maybe things would have gone differently. I failed you before you ever failed me." She reached for Ami's hand. "You came back in the end. That's all I care about. You and Ren, and even Kasper, are safe. You'll always be my best friend. My Ami."

Ami nodded through her own tears. "I think I'd like to be your Ami again. Very much. Thank you, Sunder. Or would you like to be called Maia?"

"I would. Maybe someday when I don't have to be Sunder anymore. You can put your armor back on if it's more comfortable," Maia offered.

Ami squeezed her hand. "I've hidden from you long enough."

"Speaking of coming out of hiding... How mad are your parents?"

Both of Ami's parents were members of parliament in the capital. Anything she did, as a Pilot or as a citizen of Inemelle, would reflect on them. Most of the world to the north thought the Reddalians lived simple lives in tents in the middle of the desert; the Reddalians were content to let outsiders think whatever they wanted. It kept them safe. None of the continental nations would ever consider them a threat.

Ami's duty to the world often brought unwanted attention to her people. She once spoke of how her many inventions, and the benefits they provided her people, helped ease tensions between her and her government. In a way, they were the currency she used to buy her way out of trouble.

What kind of wondrous contraption would Ami have to build to make up for attacking Noctis when she came to Maia's rescue?

Ami smirked. "My parents are working to mitigate the damage I've caused."

All to save me. I can't even die right. Maia let her hand slip from Ami's grasp and slumped back onto her bed. "So. Ten days left to live. You're sure of that?"

"Yes. I've spent the better part of these last few years in training. I've vastly improved the strength of my Perception and I'm better able to interpret what it tells me. I can say with certainty that you're afflicted with a complex spell that shares similarities with a necromantic curse. The structure is ancient and resembles Tressille spell craft. It manifests in the form of a hand crushing your chest."

"A hand? With fingers?" That was exactly what it felt like when it attacked Maia: five fingers squeezing the life from her like she was an orange, and someone dearly wanted her juice.

"There's also a tether, barely perceptible, that extends toward the originator of the curse." Ami traced a finger in the air. "Somewhere far, north by northeast from here."

"Noctis." Maia ground her jaw. "It's not enough for them to take my parents. They have to curse me, too? I wish I could return the favor. Take the entire Empire down."

"It's not productive to hate an entire people for the actions of a few. That makes you no better than their worst. Blame their government if you must. Most of the corruption in the Empire can be traced to the nation's leadership. Focusing instead on the problem at hand, I may be able to find a way to break your curse. I'm afraid that it'll take time, and we would need to know who you're bound to so that I can—"

Maia held up her hand. "Wait. You said this curse looked like something the Tressille used, right? And you said *who* I'm bound to. Not what."

"That's right. Curses always exist between two living things. The caster and the recipient."

"Fuck." Words she had spoken years ago came flooding back to Maia. Each syllable pounded like a hammer, matching the quickening thumping of her panicked heart.

My heart belongs to you, Leona, and no other.

"Ami?" Maia said as she fought to keep from trembling. "I think I know who cursed me."

Chapter 35

Two Hearts

When she finished her explanation, Maia watched the gears turn in Ami's head as she worked through what she had just heard.

"I want to be certain that I understand." Ami reclined in her wheelchair and steepled her fingers, tapping them against her chin. "You believe that the Tressille bonding rite Leona persuaded you to undergo was actually a curse that bound your hearts together in life and death. Your evidence for this is the wording of your vows and the onset of your symptoms, which began after Leona died, as well as the fact that your tether points in the direction of Noctis, where, if General Valerius is to be believed, Leona's remains are supposedly being held."

"Yes," Maia said. "That's about right. Leona was half Sinadarian. She had more magical talent in her pointer finger than the average mage has in their entire body. A curse like this would be nothing to her."

Ami stared at the cavern wall for some time. "I'm willing to entertain your premise. Please wait here for a moment."

"Where would I go?" Maia said as Ami left her in the quiet candlelight. For once, she wasn't looking forward to being right. If she was, then she was doomed.

A short time later, Ami returned with a thick tome resting in her lap. She flipped it open to a page bookmarked by a thin strip of wood. "I believe I've found the spell in question. Do you remember any of the incantations?"

"It was all in a language I had never heard. Except for the end. I had to say 'my heart belongs to you, Leona, and no other' in my own tongue. Then she said the same to me, in Sinadarian."

"Your experience is consistent with what I'm reading."

"Why do you have a book of ancient Tressille spells?" Maia asked.

"Why would I not? Knowledge is power." Ami leafed to the next page. "The spell's name directly translates to 'Heart's Oath' in the common tongue. For all intents and purposes, it functions as a curse does, though it appears to be a two-way curse. Quite fascinating. It binds two souls together. When one dies, the other follows. Some might consider that romantic, I suppose. You know, there's a good reason that even the Tressille still living in the Freelands rarely practice their native tongue. It's obscenely complex and prone to misunderstandings. Leona likely mistook it for a similar ritual meant to aid in the creation of new life."

The thought of the barbed, tentacled mess that Leona had later made from their blood brought bile rising in Maia's throat. "She wanted a child."

"That would explain her error, then. From what I can gather, Heart's Oath belongs to an ancient school of living magic. It changes and grows as it meets resistance. If you were a normal human, you would have likely died instantly once Leona passed. Your Pilot augmentations and the presence of your bonded sliver seem to have delayed it considerably. Though, your sliver appears to be far weaker than it once was. Heart's Oath is gradually overtaking your remaining defenses."

"Arcturus damaged my sliver, somehow. It felt like he ripped away a piece of it. But why would it keep getting weaker?"

"As I said, Heart's Oath grows in relation to resistance. It's a clever thing. It seeks the holes in your defenses and attacks when it's able, all to fulfill its singular purpose. Namely, killing you. Our slivers greatly strengthen our other Pilot gifts. Though Heart's Oath has been overcoming you gradually over time, I believe the damage Arcturus did to your sliver has tipped the balance. The curse appears to have shifted its focus to suppressing your damaged sliver, restricting your access to your flames and weakening your other abilities. Primarily, your Regeneration."

"So, you're saying this spell is eating my sliver?"

"'Eating' is inaccurate," Ami said.

"How do we kill it?" Maia said. "The curse, I mean."

"You can't 'kill' a curse." Ami flipped back a page. "The originator of the curse can dispel it, however—"

"She's dead."

"Correct. In the absence of willful termination of the spell by the original caster, I can devise a way to dispel the curse myself now that I know the originator. It takes the average magically attuned individual months, even years, to learn a single spell. My Perception, combined with my experience in the arcane arts, will cut that time considerably."

"That's my Ami." A smile born of a mix of joy and disbelief spread across Maia's lips, but Ami shook her head, causing it to slip away.

"I'll need weeks, at minimum, to dispel Heart's Oath, provided I'm successful on my first attempt. When it comes to new magic, I rarely am."

Maia only had ten days left to live. That was it, then. She had already prayed for more time. Asking for a further stay of execution would be stretching her threadbare luck so thin it would probably snap. "Can we slow Heart's Oath down? What about that Amplifier you stuck me with?"

"I have administered three more doses while you were unconscious. That has afforded you the extra time you currently have. Amplifier is toxic if used in excess. We would need to wait a month before administering more, after what I've given you has worked through your system. I'm afraid that the only other way to slow Heart's Oath is to find a way to repair or replace your fire sliver. That would strengthen your Regeneration and help combat the curse. However, that would merely slow Heart's Oath, not defeat it. I'm sorry, Sunder."

Maia waved the sentiment away and continued staring at the ceiling. "So, I'm dead in ten days, and there isn't anything we can do about it."

"That's not entirely true. There is another matter we should discuss that pertains to your condition." Ami closed the tome and placed it on the floor next to her. "We need to talk about Ren."

Ren set down the caged globe of glass on a flattened stalagmite, marveling as the soft light it cast caressed the walls of the narrow passage, twinkling like starlight as it touched the mineral deposits sprinkled throughout the dense stone.

The globe produced light through something Ami called 'electricity.' "Think of it as lightning, directed and given purpose," Ami said when she gave Ren the globe of light to help her navigate the tunnels of the Hollow. Shortly after recovering from her injuries, Ren had spent most of her time wandering the myriad tunnels, trying not to think of what had become of her father or Maia's declining condition and succeeding in little more than dirtying the clothes Ami had given her.

Every step she took made her painfully aware of the way the fabric moved around her skin instead of with it, making her feel exposed and vulnerable. She missed the security of her breeches and officer's jacket, whose snug fit clung to her like a suit of armor.

Neither garment had survived Lion's Roar. The purple shirt Maia had helped her dye had likewise been too torn and bloodied to salvage. The loss of that treasured garment, a gift from Maia, had hurt more than she expected, even considering Ren and Maia had tried to kill each other a little over a week ago.

Ren flexed her hand, the one she had shattered during their fight. Whatever was in the concoction Ami had injected her with, it had spurred her Regeneration further than she thought possible. Her broken knuckles, destroyed eye, and the many other injuries she suffered when Lion's Roar fired upon her had healed in mere days.

She should have been grateful to have her body restored, but the Amplifier could only help with her physical wounds. Every time a piece of stone slipped from a cavern wall near her, the sharp noise brought her back to Scarlet's cabin. Over and over in her head, she could hear the screech of Lion's Roar raging to her side, its radiant heat melting half of her face as its fury shattered Scarlet's viewport and sent a spear of black glass plunging into her chest.

After a dozen or so waking nightmares, Ren found it hard to be grateful for anything.

A dark shape twitched in the shadows to her side, skulking beyond the electric globe's light. Ren's heart clenched, pumping dread to her extremities. She turned and kicked, connecting with something solid and propelling it into the tunnel wall.

"That one's on me," Kas groaned.

"Blue Hells! I'm sorry!" Ren gasped. She hauled him to his feet, and for a moment, she lost herself in his eyes. She hadn't taken the time to catch her breath, so when Kas kissed her, deep and full, there was little wind left in her to steal.

"I need to start scuffin' my boots when I walk, so you know I'm comin'," he said.

"Not a bad idea. That, or maybe we tie a little bell around your neck." She ran her hands along his toned forearms. The scars marking his skin were old and thin. "I've been meaning to ask. You were in the corner of the cabin where Lion's Roar struck." Ren closed her eyes. She could still feel the heat charring her skin. "How did you survive without injury?"

He scratched the nape of his neck. "This is embarassin'. See, I ran to you. Tried to shield you. Didn't make it, though. Ended up trippin' and fallin' clear of the blast. Then I go and lose my footin' and fall over the edge. Barely managed to throw my grapnel and get a good grip before I tumbled. Even when I'm unlucky, I'm lucky, I guess."

Kas grinned and kissed her again, leaving a lingering warmth like a summer breeze swirling through Ren's stomach.

"I'm the lucky one," Ren said. "You came back for me."

"Of course I did. You come back for people you...well, you know."

"No." Ren looked up at him. "What do you mean?"

"You know. People you care for. A lot."

"You mean people you love?"

Kas' eyes met hers. He reddened, stifled a nervous laugh, and nodded.

"I feel the same way, I think." Ren rested her head on the worn black leather of Kas' jerkin and let him envelop her in his arms. She allowed herself a few breaths of bliss before she pulled away. "Have you heard anything?"

"Ami told me that she was headed to check on Maia. Said she should be awake soon."

"I need to see her."

"Yeah," Kas sighed. "I thought you might. Just... Don't get your hopes up, okay? Not until you see her, at least."

They walked hand in hand through the stone tunnels until they arrived at the antechamber leading to the cave where Maia rested. A voice carried from the entrance of the cave as they approached.

"We need to talk about Ren."

Ami's words stuck Ren in place. Slowly, she crept down the passage toward the cavern entrance. Eavesdropping was wrong, but her curiosity pulled her closer. Whatever they would say about her behind her back, she had a right to know.

"What about her? She's safe. That's what matters," Maia said.

Ren peeked around the corner. She hadn't been allowed to visit Maia while she slept. She assumed that when Maia awoke, she would be fully healed, just as Ren was.

But there was still a bandage covering Maia's ruined right eye as she lay on a bed of blankets. Her pallor was so pale and shiny with sweat that Ren could have mistaken her for a corpse.

"She has two hearts," Ami said.

"Yeah. You mentioned. Must be something the Emperor did to her."

"That's a definite possibility. Her organs have been shifted slightly to account for it. The configuration is nearly identical to Feral physiology. Considering Noctis appears to be aligned in some way with the Kith, it's possible that she isn't entirely human."

Ren's hand trembled as she brought it to her chest. She focused until she found the strong, singular pulse pounding beneath her fingers. There, she felt it. Beneath the thundering of her heart, another beat followed so closely behind its rhythm that she only noticed it by knowing to look for it. Something deeper and more distant, like a bass note, added its strength to the thumping drum beating beneath her sternum.

A shudder rippled over her shoulders. She didn't hear Maia's response, what she had yelled. Her twin heartbeats filled her skull. The sound was unnatural. Wrong. In returning her to life, the Emperor had turned her into a monster. Something less than human.

Kas put a hand on her shoulder. His touch was red hot, even through her shirt. She shrugged him off and hugged herself, wanting nothing more than to shed her skin and leave her filthiness behind.

"There are other anomalies," Ami said. "She has a sliver, though it's been, for lack of a better term, 'confused' into thinking it's two things at once."

"What the fuck does that mean?" Maia said, right as Ren thought the same.

"It's been attuned to both fire and lightning, simultaneously. That shouldn't be possible. It's fascinating."

"I'm glad you're intrigued. What does it all mean, though?"

"What was done to her sliver appears deliberate. With her sliver split between fire and lightning, Ren could theoretically pilot a Vanguardian attuned with either element."

"Cobalt was taken from Thenmar's Crater, along with what was left of Onyx and Pearl," Maia said. "I buried Cobalt with Leona. I thought he died when she did. If he survived, Noctis would want a Pilot who could control both remaining Vanguardians."

"That's my fear, yes."

"It hurts," Maia said after a long silence.

"What does?" Ami said.

"When she pilots Scarlet. It hurts her." Maia's voice rose as she spoke until she was shouting. "I bet her confused sliver is responsible. Either they didn't know it would hurt, or they didn't care. Nobody ever fucking cares!"

"Sunder, please remain calm."

"Fuck calm!" Maia's voice cracked as she shouted. She hacked and wheezed until the fit subsided and she found her breath. "Fuck calm. Ren's already been through enough pain for two lifetimes. How could Arcturus do this to his own daughter?"

"It may have not been so difficult for him, considering the fact that Ren isn't his daughter."

In the corridor, Ren's entire body stiffened. She willed her legs to carry her into the room, so she could tell Ami that her joke wasn't funny, to stop saying such terrible things about her. But her legs wouldn't listen. Ren became one with the cold rock of the wall, calcified and unmoving.

"Her body," Ami said, "which has been augmented with the addition of a second heart and the magics and treatments necessary to create a Pilot, is likely not the body of the real Serenia Valerius. There's evidence of grafting in her mind. Masterfully done, but not entirely unnoticeable when I examined her."

"Grafting?" Maia said.

"I theorize that, despite their best efforts, the Empire was unable to revive Serenia Valerius. I believe that someone has transplanted her memories into another body in an effort to preserve her experiences. So, in essence, she's Serenia Valerius, and at the same time, she isn't."

While Ami went on to wax philosophical about the dichotomy of the mind and body, a storm of numbness rained down on Ren. The Emperor had told her that the change in her hair color, which seemed so odd to her, was simply a side effect of her transformation.

But she hadn't transformed. Not really. They had carved her out of her body and put her in someone else's. What happened to the mind, the soul, that belonged to the girl she displaced? Or had her soul not made the leap with her? Where did she end, and where did the girl whose body she had stolen begin? Ren's nails dug into her forearms. She couldn't feel them biting into her skin. Was it even her skin? Who did it belong to? Where had they put hers?

Strong hands gripped her wrists. Ren looked down at the bloody scrapes on her arms, then up at Kas. What would he think of her now? Would he still want her? Was it this body he was attracted to? Or the person sewed into it? She had asked to be called Ren in lieu of Serenia when she awoke. Had she always known, deep down, that she was somebody else?

Who was she, then? *What* was she?

"Say all of this is true," Maia said, her tone low. "Say I believe it. You said this has something to do with my condition."

"I've suspected for some time that the Kith have allied with Noctis, but I haven't been able to prove it," Ami said. "You've likely seen the five stone towers surrounding the capital. They are a somewhat recent addition. Through Perception, I have identified arcane machinery within them that does not originate from any known culture."

"And? What does this have to do with Ren and with my condition?" Maia said.

"The long-distance umbral portals that the Kith use to send Ferals and Behemoths to our world appear temporary and only function in one direction. They are also somewhat inaccurate over longer distances. Based on what I've gleaned, I believe that these new towers around Noctis are part of a complex mechanism designed to sustain a different kind of gateway, a more permanent bridge between our world and the Kith's. The towers are gathering energy. They will likely activate soon. When they do, and this new portal opens, we'll need as many Pilots as we can muster to defeat whatever emerges."

"Ami, I'm going to need you to get to the point."

Ami held out her hands. "You have significantly more combat experience than

Ren. You're bonded to a Vanguardian. Ren isn't. To that end, I propose that we remove your heart, the heart that Heart's Oath is bound to, to free you of the curse. Then, we will replace it with one of Ren's."

"I'm not trading her life for mine," Maia growled. "No matter how good a surgeon you might think you are."

"It's likely that her second heart will sustain her, though she'll likely suffer a reduced life span, and her sliver will need to be removed as a precaution prior to the surgery. She will no longer be a Pilot. We may be able to repair Scarlet, as well, but we still need her Pilot. We need you, Sunder. I can't fight this fight alone."

"Then fix Scarlet!" Maia cried. "Fix Scarlet and transfer my bond to Ren!"

"As I explained before, a Pilot's connection to their Vanguardian persists in death. Even if you die, you'll still be Scarlet's Pilot. I'm not certain that another Pilot can ever take your place. Understand that if we don't attempt a transplant, you *will* die in ten days. Of that, I'm certain."

A long pause followed. Then, Maia cleared her throat and spoke in a monotone, devoid of even a hint of emotion.

"I understand. Let's get on with it, then."

All stiffness left Ren's body, replaced by electric panic. Her feet carried her through the Hollow's tunnels, around bends and twists, until reality's hounding gait finally caught up with her.

She collapsed back-first against the flattened stalagmite where she had left her light globe. Her arms braced against the frigid stone. Kas emerged from the dark, but when he approached her, Ren screamed in his face and stumbled around the rock, putting it between them.

"It's okay. You're going to be okay," Kas panted.

"Nothing is okay!" Ren shrieked. "They mean to cut me open and harvest me!" Was it even *her* heart they wanted? Did it belong to her, or the girl who used to live in this body? Ren let out a pitiful whimper. Nothing made sense anymore. "What else did the Emperor do to me? Maybe Maia was right. Did I ever really want to be a Pilot? Or was that something they put in my mind when they were stuffing *her* into my skull? Her skull? Is she… What am I?"

Kas' eyes hardened. "You're Ren. *My* Ren. Nothing else matters. I won't let them hurt you. Okay?"

She considered him for a long while. She wanted to believe him, so she made herself believe him. "Okay." She slid around the stalagmite and held his gaze. "What are we to do, then?"

"We run. We leave here, and we go somewhere far, far away. Somewhere they won't find us." Kas stroked his chin. "The Fen Islands. Ships leave from the coast of Brimholme all the time."

"We're in the Southlands. How are we to cross the Shining Sands, make our way through the Freelands, and cross Brimholme? It's such a long way."

His fingers laced hers. "We'll grab some of those long-legged desert birds I saw on the flight in. They use them as mounts, I think. We'll make it—together. You trust me, don't you?"

"I do."

He kissed her forehead and traced her cheek with his thumb. "I need to take care of somethin' before we leave. We'll meet at that big entrance we flew in through. We can gather what we need on the road."

"I can't leave without my belt. I need my wolf. My revolver, I mean." Ren's father—Serenia's father—had given it to her as a sign of his affection. Even if he wasn't her real father, that gun was the only thing left in the world that was hers alone.

"I'll get it." He planted another kiss on her forehead and dashed off into the darkness.

As she watched Kas disappear, Ren understood why Maia lied so often. Lies were powerful tools, like her revolver. In the wrong hands, they brought tragedy. When aimed with care, at the right target, so much pain could be avoided.

What she told Kas hadn't been a lie. Not really. Ren did want her revolver. The comfort of its weight at her back would make the rest of her journey more bearable.

But what she really wanted from her belt was her Snapstone. When it was dust in her hand, she would be transported back to Noctis, to the military sector where she lived alongside the rest of the cogs of the grinding, pervasive machine of oppression that was the Noctean Empire.

From there, all she had to do was make her way to the Imperial Palace and find the Emperor. A man of his considerable arcane prowess would be able to defeat the curse crushing Maia's heart if she provided the right motivation. Then, Maia wouldn't have a need to take Ren's heart. Perhaps Ren could kill the Kith she had sensed, as well. Its needling presence had faded when they left Noctis, leaving only Grimclaw's ever-present pulse in the back of her mind, but she was certain the sharp sensation would return to guide her to her foe again when she was near enough.

What she planned to do wasn't fair. Neither was life. She vowed to make it up to Kas once everyone was safe. He would understand. He had to.

After all: they were in love.

Chapter 36

Heartbreaker

"I understand. Let's get on with it, then," Maia said, her voice cold and even.

Ami inclined her head. "I can begin preparations for surgery immediately."

"I'm talking about transferring my bond with Scarlet to Ren. Didn't you hear me the first time? She lives, no matter what."

"As I explained, her second heart would likely—"

Maia struck the wall. It was a feeble blow that hurt her more than the unyielding stone. "No. I need to save her. You find a way to bond her with Scarlet. I don't want this life for her, but it doesn't look like we have a choice anymore. Do whatever you have to do. Whatever it takes. And when the fight is over, when I'm gone, you keep her safe."

Ami wheeled toward the door. "I understand. If that's what you want, that's what I'll do. I still think it's too great a risk. If the bond can't be transferred, the world will suffer."

"You said you might know a way to fix Scarlet," Maia said. "Let's focus on that. We'll worry about the rest later. We have ten days to figure it all out."

"It's not that simple. I—" Ami went still. "Hmm. Someone is at the entrance to the Hollow."

"How can you know that?"

"I have placed enchanted sigils throughout the caverns in key locations. When something of sufficient size steps near one, I'm alerted. I need to investigate." Ami crossed her arms above her head and brought them down to her chest.

A blast of swirling wind and green light blew the wheelchair across the cave floor. When Maia opened her eye, Ami was gone.

Metal footsteps echoed through the tunnel. Their slicing rhythm cut through the dull white noise thrown from the frothing river below. Ren spun on her heels, putting the mouth of the cavern and the raging river at her back.

Purpose flooded through her, filling her lungs with heat and tightening her limbs. As the Green Pilot of Wind rounded the corner, Ren fell into her fighting posture.

Ami was taller than she was by far, with thicker muscles than hers, and she was wearing her shining green suit of armor. If they came to blows, Ren didn't stand a chance, but she didn't falter. She meant what she told her father. She was a daughter of House Valerius. Surrender wasn't an option. Not anymore.

The Green Pilot of Wind slowed her approach and raised her hands. "I'm not here to harm you." Her helmet and visor broke apart into small segments that scurried away behind her head, revealing her scarred face.

"That's not what I heard. If you want my heart, go on. Try to take it. But I promise you this: I will not make it easy." Ren was proud of the way her voice only cracked once as she spoke.

"As I said, I'm not here to harm you. If you come back with me, we can talk."

Ren heard the slight wavering in Ami's voice. "You seem nervous. I would be, too, if I were you. If you face me, you won't get away unbloodied."

"Oh, that's not why I'm nervous. If we fought, you would most definitely lose. I'm still flustered from Maia yelling at me. I'm also worried about how close to the edge you're standing."

Ren looked back. The back of her heel was touching the open air. She stepped away from the edge. "I heard you, back in Maia's room. You're going to take my heart and give it to her."

"That was my intention. However, Maia is firmly against it. We're exploring other options."

"You would kill me, though. If it meant saving Maia."

"No." Ami shook her head. "If it meant saving the world. That's the duty of a Pilot. To do what others can't. Or won't."

In all the time she had spent fantasizing about becoming a Pilot, Ren had always known there would be costs. Was she naive to think she would have to pay them all herself? What if she had to sacrifice others? Could she do that? Could she make the difficult choices?

"Why did you say those things about me?" Ren asked. "About me being a monster?"

"I didn't say that. You're not a monster," Ami said. "No more than I am. You've been taken from a comatose state and placed in an augmented body, from what I can observe. I've had every fiber of my being rewritten and infused with magic. I've also suffered critical injuries that I will never recover from. We've both been irreversibly altered. I don't believe that makes us wrong in any way. Merely different. And it certainly doesn't make us monsters."

The sentiment was appreciated, though the idea that Ami would have gone through with her plan lingered in the space between them. "What is the other avenue we're exploring?"

"It's best if we discuss it as a group. Please, follow me." Ami motioned toward the side tunnel she had emerged from.

"Forgive me if I don't trust you just yet. I'm not going anywhere with you alone. We'll wait until Kas gets back."

Ami tilted her head back and narrowed her eyes. "Kasper Carver is with Maia. There are two people in the room where she's resting. I have sigils placed throughout the Hollow. Their design borrows from the woven magic that forms our Hunter Sense. I'm quite proud of them. If you like, I can teach you how—"

"Oh no." *I need to take care of something before we leave.* That was what Kas said before he left.

And now, he was in Maia's room.

"We have to hurry."

"Why?" Ami asked.

"Because I think Kas is going to kill Maia."

A blunt length of cold steel pressed into the top of Maia's head. "I knew you would try to finish me off, eventually," she said as she opened her eye.

"You did?" Kasper pushed the barrel of Ren's revolver harder against her skull.

Maia forced a smile, careful to keep her voice from trembling. "I had even odds on whether it was you or Ren. You both have reasons for wanting me dead." Maia coughed, spitting up a trickle of blood onto her chin. "Sounded tough, right?"

"Sure, Sun. Sure." Kasper spared a chuckle. "She could never pull the trigger, though. She loves you too much."

"More than she loves you?" Maia said. "Sounds familiar, doesn't it?"

Kasper whipped the side of her head with the revolver's barrel. "If Leona loved you more than me, she wouldn't have tried to kill you."

"Keep telling yourself that. What are you planning to do here? Is it worth losing Ren just to settle things with me?"

"These caverns are huge. She's next to the river. It's noisy. I doubt she'll hear a thing."

"Such a smart kid. Where were those smarts when you led Leona to your family's altar and got her tangled up in necromancy?"

Kasper leaned down so that his face hovered inches from hers. "I've got a secret to tell you, Sun. I knew exactly what I was leadin' her to." He allowed his words to settle and send her mind spinning. "I never told you what my parents were really executed for, did I? Necromancy has its roots in old, forbidden Tressille magic. My folks were practicin' from the source. Pure, unfiltered. Same shit our Emperor uses to keep himself young and lively. And he's not one for competition.

"Before the Emperor had them slaughtered, my folks dug deep, found the rituals to make flesh monsters from their own blood. Soldiers, for the next War of Bones. Leona wanted a kid. You didn't. I convinced her that if she had one, you would stay. I showed her the wrong passages, the wrong spells, on purpose. I knew what would happen when you saw what she made. You thought I was just some dumb kid, but I showed you, didn't I? I wasn't about to let you have her. She's mine, Sun. Always will be."

"I always knew you were up to something," Maia said. "It's tiring, being right all the time."

"Get over yourself. You think, what, because you're a Pilot, you're better than the rest of us?" He pivoted so he was crouching over Maia's chest. "You're not.

I'll show you. I'm going to avenge Leona and everyone else you've wronged. I wasn't supposed to try to kill you myself. They didn't think I could ever get close enough. Oh well. Fuck orders."

"Orders? From who?" Maia said.

"Don't worry about it."

Kasper squeezed the trigger. The revolver's hammer fell with a clink.

Maia tensed. She expected horrible pain, searing red, but it never came. She let out a relieved gasp.

Kasper squeezed again and again, but nothing happened.

"Answer the question." Ren's voice sliced into the room as she stalked in. Ami remained at the entrance to the cave, blocking it with her armored body. "Who gave you orders?" Ren said.

Kasper cracked open the revolver. His face pulled into a grim grin. "No shells."

"I only had two left after the dead woods," Ren said. "I spent one during my duel with Maia. After the fight, I took the last one and threw it into the ravine." She wilted a little and angled her head away from Maia. "Now, I ask again: where do your orders come from?"

The revolver dropped from Kasper's fingers. He stood and let his head tip back. "The same place as yours, love. When you took off and we found out Maia took you on as her apprentice, I was sent to keep an eye on you. I thought I would drive a wedge between you while I was at it." Kas shook his head. "It wasn't even hard. All I have to do is breathe near Maia to make her remember how much she hates me. The hard part was gettin' you to fall for me. Fallin' for you, though…that was easy. You remind me so much of her, you know. Leona. She was everythin' to me. If I bring you home, I can see her again. They promised me."

He reached into his belt pouch and pulled out his Farspeaker, the one he used to contact Brave Dawn. Then, he drew another, identical save for the pattern of the runes. "The Emperor wants you home, Ren."

"You were working with my father all this time. That's how we were discovered at Castle Blackwood. But he stabbed you."

"Actually, I did that to myself," Kasper said. "Wouldn't have been convincin' if I walked out of a fight with the great General Valerius without a scratch."

Ren pressed her palms against her temples. "I don't believe this. I can't. Tell me you're lying. Tell me this is some twisted joke, or a bad dream."

"It's not a dream, but if you do what I tell you, it could be. A good one, even. The Emperor wants you home. I don't want to take you to him." Kas slipped the stones back into his pouch and advanced on Ren, hands held wide. "At first, gettin' close to you was just a way to twist the knife in Sun's back. A way to be with Leona again. But it's you I want, Ren. Gods, you're everythin' she was and more. I love you. You know that, right?"

"I do," Ren said as she balled her hands into fists. "That's why this hurts so much."

"Come on, Ren." He held out a hand for her to take. "If you come with me, we can be happy. You'll see. Once Maia's gone, things will be better. She has to die. It's for your own good."

"No. It's for *your* own good. *This* is for my own good."

Ren's fist cracked Kasper square in the nose and sent him stumbling. The next punch rocked his ribs and doubled him over. He tried to draw his daggers, but that only earned him two dislocated wrists for his efforts.

It was the most one-sided fight Maia had ever seen. She expected to feel some satisfaction, watching Kasper get pummeled, but seeing the way Ren's face twisted in anguish as she climbed on top of him and rained fists down into his face didn't bring Maia any joy.

Maia had only ever felt her own heart break. She had never watched someone else's shatter. It was just as painful.

Shortly after Kasper lost consciousness, Ami stepped in and pulled Ren off him. Ren pulled free of Ami's grip and fled from the room. The first of her sobs came just as she moved out of earshot.

The revolver was within arm's reach. Maia picked it up. It didn't burn to touch, now that she knew it couldn't hurt her. She turned it over in her hand. Red flecks of Kasper's blood marred the wolf carving emblazoned in the purple sheen of the gun's barrel.

"That was unpleasant," Ami said. She was standing by the door with Kasper's limp form slung over one shoulder. "What would you like to do now?"

Maia gestured with her chin. "Can I borrow your chair?"

After Ami helped Maia cross the most precarious parts of the tunnels outside her room, she left Maia to navigate the rest of the way on her own while she tended to Kasper. According to Ami and her sigils, Ren was in Ami's workshop.

Each time Maia rolled the wheels of her chair forward, more weakness crept up her arms. By the time she reached the end of the tunnel, which opened into a wide cavern with worked floors and a ceiling so high Maia couldn't see it, she could barely lift her arms.

Several glowing globes provided light for the shop's wooden worktables. The tables themselves were covered with a mess of pages, scattered tools, and half-finished apparatus Maia couldn't begin to comprehend. What looked like a large metal decanter filled with glowing red wine rested in the corner. On the table nearby, empty needle-topped vials like the one Ami had plunged into Maia's chest sat in a clumsy pile.

Ami's inventions were impressive, but they couldn't compare to the sight of Viridian, the Green Dragon Vanguardian, who huddled against the far wall of the massive cavern. Had Ami built this new Vanguardian herself?

"Hey," Maia called to Ren. She was sitting on the ground, hugging her knees, next to what remained of Scarlet. "Can you believe those globes? What do you think they're lit with? Fireflies?"

"Electricity," Ren said after hurriedly wiping her face with her shirt. "A Reddalian invention. Essentially, harnessed lightning, directed and given purpose."

"Amazing."

"Quite. Now please, leave me alone."

Maia rolled closer. "Hey. I know what you're feeling right now. First heartbreak is always the roughest. You'll get through it. We're here for you, okay?"

Ren looked up at Maia through wet, bloodshot eyes. "Spare me. You're thrilled, and you know it. You were right about Kasper, and I know how much you love being right. I heard everything he said." She buried her head in her hands. "Blue Hells, I'm such a fool."

"It's not foolish to feel for people." Tremors flitted through Maia's hand as she reached for Ren's shoulder.

"Don't touch me!" Ren shouted and pulled from her touch. "I don't deserve your pity. I'm a weapon, crafted from parts of a dead girl. I'm not real."

"You're real. And even though you can be a royal pain in my ass, I care about you, Ren."

Ren scoffed at that. "Why would you care about me? I was made to replace you. I've brought you nothing but pain, all because I wanted so badly to become a Pilot. Blue Hells, did *I* ever want to become a Pilot? How do I know which thoughts are mine and which were carved into me?"

"I don't know." It wasn't the comforting reassurance Maia meant to offer, but it was the truth. It was time she got used to telling it. "I don't know if there's a way to know for sure. What I do know is that you're Ren, and whoever you are, I don't regret taking you on as my apprentice."

"Even though I tried to take Scarlet from you?" Ren sniffled. "Even though I killed a man? And lied to you? And cost you an eye? And tried to kill you?"

"Even then," Maia said. "It's been a long time since I've let somebody get this close. Every time I do, it goes to shit. I thought keeping people at a distance would be easier. But it's not. It's a slow, lonely death, and I don't want that anymore."

"I don't want that for you either," Ren whispered.

"I haven't been the best to you, either. I killed your mother and put you in a coma. I tried to kill your father. I lied. Broke promises. Kept things from you. And I never apologized for any of it. I'm sorry, Ren. I can understand why you hate me."

Ren pushed to her feet. "Maia. I don't hate you. I don't know if we can go back to the way things were when we were at our best, but I've never hated you. I wanted to *be* you so badly that it hurt. I placed you on a pedestal and thought you infallible. From such a height, how could you do anything but fall?"

"I'm not someone you, or anyone else, should ever look up to. You were right about me, you know. I'm nothing without Scarlet."

"I was trying to unbalance you," Ren said. "I didn't mean that, and I'm sorry I said it."

"No. You were right. When I was given Scarlet, I hated that I wasn't asked if I even wanted her. But once I had her... I was *somebody.* I dyed my hair and clothes red, even though I fucking hate the color. I did it because it made me somebody important. Somebody worth loving. Without Scarlet and my powers, I'm nobody. And I think I've known that all along. When I saw you piloting Scarlet for the first time, it hurt me. Here was a girl, brighter and more capable of becoming a great Pilot than I ever was, coming to take away the only thing that made me special. I took you on to discourage you. I wanted you to feel how I felt, to tell me I was right in not wanting to be a Pilot anymore. I wanted you to quit and choose a different path. I never got to choose. You didn't have a choice either, but I thought maybe I could do one thing right in my life. I could save you, the way nobody tried to save me. But more than anything, I think I wanted to be right."

With arms crossed, Ren nodded. "I understand," she said. "But I don't think you do."

"Enlighten me, then."

"You say you never had a choice," Ren said. "But you did. Every step of the way, from the day Heretic drafted you into her war, until now, has been a choice. You could have given up at any point. You could have scuttled Scarlet. That would have been a silly choice, one that would have plunged the world into despair, yet it was still a choice. I believe you chose correctly by continuing to fight when you were truly needed. And that's not the only decision you've made. You said you wanted to save me. Yet not once did you offer me the chance to refuse you as my savior. You made that decision for me, just as Heretic decided for you."

Maia blinked. "You're right. Blue Hells, you're right." She braced her forehead against her palm. "All this time, I never asked. Did you even want to be saved?"

"No!" Ren shook her head, laughing against fresh tears. "No, Maia. Even now, when I don't know if my thoughts are my own or who or what I really am, what I want more than anything is to be a Pilot. I want to help people. All of them, from Kaldrsteinn in the north, down to the Southlands and wherever else I'm needed." She took Maia's hand in hers. "I won't be anyone's weapon. Not Noctis', or Heretic's, or anyone else's. I will be my own weapon. Nobody will place a finger on this trigger ever again."

Maia looked up at Ren, who had become so much more than the upstart girl she had shaken hands with on a distant beach half a year ago. "Here." She pulled

Ren's revolver from where she had wedged it against her back and handed it to her. Ren turned it over in her hands as if she was seeing it for the first time. "If you're going to save the world, you'll need this."

The revolver fell from Ren's hands and clanged against the stone floor of the cavern. Maia jerked as Ren bent down and wrapped her up in her arms, squeezing her so tight Maia thought she might snap.

"I'm so sorry, Ren," Maia said.

"I know. So am I."

"I beg your pardon." Ami's voice carried through the hollow chamber as she approached.

"Hey Ami," Maia said, coughing to hide the waver in her voice as they separated.

"I'm sorry to interrupt. I've tended to Kasper's many wounds and have placed him in a crevasse for the time being until I can turn him over to the authorities in Inemelle."

"Thank you for letting us know," Ren said.

"I also came to apologize." Ami crossed her arms over her chest and hugged her armored shoulders. "I've been told on more than one occasion that I don't always consider the feelings of others when I speak. It's something I'm still working to improve. I'm sorry for suggesting that we harm you to save Sunder. Regardless of the number of extra organs you possess, you're a living creature and worthy of love and respect. I apologize."

"Thank you," Ren said, though Maia didn't miss the edge in her voice. It would take time and effort to file it down.

"You're welcome. Oh, Maia. I've given more thought to your plan."

"What plan?" Ren asked.

Maia stiffened. "We don't need to talk about that right—"

"The plan to bond you with Scarlet following Maia's death, which will occur in roughly ten days." Ami looked at her feet. "I apologize. I could have phrased that less bluntly."

Maia caught Ren's stern glare. "I know. I should have asked you first. I'm sorry. We'll come up with a new plan together. Okay?"

A few heartbeats later, Ren nodded. "Okay. First, I need to know what's going on."

Maia told her everything, from Heart's Oath and Maia's impending demise, to the strange towers around Noctis. "Those towers are important," Ren said when Maia had finished. "I overheard my father speaking about them, as well as something called the 'Aperture' on the day I left to…" She twisted her lips. "To steal Scarlet."

"The name 'Aperture' is consistent with my belief that these towers are meant to open a portal," Ami said.

"Then, how about this for a plan," Maia said. She tapped a finger to her jaw as she worked her thoughts. "Ami says there's a way to repair Scarlet. So, we do that. Then, we go to Noctis. We destroy those towers to keep the portal from opening. The Emperor is probably the strongest necromancer alive, so we make *him* remove Heart's Oath. We kill Grimclaw, along with that Kith working with your father. Then we get Leona and Aurelia's remains, along with Cobalt and whatever's left of Onyx and Pearl, and we leave. Oh, and we have the Emperor call off the invasion of the Freelands after he explains why Ren has two hearts. Simple."

"There's nothing simple about what you're suggesting," Ami said. "Further, it's less of a plan and more of a loose series of objectives with a low chance of success."

"Don't be negative," Maia said.

"Ami's right," Ren said. "Even if Scarlet can somehow be restored, bringing her to Noctis will draw too much attention, and you're in no condition to pilot her."

"You can't get to Noctis without me."

"Not true. I still have my Snapstone. Let me go to Noctis alone. I can find my father and make him see reason. There's still good in him. He simply lacks the strength to stand against the Emperor on his own. I will help him find his footing. Together, we may be able to end this without further loss of life."

"This is Castle Blackwood all over again. What if you can't avoid a fight?" Maia said.

"Ami, you said that my sliver is attuned to both fire and lightning, correct? That means I can pilot Cobalt without a formal bond, same as I've piloted Scarlet.

We stand a better chance at victory with another Vanguardian on our side."

"And what if Arcturus won't listen to reason? What if he tries to take you again, like he did before?"

By the way Ren hung her head, she clearly hadn't cut through her youthful optimism to see the ugly reality waiting on the other side, a reality in which she might need to cross blades with her own father.

"I don't like this new loose set of objectives any more than the last one," Ami said. "It's too great a risk to send Ren to Noctis unsupported. With either approach, you won't be able to count on my assistance, which means you're not likely to succeed."

Maia reeled like she had been slapped. "Wait. What? You were the one who said that we'll need all the Pilots we can get. Doesn't that include you?"

"You misunderstand." Ami clasped her hands behind the small of her back. "I said that we'll need the help of every Pilot to defend against the Kith invasion when the portal opens. Before that time, any preemptive action against Noctis would be considered an act of war. I can't put my people in jeopardy."

"You already took action! You stormed Noctis to save us," Maia said, throwing her hands in the air. "Remember?"

"In that instance, I was pursuing a Behemoth."

"Then go back and defeat Grimclaw! He's still alive!"

"I can't. I've been ordered to stand down, effective immediately, following my 'invasion' of Noctis. Soon, I'll be summoned to appear before parliament for a formal hearing. Once the Aperture opens and the Kith enter our world, my government will vote on the best course of action. It may be that they decide not to involve themselves at all, in which case, I may be unable to join any effort against the Kith."

"Fine," Maia said. "You could have abandoned us in Noctis, but you came back to help anyway. If anything, we owe you. I won't ask you to put your neck on the line for us again. Ren and I will handle this ourselves. Maybe we'll see you when the Aperture opens."

"I'm sorry, Maia. Though I can't aid you directly, I'll still help you restore Scarlet. We can begin in the morning if you like."

"Tomorrow, then. Come on, Ren. We have a loose set of objectives to go over, then I need another nap. Mind pushing me?"

Ren retrieved her revolver, took the handles of Maia's wheelchair, and guided her out of the workshop, stopping to pick up one of the smaller light globes from a table to guide their way. When they were alone in the tunnel, Ren spoke. "You know, Ami's plan may have worked. Taking my heart, I mean."

"Doesn't matter. It's a terrible idea. I would never ask that of you," Maia said.

The wheelchair stopped. "You could, though," Ren said, her voice barely above a whisper. "Ask, I mean."

Maia grimaced and reached up to squeeze Ren's hand where it rested on the handle of the wheelchair. "It's your heart, Ren. It's special. Don't give it away so easily."

"Mmm."

They continued in silence, leaving Maia to wonder if she would ever follow her own advice.

Chapter 37

The Wolf Bares His Fangs

Ash knocked the thick metal door of Slate's bay open with a single thrust of her palm. Arcturus' head snapped up at the dull thud of the door slamming into the bay wall. At the far end of the cavernous bay, shrouded in darkness, Slate's pained moans sent little rumbles reverberating through the platform.

It had taken days for Ash to calm Slate's frenzy after Scarlet's arrival in Noctis had riled him up. While she couldn't bring lasting peace to his tortured mind, his pathetic, mournful cries were preferable to tunnel-shaking roars.

"Where am I?" Arcturus slurred. He twisted against the thick chains binding him to a steel chair. The bindings dug into his bare, methodically scarred chest as he struggled.

"This is where I keep my disappointments." Ash grabbed Arcturus' head and tilted it back. "It looks like the paralytic has worn off. How are you feeling? What do you remember?"

"Scarlet. Lion's Roar." His drooping eyes shot open. "Serenia!"

"Serenia, yes. You tried to warn her of our trap and then refused to help me rescue her. Then, I had Professor incapacitate you. Is this coming back at all?"

Arcturus' head lolled. "Is she safe?"

Ash wrapped her taloned fingers around his throat. "I don't know! A Vanguardian I've never seen swooped down, disabled Lion's Roar, tossed my Behemoth around like a fucking rag doll, and left with Scarlet in its claws. Kasper hasn't reported to the Spymaster in over a week. Serenia could be dead, and there's no way to tell."

When she released him, Arcturus bowed his head. "Whatever her fate, she's far away from you. That is all that matters."

"I want you to understand me." Ash crouched in front of him, just beyond the range of his legs. "I could have killed you. Perhaps I should have, as punishment for your betrayal. Instead, I elected to spare you. I still believe that you're a good man. A man who cares about the justice we want to bring to the world. Do you remember what we talked about when we set out on this journey together?"

"I do." He grimaced and nodded. "The Empire must fall."

"It must fall." Ash closed her eyes and smiled. "So why, then, are you resisting me? If the Kith cross us, only I alone can stop them, and only after Serenia and I have become one. I can be everything that the Pilots weren't. I can keep the new peace we're making. Why would you jeopardize that?"

"Because I see, now, that you cannot keep any peace, old or new," Arcturus said. "When you were brought back from beyond the Veil, your heart did not make the journey with the rest of you. I was a fool to trust you. What you desire is wrong and no better than the atrocities the Empire has perpetuated throughout its history. If I must choose between your new world and Serenia, I choose Serenia. Every time, I choose Serenia. And that means keeping her far from your grasp."

"How many times do I have to tell you that she won't be harmed? She's my daughter! What kind of a monster do you think I am?" Ash held up her hand. "Don't answer that. I'm not in the mood for pithy retorts."

She rubbed her temples as she had in life whenever she was frustrated. "With two hearts, she can sustain both of our souls. Please, Arcturus. See reason. Without Serenia, I'll die. If I'm not around to keep them in check, the Kith will overrun this world. I need you. Help me find a way to bring our daughter home safe. Please."

He regarded her for a moment, his forehead puckered in a mix of disdain and confusion. Finally, he settled on something mournful. Pity, perhaps? "I forget sometimes that you, too, are a victim. I hope that one day, you can find peace. But it won't be through *my* daughter."

Ash cupped Arcturus' cheek in her hand. She was moments from twisting his head off when she felt another presence enter the bay. "And where in the Blue Hells have *you* been?"

Near the door to the bay, Professor floated. "The preliminary activation of the Aperture will proceed tomorrow as planned. One additional Behemoth and a thousand Ferals will cross over to prepare the city for our arrival. I have been seeing to the final preparations."

"If I didn't know any better, I would think you've been hiding from me," Ash said. She closed the distance between them with careful, measured steps. "Probably wise."

"You are acting like a petulant child. I saw an opportunity to defeat our mutual enemy and acted accordingly. This farce of yours has gone on long enough."

"You could have killed Serenia! Perhaps you've forgotten. No Serenia, no Exodus. Or, maybe, you thought you didn't need me anymore? The Aperture is complete, after all. I've held up my end of the bargain. What's to hold you to yours? Oh! That's right! If I reverse what I've done to the Emperor's mind, your plans are ruined! You can explain to your people that your inability to follow instructions and keep your bloody trigger finger in check is what doomed them. Provided any of them survive long enough to hear your words, of course."

The air around Professor rippled with a violence Ash had never felt from him, and she had seen him tear people in half with his gravity magic. As quickly as it had stirred, the air calmed. "I assumed that if the vessel was destroyed, you would settle for another," he said.

"You assumed wrong."

"Clearly. In my defense, the vessel was threatening us. The alternative was my own destruction at the hands of the Pilot. Yours, potentially, would have followed. I acted accordingly."

He had a point. Serenia might very well have killed them both. Ash had a hard time convincing herself that she would have acted any differently in his place.

She extended her hand. "Perhaps I've been too harsh. Your people have suffered greatly, as have I. Let's move forward toward the future we both envisioned when we made this pact." A few moments later, her hand bobbed in rippling air, the closest thing to a handshake Professor would permit.

"Agreed. That would be prudent. The Kith will adhere to the terms of our agreement, as promised. I bring news."

"If it's about the uprising, I don't have time for that." After Scarlet's appearance in Noctis and Serenia's impassioned, very public speech to her father, many citizens of the capital had taken to public protest once the revelation that the Emperor was collaborating with the Behemoth's masters had spread. Many Imperials had since denounced the Emperor, which resulted in unnecessary bloodshed and public executions, which only brought further protest.

At least the Iron Wardens were being put to good use quelling the rebellion, though the dissidents were fast finding, as the Kith's Ferals had long ago discovered, that the Wardens were too slow and cumbersome to stand up against a mob of agile fighters.

"I have word from Kasper," Professor said. An envelope drifted from the sleeve of his cloak.

Ash snatched the envelope out of the air. The seal was already broken. Inside, she found two letters. The first was a short report from Kasper. Amisrala Illandres lived. She was the pilot of the unknown Vanguardian, named Viridian, who had taken Maia and Serenia to a hideout in Reddalia.

Ash kept reading, pausing at the mention that Serenia was now aware that her body wasn't her own. She let out a deep sigh, a remembered behavior from her past life that served no purpose now that she barely had to breathe. The low growl that escaped her throat as she read the second letter, however, still served to express her anger.

It was a transcribed conversation that started mid-sentence, the result of Kasper activating his Farspeaker while being interrogated, followed by what sounded like quite a beating.

"That fool." Ash reached inside herself and channeled fire. Flames from her fingertips consumed the two letters. "It doesn't matter if Sunder knows what we're planning. When the Aperture opens, the Pilots will come. And we'll be ready. We're not finished yet."

"What if the vessel does not return with them?" Professor said.

"Hopefully, her loving parents can find a way to convince her to return home. Perhaps we can offer her the truth of who she really is as incentive." Ash hoped that her words carried the confidence she struggled to maintain in light of this new hole that had been punched into her plans.

"Lion's Roar cannot be repaired in time, and its power source cannot be safely retrieved. I will see to our other defenses," Professor said. "Once the Exodus is underway and the vessel is retrieved, we will cleanse it and prepare you for transfer, as promised."

The Kith drifted from the room. Chains jingled behind her, reminding Ash that she still needed to deal with Arcturus. "Now then," Ash said. "We should discuss how we're going to—"

Something hard smashed into her jaw as she turned to face him. Since she had last channeled fire, Ash instinctively brought a wall of flames up before her as protection.

While she reset her dislocated jaw, a length of chain slithered back through the flames. The Blacksteel of Arcturus' right arm glistened in the glow of its many runes. The mangled remains of the lock binding his chains fell from his grasp. Slowly, he wound the length of chain around his other arm, leaving a length of it in his grasp.

"You should know," Arcturus shouted through the blaze, "that I was always prepared to kill you if the need arose. Who you were in life no longer matters. That woman is long dead. What stands before me now is nothing but a violation of all that is natural and good in this world. I've only stayed my hand this long for Serenia's sake. You saved her and gave her life back. You and that pet Kith of yours. For that, I'm grateful. Allow me to repay that kindness. I meant what I said: you deserve peace. I will grant it to you, here and now."

"What changed?" Ash extinguished the flames. She thought to channel lightning but hesitated. The enchanted metal melded into Arcturus' bones granted him the benefits of dozens of potent spells; it also made him an excellent conductor.

She had meant what *she* said, as well. Despite the atrocities he had committed at the Emperor's behest, Arcturus was a good man. He didn't deserve to die for wanting to protect his family.

Ash reached for water instead. Arcturus shortened the length of chain in his grip and set it whirling at his side. "Your Kith said it would 'cleanse' Serenia. I've listened to its prattle many times. Your pet chooses its words carefully. I highly doubt it was looking to give my daughter a bath. You were never going to share her body with her, were you?"

Ash shrugged one shoulder. "It's simply not possible. Two minds, two souls, can't occupy the same body. I'm sorry, Arcturus. Truly. I'm the only chance this world has. Between Serenia and the world, I choose the world. Every time, I choose the world."

"You are a wretched thing. The Kith was right. Your farce has gone on long enough, as has this Empire. I will bring ruin to both."

"Don't make me kill you." What weakness had worked its way into her voice? Guilt? Fear? Where had it come from? The woman who was capable of those emotions was long dead.

"You're not as mighty as you believe. I looked to you for strength, once, when I was too weak to fight back against the Emperor's corruption. No more. Serenia has shown me the depths of my failure. It's far past time for me to stand on the right side of history."

"As if anyone will remember you." Ash sighed and spread her fingers. Daggers of ice ripped through the air from an expanding sphere of frosted air. Arcturus shielded his face with his Blacksteel arm. Most of the icicles dug into his right leg and flank, where Ash had directed the brunt of her attack.

He strode through the barrage, never slowing. The silent runes on Arcturus' arm glowed, empowered by the icicles shattering against them. He thrust his metal palm forward, releasing the stored magic in a cone of angry, swirling frost. With a flick of her wrist, Ash called to the ice and redirected it around her.

When the storm cleared, Arcturus was gone. Ash fell back right as he dropped from the sky and drove his metal fist clean through the platform where she had been standing.

Though Ash was no longer sure what could kill her, the force of Arcturus' blow gave her pause. She needed to avoid his bothersome Blacksteel arm as if her unlife depended on it.

Ash felt around her belt and found one of the vials she had Professor prepare for her as insurance, should Arcturus ever turn on her. His Blacksteel arm could absorb almost any offensive magic she threw at him, save lightning, but there were other ways to harm metal.

Ash tore her cloak from her shoulders and threw it into the space between them. As it unfurled to block Arcturus' view of her, she leaped straight up, opening the vial and magically coaxing the searing, bubbling acid into a sphere in her hand.

The cold metal chain whipped up and wrapped around her ankle, jerking her back down. The glob of acid slipped from her control and devoured a section of the platform's railing with a furious hiss as she fell. Ash's back cracked against the platform, though she barely heard it over the sound of Slate's deafening roar. Their fighting had excited him. The bay shook as the gray giant charged the platform and strained against his taught bindings.

Another jerk of the chain sent Ash careening into the wall. Ribs cracked. She could feel blue ichor pooling in her lungs. As soon as she hit the ground, she was wrenched back into the air, straight toward Arcturus' fist.

Ash barely got her own arms up in time to block his wild haymaker. Her head snapped forward as the blow launched her back the way she came. The dull crunch of bone told her that her left arm was broken. As she flew, Ash reached for her backup vial, flipped the stopper off with a taloned thumb, and flicked the vial toward her ankle.

This time, when Arcturus pulled, the chain whipped harmlessly past him, trailing acrid smoke. Ash landed in a tumble. She only knew she was staring at the ceiling by the sting of the floodlights burning holes in her vision. She spit up a gout of luminous blue blood and rolled to the side. Before she could get to her feet, a metal hand closed around her throat and hauled her up from the ground.

Ash dangled at the end of Arcturus' grip. He slammed his chain-wrapped fist into her chest, over and over. "You have lost." Dark fingers clenched harder around her neck. "And now, I will unmake you and correct the Emperor's mistake."

For the first time since she had been brought back from beyond the Veil, Ash knew terror. The quiet runes on Arcturus' arm shone, and a swell of agony burning brighter than her blood flooded through Ash as Arcturus began consuming the magics that gave her unlife.

The pain of being unraveled twisted her stomach. The necromantic forces binding her to her body were strong enough to resist Arcturus' pull, but she could feel their rent edges beginning to fray from the strain.

Among the augmented nobles of the Noctean Empire, Arcturus' power had no rival. But it couldn't hold a candle to the sheer desperation of someone who had already tasted oblivion once. Someone who would do anything to keep from fading away a second time.

A hundred spells flitted through Ash's mind. Blacksteel was a rare thing, an alloy that was as difficult to destroy as it was to make, leading Ash to commission Professor to prepare a special acid designed specifically to devour it. With her vials spent, breaking free would prove next to impossible. Never one to shy from a challenge, Ash brought her shaking right hand up and placed it on Arcturus' forearm, channeled earth, and told the metal to break with every ounce of her will.

His other hand closed around her wrist and yanked her arm to the side, spoiling her aim right as she channeled her wordless intent. Somewhere in the darkness of the bay, a high-pitched clash, like a titanic hammer striking a giant anvil, echoed back at them.

Slate's roar shook her entire body. The beast's left hand, free of its shackles, rose and fell on them. Gray, jagged metal claws sheared through the platform, leaving Ash and Arcturus balancing on a wedge-shaped length of latticed steel that quickly collapsed under their weight. They only fell for a short distance before they smashed against the back of Slate's rising hand.

Ash's fingers found a jutting edge along Slate's knuckle. Arcturus found nothing but air. He met her gaze for a split second, eyes wide with shock, before he fell several hundred feet to the dark floor of the bay.

Ash sent her will screaming into the jagged mass of murder beneath her fingers. Slate shuddered under her psychic attack, screeching in defiance. When his hand rose, Ash rolled off it and landed on what remained of the ruined platform. She lay there, unmoving, until the thumping of footsteps retreating into the darkness subsided.

The floodlights above flickered. Ash closed her eyes and turned her attention inward, to the life-giving ichor in her veins. Cracked bones mended and popped back into place. Flesh fused and pulled wounds shut. When it was over, a wave of exhaustion fell on her. She would need to feed to replace that sudden loss of life force.

Her mind snapped back to Arcturus. She pictured his body down on the ground below, twisted and mangled. A curious surge of heat hit her chest. "Arcturus," she whispered.

"He is breathing." Professor looked down at her, his face unreadable in the flush of light pouring down from above.

"Save him," Ash said. "Please. He doesn't deserve… He can still be of use to us. Do whatever it takes. Save him."

"Understood." Professor floated away and descended into the darkness. Ash pushed to her feet and immediately started barking orders to the guards who had accompanied Professor back to the bay.

"Tell the engineers we need new manacles for Slate's arms. Call the next watch and have them wait for me in the next bay." She scowled, baring her fangs. "And you! Don't you ever look me in the eye again! That goes for all of you!"

Ash stomped across the uneven platform as she left the bay, filled with a growing worry that if she stayed any longer, she might rescind her order and leave a good man to die on the off chance it might quell the rage that never stopped burning in her breast.

Chapter 38

Scarlet and Sunder

Sharp, wrenching chest pains woke Maia sometime during the night. The lingering effects of Ami's Amplifier had allowed her to sleep through the last few times Heart's Oath came to prod at her weakened defenses. Now that the Amplifier had run its course, there was nothing left to protect her from the curse's grasp. Ren scrambled over to her and held her until the convulsions stopped, then wiped blood from her mouth with a damp cloth.

Maia was thankful that her former apprentice had made the restless night more bearable by insisting on sleeping nearby. She was far less thrilled the next morning when she had to rely on Ren to push her wheelchair into Ami's workshop. Every part of her body felt leaden, piled on by thick weights that she feared would never lighten.

Ami waved to them from one of Viridian's clawed feet. She dismissed her helmet, revealing a wide smile.

Maia offered a weak wave of her hand. She tried to return the smile, but the beginnings of it felt foreign on her face, so she let it drop. Her gaze drifted up to Viridian's razor fangs and sleek, articulated neck plates. "Since I'm going to die soon, I might not have time to ask later: how did you build a second Vanguardian?"

"That's related to why we're here," Ami replied. "The short answer to your question is that I did not build a second Vanguardian."

"Oh." Maia rolled her lips. "That explains nothing."

"I'll elaborate." Ami swept her hand over Viridian. "This is Emerald. More accurately, this *was* Emerald. When she and I spoke following our defeat at Thenmar's Crater, we discussed whether she would be happier repairing her previous form or choosing another. She said that she never really felt comfortable in the form Heretic had assigned her and elected to resemble a dragon instead of an eagle. She reshaped as she repaired herself. We decided on the name Viridian together."

"She said all this to you?" Ren said. "Vanguardians possess their own wills?"

"Yes, and yes, respectively," Ami said. "How did you think they move?"

"Well, you know." Maia made an O with her mouth and waved her hands. "Magic?"

"Yes, and no. As I mentioned previously, I've spent most of the past several years in study. From connecting with Viridian, I've learned many things. Each Vanguardian's frame is made of a living metal that can repair itself over time. Our weapons and armor are constructed from the same material. Vanguardian cores are complex magical cages that contain living souls bound to an attuned elemental sliver, much like our own. This is what allows us to resonate with them."

"Living souls," Maia wasn't a magical genius by any means, but she knew enough about the arcane arts to know that a soul was one of the few things a wizard couldn't create.

They had to come from somewhere. From someone.

"Necromancy," Ren said, finishing her thought.

"The magical principles are remarkably similar, yes," Ami said. She placed a hand on Viridian's foot and curled her mouth in a curious frown. "Whether these souls were offered willingly or taken by force, I'm not certain. Neither is Viridian. She doesn't recall who she was before, though she's much happier now as a dragon than as an eagle."

"She's happy," Maia said. "She told you that."

Ami nodded. "That, and much more."

She guided them to one of her large workbenches, where a long roll of parchment had been unfurled and weighed down at the corners with smooth stones. It was a drawing of what looked like Scarlet with a thick black cuirass encasing her chest and topping her shoulders. Short black tubes extended from her back, with what looked like blasts of wavy steam ripping from their ends. Great green wings, like an eagle's, spread behind her, and an open-faced helm of the same color fit over her head. One of her blue arms had a flared buckler attached to the vambrace, while the other clutched a white and gold glaive that matched her armored greaves.

Something floated near her shoulders. Maia pushed the parchment flat. They were claws. Black crab claws.

Onyx's claws.

"What in the Blue Hells is this?" Maia said.

"Her name is Legion," Ami said. "Viridian told me that while there were no rules prohibiting her from choosing a new form with her Pilot's permission, she had to ensure that her new form was still compatible with Legion. She hadn't been aware of this directive until it became relevant. This is our ultimate weapon. When the Pilots come together, our greatest strength is revealed."

"Wouldn't Heretic have told you of this herself?" Ren said. "Why keep this 'Legion' a secret? And why have five Vanguardians at all? Why not one Pilot, with this Legion at their command?"

"Excellent questions," Ami said, beaming as she turned to Maia. "I like her. She has a curious mind. While I don't have definitive answers, I have theories. As to why there are five Pilots instead of one, I would assume that division of power and responsibility is the primary reason. Regarding keeping Legion a secret, I can't say. According to Viridian, forming Legion is only possible when Pilots act as one. This is useful information that Heretic should have provided us with."

Maia traced her fingers over the drawing. She could see where each Vanguardian began and ended, where each had broken apart and shifted to become armor and weaponry for Scarlet.

Leona. Dalzin. Edgar. Ami. They were all meant to join with her, to align to a common purpose and become the ultimate weapon. Instead, they slaughtered each other.

"We killed Legion before she was ever born," Maia said. "She's just a dream, now."

"How did you speak with Viridian to learn all of this?" Ren said. "Vanguardians do not talk."

"Scarlet does." Maia looked up at Ren. "She has. At the crater. Right before she stepped in to stop us from fighting, she spoke to me. It was one word, but that's the only time she's done that."

Ami pressed her palms together and tapped her chin with her fingers. "I don't think that's accurate. Sunder, you refer to Scarlet as 'she,' correct?"

"Yeah." Maia furrowed her brow. "Scarlet prefers 'she.' How do I know that?"

"You and Scarlet are bonded. Even if you only issue orders and don't listen for her responses, you likely hear some of what she says back, whether you register it or not."

"I never knew she was trying to talk to me." Maia looked up at Scarlet's ruined husk. "I never thought to listen. I suppose that's why she had to yell to get my attention."

Ami spread her arms wide. "We've arrived at the reason we're here today. I believe that if you can speak to Scarlet, you may be able to learn the reason why she's no longer Regenerating. If we can discover the source of the problem, we may be able to work toward a solution."

And maybe, Maia thought, *a way to transfer my bond to Ren.*

"This may lead to the restoration of your armor and weapons, as well, as they're actually stored within Scarlet's body. We won't know until we try. Will you try?"

"I don't have anything else to lose at this point. What do I do?" Maia said.

"If you can, summon what remains of your armor. Through it, you'll have an easier time establishing an initial connection."

They brought Maia away from the flammable wooden tables to an open stretch of the workshop. Ren helped Maia out of her chair and laid her down on her back. Though Maia could barely get her arms above her head, she finally managed to bring them down to her chest, calling her armor with a flash of fire and light.

Energy surged through her like a wave. Her legs tingled. For a moment, she thought she could walk again, that her armor would support her as Ami's had. Before Maia could stand, the wave broke, leaving her with just enough strength to push into a crouch.

So much for that, she thought.

"May I help you?" Ami said. Maia nodded. Calling upon her wind sliver, Ami bent down and lifted Maia in her arms. As she leaped into the air, swirling winds gathered beneath her, pushing her higher and higher until they came level with Scarlet's shattered visor. The gale guided them inside and gently set them down inside the cabin.

"Now, concentrate." Ami placed Maia inside Scarlet's flickering control beam.

She took Maia's hands and pressed them against the floor. "Reach out to her as if you were going to ask her to move, but don't issue a command. Remain open. You're on a beach, waiting for the tide to come in. Don't will the tide to come. Accept that it will come. See what it brings."

Ami leaped out through the broken viewport. Maia shut her eyes and tried to think about nothing, which only made her think about everything. What fire was left inside her flared, stoking her rage.

I'm going to die, and Noctis is going to win, and there's nothing I can do about it. The thought seeped through her, scattering her mind and leaving a trail of dread in its wake. Despair dripped through her, gradually numbing her to the world. When it reached her heart, Maia fell away. A haze covered her vision, dulling the world and leaving her amid blurry shapes and ambient noise.

There, in the depths of herself, Maia heard it. A whisper. When she realized what it was, she allowed her heart a few extra hard thumps and didn't chase the thought any further.

The whisper came again. It tugged. Maia went limp and let it take her, light as a feather, away from her body.

A field of pure white grass spread to infinity in every direction, plain and perfect beneath an endless sky of dull pearl. It took Maia a few steps to realize that she was walking on her own two feet and a few blinks to realize she could see through both eyes. She rejected the swelling rise of joy. It wouldn't last. This was a dream. A vision. It wasn't real. Neither was the odd compulsion in her gut telling her to turn around.

She turned anyway. What she found was less a shape and more of an absence of form that had been cut from the open air. Whatever it was, it was dark, the color of smoke and ash. It stood upright, like a person, but its details were so soft that it looked more like a smudge than a silhouette or a shadow. A long, flowing trail, like hair, wafted in the windless calm. The distance between Maia and the smudge felt like it stretched for miles packed into a few feet.

"Scarlet?" Maia said.

She didn't see the smudge move so much as she felt it. How could she feel it?

"Maia." When Scarlet spoke her name, the word came from inside her own chest, as if she had whispered it directly into her soul. Maia felt a warm flush that she interpreted as a smile. "After seven years of fighting side-by-side, we finally meet."

No matter how far Maia reached for the cloud, the distance between them stayed the same. "Is this you? The real you?"

"I don't know. Maybe? I've never seen myself like this. How do I look?"

"You look great." Maia tried to smile, though she wasn't sure she still knew how to. She doubted she had gotten it right.

Scarlet's soft edges quivered. "You're upset."

"It's not right," Maia blurted out. She hadn't said that. Had she thought it? "What Heretic did to you, I mean."

"Don't feel bad for me. I like living this way. Being with you. I don't remember much from before, but I think I chose this? What I am now is more than I was. I think."

Maia straightened. "I don't think I'm much of anything without you. That's why I'm here. I need to know if there's a way to give Ren my powers. I want her to become your Pilot."

"Ren." Scarlet's edges prodded at the air like little needles. A shiver hit Maia's spine. "She can't ever be my Pilot."

"Why? She's rough around the edges, sure, and it'll take all the Emperor's men, working in teams, to remove that stick from her ass, but she can do it. I know she can."

"If a Pilot dies, and a new Pilot is properly prepared, it's possible for a Vanguardian to forge a new bond. There isn't a rule against it. I can't bond with Ren, though. She has fire *and* lightning inside her. I have to obey the fire, but the lightning is too loud." Scarlet shrank a bit. "It hurts us both. Don't let her connect with me again, please. I can't stand it."

"I didn't know. I'm sorry, Scarlet. I won't let her pilot you again." That settled that. Even if Maia died, Ren would never be Scarlet's Pilot. "But could she become Cobalt's Pilot?"

"I thought I felt him during our last battle, but he was distant. A whisper. With

Leona dead, it may be possible. If there was a way to somehow silence the fire inside of Ren, she might be able to bond with Cobalt." Scarlet shifted. "I miss him. I would like to see him again."

"Maybe you will, if you can ever move again." Maia tilted her head. "I'm sorry I made you fight him. And the others."

"I'm sorry too. But I would rip all my brothers and sisters to pieces a thousand times over if it meant keeping you safe."

In the end, Scarlet had ended up in pieces, too. "Why did you stop repairing? You always used to fix yourself. Was it the curse? Was it me?"

The image of Scarlet sharpened. Harsh edges formed the vague shape of a woman with hair flowing down to her hips. "A Pilot's duty is to fight the Kith. That's what you're meant for. A Vanguardian's duty is to protect and aid their Pilot. Between the two of us, you come first. Without you, I'm useless."

"Bullshit. I've seen you move on your own. You saved us at Castle Blackwood and busted a hole in the ice at Thenmar's Crater."

"Yes, well. I'm afraid I've been naughty. I needed you to know that I couldn't feel my brothers beneath the ice, where we left them. I needed you to see. I needed to help you." Scarlet smiled again, filling Maia's heart with warmth. "The Maker's word is law. It's etched into our cores. We can't go against it. But rules are funny things. You can interpret and bend them in so many ways. Without a Pilot to guide us, our movements are sloppy. Dull. Incomplete. But if I must, I can act independently, if I believe deep down that I'm acting in a way that protects or aids you."

Maia looked down at the rustling white grass. "You stopped repairing on purpose, then."

"That's right." Scarlet paused. The empty space behind her words dragged on for hours, days, before she spoke again. "Being my Pilot brought you nothing but pain. You lost everyone you loved. I wanted to save you. But I couldn't. The Maker's words won't let me."

"The Maker. Heretic?"

"That's your word for her. It's not for us to use." Scarlet's edges blurred. "I can't stop you from being my Pilot. I thought that if I broke, if I wasn't useful anymore, maybe you would leave me. Maybe you would find a better life. I wanted to protect you. That's all I've ever been for."

"I understand." Maia sat down in the grass and toyed with the white strands, winding them around her fingers. "You did what you had to do to keep me away from danger."

"Yes."

"Even if it meant taking away my ability to choose for myself."

"Yes." A rush of something. Unseen tears?

"It was wrong."

Scarlet flickered. She was close now. "I'm so sorry, Maia."

"I'm sorry I didn't listen to you. Or her. Ren, I mean. We're two of a kind, you and I. So very good at meddling. It's time we stopped making choices for other people."

"Yes. I think so."

"I can't give up. Not yet. In nine days, the world's going to end. Can you help me save it one more time?"

A calm glow radiated from Scarlet's edges. "I'll fight by your side. Even if it means our deaths. It'll take time for me to repair. I won't be what I was, but I'll try to be enough."

"You're always enough. You're my partner. I should have treated you that way from the very start."

"You're enough, too," Scarlet said. "Even without me. You're still Maia Sunderland. When our final day comes, when we have to say goodbye, I hope you'll remember that."

"I'll try. Thank you, Scarlet. For everything."

Maia felt the beginnings of Scarlet's reply. The dark form twisted to the side, bending toward some distant call. "She's here," Scarlet said.

Before she could ask who Scarlet meant, an invisible force ripped Maia from her feet and pulled her into the endless white sky. No wind whipped against her face as she rocketed through alabaster heavens. The next time she blinked, she was crouching in a circular room of polished metal lined with sheets of glass, each painted with a moving image of a place Maia had never seen before.

In the center of the chamber, a woman wearing a loose white coat over a high-collared bodysuit darker than night itself worked furiously at an instrument that looked to Maia like a tiny piano. She attacked the keys in a frenzy with the blue fingers of one hand while the other conducted a complex symphony over an ethereal globe woven from thin strands of light.

Maia's fists tightened. Her teeth ground so hard that she thought her jaw would shatter. Iron rigidity set into her shoulders. Her breath ran away from her, rising and falling in haggard gasps.

When the figure looked up from her work, her blood-red eyes flashed in recognition. She grinned, revealing sharpened fangs that, combined with the curved horns sloping back over her head, the bone-white of her short slicked-back hair, and the powder blue pallor of her skin, gave her the appearance of a demon.

To Maia, that's exactly what she always would be.

The lone Kith approached in calm strides. When she was a few steps from where Maia crouched, it took everything Maia had to keep from knocking her unconscious.

Maia wasn't willing to give everything she had. Not for her ruiner. As she rose, she slammed her tormentor in the jaw so hard that the Kith spun into one of the thick glass panels and sent a spiderweb of cracks running through it.

Heretic straightened her suit and worked her jaw back and forth. The corner of her mouth quirked, revealing a single sharpened canine. "Now that that's out of the way, shall we get down to business?"

Chapter 39

Meet Your Maker

"Thirty-First Pilot Cohort. Designation, Red-31. Welcome." Heretic picked up a square length of glass edged with shining metal from the desk she was working at. Maia fell into a fighting posture, ready for whatever attack Heretic was preparing.

"Calm down, you big baby," Heretic said. She traced a series of glyphs onto the surface of the glass.

Something shifted inside Maia. When she looked down at her arms, she could see the floor through her translucent skin. "What did you do to me?"

Heretic's blue finger pointed up, and Maia followed it to a strange crystalline chunk surrounded by bands of moving metal bobbing over her head. Strands of light extended like puppeteer strings to Maia's head and shoulders.

"That device is powered by magic," Heretic said, raising her voice and drawing out each syllable the way you would talk to a small child if you were an absolute asshole. "I tapped into your connection to your Vanguardian and transmitted your consciousness here." She pointed to the floor. "Here. Understand?"

Two quick strides brought Maia close enough to strike. Her fist went clean through Heretic's head without harming her.

"You're just a magical projection now. Not solid." Heretic waved the length of glass and slid it into a holster on her hip. "Sorry. No more punching. And don't ask me to explain how the projector works. It would break your little mind."

"I'm not really here," Maia said.

"Correct. You're learning!"

"Where are we?"

"Oh, I think you know. Come along, Red-31." When Maia didn't immediately move to follow, Heretic sighed and floated away, carried by the gravity magic all elder Kith could channel at will.

After a moment spent trying to make sense of what was happening and coming up severely short, Maia followed. The floating crystal above her head kept pace as she walked, dipping to clear the doorway. She entered a rounded metal tunnel with a flat, smooth bottom. Along the inside curve of the tunnel, metal doors like the one she had passed through lined the wall. Around the bend, Heretic beckoned Maia to follow her through an open doorway.

It took Maia a few moments to remember she was a projection, that she wasn't really there in that room, staring at a steel table fitted with straps, surrounded by trays and shelves covered with vials and bottles and inscribed lengths of glass, and that she wasn't really gasping for air.

Being back in the room where she had been pulled apart and pieced back together was something Maia never thought she would have to prepare herself for.

"Now, do you remember?" Heretic said.

"I'll never forget. This is your ship. This is where you took my life from me."

"Oh, don't be melodramatic." Heretic sat on the table, the same table where she had strapped Maia down and mutilated her seven years prior. "Power doesn't come from nothing. All the spell-forging and alchemic treatments you underwent worked together in an extremely specific and, dare I say, genius way. It was necessary to break you apart and remake you into a version of yourself that could be attuned with magic so that your body could accept permanent enhancements. Magic is a part of you, Red-31, and it always will be. That's a beautiful thing. You should be thanking me, not taking swings at me."

"You want me to thank you for butchering us? We were kids when you took us! You gave us nightmares to last a fucking lifetime!"

"It had to be done. Adolescents are ideal candidates for Pilot conversion. Sixteen, for almost every sentient species, is such a fun age. Emotional turmoil is the key. It increases the success rate of the conversion process. As for the nightmares, extreme emotional reactions like terror or rage are needed to produce the required rush of adrenaline that serves as a catalyst for the magics and treatments."

"That's why we were awake when you ruined us. You needed our screams. Our pain."

"Yes. I would have avoided that if I could. I'm a pragmatist, not a sadist. And 'ruin' isn't the term I would use. I made you into your best self, Red-31. A consummate warrior. More than anything you could have ever aspired to become on your own. I still say you should all be grateful. Especially that aberration of yours. Serenia, right? From what I was able to pull from Scarlet, Professor did a fine job, copying my work to create that little monster."

"Call her that again, and I'll end you." Maia held her forehead in her hands. "And stop calling me Red! Gods, I hate that color. Of all the colors, you had to make me the Red Pilot. Why not blue? Or better yet, no fucking color at all? Why couldn't we have been *asked* if we wanted this?"

"Not everyone has what it takes to become a Pilot. Few are compatible with the treatments. I have to make heroes where I can find them. You're passionate. Driven. Full of anger. You had the makings of a perfect killer before I ever touched you."

"Every time a Feral or Behemoth gets close, I want to rip it to pieces more than anything. You put this bloodlust in me. You ruined me."

"The Hunter Sense I gave you might tell you where your enemy is, and it might give you a nudge in their direction, but I'm afraid it doesn't tingle anything that wasn't already there. The anger is yours. That's why Red seemed like an appropriate fit for you. The Red Pilot is meant to lead the cohort and set its pace. Of all the Red Pilots I've made, you were my favorite." Heretic crinkled her nose. "'Were.' Unfortunately, you've become something of a disappointment as of late."

"There were other Red Pilots? Before me?"

"Before, and after, as well. Story time! Come." This time, when Heretic floated from the room, Maia stayed hot on her suspended heels. They traveled through more same-looking halls until they arrived at what looked like Scarlet's cabin, but longer than it was wide, with a large glass tablet like the one Heretic carried splayed out in front of a cushioned chair seated before a massive, curved viewport. Outside, shining in the light-specked blackness, a sphere of purple floated near a larger globe of the same shade, whose full breadth expanded beyond the scope of the viewport.

As a child, Maia often looked up at the night sky and tried to count the stars floating in the sea of night so high above. Her favorite nights were the ones when the moon came out to play, casting its soft glow down on her. She used to cover the moon with the tip of her thumb, pretending that she had the power to make it disappear. But Maia's moon was far away, on another world, always chasing the tail of the sun. The moon that Maia was staring at now was close enough that she needed her whole fist to cover it.

Maia found herself smiling. "I knew there were other worlds out there, somewhere. And that they would be round, too."

"In this dimension, at least, worlds are mostly round. Magically propelled vessels, like mine, can travel between them. So can those." Heretic pointed to a shifting shape moving through the dark expanse. It grew closer, filling up most of the viewport with its sheer size. The creature looked to Maia like a purple whale that had eaten ten other whales before turning itself inside out and wearing its skeleton on the outside. The two eyes on each side of its gargantuan body blinked as it approached.

"A Leviathan," Heretic said. The beast banked and floated past the viewport. "Not the most elegant Kith creation, but they're built for transport, not aesthetics."

"The Kith made that?" Maia said.

"Yes. The designer is long dead. His kin, what's left of my people, are down there on that world." Heretic waved to the purple sphere. "They know we're up here, but don't worry. We're safe."

As Maia moved closer to the viewport, another Leviathan curled out from behind the cover of the moon and drifted toward the planet below. Somewhere, down there, waited the enemy Heretic had forged Maia to fight.

And Heretic was floating in the sky above, watching them. Doing nothing to stop them.

"This isn't the first world the Kith have visited. Far from it. I'm hoping it's the last." Heretic waved her hand, causing the air around the cabin's lone seat to ripple. The chair swiveled, pushed by her gravity magic. She sat down and crossed a leg over her knee.

Maia had been made to fight a war with the Kith, but that was the "what." It wasn't the "why." She had sacrificed so much without ever knowing why.

She deserved to know. She deserved the truth.

"I want you to tell me everything," Maia said. "Why you want your own people dead. Why *we* have to fight them for you. And, most importantly, why you brought me here."

"Since you've survived this long, why not?" Heretic propped her head up with her hand. "You should know that the Kith, as a species, aren't that old. Two thousand years, give or take a few decades. And we didn't evolve from some other species the way you did. We were made."

Seated in her chair, Heretic looked smaller. Less punchable. Maia could clearly make out the dark bags under her sagging eyes. She wondered just how long someone had to live to look that tired, that detached. Maia crossed her arms and waited.

"Our creators were hunters," Heretic continued, "a perfect example of what happens when you let a warrior culture become dominant. Their hunger for the hunt grew until no creature on their home world could satisfy them. That lust defined every aspect of their society. It drove them to learn how to travel to other worlds, so they could scatter themselves through the heavens in search of new prey. Too many hunters failed to return, lost to the stars or killed in transit. The elders sought a better way to seek the glory they craved, something more efficient, local, and controllable. So, they used their knowledge of fleshcraft to—"

"They were necromancers?" Maia interrupted.

"Close. They didn't bind existing souls to their creations. They just...created life. As we do." Heretic slapped her thighs. "At any rate, they created us and gifted us a nearby world to call home. They called us 'Kith,' which means 'unloved' in their language. No wonder we turned out the way we did. Even our own parents hated us from the moment we were born."

Maia scoffed. "They made you so they would have something new to hunt."

"No. We weren't the prey. We were created to *build* prey. And we did. We learned how to forge horrors. Before we replaced our bodies with the ageless shells we now inhabit, we taught ourselves how to transfer our minds and souls into fresh copies of ourselves, so our knowledge and experience wouldn't be lost. So we could create even better nightmares for our gods to hunt in their games." Heretic turned her chair and swiped a nail across her glass tablet. The larger tablet darkened as an image of a familiar figure spread across it.

Tough, corded muscle wrapped around exposed bone. It had a lanky posture, hunched forward, always prowling. The mask of bone with a single off-center eye hole covering its face split at the bottom, revealing its fang-filled maw.

"Not my finest work, but I was only a hundred years old. Still, they made good fodder for the games. Easy to produce using readily available materials."

Suddenly, Heretic's face seemed more punchable than ever. "You made the Ferals?" Maia said. "Do you know how many lives they've taken? I doubt you even care."

"I do care." Heretic bit her lower lip and nodded, more to herself than to Maia. "I do. Ferals and Behemoths, and all our other creations, were meant for sport and utility. Not waging war. It's a shame, what they've been reduced to."

The smile Heretic donned was clearly forced. She swiped the glass. A myriad of giant beasts spread across the viewport. "The development of Behemoths elevated the games to a whole new level. Our creations drove our masters to even greater heights of violent design. They adapted their bodies and created new weapons to face our monsters. With time, they started to win more battles than they lost. We worried that soon, the games would grow stale. My people were running out of ideas. We feared our creators would destroy us and make new sons and daughters who could please them better if we couldn't hold their interest. After seeking counsel from one of our creators, I came up with a new direction, one that would save my people and show our gods that, among all the Kith, I loved them best."

Another swipe across the glass. Maia stood and moved closer to the image, unsure if she was seeing it clearly.

She was. The colorless outline of a Pilot clad in a variation of the same armor she had been forced into seven years ago stood there on the darkened glass, clear as day. "I don't understand."

"The Kith were master fleshcrafters. But flesh wasn't enough anymore. So, I learned how to bend steel. I learned how to make it move. I created the first Vanguardian for my masters to fight, and to command it, a Pilot."

Heretic tapped her tablet, dismissing the image and lightening the glass so they could see the purple world once more. "I thought my gods would be happy. They weren't. We were meant to work with flesh and bone and muscle. Living metal was theirs alone. They told me that what I had made qualified as heresy and that as punishment for my sin, all Kith would be cleansed from the universe."

Heresy. So that's where she got her name.

"A Kith can't harm or kill a Kith," Heretic continued. "It's our oldest law. My people had the good sense to postpone the exile of my supporters and I until after we struck back against our creators, at least. My efforts bought us time, enough to split into tribes and scatter across the stars. We thought we could hide until we found a new home, a place our pursuers could never find. We thought the inhabitants of the worlds we visited would help us. All we found in our travels were people who saw us as monsters."

"So, you took to conquering," Maia said.

"What else could we do? The Kith deserved to live. At least, I thought we did. As it turns out, we're just as terrible as our creators. Maybe worse. We don't ask for help anymore. We take what we need. For over two hundred years, the Kith have moved from world to world, jumping to the next when our hunters catch up to us. Though our numbers continue to dwindle, my people were mostly successful in evading destruction until I stepped in."

Heretic rose from her chair. Maia walked beside her, out of the cabin, down twisting and turning tunnels and stairs, to an expansive factory floor. Large metal claws, wide as houses, dangled at the end of hinged arms fixed to the walls and ceiling. A pair of giant, black-visored beasts peeked over the top of the hinged doors locking them into two of the many compartments lining the wall on the far side of the factory.

"You couldn't take revenge on the Kith yourself," Maia said, "so you made us, and the Vanguardians, to get it for you."

"That's right. I calculate where the Kith will go, using predictive algorithms, and I—"

"You use what?"

"Very. Complex. Calculations. I do the math, I beat the Kith to their most likely destinations, and I draft five Pilots from the local population to fight any Kith creations that cross over."

"How many times have you done this?"

"You're a part of the Thirty-First Pilot Cohort." Heretic gestured to the looming giants. "These two are for the Thirty-Fourth. The last defense. Once we're done here and I release you back to your broken body, I'm off to complete and deliver this final batch. Then, maybe, I can finally rest, once my people are no more."

"The Kith are working with Noctis. They're building something on my world," Maia said. "I've seen it. Five big stone spires. Ami says they're for opening a portal, and I believe her."

"You should. Green-31 is brilliant," Heretic said. "Magic comes in so many flavors. Without expending rare reagents, the umbral portals my people use to send monsters to your world become less accurate as the distance traveled grows, and the bridge is only temporary. To create a permanent pathway between worlds, the Kith use a different solution, one that requires both sides to build specific attuned structures. We call it an Aperture. Your world is special, you know that? Of all the places my people have tried to conquer, yours is the first one to welcome them and work *with* them. You have a knack for destroying yourselves. It's a miracle any of you are still alive."

"If you knew what they were up to, you could have done something to stop it."

Heretic floated closer, tilting her chin upward and peering down her nose at Maia. "I'm doing something about it now. I've been a little busy." She jutted her finger toward the two Vanguardians. "I can see and hear anything one of my Vanguardians does if I make an active connection. I admit, it's been some time since I checked in with your cohort. I thought your world was under control. The final Kith tribe, barred from their most direct path of escape. Three more cohorts would be enough to box them in, preventing that last tribe from escaping to the most probable worlds they could reach. After activating two of the three remaining cohorts, I returned here to check on my people, only to find them constructing an Aperture. I didn't realize you had failed and that the Thirty-First Pilot Cohort members had killed each other. That rarely happens."

Though she was only a projection of herself, cast across the stars through a magical connection she couldn't begin to understand, something hard and coarse stuck in Maia's throat. It was her pride. With great effort, she swallowed it.

"Help us." Maia said. "Make more Pilots. Give us more Vanguardians. We can still stop the Kith like you wanted. We'll win your war for you."

"I'm too far away. I wouldn't arrive before the Aperture opens." Heretic grinned, revealing her white fangs. "Don't worry. Your fight isn't over yet. I'll tell you exactly what you need to do."

Tears pressed at eyes that weren't real. Maia wrung her hands. "What can we do? Scarlet is ruined, and even if she wasn't, I can't pilot her in my condition. How can I save my world?"

Heretic rubbed the blue skin of her forehead. "I never said your duty was to defend your world. You were created to defeat the Kith. You're weapons, not shields. Whether your world survives is incidental to winning the war. Did you know that on more than half the worlds I visit, the Pilots end up subjugating their own people? That tends to lead to success more often than not. At any rate, to defeat the Kith, once and for all, you need to wait for the Aperture to open."

"You want us to wait?" Maia said. "Let the portal open, let the Kith come through, and then what? Have a glass of wine with them before they murder us all?"

"Oh, sarcasm! Fun!" Heretic leaned forward, putting her face in line with Maia's, and rested her hands on her knees. "The towers are close to activation. Based on what I'm seeing on the world below, you have nine days remaining until the Exodus begins. The towers on your world are designed to draw vast amounts of magic from beyond the Veil and store it. Destroying the towers now would release that stored energy without a proper focus, potentially tearing a hole in reality to who knows where. Or when. No. When the Aperture is open, the energy will be safely directed into the portal. Then, all you need to do is destroy the towers on your side while one brave soul travels through the portal to topple the master tower on this side. If you don't, the Aperture will become unstable and potentially destroy time and space anyway. Toppling the towers on both sides will safely close the portal. My people won't be able to replace the master tower before our creators arrive, which will prevent their escape. Simple, yes?"

"Scarlet might not be repaired before the Aperture opens," Maia said. "Neither will I. And I'm all we've got."

"Figure it out. Thirty-First Vanguardian Cohort, designation Cobalt-31, is still functional. He's being held underground, based on what I can see when I connect to him. Get that Serenia of yours to commandeer it. Get Green-31 to assist you, as well. The Aperture will appear in the sky, at the center of the channeling towers.

Green-31 can fly through and disable the master tower."

Maia's heart dropped to her stomach. "Then what? What happens to Ami?"

The Kith gave her a nonchalant shrug. "Your Teleport function works locally. It used to allow travel between worlds, but I learned from that mistake and made some changes to future cohorts. Green-31 won't be able to use her Teleport to return once the Aperture is destroyed, so she'll likely be overrun by the remaining Behemoths down on the planet. If she's the only casualty of this final battle, I'll be incredibly surprised. I would worry about yourself first. Without a complete sliver of fire, you're not going to be able to counter that spell wrecking your insides long enough to win this battle." She rolled her blood-colored eyes. "And before you ask, no, I can't break your curse from this far away, and I don't have a spare sliver of pure, primordial magic from beyond the Veil laying around for you to use. They're all spoken for. As I said: figure it out."

Learning that Ren wouldn't be able to inherit Maia's powers and that Maia herself couldn't be saved hadn't bothered her much. She hadn't put much hope in either possibility, even before attempting to connect with Scarlet. Being told that Ami would have to follow Maia on the road to oblivion pained her.

"There has to be another way. What about Legion?" Maia said. "Ami said Viridian told her we can combine our Vanguardians."

"Your true power lies in unity. When the Pilots come together, your greatest strength is revealed. You *could* form an imperfect variation of Legion with the Vanguardians you have left. The problem is, if you know what you need to do, and haven't done it yet, then you're not going to achieve it." Heretic crossed her arms and leaned against the bulwark. "I didn't tell you how to form Legion because a genuine attuning of heart and purpose is required for the Resonance spell baked into all of you to activate. If I tell you not to think about a giant pink lizard, that's all you're going to think about. If I tell you to attune your purpose to Green-31's to resonate with her and unlock your greatest power, you'll be aware of what you're trying to do, and it won't happen naturally. Forget about Legion. What *would* work, on the other hand, is detonating Scarlet-31's core."

Maia remembered the ocean of water ripping from Onyx's ruptured core after she drove Pearl's horn into it. She tried to imagine that much fire bursting from Scarlet's chest. What would be left of Noctis? Maia had no love for the Empire, but to Ren, it was home. What would happen to the other good people living beneath the Emperor's thumb if she scuttled Scarlet in the middle of the capital?

"A sliver released from magical containment tends to return to the sea of magic beyond the Veil rather explosively," Heretic continued. "You could detonate Scarlet's core and topple all five towers at once. Or have Green-31 carry you through the Aperture so you can explode next to the master tower. Far be it from me to tell an artist what to paint. Either way, you're going to die. Might as well make it meaningful, yes?"

"I'll think about it," Maia said. As if she would be able to think about anything else for the next nine days. Her life hadn't amounted to much. Maybe her death could.

"Time for you to go," Heretic said as she traced glyphs onto her glass tablet.

"Wait," Maia said, stopping Heretic in the middle of her scribbling. There was one more burden weighing on her heart that needed addressing. "Scarlet told me that before she was a Vanguardian, she was somebody else. You said you had supporters who went into exile with you. I didn't get a good look at the size of this ship seven years ago. It's pretty big. And it seems awfully empty, now. Scarlet was a Kith. All the Vanguardians were, weren't they?"

A pained look crossed Heretic's brow. Her gaze flitted to the floor. "They knew what they were agreeing to when they sided with me. It wasn't easy for me to do what had to be done. I cared about each and every one of them. Especially the woman who became Scarlet-31. She and I—"

"Never speak her name again," Maia seethed. "Ever."

Even though she was nothing but a projection of soft light, Maia was surprised to see a flicker of genuine fear in the widening depths of Heretic's red eyes.

"Thanks for the story," Maia said. "If, by some miracle, I survive this, know that I'll find you. I'm going to make you pay for every single life you've ruined."

Heretic offered a sad, tired smile. "I hope you do. Our creators were right, you know. What I did, what the Kith have done, was wrong. The whole of creation needs to be cleansed of us. I can't rest until I've seen that taint wholly eradicated. Once that's done, I'll gladly follow my people into oblivion. Now, off you go. Prove to me that you're not a total disappointment."

With another flick of her nail on the glass tablet, Heretic sent Maia hurtling back into herself.

When Maia's mind slammed back into her body, Ami called upon her wind magic to help Maia down to the workshop floor. She and Ren gave Maia space to dismiss her armor.

"Did it work?" Ren asked.

"Yeah," Maia said. "Unfortunately. How long was I gone?"

"Minutes," Ren said. "Tell us everything you learned. Start with the good news."

Maia lay motionless for some time. She had no idea how to tell her friends that there was no good news. There was only bad and worse.

Chapter 40
Change of Plans

Ami and Ren listened attentively while Maia recounted her experience connecting with Scarlet, of meeting her Vanguardian in a strange, colorless dimension, and the reason why Scarlet had stopped repairing herself. She told them of her encounter with Heretic, and her tale of the Kith and the other Pilots she had created. She touched on Legion and what they needed to do to prevent the Kith from crossing over.

She left out certain details, like Heretic's proposal of scuttling Scarlet or the fact that the master tower beyond the Aperture could only be reached by the one Pilot who had a Vanguardian that could fly. Ami wasn't willing or able to help them, so Maia saw no point in telling her that if she did change her mind, it would mean her death, too.

When Maia finished her story, a long silence fell over the three women. It hung heavy in the air until Ren decided to cut it down.

"Fuck," Ren said.

Maia thought that summed things up quite nicely. "On the relatively bright side, Cobalt is alive. We can use him."

"If Cobalt will even have me." Ren pulled her crossed arms closer to her chest. Maia wished she had omitted even more from her story, including the fact that Scarlet also felt pain like Ren did every time she piloted her. Cobalt might react the same way. Unless there was a way to separate the fire and lightning swirling in her chest, Ren likely wouldn't be able to bond with Cobalt, either.

"One problem at a time," Maia said. "Right now, we need to prepare as best we can while Scarlet repairs herself. When the Aperture opens, we need to be in Noctis, with Cobalt in hand, ready to fight. That's our duty. Getting Aurelia and Leona's remains, and breaking Heart's Oath, comes second."

"We can get Leona and my mother back, and break your curse as well, if you allow me to go in alone," Ren said. "If I can speak to my father, we may be able to gain his aid. We may be able to stop the Emperor from opening the Aperture at all."

Not this again. "Arcturus can't be trusted, and we can't risk you getting captured."

"What happened to allowing me to make my own choices?" Ren said.

"You can, so long as you're making a choice that isn't sure to get us all killed."

"Fine." Ren threw her hands in the air. "If I had to hazard a guess, and you've left me with no other choice than to do just that, I would assume that Cobalt is being held somewhere beneath the Imperial Palace. There is a network of old catacombs and tunnels running through the mountain. We keep our honored dead there. The trouble is knowing where to look."

"Hopefully, we'll get lucky," Maia said.

"Even if we are, in your current state, you're not fit for combat. How do you expect to accompany me into the catacombs?"

"I don't know!" Maia's voice cracked, and she fell into a coughing fit that left her panting. "Getting me into the catacombs comes after we get past Grimclaw and Lion's Roar."

Ami raised a finger. "Lion's Roar is no longer functional. It's unlikely Noctis will be able to repair it before we arrive."

"They won't need it," Maia said. "Grimclaw is enough. I'm not going to lie to you, Ren. We have an impossible task ahead of us, and I don't know how we're going to win. But we have to. Somehow."

Ren touched Maia's shoulder and smiled. "I have one more suggestion if you're amenable to hearing it." She waited for Maia's nod. "We may be able to use Kasper's intelligence to our advantage."

"Indeed. Kasper may have useful information," Ami said. "He was a Noctean spy."

"It's as good an idea as any," Maia said. "Ami, can you take me to the hole you put Kasper in?"

"It is a crevasse," Ami said.

"What's the difference?"

"If it's not too much trouble," Ren cut in, "I feel I should be the one to interrogate him."

The thought of Ren visiting Kasper brought a frown to Maia's face. "Are you sure that's a good idea?"

"I want to be of use. I may have a chance at getting through to him, given our connection. And he likely won't speak to you. If he does, you'll just hit him again."

You hit him way more than I ever did. "You don't have to do this, you know."

"I know. I want to. Where might I find him?"

Ami walked to one of her worktables, tore a strip off the drawing of Legion, and sketched a quick map. Ren took it, grinned in thanks, and headed off into the tunnels.

"Do you think this is wise?" Ami said when she was gone.

"Not at all. But I don't have any better ideas." And far be it from her to deny her apprentice a chance for some much-needed closure.

The long, curling tunnel opened into a chamber with a low ceiling. Near the center of the cavern, the floor cut away to a deep gash in the rock roughly ten feet across. Thick bones belonging to an unknown animal had been lashed into a lattice over the hole.

With one of Ami's lanterns in hand, Ren moved closer to the covered maw. The light carved twenty feet down into the blackness and landed on Kasper's head and sagging shoulders. He sat cross-legged against the wall of the crevasse with his splinted and bandaged wrists splayed on his lap.

Kasper offered a weak wave without looking up at her. Seeing him so utterly defeated sent a pang of guilt through her. Then she remembered what he had done and why she had come, and anger burned her pity away. "Kasper. It's me."

"Kasper?" He twisted his head, turning a purple, bruised cheek up to her. "What happened to 'Kas?'"

"What indeed." Ren gulped. She left her light near the base of a stalactite where Kasper's belongings hung on a sharp sliver of rock. She dug through his pouches and found both of his Farspeakers. Since she couldn't tell which one belonged to Brave Dawn and which to Noctis, she left them on the ground.

In one of the back pouches of his belt, Ren felt a familiar cold steel box. When she pulled her hand from the pouch and looked at her fingers in the light, purple dust clung to them. "You had a Snapstone," she said. "That's how you survived Lion's Roar without a scratch. Its twin must have been close by, if you were able to return to us so fast."

A chuckle echoed from the pit. "That's my girl. Sharp as ever."

"I'm not a girl. I'm a woman. And I'll never be yours again," Ren said.

"Don't say that. I really do love you, Ren. I wasn't lyin' about that."

The sound of her name on his lips burned her ears like poison. "I came to ask you some questions, mostly pertaining to Cobalt's whereabouts. However, we both know you're not going to tell me anything of worth. So, I suppose I won't waste my time."

When Kasper spoke again, his voice was unsteady. "Then why are you here?"

Ren took one of Kasper's stilettos, along with its sheath. "I'm not going to hurt you again if that's what you're thinking." She slipped the dagger into the leather loop on her belt that once held the scabbard of her rapier. Inside the empty pouch where she would have kept shells for her revolver, she packed the rune-inscribed walnut grenades Kasper favored. "You have things I'll need on my journey. I don't fancy myself a liar or a thief, but I have no other choice, I'm afraid."

"You're going to Noctis alone, aren't you? That's awfully brave of you, considerin' you have no idea what—and who—is waitin' for you there."

"Then tell me. Or don't. I don't care. I'm not playing your games."

"Then let's stop playin'. You're not going to make it alone. Let me out, and I'll help you."

A part of her wanted to. It might be the only way to find out where exactly Cobalt was being held. But the longer she spoke with him, the more the warm, flowing tone of his voice would pull at her. She worried that she might do as he asked, if only for the slim chance that his intentions were genuine, that the Kas she had loved so fast and so hard had come back to her.

"Right now, I want nothing from you except your bombs and blades. That's all you're worth to me, now."

"That's all I was ever worth to Noctis, too." Kasper slipped lower into the pit. "That's all I seemed to be worth to your mother."

"What?" Ren moved closer to the hole. "What did you just say?"

"Nothin'. Forget about it."

Ren knelt on the bone grate and peered into the darkness. "My mother is dead. You're lying."

"Am I?"

The echo of his words remained in Ren's head long after the cavern walls had swallowed their sound. "Kasper. If you ever loved me, answer me truly. Is my mother alive?"

"In a manner of speakin'. If you let me out, I can take you to her."

"Tell me where she's being held and where Cobalt is."

"Let me out, and I'll tell you. Come on, Ren. I want to help you, but how can I trust you?"

"How can you trust *me?*" She stomped the bone grate. "After everything you've done, you have the audacity to question *me?* Fine, then. Rot in that crevasse, for all I care. Goodbye, Kasper."

"Wait!" he called. "Okay, Ren. You win. If you enter the catacombs from the Imperial Palace's basement, there's a long stretch of tunnel. It's lit with small glass lights. Follow them. Don't veer from the path. At the end is the Kith's workshop. Facing the door, if you go right, you'll find Cobalt. Don't go left. Whatever you do, do *not* go left."

"What's to the left? Is that where my mother is?"

Kasper sighed. "She won't be far. There. I gave. Now, it's your turn."

She cursed her hearts for betraying her. This wasn't right. Kasper shouldn't be locked in a pit. He loved her. There was something sincere entwined with his words when he said as much, something too raw to be a lie.

Maybe he could be saved. Some day.

With all the information and equipment she could gather in her possession, Ren set herself to purpose. She had concealed the counterpart to her Snapstone in a special place back in Noctis, somewhere even her father didn't know about. Those had been his instructions when he told her to hide it.

In seconds, she would be home. In hours, the war might be over, and Maia might be saved. It could be done. She had to try.

"I can't let you out, Kasper. Not yet. If you're telling the truth, then we'll speak again when I return."

She fished her Snapstone out of the small box in her back pouch. She almost dropped it when Kasper's splinted hand shot up through the grate, reaching for her. How had he scaled the wall of the pit without her hearing him?

"You need me, Ren! Ami was right about everythin'! You don't know who you really are. If you go back alone, you'll die. I can save you. Please, let me save you!"

"I am thoroughly done with people attempting to save me."

Kasper's curled fingers clawed at the bones caging him. "Ren, I'm all you've got. Who else could love you, knowin' what you are?"

"If this is what your love really looks like, I no longer want it." Ren clenched her fist around the Snapstone. "Goodbye, Kasper."

The cool, soft rock crumbled in her hand. The air around her grew cold, and a shiver bolted up her spine. As the dust swirled, the world rent and spiraled away, and a sudden pull sent her flying backward through a tunnel laced with swirling strands of violet and black.

Panic heaved in her chest. Ren had never used a Snapstone before. They were too rare, too valuable, deigned only for use in absolute emergencies. Was the trip supposed to take so long? Had she done something wrong? What if the stone's sister had been destroyed? Would she be lost to the void for all eternity?

When she opened her mouth to scream, her voice pulled from her mouth and slipped behind her, swallowed by the swirling walls of the dark tunnel as she flew at speeds she never thought possible. The next time she blinked, she was standing before a wall of stone. Purple dust wafted into her face and stung her eyes. Sickness rolled up through her and forced her to double over and wretch.

After wiping her mouth with the back of her hand, Ren took in her surroundings. Her panic returned when she realized she wasn't in the place where she had left her second Snapstone. Someone had relocated it to an empty cell, a perfect cube of quiet stone lit by a single caged, glowing globe of glass affixed to the ceiling. There was a flat steel door with a small slat at eye level and another at the base.

That was where food would come in. Between that and the bucket placed in the corner next to the door, Ren surmised that wherever she was, she was meant to be there for some time.

After bruising both shoulders trying to break the door down, Ren jumped when the upper slat of the door slid open, revealing a pair of narrowed eyes framed by a guard's helmet.

"Get comfortable, miss. You're not goin' anywhere," the guard said. The slat shut with a clang. Ren pressed her ear to the door and listened to the guard's muffled voice.

"...that Pilot Valerius has returned. No, go straight to Professor. Well, it's your bloody decision, then! Up to you whether to interrupt him durin' his work."

Footsteps, then silence. With nothing else to distract her, Ren could no longer ignore the incessant draw of Grimclaw thudding at the base of her skull, ever-present since they left Noctis. It was joined by the sharp, twisting pain of the Kith. Wherever he was, he was close.

She sat against the wall, allowing the cold stone to quench the heat rising through her back. Once she had drained a spot of its coolness, she shifted to another until she worked her way around the entire room.

The cell seemed to have shrunk since she first arrived. That wasn't possible. How long had it been? Hours? Days? With her anxious hearts threatening to blast her chest apart, Ren focused on devising an escape plan. Her Pilot strength clearly wasn't enough to take a steel door from its hinges. Kasper's grenades were too weak for the task. And even if she knew how to pick a lock, she would need more than a stiletto to do it.

The hot sting of tears welled in her eyes. Maia was right. Coming alone had been a mistake. All that Ren had left was the hope that if she was very lucky, she would live long enough to hear her mentor gloat.

When the cavern shook, she barely felt it.

As Maia stared at the dusting of purple powder covering the cavern floor, she thought to herself that, for all the strides Ren had made in the months they had spent together, she hadn't learned a bloody thing from their experience at Castle

Blackwood.

"Stupid. Impulsive. Stubborn." Maia searched for the right combination of insults that would bring her apprentice back. No matter how much Maia fumed, Ren did not materialize before her to accept a sound verbal thrashing.

"I apologize," Ami said. "I should have anticipated this. I saw her breathing and heartbeat elevate when she left us and assumed it was brought on by the thought of seeing Kasper."

Maia cradled her face in her hands. She spread her fingers wide enough for her voice to carry through the gaps. "It's not your fault. It's mine. I should have taken that Snapstone away from her the second I found out about it."

"I assume you're thinking of going to Noctis to rescue her," Ami said. "I would advise against it."

"Listen to Ami," Kasper said from the hole.

"Ami? Get me out of here before I kill him."

"I'd like to see you try, Sun," Kasper called as Ami wheeled Maia from the room. "I'm going to get out of here, and when I do..."

His hollow threats trailed off as Ami lifted Maia, chair and all, and carried her through the uneven ascending section of tunnel. Maia waited until they were back in the workshop before she spoke again.

"I have to go," Maia said.

Ami shook her head. "If you go now, you'll be defeated. We..."

Their eyes locked. Grimclaw had lived longer than any Behemoth to date. Maia had learned to live with its distant pulsing presence in the back of her mind as just another unavoidable discomfort of her continued existence. The sudden onset of a second Behemoth pulsing in her skull, along with the ache of a horde of Ferals that dwarfed any she had ever felt before, nearly doubled Maia over in her chair.

"The Aperture," Ami said.

"I have to go, now!" Maia gripped the wheels of her chair, angled toward Scarlet, and pushed as hard as she could. She made it only a few feet before her arms went numb.

With calm steps, Ami rounded the chair and stood in her path. "I'm sensing one additional Behemoth and too many Ferals to accurately count. Based on their central location in Noctis, I believe this is merely a bolstering of their forces. If the

Aperture had opened fully, we would likely be faced with an army of Behemoths."

"Ren's there, alone. If they haven't found her yet, they will soon. I have to get to her. She needs me!"

"Maia." Ami knelt in front of her and took her hands in hers, pressing them to her own forehead. "I'm not suggesting that we abandon Ren. You can't help her in your condition. That doesn't mean that we're out of options."

"Then tell me what to do, Ami. How do we win? Because I haven't a single idea beyond taking Scarlet to Noctis and threatening to rupture her core if the Emperor won't give Ren back."

"I have a proposal. You may not like it," Ami warned. "While we wait for the Aperture to open, I suggest that we spend the next nine days training, providing time for Scarlet to complete repairs. You've suffered more than most. I ask that you suffer a little longer. Then, in nine days, we'll get Ren back, destroy the towers, and end this war. I promise you."

"We?" Maia said.

Ami turned her gaze up to where Viridian rested at the other end of the workshop. Her breath rose and fell, calm as a cool ocean breeze. She closed her eyes and nodded. "Viridian and I have decided. Whether parliament grants us permission to act or not, we'll go to Noctis to close the Aperture. You were right. This fight is too big for any one of us. I can't leave you to fight it alone."

"Are you sure? What about your injuries?"

Ami donned a sad smile. "I will have time to mend once our duty is done."

The thought of spending the next nine days wondering if Ren was alive or dead sounded like hell, but the solid grip of Ami's hands on hers kept Maia from slipping back into a void of dark thoughts.

"Thank you, Ami." Maia grimaced. If Ami was going to ride to hell with her, she needed to know exactly where the road led. "There's...something I left out earlier. Something Heretic said about the towers. We can't just destroy the five towers on our side of the portal. Someone has to go through to the other side and knock down the master tower."

Ami blinked. "I understand. Viridian is the only Vanguardian capable of flight."

"I'm not asking you to die for me or anyone else. You already did, once."

"I appreciate that. Give me time to consider our options." Ami raised a finger. "In the meantime, we should discuss our training plan for the next nine days."

"Ami. Look at me." Maia patted her thighs.

"I am, and I assure you, I have taken your current condition into account. Physical motions help guide a Vanguardian's actions. However, they aren't strictly necessary for basic movement. Do you think I guide Viridian by craning my neck, walking on all fours, and flapping my arms like wings?"

Maia did think that. She shook her head anyway.

"It's important that we focus on what strengths you still possess. You can't walk. You can't fight. You no longer have reliable control of your fire sliver. However, there's one tool you have at your disposal that may still prove useful."

"My harsh language?"

Ami tapped her chin. "Two tools, then. While Heart's Oath is working to suppress the magic inside you, weakening your fire and your physical abilities, there's one gift it hasn't touched, likely because it's underdeveloped."

"Wait," Maia said. "Are you talking about my Barrier?"

"Correct. It's weak, yet I believe it can be strengthened and improved, much in the same way I trained my Perception. Obviously, you won't be able to attain that same level of mastery in such a short time, though I believe great improvements in the quality and durability of your Barrier are possible."

Maia was about to ask Ami how she meant to go about strengthening her shield when the shards that made up Ami's green helmet and black visor slid into place. Ami fell back into her fighting stance, with her open taloned hands extended like knife blades.

"Oh. Right, then." Reaching within herself, Maia found the thinnest of the many threads of magic sewed into her and pulled on it. A screen of crimson light shimmered into existence. She projected it as far forward as she could.

Ami walked up to it and thrust her taloned fingers clean through the Barrier, shattering it into glistening fragments.

She didn't often use it, but in the few times Maia had employed her Barrier in combat, it had never been broken. That jarring feeling of focusing on a single thing that suddenly became a hundred things rattled her.

"We'll train your Barrier as we would train a muscle, by breaking it down, then allowing it to recover stronger than before. Again," Ami commanded.

Maia summoned another shield. Sweat formed on her brow as she willed the Barrier to thicken.

Ami drove her fingertips through like it was made of paper. "Again," she said.

Maia pursed her lips and nodded. Nine days. If she only had that long to live, to gain what she needed to win, it had to be enough.

It had to.

Chapter 41

Cobalt

Ren gripped her wolf-emblazoned revolver by the barrel and dragged the edge of the hammer down the stone wall of her cell. The stiletto she took from Kasper would have done a better job, but she wanted to preserve the fine point of the dagger in case she needed it. Without shells, the only purpose her revolver served was marking the passage of time.

Once the guards started bringing her meals, Ren found it easier to count the days. Since then, she had carved four gashes, one for each day spent in her compact box. Four gashes meant five days until the Aperture opened. Five days until Heart's Oath took Maia's life.

Five days left to escape and save the world.

After her meals, when the quiet hum of the glass globe lighting her cell grew too loud, Ren passed the time by training. Like Kasper's dagger, she needed to maintain her own keen needlepoint if she intended to flee when the door to her cell inevitably opened. She worked her stiletto through knife drills she hadn't practiced since her early days of Pilot training and repositioned the black walnut grenades she took from Kasper to a pouch at her side, practicing her draw and release with pebbles until the motion was fluid. Effortless.

The repetitive training helped keep her mind off the aches in the back of her head that she couldn't do anything about. Two Behemoths. More Ferals than she could ever face alone. And the sharp twist of the Kith, ever-present and rarely still.

Today, that particular ache was closer than ever and growing nearer by the second.

Ren hopped and swung her revolver at the glass ceiling light, cracking it and bathing the room in darkness. She shoved her revolver back into its holster, drew her stiletto in a forward grip in her right hand, and curled the fingers of her left around a walnut grenade. She dragged the soles of her boots across the flat stone floor to scrape off clinging dust and ensure her footing was solid.

The lock turned, and the door opened outward. As soon as the light from the hall outside her cell sliced through the shadows and touched her feet, her left hand whipped forward. The grenade snapped in a burst of light and flame. Ren kept low as she sprinted for the door, driving the stiletto through the lingering cloud of smoke left in the grenade's wake.

The air around her rippled. Something grabbed her arm and wrenched it across her body. A gentle pressure lifted her into the air, holding her a foot off the ground.

Gravity magic. Few mages had ever been able to command it to any real effect without destroying their own bodies. Whoever was employing it against her possessed a level of deft control and masterful casting speed she had never thought possible. The unseen force plied her blade from her hand, then pulled her into the tunnel beyond the cell door.

The Kith's dark blue skin swallowed the light pouring from the caged glass bulbs set into the misshapen tunnel walls. With a flick of his wrist, the stiletto snapped in half and tumbled to the ground. Ren's weapon belt untied itself and floated to him. The Kith drew her revolver from its holster as the belt drifted past him and into the grip of one of the two armored guards who accompanied him.

The Kith turned the purple-hued revolver over. "You were meant to execute Sunder with this. Explain why you failed in your assigned duty."

The strange force holding Ren aloft deposited her on her feet. Ren resisted the urge to charge, fearing that the outburst would only get her thrown back in her cell. Or worse.

"I ran out of shells," Ren said. "If you can procure me some ammunition, I can demonstrate how I would have done it. Your skull, though a little on the small side, should suffice for a demonstration. What's your name, by the way? Quite rude, failing to introduce yourself to the woman who's going to end your life."

Even if she had no weapons, there were other ways to attack. Maia had taught her that much.

"A childish response. As expected." The tip of a gleaming white fang poked through the slit of the Kith's smirk. "The closest approximation to my title that

I can muster in your ridiculous language is 'Professor.' I will now take you to be examined and prepared. If you resist, I will use force."

"Prepare me for what?" Ren retreated a step back toward her cell. The air around her wrist rippled, and the unseen presence jerked her toward the Kith.

"Come. Now. I do not want to explain to your mother why I have damaged your body if we can avoid it."

Mother is alive. Ren's mind latched onto her last memory of her, when she threw herself on top of Ren to shield her from the wave of stone and wood rushing down to end them both.

She imagined what her mother would look like as a broken, desiccated corpse, shambling through the catacombs in the dark, and squinted hard to dash the image from her mind. If Kasper was telling the truth and her mother was alive, Ren had to cling to any hope that she was still herself and not a mindless ghoul. Otherwise, Professor wouldn't feel the need to explain himself to her.

The Kith handed Ren's revolver to the guard holding her belt. The other guard walked behind her as they followed the tunnel's bend, past shelves cut into the walls that held the shroud-covered remains of countless Noctean nobles.

Her attention flicked between the light, constant pressure Professor was applying to the small of her back to keep her moving forward, and the caged spheres of light set into the walls. *Follow the lights. At the end is the Kith's workshop.* Is that where they were headed? Was that where he was keeping her mother?

Professor pointed to one of the caged lights. "You are curious about these. These are called 'light bulbs,'" he said.

"Interesting," Ren said. They weren't. Ami's were bigger and brighter.

"They function through electricity."

"Lightning, directed and given purpose."

"One of the many advances the Kith have brought to your people, along with the design for both your cartridge-based revolver and Lion's Roar."

"Your blasted cannon almost killed us," Ren said.

"That is its purpose. It draws electricity from a stabilized sliver and channels it into a battery for later use. The effects are quite pronounced."

"You bring us such wonderful toys."

"We bring you gifts. To elevate you. We adopt the advances of the people we conquer and spread them to each world we visit. Your people are thieves. You steal from other nations and claim their works as your own. You do not deserve our gifts."

Ask him, Ren told herself. *Ask him if he had a hand in what was done to you. If he knows whose body you stole. Who you really are.* She almost found her nerve by the time they arrived at a branch in the tunnel. Paths cut off to the left and right. Ahead, at the abrupt end of the tunnel, a steel door waited.

The Kith's lab. That meant that the right path led to Cobalt, and the time for talking was over.

As Professor floated ahead toward the lab, a distant roar shook the stone around them. Bulbs clinked in their cages as dust fell from the ceiling and cut into the rays of light they cast.

That will do nicely for a distraction. Ren spun on the guard behind her. Though she had only seen Maia perform the technique once on Kasper and had only felt it once herself, Ren prided herself on being a quick study. She shoved the guard, sending him flailing back, and snatched one of his outstretched hands.

A bend, a twist, and a turn of her hips sent the guard flipping forward and crashing into his colleague's back. She took a moment to appreciate how easily she could have twisted the man's hand clean off if she applied any of her Pilot strength and silently thanked her mentor for yet another valuable tool as she cut down the right tunnel.

Professor's magical assault barely missed her as she rounded the corner. Rock exploded from the wall behind her, crushed to powder in the span of a blink. Another metal door set with a large lever waited at the end of the hall. Ren brought her arm down hard on the lever, threw her shoulder into the door, and blasted through. She dodged to the side as Professor sent a rippling wave of force rolling past her. When she got the door closed, Ren pushed the lever up into place, wedging her body beneath it to keep it from opening.

The lever dug into her shoulder as Professor tried to work the door open. Ren surveyed the room, looking for cover, when she saw what was waiting on the raised dais set next to the metal platform she was standing on.

Large lights from the ceiling cast white beams that danced across the deep blue sheen of a metal panther that had to be well over a hundred feet long. Though thick runic chains bound him to the dais and forced him to lay on his stomach, not a single scratch marred his perfect, violent frame. He was smaller than Scarlet, but if he could stand, he would still be large enough to crush Ren underfoot like a mouse.

She focused on the black visor, stretched across the space where his eyes would have been, and lost herself in the darkness she found there. Vanguardian visors doubled as viewports. A viewport meant a cabin.

A cabin meant a control beam.

If she moved, Professor would be upon her in seconds. She had to be quicker. The door's level jammed down into her shoulder in a slow rhythm. Ren's hearts hammered in her ears as she waited for the lever to rise. When it did, she bolted across the platform.

Ren mounted the railing at the end of the platform and sprung off, throwing herself across the gap and onto Cobalt's bowed head. She landed hard on her chest, blowing the wind from her lungs as she crashed onto the panther's snout.

Pressure gripped her legs before she could stand. Ren's fingers spread wide, pressing hard onto cool blue metal. She shut her eyes and tensed against Professor's pull.

I did my best. I'm sorry, Maia.

A warm tingle rushed through her fingertips and up into her chest, first drawing Ren further into herself, then beyond, sending her hurtling into an endless expanse of nothingness.

Ren expected to awaken in an open field of colorless grass beneath a blank sky like Maia had described. Instead, hard surfaces surrounded her, connected at odd angles, white like chunks of pure uncut marble.

She was in a tunnel, though one completely devoid of shadow or texture. When she turned to take in her surroundings, the scabbard at her belt pressed against the wall, halting her. Looking down, Ren saw that the rapier her father had given her, the one Maia had destroyed, had made the trip with her to this dreamlike realm, along with the revolver waiting at the small of her back.

Ren swallowed hard and descended, feeling her way around corners and bends until she came to an opening lined with tooth-like stalactites and stalagmites. Droplets of white water pattered into a still pool beyond, sending little echoes bouncing around the cave. Ren crept between the fangs and into the maw. When she stepped from the milky puddle and onto the island in the middle of the cavern, her feet were bone dry.

"Show yourself," Ren called to the odd presence that had been watching her since she entered the cave. She turned about, trying to locate where the sinking feeling of dread was coming from.

Something slammed into her from above and pinned her onto her stomach. Dark, smoky claws dug into her upper arms.

"You're a strange thing," a deep voice full of hunger growled, a voice that rose from inside her own chest. The shadowy mass sniffed at her neck. "What are you?"

"I am Serenia Valerius. Ren, to my friends," Ren said. "You must be Cobalt. I—"

"Be quiet!" Cobalt roared. "I know what your hearts want. I invited you in because I was curious. You smell like ashes and the tang of the warm night air before lightning strikes. You shouldn't be both."

Cobalt's weight left Ren's back. She rolled to her feet and kept her eyes trained on the soft four-legged shape prowling around her in a lazy circle.

"I have both fire and lightning bonded to my soul," Ren said.

"Your soul is confused, then." Cobalt chuckled, a dark rattle that knotted Ren's stomach. "It doesn't know what it wants to be. What it should be."

"That much is true," Ren said. "All I know is that right at this moment, I need to become your Pilot."

"I already have a Pilot."

"Leona Carver. Yes." Ren paused. "She's dead, I'm afraid."

"I know!" Cobalt boomed. "I was there when she passed. Her pain. Her suffering. Her last moments. I saw them all!"

The hot wind thrown at her by the beast's rage forced her to her knees, gasping for breath even though she had no need for air in this secret inner place. "You should consider making me your new Pilot. I have something you want."

The blurry mass sharpened and bristled. "You have nothing I want, girl."

"Perhaps you didn't hear me. My name is Serenia. Or Ren. Not 'girl' or 'Princess,' or anything else. And you're mistaken. I have something to offer that I suspect you desire very much. Freedom."

"You think you can give it to me?" Cobalt said. "Others have tried. So many have come to replace her. None of them could. No one ever will."

Ren's hearts skipped. She recalled what Maia had said to her during their argument at the tavern. *I wonder if they told you what happened to all the failures that came before you. Or where their bodies are buried.* "Then why bring me here? You said you were curious. Curious of what, exactly?"

Cobalt lowered his mass. "You don't get to ask questions."

"As a matter of fact, I do." Ren took a heavy step forward. "I'm your guest. You invited me in and proceeded to attack me. You're a proud beast, to be sure, but a poor host. At the very least, I feel I'm owed an explanation as compensation for your rudeness. Since you don't wish to oblige, I'll tell you where I think your curiosity comes from. I would say that you're wondering whether I'm worthy of being your Pilot and whether I can deliver you from your chains so that you can do what you were meant to do. The answer to both is yes."

Another low chuckle. "You're confused and strange. But interesting. You say that you want my freedom, but what you're asking is for me to bind myself to you. You want to be my new master."

"Not a master. A partner. I want us to work together to save the world."

"And what if I don't want to save the world? What if I never wanted to? What if I only did what I was told because I was made to? What if all I want in this world now is to feel the Red Pilot's throat tear between my fangs so that I can slake myself on her blood?"

"Then you're a coward, and horrible, and not worth my time and attention. I'll find another way to stop the Kith from invading our world. Stay in your chains, proud beast. This is clearly where you belong." Ren turned to leave.

When she looked up, Cobalt had slipped in front of her. He rested on his haunches, still and unmoving on the puddle's surface. His form shifted. For a moment, he looked like a silhouette of a crouched man with broad shoulders and a shorn head. "I would never hurt Sunder. She was only defending herself.

I don't hold any hate for her." He shrank a little. "I had to fight her. My Leona commanded it. I had no choice."

"With me, you would have a choice. I won't make you do anything you don't wish to do."

Cobalt tilted his head. "You said the Kith are invading? There will be more than just the little one slinking around in the dark?"

"They're coming. Nothing can be done to stop that now." Ren held out her hand. "But when they arrive..."

Cobalt padded across the puddle. He sniffed her hand and pulled away as if she had burned him. "Even if I accept you as my Pilot, we can't bond. Not while your soul is confused. You need to choose. Lightning or fire? You can't be both."

"I choose lightning," Ren said without giving it a second thought. She nodded after the fact. "Lightning is direct. Decisive. That's what I wish to be."

"Lightning it is," Cobalt said, his voice lifting and smoothing out. "I can help with that, but it won't be pleasant."

"I'll do whatever it takes. For Maia. For the world. When do we begin?"

Cobalt's head tilted toward the ceiling of the cavern. "Time passes differently here. Out there, you've run out. Survive, Serenia Valerius. Free yourself. When you return, I'll be ready."

"I will return. I swear it." Ren felt her body grow lighter. "One more thing, before I go. I was told that if a Vanguardian chooses, they can assume another form. The Vanguardian you once knew as Emerald lives, though she became a dragon, and now goes by the name Viridian."

"You want me to become a dragon?" Cobalt said.

"No. Though, if you wish, you can take on another form. There's nothing wrong with you the way you are, but you're free to assume another form if it pleases you."

"One form is as good to me as another. Though, the Maker wouldn't approve of me changing my frame." Cobalt's grin sparked from within Ren's breast. "I'll do it."

"How long will it take you to change?"

"Days. I'm not damaged, and you're not asking me to become a dragon. It can be done."

"Then I'll see you in a few days," Ren said moments before she rocketed through the roof of the cavern and into the void beyond.

Ren's back crashed onto the metal platform, leaving her gasping for breath. With a flick, Professor lifted her. Rippling waves rotated Ren like a pig on a spit until Professor seemed satisfied and placed her back on her feet.

"You are uninjured. Do not attempt escape again."

The guard Ren had thrown grabbed her by the arm and hauled her through the metal doorway. She could have easily overpowered him but decided against it. She doubted she could take Professor in a straight fight without her revolver, which was currently resting empty in her belt, slung over her guard's shoulder.

The time wasn't right. She had a few days left to plot her escape, to be ready in case Maia somehow mounted a rescue. In that time, she would wait, watch, and listen.

With a waggle of his finger, Professor threw a toggle on the wall of Cobalt's prison, leaving the chamber bathed in darkness. He took her to his workshop, where he strapped her into a smooth metal chair that appeared to be freshly smithed. Professor drew her blood, passed strange crystals over her body, and pressed down on her tongue with a thin piece of wood while he examined her mouth.

She tried to ask him about her origins and where her mother was being held, but he ignored her questions. When the opportunity presented itself, she would make him answer, she decided.

When Professor and the two guards deposited Ren back in her cell, she found the broken light replaced. That was kind. She might have gone mad, spending five days alone in the dark. Though Professor meant to keep her for some unknown purpose, he clearly needed her alive and well.

The door closed behind her, but the lock didn't slide shut. She heard movement in the tunnel beyond. Heavy boots thumped. The door opened again, and Professor glided in. Behind him, a massive Feral loomed, taller and wider than any Ren had encountered. Its head and arms were hidden by the door frame. More troubling, it didn't trigger her Hunter Sense at all.

"To ensure you do not attempt escape again, I am assigning an additional asset to guard you," Professor said. His lips curled into a sneer. When he left, the Feral entered, stooping as it crossed the threshold and unfurled to its full eight-foot height.

Ren's breath caught in her chest. She fought to keep from screaming as her eyes darted over the Feral's dense, exposed muscle to its Blacksteel right arm, blazing with arcane runes that shone through thin strands of taught, binding ligament.

When she looked up at the misshapen, drooping face the oversized Feral wore, a face that had once belonged to Arcturus Valerius, Ren couldn't contain her scream any longer.

Horror ravaged her voice and burned her throat. Any hope of escape fled Ren's hearts. A dull haze seeped into the cracks left in her mind by the sight of the abomination leering at her through her father's eyes, leaving her mired within herself.

The last thought Ren had before she stopped thinking altogether was that the light hanging from the ceiling of her cell, which allowed her to perceive her father's fate, wasn't much of a kindness after all.

Chapter 42

Heart of Fire

On the day she was meant to die, and the Aperture was meant to open, Maia awoke before the sun rose. Sleep hadn't been kind enough to take her in its gentle arms for longer than an hour at a time, so she stopped chasing it and embraced exhaustion. The sheer exertion of summoning her armor and climbing into her wheelchair left her panting and shaking.

Ami came to fetch her clad in her own armor, wearing a small metal case strapped to her lower back beneath her collapsed bow. She had watched Ami fill the case the day before. It contained needle-capped vials—"syringes," Ami called them—filled with glowing red Amplifier.

Seeing Ami wearing her helmet made Maia envious. She wished her own helmet was intact, so she could hide the dour look she knew she was wearing.

Ami had taken Kasper from his hole—his crevasse—a few days prior and delivered him to a jail in Inemelle. That left Maia with one less distraction. In between bouts of worry over Ren's safety, and a desire to see Elizabeth one last time that pulled harder than her Hunter Sense ever could, Maia spent her dwindling days focusing on strengthening her Barrier while working with Ami to connect Scarlet and Viridian into an incomplete Legion.

She had some success with the former. The latter had left her feeling frustrated and far from connected. Scarlet had repaired most of her head, as well as her right arm and shoulder, but Maia couldn't blame their failure to form Legion on Scarlet's lingering battle damage. It wasn't Scarlet's fault. It was Maia's.

Even though Heart's Oath curled around her sliver and diminished its fire, it did little to stop Maia's blood from boiling with every setback. The way Ami corrected her mistakes and reassured her in the same way every time she failed quickly started to grate on the thin threads of patience Maia was struggling to keep from fraying. The ticking clock and her many injuries didn't help, but they weren't the true cause of her frustration.

No matter how hard she tried, Maia couldn't stop being angry. At Ami, for refusing to help until it was too late. At Ren, for putting herself in danger and making the situation worse. Mostly, though, she was mad at herself for her countless mistakes. She decided that that was likely what kept Legion from forming. In the end, all she had to show for nine days of effort was the ability to make Scarlet walk without moving her own feet and a thicker Barrier, which Ami had to strike about ten times to shatter. It wouldn't be enough to save Ren if she was still alive.

Maia and Ami decided together the day before that once the Aperture opened, Maia should remain in Scarlet, using her to draw the Behemoths away while Viridian struck at the towers on her own. The dual distraction would hopefully provide the cover Ami needed to sneak into the Imperial Palace, secure the Emperor, and locate Ren. After that, all that was left was to sacrifice Viridian by sending her through the Aperture to destroy the master tower.

It wasn't a great plan, but it was better than nothing, though not by much.

"I can't tell for certain how much time you have remaining," Ami said. She wheeled Maia in front of Scarlet and took her place by Viridian. "I estimate half a day. Likely less. It's like watching a coiled cobra waiting to strike. I don't know when Heart's Oath will attack or if the Aperture will open before it does."

"Great." Maia had already considered that she might die before her duty was done. It had taken a lengthy back-and-forth with Scarlet to convince Scarlet to rupture her own core if Maia passed on and it looked like there was no other way to win.

Ami didn't need to know about that. Not yet. It would only upset her. Maia had no right burdening her with anything, given that her best friend was ready to put herself in peril for their common cause.

Maia reached down and concentrated. Her Barrier formed beneath her like a platform, and she willed it to rise. It took several minutes and much of Maia's strength to ascend to Scarlet's viewport, which had not fully repaired. Maia and her Barrier floated through the smooth-edged hole in the black glass and settled in the cabin's control beam.

Ami's voice entered Scarlet's cabin. "It's time. Are you ready?"

"Not in the slightest," Maia said. "A fancy shield isn't going to be enough, but it's all I have."

"That's not all you have," Ami said. "You have a Tressille curse shortening your life span. And a spinal injury. And a missing eye."

"Right. You're right. I forgot about all those things. Yes. It's going to be fine."

"What I mean to say is that despite everything that ails you, you haven't given up, though you did become a common drunk for a time."

"Nothing common about the way I drink," Maia said.

"Regardless, you're here, now, ready to fight a battle you may not win. Your sliver might be damaged and suppressed, but your true fire, the drive that defines you, remains. It's like a never-ending blaze that burns without fuel to feed it. It's what I've always liked best about you, Maia."

"Wait. A never-ending blaze." Maia gasped. How could she have not seen it sooner? "Ami. That's it. You're a genius."

"I agree. Would you care to elaborate?"

"No time to explain."

"There's nearly always time to explain."

"I will, later. Change of plans."

"I don't like the sound of this," Ami said.

Maia threw an arm across her body, beginning her Teleport spell. "I'll meet you in Noctis. I have somewhere to be."

"Are you going to see Elizabeth?"

Maia nearly lost hold of the spell as she threw her other arm across. "How do you know about Elizabeth?"

"You call out to her in your sleep," Ami said. "Do you love her?"

"Yeah," Maia said. "I'm pretty sure I do." She grasped the magics threatening to slip away in her moment of distraction. Her fist slowly rose as the red whirl of magic whipped past Scarlet's viewport.

"I understand," Ami said. "Good luck. I'll see you soon."

Maia wanted to correct her, to tell her that even though her heart ached to see Elizabeth one last time before the end, she had another destination in mind. Maia would have said as much, but the Teleport spell demanded her absolute focus.

It was just as well. There was a chance that Ami would try and stop her. And what Maia had planned to do was most definitely something that she would be against.

Despite the danger, Maia couldn't help but smile for the first time in over a week as Scarlet lifted into the air for a shred of a moment before the Teleport spell threw her across the continent.

The morning sun peeked out from between rolling green hills as if it was afraid to bear witness to what Maia was about to do.

If she were the sun, she would be scared, too.

Maia kept her lone eye locked on it. With its blazing orange glare burning into her vision, she couldn't see the ruins of Bracken in the distance. She focused on the copses of trees crunching underfoot with each step and pictured herself back at her family's vineyard, stomping through a wide barrel of Brackenberries. Her parents had invested in a press early on in their venture, but Maia's father insisted that they produce at least one batch a season the traditional way.

The traditional way wasn't even their way. Lucius and Galeria Liberalis of Noctis knew nothing of wine making. As Alain and Bianca Sunderland, they fared only slightly better. They had to know how terrible their wine was. They seemed happy enough, though, stomping berries with Maia in the waning autumn light, listening to her squeal with delight as she pretended she was a giant monster rampaging through a great city in search of food.

With Bracken behind her, Maia brought Scarlet across the fields, arriving at the few unkempt trees left in her family orchard. They splintered as she strode, taking a piece of her childhood away with every step. She would have preferred to take her time and veer around them, but there was no time left to take. And if she slowed down for a second, good sense would force her to turn back.

Beneath the rising sun, an inferno raged at the base of a shallow crater. Even without fuel to feed it, the flames roared at the sky.

Maia guided Scarlet into the fire, closer than Maia had ever dared approach the inferno before. Flickering flames curled into the gap in the viewport. Beads of sweat sprouted all over Maia's body.

Then, she felt it.

Maia often wondered what spell Noctis had cast to conjure a blaze that would never die, one that always returned the moment she stopped forcing the flames down. But it wasn't a spell at all. It was pure magic from beyond the Veil, drawn into their world through some arcane ritual and convinced that it was fire.

I don't have a spare sliver of pure, primordial magic from beyond the Veil laying around for you to use, Heretic had told her. *As I said: figure it out.*

It took some time, but Maia had.

Though her own sliver was damaged, it recognized its kin languishing alone in the ruin of her family home and tugged her closer. Like her, it wanted to be whole again.

Are you sure you want to do this? Scarlet said, speaking directly to Maia's heart.

"I need to slow down Heart's Oath. I don't see another way. If you don't want to be a part of this, now is the time to say so."

Silence. Maia smiled in quiet thanks and asked Scarlet to bend down. As the cabin tipped forward, she formed her Barrier at an angle and used it to stop herself from rolling through the viewport.

The sliver beckoned to the weakened flame in Maia's fragile chest. She answered by having Scarlet plunge her face into the fire. Screeching tongues of flame ripped across the cabin, coating the walls in orange fury. The firestorm swirled around Maia, enveloping her in its searing embrace. Buffeting blasts of hot wind stung her skin, forming blisters that bulged and popped in seconds.

Losing an eye had been the worst pain Maia could think of. In that moment, she was thankful for her lack of imagination. Had she even considered how hot a sliver of pure magic fire could burn, she never would have guided Scarlet into the blaze to begin with.

Maia screamed to keep from blacking out as the fire rolled over her body and consumed her. She thrust her hand out, willing, pleading, begging. Not for release, but for more.

The fire obliged. She pulled at it, desperate, until the sliver broke free of whatever had been containing it for so many years. The ravaging flames swirled toward her hand, igniting her blood and bursting through every inch of her body. They found her broken sliver and intertwined with it in a swirl of rising light.

Maia could have sworn she heard a second scream join hers as Heart's Oath tore apart, scattering black phantom fragments deep into the darkest depths of her soul.

Her cry grew louder, building in power. The unspeakable pain fueling it had dried up. Now, her roar fed on the swell of raw emotion booming in her chest, a nameless, formless thing carved from pure want.

She saw faces in the raging flames. Her parents. Leona. Elizabeth. Ami, and Dalzin, and even Edgar.

And Ren.

All those she lost. All those she loved. And the ones she could still hold onto if she was brave enough to try.

The flames coalescing within her soul dripped from her skin and flowed into Scarlet, seeking a path to the sliver bonded to her core. Tongues of flame wrapped around them both, binding them even tighter together. The flames slipped through every thread of magic woven into both of their bodies, igniting and flaring them until Maia couldn't find the gaps between the stitches.

A comforting hand settled on Maia's shoulder. She turned to its owner. For the briefest of moments, Maia lost herself in the crimson gaze of a tall, blue-skinned woman with long flowing hair the color of molten metal splitting around her curved horns and pouring down onto her armored muscles.

Then, Maia exploded.

The flames robbed her of sight, sound, and feeling. When the cabin stopped shaking, Maia was crouching next to the smoldering, melted remains of her wheelchair. A surge of energy billowed through her as the new sliver wound itself around the old, churning and blazing with an intensity she could barely contain.

Maia dismissed her reforged helmet and touched her face, tracing the familiar scar that even an extra sliver of fire would never heal. When she touched the right side of her face, she lost a fight against a shuddering wave of relief that rippled over her entire body.

Maia blinked her right eye a few times, just to revel in the act of it, and brushed her tears away with her fingers. Scarlet mimicked her motions and raised her hands up to the viewport. A splinter of a laugh forced its way from Maia's chest.

Scarlet had two hands. Both of them had been made whole again.

A quick knifing pain shot through Maia's chest, reminding her that Heart's Oath would not tolerate being ignored. She could feel the scattered fragments reforming into a cage of long, wispy fingers, probing at the new challenge the second sliver had issued.

This new vigor hadn't defeated it, but it had bought her time. And Maia intended to use it well. She reached into her core and found her Teleport, refreshed by the sliver's sudden rush of energy and waiting to be unleashed. It should have taken an hour to recharge, but Maia wasn't about to question her good fortune.

"Goodbye, Father. Now, you can rest in peace." Maia thrust her hands across her body, then pumped her fist into the sky as the swirling energy cascaded across Scarlet's body, lifting her up and taking her away from Bracken for the last time.

Part Five

Convergence

Chapter 43

The Invasion of Noctis

The days Ren spent locked in her too-small cell, staring at the monster her father had become, passed by quicker than she expected. She wasn't there for most of them. The mere sight of that twitching mass of skinless muscle and bone towering in the corner forced Ren to fall inside herself where his piercing gaze couldn't reach her. A few times, she returned to the waking world when one of her guards entered and shook her until she was present enough to eat. Otherwise, she barely spent any time conscious of her too-small cell.

On the final day, when the Aperture was meant to open, Ren returned to herself. She stole cautious glances at her father, hoping each time that she would blink the sleep from her eyes and see someone different.

The bulbous muscles of his neck and shoulders fused with his cheeks, pulling his melted grin wide. His Blacksteel arm, once his greatest weapon, had become the smaller of his arms. Thick bands of sinew crisscrossed over its length, pulsing faintly. His other arm was half as wide as his trunk, a spiral mass of flesh whose weight should have toppled him.

When she looked into his jaundiced, yellow eyes, hollow save for a small spark of remembrance when their gazes met, she wondered how much of Arcturus Valerius remained in the distorted shell Professor had made of his body.

The cell door swung open. Professor entered along with one of the two guards. The other pressed against the door frame, glancing nervously at the monster in the corner.

"It is time," Professor said. He led them all, including Ren's father, through the twisting catacombs. The pounding of Ferals and Behemoths and her Kith captor beat in Ren's mind like distant footsteps rumbling through morning fog.

"Time. For what?" Ren said.

Professor turned to her. "What?"

"You said it's time. Time for what?"

"I said that several minutes ago." He floated closer, used the tips of his thumbs to open her drooping eyelids, and glared directly into her eyes. "No matter. Whether you are cognizant or not, it makes no difference."

They emerged from a crude stairway that led from the catacombs to the deepest level of the palace basement, followed by a spiral staircase coiling up to the castle proper. Ren had never seen the palace's main hall so empty, so quiet, as if it was a preserved husk of a thing that had long since passed away. Thick pillars of polished white marble fed into a high, arched ceiling, capped with a dome of colored glass. A horrible defensive choice, easily breached during a siege, but who would ever try to storm the Noctean Imperial Palace?

She waded through the rainbow-tinted sunlight painting the long carpets of the hall, all the way to the thirty-foot wide stairway leading to the throne room. There should have been two guards on each step, but like the main hall, the passage was empty. Professor glided ahead of the group. When they caught up to him at the top, the massive gilded doors stretching from floor to ceiling were already open. The four honor guards stationed there parted to let them pass. Each one wore full plate armor, and two gripped the hexagonal barrels of massive rifles forged of Blacksteel.

"Pilot Killers," Ren whispered as her guard dragged her across the threshold. Professor hovered at the end of the chamber near the golden lion-shaped throne of Emperor Caelus Noctis III, Sovereign of the Immortal Noctean Empire. The Emperor reclined in his seat of power, dressed in flowing whites and golds, his crowned head tilted to the side in boredom.

Professor flicked his fingers, and the Emperor tumbled from his seat, rolling down the stairs of the dais elevating him above all others. He came to rest at Ren's feet, looking up at her through bloodshot eyes, his face frozen in a grim rictus.

Emperor Caelus Noctis III, immortal ruler of the Noctean Empire, was dead. Seeing a god still and unmoving should have shocked Ren to her core, but from where she was standing, she wondered how she could have ever thought him divine. He was just a man, small and fragile as any other. And somebody had broken him.

Professor bared his fangs and let out a low, rumbling growl. "Take that thing away." Ren's guards dragged the Emperor's corpse from the room as Professor's magic lifted Ren and guided her onto the throne.

"Maia will come for me," Ren said.

"We are expecting this. You will remain here," Professor said. The hulking mess of muscle that used to be her father stomped over and took his place at her side.

"What am I?" Ren said when the guards had left the room, closing the doors to the throne room behind them.

"You are a vessel," Professor said.

"A vessel for what? Or who? What do you want with me?"

"Remain here. I will return in a short time with your mother. If you attempt to escape, Arcturus will hurt you."

Arcturus. That name didn't belong on a Kith's lips. Ren pushed to her feet to follow Professor as he disappeared behind one of the smooth white marble pillars framing the throne room. A large hand shoved her back down.

Her father grunted something that sounded like "stay." She found herself in no position to argue. Even with her Pilot strength, she doubted she could best him if he turned violent.

Ren stayed where her father had placed her, stiff as the gilded metal at her back, too numb and withdrawn to contemplate whatever obscene shape Professor might have twisted her mother into.

✕

Scarlet materialized at the base of a green hill next to Viridian. Maia opened Scarlet's hatch plates and slid down the length of Scarlet's arm, throwing a spray of crimson sparks from her armored boots.

Ami approached with her hands wide, feeling the air between them. "What have you done?"

"Found more fire," Maia said. She dismissed her helmet so Ami could see her healed face. In the past, Ami had said that Pilot armor was resistant to most magic, including her Perception, and she wanted her friend to share in her proud moment.

"You absorbed a second sliver of fire. That was ill-advised," Ami said.

So much for shared joy.

"You don't seem shocked," Maia said. "You knew, didn't you? What the fire that took my father from me really was?"

"I suspected it was a sliver contained in a device designed to vent its power without allowing it to disperse and consequently return to its home beyond the Veil, yes. And I didn't tell you because I feared this exact outcome. The new sliver is entwined with your own, yet it's not properly bonded to you. You're in great danger."

"When am I not?" Maia slapped Ami on the shoulder and started the long walk to the top of the green hill their Vanguardians had crouched behind.

"You don't understand," Ami said, running to catch up with her. "The excess fire you've absorbed has pushed all your magical enhancements beyond their original limits. Though they appear to be returning to normal over time, you've greatly increased your destructive capability."

"That doesn't sound so dire."

"It's *very* dire," Ami said. "We weren't meant to contain this much raw, primordial magic. It wants to be released, to return to its home beyond the Veil. And it will not be a pleasant passing. Essentially, you've turned yourself into a bomb."

"A bomb that can win this war. Besides, I feel fantastic. Never better."

"For now. You're filled with adrenaline. It will wear off. Our slivers grant us an affinity for and protection from a particular element, to a point. You've crossed that line. That's not to speak of the fact that Heart's Oath, by its design, may return even stronger now that it has a more powerful foe to contend with."

Ami sniffled beneath her helmet and turned away from Maia, shaking her head. "How could you do this to yourself? I don't know how to fix this. Even if we're able to convince the Emperor to undo Heart's Oath, I can't save you."

Maia summoned her helmet and placed a gauntleted hand on Ami's shoulder. "I needed to do this, so I could fight. I couldn't leave it all to you. I didn't have time to think about consequences. Those can wait until after the battle is won and Ren is back safe with us. I'm sorry, Ami. Okay?"

They walked the rest of the way in silence.

At the top of the hill, they crouched by a small herd of grazing goats. Noctis loomed in the distance, its walls gripped by five stone claws that pulsated and crackled with arcane energy. Black, hateful smoke curled up from several sections of the city. At this distance, Grimclaw was barely larger than her thumb. It stood at attention near the base of the mountain beneath the Imperial Palace. Another Behemoth, a black and yellow mass Maia couldn't quite make out, prowled beyond the town wall.

"A humanoid spider hybrid," Ami said, likely making use of her Perception. "Lightning attribute."

"Name?" Maia asked.

Ami's finger clinked against her chin. "Boltspinner."

"Good one," Maia said. She knew that beneath her helmet, Ami shared her smile.

For a moment, things felt like they used to, back in the days when they gave Behemoths silly names before they set off to crush them with their giant war machines, together, as a team.

For a moment, Maia felt a second beating in her breast, a resonating thump right next to her own proud heart. It was gone before she could open her mouth.

"What else do you see?" Maia said, ignoring the lingering echo beneath her sternum.

"Multiple bands of Imperial citizens engaged in active protest," Ami said. "Some Iron Wardens stand with them."

"Really." Maia leaned in. *They finally stood up. Good for them.*

"I also see packs of Ferals roaming the streets. Lion's Roar appears inactive, as expected. We'll adjust our strategy. Since your condition has improved, you should accompany me. I suggest we employ a stealthy approach. They'll still expect us to be piloting our Vanguardians. Scarlet and Viridian will distract the Behemoths while we infiltrate the Imperial Palace. We will return to aid them in defeating the Behemoths once we have secured Ren and Cobalt and, if possible, the Emperor."

Are you going to be okay on your own? Maia thought, directing her thoughts at Scarlet.

I would be better with you guiding me. We'll manage, Scarlet replied.

"Stealthy it is," Maia said. She and Ami climbed into their Vanguardians.

Viridian took to the sky, swooping back on verdant wings to grab Scarlet by the shoulders with her four clawed limbs. With a mighty flap, they took off toward Noctis.

This time, no projectiles, magical or otherwise, assaulted them as they crossed over the outer wall in the morning light. After Viridian cleared the parapet atop the massive barrier, she took a sharp dive and leveled out into a steady glide over the city streets. Maia and Ami dropped from their Vanguardians, veering their fall toward a narrow alley.

Two Ferals, concealed by her angle of entry, looked up at Maia as she descended. She landed in a roll and ripped her newly restored falchions from her back. A quick leap brought her to the pair. As she passed, she lashed out, taking both of their heads in a flash of steel.

"Stealth isn't so bad," Maia said as the Ferals quietly burned to nothing. "I still get to cut things." But what she really wanted was to release her flames. They growled and rumbled inside her, begging to be set free. Her arms and legs tingled. If Ami was right, and she nearly always was, that tingling would likely become a burning heat before long.

Ami leaped onto the closest rooftop. Maia joined her. From their vantage point, they watched Scarlet touch down in the part of town where Ren had fought Grimclaw. Viridian landed next to her and let out a keening cry.

Grimclaw stayed where it was. Gashes covered its chest, and its forehead horn was missing, likely broken during its tumble through the outer wall. The sight of its remaining pincer caught Maia's breath in her throat, forcing her to look away.

Long, spindly legs brought Boltspinner over the outer wall from the opposite direction. Its body was covered in mottled black flesh, cracked and broken, with shiny yellow carapace gleaming through the gaps. It reared and walked upright on its four back legs while the front four, each capped with a jagged spike, swayed through the air as it moved. Atop its gigantic abdomen, Maia spied a fleshy volcano molded onto its back, studded with spinnerets.

It stopped and screeched at the Vanguardians, mandibles crackling with sparks.

"So, all we need to do is get by that," Maia said, pointing to Grimclaw, "after we find a way through that." She gestured to the throng of roughly four dozen Ferals milling in the streets ahead. "How do you propose we stealth our way through?"

Ami drew her collapsed metal bow from her back. With a flick of her wrist, the green limbs snapped into place and the metal bowstring tightened. She reached to the quiver at her right hip, drew a thin, metal arrow from the dozens waiting there, and nocked it.

Ami raised her bow to the sky and loosed, blasting them both with wind as the missile whistled into the air and vanished in the light of the morning sun.

"You missed," Maia said.

"No. I didn't."

She followed Ami's pointing finger to the throng of Ferals. One went stiff as the arrow descended from the heavens, entered the top of its head, and passed clean through to the ground. It toppled onto its back as its body burst into flames in death. The rest of the Ferals jerked their heads about, braying and squealing.

"They will soon disperse in an attempt to locate us," Ami said. "With me." She took off into a dash across the roof.

"'With me,' huh?" Maia grumbled. "I'm supposed to be the leader."

They darted and leaped across the rooftops of Noctis, cutting down to street level to avoid detection when they neared the black mage towers peppered around the city. Ami launched arrows to distract or scatter gatherings of Ferals, keeping their presence as slight as possible. They had to backtrack more than once to avoid crowds of rioters banging weapons on shields and crying for the dissolution of the Empire.

They were entitled to their anger, so Maia and Ami left them alone to sweep through the capital.

When they neared the edge of the last residential block before the markets, Maia and Ami rested atop a flat-roofed townhouse while Ami plotted their route. Maia spared a moment of her attention for their Vanguardians, who were locked in combat.

Scarlet swung wide at Boltspinner while Viridian swooped down in lazy arcs. The spider-thing weaved around the blows, screeching back in defiance.

After a few short exchanges, Boltspinner retreated. It dropped down, using its front legs to support its body, and inverted into a handstand. The fleshy mound on its back, now aimed at Scarlet, pulsated as a cone of thin, crackling web strands spun toward her. Scarlet sidestepped it, but a second spray followed, catching her and clinging to her chest.

Boltspinner bounced back onto its rear legs. Viridian swooped down from the rear. Another funnel of webs fluttered into the air, tangling Viridian's wings as she passed and sending her into a nosedive. Her crash dug a long rut through three city blocks before she came to a rest on her stomach, neck and head twisted beneath her body.

The spider reached around to its back, grabbing more strands of glistening web and casting them at Scarlet. When Scarlet was fully wound up, Boltspinner pressed its sparking mandibles to the strands in its claws. Bolts of lightning arced through the web and over Scarlet's red metal frame. The ground shook as Scarlet collapsed in a rumbling, smoking heap.

"No!" Maia cried, loud enough to draw the attention of a nearby trio of Ferals. They screeched in their gargled pitch. In the distance, others took up the call until most of the Ferals in the city had joined the mournful chorus.

Grimclaw turned, following the disturbance back to the source of its cousin's cries, and started a slow march across the courtyard toward the markets.

"We're compromised!" Ami shouted. "Run, now!"

Maia spared one last look at Scarlet. *I'm sorry. I'll come back for you. I promise.*

They rolled from the roof and took off through a side street that ran at an angle to Grimclaw's trampling path. The earth raged with each of the Behemoth's steps. Around the next bend, roughly a dozen Ferals waited for them. The time for stealth had passed. The fire blistering within Maia demanded release, so she gathered a fist-sized ball of flames in her palm, just enough to clear the path. With her hand ablaze, she leaped into the air, slamming the fireball into the ground in front of the gathered Ferals.

Cobblestone and dirt exploded in every direction as a wave of rolling flames split to either side of her. When the dust settled, Maia was crouched in a shallow trench that extended through the crumbled remains of at least two buildings on either side of the street. Nothing remained of the Ferals but floating flecks of ash.

Maia clenched her trembling hand to keep the screaming heat inside her at bay. Searing pain shot through her arm, as if it was cooking from within. She had only meant to release a little fire, but a torrent of heat flew through the gates keeping her slivers in check. If she hadn't closed them in time...

Grimclaw's shadow spread over them before she could chide her carelessness. Ami slapped Maia on the shoulder as she zipped past her. Maia followed her in a zig-zag path that took them through the outskirts of the market district. The Green Pilot's bow thrummed over and over, sending arrows through Feral masks and clearing paths through their lines. When the encroaching, thrashing mass of skinless muscle and yellowing bone grew too thick at the end of one avenue, Maia pulled out in front and threw herself into the bottleneck. She ignored the angry claws scraping at her armor as the glowing edges of her falchions separated limbs and heads from bodies.

When the horde spilled past Maia, Ami stowed her bow and laid into the Ferals with her taloned gauntlets, thrusting into their flesh with precise knife-hand strikes.

"Too many!" Ami shouted as another rush of snarling Ferals poured around the corner. "Jump! Now!"

Maia crouched and leaped high into the air at Ami's command, throwing off any Ferals who had clung to her. A furious gale of rippling wind tore down the street and slammed into the pack, throwing the entire mob back the way it came. The monsters careened like leaves in a hurricane, bouncing and splattering against the sides of buildings until the street was lined with broken and burning bodies.

Maia landed next to Ami. "Why didn't you lead with that?"

Ami hunched over, supporting herself on her knees. She was panting. "My injuries no longer permit me to exert myself the way I used to. Large efforts leave me winded."

"Was that a joke?" Maia said.

"Oh, no…"

"Really? Because it was—"

"No. Look."

Maia followed Ami's gaze. Grimclaw broke into a short thundering run and drove its shoulder into the side of a sky-scraping mage tower. The structure groaned and started to topple, blocking the sun's light as it sped toward them.

"Can't outrun that." Maia set her blades on her back and widened her stance. Her Barrier, strong as it had become, couldn't stop a falling tower.

But her fire could. One concentrated burst from her twin infernos would be enough to shatter the falling tower and throw the debris clear. That debris would have to land somewhere, but hot raining stone would be the least of Noctis' problems if she was unable to put the reins back on her rampaging flames.

While Maia debated whether to give in to the fire's call, something hard slammed into her back and sent her flying. Her head whipped back as wind whistled in her ears. When she looked down, she found two green metal arms gripping her around the waist. Maia couldn't even begin to fathom how much wind Ami had to summon to hurl them both so high into the air.

Grimclaw reached up and swung as they cleared his head. Maia's heart seized in her chest. Another blast of wind hit them at an angle, sending them veering past the black claw's arc.

They flew over the market, past the courtyard, and over the Imperial Palace, where they reached the zenith of their flight and started to descend. Maia slapped Ami's forearms until she released her grip. A wide dome of beautiful stained glass framed by white stone rushed toward them.

As Maia's armored body shattered the glass like a bullet, she called her Barrier, placing it at an angle against the ground. She landed on her makeshift ramp feet-first and skidded down its length and onto carpeted floor, her metal boots and fingers tearing long ruts in the fabric as she ground to a halt. A moment later, Ami sailed through the hole Maia had made and threw her palms forward. A steady stream of air slowed her descent and threw her back into the air. Touching down near a pillar, she dismissed her helmet, retching up blood as she leaned on the sturdy marble for support.

So that's what that looks like. Maia moved to help her, but Ami waved her away. She reached into the case she carried at the small of her back, drew a syringe of Amplifier, and jammed the needle into her neck. She winced as the luminous red drained into her.

"Are you okay?" Maia said.

"I've re-opened several of my internal wounds. I'm approaching my limit." Ami gestured to the long stairway at the end of the hall and summoned her helmet. "I'm not familiar with the Imperial Palace's layout. However, if I were a tyrannical dictator, I would place my throne room atop a set of stairs like this."

"The place looks deserted. Are we sure the Emperor is still here? And why haven't any guards come?"

Four shapes descended the stairs in unison, each clad in white-enameled plate armor and large, crested helms. Two hauled huge rifles identical to the one Maia had stared down at Castle Blackwood.

Ami sighed. "I would have preferred if you hadn't asked that question."

Maia's right eye tingled. "Those rifles can punch through Pilot armor. Whatever you do, don't get shot."

"I don't intend to," Ami said, her tone low and polished.

They drew their weapons as the armored guards rested theirs on their comrade's shoulders for support. Maia pushed her flames deep into her chest and gripped her falchions tighter.

Four honor guards. That was all that stood between her and the Emperor, and beyond that, an end to the war she had waged for seven long years.

Hold on, Ren. I'm coming. Just hold on a little longer.

The sound of grinding stone and low voices brought Ren from her haze and dragged her back to the throne room. How long had she been away from herself this time?

Professor's voice dropped like a dagger's tip aimed at a tender stomach. "I did as you asked. The results were...unexpected."

"I didn't want this!" The voice belonged to the cloaked woman stomping behind Professor as he appeared from behind a pillar. She was the one Ren saw standing with her father when they came to Noctis to fight Grimclaw. Her voice held two separate tones, one dragging slightly behind the other. "Couldn't you have just healed him?"

"General Valerius would have defied us again. I improved him. I made him more compliant."

"What did you do to him?" Ren said, interrupting their bickering. She gripped the edges of the throne and straightened.

The cloaked woman knelt at the base of the steps leading to the throne and bowed her head. Hair whiter than fresh snow spilled from beneath her tattered hood. "My apologies, Ren. It's Ren now, isn't it? I prefer that to Serenia, if I'm being honest." Her words dripped like honey tinged with a hint of poison. "To answer your question, there was an accident. Professor made some...drastic decisions in order to save your father's life. He's not quite a Feral and not quite what he was. But he's alive, and that's what matters. I want you to know that this isn't what I intended. Your father was a good man. Despite the atrocities he committed in the Emperor's name, he deserved to be forgiven. He deserved better than this. I'm sorry. Truly."

"Who are you?" Ren seethed through gritted teeth.

The hood shifted as the ghostly woman lifted her head. "I'm your mother, Ren."

"No." Ren pressed her back into the throne. "How? I saw you die. The roof came down on you, it... How are you alive?"

"Well, not alive, I suppose. Not really." Lithe fingers pulled the hood back, revealing a sharp jaw, jet black eyes, and gray skin. Her veins pulsed with an otherworldly blue glow. "And I'm not who you think I am."

"I don't understand. You said you were my mother."

"Aurelia Valerius is dead. And dead she will remain. The Emperor kept what was left of her frozen in a tomb in case she could one day be revived. She was too powerful, too important to be left to rot in the ground. The damage done to her body, though...she could never be like me." Black eyes drifted to the floor. "You should know that Serenia Valerius is dead, too. She slept for so long, she became her own dream, and then she...she..."

The horrid creature shook her mane of ghost-white hair. "Sorry. I'm running out of...me. I unravel a bit when my blood gets thin. What I'm trying to say is, I'm not who you think I am, and you're not who you think you are. But I *am* your mother, Ren." She grimaced, baring white fangs. "Here. This will be easier than words."

She stood and removed her cloak. When she saw what was beneath, Ren's hearts slammed into her sternum, as eager to escape her chest as she was to flee the throne room. Ginger steps brought the woman up the stairs. She reached out and placed her hand on Ren's forehead, gripping her skull to keep her from squirming away.

Ren's back arched as images and colors and smells and sounds pressed their way through the cracks of her mind. She struggled against them, but the woman claiming to be her mother pushed harder, overwhelming her with memories that weren't her own.

She wanted to scream. She wanted to run. In the end, all she could do was shatter against the wave.

Shh. It's okay. A voice, frosted and close, drifted through Ren's mind. *It's a lot to take in, but I promise I'll show you everything. Who you are. Where you came from. Before that, how about introductions? This is the first time we've properly met, after all.*

The ashen ghost let go of Ren's head, keeping her mental hold on her as she sat on the throne's armrest. *I've taken so many names in death. Lately, I've gone by Ash. That's all that's left of a person when their life's spark has burned and faded to black. It seemed fitting. My own name didn't suit me anymore. I was no longer the woman who owned it. But now that you're here, with me, I'm finally starting to feel like my old self again.*

She reclined, letting the weight of her blue, gold-trimmed armor settle, and traced her fingers along Ren's cheek.

Hello, Ren. My name is Leona Carver. And I'm so very glad that you've come home to me.

Chapter 44
Puppeteer

After dealing with the Emperor's honor guard, Maia began the long climb to the throne room, taking the stairs in threes. The twisting pinch of the Kith prodded the back of her skull with every step, and Maia regretted not asking Heretic anything about the threat she was about to face.

Having never been so close to the Emperor's seat of power, Maia didn't realize that the throne room doors were meant to open outward. When she kicked one of the golden portals as hard as she could, the force of the blow sent it twisting off its hinges. She yelled, "knock knock!" as she and Ami stepped over the fallen door and entered the dim-lit throne room, weapons drawn. Her eyes darted about, looking for threats.

She found three. The Kith, hovering a foot off the ground near the throne dais. A creature that looked like a Feral, but twice as large and wearing the face of a man. And lounging on the throne next to Ren, a Pilot encased in the same deep blue armor and panther-styled helmet, all trimmed with gold, that had once belonged to the love of Maia's life.

"What the fuck?"

The words had barely left Maia's lips when three arrows whistled past her head from behind. The Kith flicked his fingers at each arrow, shattering them with short bursts of rippling air. He made a fist and jerked his hand. Ami smacked into Maia's shoulder as she flipped past her and crashed onto her back. Maia dropped into a fighting stance as the hulking Feral-thing charged at her with thumping steps.

"Stop!" the Blue Pilot boomed. The beast paused mid-charge. "Arcturus, to me."

"Arcturus?" Maia searched for his face in the beast's stretched features and permanent grin. Her stomach tightened. "What did they do to you?"

"Don't worry about him." The Blue Pilot patted Ren, whose vacant stare made Maia's heart sink. "Worry about me."

Blue metal and black, hardened glass separated and slid behind a smooth mane of ghostly hair. The face beneath the helm sent a wave of numbness rolling from Maia's head down to her toes. "Hello, my love." Leona curled her cold, gray lips into a grin. Faint blue strings of light pulsed under colorless skin that had once born an olive luster, warm and full of life.

Maia's mind raced, trying in vain to catch up to what she was seeing. It faltered, tripping over itself and collapsing in a tangled mess. "You're dead."

"Clearly, I'm not, though not for your lack of trying."

"How are you here? I don't..." Maia's falchions dangled in her grip.

"I knew you would come for the Emperor to force him to put an end to all of this. You'll be happy to know that Noctis is now free of Caelus' reign of tyranny. I was worried that killing him might unmake me since he was the necromancer who raised me, but it looks like the rules don't apply to me anymore." Leona studied Maia hard. "Speaking of breaking rules... What did you do to yourself? You're practically exploding with energy."

Leona reached for the smooth blue metal spear affixed to her back and turned it over in her palm. It extended to its full six-foot length, placing its razor tip against Ren's throat. "Throw down your weapons and take off your helmet."

Maia looked to Ami, who shuddered against a flickering wall of force holding her on the ground, and to Ren, who hadn't reacted to the line of blood trickling down her neck. She hurled her falchions at the ground, sending them bouncing and clanging off to the sides, and broke apart her helmet.

"Thank you, love." Leona collapsed her spear and replaced it on her back. "Thanks to the Emperor's efforts, and due in no small part to the knowledge I've brought back from beyond the Veil, I'm stronger than ever. I could probably reach you with my Telepathy through your helmet without touching you if I focused, but I've taken enough chances with you already." Leona looked down. "Amisrala? Is that you in there?" She tapped Ami with her foot, then stomped her chest plate. "I'm very curious to know how you survived all this time without my knowing. Unfortunately, we don't have time to catch up. I need to speak to my wife."

With uncanny speed, Leona sprung at Maia and slapped her palm down on her forehead. The full weight of her Pilot gift of Telepathy bore down on Maia like a landslide, battering her until she collapsed under the assault.

Maia cringed as Leona sent her will slithering into her mind. *I'll show you what I showed Ren,* Leona said, her words echoing in Maia's brain. *It broke her, I'm afraid. Let's see how you fare.*

On occasions where words failed her, Leona often asked Maia to connect with her like this. She would gently push images and shadows of sentiments to Maia so she could be better understood.

There was nothing gentle about the thick needle of light and color thrusting through Maia's mind. It unfurled into sights. Sounds. Pain. She fought back the queasiness rising in her stomach, unable to do anything but see what Leona wanted her to see.

First, there was darkness. She found herself floating in endless warm night flecked with distant lights. The nothingness bore down on her, so heavy. So full. Crushing despair blended with the tingling of countless threads trailing off her spark-like self to the whole of infinity, to every other wandering soul returned to the wellspring of creation.

The warmth turned to a cold so harsh it burned her heart in her chest. She opened her eyes and screamed. Bolts of torment punctured her smooth edges, pinning her into a body that was no longer hers. Her limbs creaked to life. Her defiant wails painted the walls. Hands scraped. Teeth gnashed. She had no control over any of it. Her mind protested, but her body *wanted.* It was only the thick chains binding her to the altar that kept her from devouring the mages gathered around her.

They labored over her, but for how long? Days? Weeks? Time blended into one unending torturous moment that made her Pilot augmentation feel like a pinprick in comparison.

Potions and spells. Luminous hate, manufactured and thick, pumping through her veins. Patches of magic sewed over what Heretic had laid, crafting seething fabric that had no right to be.

Finally, when their work was done, she spilled out through herself. The pain fell away like a curtain. Cool air touched her lips. She could taste it. It had been eons since she had tasted anything.

It was sour. Wrong. No matter how hard she prayed for oblivion to sweep in and take her back into its warm bosom, she remained.

Occasionally, her heart shuddered. Boundless energy came in waves from the sloshing bright blood they filled her with. She followed its flow to her core, to the sliver of magic Heretic had driven into her soul when she remade her into a goddess. Crackling lightning whispered to her. *Friend,* it said, recognizing her as one who also came from its home beyond the Veil. She spoke to it in a tongue lost to the dawn of time, a language she had no way of knowing, and told the sliver what she wanted.

Since they were such good friends, it shaped to her needs in moments. Lightning became fire. The robed necromancers encircling her lit up like candles in the dark, waxing and waning until they were nothing. She found the strength she always had in life, the rush of purpose that had allowed her to withstand every hardship the world could throw at her, and used it to break her bindings.

"What am I?" she said to the one mage she had spared, resplendent in his crown and flowing white and gold robes adorned with the emblem of a lion.

"A Lich." The man's voice wavered despite its commanding silver tenor. "In life, you were Leona Carver. Now, you are my greatest creation. I've brought you back from beyond the Veil, uniting your mind and soul with your corporeal form. Yet you are no mere undead beast. You are the harbinger. The first of many. The cure for death itself. You are perfect."

She reached down to the weave of magic inside her and found that she very nearly was. She could read the spells sewn into her, saw them splayed out in the oldest tongues. She pronounced their true names. The magics bound to her body flared inside her like blazing suns. She persuaded her sliver to become lightning once more, awakening the gifts granted to her through her Vanguardian bond.

Her Telepathy grabbed the man's mind without her having to touch him. Before, drawing a single memory from him would have taken everything she had. With her newfound skill, she peeled away his layers and read his mind like pages in a book.

This pathetic, trembling thing was Emperor Caelus Noctis III. He pushed back against her. She took hold of the thin line binding him together and snapped it like a twig. She pressed the ends together, leaving her touch on them. He belonged to her, now.

"Why?" she asked. He opened to her will, allowing her to delve deeper.

Cobalt. She was meant to command him and lead Noctis' armies across the continental nations like a scythe threshing through wheat and chaff, culminating in a grand battle against their greatest foe, the only true threat standing in their way.

"Maia." A ripple of longing tinged with hatred fell over her. Was that name always such a hideous thing to her?

Caelus led her deeper into the catacombs beneath the Imperial Palace to where Cobalt waited for her in his steel prison. She had no intention of being anyone's puppet ever again, but the Emperor's plan wasn't without merit. Every inch of her body screamed for revenge against the one she loved, the one who stole her life.

Though she had coaxed her sliver to become lightning again and found she could still summon her armor and use all her Pilot gifts, the blue panther ignored her. *Get out,* he told her. *You're not my Leona. Not anymore.*

She wasn't anyone's Leona anymore. Her pieces didn't line up the way they once had. How much had she changed that her own Vanguardian could deny her?

When she had gathered enough shards of her broken nerve to act, she commanded Caelus to offer his curved ceremonial dagger to her so that she could end her suffering on her own terms.

The blade barely started its work when a sharp twist in the back of her mind stayed her hand. Like her other Pilot abilities, her Hunter Sense had persisted in death. As she wandered through the dusty catacombs, the foreign bite grew keener until, at last, she found him.

She summoned her armor in a great flash of lightning and set upon the Kith with her spear, driving him back through the tunnels and up into the annals of the white marble palace resting atop the catacombs like a tombstone. She spent all her rage on him until only grief remained, and only then was she able to hear him.

He told her that his people often sent a single envoy to worlds they sought to conquer. Like their Feral foot soldiers, they couldn't gather in numbers for fear that Heretic's Pilots might discover them. Upon his arrival in their world, he approached the Emperor and offered his services as an adviser a short time before she was ripped from beyond the Veil. Caelus never knew what he really was, only that the gifts and knowledge he brought would lead to power beyond the Emperor's wildest dreams.

But she saw the truth of him. And though he was her enemy, the Kith known to his people as Professor had much to offer her: new blood to replace the weakened sludge in her veins and a way to regain the life that had been stolen from her.

All the would-be puppet had to do was become the puppeteer by taking control of the Empire and seeking the revenge she had already set her mind on. With the resources of the Empire at their disposal, the Kith had a hope of survival. Didn't they deserve that? Didn't everyone deserve a new beginning? She knew she did. The Nocteans had squandered their many chances. Their dark work had perverted her into a creature of nightmares. Didn't the Empire and its people deserve to be punished for that?

Maia gritted her teeth. "You sold them the world."

"I did," Leona said. "Part of it, anyway. The Kith will occupy the Noctean Empire, and we'll leave them to their devices until it's time for them to flee from their makers yet again."

"And the people of the Empire? What happens to them?"

Leona shrugged. "Labor. Raw materials. I wouldn't worry about it. They chose to follow a tyrant. This is their reward for being too weak to stand up and say 'no.' Their lives are a small price to pay for peace, and with them, I'll buy back everything you took from me. Everything I deserve. I'm doing this for us. For her."

Maia's eyes flicked to Ren. She still hadn't moved to wipe away the spot of blood on her throat.

Yes, Maia. Leona's voice hissed inside her mind. *For her. For my daughter. Rather,* our *daughter.*

The memory of the thing Leona created from their shared blood in that sunken altar filled her mind with tentacles and teeth.

No. Leona pulled that recollection from her focus and thrust something from her own mind in front of Maia.

Hooves thundered through a forest bathed in moonlight. The rider didn't slow as he tossed a wrapped bundle at her feet and charged away as fast as his lathered horse would take him.

The bundle contained knives. Swords. Arrows. Crossbow bolts. All ruddied with crusted blood. Maia's blood.

She brought them home, to a circular chamber in the catacombs. There was a cylinder of steel and glass fed by vats of frothing liquid perched on metal struts. Scrapings from the recovered weapons mingled with the drained blood of a dead woman. So much more went into that container, but the blood had been the key, the most important part.

"You made her. You made her from us." Maia shivered despite the hot slivers blazing inside her. She could see the resemblance now when she looked at Ren. The blue ferocity of her eyes. The ruddy red of her cheeks. She looked so much like her mothers.

"Noctis has been trying to make new Pilots for years," Leona said. "None of the candidates became successful replacements for you, so they were discarded. Professor showed us where they went wrong, using me as a map to Heretic's secrets. We had everything we needed, but we couldn't wait sixteen years for Ren to grow up. We gave her two hearts, like a Feral, so she could handle the stress of accelerated growth."

"How could you do this? Why? Why would you... *Why?*"

"Because I deserve to live, Maia!" Leona screamed. "The world took *everything* from me. It's taken from you, too. The difference between us is that I'm willing to do something about it."

Leona's hand drifted from Maia's forehead down to her scar. "The Kith learned long ago how to transfer their consciousness into copies of themselves. They promised to place me in a new body to keep my soul from being torn apart when my artificial blood runs dry and I finally die for good. They even let me choose the body." She pressed her thumb along the crease of Maia's scar. "How could I choose anything but her? A perfect union. You and I, in equal measure. The family I always wanted, one that can *never* be taken from me. We were gods, Maia.

But despite all we do for the undeserving wretches of this world, we're treated like the lowest of the low. Shouldn't we be allowed to have one thing for ourselves? Don't I deserve this one thing for all I've done for this world?"

"You had one thing! You had me."

"For how long? Another year? Two?" Leona sneered at her. "You're like a burning brand. Nobody can hold onto you forever. Edgar tried. You burned him and left him for me. You would have left me, too, like everyone else. I needed something that would make you stay. A child. A family. You wouldn't leave, then. But you had to go and ruin everything."

"That thing you made, back at Kasper's altar, it was hurting you," Maia said. This time, Leona let her linger on the nightmarish mass of teeth and tentacles, and the way it tore into its mother's flesh as she tried to hold it to her breast. "You made that thing for me. I killed it for *you.*"

"That time, I failed. This time, with Professor's help..." When Leona looked at Ren, her lips pulled into an awed smile. "She's *perfect.* You wouldn't believe how much potential her body holds. But I couldn't occupy her right away, not until the Kith arrived with what we needed. Serenia Valerius never would have woken up from her coma. I needed Arcturus' support, so I told him I would give our daughter's body to her. Her mind and soul would live on, and when I joined with her, she would be preserved."

Arcturus ground his exposed teeth. His muscles flexed and twitched, but he didn't move from where he was standing near the dais.

"In the end, I could only pass on her memories. The rest had to be thrown away. And when I join with Ren, those memories will have to make way for mine. Her soul, replaced by mine. It's been a kindness, letting Serenia live on this long. It's time for her to finally rest."

"You're a monster," Maia said. "Maybe dying made you this way. Maybe you were always this horrible, and I was too blinded by love to see it. All I know is you had a hundred chances to kill me. You shouldn't have wasted them."

"I didn't," Leona said. She slid her thumb across Maia's right eyebrow. "Last I heard, you stopped healing, but look at you now. I can't even see where my bullet tore you apart."

The remembrance of a flash of red stole Maia's breath. "That was you."

"I got impatient. The goal was always to kill you, of course, but this? This is what I really wanted." Leona leaned in closer, placing her lips next to Maia's ear. "When you cross over to the other side, you bring everything with you. All your memories. I wanted to fill you with pain. I wanted you to know it was me who undid you before I sent you to the other side. Attacking you head-on was too much of a risk. Ren was supposed to remind you what it was like to be a Pilot, so you would go back to being a good little defender of the masses and I could lure you into a trap. Either that, or she would kill you. The fact that you two grew so close is more than I could have hoped for. Now, I have something more to take from you. She's become a better weapon than I had ever planned."

"She isn't a weapon! She's a person! And I won't let you take her from me."

Leona's face twisted. Her voice projected into Maia's mind. *It's not too late, you know. You could come back. Be with me again. With her. If you side with me, with the Kith, then you don't have to die.*

Maia shook her head, straining against Leona's mental grip. "But she would. You want to take away everything she is and replace it with...*you*. I can't let her die. I..."

"Love her," Leona finished. "You gave your heart to *me*. You said the words. You belong to me. If you truly want to give me up, if you want to throw away your chance to make amends, fine. I'm going to take Ren's body, and with her dual-natured sliver, I'll take control of Scarlet and Cobalt. Then, I'm going to send you screaming to the other side of the Veil. If I can't have all of you, I'll have to settle for the bit of you that exists in Ren."

"You. Can't kill. Maia," Ami gasped. The rippling waves of force drove her harder into the ground, cracking the floor.

"And why not?" Leona motioned to Professor. The air around Ami went still. "Speak. Do you know something I don't?"

Ami coughed and wheezed beneath her helmet. "Quite a few things. For one, I know about Heart's Oath. The curse you placed on Maia without realizing. When one of you dies, the other will follow. It's killing Maia because it believes you're deceased. I believe it's taken this long to run its course due to you not being completely dead. If you kill Maia, *she* will be completely dead. You'll die too, shortly after. And when Maia dies, the unbound sliver within her will release.

Everyone in the capital will be destroyed."

Leona squinting at Maia as if she was looking clear through her at something else beyond. "She's right. Huh. That explains so much." She kicked Ami in the side, sending her skidding across the floor and into a marble pillar. "Well, we all make mistakes."

"Then make it right. Break the curse," Maia said. "I know you can. Break it and fight me. If you want me, here I am. Take your anger out on me. Leave the rest of the world alone."

"The world is the point of it all, Maia! You should be grateful. I'm going to save us all from the Noctean Empire. I'm going to march up to Sinadaria and grind the elves living there to dust for what they did to my father. I'm going to sweep through Kaldrsteinn, find Edgar's people, and wipe them out as atonement for the way he treated you. I'm going to every nation on this fucking continent to find everyone who thought that trade sanctions and political posturing would be enough to stop the Empire from perverting the laws of nature. I didn't ask to come back. But I'm here. And with the Kith's help, I'm going to make the world a better place. You'll see."

"It is time," Professor said. "We must go. Now."

Leona tilted her head to Arcturus. "Keep Maia here, but don't kill her yet. Feel free to tear the green one in half if she tries to follow us. Make sure Maia watches. I'm off to slip into someone a little more comfortable."

Ren stood and trudged after them, eyes rimmed with tears, hurried along by the undulating force of Professor's magic.

"Before I go," Leona said, "I have a question for you."

"Why not just pull the answer out of my head?" Maia snapped.

"I could. But I want to hear it from you. Tell me: what happened to Kasper?"

"Let Ren go, and I'll tell you."

Leona shrugged. "I know you didn't kill him. You're not that kind of person. He'll find me when this is all over. He adores me. I just wish that his love was enough. Goodbye, Maia."

Her hold remained, though Maia could feel it weakening as Leona moved further away. "Ren!" Maia shouted as they disappeared behind a row of pillars. "Don't let them tell you who you are! You can be whoever you want to be! You're not their weapon! Remember what you said! Don't let anybody place a finger on your trigger ever again! I'm coming for you, okay? Hold on!"

The sound of grinding stone, followed by a thud, reached Maia as she fell free of Leona's grasp. She ran to where Ami had fallen, but a thick muscled arm bashed her in the chest and threw her to the other side of the throne room like she weighed nothing.

A mix of pity and rage swirled inside Maia as she looked upon the thing Arcturus had become. He took two thumping steps toward her, then stopped. His shoulders and neck were fused together, so he had to bend at the waist to look down at the green metal arrowhead protruding from his thigh.

"Good shot," Maia said.

"I was aiming for his head. I missed," Ami said. She braced against the wall, her breath heaving and her bow quivering in her hands. "I never miss."

Maia threw herself into a roll, scooping up one of her falchions from the ground and summoning her helmet. "Arcturus! If you're still in there, I'm sorry! What they did to you... Even you don't deserve this. I'll end your suffering. I promise. I—"

The rest of her words seized in her throat as familiar phantom fingers darted in and clenched her heart. Her vision went red, then white. Arcturus' primal roar cut into her ears, scattering the stardust in her eyes. She convulsed against the tightening in her chest and collapsed onto her side.

When Arcturus turned from Maia and started a slow trudge toward Ami, two arrows sped past his head, striking marble. The third stuck in his neck, but Arcturus tore it out, bent it in his Blacksteel grip, and roared in wild defiance.

As convulsions wracked her body, all Maia could do was watch Arcturus' advance, knowing that there was nothing she could do to keep from losing her best friend a second time.

Chapter 45
Desperate Measures

The catacomb walls seemed tighter on Ren's return trip through the worn tunnels. Her legs had turned to cold jelly, like a newborn fawn taking its first steps, and she only kept pace through Professor's magical nudges at the small of her back. All the while, her captors bickered.

"*Song and dance?* That's what you think this was? You're so fucking rude," Leona said.

"The description is apt," Professor replied. "We have wasted too much valuable time catering to your infantile whims."

"As a result of my whims, we have two Pilots cornered, their Vanguardians have been captured, and we got to twist the knife a little. How can you be unhappy right now?"

The Kith turned to face her, though he continued to float down the tunnel. He jabbed a finger at Leona's armored chest. "You did not notify me of your plan to dispose of the Emperor prematurely."

"I thought you would be pleased. I meant it as a show of good faith. I've been holding him over your head for so long."

"Now I am left to wonder what axe has been left dangling in the Emperor's place, ready to descend on me."

"I think that's the first time you've used a metaphor! This calls for a celebration!"

Their threats and shouts faded into dull braying noise. Ren fell back inside herself again, so she wasn't there to hear them. Had she ever been anywhere? Or anyone?

She couldn't call herself Serenia. Perhaps she carried that girl's memories, but she wasn't her. And "Ren" was just a derivative of a dead girl's name, a reference to someone she never was and could never be. Still, she had grown quite attached to it. Hadn't she lived with it long enough to lay claim to it?

Did it matter? Could she even call herself human? Humans didn't have two hearts. Humans weren't built. Humans weren't *designed*.

Whatever came next, Ren didn't care. She was a thing. A vessel. She could only hope that her passing would be relatively painless.

As if anything in her life ever was.

They passed a familiar branch in the tunnel. The right path led to Cobalt, who was waiting for his new Pilot, one who would only disappoint him. The left led to danger if Kasper was to be believed. Professor's prodding brought her past the intersection and across the threshold of his laboratory before she could find the will to flee.

You wouldn't like what's down there, Leona said into her mind. *My advice is to give in. Don't fight. It'll only hurt more. Besides, this is best for everyone. Professor and the Kith are going to betray us, you know.*

Out of the corner of her eye, Ren idly watched Professor fiddle with the banded crystal apparatus sitting on a table far from the entrance to the laboratory. *How do you know?* she thought.

It's what I would do. Leona quirked a grin at her. *Once I take your body and regain control of Cobalt, I'll be able to fight back. I'm the only hope the world has. Besides. When my soul is back in a living body, the curse I cast on Maia won't hurt her anymore. She'll be saved. Don't you want that?*

Leona didn't wait for her response. She could feel what Ren wanted and knew that it hadn't taken Ren a fraction of a second to give up, to offer her life up if it would save Maia's. Seemingly satisfied, Leona let their connection fade and joined Professor by the projected image of Noctis that his crystal apparatus sketched onto empty air with strands of light.

Professor scratched a few symbols into a square-cut piece of flat crystal produced from his robes, and that was it. That was all it took to begin the end of the world.

Ren watched Noctis through the projected image. The five towers enclosing the capital crumbled, revealing intricate machinery like nothing she had ever seen before. Gears whirred. Long metal protrusions expanded and locked into place.

Arcane energy flowed up toward the tip of each curving tower, crackling and eager.

In perfect unison, five searing rays of light ripped into the sky. They traced a circular pattern in the air, inlaid with strange glyphs, then pulled back to settle at the edges of the carved sky.

The beams darkened, spitting haphazard gouts of purplish black that oozed over the pattern like congealed ink. The floating lake of dark magic bent into itself, pressing deeper into the sky until it tore upward, spilling into a swirling maelstrom of violet light and black smoke.

The Aperture had opened.

A gargantuan creature slithered down from the hole in the sky. A fresh pain, duller and more bludgeoning than anything her Hunter Sense had registered before, pulsed in Ren's mind. The whale-like monster blinked each of its four eyes in sequence, showing a complete disregard for the laws of nature as it swam through the sky in slow descending circles.

It dipped low, flattening a stretch of farmland far beyond the city's walls when it landed. Its sides pulsated. Flesh separated, revealing several puckered holes along its flank. From these expanding openings came a group of smaller Behemoths. Each looked like a half-formed, veined heart striding on four stilt-like legs, with two thin, many-jointed arms placed on either side of a hollow, toothless maw.

"What are those for?" Leona said.

A grin slipped into the edges of Professor's voice. "They are tasked with gathering the citizens of Noctis. We must replenish our forces."

Large, distended dragonflies the size of Ferals streamed around the smaller Behemoths, chattering and twitching the cruel stingers attached to their long abdomens. They swarmed over the city, joined by thousands of Ferals spilling forth from the whale-thing's sides.

Professor swiped his hand. The image shifted. Ren saw Grimclaw holding a silent vigil in the courtyard below the Imperial Palace. Another Behemoth, a strange spider monster, stood over two tangled masses of web. Splashes of red and green poked through gaps in the webbing.

Scarlet and Viridian. It was Ren's fault they had been captured and were now unable to help Maia and Ami as they fought for their lives against the monster that had once been her father.

No. Not *her* father. Serenia's father. Who was her father, then? Professor? Or did she only have mothers? Was that what Leona and Maia were to her?

Did a made thing even have parents? Or just engineers?

"I've delivered, true to my word," Leona said. "How long until your people arrive with whatever you need to fulfill your end of the bargain?"

"Come with me." Professor floated to the back wall of the chamber, where a thick black door was set seamlessly into the wall.

"I've always wondered what was back there," Leona said.

Professor scraped a nail across the door's surface, sketching glyphs that faded as soon as he completed them. When the final symbol vanished, the black door warped and rippled, slowly melting and spreading into an inky, circular puddle.

"What in the Blue Hells is this?" Leona said.

"You have seen our umbral portals before. This one has been suspended for immediate activation and calibrated for perfect accuracy. It leads to a secondary facility. I have what we need there."

"You lied to me." Leona's mailed fists shook at her sides. "You said the Kith would bring what you needed to perform the transfer. You could have put me in Ren's body at any time!"

"Had I done that, you would not have aided us."

"You know what I think? You were never going to help me." Leona reached for the spear at her back. "Nobody ever wants to help me. I should have killed you the first time we met."

The spear telescoped to its full length and froze in place, held fast by rippling air. With her free hand, Leona slapped a wire vial holder off a nearby table. Professor raised his hand too late to deflect it. Glass shattered against his scalp, drawing thin lines of blood.

Glowing, blue blood.

"Lying bastard." With Professor's gravity magic disrupted by the distraction, Leona hurled her spear into Professor's chest. "It's been your blood flowing through my veins all this time, keeping me alive. Empowering me. You never ran out. You just decided to stop sharing."

Professor snarled, revealing his white fangs. He panted as he spoke. "Correct.

Further: while I do have the equipment necessary to transfer your mind and soul into a new body, your assessment is accurate. I would have killed you before the transfer was complete."

His words sent an electric shiver through Ren. The haze parted, leaving her reeling in the light. "I was never going to be your vessel. I never truly had a purpose, after all."

Leona and Professor turned to look at her.

"I've been a fool." Ren pulled her attention from the banded crystal and the horde of nightmares flooding through the city walls and focused instead on the purple sheen of her revolver, resting in her belt on one of Professor's workbenches. "I was told when I awoke that I was to be a Pilot. I was given a path. A purpose. Then I was told that my purpose was to retrieve Scarlet for the Emperor and make my nation proud. You say that that was all a lie, that my design, my sole reason for existing, was to be a vessel. To sacrifice myself. Now, I learn that I was never even meant to serve that end. I was never truly meant for anything.

"All this time, I've been blindly following the destiny others have placed in front of me. And like you, Leona, I was ready to trade the world to save a life that mattered to me. The difference between us is that the life that matters most to you is your own. You care for nothing else. It seems that we're both failures, mother. But there's still time for me to make things right. If I have no purpose, no destiny, then I'm free to choose my own. That being the case, I'm choosing to end this madness."

Pitch-black eyes narrowed. Leona bristled. "No. You're still my weapon. You're my creation, and you *will* obey me. This walking piece of shit is going to keep his promise once I put a few more holes in him. You want to save Maia? Be a good little girl and *come here*."

"I'm not a little girl. And I'm not your weapon. Not any longer."

Ren dashed for her belt. She made it halfway to it before Professor plucked it up with his gravity magic and drew it into his waiting hand.

That was exactly where Ren needed it to be. She hadn't been making a move for her revolver. It had no shells left. But Ren's belt held more than that masterwork of Noctean craftsmanship.

She reached out to one of the compact bursts of flame trapped inside Kasper's many grenades, just as she had reached out to quell Maia's wall of fire in Thenmar's Crater. Instead of pushing the flame down, she pulled on it with as much might as her confused sliver would allow.

The grenade burst, setting off the others packed neatly in the pouch. The staccato beat of a dozen magical explosions threw Leona to the floor and propelled Professor backward into the spreading pool of shadow on the back wall. The portal bent inward and snapped, swallowing him. He writhed and slapped at his flaming robes as he sank into the dark portal. As Leona summoned her helmet and rose, Ren fell into a fighting stance, ready to receive her.

Before Leona could move, waves of rippling air rolled over her body. Professor's mangled hand protruded from the portal, trembling as he anchored himself to her.

"Help me!" Leona folded forward and gripped the edges of one of Professor's stone tables. "Without me, the world is doomed! Join me, and we can defeat the Kith together!"

"If I do, will you release Maia? Will you break the curse?"

Leona lifted her chin. Her fingers drew gashes in the stone as Professor pulled her toward the portal. "Never."

"Then you're on your own. I wish you good luck, mother."

Ren turned on her heels and fled from the chamber. Leona's furious screams beat against her back as she ran. As she rounded the corner, threw open the door to Cobalt's bay, and stumbled through the dark to the railing at the edge of the platform, Ren hoped that Leona would be a match for Professor in his injured state.

If not, and he ended her life for good, then Maia only had minutes left to live.

Heart's Oath relaxed its grip on Maia's chest, retreating as her flames coiled around it. She gasped and rolled onto her side, reaching for her falchion as the bite of her fire nipped at her from within, replacing the pain of a phantasmal grip with uncomfortable heat.

Though the curse's latest assault had left her winded and dizzy, it was far from the worst attack it had thrown at her. And since it hadn't killed her, it wouldn't be the last. Her flames would only delay it. The worst was yet to come.

As Maia stood, the earth trembled. Dust shook loose from the ceiling of the throne room and fell in thin curtains. Arcturus stopped pursuing Ami and looked upward as if staring through the marble ceiling and into the sky beyond it. Ami reeled and held her head. "So many," she said.

Maia felt it, too. A new presence, blunt and overwhelming. Smaller tingles in the back of her mind, like a swarm of fireflies across the night sky. Countless Ferals. And several Behemoths, smaller than usual.

Based on the sheer number of new threats lighting up her Hunter Sense, Maia was fairly certain that the Aperture had opened.

Three more arrows thudded into Arcturus' chest and snapped him out of his daze. He swept his Blacksteel arm over the shafts, bending and dislodging them. He ambled after Ami, whose hand worked furiously over the mouth of an empty quiver, lowered his shoulder, and charged. A summoned gust of wind threw Ami clear of his path, but he diverted his rush abruptly as she passed.

The trunk-like mass of his left arm caught Ami in the side of the head. She spun like a top and crashed into the Emperor's throne, toppling it.

"No!" Maia thrust her free hand out, reached inside herself, and drew upon her Barrier. A curved shield of red light sprung into existence at the center of the throne room.

Arcturus walked past it without stopping. Maia blinked against rolling nausea and dizziness and let her shield dissipate. No matter how sturdy it had become, her Barrier spell wouldn't do her any good if she was too dizzy to aim.

With what little remained of her fight trickling away, Maia collapsed to her knees. She couldn't save Ami from Arcturus. Ren might already be lost to her. And soon, Heart's Oath would send Maia to join her.

She clenched her falchion's handle tighter. For a fleeting moment, she thought of turning it on herself. In one precise thrust, she could stop Leona and end the Kith invasion. Without her constant pushing to keep her slivers at bay, her death would release them with enough force to destroy the capital and the five towers surrounding it.

Without anyone left to travel through the Aperture and destroy the master tower on the other side, the portal wouldn't close. If what Heretic said was true, that could mark the end of reality itself.

The blade fell from Maia's fingers. She dismissed her helmet and breathed in the stale air of the throne room. Squinting, she raised her hands and pointed them at Arcturus. If a precise thrust with her falchion wouldn't do, then she would make use of her other tools.

Flames wreathed Maia's arms. Tremors wracked her muscles as she struggled to keep the inferno raging inside her from spilling out. The strain of holding back so much screaming power caused her vision to waver even more. She hadn't kept a tight enough reign on her flames when she turned them loose on the streets of Noctis. For her attack to succeed, she would need to maintain control.

If she let the gate open too wide, Ami would be consumed by the spreading wildfire. If Maia didn't open them enough, Arcturus would stroll through her flames unhindered and crush Ami before she could recover.

No pressure, Maia thought. She shut her eyes, spread her fingers wide, and tried not to imagine what Ami's screams would sound like if she failed.

Chapter 46

Bonds

After feeling around in the dark for what seemed like an eternity, Ren found the hatch plates at the back of Cobalt's head. The low swishing sound they made when they unlocked coaxed a sigh of relief from her. Once inside the cabin, which was much smaller than Scarlet's, she dashed into the brilliant white beam of light shining at its center.

The world fell away. When her senses returned, Ren found herself back in the colorless cave. She didn't hear Cobalt approach from behind so much as she felt him peering at her.

"Serenia Valerius," the smoky beast purred. "You're back."

Ren scrunched up her face. "That's not my name. I... Please do not call me that."

Cobalt tilted his head. Shadowy ears perked. "You're distressed."

"An understatement." Ren felt heat welling up in her cheeks.

"Are you prepared?"

"I must be. I don't have a choice."

"Yes, you do. And you need to be certain that you want this. It *will* hurt, more than anything you've ever felt."

Ren shrugged one shoulder. "You don't know what I've felt."

"This won't fix it, you know," Cobalt said. "If anything, it will make it worse. Still, whatever hurt you... If it has a throat, we'll tear it out. If not, well. You'll still have me. We'll find *something* to tear."

"You were reluctant to make me your Pilot before. Did the pending destruction of the world change your mind?"

"I've had time to think. You confused me before. You have Leona's scent and traces of Sunder's as well."

"Blue and red, in equal measure. You knew what I was?"

Cobalt nodded. "I wasn't sure if you did. Though, there's more to you. More than the subtle whispers of your heritage. You're blue and red, but something more. Something new."

"I'm more?"

"You are. I can feel it, even now. I wasn't sure you were coming back. I told myself that if you did, I would go with you. I'm curious to see what happens next. For you to escape twice is a feat. That tells me you fight to keep your word. That's why I know I'm making the right choice by bonding with you."

"Even if it means facing Leona? What will you do, then?"

"My Leona is gone. What remains... I'll set her free, if it comes to that."

"It very well may." Ren shut her eyes as tight as she could and tipped her head back. She couldn't spare a single tear, even in that phantom realm. Not until the work was done. "So, what happens now?"

"Bonding isn't so complex, but in this case, we need to go a step further. Your soul is teetering on a precipice. It could go either way. We need to tell your sliver to choose lightning while making it forget that it ever thought it could also be fire. There's a good chance you won't survive. Even if you do, you might wish you hadn't."

"I see. What does the process entail?"

"I'm going to have to electrocute you."

"Oh." Ren had only learned what electricity was a short time ago, but she could gather what the word "electrocute" meant by the severity of Cobalt's tone.

"I'll ask again: is this what you want?"

"The purpose I was given was a lie. Everything about my life is fiction. That doesn't mean I can't take pieces of what I was given and forge something new from the scraps. I don't know who I truly am. Not anymore. Yet, when I'm still, when I listen to my hearts telling me what they want most, they're quite clear. My want is no longer born from honor, or glory, or some a sense of duty to a higher power. I want this because it feels right, more than anything ever has. I want to fight for the people who can't. And I'm ready for what comes next."

"No," Cobalt said. "You're not. You may want to bite down on something."

Ren snapped back into her body. She was floating, suspended in the calm embrace of Cobalt's control beam.

Then the lightning came, and the screams it tore from her chest filled the cabin.

Her body seized, clenching into a single twisted knot of agony. She couldn't shut her eyes against the hot, crackling flashes painting her vision white and red and gold. Darkness took her, and in the blackness, she found no peace. The searing arcs darted through her body, boiling her blood and burning her soul and forcing her back to the waking world.

Deep within her chest, her twin hearts jerked in spastic rhythms. She couldn't taste anything but smoke and copper. When she awoke from her second blackout, the storm continued to rage through her, joined by a surge that brought fresh torture to parts of her that she never knew existed. All the while, Ren prayed to the heavens for the pain to end.

A thundering boom stole her hearing. The cabin darkened as the lightning storm died in an instant, leaving bright shadows in her vision. Something in her chest shifted. Her hearts pounded in one singular beat, united in their shared purpose. The tingling remnants of the electricity faded with the ringing in her ears.

Ren felt the pressure of her new armor against her skin, heard it clink as she stood, but couldn't tell if it was warm or cold. It was nothing but weight pressing on her skin.

It's done, Cobalt said, speaking directly into the core of her being. *How do you feel?*

"I don't," Ren said. "At all. No pain, no sensation. I feel nothing."

That was the cost, then. Shocking the fire from her soul had taken away electricity's ability to bite her. It also took her ability to feel anything else.

Cobalt was right. She hadn't been ready.

But she asked for this. She accepted the risk. Now, it was time to see what she had bought for such a high cost. Like Scarlet's viewport, the tinted glass of her helmet did nothing to hinder her vision, so when she looked down at the metal covering her clawed hands, she could plainly make out its color when the light of the control beam returned.

Her hearts skipped a beat. She used one of her sharp claws to trace the gold trim shining at the edges of the curved plates of deep, royal purple encasing her.

She felt Cobalt's grin within her chest. *You're the Purple Pilot of Lightning. The first and only. Not red. Not blue. Both, and more.*

"I'm a Pilot. A real Pilot." Half of a laugh slipped from Ren's throat. "I can Teleport?"

You can. You also have the gift of Telepathy, as Leona did. As for your weapon… Leona favored the spear. I've given you something I think will be more to your liking.

Ren reached her left hand to the small of her back, rolling her fingers around her weapon's handle, and drew it. The firearm, forged of purple metal that matched the hue of her armor, had a cylinder much like her revolver, but she couldn't see a way to access it. The weapon's handle extended at an angle much shallower than what she was used to. Though the grip was a little longer than she preferred, no weapon had ever fit her hand so well. Attached to the underside of the gun's barrel, which was almost as long as her forearm, a keen blade of shining metal extended past the tip of the muzzle.

This isn't the kind of firearm you're used to. It draws power from your sliver and compresses it into magical ammunition. Much more accurate than if you called lightning with your sliver. The weapon will reload itself so long as it's still touching you, but it takes time to charge. Six shots. Fire too fast, and you'll be in danger.

"And what am I to do in the meantime?"

I did keep one aspect of Leona's spear intact. Use your will. Tell the weapon to extend.

With nothing but a thought, Ren bade the weapon to grow longer. The bayonet extended, telescoping to its full three-foot length.

"A sword!" Ren passed the weapon to her right hand and turned it over, marveling at its perfect balance. It was thicker than her rapier, equally suited for cutting as it was for thrusting, though if it was heavier than her lost blade, she didn't notice.

Not a sword. Not a gun. Something different. Like you. Cobalt paused. *I don't remember who I was before all this. I think I might have been good at making weapons.*

"I should think so. This is a masterpiece." She willed the blade to retract and set it at the small of her back, where it held fast without the need for a holster. "Thank you, Cobalt."

I think we'll need to decide on a new name for me. Return to the platform. Along the back wall, there are levers. I've seen what they do. Throw them all.

The cabin hatch plates opened. Ren left Cobalt and searched the bay until she found three levers built into a square gap cut into the wall. When the pulled the first lever, the thick runic chains binding Cobalt sloughed off his body, slithering off the edge of the dais and thudding onto the floor below. The next lever woke up the electric lights and illuminated the bay.

Cobalt, the Blue Panther Vanguardian, was no more. In his place on the dais, a wolf forged of purple metal crouched, sharp blades of mock fur sweeping across his back, razor fangs and claws gleaming in the light.

The wolf wasn't her symbol; it belonged to House Valerius. To a dead girl. And yet, it seemed fitting. The wolf, and Serenia's memories, were all that remained of her. Ren would bear them both as a tribute to the girl who became her own dream.

"You're right," Ren said. "Cobalt won't do anymore." Compared to other colors, purple was a rare thing. It didn't have as many names. She needed to choose the right one. "How does 'Indigo' sound to you?"

Perfect. Indigo growled. The low rumble set Ren's hearts leaping and skipping. This wasn't the turn of events she had envisioned, but in the end, she finally achieved her goal. She was a Pilot with her own Vanguardian. In purple, no less.

There was one more lever on the wall. Ren pulled it. It set in place with a dull crunch. Beyond Indigo, the back wall of the chamber split, revealing a dim-lit passageway. While the shuddering metal doors parted, Ren took off in a running leap and landed atop Indigo's head. She slid off the back, grabbed onto the edge of the open hatch plates, and flung herself inside his cabin.

"This tunnel must have been how they brought you down here. No doubt, it leads to the surface." Ren stepped into the control beam. "Do I need to run on all fours?"

No. That would be silly. Just run normally, and concentrate. Intention is what matters most.

"Let's hope so." Ren turned Indigo toward the tunnel and broke into a run. Indigo's metal paws thundered against the floor of the bay, driving him through the mouth of the tunnel much faster than Ren expected.

We're coming, Maia. Please, hold on.

Leona's fingers dug into the floor of Professor's laboratory, carving long ruts in the stone. His magical grip tightened, tugging at the back of her armor as he dragged her toward the black portal spread across the wall behind her.

She was no stranger to having things taken from her. When she was a child, the Sinadarians took her father from her for tainting his bloodline by fathering a child with a human woman. Then, Leona's stepfather made her the focus of his razor-thin temper, and when she stood up to him, he came for Leona's life. When her mother intervened, he took hers instead.

When Leona found Kasper, and Maia, she thought her days of loss were over. Then Maia took the child Leona had created for them. When Leona lashed out at her in anguish, Maia took the world from her. Now, Kasper was gone, too, possibly dead. Or worse.

Leona had no more room for loss. She wasn't about to let Professor steal her only chance at revenge, the only thing she had left that held any meaning.

And then a sudden jolt of blinding pain reminded her that she still had more to lose.

The color bled from her brilliant blue and gold armor, rendering it a dull, cold gray. Her visor cracked. Then, her chest plate. Her armor slowly peeled from her body in shattered chunks to be sucked into the dark portal by the flow of Professor's gravity magic.

Death and rebirth had changed her, given Cobalt cause to defy her, but they hadn't been enough to undo their bond. Why now? Why was this happening to her? What had she done to deserve this latest cruelty?

Ren. Leona thought she had gone straight down the tunnel, toward Maia, when she fled Professor's laboratory.

But she hadn't. She must have turned, toward Cobalt.

The last piece of Leona's armor flecked from her back and vanished into the portal. Professor's grip no longer had to contend with the added weight of her protective metal shell blocking the full might of his magic. The rippling force pressed against her sides, squeezing and pulling and twisting all at once. Leona counted her ribs as they cracked. She would need to expend more of her blood's dwindling energy to heal her injuries. That might leave her with only hours left to live, at most.

That was all the time she needed to see Maia and Ren pay for everything they had done to her.

Attuning her sliver with anything but lightning would have denied her access to Cobalt's gifts, including her armor. Since that was no longer a concern, Leona convinced her sliver it was one with the earth. She let go of the floor and rolled onto her back as Professor drew her across the lab. She reached out, grabbed the ceiling with her earth sliver, and pulled as hard as she could.

The worked stone crumbled. Chunks cascaded down, sealing the portal behind a wall of debris and blocking Professor's grip from reaching her. Leona sprung to her feet and stumbled from the crumbling laboratory as the cave-in followed her into the tunnel beyond. She stopped at the intersection, hesitating. One path led to Cobalt, who was now completely lost to her. The other led to her other child, who would rip her apart now that she didn't have her Telepathy to keep him in line.

A blast of air and rock threw her straight down the tunnel, past the intersection. When the world stopped shaking and the tunnel walls stopped groaning, Leona brushed herself off and channeled some of her blood's power to hasten her Regeneration.

The way behind her was blocked. She could move the rock easily with her attuned sliver, but there was no guarantee that shifting that much stone wouldn't bring the rest of the catacombs down on top of her.

She had been patient for so many years. Aside from losing Cobalt and her Pilot gifts, being betrayed by Professor, and learning that she couldn't kill Maia without destroying herself as well, it was still a good day.

The long way suited her just fine. The detour led past an armory stocked with Pilot Killer rifles and enough ammunition to kill Maia a hundred times over.

And when the path eventually wrapped back around to the place where she kept her perfect mistake, her final revenge would be within her grasp.

"Ami! Brace yourself!"

Maia closed her eyes and opened the gates to her flames. A screeching tongue of fire lanced from her hands, widening and curling as it swallowed Arcturus along with half of the throne room. He roared and thrashed against the flames' embrace. Maia counted to five, shaking as she fought to stem the flow of fire, then pushed with all her might to will the flames away. The effort left her panting, and the infernos within, denied further release, took their fury out on her instead. She could feel the skin on her hands blistering and blackening underneath her red gauntlets.

Arcturus took a knee. His curved back, charred and cracked, rose and fell with labored gasps. Ami stumbled from the smoky haze, her armor slightly blackened. Maia was about to call to her when Arcturus rose with a furious bellow. He thrust his fleshy arm, wrapping Ami's torso in his thick fingers, leaving her arms and legs dangling helplessly as he lifted her into the air.

Maia grabbed her falchion and rushed Arcturus. Her blade was halfway to his neck when a Blacksteel fist crunched into her chest and heaved her back. She couldn't shake the stars from her eyes. The runes on Arcturus' arm were still glowing, and when she looked closer at gaps in his burned flesh where exposed bone peeked through, she saw the strips of metal banded to parts of his skeleton.

He still had his runics bolstering his strength and speed and endurance. Her fire had hurt him, but could it kill him? She couldn't risk another blast, not without hurting Ami or herself. If she had a sliver of lightning, like Leona, the metal laced into Arcturus' bones would carry its sting through his entire body.

That would fry him like an egg. It would also kill Ami, who he held firm in his unrelenting grasp.

Maia wasn't sure where her other sword had gotten to. That left her with an arsenal consisting of one blade and a Barrier she couldn't properly aim.

Arcturus squeezed harder. Ami's chest armor creaked. His metal hand snapped out, grabbing her face. With a clench and a pull, he tore the front of her helmet off. The rest tumbled to the ground to join it.

As Arcturus' Blacksteel hand cocked back and curled into a tight fist, a hurricane ripped from Ami's outstretched hands, blasting him and pushing Ami to the end of his grasp. The metal fist trembled as Arcturus fought against the storm's rage.

"Maia. Go find Ren. I can't hold General Valerius for long!" Ami shouted over the ripping winds. "Go!" she said again when Maia didn't move.

"No! I can't leave you!" Maia called back.

"Why not? I left you!"

Maia winced. *If we're always keeping score, we'll all end up dying for each other.* "Ami, listen to me! You did what you thought was best. I don't blame you for leaving me!"

"But I do!" Ami's voice wavered, on the verge of cracking.

"Well, stop it!" Maia shouted. "Maybe you should have stayed and fought. But you're my best friend, and I should have trusted you. We failed each other. Getting yourself killed for me won't make it right! I forgive you. I forgive *us.* And I love you, Ami! I love you so much. I'm not letting you go! Not now, and *not ever again!*"

Something swelled in Maia's chest, filling the space where bitterness and despair had made their home. The roaring winds died. Ami's body slackened. She had pushed herself too far. The moment that followed stretched, as if Arcturus' arm was moving through cold molasses. Maia saw the path it would eventually take, clean through Ami's head, once the endless second ended.

She couldn't trust her blurry vision to guide her aim, so Maia shut her eyes, called upon her Barrier one more time, and hoped it would appear where she needed it. The sound of a massive hammer striking an anvil resonated through the throne room, followed by a sharp grunt.

Maia opened her eyes. At the far end of the room, the edges of her glimmering red Barrier protruded from a pillar, having missed the mark completely. She followed Arcturus' fist to a second, cracked Barrier, angling into the path of his blow.

A Barrier woven of soft, green light.

Maia blinked. "How in the—"

"Strike! Now!" Ami cried. Maia's vision cleared. The world stopped listing. She burst into motion, lifting her blade high for a decisive blow.

No. That wasn't right. The overgrown deltoid muscles on Arcturus' left side shifted. He was going to drop Ami and strike with that huge arm of his. A haymaker. No. The faint silhouette changed with her next step, like a visible echo of something that had yet to happen. A cross. It would snap her head back and drop her. Three broken vertebrae. Blood pooling in her skull. Death soon after.

Another step. The ghostly path of Arcturus' blow remained unchanged. He released Ami, turned, and threw the exact cross Maia had expected. She dropped to her knees, twisting her hips to spin as she skidded underneath Arcturus' arm. At the end of her short spin, she extended her blade and drew its hot edge across his hamstring.

Sliding to her feet, Maia took her falchion in both hands and chopped right where she *knew* Arcturus' flailing arm would be. The blade slipped clean through the elbow joint like a leaf gliding down a stream. He grabbed at the gout of sparking blood spewing from what remained of his arm and fell onto his back.

Ami stumbled to the side, clear of the falling mass of twisted flesh and bone. "You accessed my gift of Perception."

"And you called on my Barrier," Maia replied.

She was about to ask how that could be when she felt it, deep in her chest. A second thumping heartbeat, just beyond her own, pulsing in such perfect rhythm with hers that it felt like her own heart had doubled in size.

"Heretic said that when we come together, our greatest strength is revealed. I thought she meant Legion," Maia said. "It's us. We're the strength."

Arcturus lurched to his feet. Even with all the burns marring his body and the loss of an arm, he showed no signs of slowing. He bellowed as he charged, shoulder lowered to press both Maia and Ami into the wall.

As Ami threw a green Barrier in his path, Maia cast her own red Barrier behind it and pushed. Arcturus hammered the shields with his metal fist. A powerful shock wave threw him back, but he reset and swung again and again, runics flaring as he called upon the full might of his stored enchantments.

The green Barrier crumbled. Cracks raced through Maia's own shield as she forced the pieces to stay together, to hold against the unrelenting assault. Before long, the stress of holding together so many fragments became too much, and the spell failed. Arcturus roared in triumph, raised his remaining arm, and prepared to deliver a killing blow.

The blow never landed. Coursing tendrils of lightning ripped from the corner of the chamber, dancing and snapping over his body. His muscles spasmed and contracted, forcing him to stand completely rigid. Maia heard the crunch of bone as his body's tension broke itself.

Maia crushed Ami in a tight hug and shielded her with her body as the lightning raged through the room, carving an errant path across shining marble and rendering it into powder. When the crackling storm ended, acrid smoke filled the air. Arcturus reached to the sky as if to cling to it to keep from falling. He collapsed onto his back, where he became perfectly, deathly still.

The lightning had to have come from somewhere. From someone. "Leona." Maia readied her falchion.

She was about to charge when Ami grabbed her arm. "Look," she said.

A Pilot stepped over the broken door and entered the throne room. Her helmet was styled after a wolf's head, and the black glass of her visor bore serrated edges, giving it the appearance of being lodged firmly between rows of sharp fangs. Instead of a cold, hateful blue, this Pilot's armor was a rich purple, trimmed with gold, like royalty.

Like a princess.

"Apologies. Lightning is harder to control than I realized," the Pilot said, her voice distorted and metallic. "It will take time to master it, I suspect."

Maia blinked. "Ren? Is that you?"

"No," the Pilot said. "Maybe? I don't know."

Her purple, wolf-shaped helmet broke apart and slid away, revealing a woman who looked like she had aged ten years since she descended into the catacombs. She ran a hand over her frazzled crown of black braids, then regarded her clawed gauntlets. "I'm purple."

"Yeah," was all Maia could think to say. "Where are Leona and Professor?"

"Leona wouldn't break the curse." The Purple Pilot reached for the weapon resting at the small of her back, a fearsome firearm that looked like a hand cannon and a sword had a child. "They turned on each other. I don't know if Professor survived their encounter. We can see to them later. Right now, we must close the

Aperture."

She didn't even acknowledge that she had just killed her own father. Serenia's father? Maia couldn't begin to fathom the turmoil churning in her former apprentice's mind.

"Wait. How are you walking?" the Pilot said. "And your eye... How?"

"Long story. I'm sure you have one, too. Another time?"

"Agreed. We have much to do."

"We do," Maia said. "So... You're a Pilot now. It's normally bad form to pick your own name, but I'd say you've earned the right more than anyone. What should we call you?"

"Not Serenia. Perhaps Ren, in time." The Pilot shook her head. "All I know for certain is what I wish to be. It's time to hold true to my word and become my own weapon, one I will aim at the heart of anything that threatens the people of this world."

The pieces of her helmet reformed and locked into place, hiding her face behind cold, blank resolve. "For now, you may call me Trigger."

Chapter 47
Legion

Trigger.

It felt good, having a name that was all her own. It felt even better than the deep purple armor hugging her body like a second skin. Though she couldn't feel the temperature or texture of the metal, the weight and pressure were a comfort, at least.

Once, as a child, a young girl named Serenia had tried on her father's armor. She could barely carry the weight of his white lacquered chest plate and gauntlet, and even then, she couldn't take two steps without falling over. What would that girl think of the woman Trigger had become?

Trigger looked past Maia and Ami to the smoldering ruin of General Arcturus Valerius. She thought to herself once, perhaps naively, that she could fulfill her duty as a Pilot without taking a life. The twisted shape Arcturus had been forced into was decidedly inhuman, a monster that needed to be put down, but christening her lightning sliver on him still laid a heavy weight on her chest.

"Trigger it is, then," Maia said.

"I'm sorry for ruining things, again."

"Don't worry about it. It all worked out. We're back together now. That's all I care about." Maia slapped her on the shoulder as she walked past.

Beneath her helmet, Trigger hid a grimace. "I'll catch up. I need a moment. Alone."

Ami and Maia retrieved their weapons and left her in the smoky haze of the throne room. Trigger bent down by Arcturus and touched his forehead. His breathing had gone so slight that the only way to notice he was still clinging to life would be to stare at him as intently as Trigger had been.

She reached down and found new threads connecting the weave of magic within her. The one she sought was within easy reach. She tugged on it.

Though the enchanted metal melded to Arcturus' skull repelled her, he guided her gently through the gaps. A warped collection of rapidly changing images assaulted her. She watched Arcturus' life flash before his eyes in his final moments.

Are you still here? Trigger thought.

Serenia. A familiar warmth spread through her hearts.

No. She's...gone. I'm the keeper of her memories.

I did it all for her, he said. *All of it.*

I know. She knows.

Arcturus trembled. *You did what I never could. You stood up. I'm so proud of you.*

Trigger swallowed. *I'm sorry for hurting you.*

You did your duty. There's nothing to forgive. One of his jaundiced eyes opened into a thin slit.

Trigger left his mind and returned to the throne room. "Do you want me to wait with you?"

"No. Let. Let go."

"I'm not sure I can. I know you were Serenia's father and not mine. Not really. But I—"

"No." His metal arm brushed her shin. "Still. Still my daughter. So proud of..."

His final breath slid out in a long, soft whisper. His metal hand clinked against the floor as it dropped. Trigger shut his eye with the tips of her fingers and brushed away the tear spreading beneath it.

Then she was running, taking the stairs in leaps, all the way down to the main hall and beyond to the open palace entrance. Ami and Maia were waiting for her there.

"Are you," Maia began, then shook her head. "Sorry. Of course you're not okay."

Trigger willed herself to become as hard as the metal encasing her. "I can fight."

"No doubt about that," Maia said. She scratched the back of her helmet. "I'm happy you're here with us. I... I missed you."

Trigger's armor clanged against Maia's as she launched into a tight embrace. She rested her helmet on Maia's shoulder and squeezed as hard as she could. *Thank you,* she thought.

I'm just glad you're safe.

The echo in her mind made Trigger pull away. She hadn't reached out to Maia with her newfound gift. "Wait. Did you just…"

"Yeah. You have Leona's Telepathy. And I guess I do, too."

"It seems that when we're aligned in heart and spirit, we can share our Pilot gifts." Ami tilted her head away. "It's good that you can share Trigger's Telepathy. It should prove valuable in the fight ahead. As Trigger and I can't… That is to say, we won't be able to…"

Without her helmet to hide behind, Ami's pained frown tugged at Trigger. "Ami. I know that you had the world's best interests in mind when you proposed your plan to Maia. Know that it may be some time before I no longer resent you for scheming to steal one of my hearts, but that doesn't mean I don't understand yours." *Let's finish this fight together.*

Ami canted her head. *I would like that very much. Oh, fascinating. Though our helmets, like the rest of our armor, diminish the effects of most magic directed at us, including forced psychic intrusion, it seems that when we resonate and share our gifts, this is no longer a concern.*

"Convenient. Also, annoying." Maia rapped the side of her helmet with a metal knuckle. "Let's keep it out here as much as we can."

When Trigger grabbed the thick golden handle of one of the palace's massive front doors, two hands joined hers. Together, the three Pilots heaved the mighty door open and charged out toward the chaos waiting in the city below.

Though Leona crept into Slate's bay as quietly as she could, somehow, the beast knew his mother had arrived. The dull red glow of his misshapen visor cut through the dark. His mouth opened with a low rumbling growl, baring row upon row of jagged, misshapen teeth as he stalked toward what remained of the platform.

Without her Telepathy, she couldn't soothe him. She didn't dare look away; she knew that if she did, he would end her.

That he hadn't already was surprising.

"Slate, I—"

The piercing keen of his roar scattered her white mane and rattled her barely beating heart. Leona set her Pilot Killer and the pouch of ammunition strapped to its stock on the ground, held up her hands, and backed away. "Slate. I'm here to help you."

She pressed her back to the bay wall and felt around, never taking her eyes from her furious son. The lever tipped slowly. Slate's remaining bindings snapped off and tumbled to the bay floor in a loud crash.

"See? I'm helping." Leona threw the next lever, starting the long process of opening the doors at the end of the bay, and stepped to the edge of the ruined metal platform. "Now, we can be together. That's what you want, right?"

Her fingers brushed his snout. Slate nudged her, almost throwing her off her feet. Even though she kept him locked in the dark, even though she had Professor contort him into a freakish mockery of a Vanguardian, Leona knew from her time spent in what broken semblance of a mind Slate had that he still regarded her as his savior.

That didn't mean he wouldn't grind her into a stain beneath his claws if she upset him. Theirs was a complicated relationship.

"My son," Leona said. She pressed herself against the jagged gray metal of his face. "We've been wronged, you and I. I know you hate me. But don't worry. Soon, I'll be gone. Nothing can stop that now. So, if you want to hurry me toward oblivion, I won't fault you for it."

A sound something like the trill of a baby lizard slipped from Slate's throat, but he didn't move to crush her.

"Neither of us asked for this. We've both lost so much, and now I... You know what? Fuck it all." Leona grabbed her Pilot Killer and vaulted onto Slate's snout, marching down its length and stopping inches from his visor. "I'm going to be completely honest with you. I'm here because I want revenge. I want to run wild and rage against those responsible for what happened to me. I know you want that, too. Join me, Slate. Join *with* me. Let's make sure that even after we're gone, this world will never forget who we were."

A moment passed. Then, the screech of sliding metal cut the quiet. Leona kissed Slate's red visor, sprung onto his forehead, and made her way to the base of his skull. Thick mist slipped out of his misshapen, blade-like hatch plates. She climbed inside, crawling through a short, twisting tunnel that opened into a lopsided gray cabin covered with lengths of thick black tubing. A control beam pulsed faintly at the center of the cabin, its light red as blood.

Leona hesitated. Once she stepped into the control beam, there would be consequences. Slate was imperfect. Concessions had been made in his construction due to Professor's lack of experience working with living metal. Slate's sliver was rendered pure, with no elemental attuning, out of necessity. Some magics had to be stripped from his core. Bonding with Slate wouldn't grant Leona a unique gift or the ability to Teleport. And from what Professor had told her, the process would be far from pleasant.

I've been through this once already. How bad could it be? Leona thought. She stepped into the control beam, emptied her mind, and waited.

Something struck her from behind. Agony, foreign and barely remembered, blossomed through her back as a length of black tubing as thick as her wrist sprung from the cabin wall and dug into her flesh. Another erupted from the dark tangled mass and bit into her. And another. They attacked like angry vipers, latching onto her back and shoulders.

A horrendous tearing sound filled the air. A piece of gray metal ripped from the cabin wall, slammed into Leona's forearm, and formed over her undead flesh, sending sharp jolts lancing through her body. More jagged shards followed, battering her from all angles until she was entombed in a bulky suit of gray patchwork mail, save for a strip across her eyes.

A corner of Slate's red viewport cracked. A chunk of red glass slammed into the bridge of Leona's nose and molded onto the crooked mass of her helmet to form her visor.

When Slate had finished remaking her, Leona looked at her reflection in the viewport, at the new perversion she had become, and let out a primal scream. Slate joined her, shaking the cavern with his roar.

Together, they charged through the tunnel at the end of the bay, one tempered will aligned against the world.

Trigger and Ami touched down in a crouch behind Maia at the courtyard below the Imperial Palace. She was happy for their comforting presence as she looked up at the swirling maelstrom of violet energy and black smoke casting a blanket of twilight over Noctis. The sun's rays veered around the far edges of Aperture, eager to stay clear of the menacing maw consuming the sky.

The sheer disarray beyond the courtyard overwhelmed Maia's senses. Thousands of Ferals chased screaming Noctean citizens toward organ-shaped Behemoths, who scooped them up with bony arms and pushed them into their wide, toothless maws. Their bottoms sagged with each new victim they swallowed. Meanwhile, buzzing, oversized dragonflies swooped down on fleeing soldiers, impaling them with long, barbed stingers the size of pikes and depositing them in the Behemoth's mouths.

"Absolute fucking chaos," Maia breathed.

"An apt description," Ami said.

"The larger ones are harvesting citizens," Trigger said. "Raw materials, Leona said."

"They seem to be ignoring the children." Ami pointed to one of the Behemoths as it shook a screaming young boy from the leg of the man it held in its grasp. The child landed on his back and groaned as the man disappeared into the Behemoth's mouth.

"Okay." Maia pointed to the organ-shaped Behemoths. "That one's a Harvester, then." She followed one of the dragonflies with her finger. "Those, we'll call Swoopers. And that," Maia said, gesturing through the hole in the city walls to the whale-like monstrosity lounging in the countryside, "is a Leviathan."

"I don't see Boltspinner," Ami said. She guided their attention across the square to where Scarlet and Viridian rocked back and forth inside their webbed cocoons.

Maia was more concerned with where Grimclaw had gone. Rhythmic thundering beneath her feet made her regret the silent question. The black beetle backhanded the last remaining mage tower in the city out of its way, then pointed at her as it approached.

She couldn't take her eyes off its massive pincer, horrible and clacking and dark, so much like the one that haunted her nightmares and turned her blood to ice at the very thought of it.

But it wasn't Onyx's claw. Onyx was dead, along with Edgar. Grimclaw wasn't the thing that waited for her when she closed her eyes at night. It merely resembled it. And unlike her nightmares, intangible and steeped in horrible memories she might never be rid of, Grimclaw was quite real.

How unfortunate for Grimclaw.

Twin fonts of fire bellowed inside Maia, rising higher until they slipped from her skin and coated her armor in broiling rage. Instead of pushing to contain them, she allowed her flames to escape in short, pulsing waves. "I'm taking my life back," Maia said. "You can't hurt me. Not anymore. Never again."

"Maia? What's wrong?" Trigger said. She and Ami fell back, steering clear of the surge of fire blasting from Maia's armor.

Ami cleared her throat. "We failed to mention that Maia has absorbed a second sliver of fire and has turned herself into a walking explosive."

"Wait, what?" Trigger said.

"Go free Scarlet and Viridian," Maia said. "This one's mine."

"What are you going to do?"

"Something ill-advised."

Fire burst from Maia's feet with each step, propelling her toward her foe in impossibly long strides.

Has any Pilot ever fought a Behemoth without a Vanguardian? Trigger said through their shared connection. *Isn't that suicidal?*

No, and yes, respectively, Ami said.

Maia ignored the voices in her mind and ripped her blades from her back. Grimclaw watched her approach with great interest. Perception revealed the pincer's diagonal path, showing Maia exactly where it would land. She waited until the foreshadow of the descending claw enveloped her.

An explosion of shrieking fire threw Maia straight into the air. Grimclaw's pincer slammed into the earth, missing her completely. She landed on the black chitin of its wrist and kicked off in another leap. The beetle screeched as the fiery blast from Maia's launch tore into its armor and released a torrent of sparks and burning blood. Touching down high on its forearm, she dashed up its length. With each step, Maia slashed. Her flame-wrapped blades sang as they sheared into Grimclaw's darkened shell, leaving a trail of molten cuts in her wake as she scaled its arm.

Grimclaw stumbled and threw its head back, mandibles thrown wide in a pained scream. Since she was already acting monumentally reckless, Maia didn't think twice about summoning one more explosion to her feet and hurling herself upward in a lazy arc that dropped her right in Grimclaw's open mouth.

In the constricting darkness of the Behemoth's throat, Maia opened herself up to a larger pulse of power from the inferno within. The world flashed white. She couldn't hear anything but her own heartbeat. When she was able to see again, she was falling. A quick turn and a burst of roaring flame from Maia's palms slowed her descent. She landed in a crouch, knees buckling painfully, and turned back in time to see the flaming, headless corpse of Grimclaw collapse and explode at the far end of the courtyard.

Maia couldn't stop herself from shaking. Her heart wouldn't stop flooding her body with haze-filled panic as she struggled harder than ever to contain the flames threatening to rip her asunder. Smoke trails snuck through the seams in her armor. Whatever damage she had done to her body, she didn't care. If Maia somehow survived until nightfall, she knew that for the first time in four years, she would sleep well.

You were right. That was ill-advised, Ami said.

I've done worse, Maia replied.

No. You haven't.

The earth trembled again, drawing Maia's attention to where Boltspinner had burst through a row of tenements to cut off Ami and Trigger's path. It turned to the side as a purple streak smashed into its chest and sent it rolling on its back.

It was a metal wolf, sleek and terrible, with metallic tufts of hair curving across its back like knives. Trigger ran at full speed toward it, lightning curling off her feet with every step. She leaped and landed on the kneeling wolf's head near the open hatch plates at the base of its skull.

What happened to Cobalt? Maia thought.

This is Indigo, the Purple Wolf Vanguardian. The glee in Trigger's projected voice coaxed a smile from Maia.

As Boltspinner scrambled to stand, a long slot on Indigo's back slid open. A burst of crackling lightning propelled something slender into the air high above the Behemoth. Indigo charged Boltspinner, rebounded from its chest into a vertical leap, and gripped the spinning object in its teeth.

When Indigo's jaws clamped down on what Maia now understood was a longsword hilt, the weapon's segmented blade extended. Indigo tucked into a roll as he fell. The longsword turned over with him three times in the air, gaining momentum with each revolution.

Full Moon Slicer! Trigger cried. The sword passed through the Behemoth's head, continued through its body, and struck the stone beneath its feet, reverberating in a savage wail. Boltspinner staggered back, furiously working with its claws to keep the two halves of its body from separating as it exploded in a shower of sparks and fire.

How was that? Trigger said.

Maia blinked away a tear. Her chest swelled with a pride she had never known before. Whatever happened to her, at least the world would have the protector it deserved. *That was perfect, Trigger. Just perfect. Wouldn't change a thing.*

By the time Maia made it to where Ami was crouched, Indigo had sliced through the webs binding Scarlet and Viridian. The green dragon rolled onto her feet and took off with a mighty flap of her wings, crashing into the ground in front of Ami and lowering her neck so her Pilot could enter. Scarlet jogged over to Maia and took a knee so she could do the same.

It seemed like ages since Maia last basked in the gentle warmth of Scarlet's control beam. *I missed you.*

I missed you too. I thought I had lost you.

Not yet. Maia pushed the angry flames down and ignored Heart's Oath tingling in her chest. She directed her thoughts to Ami and Trigger. *Are you two ready?*

For what? Trigger said.

Legion, Ami said.

Indigo's sword blade retracted. He tossed the handle and caught it in the open slot on his back. *How do we begin?* Trigger said. *Do we perform a particular series of hand gestures? Do we need to yell something?*

Relax, and open your hearts, all three Vanguardians said in one harmonized voice.

Maia knew, somehow, to duck. Viridian's lower jaw unhinged as she leaped onto Scarlet's back. Her upper jaw slid over the top of Scarlet's head, capping it like a helm while the rest of Viridian shifted and locked into place, melding with her back. It seemed like thrusting Scarlet's arms forward to catch Indigo in the middle of his backflip was the right thing to do. The wolf split in half down the middle in mid-air, each half sliding over Scarlet's forearms like armored sleeves.

Machinery whirred. Gears ground. Through her connection to Scarlet, Maia could feel the breadth of the green wings on Scarlet's back and the weight of the purple gauntlets covering her arms. The cabin floor on either side of Maia split open. Soft beams of light painted the Green and Purple Pilots as they rose on platforms from the holes in the cabin floor, locking into place with a metallic crunch.

Maia steadied her breath as she looked to each of her dearest friends in turn. "Three of five isn't bad."

We agree. The blended harmony of Legion echoed in her head.

Beyond the walls of Noctis and the shadow of the Aperture, the Leviathan wailed and pitched in the light of the afternoon sun. A swarm of Swoopers in the sky above coalesced into a thick mass, seemingly driven by the urgency of the whale's cries, and descended on Legion. They pinged off her hull, unable to find a vital point to sink their stingers into. Maia flexed Legion's arms and willed Scarlet's blades to extend.

She expected two long lengths of hot-edged metal, so Maia was more than surprised when two tapered streams of raw magical energy erupted from Legion's purple gauntlets.

Maia whistled. "Well. That's even better." The energy blades hummed twice through the air, disintegrating dozens of Swoopers with each slice and scattering the swarm.

"We must destroy the towers," Ami said.

"I think we'll need to attend to that first," Trigger said. The Leviathan shifted. From fleshy holes in the titanic whale's flank, five Behemoths emerged, closer to

Legion's size than the smaller Harvesters.

Maia sized up her new opponents as they appeared. A skunk walking on its hind legs, fire bristling up and down its body, led the group, followed by a lizard man with snake heads for hands, a sword-toting eagle with armored limbs instead of wings, some kind of red demon with a spear, and a floating jellyfish with flailing, barbed tentacles.

"Who gets the honor of naming those?" Trigger asked.

Maia smashed Legion's energy blades together, delighting in the way they crackled and repulsed each other. "They won't live long enough to need names."

Chapter 48

Ravager

Maia guided Legion through the hole in the city wall, blades held wide and ready to receive the charge. The flaming skunk Behemoth came first, so it had the honor of being the first to fall. Legion waded unabated through the plume of curling flame spewing from its mouth and buried both of her blades in its chest. Maia jerked them free, tearing the Behemoth apart in a spray of burning sparks.

A quick hop and a flap of her great green wings brought Legion soaring through the explosion left in the wake of the Behemoth's destruction. Maia glided away from Noctis, drawing the remaining four Behemoths further into the fields. When they were gathered beneath her, she folded Legion's wings and dropped like a rock, landing next to the Behemoth with snakes for hands and driving one of her crackling arm blades into the earth.

The hissing, charging Behemoth caught a spew of dirt and sod in the face as Maia ripped Legion's blade up from the ground in a wide arc. The snake heads at the end of each arm shut their eyes and warded against the spray. They did little to defend against a spinning backhand slash that took all three heads from its body.

Legion marched past the dying Behemoth. The eagle-man with the sword and the red devil with the spear flanked her in a slow circle, working their weapons through spins and flourishes meant to intimidate.

"I wouldn't mind a turn," Ami said.

Even if Ami had yet to fully recover from their last battle, she deserved to revel in Legion's glory. Maia relaxed her shoulders and willed the weight of her control beam to lighten, shifting command to Ami. "You're going to love it."

Though she had yet to find her breath after the fight in the throne room, Ami slipped into a fighting stance and folded Legion's wings over her body. The two Behemoths tightened their circle, bobbing their heads as they searched for a way through the shielding wings.

"What stopped you from doing this before?" Trigger said. "Forming Legion, I mean. Weren't all the Pilots united in their purpose?"

"Yes, and no," Ami said. She pivoted to keep the two Behemoths in her peripheral vision. "We were five weapons pointed at the same target. We weren't one weapon. There was always mistrust and discord between us, even if we never admitted it."

Maia scoffed at that. "There was never anything like that between you and me."

"That's not entirely true. I didn't approve of your relationships with Edgar and Leona."

"Oh. You thought Pilots shouldn't get involved with each other."

"No. Neither of them treated you well. I was too afraid to tell you that you deserved far better. I didn't want to upset you or drive you away from me."

It was too dangerous for Maia to hug her dear friend in the middle of battle. She settled for feeling thankful that she would get to spend her last few hours—or minutes, if that was all that fate would afford her—fighting alongside two of the best people she had ever known.

When they got tired of circling, the two Behemoths attacked as one, closing in from either side like a pair of scissors. Legion stepped back as sword and spear struck the sheer surface of her folded wings, gliding off and driving into the ground at Legion's feet.

Her wings unfolded, catching each Behemoth in the chin and throwing their heads back. Legion raised her arms, stepped past the Behemoths, spun, and brought her blades to bear. The headless Behemoths toppled, shaking the earth as they combusted.

"Two left for me?" Trigger said as she cracked her knuckles.

Maia pointed to the remaining Behemoth, a bloated jellyfish hovering in the distance. "There's only one left."

Far behind it, the Leviathan let out an ear-splitting roar. With an arch of its back, the great whale took to the skies, moving through the air as if it were water.

"I count two," Trigger replied.

Ami visibly relaxed, and Trigger took over. She slammed her palms together and dashed for the last Behemoth, arms pumping and blades scything through the air as she ran.

The red three-lobed cluster suspended within the jellyfish's milky body stirred. The air around the Behemoth lit up with glowing flecks that shimmered like falling snow. Trigger made it halfway to the Behemoth when a thin ray of white light screeched from the jellyfish's core and lanced through Legion's chest.

"Shit!" Trigger cried as Legion tumbled onto her back. Maia's heart seized, and she shut her eyes, waiting for the end. She let out a relieved sigh when she realized that the piercing beam had missed Scarlet's core.

"I saw that attack coming," Ami said.

"Well, speak up next time!" Trigger said. "I'm not yet accustomed to my own powers, let alone yours!" She pushed Legion to her feet and slipped to the side, narrowly avoiding a second ray cutting into the ground.

"I'll finish this," Maia said. "We can't risk taking another hit like that."

"Trust me! I know what I'm—"

Trigger didn't get to finish her sentence, and the jellyfish didn't get a third shot. It folded like a sheet on a clothesline during a windstorm as something much larger slammed into it and bore down. The Behemoth's tentacles flailed against its new aggressor. The gray, twisted mass atop it drove its claws through the jellyfish's skin, scattering sparks in wide gouts.

With its arm buried in the jellyfish up to its elbow, the gray thing grabbed the Behemoth's core and ripped it out. Its claws closed into a fist. The core, and what remained of the deflated jellyfish, erupted in a fiery explosion.

The hulking shape strode through the smoldering blaze. It looked like a bulky, saw-toothed lizard, covered in thick armor plates, walking on its hind legs like a person. Its long, swaying tail slapped the earth as it plodded forward.

A Ravager. Maia had encountered them more than once in her travels through the Therion Kingdoms far south of Reddalia. The typical Ravager was only a few feet taller than a human. She had never seen one large enough to dwarf Scarlet's size, and she definitely hadn't encountered one forged of misshapen hunks of jagged gray metal with a bent piece of red glass where its eyes should be.

"It's a Vanguardian," Maia breathed. The Leviathan bellowed and veered away, sailing toward Noctis. It clearly didn't want any part of whatever was to come.

"Hello, lover." The scraping voice projecting into Legion's cockpit carried the roughness of a saw biting into a hunk of metal.

"Leona?"

"Ren took Cobalt from me and left me to die," Leona said. "I had no choice but to make use of my last remaining weapon. What do you think of my son?" A discordant chuckle rattled through the cabin. "The Emperor sent engineers to recover the remains of all the fallen Vanguardians from Thenmar's Crater. Cobalt survived, as you know. But so did Pearl. As it turns out, Vanguardians can survive having their heads torn off so long as their cores remain intact. We combined him with Onyx's remains, just as we combined your blood with mine to make Ren."

The colorless mass of serrated violence, all odd angles, stretched his arms back and pushed out his massive chest. "He chose this form from his shattered memories, but unfortunately, he didn't get the shape quite right. Please welcome to the stage, Slate, the Gray Ravager Vanguardian."

Maia could feel Legion's tension through the weight of the control beam. *Our brother,* Legion said. *We can hear him, crying out for release. We must free him. His mind is tearing itself apart.*

Maia's hands trembled as she beheld Leona's final play, a walking defilement of her lost friend's memories. Despite all the rage and fire billowing inside her, bellowing for action, Maia couldn't move.

It wasn't the reservations she had about striking Leona down a second time. It wasn't the shock of seeing remnants of her friends' Vanguardians, mangled and perverted, coming back to haunt her in the waking world. Those things gave Maia pause and made her knees lock and her stomach twist, but they weren't what made her go as rigid as a block of granite.

It was the trembling phantasmal fingertips slithering across her heart, preparing to squeeze one last time, that stopped her from acting.

Heart's Oath clamped down, bending Maia and throwing her to the ground. She tried to cry out, to scream, but her breath caught in her throat as every muscle in her body clenched at once. She shuddered against waves of knife-like spasms, praying that she could hold on long enough to keep from killing her friends when she breathed her last and her slivers ripped from her body.

"Help Maia," Trigger said. "I'll handle Leona."

Ami left her control beam and pulled Maia clear of hers. She studied Maia briefly, then shook her head. "Maia has only a short time left."

"Leona! Stop this, now!" Trigger cried. "Break the curse!"

"Ah, Ren. I have a bone to pick with you, as well. A sharp one. How about I drive it through your chest?"

"My name is Trigger. Listen to me, Leona, and listen well. Though I would love nothing more than to make you answer for the grief and pain you've caused, I've already laid one member of my family to rest today. I don't wish to lose any more. Not Maia, and not you, either."

"That's too bad. I'm afraid we don't always get what we want," Leona said. Slate hunched forward. The brutal claws at the end of his long arms scraped at the trampled grass at his feet. "You stole Cobalt and turned him against me. You took away my only chance of getting back the life that was stolen from me. If Maia can't face me, then I'll have to settle for taking my revenge on you instead."

"If I face you, and win, will you remove Heart's Oath?"

"Oh, maybe," Leona purred. "Why don't we see if you can make me?"

Trigger couldn't refuse her challenge. Leona wouldn't let her stroll back to Noctis and close the Aperture without resistance. She had to be stopped, somehow. Trigger flourished Legion's magical blades and told herself that though she was a made thing, she had been crafted from the two fiercest women to ever live. With their combined might coursing through her veins, she couldn't lose.

Slate moved first, dropping onto all fours and breaking into a mad dash. With Perception, Trigger saw his pounce just before he left the ground. Legion stepped aside and brought a shining blade sparking across his back as he passed.

Vanguardian armor wasn't Behemoth flesh. The energized edge bit into Slate's ridged back, scoring a thin glowing gash along his spine that caused no real damage. He spun on Legion as he landed, raking with his claws. As Legion slipped away, Slate leaned into his next wide swing and continued his rotation.

Trigger watched his claws, waiting for Perception to reveal his intention. No projections came from his hands. Instead, she saw the foreshadow of a long, gray length rising from below too late to react to it.

She had never fought anything with a tail before.

The blow rocked Legion, sending her reeling. Slate followed hard and fast with claws and fangs, keeping Legion's weight on her heels and driving her toward Noctis. Every time Trigger found an opening and drew one of Legion's blades across his skin, Slate didn't bother evading or guarding. He accepted each brilliant slash and answered with a fist to Legion's head or chest before she could recover.

Almost all of Trigger's combat training in Noctis had assumed that she would be facing another duelist, someone who sought victory while avoiding their own injury and death. Fighting Leona was nothing like dueling. It was brawling. And Leona clearly didn't care how much her Vanguardian suffered, so long as she won that brawl.

After what Trigger thought was a quite cunning cross cut with both of Legion's arms, Leona punctuated the gap in their experience by throwing Slate inside her reach with perfect timing. He gripped her torso, pinning her arms to her side. With a pivot of his weight, he threw Legion like a sack of wheat.

Legion twisted in the air and landed hard on her back. When Trigger's vision stopped spinning, she rolled the combined Vanguardian onto her stomach.

"You fight like her, you know that?" Leona's voice boomed, filling Legion's cabin. "Get up. I'm starting to enjoy myself."

Think! Trigger screamed at herself. Attacking this twisted amalgamation of two Vanguardians head-on, the way Maia would, wasn't working.

Don't do it my way, then. Maia's voice rasped through her head. *She knows my way. Do it your way.*

What do you mean? I am you!

No, you're not. When I used to look at you, I admit, I saw some of myself in you. Some of Leona, too. Maybe that's really why I took you in, why I trained you. Maia gasped and coughed. "Now. When I look at you. I don't see me. Or her. Just you. Someone different. Unique. Forget everything I taught you. Do it your own way."

With a mighty push, Trigger forced Legion to stand. She extinguished Legion's left energy blade and fell back into a fencer's bladed posture, right sword leading, left flank pulled back.

"Come at me, then!" Trigger yelled.

Slate answered her challenge with a sky-splitting roar and ambled in. Trigger waited, fixed in her perfect receiving posture.

When Slate swung wide, Legion retreated. The Ravager's tail came whipping around, and she slipped under it, scored a hit on his flank, and backed away.

Dodge and counter. Slip and move. Instead of trying to match Slate's ferocity with her own, Trigger moved with his tempo, using her agility to strike in the gaps behind his actions.

A dozen thrusts later, Slate's posture grew more rigid. Leona started mixing feints in with her punches and shoulder charges. Trigger's approach had forced Slate to change his. When she was sure of the pattern, she inserted herself into it, thrusting as Slate recovered.

The Gray Vanguardian stumbled back, reeling from what Trigger thought was a superficial jab into his armpit. Perhaps she had struck something vital. Perhaps his injuries would finally compromise him.

Legion's arm blade flared harder. One thrust between the crooked seam of his neck, followed by a hard wrench to remove his head, and the fight would be over. She shifted her weight forward to close the distance when Slate straightened from his daze, sizzling vapor rolling from his shoulders as they split open to reveal rows of thick cannon barrels.

Shit.

Trigger threw Legion's left wing up as a makeshift shield right as the cannons lit up in an off-beat rhythm. The tips of over a dozen serrated gray spikes thumped into Legion's wing, piercing and lodging there. Trigger braced, expecting Slate to close the distance and strike, but when she parted her wing, Slate was gone.

Or rather, he wasn't in front of her. A sudden jerk sent Legion listing to the left as the keen of tearing metal assaulted Trigger's ears.

The green wing, still covered with jagged gray spikes, hung from Slate's jaws. He dropped it and stepped inside the arc of Legion's swing as Trigger brought her blade down on him. His arm snaked around her forearm. With a twist of his hips, he sent Legion spinning onto her back. Before she could recover, he stomped on her chest with a clawed foot for leverage and jerked the purple gauntlet, and its blade, clean off.

"I had no idea we could have joined our Vanguardians like this." Leona chuckled. "Slate may be an abomination, but do you know what your brother has that you don't? He's complete. Unbreakable. You're just pieces, pretending to be whole. You don't have the power to save anyone."

Trigger ignited her other energy blade and punched up, but Slate caught it in both hands. Another jerk. The other half of Indigo sailed through the air to join its discarded twin with a loud crash.

Without Indigo, Trigger had no connection to Legion. Her control beam lifted, and she tumbled to the back of the cabin.

Slate's foot rose and slammed down, driving Legion into the earth. Trigger's upside-down view of Noctis through Legion's cracked viewport shook with each of his stomps.

"What a disappointment." Leona ground Slate's heel into Legion's chest one last time before turning the gray lizard's attention skyward to the churning maelstrom above. "It won't be long, now."

"She's. Wrong." Maia coughed between labored, shivering gasps and spit up a glob of blood. "We're whole. We're one."

Trigger turned herself over. "No. She's right. You're *both* right. Together, as a whole, we're strong. But we're also pieces. Individual, and unique. And there's more than one way for pieces like us to work together."

Her frantic gaze settled on Lion's Roar. Viridian's attack had bent its barrel and left the whole domed structure leaning to the side. It didn't look at all imposing anymore. It was nothing more than shaped metal designed to channel electricity.

Lightning, directed and given purpose.

"Ami, assume control of Legion. I have a plan. Since I'm better suited to fighting from a distance, I will support you from Indigo." Trigger ran to the cabin's hatch.

"Understood." Ami moved from Maia's side and stepped into the control beam. *What ranged weaponry does Indigo possess?*

Hmm. About that. Trigger hit the ground in a tight roll. She covered her head with her arms and stayed low as she ran to where Indigo lay. He had just finished pulling his halves back together when she reached his bowed head. *As far as I know, aside from projecting short-ranged bolts of lightning, Indigo doesn't have any.*

I need to go fetch something. Hold Slate at bay until I return.

I don't understand.

Trigger crouched on Indigo's snout and sent her intention through the purple metal at her feet, spurring him into a bolting rush back toward Noctis.

A smirk spread across her lips. *I'm taking one last bit of inspiration from Maia. You won't like it.*

Chapter 49

Something Ill - Advised

Indigo's paws drummed against the streets of Noctis as he ran, knocking chunks of masonry from each building he brushed up against. Trigger rode on his back, leaving him to navigate while she focused her attention on the Ferals, Swoopers, and Harvesters overrunning the city.

Despite her lack of familiarity with Ami's shared gift of Perception, Trigger had no problems aiming with her new weapon, which she took to calling a "gunblade." By the time Indigo cleared the large channel separating the two halves of the industrial sector and entered the market, she was already getting a feel for the weapon's handling.

Each squeeze of her gunblade's trigger discharged like a booming thunderhead, sending a thick shell of purple, piercing magic slamming into the head of a Feral or the body of a Swooper. When electric smoke drifted from the weapon's barrel and its hammer clicked empty, she swapped it to her right hand, extending the blade and slicing through anything foolish enough to mount Indigo's back as he passed.

Soldiers, citizens, and Ferals threw themselves aside as Indigo charged on. Trigger didn't fool herself into believing for one second that they had all successfully cleared the way. If she tarried and treaded with care, countless more would die, so she kept Indigo moving at his fevered pace. The only solace she found came from firing at the thin legs of any Harvester they passed, hoping to stumble them so the captives inside had a chance to escape.

Indigo took a sharp corner and slid, paws scrambling for purchase, shredding the face of a polished stone building as he recovered. Debris smashed into Trigger's back and shoulders. If the impact injured her, she couldn't tell. She wouldn't know she was hurt until a part of her stopped functioning.

Such was the price she paid for power, and yet, Leona was right. Her power wasn't enough. That was why she asked Indigo to take her through the city and beyond, to the sheer mountain face where Lion's Roar lay dormant and broken.

Trigger stowed her gunblade and gripped a seam at the base of Indigo's neck to keep from falling off as he scrambled up and over the city walls, approached the mountain, and bounded up its sheer rock face. With a push and a twist, Indigo leaped and wrapped his front legs around Lion's Roar's barrel. The structure groaned, protesting against his weight. Trigger ran up Indigo's neck and leaped onto the barrel just as his claws slipped free with a resounding screech.

She watched him crash against the steep cliff and roll down its face, kicking up dust as he tumbled. Looking to the distance, she saw Legion throw herself to the side as a stream of metal spikes from Slate's shoulder cannons cut into the ground where she had been standing. She barely made it to her feet before Slate unleashed another barrage.

"Hold on just a little longer. I'm coming." Trigger sprinted along the barrel until she reached the ruined dome. She slipped into a gap torn in the housing and dropped a short distance to a raised, uneven walkway.

A single source of light flickered in the darkness. Her metal boots clinked along the walkway as Trigger made her way to what she could only describe as lightning in a bottle, set into a twisted machine fed by blackened, curved pipes of a material she had never seen before.

Her own sliver pulled her toward the crackling spark suspended in the glass container. Trigger fumbled around the machine's base until she found a flat disk that felt like it could be twisted. She dug her clawed, metal fingertips into the grooves along its surface and turned it.

The whole machine shook. Sparks bit the air. Pieces of the metal housing retracted. With a ginger grasp, Trigger plucked the glass cylinder from the pedestal and nearly dropped it when the sliver inside went wild in her hands. The spark bounced around the glass cylinder like a deranged firefly. Yellow tendrils of lightning licked at the side closest to Trigger, trying to touch her fingers through the glass. She briefly considered answering the sliver's silent scream and allowing it to bond with her own lightning, which she struggled to keep calm.

She kept the cylinder at arm's length. When Maia drew a second sliver of fire into herself, she had become a living explosive in the process. Noctis didn't need to deal with a walking storm front, as well.

When Trigger left the shadow of the dome, Indigo was clinging to the cliff face beneath her. He jerked his head toward his back and opened the hatch at the back of his head.

"Don't break the glass. Don't break the glass." Trigger repeated her new favorite phrase over and over as she stepped from the edge of the rent cannon. She intended to land on the top of Indigo's head and slide over the edge and into the cabin, but she was preoccupied with the glass container in her hands, which held enough destructive energy to wipe out an entire city, and landed on his snout instead.

She curled her body around the sliver as she bounced and rolled until she collided with something solid. The dull crunch of glass stole her breath. She allowed herself a deep sigh of relief when she realized the sound had come from Indigo's visor, which she had crashed into and cracked.

Then Trigger looked down at the broken cylinder cradled in her arms. She moved without thinking, closing her left hand around the spark before it could expand.

It slipped through her armor and flickered through her forearm. A blinding flash preceded a deafening boom of thunder. Webs of lightning arced from her armor in zig-zag patterns, striking the side of the cliff and raking destruction down its face. Indigo scrambled to right himself as his footholds crumbled, turning in mid-air and breaking into a dash down the crumbling face of the cliff. The speed of his descent pressed Trigger flat against his cracked visor while she struggled to keep the raging lightning contained in her arm, so it wouldn't enter her chest and tangle with her own sliver.

Get us back to Legion! she mentally screamed at Indigo. He grunted in response and tipped his head back to keep her level as they rounded the bottom of the slope and took off across the plains, seconds before Lion's Roar heaved and tumbled down the side of what remained of the mountain beneath it.

Heart's Oath relaxed its grip, almost as if it was toying with what remained of Maia after its latest, most vicious attack. Through a black-ringed haze, Maia watched Ami work Legion through a flurry of punches and kicks. Since she usually had her own opponents to contend with, Maia didn't often have a chance to watch Ami ply her craft.

Under different circumstances, she would have delighted in the opportunity. Instead, she watched helplessly as Ami's steam slowly ran dry. Ami struggled to dodge Slate's blows, panting and grunting every time she had to move suddenly. Too often, she stopped to spare a glance back at Maia, leaving herself open to attack.

Ami was pushing beyond her limits. Worse, she was distracted.

Slate set his clawed fists next to his jaws and weaved in, taking Legion's upper-cut without flinching and smashing her chest hard enough to throw her back on her heels. This was the Leona few people knew. As a hunter, she was an ambush predator, relying on traps and favorable terrain to set up cunning kills. In a fight where Leona failed to seize the advantage early, she didn't fall into the graceful, poised dance one might expect of a half-elf who grew up in the forest, floating away and relying on deft counterstrikes to win.

In those instances, Leona became a scrapper, shrugging off blows and using every single tool at her disposal to deliver as good as she got. With a lifetime spent bearing the blows of so many misfortunes, some might have called her style suicidal, though in truth, it was anything but. There was a conviction in the way she stood her ground, a firm belief that she would never, *could* never lose. Life had forged her into something as hard as the giant metal lizard under her command and equally as capable of outlasting any opponent. Even Ami.

Maia forced air into her burning lungs. Her head grew lighter and she fought the urge to shut her eyes. If she did, Ami would be the first to die when Heart's Oath took her.

"Stay with me," Ami said as if reading her thoughts. Perhaps she had been. "Tell me what you're going to do when this battle is over."

Maia couldn't find enough air to speak. *I'm going to take Scarlet to the center of Noctis and detonate her core,* she thought. *I'll take all the towers out myself.*

"No. After Slate has been dealt with and we force Leona to break the curse. After the Leviathan is defeated and the Aperture is closed. What will you do? Focus, Maia. What will you do?"

Find Elizabeth. She pictured her face and the warm tawny glow of her skin, and her brown eyes, always heavy with concern and longing. *I'm going to the Hinterlands. To Steadbrook. I'm going to find her.*

"And then what?" Ami ducked under Slate's wild haymaker and pushed his knee down as it rose toward Legion's chin.

Then I'm going to be with her. I'm just going to...be. No more Sunder. Just me. Just life. With her.

"Then don't give up! We'll find a way through this." Ami struggled for breath, and for a moment, she looked like she might collapse.

Slate rocked Legion with a short hook to the stomach, then reared back and launched a cross that threw Legion's head to the side. From that angle, through a small crack-lined hole in the viewport, Maia saw a streaking form bounding across the field.

"I'm back." Trigger's voice trembled as it filled Legion's cabin. "I need you to hold Slate still so I can get a clean shot."

"A shot with what?" Ami said.

"Lightning, directed and given purpose."

Indigo took up a flanking position atop a hill roughly a mile away. With Perception, Maia could barely make out Trigger as a purple smudge standing inside her wolf's open jaws. Lightning poured from her like water from a fountain. The bolts arced forward from her braced left hand, gathering near the tip of Indigo's jaws in an ever-growing sphere.

"I obtained another sliver of lightning from the remains of Lion's Roar," Trigger said. "I think I can direct its release. Hold Slate still however you can!"

Ami had her hands on her knees. Legion matched her posture. Slate looked his opponent up and down, made a dismissive gesture, and began a slow, trudging walk toward Indigo.

Ami, can you open a connection to Slate? Maia said.

Ami shook her head. "He is resisting. Leona doesn't wish to speak anymore."

If Maia could get through to Leona, she could explain everything. That the deaths of their friends, and her own death at Maia's hand, had been an accident. Barring that, she could distract Leona long enough for Trigger to end her.

If Leona wouldn't talk to her through their Vanguardians, maybe she would be more open to an in-person conversation.

Ami. Do you trust me? Maia thought.

"I do."

Then give me some Amplifier.

The Green Pilot's hand went to the case strapped to the small of her back. "Neither of us can handle another dose right now. If you take more, you'll die within an hour."

I don't need an hour. I only need a few more minutes. Come on, Ami. I'm out of time. Give me the Amplifier, take Viridian, and start running. We're far enough from the city. The explosion might not reach. I need to get to Leona and stop her. If I fail, the blast might be enough to destroy Slate. If not, it'll disable him long enough for Trigger to take her shot. Please, Ami. I'm done for. Let me help. Let me go out fighting.

The case of Amplifier thudded to the ground. "Take a quarter dose. No more."

Maia dismissed her helmet and fought her quaking muscles and smoking insides as she crawled to it. She undid the clips. Inside, there were three vials. With trembling fingers, she reached for one.

Her fingers closed around all three. She jammed them into her neck, pushing the plungers down with her palm before Ami could stop her.

"Maia! No!"

"Maia, yes."

A new burning pitch pulsed through her veins. The floor blurred and rushed toward her at least eight times before her vision sharpened to a razor's edge. Heart's Oath's grip fell away, a whipping surge of power prying its fingers back.

"Go, Ami. Get out of here."

Maia rolled to her feet as Ami's platform sunk back into the floor. The hole sealed shut with a loud bang. Moments later, Viridian fell from Maia's back and, missing a wing, settled for running back toward Noctis.

I hope you know what you're doing, Ami said.

Already, Maia could feel the Amplifier turning on her like a million little knives carving at her veins. *Scarlet. I have a favor to ask. I need you to throw me at Slate. Really, really fucking hard.*

She could feel Scarlet's hesitation. *Are you sure?*

"Yes!" Maia shouted. "You won't make it there in time. I need to help Trigger! Please, throw me! Now!"

Scarlet's hatch slid open. Maia slipped from the cabin and made her way to Scarlet's palm. "Leona!" she screamed. "Don't walk away from me! I'm the one you want!"

Slate turned his head. Had Leona heard her from that far away? It didn't matter. Slate's attention was on her. That's what mattered.

Maia summoned her helmet as red fingers curled and shuttered her in darkness. Scarlet's joints groaned as she reared back. Before Maia could blink twice, she was careening through the air like a bullet from Trigger's revolver.

With a roar, Slate cracked open his shoulders. Steam spilled out in lazy clouds as a dozen lengths of metal reached for her.

The cannons fired. Maia called upon Perception and angled her body against the storm of metal shards flying her way. When her legs touched one of the missiles as it passed beneath her, she kicked off, diverting her flight. Wind buffeted her and filled her ears. She ignored the swarm of tree-sized shards and picked out the projectiles most likely to shred her to pieces.

She turned and twisted, pushing with her hands and feet, bouncing between spikes. One slipped against her side, drawing a long line of sparks and sending Maia spinning to the left. Her view flipped between the ground and the sky, and when she righted herself, she found she was clear of the storm.

That would have been cause for celebration if not for Slate's clawed arm speeding her way.

Maia called on Perception, but all it showed her was that no matter how she moved, there was no way to avoid reenacting Leona's death in Thenmar's Crater, with Maia as a stand-in.

Reaching to the magics inside her, Maia summoned a Barrier ahead of her path and angled it upwards. She shut her eyes, blocking her access to Perception, refusing to believe that there was no way forward. Her hands slid across the suspended Barrier. She pushed off into a vault and twisted like a javelin in flight. A gale smacked into her and pushed her into a slow, sidelong spin.

When Maia opened her eyes, she found that she had slipped through Slate's grasp, literally. The Ravager's visor sped toward her. She landed on his snout and rolled onto her right shoulder hard enough to crack her pauldron. Maia found her feet and broke into a run. Rising heat swelled in her breast as she neared Slate's crimson visor. Her twin slivers swirled and gathered, ready to unleash their furious rage as soon as she opened her gates to them.

Maia had barely touched her knuckles to the visor when Slate pitched his head back, throwing her into the air. Halfway to the grass below, darkness curled in around her. Slate's clawed hand groaned as it closed into a fist. Maia's eyes flicked through the dark, frantically looking around for a gap in his grip.

When she pressed flat against Slate's palm, she felt something flowing from the gray metal, like a tangible scream. Legion said she could hear her brother's torment. From so close, the malice and agony pouring from Slate's metal skin deafened Maia's insides.

Before she died and came back with frightening powers, Leona had difficulty reaching Maia with Telepathy while Maia had her helmet on. If Maia was willing to receive it, or Leona was able to make direct contact, only then could her Pilot gift reach through the strange metal that made up their armor.

The same strange metal that Vanguardians were made of.

Maia whispered an apology to Pearl and Onyx for failing them, grabbed hold of the gift she had borrowed from Trigger, and pushed. She sailed through the frayed edges of Slate's meager defenses and entered his fractured mind so quickly that it jarred her. From there, she reached for the swirling void in the back of her own mind, where she kept her worst nightmares, and hurled them at Slate.

She found her memory of Onyx's claw gripping and twisting Pearl's neck, wrenching his head off. She watched him spear Pearl's head with his legs, killing the beautiful, innocent soul trapped inside. She saw Onyx's cabin fill with flames, heard Edgar's dying screams, and felt Pearl's horn slip through the seam of Onyx's chest, a torrent of ice water erupting from the scattered remains of his shattered soul.

And Slate watched with her. As his hand relaxed, the sun peaked through between his fingers. He stared off into the distance, locked within memories of both his own deaths and his Pilots'.

Maia didn't know how long the moment would last. She had played her part. She redirected her Telepathy back to the shared flow that connected her with her friends and yelled into the void as loudly as she could.

Trigger! Now!

Trigger's knees buckled. She had no way of knowing the extent of the damage her body had suffered by letting an unbound sliver of lightning run rampant inside her arm. The smoke rising from the seams of her armor told her it was probably worse than she estimated.

Maia's voice blasted into her brain. *Trigger! Now!*

The sphere of swirling destruction had grown so large, it blocked her view of the fight. *Aim for me, Indigo. Avoid Slate's core and cabin. Fire! Now!*

With all her might, Trigger pushed. She didn't have time to think of a name for the spiraling column of lightning that screamed from the tip of Indigo's maw with such fury that it stole all the sound in the world. The riot of color was gone in the blink of an eye, as was Slate's right arm, half of his head, and a good portion of his torso. Trigger fell to her knees as Slate toppled backward, his impact kicking up a large cloud of dust mixed with singed grass. As numbness set in, she barely managed to crawl out of Indigo's mouth and onto the grassy hill before slipping into unconsciousness.

The last thought that flitted through her mind as she looked past the tendrils of smoke snaking from her body was a prayer, a hope that her sacrifice had been enough to end the fight.

Chapter 50

Last Dance

It took Slate so long to collapse, Leona wondered if that horrible blast of lightning had stolen time itself when it cut through him. The black tubes binding her to Slate's cabin walls tightened, absorbing the impact as the Vanguardian crashed to the earth. He had fallen beyond the edge of the Aperture's shadow, allowing the blinding light of day to rush in through the shattered viewport and twinkle in the wicked fragments of red glass strewn across what was left of the cabin.

This wasn't how Leona expected the day would end.

The mass of thick black tubes tensed further as if Slate sensed that she meant to leave him. She had to. Maia was still out there. Alive, for the moment. She had more suffering left in her. There were too many things she still had to answer for.

It was the only reason Leona still lived. She had merged her body with this mechanical monstrosity for the sole purpose of buying more time, more power, so she could finish this fight.

Leona wasn't about to let Slate stop her. Not when she was so close.

She reached down to her sliver and, with kind words, coaxed it into becoming lightning, the element she had worn the longest and knew best. Bolts danced from her spread hands, striking the ends of the black tubes where they connected to the wall. When she stepped from the control beam, the mass of severed tendrils dragged behind her, streaming from her back and shoulders like a mantle of flowing darkness.

She hefted her Pilot Killer, pulled the charging handle, and let it slide back with a chunky metal clang. Her mantle of tendrils spread out to either side, responding to her will. Frayed black tips hooked onto the sharp edges of the shattered viewport and pulled her out into the daylight.

By the time Maia crawled out from beneath Slate's severed right hand, the three doses of Amplifier had worn off, leaving her in a fuzzy daze. Her seared veins throbbed against the ravaging effects of the liquid fury she had pumped into her body, a pain that paled in comparison to the rhythmic clenching of Heart's Oath and the twin slivers of fire burning her from within. She pushed on with what strength she had left, forcing one foot in front of the other. She couldn't quit. Not yet. Not while Leona was still alive.

Maia climbed onto Slate's prone leg and began her ascent toward his cabin. *Ami. Trigger. Are you there?*

I'm here, Ami said. *The Harvesters are gathered at the city gates. They're capturing any Nocteans who try to flee.*

Maia nodded to herself. *Trigger?*

I'm hurt. Her words sent a shiver up Maia's spine, and she almost turned back. *Don't worry. I just need some time to recover. Ami, we need to deal with that Leviathan.*

Viridian can't fly with only one wing, Ami said. *Even if we defeat the Leviathan, we no longer have a way to close the Aperture safely. We cannot prevent the Kith from crossing over. We should regroup so we can formulate a new plan.*

Maia pulled her shoulder blades tighter and kept walking. *Save as many people as you can. Get the city gates open. Keep focusing on the Harvesters for now, and pray to whatever goddess you prefer that the Kith don't have any more flying whales to send our way.*

What are you going to do? Trigger said.

What I have to.

If you kill her, you'll die as well. I've already lost a father today. Don't take...only fami...have...

Trigger's telepathic voice became a scratchy whisper, then faded entirely. Reaching inside herself, Maia realized that the threads of magic that had once glowed with Telepathy and Perception had gone silent. The fact that Maia's decision to put an end to Leona had gone so far in opposition to her friend's wishes that it severed their connection only punctuated the fact that this was her duty alone.

Maybe, by the time she made her way around the smoking gap where a quarter of Slate had vaporized in the span of a breath, she would have some idea as to how she was going to fulfill that duty.

Scarlet's pounding footsteps shook the earth as she approached. Maia reached out and pushed back. *No. Go to Trigger. Protect her. Make sure she's okay. I don't want you near me, in case...*

Scarlet didn't argue. She turned and ran toward the distant hill Indigo was couched on.

When Maia finally dragged herself to Slate's skull, a strange slithering sound slipped from his cabin. Dozens of thick, snake-like tendrils latched onto the edge of the shattered viewport. They flexed and followed in a trail behind the indistinct shape that flung itself from Slate's cabin.

The figure slammed down in front of Maia. The writhing mass of tendrils flattened against the back of a misshapen suit of armor built from rent chunks of jagged gray metal that looked to be fused to Leona's flesh. One pauldron, larger than the other, sported wicked spikes that curved away from the rest of the Pilot's mess of a body as if trying in vain to escape the horror they were a party to. The armor darkened near the right gauntlet, abandoning the shape of a human hand for something resembling a crab's claw. Thin lines of glowing blue blood ebbed through gaps in the patchwork armor. Ghost-white hair spilled through the back of a misshapen helmet. A single piercing eye, black as midnight, bore into Maia through a hole in the crooked crimson visor, right beneath a curved white horn thrusting from the helmet's forehead.

A rush of panic sharpened Maia's vision. She drew her flame-edged falchions. "What in the Blue Hells have you done to yourself?"

Leona hefted her rifle with her left hand. She flexed the dark gray claw and regarded the mangled shape it formed. "This is what it cost to gain the power I needed to kill you. It's a price I pay gladly."

When she saw the full extent of the horrific lengths Leona's lust for revenge had driven her to, what she had twisted herself into just to get one step closer to tasting victory, Maia's own taste for battle soured in her mouth. She couldn't tell if the tightening in her chest was due to the Amplifier's toxic touch, Heart's Oath preparing for its final strike, or simple disgust. "You don't have to kill me. And I don't have to kill you. We can walk away. I only destroyed the thing you made from our blood because it was hurting you. I killed Edgar because he killed Dalzin, and I thought he had killed you and Ami. He would have killed me if I didn't stop him. And you... I never meant to hurt you. I just wanted you to *stop*. I never wanted to hurt you."

"I know."

The tips of Maia's falchions touched the gray metal at her feet. "You know?"

"I knew that our child was a monster. It couldn't be allowed to live, but I was too weak to do what needed to be done. And I know that Edgar struck first, and you were just defending yourself. I know that what happened after he fell was my fault, along with a thousand other things I can't begin to apologize for. My anger brought ruin to us both. I paid for my mistakes. I lost you. I lost my life. I paid."

Leona leveled her rifle. "But you haven't. You killed me. You killed our child. You killed our friends. You broke your promise to me and gave your heart to somebody else. And now, you've turned my own daughter, my only salvation, against me. Regardless of the circumstances, you're just as guilty as I am. And you need to be punished."

The rough edges of Leona's words formed a barbed barricade between them. Maia didn't need Perception to see that there was no way through without suffering wounds she didn't need or deserve.

Maia laughed, sending pain radiating through her chest. "You know what? Fuck this." She gestured back toward Noctis, teeming with horrors, while a whale monster floated impossibly in the sky above. "I should be back there, dealing with this mess you made. Not sitting here, wasting what little time Ami's juice bought me. This fight is pointless. You've lost. You're stuck in that body, and since you won't break the curse, you'll go when I do. It's over, Leona."

"You think I'll just let you walk away from this? From us?"

"I already have. And you know what the funniest part is? I don't even hate you. Hating you would mean holding you in my heart, and there's no space there for you. My heart doesn't belong to you anymore. I'm taking it back."

As Maia turned to walk away, Leona stomped after her. "You can't take it back!

It's mine!" she shouted. "You're leaving me. Again. Just like everyone else. I won't let you. This only ends when we're both dead! That was our promise! You can't walk away from that!"

"Can, and am. You want to end it? Shoot me in the back. Or shoot yourself. I don't care anymore." Maia put her falchions away and waved dismissively. "I have work to do. I need to make the time I have left matter. Goodbye, Leona."

As the words left her lips, four years of grief sloughed off her shoulders. Letting go of the ghost of her dead wife and everything she had suffered in the years since Thenmar's Crater left Maia feeling lighter than ever. She kept walking, expecting a bullet in the back of her head by the time she made it a dozen paces. Maia even counted them.

At ten paces, Leona struck.

"Then your father's death will go unanswered."

Maia's resolute march ground to a halt. "What?"

"When I came back from beyond the Veil and made Caelus my slave, I gained access to the Noctean intelligence network." Leona paced behind her, boots thumping. "We kept a close eye on you while I came up with a plan to make you suffer for your crimes. Taking you on directly was too risky, so I decided to use precisely placed Behemoths to lure you into a trap and finish you off with Lion's Roar. Ren—Trigger—unwittingly aided in that plan's success, to a point. But before that, we tried other methods to motivate you, to bring you to Noctis."

Maia's hands trembled at her sides. "The sliver of fire."

The corner of Leona's exposed eye turned up. She was smiling beneath her patchwork helmet. "There are places in this world where the Veil is thinner. With the right rituals, you can reach through and pluck a sliver of pure magic and bring it back to our world. It's extremely difficult, but from there, it's a simple matter of telling the sliver that it's a raging inferno before you contain it within an enchanted Blacksteel device designed to allow the flames contained within to vent for years without releasing the sliver entirely. Arcturus would have been against the use of such a weapon and would have wanted no part of it, but I'm no stranger to taking matters into my own—"

She expected Leona to say "hands," but it was hard for her to say anything when Maia's scarlet metal fist slammed into her stomach like a missile, unleashing a deafening explosion that threw her from Slate's chest.

Maia's flaming leap brought her to the far end of the shallow ditch Leona's smoking body had carved into the verdant field. She leveled her hands and opened her gates. Torrents of flame rolled from Maia's palms, drowning out her own screams. She stopped just short of releasing both of her entangled slivers and pushed the twin infernos down, hoping that what she had unleashed was enough.

The flames shifted. Movement. A thundering boom hit Maia's ears, followed by a thin whipping crack. She fell to the ground, clutching her head, and blinked both of her eyes just to be sure they were still there. With frantic fingers, she traced the thin scratch in her helmet. The shot hadn't penetrated. It had only skimmed her.

Her moment of relief dissolved as Leona emerged from the conflagration, armor glowing orange like an ingot fresh from the forge. The burning pouch strapped to her rifle's stock exploded, ripping the weapon to pieces and flinging her sideways through the air.

Leona staggered to her feet. Her left arm hung at her side, mangled and useless. She paused for a second, concentrating, then relaxed. "That's better. I've attuned my sliver to fire. You can't hurt me with your little flames anymore."

"Bold of you to assume that I wasn't planning on tearing you apart with my bare fucking hands!"

Maia worked to control the rising blaze inside her as she let every other part of her run wild, flooding her body with rage and grief and purpose. A wave of black tendrils whipped her as she charged, throwing her into a roll. She ignored the new pain in her side and gained her feet, launching two quick punches as she rose. They rang against the left side of Leona's helmet, where she couldn't defend, flecking sparks and bits of semi-molten metal. Maia kept punching, filling the air with the pinging sounds of a hammer striking an anvil.

Leona's tendrils closed around Maia from either side, weaving into a cage. Maia leaped to escape it, but Leona caught her foot with her misshapen claw hand and slammed her onto her back. As she rose, Leona drove on with a short uppercut that snapped Maia's head back.

Her arms and legs grew heavy. Leona grabbed her shoulder and drove her knee into Maia's stomach. Something cracked inside her, and she was coughing up blood when a second blow threw her against the writhing tentacle wall.

Leona followed her to the shifting mass and rammed her claw into Maia's stomach, over and over.

"You took everything I had!" Leona screamed. "We were goddesses! We could have ruled this world. We could have had any life we wanted. Instead, we resigned ourselves to serving, groveling for whatever scraps of affection the chattel of this world could spare us. We deserved more!"

The hail of punches stopped. The tentacles slackened. Maia let them support her body weight as she tipped back. "We deserved better than we got. That doesn't mean we were better than any of the people under our protection. It doesn't give us the right to hurt them like you're doing right now."

"Look what they did to me! Do you think I wanted to come back like this? Every waking moment feels wrong in a way I can't begin to describe, and waking moments are all I have, Maia. I can't sleep, or rest, or know even a moment of peace. And when I finally expire, my soul will be dashed across the cosmos. Nothing can stop that now. All I have left is *this*. You, and I, and all the pain I can carve into your soul before I send you screaming to the great beyond."

The tentacles heaved suddenly, throwing Maia back toward Leona. She saw Leona's claw poised to deliver a haymaker that would likely end her life. Instead of ducking, she continued walking right into its path.

I don't need strength to win.

She caught Leona's claw and turned it over. Leona ducked and turned in place, unwinding her torqued wrist. The twisting motion broke Maia's grasp. She clamped her claw around Maia's elbow and jerked, flipping Maia onto her back with a sudden burst of strength and speed.

Leona stomped on Maia's chest. "Give it up. I know all your moves."

Not all of them. There was one technique in particular that Maia had learned during their time apart, one she was certain Leona wouldn't be prepared for. In a moment of weakness, she had almost used it on Trigger at the end of their duel in Thenmar's Crater.

Maia had stayed her hand, then. This time, she had no reason to. With time to prepare, she could land a death blow. From this range, there was no way Leona would survive.

When Leona slammed her foot down again, Maia rolled away from it and rose. A darkened claw crunched into her helmet and threw her back down.

"You can't win. I'm not just a Pilot anymore. I'm a Lich, with powers you can't even begin to fathom. Even with that second sliver, your strength is *nothing* compared to mine!" Leona said.

"Really?" Maia's arms quivered as she pushed off the ground with her knuckles, straining to hold onto the last fleeting ounces of her strength. "Then how come I keep getting back up?"

With a steely roar, Leona charged. Maia leaped and reached for her falchions. As soon as Leona's claw wrapped around her ankle and pulled, she brought both curved blades down as hard as she could. Aided by the pull, the glowing edges of Maia's falchions sheared through the black tendrils on either side of her.

Taking advantage of Leona's moment of confusion, Maia brought both falchions crashing down onto her, one after the other, over and over. When the edges of her swords chipped and cracked from her furious abuse, she smashed Leona in the visor with both handles before she could stumble away from Maia's rage-fueled assault.

If Leona wanted a brawl, then Maia would oblige.

Maia dropped her ruined weapons and followed Leona's stagger, never letting the pressure off. There was no technique left in her movements, no art or style, just a question of which one of them would break first. She threw her whole weight behind every punch, only stopping when her gauntlets cracked and her blistered knuckles broke.

"You told me before, in the throne room, that the difference between us is that when the world shits on us, you're the one willing to do something about it." Maia slammed Leona in the helmet with her elbow until her horn snapped and a dull crunch left Maia's right arm hanging at her side. "But you're wrong. Do you want to know what really sets us apart? Why I can win when you're so much stronger?" She drove her knee into Leona's face until the gray mask buckled, and Maia had to limp to keep up with her as she staggered and backpedaled.

Grabbing Leona by the back of her neck, Maia pulled her in sharp and fast, ramming what remained of her helmet into Leona's. "I have people counting on me, people I can't afford to let down." She bashed Leona's face with her armored forehead, over and over, until both of their helmets cracked and fell away. "I don't care what power you brought back from beyond the Veil. It's nothing compared to my love for them."

With one last headbutt, Maia sent Leona crashing to the earth. Leona's head lolled from side to side. When she coughed, blue blood dribbled from her cold, dead lips. "Go on then. Finish me off. Send us both to oblivion. Do it."

Maia stood astride Leona's prone body, her fingers curled into talons. She brought her left arm back, twisting her wrist so all the muscles in her forearm wound tight like thick rope. She took aim at Leona's face and prepared to unleash her deadliest technique, one Leona could never hope to dodge from such a close distance.

As she prepared to release, something inside Maia popped. Her arm uncoiled and hung at her side. She expected it to hurt more. A great clench in her chest. The feeling of her heart crushed into paste beneath her sternum. Something grand and violent and painful.

In the end, Heart's Oath didn't have to grip hard. With her flames pushed so far down and the Amplifier's effects long gone, there was nothing standing between the curse and its prey.

Its touch was cold but kind, a light caress that stole the warmth from Maia's tired, broken heart.

She smiled as she fell. "I would have had you."

From a bed of grass that felt as soft as a down mattress, Maia stared up at the sun, blinded by its brilliance, until Leona's grim shadow rose to block its light.

"Yes," Leona said. "You would have had me."

Sorry, Dad, Maia thought as a jagged metal claw closed around her throat and squeezed. *I couldn't make it right for us.*

Chapter 51

Compassion

Trigger rolled away from whatever was nudging her side. Though her visor filtered out the sun's angry glare, she raised her hand and splayed her fingers to catch as much of its light as she could. She could only hold her hand to the sky for a few moments before the shuddering in her limbs became too great to bear.

Indigo prodded her again with the edge of his snout, pushing her arm across her chest. "I'm okay," Trigger said and forced herself onto her feet. Scarlet loomed a short distance away, watching her through a cracked visor.

Maia. Are you there? Where had she gone that Trigger couldn't hear her anymore?

Scarlet's head jerked to the side with a metallic whine. Trigger followed the motion to the massive stretch of burned grass halfway between Indigo and where Slate had fallen.

With Perception, Trigger looked across the distance, taking a few moments to focus her enhanced sight. She watched Maia drive her forehead into Leona's face. Both of their helmets crumbled and fell to the grass in chunks. One more headbutt sent Leona onto her back. Maia stood over her, cocked her arm back, and prepared to strike.

Then she went limp, like a puppet with its strings cut, and folded to the ground.

"Indigo!" Trigger yelled. "Get me to Maia. Now!"

She leaped as high as her trembling legs could take her. Indigo ducked to meet her halfway, but red fingers intercepted her, snatched her before she could reach Indigo's back, and carried her into the sky.

"Scarlet, what are you doing?" Trigger said. "Put me down! I need to get to—"

Scarlet took three running steps, twisted at the hips, and flung Trigger into the air like she was skipping a rock across a lake.

"Thank you!" Trigger cried, but the whipping wind stole her words. As the arc of her flight waned, she ripped her gunblade from her back, took aim, and squeezed the trigger.

For almost four years of sleepless nights, Leona thought of nothing but what it would feel like to finally defeat Maia. Some nights, she pictured herself standing over Maia in Scarlet's cabin, looking down at her mangled, beaten body, and saying something clever before crushing her sternum beneath her boot. Other times, they were in Noctis, high on the parapet of the outer wall. Maia would be dangling from the tip of Leona's spear, convulsing as the unbridled fury of Leona's lightning ravaged her insides.

A thousand nights. A thousand variations that ultimately ended the same way, with Maia dead and Leona victorious. Now that she stood over Maia and watched her breaths come in short spurts, Leona found no joy in victory.

She hadn't won. Maia had lost. Their fight hadn't reached its end. Now, it never would.

Leona bent down, curled her claw around Maia's neck, and lifted her from the ground. As she hung from Leona's grasp, the corner of Maia's mouth quirked in a final show of defiance. A surge of hot anger spread to Leona's arm, urging her to clench even tighter, even if it meant her own end.

But she didn't. She thought she wanted to. Squeezing the breath from Maia's throat was one of her favorite daydreams. It was the greatest purpose her claw could fulfill. Why wouldn't it close?

Her rage drained away. Was Maia right? Did their fight have any meaning? There could be no winner, and not just because of Heart's Oath's equalizing presence. No matter the outcome, whether she won or lost, Leona would have to say goodbye to the woman she had vowed to spend the rest of her life with.

Leona deserved her revenge. But hadn't she taken it already? Hadn't she done enough already?

A whisper reached her on the wind. She followed it to the sky above, where it grew from a gentle murmur to a piercing scream as its owner descended like a furious angel from the heavens.

A blast of purple struck Leona in the arm, blowing a piece of her vambrace clean off. Maia fell from her grip. A second bolt struck her in the abdomen, tearing through armor and flesh and ushering a gush of sparks and bits of gray metal. Trigger passed her gun to her other hand as she descended, where its crackling, electrified blade extended to the length of a sword. As she landed, she thrust.

The blade slipped through a gap in Leona's armor, passed between her ribs, and punched out her back, narrowly missing her deadened heart. She grabbed the blade and pulled herself along it until the hilt pressed against her chest and the tip of her nose touched her daughter's visor. "Haven't you taken enough from me?"

Trigger's helmet broke away, revealing the scowling young woman beneath it and the fresh burns covering her cheeks and brow. Exhaustion tugged the corners of her eyes. "It's nothing compared to the pain you've wrought. You made me to be nothing more than a weapon. You forced the man I looked to as a father to lie to me. Then you had him twisted into an abomination of who he was, what he stood for, and set him against my friends. And now, you want to take away the person I love most in this world."

With a wrench of her blade, Trigger dragged Leona in a sidelong shuffle back to where Maia lay. "I should hate you. I should want you dead. But I don't." The corner of Trigger's mouth quirked, as Maia's had.

Leona spat a mouthful of barely glowing blue blood onto the grass. "Why not? You deserve vengeance as much as I do."

"Perhaps." Trigger's leg swept Leona's out from under her, driving her down onto her back. She clamped one hand down on Leona's forehead and touched Maia's with the other. "But I don't long for it the way you do."

The mental attack lacked subtlety and nuance. Trigger drove into Leona like a dull knife, spreading her mind wide with a rush of urgency. Leona waited for her daughter's pitiful attempt to break her will and bind it to hers, but it never came.

Life has been unkind to you, Trigger said, her voice reverberating in a soft echo. *Why would you inflict that same pain on others? You're no better than those who took from you.*

A growl rumbled in Leona's chest as she ground her teeth. "No. I'm not like them. I'm only taking back what I lost. What I'm *owed*. I'm making a better world for everybody!"

By forcing others to live through the same hardships you've endured?

"What are you..." Images from Trigger's mind flowed into hers.

Leona saw one of the harvesting Behemoths plucking Nocteans from a fleeing crowd and shaking free any children that clung to their screaming parents. In the next instant, she was riding on the back of Trigger's Vanguardian, who had once been her Vanguardian. As she blew through the streets of Noctis like a wild storm, Leona saw the carnage and destruction the Kith had brought to the city, the way the Ferals and their swooping insect cousins murdered or made off with parents and older siblings, ignoring the young and their weak attempts at resistance.

And in each screaming, grief-stricken child's face, she was reminded of all the times she wondered, in her youth, if she would die from crying too hard. So many orphans, just like her, doomed to the same nightmare she never woke from.

I know this isn't what you intended, Trigger said. *It's not too late. We can stop it here and now.*

Leona let out a bitter laugh, half snicker, half sob. "You can't stop this. Nobody can. Not even I'm strong enough to beat back the Kith alone. What makes you think you can?"

Because I'm not alone.

A warmth radiated from the grass next to her, calling to her like a beacon in the night. *Maia.* Trigger had somehow connected Maia and Leona's minds through her gift of Telepathy. It never occurred to Leona that such a thing would even be possible. As Trigger clumsily plucked memories from a blurred mess of colors and shapes, she presented them to both members of her captive audience.

A handshake on a cold beach at the edge of the Freelands, filling her with determination. A Feral stomping across a field, and the smell of sizzling bacon. A crumpled red shirt clenched in her hand and the way it made her heart sing. The weight of Maia's armored body in her arms as a wall of fire blasted their backs with heat and the world crumbled beneath them. A song in a tavern and the roar of an excited crowd. A robed man thrown from his feet from her revolver's bark. The crunch of snow under her boots. The barrel of her gun aimed where it shouldn't be. An embrace, tight and desperate and fleeting.

In every moment, Maia was there. Whether they were fighting the Kith or each other, they were together.

They were family. The family Leona had longed for. The warmth and weight of their bond projected from Maia and Trigger's hearts, overwhelming her. That light bloomed from the ashes of loss and rose defiantly toward an uncaring sky, refusing to bend or break as misery rained sickly black upon them.

A spark flickered in Leona's chest, a remembrance of the woman she might have become had circumstance not sharpened her edges. Though that woman lay buried beneath a thick, frothing morass of hate and rage that all but consumed her, the memory of the woman who never was and what she wanted remained.

If Leona focused hard enough, if she pushed through and clung to that fading spark, maybe she could become that woman, even if just for a moment. Maybe, she could find it within herself to be kind, the way the world had never been kind to her.

Maybe, she could preserve the family she always yearned for, even if she could never be a part of it. Because eventually, that bond would break, and that warmth would die, as all things were destined to. And all the joy it brought Maia would be taken from her, inflicting far greater pain than anything Leona could ever visit on her.

The world had to survive. Maia had to go on living. That would be Leona's ultimate revenge.

The telepathic pressure lifted. When Trigger drew her blade from Leona's chest with a gurgle of Kith blood, Leona shifted to her knees, shaking the lingering wisps of the psychic assault from her head.

"You have a choice," Trigger said.

"I never felt like I did. But you're right." Leona slid her good arm around Maia's shoulders and pulled her close. The curse that bound them had been birthed from words and blood and will. She would dispel it with the same. "You gave your heart to me once," she whispered into Maia's ear. "I'm giving it back."

Leona pressed her bloody lips to a shallow cut on Maia's forehead and left a cool, gentle kiss there. Her own heart jumped in her chest as ghostly fingers she never noticed faded back into the abyss that had borne them. Maia gasped and thrashed against Leona's embrace. Her eyes shot open.

Heart's Oath had been defeated, but there was still more to do. Leona placed her claw on Maia's chest and held her down as she struggled. "Trigger. I need your help. Lay your hand on mine."

Trigger scrambled to her side and covered Leona's hand with her own. As Leona drew strength from her daughter, mixing it with the dwindling power left in her own veins, she set it to work mending bones, stitching tissue, and burning toxins. Maia's skin glowed as the hollow orange light crept through her.

Leona didn't dare try to withdraw the second sliver of fire Maia had taken into herself. It was too tangled, too interwoven with the one Heretic had given her, to safely extract.

In a way, it made her efforts entirely pointless. When the twin slivers finally became too much for her body to bear, Maia would die. And soon.

The glow receded. Light returned to Maia's eyes, and she rolled away into a crouch. Her breath came in hungry gasps. "What did you do?"

"Whatever I could." Leona smiled. She imagined how crooked it looked, as she was very much out of practice. "I've bought you a little more time. I can't remove the second sliver without tearing the other out along with it. Even if I did, there's no way to safely disperse that much power in my current state. Without a more skilled hand than mine, you'll die. I had hoped to give you a long life, full of suffering and loss, but a little time is better than none, yes?"

With a grim nod, Maia staggered to her feet. Sweat trickled down her face in thick rivulets. The heat rolling from her cracked armor caused the air around her to waver. "Thank you, Leona. But this doesn't change anything between us."

"No. It most certainly does not."

The earth shook with Scarlet's approach. The purple wolf at her side cocked his head and peered at her.

Leona turned away from his scrutiny. Maia and Trigger were already walking away, leaving her alone to dwell in the hell that she had made for herself. "What will you do with the time you have left?" she called after them.

Trigger summoned her helmet. She cast one last glance back over her shoulder and shrugged. "Whatever *we* can."

Chapter 52
A Vanguardian's Duty

Scarlet's fevered strides tore large tufts of sod from the earth as she charged toward Noctis. Indigo kept pace at her side, head bobbing frantically with each awkward gallop.

Maia's sweat-drenched hair clung to her forehead as she drove Scarlet on. Stinging, salty droplets trailed down into her eyes. She dismissed her helmet, resisting the urge to dismiss her armor, if just to cool her body for a moment. It likely wouldn't help. The rising heat itching its way through her skin wouldn't stop. She had held her flames in for too long without release. Like a stifled sneeze, they would come out eventually, and she had no doubt they would tear her apart.

Ami's voice crackled through Scarlet's cabin. "I'm in need of immediate assistance!"

"Ami, we're on our way!" Trigger shouted, sending her voice to both Scarlet and Viridian. "Where are you?"

"I'm headed in your direction!"

Viridian's remaining wing clipped the edge of the city wall as she dove through the gap Grimclaw had left. The Leviathan dipped down from above, letting out a dull roar that reverberated deep in Maia's chest as it chased Ami into the field, its gargantuan maw open and waiting.

"Keep running!" Maia leaned forward and drove Scarlet harder. "I have an idea!"

"If your plan involves jumping into its mouth and exploding, I don't want to hear it," Trigger said.

"You heard Leona. I'm done for, and there's nothing we can do about it."

"I didn't go through the trouble of saving you just to watch you die!" Trigger snapped. Indigo dug his forepaws into the ground and skidded to a stop. "Besides, you're not the only one with a reckless streak. Do you remember the Sea of Knives? When I asked what would happen if Scarlet's Teleport placed her inside something much larger than herself?"

"Trigger, don't even think about it!"

But Indigo was already floating in place, surrounded by a swirling vortex of purple light. One second, he was there. The next, his luminous frame collapsed into a thin ray of light and ripped into the sky. Half a breath later, the returning beam cut down from the heavens, shearing through the Leviathan's back and depositing Indigo somewhere inside it.

The Leviathan tore along a vertical seam as it burst from within, showering the field with flaming blood and viscera. Its remains flopped to the ground with a sorrowful bellow and erupted in a titanic mushroom-shaped cloud of fire.

Viridian stumbled from the blaze, her green body still smoldering. Scarlet dashed past her. At the center of the mile-wide scorched circle, she found Indigo, unmoving, his visor destroyed and his purple body blackened with ash.

"You bloody fool!" Maia cried. "Why? Why did you do it? It should have been me! I was going to die anyway!"

"Not. If I can...help it."

"I'll see to her," Ami said as Viridian limped to Scarlet's side, joints groaning as she braced on her front legs. "I can't fight any longer. I'm sorry, Maia. The rest is up to you."

Maia closed her eyes to temporarily break her connection to Scarlet. She held her head in her hands, took a deep breath to steady herself, and opened her eyes. "Did you get the gates open?"

"Only two of them," Ami said. "The Leviathan turned its attention to me before I could clear the Harvesters from the city's main gate."

"How many people escaped?"

"Not nearly enough."

The taste of sulfur filled Maia's mouth with every burning breath she took. She weighed her options. She could Teleport somewhere far away, sparing the remaining population of Noctis the instant yet horrifying death that would come when she exploded. Of course, that would leave them, and the rest of the world, to suffer at the hands of the Kith. Her other option was to detonate Scarlet in the center of the capital, killing hundreds of thousands and taking the whole world with her if Heretic was right about the importance of the master tower.

It was like choosing which fist to be punched with. No matter which she picked, it was going to hurt.

A pained voice scratched through Scarlet's cabin like a loose grindstone "Maia. Get out of my way." With off-rhythm steps, Slate thumped toward her, his mangled body pitching to the left with each step and causing his knuckles to draw ruts in the torched countryside.

Maia seethed through gritted teeth. "I don't have time for this."

"Neither do I," Leona said. "Move."

Scarlet shifted, allowing him to amble past her. "What, you think you can fix all of this?"

"No. But I can stop it from getting any worse. The Kith betrayed me. It's time I reminded them just how dangerous I am as an enemy."

"Unless you can fly through the Aperture and destroy the tower on the other side..."

She could practically hear Leona's smirk. "As a matter of fact, I can."

Slate bent at the waist. His gnarled back and calves cracked open. Magic-tinged vapor erupted from the ends of the rockets concealed within, lifting the gray metal monster into the sky.

"Of course! Slate is composed of parts of both Pearl and Onyx," Ami said. "Onyx was meant to act not only as chest armor for Legion, but as a propulsion system, as well. Do you recall the rockets in my drawing?"

Before Maia could even think of thanking her, Leona's voice cut back. "Remember your words, Maia: this doesn't change anything between us. If, somehow, we both survive, and our paths cross again, let's kill each other properly."

The drone of the rumbling rockets would have drowned out anything she had to offer in response, so Maia saved her breath. She had wasted too much of it on Leona already.

Still, she spared some of the precious little time she had remaining bearing witness as Slate took off in a careening arc toward the swirling maelstrom above. For giving Maia what remained of her life back, she owed Leona that much.

The thrum of Slate's rockets rattled what remained of his cabin. A rush of air swept in, washing away the black and purple smoke clouding Leona's view. Slate emerged from the other side of the Aperture upside down, right above a gargantuan obelisk that pulsed with dark energy, a stark contrast to the pristine city carved of shining crystal that sprung from purple sands a few miles away. Leona willed the fresh tendrils connecting her to Slate's cabin walls to pull tighter so she wouldn't fall through the shattered viewport as they fell from the sky.

The back of Leona's mind lit up all at once. Thousands of sharp, twisting aches drew her focus to the ground below, to the sea of blue faces looking up at her amid an army of Behemoths, Ferals, and other monstrosities. Even the six Leviathans gathered around the tower turned their attention skyward as Slate thundered from the heavens, his one remaining fist leading the way.

Leona kept her eyes open as long as she could, not wanting to give one more second to oblivion than she had to. When Slate collided with the upper half of the master tower, and a rush of stone cascaded into the cabin and over her ruined body as, Leona smiled, delighting in the knowledge that her vengeance against the Kith was complete.

As far as Maia knew, Noctis was the only city in the world that had flushing toilets. The first time she used one during her time in the Imperial army, she developed an irrational fear of being sucked down the bowl while it emptied.

A short time after the Aperture swallowed Slate, it stopped moving. Its edges undulated and flexed, stretching beyond the beams of dark energy carving it into the sky.

Then it started swirling in the opposite direction. Clouds bent over the widening edges to be devoured by the maelstrom. Dust and debris swirled up from the streets of the ruined capital city and floated toward the chaotic churning mess. It reminded Maia of that silly fear of hers, but on a scale she could never have fathomed.

Leona had done her part. The master tower was destroyed. It was Maia's turn to die.

Scarlet bent down, reached into the broken seam running down Indigo's back, and took the purple longsword handle resting there. She gripped it hard, causing the blade to extend to its full length. "It's time," Maia said. "Ami, take care of Trigger. Keep her safe. You're all she has left."

"I will. I promise you." Ami sniffled. Maia heard her breath shudder. "I love you, Maia."

"I love you too, Ami. Now get as far from here as you can."

Viridian's jaws closed around Indigo's neck and pulled. Hopefully, Ami would be able to get them both clear before Maia and Scarlet exploded, bathing the city in a conflagration like nothing the world had ever seen.

"This is the spot," Maia said when they arrived at the courtyard at the center of Noctis. The black, acrid smoke rising from the seams of her armor sent her into a coughing fit. "This is where we die."

What about the people still trapped inside the city? Scarlet said.

"We don't have any more time. I can't hold on any longer." Maia dropped to her knees. Above them, the Aperture swirled faster and faster. Throngs of Ferals, Swoopers, and even a Harvester lifted into the air. Chunks of destroyed buildings battered them before the raging maelstrom ground them into nothing. "If we don't destroy those towers, that portal is going to rip the whole world apart."

I understand.

Scarlet's chest creaked as it opened. The dancing glow of her core bathed the courtyard in a soft orange light. At Maia's command, Scarlet reversed her grip on Indigo's sword and angled it toward her chest.

Maia coughed and spit, but the taste of ashen death wouldn't leave her mouth. Hot plumes of fire pushed up her throat with every other breath. "I'm sorry, Scarlet. For all of this. For so long, you've been my biggest burden and my greatest strength. And, at times, my only friend. I couldn't have come this far without you. You made me what I am. Without you, I'm nothing. If I have to go, I'm glad we're going together. Thank you for getting me this far. And for everything."

A few moments passed. Scarlet was considering her response. *Maia. We should join our slivers. With all three combined, we can make sure the explosion destroys all five towers.*

Scarlet shuddered as long, winding wisps of fire drifted from her core and curled into her cabin through the small hole in her visor. Maia felt them calling to her. Begging her. She reached for the strands, shut her eyes, and focused. An ebb of twirling flames danced from her fingertips, bending toward the wisps extending from Scarlet's core.

When their flames touched, a new rush of power struck Maia with such force that her head rocked back. When she looked down inside herself, she couldn't tell where each sliver began and ended. One continuous flow of raw, searing potency entwined her soul to Scarlet's. The presence of Scarlet's sliver pushed the spells woven into Maia even further than her second sliver had, mending her cracked bones and burned flesh in a few breaths. For a short time, Scarlet and Sunder were one seamless, perfect being.

Maia opened her eyes and smiled at the blue-skinned woman kneeling across from her, the same horned, lava-haired goddess she briefly glimpsed when she absorbed her second sliver and turned herself into a walking bomb.

"It's you." Maia reached for her.

"It's us." Scarlet guided Maia's head onto her shoulder and held her close enough that she could feel her heartbeat.

Then she sunk her fingers into Maia's chest, grabbed her fire, and pulled.

"Scarlet, stop it!" Maia was alone in the cabin again. Her hands worried at the stream of flame slipping from her chest. A sharp pain bit her spine. Her chest compressed, like she was being pulled inside out. The red and gold drained from her armor and slipped into the torrent, leaving Maia clad in a shade of gray so dull and lifeless, it made Slate's armor look vibrant. "What the Hells are you doing?"

Scarlet's voice projected from the walls of the cabin. "A Vanguardian's duty is to protect and aid their Pilot. I'm glad that, in the end, I could finally fulfill my purpose."

The last flicker of Maia's flames slipped into Scarlet's core, leaving her feeling weaker, colder, and more naked than she had ever been in her life. The shadowy thread always present in the recesses of her thoughts was gone. She shivered against the sudden chill biting into her as lifeless gray armor crumbled from her chest and shoulders. When she touched the handles of her falchions, they turned to dust in her hands, joining what remained of her armor on the cabin floor.

Shimmering red lights swirled around her, gaining speed.

"I am sending you away, to somewhere safe," Scarlet said. "Somewhere you loved, once."

Maia clawed at the lights whipping around her in a tight tornado. "No. You can't do that. I'm your Pilot. I... You can't. This isn't fair!"

"Life isn't fair, so why should we fight as if it is?"

Maia grabbed a handful of the dust that used to be her weapons and armor and clenched her fist so tight, her fingernails cut into her palms. "You can't do this. Don't make me live without you. Who would I even be?"

"You'll be Maia Sunderland. And you'll be glorious."

The swirling lights swallowed her scream. When they dissipated, Maia was utterly alone. She opened her hand and watched the grains of her past life slip from her grasp and mingle with the cool beach sand beneath her.

She reached again for Scarlet, hoping that some lingering thread remained to bind them together. Maia found only a hollow space, an empty part of her that she knew could never be filled.

And so, Maia crumpled on the beach, curled her knees into her chest, and let the crashing waves drown out the sound of her weeping. There was nothing else she could do.

Her war was over.

The three slivers gnashed and snarled at the bars of the magical cage binding them to Scarlet. They had been so eager to be reunited, but now that they were one, they were restless, climbing over each other, desperate to leave their new prison and return to their home in the endless infinity that waited beyond the Veil.

Though her core hummed with more power than Scarlet could handle, the hollowness that Maia left behind boomed even louder. But that wasn't possible. Her core wasn't a thing you could carve a piece from. It couldn't be broken like a heart could.

It could only be destroyed.

The Aperture's pull increased, lifting Scarlet into the air. She turned so that her chest was facing the earth and pressed the tip of Indigo's longsword to her heart.

One thrust, and the world would be saved. One thrust, and the Kith would finally be defeated.

One thrust, and Scarlet would never see Maia again.

In the span of a single, selfish thought, her fingers betrayed her intentions. Indigo's blade slipped from Scarlet's grasp and bounced off her shoulder as it flew up into the sky to be consumed by the raging Aperture. She scrambled after it, pushing off the rising stonework torn from the city below until she had it back in her grasp.

Scarlet jerked the tip of the sword into her chest. It recoiled, flying from her clumsy grip once more. She could feel a small crack spread through the cage binding her together, just wide enough for the slivers to escape.

She let her arms float out to the sides, spared one last thought for that fiery young woman she had loved so well, and let go.

Trigger felt the blast before she saw it and saw it before she heard it. It started in the sky above Noctis as a thin beam of flame that raced to the ground with such speed, a bolt of lightning would have paused to take notice. Flames curled and billowed outward across the capital as the beam burrowed into the ground, sending an elaborate filigree of molten red fissures expanding through the earth.

Then the city of Noctis, most of its several hundred thousand residents, the entire Kith invasion force, and the ground beneath them all pitched into the air and tore asunder in an explosion so furious, it took the earth minutes to stop shaking. An expanding wave of dirt and ash rolled over the unyielding metal of the two Vanguardians standing vigil on a lonely hilltop, so very far away.

With the towers destroyed, along with miles of countryside beyond in every direction, the Aperture closed in the time it took Trigger to blink. One moment, the swirling hole in the sky was swallowing everything it could grab. The next, the sun, visible once more, painted the sky orange and brown as it struggled through the thick haze of vaporized debris clouding the air.

They waited on that hilltop for hours, watching the burning crater for any signs that something had survived its hellish birth. Then, after the sun had given up and left them to their grief, a dark spot appeared at the edge of the blaze.

Indigo was already bolting toward the crater where Noctis had been before Trigger could ask him to. He moved like a dart, weaving through boulders and sodden chunks of smoldering earth, his gears and bent joints grinding and screeching with each leap and stride. Trigger didn't need to look back to know that Viridian wasn't with her. With one wing missing, she could never keep up with Indigo's speed.

A mile from the edge of the flames, Trigger willed Indigo to climb onto a large mound and tilt his head down. She reached for Ami's Perception to get a better look at what had emerged from the fire. She shut her eyes, shook her head, and tried again, not trusting what she saw.

Scarlet lurched from the fire, though she had left her namesake color behind in the flames. A lifeless gray covered her from head to toe, giving her the look of an empty suit of plain ornamental armor. Her chest panels were pulled wide. Inside, a faint, colorless light pulsed, like a candle at the very end of its wick, one whisper away from darkness.

The Vanguardian raised her smoking arms and forced the panels shut. Her head canted slightly as if she could somehow see across the distance, to the girl who had once shared her cabin, and was struggling to remember her.

A few heartbeats later, the gray titan turned and wandered away, each step slow and laborious. Trigger didn't need Perception to know that Scarlet's cabin was empty. A sudden and overwhelming urge to sink into the floor and never rise again struck her, but Trigger pushed her shoulders back and forced herself to remain standing tall.

Rest could wait. She remained on that mound, eyes watering from the bright brilliance of Maia's funeral pyre, until Ami and Viridian were able to join her.

They stayed there until dawn, sharing their grief in silence. Then, with the rising sun, they were gone in a flash of purple and green light, never to return.

Chapter 53

Separate Ways

After five months residing in Inemelle, Trigger had yet to get used to the heat. Ami suggested she wear a head wrap to protect against the sun, and though it hid the thick white and purple braid she had spent so much time styling and perfecting, Trigger relented after her second bout of heat exhaustion.

The afternoon had been particularly warm, so Trigger retreated to the water gardens just outside of the city to wait out the heat. She couldn't feel the sun's touch directly, or anything else for that matter, but the dizziness fogging her mind told her that a trip to the cool waters of the temple-like gardens would only help.

Despite the stifling climate, Trigger tried to make the most of her time in the Reddalian capital. Ami had yet to run out of new eateries to bring her to, and though none of the delights she sampled could shake the remembrance of a particularly terrible sandwich and the company she had shared as she choked it down, Trigger enjoyed indulging Ami's attempts to cheer her up. Their lunches provided a much-needed distraction from the many political hearings they had both been forced to attend regarding their actions in Noctis.

When she had time to herself, Trigger wandered the city, taking great interest in the complex water wheels scattered throughout Inemelle. She studied the way they aided local industries, powering trip hammers and mills so the workers didn't have to slave as hard to provide for their families.

Unlike the Freelands, Inemelle had a centralized government, which brought with it laws that served the wealthy more than those less fortunate, but for the most part, Trigger could find far worse places to settle down.

If only she could settle.

She undressed and let her bare legs dangle over the edge of a marble fountain. With nothing else to occupy her mind, her mind drifted, as always, back to her duty. The day before, she and Indigo had stumbled upon a group of Ferals during a random patrol in the reaches of Kaldrsteinn. Her surprise at discovering such a large gathering of Kith foot soldiers so far from Noctis was eclipsed by the fact that not a single one of them had triggered her Hunter Sense.

The day before that, Trigger had traveled to Brimholme to aid the forces gathering there, preparing to march into the Empire to face a group of necromancers who were attempting to fill the power vacuum left by the Emperor's death.

She thought the gathered freedom fighters might welcome her presence as a deterrent against any resistance. She was mistaken. Like everywhere else she or Ami went in search of rogue Ferals and Swoopers and the odd Behemoth that escaped Noctis before Maia's final sacrifice, the people of Brimholme had set upon her with rocks and arrows and spears. One of the angry Granrum dwarves screaming for her blood had gotten her hands on a Pilot Killer rifle, the same make and model that had cost Maia an eye. After the first shot narrowly missed her, Trigger retreated, wishing the gathering forces luck while trying not to take their anger personally.

The web of the Noctean intelligence network spread far beyond Noctis, and the destruction of the capital didn't seem to have hindered its reach in any meaningful way. Agents and spies loyal to the Empire wasted no time letting the world know that Scarlet and Sunder had turned on the people they swore to protect, invaded Noctis, and burned it to cinders for no reason other than a severe, irrational hatred for the Noctean way of life.

Only those that Ami had helped escape knew the truth, that though the city had been reduced to a flaming scar in the earth so wide and deep that it made Thenmar's Crater look like a pothole, the Pilots hadn't acted out of malice. By sacrificing Noctis, Maia had saved the rest of the world from destruction.

That didn't mean Trigger's duty was complete. She still ventured out to hunt a few times a week, combing the continental nations for any of the Kith's creations that could now apparently escape her detection. She used those hunts as an excuse to track Scarlet, who people took to calling the Smoldering Titan, as she meandered endlessly about the continent. The few times Trigger caught up with Scarlet and found the courage to approach her, the gray giant kept walking without stopping to acknowledge her presence. It was almost as if she was sleepwalking, forever caught in an endless waking dream.

Between undetectable threats, the ire of an entire continent, and Scarlet's odd behavior, there was still the matter of Kasper's disappearance. A few days after she and Ami returned to Inemelle after Maia's sacrifice, Trigger summoned the nerve to visit Kasper in prison. She apologized for losing control and hurting him. Then, she cursed him for betraying her, manipulating her, and making her question whether what she had felt for him had been real, or just one of the many ideas she had let somebody else plant in her mind.

Through it all, Kasper said nothing, staring at her through the bars of his cell with a look of blank detachment that didn't shift once, not even when she told him about Leona's resurrection as a Lich, and her fight with Professor, and the way they both died. He had a right to know.

The next day, Kasper was gone, having somehow escaped captivity without a hint as to how he had accomplished such a feat. He would have a hard time crossing the Shining Sands to escape Reddalia, but he was clever. Perhaps he had made it all the way to the Freelands. Or maybe, he was still in the Southlands, waiting for the right time to steal into her bedroom at night and take his revenge on her.

From that point on, Trigger took to sleeping on a thin bedroll in Indigo's cabin and rarely left without summoning her armor. She chose to forgo wearing it that day. Even if a knife found its way into her back, it was worth taking a rare risk. She deserved a single day of reprieve from her never-ending, thankless duty.

The smooth sound of wheels rolling over wet stone caught Trigger's attention. She swung her legs out of the fountain's rolling waters and let them drip on the marble floor. "Come for a swim?" she said.

Ami locked the wheels of her chair and offered a wide smile. She was holding a small box in her lap. "Something came for you today. I took the liberty of inspecting it before opening it. It's safe. I only read the letter addressed to me. What remains in the box is for you. Happy Birthday, Trigger."

"Thank you, Ami. Is it from Tobias?" How he had discovered that she was living in Inemelle, or how he was able to afford the cost of sending news across the Shining Sands once a month, Trigger couldn't begin to guess.

Ami placed the box in her hands, unlocked her wheels, and gave Trigger some space.

The lid of the worn pine box stuck in its grooves. Trigger nearly broke it attempting to slide it open. Inside, a smooth black stone covered in runes rested quietly. Beneath it was an envelope sealed with wax, in the fashion of Imperial nobles.

Her hearts seized. She didn't recognize the seal at first. It didn't match any of the noble houses she was aware of. Was this a newly formed family seeking revenge for what happened to Noctis?

Then Trigger realized it was a pair of curved swords crossed over a bushel of berries, and the letter was addressed to "Princess," and she almost fell backward into the fountain.

She snapped the seal in half, withdrew the folded letter inside, and began to read.

Dear Trigger,

Sorry about "Princess." I didn't want anybody to know who I was sending this to and who it came from.

I don't know where to begin. Mom and Dad taught me how to read and write, but we never got around to letter writing. Do I write that I hope this finds you well? I've heard that in plays, and it always sounded nice. I do hope you're well. I really do.

I suppose I should begin by saying I'm sorry for not writing you sooner. I bet you're wondering how it is that I'm still alive. Right before Scarlet destroyed Noctis and wiped out the towers, she stole my fire slivers, combined them with her own, and Teleported me to the Freelands. I didn't know she could do that. Remember that beach from way back, when we first became mentor and apprentice? She sent me there.

I miss her a lot. About as much as I miss you. I ran into her in my travels once, but she didn't seem to recognize me. Maybe that's for the best. She deserves some peace after everything I put her through.

It seems that in saving me, Scarlet unmade me. Our connection is gone. I'm not a

Pilot anymore. I've lost my fire, my weapons and armor, my Barrier, and my ability to Teleport. That one hurts the most. You tend to forget how big the Freelands are until you have to walk them on foot. I have a newfound respect for cobblers, now.

Things haven't been easy since then. I've been recognized a few times, and that never ends well. I had to start cutting my hair and disguising myself to keep people from discovering who I am. I've also had to do some things that I'm not proud of. Maybe I'll tell you about them someday.

Trigger, I need to be honest with you. The reason I haven't written sooner is that I was afraid. I destroyed the city you called home and all the people you swore to protect. Not a day goes by that I don't wish I could have found another way to stop the Kith. I'm sorry for laying the world's hate on your shoulders. If you blame me for what happened, and for leaving you, and for being the one who turned the world against you, you have every right to.

We can talk about it when you're ready. The Farspeaker I sent you works, and I have its twin. Don't ask where I got it from. It's another long story.

By the time you get this, hopefully I'll be in Steadbrook. News takes a long time to get there, and the people there like to keep to themselves. I should be able to hide, for a while, at least. There's someone waiting for me there. If she's patient, and I'm lucky, then maybe I'll have a chance at making a new life. A life beyond Scarlet and Sunder.

I'm curious to see what that looks like. Scared, too.

In time, the world will forgive us. When that happens, they may need you again. It's up to you if you want to answer the call. I know you'll do what your hearts tell you to do, and I pity anybody who tries to stop you.

Just remember that you're never alone. This fight is too big for any one of us. If you ever need me, call me, and I'll be there. Always.

Yours,

Maia

Trigger folded the letter, slipped it back into the box, and slid the lid shut. She laid it in her lap and rested her hands atop it.

Ami waited for some time before drawing closer. Trigger smiled and handed Ami the box while she dressed. Then she placed her hands on the carved handles of Ami's wheelchair, waiting for Ami's nod before she started pushing her in the direction of the Hollow.

"Is everything okay?" Ami said.

With a sniffle, Trigger blinked away the first of many relieved tears. She took a deep breath. "I think it will be."

It wasn't the first time Elizabeth Barlowe had torn one of the many blisters lining her upper palms, but it was the first time she had torn two in one day.

The tree before her shook, scattering the freshly fallen snow clinging to its branches. The rope she had wound around the trunk to soften her longsword's blows was fraying. It would need to be replaced soon. But not yet. There was still a bit of lingering daylight left, and Elizabeth intended to make the most of it.

Steadbrook wasn't anything like she had imagined. It was less of a town, like she had been led to believe, and more of a loose association of families and tradespeople gathered in a shallow valley in the mountains bordering Kaldrsteinn, where the winter was almost as fierce and everlasting as it was to the north. Everyone traded for what they needed, but that didn't mean they were always friendly about it. Her parents still refused to speak to her. That left her with nobody to rely on but herself.

Elizabeth briefly considered offering her expertise to the sole watering hole in the region. Ultimately, she decided against it. She came to Steadbrook for a fresh start. Falling back into her old profession would defeat the purpose of fleeing to the intersection of nowhere and nothing to begin anew.

Instead, Elizabeth took to tending goats. There was always a demand for meat, milk, cheese, and wool. Though she wasn't an entrepreneur anymore, that didn't mean she couldn't find her place in the wheel. Tending to her flock and preparing the products she gleaned from them took up most of her daylight hours, leaving little time to train before harsh night descended upon the valley.

She spent those nights furthering her study of herbalism and medicine. The books and materials she had picked up from a chance caravan visit had cost her dearly, but Elizabeth gladly paid the price on the off chance she could succeed where so many healers had failed by finding a cure for Maia's condition, should Maia ever find her way back to her.

The days remained short. Winter in the valley persisted well into spring, so Elizabeth spared time for a second practice session, not knowing when she would get another chance to train in the daylight. Without a teacher to guide her practice, she could only hope that the effort she put in would be worth something if a bandit ever came calling.

As she poked at the blisters that had yet to tear, one of her goats bleated in alarm. Elizabeth wasn't expecting any trade. She spun, brandishing her longsword at whatever had startled her livestock.

When she saw who was coming up the hill, the blade slipped from her fingers and tumbled to the snow.

The traveler was wrapped in worn hides and a ratty cloak that looked like it had been sewn together from patches of far worse cloaks. She looked leaner than Elizabeth remembered her, with an uncharacteristic thinness to her ruddy, windburned cheeks. That carefree, easy smile she always wore was gone, replaced by a thin-lipped grimace. The steady way she moved told Elizabeth that though she had suffered in her travels, what remained of her was forged of the same taught steel and filled with the same fire that set Elizabeth's heart ablaze the very first time she gazed into those brown, bold eyes, and that smooth, deep scar drifting down the left side of her face like a calm river.

When her eyes met Elizabeth's, she froze like a deer caught in a clearing. Slowly, she removed her hood. Close-cropped brown hair covered her head, free of any trace of red. She stayed where she was, stiff and tense, as if she didn't know what to do next. Her eyes flicked to the sides. Elizabeth wanted to run to her, wrap her up in her arms, and never let her go, but she worried that any sudden movements might scare her off.

Instead, Elizabeth put her hands on her hips and turned her chin up, mostly to keep the tears welling up in her eyes from spilling. She cleared her throat to test her voice, took a deep breath, and smiled.

"So. What in the Blue Hells took you so long?"

Author's Note

Thank you for reading *Scarlet and Sunder*, and for supporting independent fiction. If you enjoyed the book, here's what you can do next:

- **Sign up for my free newsletter** at www.mikerousseau.com to receive updates about current and future releases. While you're there, be sure to check out my other work!

- **Leave a review** wherever you purchased this book, or anywhere else you like. Honest reviews help me reach even more readers, which allows me to keep publishing books! Thanks in advance. I really appreciate it.

Acknowledgements

My biggest thanks to my parents, who encouraged me to explore my creativity at a young age and never stopped believing in me.

To my early readers, for helping me work through some of the more delicate subject matter, providing feedback and notes, and hyping me up all the times I needed it: Laureen, Erin, Montana, Zach, Heather, and Anton.

To my editor, Charlie Knight, for their thoughtful, sensitive, and professional line, copy, and developmental edits. To Félix Ortiz, for his fantastic cover illustration, and Shawn T. King, for turning that art into a killer cover.

To Dan, for taking all those late-night phone calls when I was in the weeds and thought I would never see this through to the end.

To Cat Rambo and the good folks at Chez Rambo, for providing the welcoming, inclusive space I sorely needed.

To Reese Hogan, Sean Grigsby, Cameron Johnston, Essa Hansen, and all the other authors who encouraged me or gave me advice along the way.

To R.A. Salvatore, whose work inspired me as a teenager and led me to my own worlds.

And, of course, my heartfelt thanks to you for reading my debut novel. I promise to put just as much heart and effort into the next one.

www.ingramcontent.com/pod-product-compliance
Lightning Source LLC
Chambersburg PA
CBHW061532190726
48289CB00004B/1014